Dorothy Simpson work
for many years as a mar.
became a full-time writer. ...en
and lives near Maidstone i. ...ne Thanet
series. *Last Seen Alive*, the t ...anet novel, won
the Crime Writers' Associatio ...agger Award.

DOROTHY SIMPSON

THE FIFTH INSPECTOR THANET OMNIBUS

A DAY FOR DYING
ONCE TOO OFTEN
DEAD AND GONE

WARNER BOOKS

A *Warner* Book

This omnibus edition first published in Great Britain by Warner Books in 2001

The Fifth Inspector Thanet Omnibus Copyright © Dorothy Simpson 2001

Previously published separately:
A Day for Dying first published in Great Britain in 1995 by Michael Joseph Ltd
Published by Warner Books in 1996
Reprinted 1996, 1997, 1998 (twice), 1999, 2001
Copyright © Dorothy Simpson 1995

Once Too Often first published in Great Britain in 1998 by
Little, Brown and Company
Published by Warner Books in 1999
Reprinted 1999, 2000, 2001
Copyright © Dorothy Simpson 1998

Dead and Gone first published in Great Britain in 1999 by
Little, Brown and Company
Published by Warner Books in 2000
Copyright © Dorothy Simpson 1999

The moral right of the author has been asserted.

A CIP catalogue record for this book
is available from the British Library.

ISBN 0 7515 3194 4

Printed and bound in Great Britain by
Clays Ltd, St Ives plc

Warner Books
A Division of
Little, Brown and Company (UK)
Brettenham House
Lancaster Place
London WC2E 7EN

www.littlebrown.co.uk

A DAY FOR DYING

To my niece, Alison, with love and gratitude

ONE

It was on a Saturday evening in late March that Ben dropped his bombshell.

Thanet and Joan had had a quiet evening at home. They'd eaten supper off trays in front of the television set and were now discussing their holiday plans before going to bed.

'Didn't you say the Dracos went Greek-island-hopping last summer?' said Joan.

'Yes. They had a marvellous time. The Super came back looking so relaxed we could hardly believe it was the same man. Of course, it was partly huge relief that Angharad was still in the clear.'

Angharad Draco, wife of the Superintendent of Sturren-den Divisional Police Headquarters, where Thanet worked, had been diagnosed as suffering from acute myeloid leukaemia four years ago. So far, she had been one of the lucky ones. The average outlook is only two years of life from diagnosis and there had been general rejoicing when she had passed this milestone and begun to put on weight, regain her spectacular good looks. Now, with every month that went by, the hope grew stronger that the danger really was over.

'I ran into her in the town the other day,' said Joan, 'and she looks wonderful.'

'I haven't seen her for ages.'

'Well, you will at the party.'

They both glanced at the invitation card on the mantelpiece.

Thanet grinned. 'There are all sorts of rumours flying around . . . marquee, top-notch band, caterers, the lot.'

'Well, you can't blame him for wanting to celebrate. Her birthday must mean something pretty special these days.'

The front door slammed and they glanced at the clock. It was only 10.30. They raised eyebrows at each other.

'Hi!' said Ben, poking his head into the room.

'You're early!' they said.

'I wanted to catch you before you went to bed. I'll just . . .'

'. . . get a snack,' they chorused, smiling. Their son's snacks were a family joke.

He gave a sheepish grin and disappeared.

'Sounds ominous,' said Thanet.

'Certainly does. Must be important. Ten-thirty on a Saturday night? Unheard of!'

'Perhaps he's finally made up his mind at last.'

'Let's hope so!'

It was decision time for Ben. He was bright enough to have been offered a place at both Bristol and Durham Universities, and had been trying to decide which was his first choice. There had been endless family discussions on the respective advantages and disadvantages and they had all reached the stage where it would be a relief when the decision was made.

Ben came in carrying his 'snack' – a triple-decker sandwich flanked by an apple and a banana.

'So,' said Thanet when Ben was settled. 'What did you want to talk about?'

Ben had taken a huge bite out of his sandwich and finished masticating before saying, 'I've made up my mind what I want to do.' He cast a swift, assessing glance at his parents before taking another bite.

Thanet felt the first stirring of unease. 'And?'

Another pause. Ben swallowed, then put his plate carefully down on the table beside his chair before saying, 'I've decided not to choose either.'

'Ah.' Taken aback, Thanet didn't quite know how to react. He sensed a crisis looming.

'What d'you mean, exactly?' said Joan. Her tone was strained. She was trying, but just failing, to conceal her dismay.

Ben sat back, folding his arms across his chest as if to defend himself from the attack he was sure would come. 'I've decided not to go to university at all.'

Thanet knew his face must be betraying something of the disappointment which welled up in him, and was helpless to prevent it. Not having been to university himself and having always regretted it, he had pinned his hopes on Ben. Bridget had not been academic and he had been happy to encourage her in her chosen career, admired the success she had made of it. But Ben . . . Ben was bright, had sailed through his exams with ease. What a waste it would be, not to take up this unique opportunity to enlarge his mind, his experience, his knowledge. Careful, he told himself. We must be careful. He glanced at Joan and could see her thinking the same thing. Safer to say as little as possible, make sure that no bridges were burned.

'At all?' he said, echoing Ben's last words.

Ben nodded.

3

'You mean, you want to defer taking up your place?' said Joan. 'Have a year out?'

Thanet could hear the hope in her voice. That could be it, of course. So many young people these days did just that after taking their A levels, eager to see something of the world before they settled down to three or four years of further study. Having missed out earlier, Bridget was travelling at the moment. Perhaps that was it. Perhaps Ben had been made to feel restless by the postcards which had been arriving from the Far East and, of late, New Zealand and Australia?

But Ben was shaking his head. 'I've made up my mind what I want to do, and I can't really see the point of wasting three years going to university.'

'What do you want to do?' said Thanet. Ben had always said he couldn't make up his mind.

Ben raised his chin and looked straight at his father. 'I want to go into the police.'

Silence.

Thanet didn't know what to say. This was the last thing he had expected and his reaction was mixed. He was touched, proud, yes, that his son was choosing to follow him. But he was, above all, dismayed. Apart from the tragedy it would be for Ben to throw away this chance, life in the force was not what it had once been. Over the last decade the problems of law and order had proliferated, slowly seeping out into the rural areas from the cities. He loved his work, had never regretted his choice of career, but of late had often wondered if, had he been starting again, he would have thought more than twice about it.

'I see. I assume this isn't a sudden decision?'

Ben shook his head. 'I've been thinking about it for ages. But I knew you'd both be disappointed if I didn't go to university, so I kept on putting off telling –'

4

The telephone rang and Thanet went to answer it, not sure whether to be glad or sorry that their discussion had been interrupted. He hoped it might be Bridget but it was Pater, the Station Officer.

'Sorry to disturb you, sir . . .'

'It's all right, it's too early for me to be enjoying my beauty sleep. What's the problem?'

'Report of a suspicious death just come in, sir. Out at Donnington. Body of a young man found in a swimming pool. There was a party going on.'

'Sounds as though he might have had too much to drink. Have you notified the Super?'

'He's out. I left a message on his answerphone, then rang you.'

'I'll leave right away. What's the address?' Thanet scribbled directions and put the phone down. No need to tell Pater what to do, the sergeant knew the routine off by heart. He returned to the sitting room.

Joan stood up as he came in. 'We heard.'

'Yes, sorry, Ben. This is important to you, I know.'

Ben shook his head. 'It's OK, Dad, I understand. We can talk about it some other time.'

'Yes, of course.' And it was probably best that way, thought Thanet. It'll give Joan and me time to discuss how best to react.

Outside the air was fresh and cool after the warmth of the house. A light breeze had sprung up, chasing away the ragged clouds which from time to time had obscured the sun throughout the day. The sky was clear and the street and driveway were bathed in the silvery light of a moon that was almost full.

Thanet shivered and turned up the collar of his coat. Donnington wasn't far, only a couple of miles from Sturrenden on the other side of the river. At this time of night it shouldn't take more than ten minutes or so to get there. A party, he thought gloomily. The place would be crawling with potential suspects.

He found the house without difficulty. It was in a country lane leading out of the village, one of several properties standing well back from the road. There was a big bunch of balloons tied to the gatepost and a patrol car parked on the verge outside. A uniformed officer waved him down as he slowed.

'Sorry, sir, there's no room to park inside at the moment, drive's crammed with cars already. There was a party going on.'

'What sort of party, do we know?'

'Engagement party for the daughter of the house. The dead man was her fiancé.'

Poor girl, thought Thanet as he parked his car. What a way for the night to end.

As he got out another car could be heard approaching along the lane and he saw with satisfaction that it was Lineham's Escort. He waited for the sergeant to join him and told him what little he knew as they walked to the entrance to the drive. Then they paused for a few moments to look around.

The wrought-iron gates, hung on brick pillars, stood wide open. Just inside them the driveway forked, the narrower arm leading off to the right in the direction of a bungalow where lights still burned. A gardener's cottage, perhaps? The grounds of the house were sufficiently extensive to warrant one; the drive was a couple of hundred yards long and the moonlight revealed wide lawns spreading away on either side, bisected by flower borders and flanked by stands of mature trees. Cars were parked nose to tail all the way along the drive and in the big parking area in front of the house. This was ablaze with light, a long, low, sprawling structure, 1930s stock-brokers' Tudor by the look of it, built at a time when domestic help was still readily available. At one end, projecting forwards at right angles to the main house, was a single storey building and as he and Lineham drew nearer Thanet could see it was a separate structure, a block of garages. Somewhere behind the house a dog was barking, a big one, by the sound of it. It had probably been chained up for the evening.

'Let's hope things haven't been disturbed too much,' he said. 'Looks as though there's quite a crowd here tonight.'

But predictably Lineham was too busy taking in the general air of affluence to respond. 'Four garages!' he said. 'Not exactly paupers, are they?'

Thanet grinned. Lineham's stock reaction to any property larger than the average never failed to amuse him. 'Fancy the place, do you, Mike? You'll have to ask for a rise.'

'Ha, ha. Very funny.'

Thanet could hear more cars arriving in the lane behind them. The SOCOs, perhaps, and Doc Mallard. 'Come on, let's get a move on, find out what's what.'

They quickened their pace. The curtains had not been drawn and they glimpsed people standing around or sitting huddled in small groups. Even from outside the air of shock was evident.

Almost before the reverberations of Lineham's knock had died away the door opened.

The woman was in her late thirties, with fashionably tousled long dark curly hair, deep-set brown eyes and a pointed nose. Her careful make-up could not disguise the hint of ill humour in the set of her mouth, the frown lines scored between the heavy brows. Her simple black dress

7

looked expensive and she was wearing a chunky gold necklace and earrings. The 'lady' of the house, Thanet assumed. But he was wrong. She introduced herself as the housekeeper, Barbara Mallis, and gestured them into a large, square hall with panelled walls and a wide oak staircase. The subdued murmur of conversation emanating from the rooms on either side died away as people craned to catch a glimpse of them.

'I'll let Mr Sylvester know you're here.'

But there was no need. A man emerged from the room to the left.

'Ah, there he is,' she said.

Sylvester was casually but expensively dressed in cashmere sweater and soft silky cords. He was around fifty, Thanet guessed, with thinning hair and the pock-marked skin of a former acne sufferer. He looked distinctly unhealthy. Heavy jowls and a protruding belly betrayed a penchant for too much rich food and the skin of his face was the colour of uncooked dough.

He acknowledged Thanet's introductions with a tense nod. 'This way.'

Sylvester obviously didn't believe in wasting time on social niceties, thought Thanet as he and Lineham followed him across the hall and along a corridor at the back leading off to the left. They were presumably going to the swimming pool.

'I gather it was you who found him, sir,' said Thanet.

'Yes.'

'And he was your daughter's fiancé, I believe?'

Sylvester nodded, tight-lipped. He had stopped in front of the door at the end of the corridor and was fishing a key out of his pocket. 'I made sure it was locked before we left.'

Thanet's heart sank. 'We?'

8

Sylvester's shoulders twitched impatiently. 'Oh, I know, I know, I've seen the films, I'm aware that you shouldn't disturb anything and looking back I can see I should have kept everyone out, but at the time . . . You're just not thinking straight. You can understand that, surely.'

'Only too well. Unfortunately it does make our job more difficult.' It also ensured that if Sylvester himself had helped the unfortunate young man on his way, it would be more difficult to isolate scientific evidence against him.

Sylvester merely grunted and turned the key in the lock. Warm moist air and a smell of chlorine rushed out to greet them. Thanet caught a brief glimpse of dark water shimmering in the moonlight before Sylvester flooded the room with light.

Thanet caught Lineham's admiring glance and knew what the sergeant was thinking. *They really must be loaded.* The pool house was indeed unashamed luxury. It must have been around twenty-five metres long and was built entirely of glass, and double glazed, too, for there was no sign of condensation on the windows or roof. Of irregular shape, the pool itself was deep enough to sport a diving board at the nearer end. Comfortable *chaises-longues* with yellow-and-white-striped cushions which would bring a hint of sunshine to the gloomiest of days were interspersed with groups of exotic potted plants, some of which were as tall as young trees. It would be a real pleasure to relax here after a hard day's work – a pleasure which from now on would no doubt be blighted by the memory of what had happened tonight.

The body lay at the far end of the pool and as they approached it Sylvester was explaining that the only way he could get it out was to tow it to the shallow end. He had found that it was impossible to lift a dead weight out of deep water without help.

'You went in after him yourself?' said Lineham.

'Yes.' Sylvester glanced down at his clothes. 'I had to go and change.'

Thanet was scarcely listening. He was bracing himself for his private purgatory, that first close look at the corpse. By now he was resigned to the fact that he was never going to overcome this weakness of his and that all he could do was grit his teeth until it was over.

And here it came.

This time it wasn't as bad as he had expected, perhaps because apart from a bruise on one temple there were no outward signs of violence. The young man lay on his back in a puddle of water near the steps leading down into the shallow end, limbs neatly arranged, eyes closed as if he were asleep. He had been in his late twenties, Thanet guessed, well built and handsome, with the sort of looks a male model would envy. His dark hair was still wet, sleeked back from his forehead, his expensive suede trousers and silk shirt sodden.

'What was his name?' Thanet asked.

'Max Jeopard.'

Max Jeopard. Thanet repeated the name in his head. Over the next days, weeks, perhaps months, he would come to know Jeopard in a way that no one else could possibly have known him. Thanet was aware that our view of the people in our lives is subjective, coloured by our own thoughts, attitudes, prejudices, life experience, and rarely do we learn what others truly think of us. But in a murder case the investigating officer is in the unique position of gathering together many different views of one person so that, gradually, a composite picture begins to emerge. Often it is only then that the true cause of the tragedy can be understood.

Thanet glanced around. There was no sign of a break-in. 'Are the doors to the garden kept locked?'

'Yes. Locked, bolted and morticed.'

Lineham was already checking. He nodded confirmation.

So, if Jeopard had indeed been murdered there was no question here of an intruder. Someone he knew, probably someone he knew well, had felt that life would be intolerable if Jeopard continued to walk the earth. Thanet shivered as the familiar *frisson* of excitement trickled down his spine. It was as if he had caught the first scent of his quarry.

He had to put another obvious question, even though he was sure of the answer he would get. 'Could he swim?'

Sylvester compressed his lips. 'Like a fish.'

There was a knock at the door and Barbara Mallis put her head in. 'Inspector,' she said, raising her voice to be heard across the intervening space, 'the police doctor has arrived. And some more of your men.'

'Right. Thank you. Show him in, would you? And the Scenes-of-Crime Officers too, if they're there. Tell the others I'll be out in a moment.' Thanet turned back to Sylvester. 'As soon as I've got things organised I'd like to talk to you again, get a little more detail. Er . . . is there a Mrs Sylvester?'

'She's with Tess, our daughter. The doctor's with them. I believe he's giving her a sedative – Tess, I mean. Naturally she's in a terrible state. Anyway . . .' Sylvester glanced at Doc Mallard, who was now approaching, accompanied by the SOCOs. 'I'll be around when you want me. But my guests – when will they be able to go home?'

'I'll be out to talk to them shortly. Perhaps you could assemble them all in one room?'

'Of course.' Sylvester hurried off.

Mallard nodded a greeting, holding back for the photographer to take shots of the body. Then he squatted down, peering at the bruise on the temple. 'Nasty contusion here.'

'He could swim like a fish, apparently,' said Thanet. 'So the question is, was he dead or unconscious when he went into the water? I don't suppose you'll be able to tell until the post-mortem.'

Mallard glanced up at Thanet over his half-moons. 'Quite.'

'Anyway,' Lineham said to Thanet while they waited for Mallard to finish his examination, 'looks as though it's a suspicious death, all right.'

'He could have been drunk, slipped, banged his head.'

'When he was all alone? At his own engagement party? You don't really believe that, sir.'

Thanet didn't. 'Unlikely, I agree. Still, we'll see.'

Mallard held out a hand. 'Give me a heave up, will you? Must be getting old.'

Thanet obliged. 'So, what's the verdict, Doc? How long has he been dead?'

'Well,' said Mallard, 'you know how I hate committing myself . . . and it's tricky because it's so warm in here . . . but I think it would probably be safe to say some time in the last three hours.'

Thanet glanced at his watch. Eleven-forty. And the phone call had summoned him at around eleven. So, some time between 8.30 and 11, then. Not much help, really. 'Right, thanks, Doc.' He glanced at the SOCOs. 'We'll leave you to it, then.'

Sylvester was waiting in the hall with DCs Bentley and

Wakeham. He looked relieved to see Thanet. 'It's a bit of a crush but I've got everyone together in the lounge.'

Mallard glanced at Thanet. 'Don't bother to see me out. I'll be in touch.'

Thanet nodded and followed Sylvester. He saw at a glance that the man had not been exaggerating. There must have been a hundred people crammed into the room, mostly standing. A few were sitting on the floor or perched on the arms of chairs. Right at the front were seated two elderly women, one of them in a wheelchair. The subdued hubbub of conversation died away and a sea of faces swung expectantly in his direction as he entered.

Thanet introduced himself. 'I'm sure you are all aware by now of the tragedy which has taken place here tonight. You must be anxious to leave but we'd be grateful if you could be patient just a little longer . . . Then, after giving your names and addresses, you can all go home. But before you do so we should be grateful if you would think hard and see if you heard or noticed anything, anything at all, which could be even remotely connected with Mr Jeopard's death. I'm afraid that at the moment I can't respond to any questions because almost certainly I wouldn't know the answers. That's all. Thank you.'

He was turning away when a young man darted forward. 'Inspector . . .?'

'This is Hartley Jeopard, Max's brother,' said Sylvester.

'A terrible business, Mr Jeopard,' said Thanet. A platitude, but what else could he say? Hartley Jeopard was a couple of years younger than his brother, Thanet guessed, and resembled him not at all. He was much taller and thinner, for a start, with the apologetic hunch adopted by so many of those who are of above average height. His clothes were nondescript, brown trousers and fawn crew-necked lambswool sweater, and he lacked his brother's striking good looks. Hazel eyes beneath floppy brown hair looked anxiously down at Thanet from a narrow undistinguished face.

'Inspector, I'm worried about my mother.' He glanced at the woman in the wheelchair. 'It's been such a terrible shock for her . . . Would it be possible to take her and my aunt home right away?'

'I didn't realise she was here. Yes, of course. I can come and see you tomorrow morning. Give Sergeant Lineham your address, will you, while I have a word with her?'

Jeopard's mother did indeed look ill. Her pallor was alarming and she was gripping the arms of her chair as if to prevent herself from sagging forward. What on earth was Sylvester thinking of, Thanet thought angrily, to have herded her in here like this? But the man had only been obeying instructions. Perhaps, before that, the two women had been given some space and privacy. Thanet hoped so, anyway. As he murmured condolences and apologies for holding them there his genuine concern must have shown because Mrs Jeopard's expression lightened a little and her sister gave a little exclamation of relief when he said that Hartley could take them home immediately. 'I will need to talk to you, though. Between 10 and 10.30 tomorrow morning?'

'Yes, of course. Thank you.' Mrs Jeopard was controlling herself with difficulty. Her lower lip trembled as she spoke and Thanet was glad that Hartley arrived at that moment to take charge of her wheelchair. Her sister, he saw when she stood up, was almost as tall as her nephew. Genes were responsible for some curious family quirks.

A buzz of conversation broke out behind him as he left

the room. A man and a woman were just coming down the stairs: Mrs Sylvester and the family doctor, Thanet guessed. He was right. Tess was under sedation, he learned, and shouldn't be disturbed. The doctor left and Thanet told the Sylvesters that as soon as he had got his men organised he would like to interview them first. 'Have you got a room we could use?'

Sylvester frowned, thinking. 'Most of them are being used for the party. There's the den, I suppose ...' He glanced at his wife as if seeking approval or suggestions.

But Mrs Sylvester wasn't really listening. She was looking put out. 'I wanted to go back up to sit with Tess. Just in case she wakes up.' She was a little younger than her husband, in her late forties, with a floaty mane of streaked blonde hair, bright blue eye shadow and a lipstick that was far too harsh for her skin colour. She was wearing a tight sequin-covered black lace dress which revealed every curve and shimmered as she moved. And she was, Thanet realised, saying one thing to her husband and trying to communicate another. The look she was giving him was fierce in its intensity, pregnant with words unspoken.

Sylvester frowned at her. Either he couldn't work out what she was trying to tell him or he was deliberately choosing to ignore it; Thanet couldn't make up his mind which.

'Perhaps a friend could sit with her for a little while?' suggested Thanet.

'Yes. How about Anthea?' said Sylvester.

For some reason this suggestion upset Mrs Sylvester even more. 'What, after –?' She glanced at Thanet and broke off.

Interesting, he thought. What was going on here? But perhaps he was misreading her. Perhaps she was simply reluctant to relinquish her role to someone else and was angry that Sylvester had suggested an alternative.

She compressed her lips. 'All right,' she said grudgingly. Then to Thanet, 'I hope this won't take long . . .'

Thanet wasn't going to be forced into giving a promise he might not be able to keep. How could he possibly tell, at this stage, how long the interview might be? 'Thank you.'

'I'll see if I can find her,' said Sylvester. He disappeared into the sitting room, returning a few moments later with an exotic creature in a scarlet satin cheongsam. Her long dark hair had been put up in a knot secured by a long wooden pin, enhancing the chinese effect, but the matching heavy make-up was streaked and blotchy, her eyes swollen with tears shed and unshed. Here, apparently, was someone who really did mourn Max Jeopard's passing.

'Are you sure you'll be all right?' Sylvester was saying.

The girl gave a determined nod. 'I'll be glad of a bit of peace and quiet.' She gave Mrs Sylvester, whose face was stony, a somewhat shamefaced look before going upstairs.

Thanet watched her go. No doubt about it, there were interesting undercurrents here. He glanced at Lineham and could see that the sergeant was thinking the same thing.

Sylvester patted his wife's shoulder. 'Don't worry,' he said reassuringly. 'Tess'll be all right with her.' He turned to Thanet. 'They've been friends for years.'

Five minutes later the Sylvesters were leading the way to the 'den'. Thanet followed with Lineham on his heels, aware of a sense of rising anticipation. This was the part of his work that he enjoyed most of all, the interviewing of suspects. It was where he would begin to understand the complex web of relationships which surrounded the dead man, the point at which, for Thanet, Max Jeopard would start to live and breathe again.

He was eager for the process to begin.

TWO

The den turned out to be a small square sitting room equipped with a huge television set and saggy leather armchairs from which it would clearly be a struggle to get up. Impossible to conduct an interview from their depths; Thanet elected to lean against the windowsill, Lineham to sit sidesaddle on the broad arm of one of the chairs. Despite their apparent disharmony of a short while ago the Sylvesters presented a united front and chose to share one, she perched on the edge of the seat, tugging down the skirt of her tight black dress which had ridden halfway up her thighs, her husband sitting on the arm beside her, one hand resting on her shoulder. They watched apprehensively as Lineham took out his notebook and flicked it open.

'Right, well, perhaps you could fill us in on this evening,' said Thanet.

The Sylvesters stared at him. It was interesting that they didn't look at each other, Thanet thought. It was, he felt, almost as if they were afraid to. If so, why?

Mrs Sylvester put her hand on her husband's knee, her painted fingernails standing out like drops of blood against the pale velvety cords.

'Where . . .' Sylvester cleared his throat, tried again. 'Where d'you want us to begin?'

Alarm bells were definitely ringing in Thanet's mind. He was becoming convinced that the Sylvesters were not simply suffering a natural distress engendered by the events of the evening. They were frightened. It showed in the sheen of perspiration beginning to appear on Sylvester's forehead, the whiteness of Mrs Sylvester's fingertips where they gripped her husband's knee with excessive force. Was one of them responsible for Jeopard's death? Or did each suspect that the other might be? He refrained from the obvious response. 'What time were people invited for?'

Mrs Sylvester visibly braced herself, removing her hand and straightening her back. 'Eight o'clock,' she said. 'But they didn't start arriving until around a quarter past.'

'And Mr Jeopard?'

'A little earlier,' said her husband. 'Around a quarter to eight, I should think.'

His wife was nodding. She was being as matter of fact as possible, but the fear still lurked at the back of her eyes. 'Must've been. I was still getting ready.' She put up a hand to fluff out her hair, unconsciously miming what she had been doing at the time.

'He lives locally, I gather.'

'Yes,' said Sylvester. 'At least, that is, his family home is here. But he and Hartley both have flats in London. Hartley came down last night, I believe, so that he could drive his mother and aunt to the party tonight, but Max drove down from town this evening.'

'How was he?'

'His usual self,' said Mrs Sylvester. Her tone was tart and she cast an uneasy glance at her husband, conscious of having betrayed rather more than she would have wished.

19

'Which was . . .?'

'Full of himself,' said Sylvester shortly. 'Look, Inspector, there's no point in pretending. We weren't too keen on Tess's choice of a husband. But not, I assure you, to the extent of pushing him into the swimming pool to make sure she didn't marry him!'

Even if someone else did. The unspoken words hovered in the air and Thanet allowed a brief, uncomfortable silence before he nodded, content to accept the statement at face value for the moment. Time would tell whether or not it were true. 'So,' he said. 'Mr Jeopard was in a good mood – why shouldn't he be? After all, it was a special occasion for him. In your opinion, then, there's no question of it being suicide?'

'Suicide! Good God, no!' Sylvester had relaxed sufficiently to appear amused rather than shocked at the suggestion. 'Max was the last person in the world to want to kill himself. He enjoyed life far too much.'

'Then could it have been an accident, d'you think?'

'Difficult to see how,' said Sylvester reluctantly.

'Oh I don't know, Ralph,' his wife protested, a hint of desperation in her tone. 'He could have slipped, hit his head on the side as he went in.'

'Oh come on, darl! Those tiles are all special non-slip, you know that. Cost us a bomb. And we know he wasn't drunk, we were talking to him in the supper queue just before he disappeared. What the hell was he doing in the pool house, that's what I want to know. He was only supposed to have gone for a pee!'

'I know that, but . . .'

'I'm sorry,' interrupted Thanet. 'Let's go back to what we were saying, shall we? So in your opinion at least, Mr Sylvester, it couldn't have been an accident, either. We won't close our minds to the possibility of course, but meanwhile we have to look closely at our third option.'

There was a brief silence. Mrs Sylvester was staring at Thanet as if mesmerised, clearly terrified of what was coming. Without looking at her husband she put up her hand to feel for his, which closed over it, gave it a reassuring squeeze. 'No point in pussy-footing around, is there?' Sylvester said. 'We all know what we're talking about, don't we? Murder.'

His wife made a little moaning sound and he leaned forward to put his free arm around her shoulders. 'It's all right, darl,' he murmured into her hair. 'Don't worry.'

She jerked away from him, twisting to look directly into his face. 'How can you say that, Ralph? Someone is deliberately killed, under our own roof, and you say don't *worry*?' Her voice went up, almost out of control, and Thanet could tell from her expression that once again she was willing Sylvester to hear what she was not saying aloud.

Thanet found himself leaning forward as if to catch those unspoken words. What was it that she was trying to communicate to her husband?

'We don't *know* that it was deliberate yet, do we?' said Sylvester.

'It's what you just said!'

'Not exactly. I said that's what we were talking about.'

'What's the difference? You're just splitting hairs! I don't –'

'There's a big difference darl, surely you must see that? Someone might have killed him, yes, but not because he intended to. It could have been murder by accident, sort of, if you see what I mean.'

Now he was doing it too, staring intently into his wife's eyes as if to convey an unspoken message. And it seemed to work because after a moment Mrs Sylvester relaxed a fraction and looked at Thanet. 'Would that be possible, Inspector?'

'Possible, yes. How likely, we don't yet know. It's all speculation at the moment. We won't get anywhere until we've established the facts, so if we could go back to what we were saying . . .? Mr Jeopard was in a good mood earlier in the evening, you say. Did you see any sign of problems with any of your guests?'

They were shaking their heads.

And they were lying, Thanet was sure of it. He could tell by the way they still studiously avoided looking at each other and by the glazing of their eyes as they strove to conceal the truth.

'We weren't exactly keeping an eye on him,' said Sylvester. 'I was moving around all the time, topping up people's drinks. And you were busy circulating, weren't you, darl?'

Mrs Sylvester was nodding. 'People were spread out through all the downstairs rooms.'

'Including the pool house?'

Again the head-shaking double act.

'No. Just in case anyone had one over the eight and fell in,' said Sylvester.

'You know what young people are,' said his wife with a false little laugh. 'Sometimes they get carried away, even jump in with their clothes on. We didn't want to risk any accidents. And even if they all behave perfectly there's always the chance of a glass or a bottle getting broken and that's dangerous where people walk around in bare feet.'

'So we locked the door and left the lights off, to show it was out of bounds, so to speak.'

'And the key?'

'Always hung on a hook beside the door.' Sylvester

shifted uncomfortably. 'Looking back, I suppose it would have been sensible to take it away altogether, but we never do. The place is only ever locked for extra security. And tonight, well, it never occurred to me to do anything else. After all, you'd have to be pretty brazen, as a guest, to ignore a hint like a locked door with the key removed.'

'Right. So you both saw Jeopard from time to time, but neither of you noticed any sign of a scene, a quarrel or disagreement of any kind?'

Once again the shutters came down. 'No.'

Thanet didn't press the point. No doubt the truth would emerge eventually. 'So how did you come to find him in the pool house, Mr Sylvester?'

Sylvester hesitated a moment, as if uncertain where to start. 'As it was an engagement party, it was arranged that the two families would sit together at supper – that is, Max, his mother and aunt, Tess, my wife and myself.'

'We had one table set aside for us,' said his wife, 'specially laid and decorated. Just to mark the occasion. It was Tess's idea.'

'So when it got to time for supper –'

'Sorry to interrupt,' said Thanet. 'But, just to be clear on this, did you have caterers in?'

Sylvester glanced at his wife. *Your province.*

'Yes,' she said. 'It was a buffet meal. Just before it was served they set up a number of small tables, in the various rooms, so people could eat in comfort.'

'Can't stand eating off my knee,' said Sylvester. 'Hopeless if it's a knife and fork job.'

'And what time was supper served?'

'Nine-thirty,' said his wife. She paused in case Thanet had any further questions before continuing. 'We all collected our food from the buffet, then found somewhere to sit. Afterwards the caterers cleared everything away, including the tables. We've done it like that before and it works very well.'

'So the six of you queued up for your food with everyone else and took it to your table?'

'Yes,' said Sylvester. 'Well, sort of. Mrs Jeopard is in a wheelchair, as you saw, so she and her sister chose what they wanted to eat, then Tess carried their plates and Max pushed his mother's chair to our table, got her and his aunt settled. Then he and Tess went back to collect their own food. About five minutes later Tess got back and sat down. We all assumed Max would join us shortly and it must have been a good ten minutes before his mother said she wondered where he'd got to.'

'That's right,' agreed Mrs Sylvester. 'We didn't pay any attention at first. Like my husband said, we assumed he'd gone to the loo – which was, in fact, what Tess told us. When Max's mother said she wondered where he was, I mean.'

'What time would that have been?' said Lineham.

'Well,' said Sylvester, working it out. 'Supper was arranged for 9.30, and I think it was on time, wasn't it, darl?' He waited for his wife's nod. 'Then it would have taken us about ten minutes to get settled. Usually, at parties, we serve ourselves last, but on this occasion there was a bit of fuss made about the special table and so on, and everyone waved us to the front of the queue.'

'So you sat down about twenty to ten?'

'Thereabouts, I should think. Then it was another ten minutes or so, like I said, before any comment was made about Max not having come back yet, and it must have been a further five or ten before I went to look for him.'

'Around ten o'clock, then?'

'It must've been about then,' said Mrs Sylvester. 'Tess had been getting restless and I think by then she felt we'd all waited long enough, so she said she'd go and see if she could find him. But my husband said no, she was to stay and enjoy her supper and he'd go instead.'

'So I did,' said Sylvester. 'Trouble was, there were so many places to look – a cloakroom and two bathrooms for a start, then tables had been set up everywhere, like we said – hall, lounge, dining room, conservatory, and quite a few of the young people had settled down on the stairs and the upstairs landing. And everywhere I went people kept on delaying me – saying what a great party it was and so on, and I had to keep stopping to chat. I even went into the bedrooms, to make sure he hadn't crashed out on one of the beds, unlikely as that seemed.'

'Did you ask people if they'd seen him, as you went around?' asked Thanet.

'No. What was the point? If he'd been there I'd have spotted him. I was sure I'd find him somewhere, talking to somebody. I just thought he'd probably got engrossed in a conversation and hadn't noticed how time was slipping away.'

'Max was like that if he was really interested in what someone was saying,' said Mrs Sylvester. 'Sort of intense.'

'Anyway,' said her husband, 'he was nowhere to be seen. The only place left to look was the kitchen and it was on way my back from there that I thought of the pool house – it's at the other end of the corridor which leads to the kitchen, you see. I didn't expect to find him there but as I got nearer the door I could see the key wasn't hanging on its hook, it was in the lock. And even when I switched the lights on in there, at first I thought the place was empty. I didn't go right in, there seemed no point, just glanced quickly around. But as you saw, the deep end is nearest to the door and the diving board obscures your view of the pool, so it was only as I swung around to turn away that I glimpsed something dark in the water. When I moved for a better view I saw that there was a body floating on the surface. I kicked off my shoes, tore off my jacket and dived straight in. I suppose I must have realised it was Max, but I wasn't sure until I got him out, and that was a real struggle, I can tell you. I don't know if you've ever tried to get a dead weight out of water, but in the deep end it is absolutely impossible – if you try to push it up on to the side you just go under. So I towed him to the shallow end and even then I had problems getting him up the steps, it was like heaving a couple of sacks of potatoes.'

'Ralph!' protested his wife.

'Sorry, darl, but that's the way it was. Anyway, I could see right away that he was dead, and it was hopeless, but I knew I mustn't take that for granted, I'd still have to make an effort to revive him. I also knew that every second counted, that I couldn't delay by going to fetch help. God, I was wishing I'd taken first-aid classes, I can tell you. I felt absolutely useless. I put him on his stomach for a few minutes first, tried to pump some water out of him, then rolled him over and tried to give him the kiss of life – to the best of my ability anyway. I'd only ever seen it done on television.' Sylvester shook his head, his face screwed up in distaste. 'Not an experience I would wish to repeat. But after a few minutes I could see I wasn't getting anywhere so I rushed back to the party, asking if anyone knew about resuscitation.' He shook his head again. 'I'm sorry. I can see now that this will make things difficult for you, but at the time . . .'

'A natural thing to do in the circumstances,' said

Thanet. 'I'd probably have done the same myself. So how many people went to see if they could help?'

'We all poured in,' said Mrs Sylvester. 'It was awful. Tess had hysterics, as you can imagine . . .'

'But nothing could be done,' said her husband heavily. 'So we got everyone back out as soon as we could. Then we rang the police.'

But by then irreparable damage would have been done as far as finding any useful scientific evidence was concerned, thought Thanet ruefully. Well, it was pointless to bemoan the fact. 'What time was it when you found the body?'

Sylvester rubbed his bald pate in a polishing movement while he worked it out. 'Around 10.30?'

'Right. Now, let me make sure I have this absolutely straight. Living in this house are the two of you and your daughter Tess. Anyone else?'

Thanet thought it an innocuous question but suddenly the atmosphere was strained again, the fear back in their eyes. The answer to his question was obviously yes, but neither of them responded.

'Is there?'

'We have a housekeeper,' said Mrs Sylvester. 'Barbara Mallis.'

'Yes, Barbara,' echoed her husband.

'She's been with you long?'

'Must be four years now,' said Sylvester. 'That's right, isn't it, darl?'

'Yes.'

'And a gardener, Ron Fielding,' said Sylvester. 'Though he's not exactly one of the household. He and his wife and daughter live in the bungalow near the gates.'

'And that's the lot?'

There was a brief silence. Sylvester's hand closed over

his wife's shoulder again and she put hers up to clutch at it, twisting her head to look at him. They exchanged a despairing glance. *We'll have to tell them.*

Thanet glanced at Lineham. The sergeant raised his eyebrows. *What now?*

'And there's our son, Carey,' said Sylvester at last, capitulating.

'Your son?' Thanet did not try to hide his surprise. Why no mention of him till now? Perhaps the lad was a late child, too young to attend the party? But if so, why all this reluctance? 'How old is he?'

'Twenty-eight,' said Sylvester with resignation. 'He's ill, so his nurse lives in the house too. Michael Roper.'

So why all the mystery? Thanet wondered. Unless it was an illness which the Sylvesters were reluctant to admit to, like AIDS. But if so, and the young man was ill enough to warrant a full-time nurse, this still didn't explain why they should be afraid, as opposed to embarrassed. Unless . . . Yes, that could be it. 'What, exactly, is wrong with your son?'

Mrs Sylvester bit her lip and her grip on her husband's hand tightened. Sylvester gave a resigned sigh. 'He's schizophrenic.'

Thanet had guessed correctly. 'I see.' And he did. This, then, was the root of the Sylvesters' fear: they were afraid that their son was responsible for Jeopard's death. Schizophrenics were notoriously unpredictable. They were not all violent or dangerous, by any means, but many were.

'How serious is his illness?' said Thanet, aware that the severity of this particular condition can vary enormously.

'Pretty serious,' said Sylvester. 'Carey doesn't go anywhere without Michael, and they spend quite a lot of time in his rooms. The doors are kept locked.'

28

'And tonight? Did they come to the party?'

Sylvester shook his head. 'We were afraid the noise and the numbers of people might be too much for Carey to cope with. They stayed upstairs.'

So what was the problem? It was time to bring the matter out into the open. 'Look, Mr Sylvester, Mrs Sylvester, it's been obvious to me ever since we started talking that you are both very worried about something and from your reluctance to tell me about him I imagine that you're afraid your son might be involved in Mr Jeopard's death. But if he was safely locked up in his room with his nurse . . .'

They stared at him and Thanet saw the tears begin to well up in Mrs Sylvester's eyes. Her lower lip began to tremble and then, suddenly, the vestiges of her control snapped and she began to weep, turning her head away and pressing her face into her husband's thigh.

Sylvester looked down helplessly at her and began to stroke her hair. 'Darl, don't,' he pleaded. 'I can't bear it. Don't!' Then he glanced at Thanet. 'Carey got out this evening,' he said, wearily, the words barely audible above the sounds of his wife's distress. 'And he's still missing.'

THREE

Thanet and Lineham exchanged a glance. *Not surprising they're worried!* 'I see,' said Thanet. 'How long has he been missing?'

Sylvester ran a hand over the top of his head. 'I'm not sure. Oh, I know that might sound crazy, but everything's been in such a turmoil since I found Max in the pool. I didn't even know Carey was missing until my wife told me, did I, darl?'

She shook her head.

'So when did you find out, Mrs Sylvester?'

'Shortly after Ralph went off to look for Max.'

'Can you be a little more precise? It could be important.'

She frowned, screwing up her face as she tried to work it out. 'Say, a quarter past ten?'

And Max Jeopard had died between twenty to ten and half-past, when Sylvester had found him. 'And who told you?'

'Michael, of course. His nurse. He was very upset, as you can imagine.' Now that the matter was out in the open Mrs Sylvester couldn't wait to unburden herself and the words came tumbling out. 'He and Carey had supper much earlier than us, about 7.30, in Carey's sitting room.

But about twenty to ten Carey said he'd like a cup of coffee, so Michael came down to fetch one. There was a lot of activity in the kitchen and he didn't want to get in the way so it took him a bit longer than usual to make it. When he got back upstairs he found the door unlocked and Carey gone.' Mrs Sylvester glanced at her husband. 'He thinks someone who'd had a drop too much must have been looking for the bathroom, turned the key without thinking it odd that the door was locked from the outside, realised he'd got the wrong room, but didn't relock the door again. And Carey . . .' Mrs Sylvester's tone became despairing. 'Well, Carey regards it as a sort of game, to escape whenever he can. He hates . . .' Her voice shook and the tears spilled over again. 'He really hates being locked in.' She shook her head. 'Oh God, you must think us absolute monsters, locking our own son up like that, but you have no idea, you can't imagine –'

'It's the bloody Government that's to blame!' exploded Sylvester. 'And their sodding Mental Health Act! Closing all the mental hospitals and dumping these sick people either on their families or on the streets! Community Care! It's a joke, a bloody joke, that's what it is, and a sick one, at that.'

Sylvester was well launched into what was obviously a long-held grievance and there was no stopping him. Not that Thanet particularly wanted to. He agreed with practically every word the man was saying. There was no doubt that in the past there had been cases where people had been wrongly locked away, sometimes for many, many years, but the Government had now gone too far the other way. Thanet had seen some of the pathetic creatures turfed out to fend for themselves, perhaps for the first time in their lives, and completely unable to cope. Only recently he'd come across the case of a man who had been supplied with money and a room of his own and who had been found virtually starving, having no idea how to budget or to prepare food for himself. Others either slept rough or persistently committed criminal offences in order to get themselves put in prison; incapable of organising themselves they were only too happy for others to do it for them. A roof over their heads, food on the table and a modicum of warmth was all they asked of life.

'They have no idea,' said Sylvester, 'they can't begin to realise what it's like to have a relative who has schizophrenia. I'd like to see Mrs oh-so-sweet Bottomley with all those statistics she reels off so pat trying to cope if *she* had a son or daughter who was a schizophrenic! We tried to manage by ourselves at first, didn't we, darl, but it was impossible. Marion was at the end of her tether, weren't you? So in the end we decided to get a full-time nurse to look after Carey. It still isn't easy, but at least now we can live something resembling a normal life and it's taken the pressure off Marion a bit. But we're lucky, we can afford to pay for a nurse. What about all those poor sods who can't, that's what I'd like to know?'

'I do understand . . .'

'Don't say you understand!' said Sylvester savagely. 'No one can understand, unless they've been through it themselves! No one! You can't begin to imagine what hell it was for Marion. She could never go out because she never knew what Carey would get up to if he was left alone. Once he slashed his wrists and she came home to find him bleeding to death on the kitchen table. Another time she found him unconscious. D'you know what he'd done? He'd stuck his tongue into an electric socket! His voices had told him to, he said! And what did the bloody doctors say? That we must make sure he took his medication! You try making a grown man take pills if he doesn't want to!'

'He hates taking them,' said Marion. 'Says they turn his mind inside out. But Michael seems to have the knack. Carey will accept things from him he won't accept from us.'

'If he's still missing, I assume someone is looking for him?' said Thanet.

'Yes. Michael is,' said Sylvester. 'And Ron. The gardener. They know most of the places he likes to hide. Fortunately he doesn't usually stray too far. But this time . . .' He glanced at his watch. 'Oh God, it's gone half past twelve. It's been more than two and a half hours now!'

No wonder Mrs Sylvester looked frantic, thought Thanet. What a disaster of an evening it had turned out to be for them. He stood up. 'You must be wanting to join the search. I'll arrange for some of my men to help you.'

Sylvester jumped up. 'No! He'll be frightened if . . . Oh, but then, I suppose . . .'

'I think it would be advisable,' said Thanet gently. 'But we'll be careful, I promise.' He glanced at Lineham. *Fix it, will you, Mike?* Lineham nodded and left the room.

Anxious to go, the Sylvesters were already at the door. Thanet raised his voice. 'Would you send Mrs Mallis in next, please?' In the course of her duties the housekeeper would have been better placed than anyone to have an overall view of what had gone on this evening.

Sylvester spoke over his shoulder. 'Right.'

While he waited, Thanet thought. Almost certainly, this was murder. But what had Jeopard been doing in the pool house? Had he arranged to meet someone there? Unlikely that he would have wandered in there alone. Thanet said so to Lineham who was soon back.

'I agree. He must have been meeting someone. But who?'

'I expect we'll find out sooner or later.'

'You didn't ask the Sylvesters why they didn't like him.'

'I was going to get around to that last of all. I thought if I asked early on they might clam up. Then when they dropped that minor bombshell . . .'

'Think their son did it, sir?'

'It's an easy conclusion to jump to. And for that reason I think we ought to be wary of doing so. It's not as though he's a homicidal maniac. How are the others getting on?'

'I put Bentley in charge of the search for Carey. Most of the guests have gone, there're just a few stragglers left and Wakeham is seeing to them.'

'Good.'

There was a knock at the door. Thanet raised his voice. 'Come in.' And then, to Lineham, 'You take this one, Mike.'

'OK.' Lineham stepped forward. 'Come in, Mrs Mallis. Sit down.' This time he leaned against the windowsill and Thanet sat on the arm of a chair.

It was interesting, Thanet thought, that Mrs Mallis chose to do likewise. She obviously didn't wish to confer a moral advantage by having to look up at them. Which perhaps meant that she had reason to be cautious. He folded his arms and studied her, remembering his initial impression that she was the 'lady' of the house. Yes, both clothes and jewellery were expensive, but if she had no family responsibilities there was no reason why she shouldn't indulge herself. She obviously cared a great deal about her appearance. Time, as well as money, had been spent on it. Her make-up was skilful and it must take hours to coax her hair into those deceptively casual tousled curls. There had been no mention of a Mr Mallis so she must be a widow or a divorcee – the latter, he guessed, noting again the impression of bad temper conveyed by a mouth which turned down at the corners, the calculating look with which she was watching Lineham. Perhaps he was being unfair. Perhaps life had treated her badly. She caught his eye and he smiled at her, disarmingly, he hoped, and was disconcerted when she responded by giving him a flirtatious glance and running her tongue slowly over her upper lip. Good grief! Did she think he was making a pass at her? Glancing at Lineham he was irritated to catch a glint of quickly suppressed amusement in the sergeant's eye.

'We think you might be in a unique position to help us, Mrs Mallis,' said Lineham.

Very neat, Mike. A hint of flattery should go down well here.

But she was wary. 'Oh?'

'You've had quite a bit of time to think about Mr Jeopard's death, and you'll understand that unless and until we can prove otherwise, we have to treat it as suspicious. In which case, whether it was deliberate or accidental, we must assume that someone here tonight was on bad terms with him. Now, you are in the position of being in the family, so to speak, but not one of them. We're hoping you'll be able to put us in the picture.'

'I've been asked to do many things in my time,' and again she flicked a glance at Thanet, 'but never before to be a police informant.' She smiled to take the sting out of her words.

It hadn't registered when she met them at the door, but her voice was husky, gravelly, almost. Thanet guessed she was a smoker and almost as if she had picked up what he was thinking she reached into a side pocket and pulled out a pack of cigarettes.

'D'you mind?'

Lineham would, Thanet knew, but the sergeant shook his head. 'Go ahead.'

She fished out a lighter – gold, by the look of it – and lit up, inhaling deeply. 'That's better.'

Lineham looked at the long plume of smoke curling towards him and Thanet could see the sergeant willing himself not to duck or wave it away.

'In a murder case we need all the help we can get,' Thanet said.

She drew on her cigarette, inhaled, blew out smoke again. 'I imagine the Sylvesters didn't say a word about Gerald Argent?'

'No,' said Lineham. 'Why?'

'They wouldn't. He's their blue-eyed boy. Until recently he was engaged to their daughter.'

'To Tess Sylvester?'

She nodded, looked around for an ashtray.

Lineham fetched one for her. 'So what happened?'

She tapped the ash off her cigarette before answering. 'Max was an old flame of Tess's, I believe, but he's been away a lot, travelling. He's a travel writer, I don't know if you knew that. Anyway, Tess and Gerald got engaged last autumn and they were planning to get married this summer. Then at Christmas Max comes back from a really long trip to South America. He'd been away about two years. When he found Tess was engaged he went all out to get her back from Gerald. And believe me, when I say all out, I mean all out – he positively showered her with flowers, presents, letters, the works. I should be so lucky! At first she wasn't having any but in the end she gave in, broke off with Gerald and got engaged to Max. Of course, you have to make wedding arrangements ages ahead these days, to book up the church, the reception and so on, so what does she do? Decide to use the ones she'd already made with Gerald, that's all! She was even going to use the same wedding dress – well, she was having it specially made, but even so it's a bit much, wouldn't you agree?'

Her attitude left a nasty taste in the mouth, thought Thanet. Where was her loyalty to her employers? Had the Sylvesters done something to set her against them? And if she didn't like it here, why stay? Competent housekeepers are at a premium these days.

'So, this Gerald,' said Lineham. 'Was he here tonight?'

'He was invited,' she said, stubbing out her cigarette. 'But he refused.' She paused, for effect. 'Originally, that is. He obviously changed his mind. Yes, he was here. But they weren't on speaking terms.'

'He and Max Jeopard, you mean?'

'That's right. In fact, I saw him deliberately snub Max.'

'What happened?'

'I wasn't right next to them, so I didn't hear what was said. But I saw Max speak to him and hold out his hand. Gerald didn't say a word, just turned away.'

'What did Max do?'

'Just shrugged and laughed it off. What else could he do?'

'Did you see either of them during the supper interval, before Mr Sylvester raised the alarm?'

'Not that I can recall. I was too busy collecting up dirty glasses to notice anyone, really.'

'Well, if you do remember, perhaps you could let us know.'

'There's more, if you're interested.'

'Please.' Lineham waved a hand. 'Go ahead.'

'Everyone will tell you that Max was a terrible flirt. The type who couldn't keep his hands off an attractive female.' Again that sideways glance from beneath her lashes at Thanet. 'You know what I mean?'

Was she implying Jeopard had made a pass at her?

'You're saying he was fooling around at his own engagement party?' said Lineham.

'I was moving around a lot, naturally, making sure that everything was running smoothly, and I saw him make a pass at least twice during the evening.'

'Was Tess around? Did she see him?'

'Once she did, certainly.'

'How did she react?'

'How d'you think? A face like thunder. But he got around her. He always could, I imagine. He had a lot of charm. But more to the point, I think his fun and games got him into some kind of trouble.'

'With the boyfriend of one of the girls he made a pass at?'

'No. With a woman. Unfortunately I didn't actually see what happened. I was in the next room, just heard this brief commotion, voices raised in anger, then an unmistakable sound.' She paused. She evidently enjoyed a little drama.

'Of?' said Lineham.

'Flesh meeting flesh,' she said with evident satisfaction. 'Then there was a brief silence before everyone started talking twice as loudly to cover up their embarrassment, if you know what I mean?'

'So what, exactly, had happened? Do you know?'

'Some woman had given the prospective bridegroom a good slap across the face, apparently. It took a while for the marks to fade.'

'So who was the woman?'

She shrugged. 'No idea. Someone he'd been playing around with, no doubt. Hell hath no fury and all that.'

She had nothing else to tell them for the moment and they let her go.

'Nice woman,' commented Lineham sarcastically.

'Ha, ha!'

'She certainly fancied you, sir!'

'You must curb that imagination of yours, Mike. More to the point, it looks as though –'

A knock at the door interrupted him. It was Bentley.

'Just to let you know we've found the Sylvester lad, sir.'

'Where was he?'

Bentley's mouth tugged down at the corners. 'In the dog kennel, with the dog.'

FOUR

'In the dog kennel!' echoed Lineham.

Bentley's face told them that this was no joke and Thanet experienced an uprush of sympathy for a fellow human being driven to take refuge in so unlikely a place. 'Think he had anything to do with Jeopard's death?'

Bentley shook his head. 'Impossible to tell. But he's pretty pathetic, I can tell you.'

'Where is he now?'

'His nurse has taken him up to his room.'

'What d'you think, John? D'you think we ought to interview him tonight?' Thanet trusted Bentley's judgement.

'To be honest, I shouldn't think there's much point. He's obviously in a bit of a state. By tomorrow he might have calmed down. And he's not going anywhere, is he?'

'We'll leave it then.' Thanet glanced at his watch. One-twenty-five. 'In fact, I think we'll call it a day.'

He got into his car carefully, conscious of his aching back, which always played up when he was tired. Lately it had been troubling him more and more and he had even begun to experience pain in his right hip. Over the years he had seen an orthopaedic specialist more than once and had undergone several courses of physiotherapy, but nothing had really worked. Lately, alarmed by the possibility that his back problem might now be affecting his hip, Joan had been urging him to see a chiropractor. Some people swore by them, she said. Tired of trying various treatments and convinced that nothing was going to do any good, Thanet had resisted. But Joan had refused to give up and finally he had been driven to make the fatal mistake of moving from outright refusal to argument.

'Do you realise just how many charlatans there are around? Anyone can put up a board and set up a practice as a chiropractor, did you know that?'

'Luke, for heaven's sake, I'm not a complete dimwit! Of course I know that! The simple answer is to make sure you find one that *is* registered.'

'There might not even be one, locally.'

They both knew that by now he was putting up only a token resistance. Joan had got out the yellow pages and plonked the book in front of him.

'"Let your fingers do the walking,"' she had quoted.

And so it was that, just to keep her quiet, he had capitulated. His first appointment was to be on Monday afternoon. Perhaps, he thought as he started the car, he would now be able to cry off, pleading pressure of work with this new case. No, there was no point. Once Joan made up her mind about something like this he might as well bow to the inevitable.

Next morning he ate a solitary breakfast and took Joan up a cup of tea before leaving for work.

She was awake. 'Oh, lovely, darling. Thank you.'

'I should have a lie-in if I were you.' Thanet sat down on the bed to be companionable for a few minutes.

'I'll see. What time did you get in? I didn't hear you.'

'A quarter to two.'

She gave a sympathetic groan. 'What did you think of Ben's little announcement last night?'

'Much the same as you, I imagine. We'll have to see what we can do to get him to change his mind.'

'The trouble is, you know what they're like at his age. Put up any opposition and it'll only make him more determined.'

'I know. We'll just have to be careful. But we must try, don't you agree?'

Joan sighed. 'There always seems to be some problem . . .'

'Bridget didn't ring last night?'

'No. I really am getting worried. She should have arrived in Adelaide by now.'

Bridget was travelling with the Experiment for International Living, an excellent organisation which arranges homestays for young people in most countries of the world, in the cause of international understanding. Bridget had heard about it through a friend. Thanet and Joan, alarmed at the idea of her travelling alone, had been happy to know that she would be moving from one family to another and that someone would be around to help her if she ran into difficulties. So far the trip had gone smoothly. Each time she arrived in a new place she had made a brief phone call to tell them of her arrival. She had stayed in both North and South Islands in New Zealand and was now in Australia. The day before yesterday she should have arrived in Adelaide but so far there had been no word. Fearsome stories of young women raped, mugged or even murdered in Australia during recent years had constantly been in Thanet and Joan's minds and now, once again, they tried to reassure each other by suggesting all the possible reasons for the delay. Finally Thanet glanced at his watch. 'Sorry, love. I really must go.'

Joan put up her face for his kiss. 'Hope it goes well today.' She knew how hectic the first full day of a new case could be.

Outside it was a beautiful day, warm and sunny, the clouds of blossom on the spring-flowering trees lighting up the quiet Sunday-morning streets. Thanet put behind him regrets that he couldn't spend the day with Joan and began to plan his priorities. By the time he reached the office he had them clear in his mind.

Lineham was already engrossed in reports of interviews with last night's party guests. He waved a sheaf at Thanet. 'Bentley and Wakeham must have sat up half the night to do these.'

'I thought I told them to go home!'

'You know what they're like.'

Thanet did: Bentley reliable and conscientious, Wakeham as keen as mustard. He shouldn't be surprised, really. 'Anything interesting?'

'Couple of things. You know what the housekeeper said about Jeopard being slapped on the face? That was a girl called Anthea Greenway, apparently. I was wondering ... Wasn't the girl Mr Sylvester sent up to sit with his daughter called Anthea?'

'Yes, she was. The one in the Chinese outfit. She and Tess have known each other for years, he said. Does anyone know why she slapped Jeopard?'

'Not what actually precipitated it. But it seems to be common knowledge that she was his girlfriend at one time.'

Thanet frowned. 'I wonder when. According to the housekeeper, it was Tess he used to go out with before he went to South America and Tess he made a dead set at when he came back at Christmas.'

'She certainly gave the impression that he launched straight into trying to get Tess back from Argent. So if it's true he used to go out with Anthea it must have been before he left.'

'But in that case . . . A bit odd, isn't it, Mike? Not only that she should still be angry with him, after so long, but that she should have saved up demonstrating it until his engagement party?'

'No use expecting logic where women are concerned. More to the point, I wonder if she was angry enough to have shoved him into the swimming pool later on.'

'He'd hardly agree to meet her after she slapped his face, surely. But I agree, it'll have to be looked into. Anything else?'

'A couple of people mention him making passes at other women, like the housekeeper said.'

'Any jealous boyfriends or husbands hovering in the background?'

'If there were, nobody's saying so.'

'That it, then?' Lineham had a tendency always to save the best news to last and Thanet suspected that the glint in the sergeant's eye denoted an interesting titbit yet to come.

'At least three people mention the fact that around nineish a note was handed to Jeopard. He glanced at it, then shoved it in his pocket.' Lineham made the statement with an air of triumph, like a dog laying a particularly juicy bone at his master's feet.

'Really? Now that *is* interesting. An assignation, you think? Meet me in the pool house during the supper interval, that sort of thing?'

'Highly likely, I should think.'

44

'We didn't find any note in his pockets, did we?'

Lineham shook his head.

'So what became of it, I wonder. Who delivered it?'

'One of the waitresses.'

Thanet glanced at his watch. Time for the specially called morning meeting. 'Get Wakeham to try and track her down, will you, find out who gave it to her. And get him to double-check Jeopard's clothes, make sure that it wasn't in any of his pockets. I suppose it's possible that we could have missed it. It might have been soaked and stuck to the lining. Anything else I need to know before I go down?'

'Only that accounts of Jeopard's movements at supper agree, so far as we can tell, with what the Sylvesters told us. Several people saw him wheel his mother to their table, then leave her. Tess followed him.'

'Did she, now? Let's hope she's recovered enough to talk this morning. We'll go out there after seeing the Jeopards, as arranged.'

Downstairs he followed the usual routine. Arriving outside Draco's door two minutes ahead of time he waited for his long-time friend and colleague Inspector Boon of the uniformed branch to join him, glad that Boon was on duty this weekend. Draco was a stickler for punctuality and recently Thanet and Boon had evolved their own little ritual to lighten their day. It was childish, they knew, but they both enjoyed it.

Boon joined him and they stood with wristwatches poised. A glance around to make sure that no one was watching and at ten seconds before one minute to, they began to chant quietly, in unison, 'Ten, nine, eight, seven, six, five, four, three, two, one . . .'

It was Boon's turn to open the door and he did so, bowing Thanet in ahead of him.

The ritual continued, though Draco was unaware that he was participating. Seated behind a desk which was a model of order and implied efficiency he glanced at the clock to check that they were not late, cleared his throat and said, 'Ah, Thanet, Boon, just in time,' and waved at them to sit down. He made a minute adjustment to the position of the pen on the blotter in front of him and sat back. 'If you're ready, then, Thanet?'

The morning meeting, one of many reforms introduced by Draco when he arrived several years ago, was an exercise designed to keep him in touch with everything that was going on in his subdivision and to ensure that each section knew what the others were up to. In Draco's view, good communications were of fundamental importance and Thanet had to concede that, as usual, the Superintendent was right. To begin with everyone had grumbled at the fiery little Welshman's crusade for greater efficiency but before long they were admitting that it had paid off. Morale had improved and the crime detection rate had shown a marked increase. At times the Superintendent had driven his staff to distraction but gradually his idiosyncracies had come to be regarded with an indulgent amusement and his staff had grown to respect him, become fond of him, even. They had all watched with dismay as Draco, who adored his wife, had struggled to keep his spirits up during her lengthy fight against leukaemia, and had rejoiced with him when, little by little, the tide had turned in her favour. Now it was hard to believe that the man who sat behind the desk, black eyes glittering like new-cut anthracite, body tense with suppressed energy, could ever have been so demoralised as to have barely been able to display even a minimal interest in his work.

He listened carefully to Thanet's report and as usual

Thanet was aware that the intensity of Draco's interest was forcing him to express himself as clearly and grammatically as possible, to present the facts as succinctly and comprehensively as he could. There was something about the man that made you want to meet the rigorous standards he imposed.

A few pertinent questions when Thanet had finished and then, 'Sylvester . . .' Draco mused. 'Sounds familiar.'

Thanet was tempted to say, 'Victor?', but restrained himself. If Draco had a failing it was that he lacked a sense of humour where work was concerned.

'Motorway construction!' said Boon triumphantly.

Draco snapped his fingers. 'That's right! On the trucks and diggers.'

'Probably has a plant-hire business,' Boon added.

'Something like that, I imagine,' said Draco. 'Right, well, I think that's it for today. We'll look forward to hearing how things develop, Thanet. Sounds as though it's the sort of thing that's right up your street.'

As they left the room he had already picked up a piece of paper from his in-tray and was reaching for the phone.

'What did he mean by that?' said Thanet to Boon when they were outside.

'Right up your street, you mean? Messy, I should think.' Boon's hands described knots in the air. 'Tangled family relationships.'

And Draco was right, of course, thought Thanet as he hurried back up to his office. As usual.

Lineham had got everything organised in his absence and was ready to leave. It was a pleasure, outside, to drive through empty streets instead of sitting in the traffic jams which invariably built up in Sturrenden during the week.

'Hope you hadn't planned anything special with the

children today,' said Thanet as they passed a family piling into an ancient Vauxhall which looked as though it might just make it to the end of the road.

'Not really. We were going to the in-laws for lunch, that's all. Louise'll still take the kids.'

'Talking about Richard, how did you get on at that demonstration on Friday evening?'

Lineham's son Richard was now a bright, lively nine-year-old. A couple of years ago, after considerable learning and behavioural difficulties at school, he had been diagnosed dyslexic. When the problem had been identified Lineham and Louise had had high hopes that now, at last, something could be done to deal with it. The difficulty was that although, theoretically, help was available, in practice specialist teachers were so thin on the ground that Richard had been receiving only twenty minutes special tuition a week. Consequently he had fallen further and further behind in his schoolwork and had become more and more convinced that he was incapable of learning. Lineham and Louise had made every possible effort on his behalf, but had got nowhere. Recently, however, Louise had read an article about the Denner system, a computer-based teaching method which was said to achieve astonishing results. On Friday the Linehams had gone to a demonstration in Folkestone.

Lineham's face lit up. 'Of course, I haven't had a chance to tell you. It was fantastic!'

'Really? You think it might be of some use?'

'Oh, definitely. In fact, Louise was so impressed – well, we both were, but this will show you how keen she was – she's thinking of doing a course and setting up a unit.'

'So what was so impressive about it?'

'The results it achieves! They claim – and there's loads of documentary evidence from delighted parents that the system really does work – they claim that on average a young pupil will catch up three to four months for every one month of study and once he has finished the course he doesn't slip back but keeps pace with his class!'

'That sounds amazing! So how does it work?'

'Well, the children work alone with a talking computer, using multi-sensory principles – touch, sight and hearing are all involved. They talk into a microphone, a voice answers, and they learn to touch-type commands. The software is individually designed for each pupil. Once they are happy about spelling – which sounds absolutely astounding, doesn't it? Imagine Richard, happy about spelling! Anyway, the claim is that their confidence then spills over into using a pen. Honestly, sir, for the first time we really do feel there's a ray of hope!'

'No snags?'

'Well, there is one – the cost. The Denners have set up a centre in Devon, but across the country the way the system works is to set up small units which have to be individually funded – you have to buy the computer and the software, for a start. We're hoping to get together with some of the other parents to set one up but if we can't, as I say, Louise is seriously considering doing it herself. It would be worth it, to be able to help Richard after all this time, and we're sure people will be clamouring to use it once the good news gets around.'

'I'm delighted, Mike, I really am.' If this system really worked, as it apparently did, it would be a major advance in an area which until now had proved an intractable problem for hundreds of thousands of frustrated parents and children.

'It just goes to show you should never give up, doesn't it?' said Lineham. 'We almost had, you know.'

'Do parents ever?' said Thanet.

The Jeopards lived a mile or so beyond Donnington and Thanet and Lineham were out in the countryside now, driving through lanes where a haze of green was misting the hawthorn hedges and young lambs bounced about as if on trampolines. At times like this Thanet wondered why on earth he lived in the town.

Suddenly trees closed in on either side and a stone wall appeared on the left. Lineham was peering ahead. 'This is it, I think. The entrance is just along here, I've passed it before. Ah, yes. Here we are.'

He signalled and turned in between two tall stone pillars linked by a stone archway. Inside the drive swung sharply to the left and Lineham drew up in a gravelled parking area in front of an ancient wooden barn which was obviously used as a garage; the tall doors were open and there were a couple of cars parked inside, a newish Volkswagen Golf and an F-registration Vauxhall Astra.

'I expect the Golf is Hartley Jeopard's,' said Lineham as they got out. He was always interested in cars. 'And the Vauxhall is probably his aunt's.'

They walked back to the path which led up to the front door, a wide path of massive stone slabs flanked by narrow beds which in summer were no doubt ablaze with colour. Halfway along they paused to admire the beauty of the old house which slumbered before them, its Tudor façade of ancient beams, leaded windows and cream-washed plaster complacent in the spring sunshine. The place had a very different atmosphere from the Sylvesters' house – old money as opposed to new. Thanet wondered what Mrs Jeopard had thought of her son's proposed marriage.

Lineham inhaled deeply as they approached the massive front door, as if he could smell the affluence in the air. 'Oh yes, ve-ry nice,' he said.

There was no doorbell, only a heavy cast-iron knocker in the form of a twisted rope. Lineham let it drop twice, the sound unnaturally loud in the hush which lay over both house and garden.

'Should be someone in,' he muttered, 'with two cars in the garage.' He knocked again.

At last brisk footsteps could be heard approaching and the door opened.

'Ah, Inspector.' Hartley Jeopard loomed over them, a mournful heron in jeans and sweatshirt. 'Good morning.' He stepped back. 'Come in.'

FIVE

Inside the house it was cool and dark after the warmth and brightness outside and it took a few moments for Thanet's eyes to adjust. They were in a broad stone-flagged passage and Hartley led them through a door on the left into a square, spacious hall which stretched right up into the exposed roof rafters. A staircase led up to a railed gallery which ran around three sides at first-floor level. Heavy linen curtains in a jacobean design hung at the windows and there were comfortable chairs and sofas and a couple of really beautiful pieces of antique oak furniture glowing with the patina of centuries of polishing. The wide oak floorboards were bare of either rugs or carpet, Thanet noticed, probably to facilitate the movement of Mrs Jeopard's wheelchair.

Hartley waved them into armchairs but remained standing. 'Sorry I had to duck out last night, but I felt I really had to get my mother home.'

'We quite understood. How is she this morning?'

'Pretty well devastated, as you might imagine. And she looks very tired, I don't think she slept too well. But she's bearing up. She's always been fairly tough. Anyway, she insists that if you want to see her, you can.' He raised his eyebrows.

Thanet nodded. 'We would like to, if she's up to it.'

'Right. I'll just go and make sure she knows you're here. Do sit down.' He left the room through a door beneath the gallery.

'I imagine her room's on the ground floor,' said Lineham. 'It'd be difficult to install a lift in a house like this.'

In a minute or two Hartley was back and this time he sat down too, stretching out his long legs and steepling his fingers beneath his chin. 'I'm afraid she'll be at least another twenty minutes or so yet.'

'Fine,' said Thanet. 'Meanwhile, is there anything you can tell us about the party last night which might help us?'

'Such as?'

'Anything at all. Did you, for instance, notice any unusual incident involving your brother? Any quarrel or disagreement?'

There was something, obviously. The expression in Hartley's eyes had immediately become guarded and he lowered his hands and looked down at them, began to massage one thumb with the other. Then he glanced up. 'Do I gather that you have decided my brother's death was not an accident?'

'It's very difficult to see how it could have been. So at the moment, yes, we have to treat the death as suspicious.'

'You mean . . . murder.' He blurted the word out as indeed most people do, when referring to the death of someone close to them. It is incredibly difficult to relate such an appalling crime to a husband, wife, brother, sister, or child, and putting it into words is a stumbling block which many find impossible.

Thanet nodded. 'I'm sorry.'

Hartley was shaking his head. 'It's all right. We – my

mother, my aunt and I – have already discussed this. And we agreed it was extremely unlikely that it could have been an accident. Even if he had fallen in, he could swim like a fish, did you know that?'

'Yes. Mr Sylvester told us.'

'I suppose there is just the remotest possibility that he could have slipped, or tripped, banging his head and knocking himself out as he fell in, but we all thought it extremely unlikely. It wasn't as though he was drunk, and there was nothing to trip over, or to slip on, for that matter. And what was he doing in the pool house in the first place? That's what we'd like to know.'

'And so would we,' said Thanet. 'In fact, these are all questions we are asking ourselves. Which is why I'm also asking if you noticed your brother having any argument or disagreement with anyone last night.'

Once again Hartley's eyes fell away from Thanet's, and again he failed to respond. He obviously wasn't going to volunteer the information.

'For instance, we understand there was an incident involving a friend of Miss Sylvester, a Miss Greenway,' said Thanet.

Hartley sighed and pulled a face. 'I suppose it was unrealistic to suppose you wouldn't hear about that. Yes, it's true. I wasn't going to say anything because I genuinely do not believe that Anthea – Anthea Greenway – could possibly have had anything to do with Max's death.'

'She slapped his face, I understand. In public.'

Hartley nodded.

'Why, do you know?'

A shake of the head this time. 'No. I was across the other side of the room.'

'She used to go out with your brother, I understand.'

A flash of fierce emotion, so quickly suppressed that Thanet might almost have imagined it. But he hadn't, he was sure.

'That was years ago!'

'When, exactly? Can you remember?'

'The summer of '92, as I recall.'

The answer had come immediately, which was astonishing. How many people have precise and instant recall of dates, especially if they are two or three years ago? Unless, of course, they have a personal reason for remembering. By now Thanet had a strong suspicion that Hartley was keen on Anthea himself.

'Before your brother went away on his last trip, in fact?'

'That's right. He came home in May of that year, for the publication of his first book. And he went away again in October.'

Hartley's tone was neutral but again Thanet had the feeling that he was keeping his real emotions well out of sight. 'I see.'

Max, Thanet learned, had always had itchy feet, ever since, in his gap year between school and university, he had spent the time back-packing alone around the Far East – chiefly in Thailand.

'Before he went away he was like the rest of us – didn't have a clue what he wanted to do for a living. It was more or less taken for granted that if we could get into university we'd go, but Max was determined to do some travelling first. And by the time he came back he'd made up his mind he wanted to be a travel writer. He was all for throwing in his place at Oxford but Ma somehow managed to talk him around, God knows how. Probably by offering to finance more travel during the vacations and even afterwards, for all I know. Anyway, he was always taking off somewhere and the minute he finished at university he left for China, this time with the specific purpose of gathering material for a book. He was dead lucky in a way, in that he arrived there at a very interesting time, in the aftermath of the Tiananmen Square massacre.'

'That would have been in – let me see – 1989, then?'

'That's right. The Western world was very keen to find out what was going on over there and don't ask me how, but Max managed to interest one of the national dailies in what he had to say. Before we knew where we were we were reading his reports over our toast and marmalade. They were very good, really gave you the feel of what it was like to be caught up in it all, and more importantly for him, they got his name known. As a result, he managed to interest a publisher in his book well before he'd even finished writing it.'

'How long was he away?'

'Almost eighteen months. He got back a few weeks before Christmas the following year, and spent the rest of the winter holed up here, writing.'

'As a matter of interest, what was the book called?'

'*Peephole into China*.'

Thanet made a mental note to try and get hold of it. Books reveal much about their writers and travel books more than most, relying as they do on the author's quirks, attitudes and viewpoint to give them their individuality. 'Was it successful?'

'Oh yes, very. Astonishingly so.'

'Enough to buy him a flat in London, I assume? That's where he now lived, I understand.'

'Yes. But the flat was actually bought with money Max inherited from Dad. It had been held in trust until he was twenty-five.'

And the same applied to Hartley, Thanet discovered. He worked as an accountant with a firm in the city, but often came down to Kent at weekends.

Max, he learned, had finished the book in June '91 and almost at once was off on his travels again, this time to South America, returning for its publication the following May.

'That was presumably when he started going out with Miss Greenway?'

Again the shutter came down. 'That's right.'

Thanet probed a little deeper. 'Was this a long-running affair? Had he been out with her before?'

'Oh no. Until then it had always been Tess. But she got fed up with him always taking off at every possible opportunity.'

'So on this occasion, the summer of '92, when he came home Miss Jeopard didn't want to have anything to do with him?'

Hartley was shaking his head. 'She was away herself, then. I imagine she thought it might teach him a lesson, if she wasn't always here waiting for him every time he came back.'

'Where was she?'

'In the States, I believe. Look, Inspector, I'm sure you know what you're doing, but is all this relevant? What possible connection can there be between Tess's trip to the United States and Max's death?'

'I'm not saying there is one. But one thing that experience has taught me is that you can never judge any piece of information irrelevant until the case is over. You simply never know what is going to prove significant and what is not, and you therefore have to try and gather in as much as you possibly can. As his brother you must know more about his life than most and know him better personally, too. So bear with me, will you?'

Hartley shrugged. 'If it'll help.'

'Anyway, perhaps we could now go back to the party last night. I believe there are some questions Sergeant Lineham wants to ask you about that.'

This was prearranged and Lineham took over smoothly. 'It's merely a question of trying to place people, sir. You'll appreciate that with so many guests present it's rather difficult to get a clear picture of who was where and when. Now so far the last sighting we have of your brother is at twenty to ten. Apparently he and Tess settled your mother and aunt at their table and then went back for their own food. That was the last anyone saw of him. According to Tess he said he was going to the toilet. Did you see him after that, by any chance?'

Hartley was shaking his head. 'I'm afraid not.'

'You weren't sitting at the family table?'

'No. It was just Tess, Max and the parents. My aunt was included, of course, but I had supper with Anthea and another friend of ours.'

'Would that have been Mr Gerald Argent, by any chance?' asked Lineham innocently. 'Miss Sylvester's former fiancé?'

A gleam of reluctant admiration appeared in Hartley's eyes. 'You don't waste much time, do you? Yes, that's right.'

An uncomfortable trio, thought Thanet. If he was right, they had a lot in common: unrequited love – Hartley carrying a torch for Anthea Greenway, Gerald for Tess and Anthea herself perhaps for Max. Very interesting.

'So you all queued up together, collected your food and sat down to eat it?'

Hartley shifted uncomfortably. 'More or less.'

Lineham raised his eyebrows.

'While we were queuing Anthea went off to the loo.'

'How long was she away?'

He raised his shoulders. 'I wasn't timing her, Sergeant!'

'Approximately, then?'

'Gerald and I were halfway through our first course when she joined us, so it must have been, let me see, about ten o'clock.'

'And she had left at . . .?'

'Around twenty to, I suppose. She said she'd had to queue for the loo. And she'd had to collect her supper too, of course.'

'But you and Mr Argent stayed together?'

'Well no, not for the whole time. I went off to the loo as well.'

A general exodus, thought Thanet. But understandable. Everyone stands around talking and drinking, not wanting to break up conversations, and then supper is announced, people queue up and some of them, seeing that they'll have to wait to collect their food, decide to go to the lavatory – where they also find queues, of course.

'And what time did you rejoin Mr Argent?' said Lineham.

'Ten minutes later, or thereabouts.'

'Around five to ten, then?'

Hartley nodded.

'And you're sure you didn't see your brother? That was where he said he was going, too, at around the same time.'

'No. I told you.' A hint of impatience there. 'He may have gone to a different one.'

'So in fact, at suppertime each of the three of you was alone for at least ten minutes, longer in the case of Miss

Greenway?' *At around the time your brother disappeared.*
The words hung on the air, unspoken but implicit in
what Lineham was saying.

Hartley sat up with a jerk and a quick, sideways glance
at Thanet. 'Hang on a minute. What, exactly, are you
implying, Sergeant?'

'I'm simply trying to get the facts straight, sir.'

'Oh come on! I'm not an idiot, you know! You're
saying you suspect one of us, aren't you?'

'Not at all. We don't suspect anyone at this point.
That's right, sir, isn't it?' Lineham glanced at Thanet.

Thanet nodded. 'Much too soon.'

It was clear that Hartley didn't believe them. 'Well, to
answer your question, each of us was alone in the sense
that we weren't with the other two, but each of us was
emphatically not alone in the literal sense of the word.
I'm sure that when you check you'll be able to find other
people who can vouch for us.'

Lineham nodded, as if to accept this statement at its
face value. 'To go back a little, did you by any chance see
anyone hand a note to your brother, earlier in the
evening?'

'Definitely not.'

'Have you any idea what it could have been about?'

'Not the faintest, I'm afraid.'

'Just one more question then, Mr Argent. How upset
was he when Miss Sylvester broke off their engagement
and became engaged to your brother instead?'

Thanet noticed that the door to Mrs Jeopard's quarters
was opening. Hartley, seated with his back to it and
intent upon the conversation, remained unaware.

'Well a bit upset, naturally. You don't ask a girl to
marry you unless you're in love with her. But if you're
suggesting Gerald could have had anything to do with

Max's death, you're out of your mind. He wouldn't hurt a fly!'

'You're being ridiculously naïve, as usual, dear.' The incisive voice sliced into the conversation.

This was a very different woman from the pathetic figure in the wheelchair last night. This morning Mrs Jeopard's back was ramrod straight and she had armoured herself against the world's pity in an elegant black silk dress. She was immaculately groomed, her greying hair framing her face in soft curls, her make-up discreet, her long, delicately-boned hands heavy with rings. Last night Thanet had put her in her early seventies but today he saw that she was considerably younger – mid-sixties, perhaps. He wondered what illness or accident had put her in a wheelchair.

Her sister was also dressed in black, though less expensively. They were really very alike, he realised, and wondered which was the older. It was difficult to tell. He soon found out.

Mrs Jeopard held out her hand. 'I don't believe we were properly introduced last night, Inspector. I am Eleanor Jeopard and this is my twin sister Louisa Burke.'

Non-identical twins, obviously, thought Thanet as he responded. Even seated it was evident that Mrs Jeopard was much the shorter of the two.

'I'm afraid you have to take everything my son says about Gerald Argent with a pinch of salt.' Mrs Jeopard gave Hartley what could only be described as a frosty smile. 'They're practically inseparable. "A bit upset", indeed! The fact of the matter is, Gerald has always been a fool over that girl. He couldn't believe his luck when she actually agreed to marry him so you can imagine how he felt when she threw him over.'

SIX

Hartley was driven to protest. 'Mother, really! You simply cannot go around saying things like that!'

'Why not, if they're true?' She turned her cool blue gaze upon Thanet. 'I assume you have come to the conclusion that my son's death was no accident?'

'Well, I . . .'

'I agree, there is no other possible explanation. Louisa, do stop hovering and sit down. I can't think with you looming over me like that!'

Louisa sat.

No doubt about who was in control in this house, thought Thanet.

Mrs Jeopard fastened her attention upon him again. 'There's no doubt in my mind. Someone must have pushed him in deliberately. Probably hit him over the head first. In fact, they must have done, or he'd have managed to get out. I'm sure that's what you'll find, when you do the post . . . post-mortem.' For the first time there was a tremor in her voice, but she recovered immediately. 'So naturally I have spent most of the night thinking who it could be. I assume you'd like to hear my conclusions?'

'Yes, of –'

'The trouble is, Inspector, everyone was jealous of Max, weren't they, Louisa?' The merest flick of a glance in Hartley's direction hinted – perhaps unconsciously, Thanet thought – that even her other son was not excluded from this accusation. 'He had everything, you see. He was handsome, intelligent, athletic, and creative, too, a most gifted writer. Have you read his book?'

'No, but –'

'I brought this for you.' Draped across her knees was a mohair travelling rug in a beautiful range of blues and greens and now she put one hand beneath it and pulled out a paperback, held it out to Thanet. *Peephole into China.* 'More than anything it will show you the sort of man he was.'

Thanet took it from her. 'Thank you.' The jacket design was striking, a typical two-dimensional Chinese landscape of high rounded mountains, misty gorges and stylised trees, glimpsed through a huge keyhole. He turned it over and Max Jeopard's face grinned up at him, assured, confident of his charm and ability to cope with any and every situation. Perhaps on that last, fatal occasion it was over-confidence that had brought about his downfall. Perhaps he had made the mistake of underestimating the strength and determination of someone known to him but to whom he had felt superior.

Mrs Jeopard was watching him and now she gave a nod, as if satisfied that Thanet's interest was sufficiently aroused for him to follow her instructions.

'That girl, of course, was besotted with him.'

'Miss Sylvester?' Thanet wondered how Mr Sylvester would have felt at hearing his daughter referred to as 'that girl'.

'Yes. We always knew it would never work with Gerald, didn't we, Louisa?' Once again Mrs Jeopard did not wait for a reply, apparently taking her sister's agreement for granted. She cast a scornful glance at Hartley, as if he, not his friend, had been the inferior suitor. 'We knew that if Max came back before they were actually married, she'd leave Gerald like a shot. I prayed he wouldn't, I can tell you.'

'You didn't approve of your son marrying Miss Sylvester?'

'I most certainly did not!'

Louisa Burke had made an involuntary movement of protest and now Eleanor Jeopard snapped, 'Oh, for heaven's sake, Louisa, why bother to pretend any more? You see, Inspector, while Max was . . . There was no point in opposing Max's wishes. He was such a determined person he always got what he wanted in the end and I'm afraid that what he wanted was Tess. The trouble was, she couldn't accept that she had to come second, after his work. She got tired of him going off on his travels. I think she thought it was pure self-indulgence on his part. She seemed incapable of understanding that if he didn't have the material to write about he couldn't make a living! She wanted first and exclusive rights in him and Max felt he absolutely could not be tied down like that.'

'Was that your only reason for disapproving of her?'

'Not at all. My reasons, as one might say, were many and various.'

'Mother, really! How do you think Tess would feel if she could hear you talking about her like this?'

'To be honest, I don't care a jot what Tess feels.'

'I thought you liked her,' said Hartley. 'You always made her welcome and –'

'Hartley. I sometimes think you're an even greater ninny than you look. Of course I made her welcome. She

64

was Max's choice, wasn't she, and I accepted her for his sake. If I hadn't, it would have driven him away, can't you see that?'

Hartley jumped out of his seat and stood looking out of the window, jingling the change in his pocket, his frustration revealed in hunched shoulders and rigidity of stance.

Thanet wondered what it must have been like for him, being Max's younger brother, probably overshadowed at school, always second in his mother's affections.

'But really, dear,' Mrs Jeopard's tone had changed. Now she was trying to coax him into agreement. 'You must admit the Sylvesters are not exactly our sort of people.' Somehow she embued the words with capital letters.

Hartley swung around. 'In your view, very few people are.'

'Well, even you will agree that it's not exactly a promising prospect, to know your son is marrying a girl with a brother who is insane!' Mrs Jeopard switched her attention to Thanet again. 'You have heard about him, I suppose, Inspector?'

'Yes, Mr Syl –'

'And they did tell you he was actually on the loose last night?' Mrs Jeopard twitched angrily at the rug on her knees. 'How irresponsible can you get?'

Thanet wondered if he would ever be allowed to finish a sentence. He was running out of patience. He caught the glint of amusement in Lineham's eye and decided that the time had come for him to assert himself.

He opened his mouth to speak but Hartley got in first. 'Mother, they did explain that it was one of the guests who –'

'I don't care what they explained, the fact remains that

Carey was roaming about last night and he's always been jealous of Max, as you very well know. He was furious when Max got into Oxford and he didn't. And he resented the fact that Max had so often made Tess miserable by going off on his travels again. He was always trying to persuade her to break away from him. You told me that yourself, years ago.'

Right, thought Thanet. He cut in, quickly. 'Do I gather that Carey Sylvester has only recently become schizophrenic?'

Mrs Jeopard was about to reply but this time Hartley pre-empted her, returning to his seat as if to re-establish his right to participate in the conversation. 'Carey was fine until halfway through his second year at university. He was taking a degree in Urban Land Management at Reading. Then suddenly he just . . . fell apart.'

Mrs Jeopard didn't like being ousted from centre stage. 'He went into a mental hospital for six months or so and he's been in and out of them ever since. Until that absurd Mental Health Act, in fact, when he was forced to stay out permanently. I don't know what the Government was thinking of, turning all those madmen out into the streets. Really, it's enough to make one think of resigning from the Conservative Party!'

'The Sylvesters,' said Hartley with a reproachful glance at his mother, 'have had a rotten time of it. In the end they hired a nurse for Carey. And I think it's downright unkind of you, Mother, to call them irresponsible. They've done everything they can to –'

'Maybe they have. But it still doesn't alter the fact that last night that maniac got out. Nor the fact that your brother was found dead in their swimming pool.'

'We don't know that there's any connection!'

'I'm not saying there is. I'm just saying that there's a

66

distinct possibility there might be! Anyway, that's not exactly what the Inspector was asking. He was asking for the reasons why I disapproved of Tess Sylvester as a wife for Max. And I'm simply saying that madness in the family was one, and one that I certainly consider valid, as I'm sure most people would. Have you got any children, Inspector?'

'Two,' said Thanet.

'Then I'm sure you'll know what I mean.'

And she was right, of course. But he wasn't going to give her the satisfaction of admitting it.

'And last but not least,' said Mrs Jeopard, 'I didn't like the idea of Max marrying a girl whose father didn't appreciate him.'

'In what way?' said Thanet.

She waved a vague hand. 'I suspect Ralph Sylvester didn't like the competition. That man absolutely dotes on Tess and he would, I'm sure, have preferred someone more . . . malleable, like Gerald, as a husband for her. Someone local, who wouldn't be liable to whisk her off to the other side of the world at the drop of a hat. Someone with a nice steady boring job who'd settle down a couple of miles away and present the Sylvesters with a couple of grandchildren in the not too distant future. Max was altogether too unpredictable, too unconventional for his taste.'

'Your son didn't get on with his prospective father-in-law?'

'It depends what you mean by get on. Louisa, do you mind? This cushion . . .'

Her sister sprang to adjust the offending article. So far she had not, Thanet realised, contributed a single syllable to the conversation, and was unlikely to have the opportunity to do so in the presence of Mrs Jeopard. He wondered how he could manoeuvre an opportunity to speak to her alone. In his experience the quiet ones often noticed far more than those who were too busy projecting their chosen image to be aware of the nuances of other people's behaviour.

'They obviously didn't get on in the sense of having much common ground or enjoying each other's company,' she went on. 'But if you're asking if there was any overt antagonism between them then no, there wasn't. Like me, Ralph Sylvester was making the best of a bad job. He didn't want to risk alienating his daughter by open disapproval. All the same, I'd be willing to wager that in private he'll be rubbing his hands together with glee this morning.'

Hartley was again driven to protest. 'Mother!'

'Don't "Mother!" me,' she said furiously. 'What is the point of pretending? Nothing will convince me that Ralph Sylvester isn't secretly delighted that Max is dead.'

Delighted enough to have helped him on his way was the implication.

From the moment she entered the room she had dominated the conversation but now, suddenly, her vitality seemed to fade away. That last spurt of anger seemed to have depleted her. The colour had drained out of her face and the skin of her forehead glistened. She produced a dainty lace-bordered handkerchief and dabbed at her upper lip. Hartley jumped up and bent over her solicitously. 'Mother . . . are you all right?'

For the first time she managed a faint smile, gave his arm a reassuring pat. 'Yes, of course, dear. Perhaps a glass of water . . .?'

He hurried off at her bidding. It was time to bring this interview to a close, thought Thanet. He wondered again what was the matter with her and wondered too how

68

much it had cost her, just how far she had had to draw upon her evidently meagre reserves, to give the performance they had just witnessed.

'Well, you've certainly given us food for thought, Mrs Jeopard,' he said. 'And if you could just bear with me for a few moments longer while I check one or two facts, we'll leave you in peace.'

She inclined her head. 'Of course.'

Hartley returned with a cut-glass tumbler of water and she took it, sipped from it gratefully before returning it to him. She verified that yes, she had last seen Max when he had escorted her to their table at about 9.40, and that it must have been around ten when Tess announced that she was going to look for him and Ralph Sylvester went instead. She had no knowledge, she said, of any note handed to Max earlier in the evening.

'One last question, then,' said Thanet. 'There was an incident before supper involving some kind of argument between your son and a friend of Tess Sylvester, Anthea Greenway. Do you know anything about that?'

When Anthea's name was mentioned there had been an immediate flicker of comprehension in her eyes, quickly suppressed. She shook her head. 'I'm afraid not,' she said.

No doubt about it, she was lying. But why? Whatever the reason, questioning her about it would have to wait. She was clearly exhausted. Thanet stood up and thanked her.

Louisa Burke rose also and spoke for the first time. 'I'll see you out.'

Thanet was pleased. The opportunity to speak to her alone had unexpectedly been handed to him on a plate.

SEVEN

Thanet suspected that there was something specific Louisa Burke wanted to say to him, but that she would be frightened off by too direct an approach. In the hall he said conversationally, 'Have you lived here long, Miss Burke?'

She plucked at her black cotton skirt, as if to gather up courage. 'Ever since my sister's marriage.'

'Beautiful house,' said Lineham, playing along.

'I don't actually live in the house. There's a little flat over the stables . . . It used to be the chauffeur's, in the days when people had chauffeurs. Eleanor's husband very kindly did it up for me. It's nice to be independent.'

Thanet wondered how much independence she actually had. 'Your sister is very fortunate, to have you to look after her.'

She gave an embarrassed little laugh, as if unused to compliments. 'I don't do it alone, you know. The district nurse comes in regularly to bathe her and of course we have help in the house.'

Thanet felt like telling her not to undervalue what she did. Eleanor Jeopard couldn't be the easiest of patients and there was little doubt that without her sister's help she would either have had to employ a full-time nurse or go into a nursing home. 'How long has your sister been' – how should he put it? – 'incapacitated?'

'Ever since the car crash in which her husband was killed, when Max was thirteen, so it must be . . . let me see . . . sixteen years now. Actually, that was what I wanted to say to you, Inspector. My sister . . . she's in constant pain, you know, and life is not easy for her. She was always such an active woman, with so many interests. So now, sometimes she . . . well, she tends to come across as much, well, harsher than she really is. I'm just saying that we have to make allowances for that in what she says.'

They had reached the front door now and they all stepped outside, automatically gravitating towards the sunshine.

Thanet paused, turning to face her. 'Are you saying that what she told us was a . . . shall we say an exaggeration of the truth?'

'Well, no, not exactly. It's just that I wouldn't want you to think less of her because she expressed her opinions so strongly. Max, you see, was always the apple of her eye. The only way she can begin to cope with what has happened is to turn her anger on to other people.'

'Yes, I do understand that.'

For the first time she met his gaze directly. 'Yes, I believe you do.' Already, her mission accomplished, she was turning back towards the house.

'Miss Burke . . .' He mustn't miss the opportunity. 'If I could just check one or two points?' But he learned nothing new and was interested to note that she, too, was reluctant to talk about the incident between Anthea Greenway and Max. She admitted having witnessed it from across the room.

'Do you know what might have prompted her to slap him across the face in public like that?'

She shifted uncomfortably from one foot to the other and glanced at the hall windows to her right. 'No idea. I'm sorry.'

Following her gaze Thanet saw that Mrs Jeopard had been watching them. She couldn't possibly hear what they were saying but Louisa Burke was behaving as if she could, edging unobtrusively back towards the haven of the front door. Reluctantly, he let her go.

'What was all that about?' said Lineham as they returned to the car.

'No idea.'

'I mean, why clam up about Anthea Greenway like that?'

'The only reason I can think of,' said Thanet as he got in and wound the window down, 'is that I suspect Hartley Jeopard is in love with Anthea and his mother is following the same policy as she did with Max, in trying not to alienate him by criticising his girl friend.'

'D'you think she might have been more open if he hadn't been there?' Lineham made a minute adjustment to the rear-view mirror before starting the car. He was somewhat obsessive about checking that everything was properly in order before moving off.

'I don't know. I doubt it, actually. I imagine family loyalty ranks pretty high with her and now that she's lost one son she's not going to risk losing the other.'

'You could have fooled me, the way she treated him! If you ask me she's an autocratic old so-and-so.' Lineham's own mother had always been something of a problem and his hackles invariably rose at the first signs of maternal domination.

'She did come over like that, I agree. But I'm not sure

how much of it was an act put on for our benefit. Or if, as her sister says, it's the only way she could cope. Didn't you notice how exhausted she was by the end of the interview?'

'Maybe. But if you ask me, there's no doubt who rules the roost. I felt sorry for the sister.'

'She can't have much of a life,' Thanet agreed.

They had reached the gates and Lineham leaned forward to check that the road was clear before moving out. 'Anyway,' he said, 'I suppose we're a bit further forward.'

'Depends what you mean by further forward. Our list of suspects is getting longer by the minute, true.'

'It certainly is! Gerald Argent sounds the most likely candidate, wouldn't you agree? He must have been really miffed at having Tess snatched away from him practically at the altar, especially if, as Mrs Jeopard claims, he's been mad about her for years. He's obviously still pretty fed up about it if, as the housekeeper told us, he originally refused the invitation to the engagement party. I wonder how she knew that, by the way.'

'I should think not much goes on in that house that she doesn't know.'

'Anyway, Gerald obviously changed his mind and went, but she did say that he deliberately snubbed Max. Not surprising, if you ask me. Did you notice, by the way, that Hartley was anxious to play down Gerald's involvement with Tess?'

'Yes. I'd guess that he and Gerald are pretty close friends.'

'But you agree, sir, that Gerald has a pretty strong motive?'

'So have a number of other people.'

'True. There's Hartley himself, for that matter. I

wouldn't mind betting that Max played the same trick on him as he did on Gerald, filching his girlfriend from under his nose. But for no better reason than that his own wasn't available at the time!'

'Possibly. Tess was away in the States, wasn't she?'

'That's what Hartley said. Anyway, it couldn't have been easy, having Max Jeopard as an older brother. I imagine he outshone Hartley at most things. And he was obviously his mother's favourite. I'd guess that's why Hartley is as he is.'

'Diffident, you mean?'

'Yes. Looking as though he's apologising for his exist-ence. And we all know how dangerous the quiet ones can be, how the worm can turn.'

'But if that is so, why wait until last night? If Hartley was going to snap over Max taking Anthea away from him, surely he'd have done that when it actually hap-pened? After all, Max has been away for a couple of years, until Christmas, in fact, and it sounds as though the minute he got home and found Tess engaged to Gerald Argent he went all out to get her back.'

'And I wonder how Anthea felt about that. I suppose we shouldn't rule her out, either. What if she'd been expecting him to take up where they left off, when he got home? And then he makes a dead set for Tess instead. It's interesting that both she and Max excused themselves from the people they were with at the same time, twenty to ten. D'you think they might have arranged to meet? That's a point, sir! That could be it!' Lineham flashed Thanet a delighted grin.

'Well? Go on!'

'I'm trying to think what time the face-slapping incident took place. Was it before or after nine o'clock, that's the point?'

'Ah. You mean that the note could have been from Anthea, apologising for the scene she made and begging him to meet her in the supper interval . . . to . . . what?'

'Apologise properly? And promising something, anything, so long as she could see him alone for a few moments.'

'Do you think he'd have gone along with that?'

'No idea. It's possible. If only to tell her that it was pointless to go on hoping he'd come back to her. Then she loses her temper, gives him a shove, he hits his head on something as he falls into the pool and she just walks out.'

'Leaving him to drown. When she's supposed to be in love with him?'

'It could have happened like that.'

'I agree. It could. But there's the same objection as there is to Hartley having done it. Why wait until now? If she were going to take any kind of revenge, surely it would have been at Christmas, when she found he wasn't coming back to her?'

'Oh, I don't know. She could have kept on hoping and hoping but then, when he finally got engaged . . . Anyway, you have to admit that to make that sort of scene in public she must still feel pretty strongly about him.'

'I suppose so. But let's face it, Mike. Some people enjoy making a spectacle of themselves, and Anthea looked a pretty colourful character to me.'

'You mean the way she was dressed?'

'It was fairly flamboyant, wouldn't you agree? In fact, I wouldn't have thought she was Hartley's type. I'd have thought he'd go for someone altogether quieter, more subdued. Still, all the signs are that he did, and if so then I agree, we have to consider him a suspect. Especially as I imagine he wouldn't exactly be the type to have a string of girlfriends, either. He'd be very much a one-woman man.'

'Unlike his brother! From what we've heard, Max just had to have a woman – any woman, in tow. And even when he had one he couldn't keep his hands off the others, by all accounts! If you ask me it's not surprising someone decided to clock him one and chuck him in the swimming pool! Oh all right, all right, sir, no need to look at me like that. I know murder can't be justified. But you must agree that occasionally it is at least understandable and from what we've heard about Max Jeopard . . . He sounds as selfish as they come, doesn't he? Never mind anyone else's feelings as long as his own were gratified. Imagine groping other women at your own engagement party! What must Tess have felt about that!'

'Quite. Or her father, for that matter.'

'You think it's true, what the old lady said about him being dead against the marriage?'

'It wouldn't surprise me. Sylvester and Max would have been chalk and cheese, I imagine. And I should think it's true that Sylvester would much prefer to have Tess settled locally, where they could see her regularly and be able to watch their grandchildren grow up. Of course, for all we know, Max and Tess were planning to settle in this area anyway, or at least to have a house here as a base. We must find out.'

They were both silent for a while, thinking. Then Thanet said, 'The fact of the matter is we're only just beginning to scratch the surface of this case, Mike. Let's find out a bit more about these people before we start trying to draw conclusions. Which reminds me, we mustn't forget that Max Jeopard actually spent most of his time – when he was in this country, that is – in London. There's too much to do today, but I think we'd better try and get up there to take a look at his flat. Tomorrow morning, perhaps.' They were approaching a pub and he glanced at his watch. Twelve-forty-five. 'Might as well pull in here for a bite to eat. Once we get to the Sylvesters' we'll be there for hours.'

The pub was quiet, the service swift, and three-quarters of an hour later they were turning once again into the Sylvesters' drive, just behind another car, a blue Nissan, which took the right fork, towards the bungalow.

'Perhaps we'll have a word with the gardener first,' said Thanet. 'What was his name? Fielding? He might have seen something last night.'

They parked in front of the main house alongside a sleek K-registration BMW convertible at which Lineham cast admiring glances. 'Wonder whose it is,' he said wistfully, running a hand along its bonnet.

'Sylvester's, I imagine. Or his wife's.'

'Or even Tess's. Must be nice to be able to afford to buy your daughter a car like that! They cost around £28,000 new, you know. Probably thirty, on the road. And this latest 325i model is holding its value well.'

Thanet laughed. 'I think you must spend all your spare time reading Auto magazines!'

Lineham grinned. 'Pretty well.'

They walked back down the drive. By daylight last night's impression of prosperity was underlined. The whole establishment was in excellent order and groomed to perfection, a place where weeds would think twice before daring to raise their heads above the soil and shrubs and trees obediently grew to exactly the right dimensions. The lawn edges were knife sharp, the block paving of the drive free of moss and algae.

'Wish my garden looked like this,' said Lineham.

Thanet laughed. 'Too much hard work.'

His smile faded as he saw why the people who had got out of the Nissan were taking so long to get into the bungalow. There were three of them, an elderly couple supporting a much younger woman who was so weak she was apparently incapable of walking alone. With their arms around her waist they were making pitifully slow progress towards the front door, which stood open.

By mutual accord Thanet and Lineham slowed down to allow them time to get themselves organised indoors.

'Think we ought to come back later?' said Lineham.

Thanet shook his head. 'Not much point in putting it off. It doesn't look as though the situation is likely to change much, does it?'

'Their daughter, you think?'

'Must be. Sylvester said they had one.'

'Wonder what's the matter with her.'

'Something pretty serious, by the look of it, poor girl. It didn't look as though she could stand unaided.'

'It must be terrible to see your son or daughter in that condition.'

Cancer, Thanet thought. Or some incurable wasting disease. He pushed away the thought of Bridget in that state. It didn't bear thinking about.

Fielding had obviously seen them heading in his direction and now he came back out of the bungalow, shutting the door behind him.

Thanet studied the man as he introduced himself. The gardener was in his mid-sixties, he guessed, short and whipcord-thin with sparse brown hair and a narrow face on which lines of anxiety were deeply etched. He was wearing a tweed jacket, shirt and tie. Sombre hazel eyes peered out at Thanet from deep sockets.

'You wanted to see me?'

'Just a few questions about last night.'

Fielding said nothing, just waited.

'I imagine you were helping in some way?'

'I was overseeing the parking. You can get so many more cars in if they're parked properly.'

'So what time did you come back down?'

'It must have been about a quarter past nine. My wife was watching the nine o'clock news when I got in.'

'We understand you helped look for the Sylvesters' son when he went missing. Did his nurse, Mr Roper, come down and fetch you?'

'Yes, he did.'

'What time would that have been?'

'Somewhere around five to ten, ten o'clock, I should think.'

'And were you indoors all the time during the intervening period?'

'No. Mr Sylvester had asked me to keep an eye open for gatecrashers. You never know these days . . .'

'So you went out, patrolled around?'

'Not exactly. I just came out and walked down to the gate a couple of times, made sure everything was quiet.'

'Did you, on any of those occasions, notice that the pool house was lit up?' A vain hope, but he had to ask.

Fielding shook his head. 'Afraid not.'

'And you didn't actually go into the main house, you say?'

'No.'

'So you saw nothing, heard nothing suspicious, the entire evening?'

Another shake of the head. 'I'm sorry.'

As they walked back to the house Lineham said, 'Pity.'

'If he only walked down to the gate he'd have been too far away to see anything useful anyway. And in any case, we're only assuming the pool house was lit up. If Max's assignation was with a woman . . .'

'True. Light would have been the last thing he would have wanted.'

Suddenly there was the sound of furious barking and a large brown dog came rushing out from the gap between the garages and the house and raced towards them. Thanet and Lineham froze. It was, Thanet saw to his alarm, a Dobermann. It approached at terrifying speed, its eyes narrowed to yellow slits, fangs bared as it continued its frantic barking. Pointless to think of turning to run. He could only hope that it would find their immobility unthreatening.

When it was only ten yards or so away a girl emerged from the same gap. When she saw what was happening she began to run. 'Jason!' she shouted. 'Stay!'

The dog skidded to a halt in front of them but continued barking ferociously.

'Tess Sylvester, presumably,' said Lineham with a nervous laugh.

EIGHT

Thanet had never seen a Dobermann at close quarters before and hoped he never would again. He was prepared to believe everything he had ever heard about their ferocity. He realised that the palms of his hands were damp.

'Jason!' she shouted again. 'Enough!'

The dog stopped barking immediately but did not change its aggressive stance, just stood looking at them, ready to spring, the whites of its eyes showing.

The girl came up alongside it and laid her hand on its head. 'Sit!' she said. Reluctantly, the Dobermann lowered its rear quarters to the ground and was rewarded by a pat and a murmured, 'Good boy!'

Thanet could see why Tess's father apparently doted on her and more than one man had wanted to marry her. Despite her red-rimmed eyes and the dark shadows beneath them she really was a lovely girl, with a clear, almost luminous complexion, lustrous dark eyes and a tumble of luxuriant hair the colour of ripe chestnuts. She was wearing the ubiquitous country uniform of Barbour and green wellington boots.

He discovered that he had been holding his breath. 'Good watchdog!' he said, when they had introduced themselves, relief infusing his comment with apparent enthusiasm.

'He certainly is,' said Tess, fondling the animal's ears. It turned its head, clearly relishing the caress. 'He's an old softie, really.'

'You could have fooled me!' said Lineham.

'Oh, but he is. Really. And once he knows you're supposed to be here, he'll be fine. In fact, just to be on the safe side, I'd better introduce you properly, then there won't be any problem. Give me your hand,' she said to Thanet.

Thanet held it out and she took it between both of hers and rubbed it before offering it to the dog. With difficulty Thanet refrained from flinching. The dog sniffed at it warily.

'You see?' she said. 'I've put my smell on it. Now, next time you meet, he'll associate your smell with mine and know you're a friend.'

Thanet hoped she was right.

'Now yours,' she said to Lineham, and the sergeant reluctantly went through the same process.

Watching, Thanet realised that they had reason to be grateful to the animal for breaking the ice. The diversion had distracted them all from the business in hand.

The aggressive light had magically faded from the dog's eyes and now it trotted around beside Thanet and thrust its nose into his palm.

'See?' said Tess. 'He wants you to stroke him.'

'Amazing,' murmured Thanet, complying.

An awkward silence fell. Somehow he had to bridge the gap between banality and tragedy. 'Miss Sylvester, allow me to offer you my condolences. This is a terrible time for you and I hesitate to say that I need to talk to you, but . . .'

'That's all right. I understand. Go ahead.' But she had

turned her head away sharply and when she looked at him again he saw that her eyes had filled with tears. She bit her lip. 'Naturally I want to do all I can to . . .' She shook her head, unable to continue.

To give her time to overcome her distress, in unspoken agreement Thanet and Lineham turned and began to stroll towards the house, leaving her to trail behind. After a few moments she blew her nose and came up alongside them. Thanet gave her a sympathetic smile and said, 'There's nothing that can't wait, if you prefer.'

She shook her head. 'I'd rather get it over with.'

'Very well.' Quickly, Thanet took her through the events of the evening. Her account agreed with everything they had been told so far. He deliberately avoided questioning her about the incident with Anthea Greenway. There had been plenty of other witnesses and it was pointless to cause her unnecessary distress. The note was a different matter, but she apparently knew nothing about it. She had taken her duties as hostess seriously and during the early part of the evening, before supper, had done her best to circulate among the guests.

Now for the difficult part. 'Miss Sylvester . . .'

'Tess, please.'

'Very well. Tess. I'm sorry, but I really have to ask you this.'

They had reached the house. She had taken them around to the back door, pausing to chain the dog up on the way, and was now removing her boots. Aware of the alteration in his tone she glanced up at Thanet sharply before straightening up. Then, without a word, she opened the door, led the way into the kitchen, stopped and turned to face him, folding her arms and hunching her shoulders as if to protect herself from whatever was coming. 'What?' she said.

'You'll have talked to your parents this morning and be aware that we are treating this as a case of suspicious death. So I have to ask you if there is anyone, to your knowledge, who would be glad to see your fiancé dead?'

The fear faded from her eyes leaving behind a strange blankness, as if she had pulled a shutter down to hide her feelings and then suddenly it was back again, redoubled. 'No!' she cried. 'Of course not!' She put her hands up to the sides of her face, pressing so hard against her cheeks that her features became distorted. Then, without warning, she turned and dashed from the room.

Thanet pulled a face. 'Well handled.'

'No point in blaming yourself, sir. It's not surprising she's a bit fragile today.'

'Looks as though she does have her suspicions, doesn't it? Who, do you think?'

Lineham shrugged. 'Father, brother, Gerald whatsisname, her former fiancé? Take your pick.'

Thanet glanced around. The kitchen was much as he would have expected, the type by now familiar to everyone through the glossy magazines: elaborate wooden units, wall-tiles whose unevenness proclaimed the fact that they were hand-made, terracotta tiles on the floor and every sophisticated gadget known to man. But there was one interesting individual touch, a cork noticeboard set into a specially constructed niche, covered with photographs of varying shapes and sizes. He crossed to take a closer look at it but before he could do so footsteps came clacking along the corridor from the hall and a woman called out, 'Who's there?'

Marion Sylvester came into the room. 'Oh, it's you, Inspector. I thought I heard voices.' She was obviously the type for whom an attempt at glamour is a way of life. Her plump thighs were encased in tight black leggings, her heels were a good three inches high and her black and white sweater sported a striking design of geometrics and swirls. But this morning her eye shadow and lipstick had been unevenly applied by an unsteady hand and the pouches beneath her eyes were testimony of a sleepless night.

'We were talking to your daughter.'

Marion Sylvester groped for a chair and collapsed upon it as if her legs had suddenly become incapable of holding her upright a moment longer. She raked a hand through her hair. 'Oh God, I just don't know how I'm going to cope with all this. Poor Tess. She's absolutely distraught. She's trying to put a brave face on it but she keeps on rushing off to her room and locking herself in. Then there's Carey. All this upset is so bad for him.'

'How is he this morning?'

She lifted her shoulders. 'Who can tell?'

'I'd like a word with him later.'

She looked alarmed. 'I don't know if that would be a good idea.'

'I'll try not to upset him, I promise. And his nurse can be present at the interview.'

She shook her head wearily, as if she had no strength left to argue. 'Oh, I suppose so, then. If you must.'

Thanet turned back to the noticeboard. The photographs had been crammed on to it, many of them overlapping. 'Interesting collection.'

She shrugged. 'It's a thing of mine. I always think it's pointless sticking them into albums, no one ever looks at them. The trouble is, I can never bring myself to throw them out. Some of those have been there for years.'

'So I see.' Thanet's eye had alighted on a group photograph and he leaned forward to look at it more closely. A number of young people were relaxing over tea on the lawn after a game of tennis. There were seven of them, three girls and four boys, some seated on deckchairs and some sprawled on the grass. He realised with a jolt that although they were much younger a number of the faces were already familiar to him. Surely that was Tess, and Hartley Jeopard, and Anthea Greenway and Max, of course, sitting at Tess's feet and looking tanned and debonair. So the others must be . . .

'What are you looking at?' Marion Sylvester's voice, beside him.

He had been so engrossed that he hadn't even noticed her move.

Obviously intrigued, Lineham joined them.

'I am right, aren't I?' Thanet pointed out the faces he thought he recognised.

'Oh yes. I took that myself. They seemed to spend most of the summer holidays playing tennis in those days. You know how it is with kids, they go through these phases. That must have been taken, oh, a good ten years ago now. Some of them have moved away, of course, Hartley and Anthea live in London and so does . . . did, Max. In the normal way of things Carey would be gone too by now, no doubt, if he'd finished his course at university and found himself a job. He was such a clever boy.'

'Which is he?'

Marion laid a scarlet fingernail on a profile beneath a shock of dark hair.

'And who is this?'

'Oh, that's Linda Fielding, our gardener's daughter.'

Thanet looked at the somewhat plain features and sturdy figure of Linda Fielding and with a shiver remembered the frail creature they had seen earlier, who could not now even walk unaided.

'She and Tess and Anthea are the same age,' said Marion. 'They were all in the same class at school, so Linda often used to make up the numbers at tennis. When this photo was taken Tess had a sprained ankle, I remember.'

Now that it had been pointed out to him Thanet could see that unlike the others Tess was not wearing tennis whites. He had been misled by the fact that her summer dress was in a pale colour.

Marion was still talking about Linda. 'Poor girl, she's very ill now, I'm afraid, which is why she wasn't at the party last night.'

'We saw her earlier, when we arrived. What's the matter with her?'

'Cancer, I imagine,' said Marion. 'I haven't enquired too closely, it's obvious it's serious. She's not been well for some time but lately she seems to have gone downhill at an alarming rate. I feel so sorry for the Fieldings. She's their only child and they've always doted on her. They were getting on a bit when she was born and I think they'd given up hope. Though I always feel sorry for kids with older parents, especially if they're only children, like Linda. They never seem to mix well. Linda was never really a part of the group in the same way as the others. I suppose it was partly because, to put it bluntly, she came from a different class, her father was only a gardener, after all, but it wasn't just that. She was always quiet, mousy, never had boyfriends or went to discos. And of course she was a real bookworm, not like the other two girls. Tess has never been what you might call academic and Anthea was always the arty type.'

Thanet wondered why Marion was telling him all this. He was much more interested in hearing about Gerald,

Tess's former fiancé, who was no doubt the other as yet unnamed male in the photograph. Unless, of course, Marion was deliberately trying *not* to talk about Gerald. Which, if true, was interesting. He decided not to interrupt the flow of reminiscence. You never knew when you might learn something useful and in his experience it was good policy, once a witness started to talk freely, to allow him or her to do so.

'I remember the Fieldings were so thrilled and proud when Linda got into Bristol. Unfortunately for her, of course, when she left university in, let me see, it must have been '91, it was right in the middle of the recession and she couldn't find a job. It was awful, really. Mrs Fielding used to be almost in tears telling me about all the job applications Linda kept on sending off, dozens and dozens of them. Most of the time people didn't even bother to acknowledge them, let alone tell her the post had been filled. I think that's terrible, don't you? I mean, they could at least have the courtesy to do that, couldn't they? And after all that education, spending all those years getting a degree, it's so soul-destroying ... And then, when Linda finally did get a job, the year before last, she'd only been in it a few months when she started getting health problems. She really has had a rotten time.'

She seemed to have run down and Thanet was just going to ask about Gerald when, still gazing at the photograph she said, 'The three girls were all so different – still are, I suppose.'

'In what way?'

'Well, Linda and Anthea were like chalk and cheese. Linda so quiet and shy, and Anthea, well, have you met Anthea yet?'

'Not yet. We did see her briefly, last night.'

'Then you'll see what I mean. The way she was dressed – typical. Anthea always has to be different, always has to be noticed.'

'Who always has to be noticed?' Ralph Sylvester had come into the room. Like Marion he looked as though he hadn't slept much last night. 'I thought I heard voices,' he said, echoing his wife.

'Anthea, dear.'

'Ah, Anthea,' said Sylvester, sitting down heavily at the table. 'Any chance of a cup of coffee, darl?'

'Of course. Would you like a cup?' she said to Thanet and Lineham.

'Yes, please.' They joined Sylvester at the table.

'What did you mean, "Ah, Anthea"?' said Thanet.

'She just doesn't know how to behave, that girl,' said Marion indignantly, clattering kettle and mugs. 'Haven't you heard about the scene she made at the party last night? Disgusting, I call it, making a public spectacle of herself like that. If she wanted to make a fuss why couldn't she have done it in private, that's what I'd like to know, instead of ruining Tess's engagement party?'

'Oh come on, darl, aren't you exaggerating a bit? She didn't exactly ruin it, did she? It was what happened later that ruined it.'

'Well you know what I mean. And you said yourself, last night, that if anyone had a grudge against Max, it was Anthea.'

'Marion!' Sylvester cast an anxious glance at the two policemen. 'Think what you're saying!'

'I'm only repeating what you said yourself!'

'Maybe. But that was in *private*, don't you see?'

'I don't care whether it was in private or not, it's true, isn't it?'

'Perhaps. I don't know. But we ought to let the police

make up their own minds, don't you think? It's hardly fair to Anthea . . .'

'Fair? *Fair*, to *Anthea*?' Marion swung around, hands on hips, eyes blazing. 'What about Tess? Is it fair to Tess that her life has been ruined? Don't talk to me about being fair to Anthea. If she did decide to have another go at him later and shoved him into the swimming pool, then all I can say is that she deserves what's coming to her!'

'All right, darl, calm down. All I'm saying is that you can't go around hurling wild accusations about people.'

'I am *not* hurling wild accusations! I'm simply saying . . .'

Thanet decided to intervene. Rows were often instructive, revealing. People said things they hadn't intended to say. But this one seemed now to be going around in circles. 'Mrs Sylvester,' he said. 'I don't think this is getting us anywhere. We had heard about the scene last night at the party, between Miss Greenway and Mr Jeopard, but so far we haven't managed to find out what it was all about.'

'Who have you asked?'

Thanet wasn't prepared to be specific. 'One or two people.'

'The Jeopards, I bet! And they wouldn't tell you, oh no. Not on your life, they wouldn't!'

'What do you mean?'

'Marion . . .' said Sylvester, a note of warning in his voice.

But she was not to be stopped. She shook her head at him impatiently. 'Why should I keep quiet? What do we owe them, you tell me that? Do you think I didn't know they never thought our Tess was good enough for their precious Max? And although Hartley never had a look-in in the favouritism stakes while Max was still alive, now there's only him they're closing ranks, don't you see? Hartley is still carrying a torch for Anthea and they don't want to upset him by saying anything that would compromise her!'

So he'd been right about Hartley and Anthea, thought Thanet. But he would like to know more, much more. 'Mrs Sylvester. Would you please explain exactly what you are talking about?

She spooned coffee into the mugs. 'Sugar?'

They shook their heads.

She plonked the mugs on to the table and sat down. 'Only too glad to oblige,' she said.

NINE

'I always did think Anthea was keen on Max, didn't I, Ralphie?'

Sylvester merely grunted and took a gulp of his coffee, so Thanet assumed he wasn't disagreeing.

'But of course Max never had eyes for anyone but Tess. Or Tess for him. Proper little pair of teenage love-birds they were, weren't they, Ralph? Oh, I know you didn't approve. You thought Tess was too young to have a steady boyfriend, but I could see there was no point in trying to discourage them. And you have to admit, they really were rather sweet together, weren't they?'

Another grunt, another slurp. Sylvester obviously had no intention of contributing to the conversation at present.

Lineham leaned forward and opened his mouth, no doubt to ask how it had come about, if Max and Tess had only ever had eyes for each other, that they had both apparently had a serious relationship with someone else. Thanet gave an almost imperceptible shake of the head. *Let her tell it her own way.* It was enough. Thanet and Lineham had worked together for so long and had built up such a rapport that the merest hint or flicker of an eyelid was enough to communicate the desired message. Lineham shut his mouth and sat back again.

Marion Sylvester hadn't noticed this little exchange but her husband had and Thanet was pretty certain that he had interpreted it correctly. The man was no fool.

'The trouble was,' Marion went on, 'Tess could never really understand this itch Max had to travel. Well, it was more than an itch, wasn't it, Ralph, it was more like a . . . a . . .' Marion groped for the word.

'A compulsion?' suggested Thanet.

'Yes, that's it. That's it, exactly. A compulsion. It took me a long time to realise that's what it was – years, in fact. For ages I just used to think he was plain selfish, going off whenever he could and never considering Tess's feelings. It upset me, to see how hurt she used to get. But in the end I accepted that that was the way he was, and there was nothing to be done about it. I mean, he was always the same, wasn't he, Ralph? The minute he was old enough he was off backpacking in the summer holidays.'

'Too much money,' Sylvester intervened unexpectedly. 'And too used to having things his own way. Spoilt rotten, that boy was. He could always twist his mother around his little finger. Pity his father died when he did.'

'Max was about thirteen then, I believe?'

'Something like that.'

'What work did his father do?'

Sylvester shrugged. 'He was some sort of high-powered civil servant, I believe.'

'Anyway,' said Marion, 'Max got a place at Oxford and decided to spend the whole of his gap year travelling. You can imagine how upset Tess was, when he told her. But you had to admire her. Once she saw he wasn't going to change his mind she decided to do a Cordon Bleu course while he was away and then do her secretarial course in Oxford, to be near him when he went up the following October.'

'I had the feeling he wasn't too pleased about that,' said Sylvester. 'We were there when she told him. I think he liked the idea of being footloose and fancy-free while he was at university.'

Marion gave her husband a reproachful glance. 'I think you imagined all that. I think he was thrilled to bits.'

Sylvester gave a cynical snort. 'Thrilled! Huh!'

Marion frowned. 'Anyway, that was what she did. And when she'd finished the course she stayed on, got a job in Oxford for the rest of the time he was there. I think she took it pretty much for granted that they'd be married when he'd taken his degree. So you can imagine how she felt when at the end of his final term he told her out of the blue that he wasn't ready to settle down yet. His year in the Far East had made him realise that he wanted to be a travel writer and if they were to have any future together she must understand that he had to be free to travel, whenever and for as long as he wished. So in a few days' time he would be leaving on a trip to China and planned to be away at least a year, perhaps longer. Imagine, all the arrangements were already made and he hadn't said a word about it till then! Well, that was the last straw! That was when she first broke off with him.'

'So that would have been in – let me see – June '89.'

'Right,' said Sylvester.

'Yes,' said his wife. 'Mind, I think she was sorry later that she'd acted quite so hastily. Particularly, I remember, when she realised she was going to miss the College Ball. It's such a very special occasion and I think she thought he wouldn't go at all if he couldn't take her. Also, I suspect she thought he wouldn't manage to find another partner. Girls are always in short supply in Oxford and most were already fixed up with partners by then. But no. She discovered later that Max had immediately got in touch with Linda, of all people, and invited her instead! Linda was in her first year at Bristol by then. He'd never looked twice at her before and never did again, to my knowledge, but I suppose beggars can't be choosers and he just wanted to show Tess she wasn't the only girl in the world.'

'Did it to spite her, more likely,' said Sylvester.

Marion sighed. 'Perhaps. I don't know. Anyway, as I say, Tess was especially upset about that. I think she thought he'd beg her to go with him, this one last time.'

'Max wasn't exactly the begging type.'

'That's not true! He certainly begged her in the end, didn't he, when she was –'

Sylvester cut in swiftly. 'I told Tess at the time, "You've only got yourself to blame. You told him you didn't want anything more to do with him, and he obviously took you at your word."'

Thanet suspected that Marion had been going to say, 'When she was engaged to Gerald'. Interesting that her husband had stopped her from doing so. Did Sylvester seriously think that the police wouldn't find out about that?

'Anyway,' Marion went on, 'off he went to China and he was gone for over a year, didn't come back until, when? The end of November, wasn't it, Ralph? He just turned up on the doorstep as if he'd never been away and nothing had ever gone wrong between them! I couldn't believe it! What a nerve!'

'I told her then, she ought to have nothing more to do with him,' said Sylvester. 'But would she listen? Oh no, not Tess.'

'But you know how miserable she was all the time he was away, Ralph. She nearly drove me mad, moping about the house. And I was worried, too. She was off her food for so long I was afraid she was getting anorexic. So although I was cross with Max, when he just turned up like that, I was so relieved to see her happy again I could have forgiven him anything.'

'Until the next time,' said Sylvester. 'It was all very well while he was living at home writing his book, but the minute it was finished he was off again!'

Lineham's frown of concentration told Thanet that the sergeant, like him, was having problems keeping up with all these comings and goings. 'That would have been when, exactly?'

'The following June,' said Marion. 'June '91. And that I do remember because it was just after Tess's twenty-first. We planned a big party for her and I know she was convinced that Max was going to propose that night. She knew his book would be finished by then and she thought it would be a sort of double celebration. But he didn't. The very next day, in fact, he told her he was planning another trip. She was, well, devastated, wasn't she, Ralph? That was when I realised that the situation was never going to change, that that was the way Max was, and if she wanted him, sooner or later she was just going to have to accept it. And that was what I told her. But she just couldn't. Accept it, I mean. Not then, anyway. Well, I suppose at that age you've got all these romantic notions. You think you've got to come first with the one you love, don't you? So this time Tess said that was it. Absolutely and finally it. She told Max that if he did go off again it was goodbye Tess. And he went. *Finito*.'

'That,' said Sylvester, 'was when I stepped in. Rather than face the prospect of having Tess drooping around the house like a wet fortnight for God knows how long, I thought it would do her good to do a bit of travelling herself, might help her to get Max out of her system. We've got various relatives dotted around the globe, so to start with I put together a package with a few frills like first-class air travel thrown in, and off she went, to Australia and New Zealand, to begin with.'

Thanet could see that Lineham was thinking, *And very nice, too! It's all right for some!* 'And did it work?'

The Sylvesters consulted each other with a glance. Then Marion shrugged. 'To some extent yes, I think so. It took Tess's mind off Max and certainly gave her a taste for travel herself. The trouble is, travel to Tess means staying in comfortable hotels, eating gorgeous food, going shopping and sightseeing, whereas so far as I can gather Max prefers to rough it, go native, if you like. So there's never been any suggestion she should go with him.'

'I imagine he feels that that kind of travel is more likely to give him interesting experiences to write about,' said Thanet.

'Perhaps. I can't see the appeal myself. Give me a bit of comfort, any day! Anyway, for the past few years both Tess and Max have been away quite a bit and when they did come home they seemed to miss each other. Tess came home for Christmas that first year, '91, but Max was still away in South America. Then he came home the following May, for the publication of his book.'

Thanet's antennae twitched. There had been a subtle alteration in Marion's tone there. Why?

'I'm getting confused,' said Lineham. 'I thought Mr Jeopard came back from South America last Christmas.'

'Yes, he did.'

'And he'd been away two years?'

97

'That's right.'

'So why did he go back there for such a long period of time when he'd already done one lengthy trip out there?'

'Oh, I see what you mean,' said Sylvester. 'Because he hadn't quite gathered all the material he needed. But he was away much longer than he'd intended the second time. In fact, at one point his mother hadn't heard from him for so long that she was afraid something dire had happened to him. And it had. We heard later that he might well have died. He'd fallen seriously ill while in the Amazonian jungle and been taken in by natives who looked after him for months until he was strong enough to be transported to the nearest hospital, which was some distance away. Even then it was some time before he was fit to travel.'

All good copy for the book which would now never be written, thought Thanet.

'Anyway, to get back to what I was saying, when he came back in '92 for the publication of his book, Tess had gone off to the States. But would you believe, the first thing he did was to come around here looking for her?'

By now this didn't surprise Thanet in the least. However many ups and downs there had been in the relationship between Max and Tess, clearly there had existed between them some magnetism which they were powerless to resist.

'Just turned up on the doorstep again, didn't he, darl?'

Marion nodded. She stood up abruptly and began to clear away the coffee mugs. 'Anyone fancy another cup?'

'Yeah, I wouldn't mind,' said Sylvester.

Thanet and Lineham shook their heads. Thanet was watching Marion closely. Her husband didn't seem to have noticed anything, but for the last few minutes she had been very quiet. Thanet was convinced that something had occurred to her which had had the effect of disrupting the earlier steady flow of reminiscence. What could it be?

'If I'd been here I'd have sent him packing,' said Sylvester. 'Anyway, it was soon after that he took up with Anthea. Now that was a new one. He'd never shown any interest in her before. Though like my wife says, she'd always thought that Anthea fancied him. Trouble was, by then Anthea was living with Hartley.'

'Ah.' So it had been that serious between Hartley and Anthea, thought Thanet. How must Hartley have felt, when Max waltzed home from wherever he'd been and in default of Tess being around, stole Hartley's girl from right under his nose? 'How did that happen?'

'It was at the party Mrs Jeopard gave to celebrate the publication of Max's book, I believe,' said Sylvester. 'Thanks, darl.' He took the fresh cup of coffee Marion had produced for him. 'We were invited but we didn't go, did we? I thought he had a bloody cheek asking us, after the way he'd treated Tess. Not that it should have surprised me. He had the nerve for anything, if he wanted it. I suppose that as Tess's parents he was hoping to get us on his side again. Anyway, if that was what he wanted he was disappointed. And the next thing we heard, Anthea and Max were being seen everywhere together.'

'It didn't last that long,' said Marion, rejoining them at the table. 'Max took off again in the autumn for that second trip to South America – would have gone earlier, in my opinion, if it hadn't been for the fact that his mother was ill and even he couldn't bring himself to be that callous.'

'So what happened with Anthea? Did she go back to Hartley?'

Marion shook her head. 'No. And to my knowledge

Hartley's never had another girlfriend, before or since. I felt really sorry for him, I can tell you. Though I must say it did surprise me when he first took up with Anthea. I wouldn't have thought she was his type, I'd have said she was too, well, flamboyant. But there's no accounting for taste, is there?'

'And what about Anthea?'

Sylvester gave a cynical little laugh. 'From what happened last night, I gather she'd counted on Max coming back to her.'

'What did happen, exactly?'

Sylvester and his wife glanced at each other. She gave a little nod. *You tell it.*

He took a sip of coffee and narrowed his eyes in thought, remembering. 'Well, Anthea arrived late.'

'Wanted to make an entrance, probably,' said Marion, unable to resist joining in, 'make sure her little exhibition had the maximum effect.'

'What time exactly, do you know?'

Sylvester frowned, thought. 'Sorry, no.'

'Could you say if it was before or after nine o'clock?' Thanet was still anxious to find out if this little episode had taken place before or after the note was handed to Max.

'No, I'm afraid not. All I know is that most of the guests had arrived by then and there was quite a crowd. I was in the same room as Max and I saw Anthea appear at the door. I happened to be facing that way but in any case you couldn't really miss her, of course, in that red Chinese outfit she was wearing. She stopped in the doorway for a minute, glancing around as if she was looking for someone – Max, I realised, because as soon as she spotted him she marched straight across to him, elbowed her way into the little group of people he was talking to, and put her hands on her hips. It was obvious she was out to make trouble and almost before she'd said a word everything went quiet.

'"Hullo, Max *darling*," she said. Then she stepped forward and quite deliberately slapped his face, really hard. It sounded like a pistol shot, and if there was anybody in the room who hadn't been aware of what was going on, they knew about it now. You could have heard a pin drop. "You bastard!" she said. "I wish Tess joy of you." Then she swung around and stalked out. You should have seen Max's face! The shock! He couldn't believe she'd actually done it!' Retrospectively, Sylvester was clearly enjoying Max's discomfiture.

'What did he do?' Thanet was genuinely interested. What did people do, in embarrassing situations like that?

Sylvester shrugged. 'Pretended to laugh it off. Rolled his eyes, grinned around at everyone and said, "Wow!" They laughed, of course, as he'd intended them to, and gradually conversations started up again. No prizes for guessing what they were talking about, of course. I was livid, I can tell you. I didn't know which of them I was more angry with, Anthea for making such a scene at Tess's engagement party, or Max for messing around with one of Tess's friends in the first place.'

'But why did she wait until last night?' said Lineham. 'I assume there would have been plenty of other opportunities for her to tackle him before then?'

'Of course there would!' said Marion. 'Max has been home since Christmas, that's three whole months. That's why we were so furious with her. She's just an exhibitionist, that's all.'

'And I suppose she wanted to cause him maximum humiliation,' said Sylvester. 'It wouldn't have been enough to do it in private.'

'Well she might have thought of Tess!' said his wife. 'She is supposed be Tess's friend, isn't she?'

'I know, I know. Don't get cross with me, darl, I agree with you, for God's sake!'

'And do you know,' Marion said to Thanet, 'she even had the nerve to stay on at the party, afterwards!'

'We didn't want to cause more unpleasantness by asking her to leave,' said Sylvester.

Thanet said, 'I'm surprised, in the circumstances, that you asked her to sit with your daughter while I talked to you, last night.' Though Marion had been against it, he remembered.

'Well,' said Sylvester, wearily, 'last night we were all so shell-shocked we weren't thinking straight. I just suggested the first person who came into my mind and it happened to be Anthea. She's been around so long she's practically part of the family.'

'Which is what makes her behaviour all the worse,' said Marion. 'I'm only thankful Tess wasn't actually there to see it. It would have been so humiliating for her.'

'Maybe if she had been, Anthea wouldn't have done it. Maybe she checked first, and picked her moment,' suggested Sylvester.

But Marion was obviously not inclined to give Anthea the benefit of the doubt. 'You're too good-natured by half, Ralph.'

Thanet thought there had been enough discussion of Anthea. 'There's one person in that group photograph we haven't mentioned yet,' he said. 'I believe it must be Gerald Argent. I understand your daughter was engaged to him before Max?'

They exchanged dismayed glances. 'Yes, she was,' said Sylvester. 'But what's that got to do with it?'

'Oh come, Mr Sylvester, don't pretend to be so naïve!

Your daughter is engaged to one man. She breaks it off and becomes engaged to another, who is then found dead in a swimming pool on the night of their engagement party.'

'You're not suggesting Gerald had anything to do with Max's death, are you?' said Marion.

'That's utterly preposterous!' said Sylvester.

'Is it? Is it, Mr Sylvester? Just think about it.'

'It is if you know anything about Gerald!' said Sylvester.

'Gerald wouldn't hurt a fly!' said Marion.

If the general public knew how often this was said about those who had committed the most atrocious acts, they would ban the phrase for ever, thought Thanet. 'How long was your daughter engaged to him?'

They exchanged glances. *I suppose we'll have to tell him.* 'Six months,' said Sylvester reluctantly.

'But they'd been going out together for ages before that,' said Marion, apparently anxious not to make Tess seem too fickle. She turned to her husband. 'When did they start?'

He frowned, and they worked it out between them. Since Tess finally broke it off with Max the day after her twenty-first birthday, they had not seen each other until three months ago, when Max came home at Christmas. Tess had spent a year in America before finally returning home in the spring of '93. Not long afterwards she had begun to go out with Gerald and her parents had heaved a sigh of relief, believing what they wanted to believe, that their policy had worked and Tess had finally got Max out of her system. The previous autumn, when Gerald had been promoted to managerial status at the bank in Sturrenden where he worked, they had become engaged.

A June wedding had been planned and everything had gone smoothly until Max's return at Christmas, when yet again he had tried to take up with Tess. But this time, to the Sylvesters' relief, Tess had said she didn't want anything to do with him. Unfortunately he had refused to take no for an answer. He had at once launched into a single-minded campaign to win her back. Letters, flowers and presents arrived daily, and on one occasion he had even hired a light aircraft to float a banner, with 'Tess, I love you' written on it, across the sky. But still she had resisted.

Then, for the first time, he proposed.

'When was that?' said Thanet.

'About ten days ago,' said Sylvester grimly. 'Marriage had never been mentioned before.'

'I think it had dawned on him that this was his last chance,' said Marion, 'that if he didn't get Tess now he would lose her for good. I tried to tell her that this didn't mean he had changed, but I could see she was weakening. "He must have," she said, "or he wouldn't have asked me to marry him." I told her I meant he would still go off on his travels when he wanted to, that I really didn't believe she would be able to stop him. And d'you know what she said? She said, "It's no good, Mum. I've come to realise that a bit of Max is better than no Max at all, and if that's what I have to settle for, then I shall." "What about Gerald?" I said. And she just shook her head. "Oh, Gerald," she said. "He'll be hurt, of course, and I'm sorry. But between the two there just isn't any choice. I've never loved anyone but Max, and I don't think I ever shall."'

Marion's face suddenly crumpled. 'I don't know what she's going to do!' she cried. 'I don't know how she's going to bear it!'

Sylvester got up and put an arm around his wife's shoulders. 'We'll see her through, somehow,' he said.

She turned her face into his shoulder. 'Oh I hope so, Ralph. I do hope so.'

Thanet caught Lineham's eye. *I think we've done all we can here, for the moment.*

It was time to interview Carey Sylvester.

TEN

On the way up to Carey's room, however, they ran into Barbara Mallis. She was carrying a pile of sheets and towels and she smiled at them over the top of them. 'Oh, good morning, Inspector, Sergeant.'

Thanet was never one to pass up an opportunity. 'Ah, Mrs Mallis. I wanted a word with you. Would now be a convenient moment?'

'Yes, of course.' There was a table opposite the top of the staircase and she laid down her burden of household linen and turned to face them. 'How can I help?'

Despite the emotional turmoil which surrounded her she appeared calm and self-controlled, and was the first member of the household Thanet had encountered this morning to look as though she'd had a good night's sleep. The care she took over her appearance was clearly habitual: her make-up was immaculate and her hair drawn back this morning into an elegant chignon which Thanet did not think suited her. It emphasised her pointed nose and did nothing to conceal the deeply etched frown lines. She was wearing tight jeans and an expensive-looking sweater appliquéd in an abstract design of whorls and zig-zags dotted with seed pearls and clusters of beading.

'Is there somewhere a little less public where we could talk? You have a flat in the house, I believe.'

'Yes. This way.' She turned and led them up a further, narrower flight of stairs to the attic floor, but Thanet had not missed the hesitation. She hadn't wanted to take them into her private domain. Why? Because of a natural reluctance to have her privacy invaded, or for some other reason?

The flat surprised him, and Lineham, too, judging by the look the sergeant gave him after a quick glance around. Stretching across the whole length and width of the house, with dormer windows at the front and velux roof lights at the back, it consisted chiefly of one huge open space with a door at one end leading presumably to bedroom and *en suite* bathroom. In one corner a compact little kitchen was divided off by a unit of open-sided shelves from a dining area with sophisticated glass-topped table and tulip-shaped chairs. The living space was comfortably, even luxuriously furnished, with thick fitted carpet, festoon blinds at the recessed dormer windows and dralon-covered three-piece suite. Perhaps efficient housekeepers were in such demand these days that lavish accommodation would be regarded as a natural perquisite of the job?

'Nice flat,' he said, and was interested to note that an expression which he was unable to interpret flickered in Barbara Mallis's eyes, and was gone. What had it signified? he wondered. Why should such an innocuous comment produce any reaction at all, other than mild gratification?

'Yes, isn't it. Would you like to sit down?' Her tone implied that she would like the answer to be no, they wouldn't, as their visit was to be brief.

She had been forthcoming enough last night and so partly out of perversity but also because he was interested to find out why she wanted to get rid of them quickly, Thanet accepted the invitation. 'Thank you.'

She chose to perch on the very edge of one of the armchairs. *I'm a busy woman. I hope this won't take long.*

'How long have you been with the Sylvesters, Mrs Mallis?' said Thanet when they were settled.

The question obviously surprised her and Thanet was interested to see that she looked wary.

'Since '91,' she said. 'Why?'

'Just interested to fill in a little background. What happened to the previous housekeeper?'

'There wasn't one. I was the first.' Thanet's cocked eyebrow forced her to continue. 'When Carey came to live permanently at home after being in and out of hospital, they found Mrs Sylvester couldn't cope. So they decided to get someone in to run the house. At that point she was still trying to look after him herself. It was hopeless, of course. Absolutely hopeless. He was so unpredictable. To be honest, if she hadn't given up, if they hadn't got Mike Roper in to look after him, I don't think I would have stayed. You can't imagine what it was like when Carey was free to roam around at will. The trouble was, he hated taking his medication – they all do, I believe, all these schizos, it's the one thing they loathe and it's the one thing which keeps them reasonably normal. That was what was wrong with that Ben Silcock or Ben Silcox, whatever his name was, who climbed into the lion's den at London Zoo. Remember?'

Thanet remembered only too well. Anyone who had seen the television footage of the unfortunate man being mauled by a full-grown lion wasn't likely to forget it. He nodded.

'You know what I mean, then. Without proper medication they go haywire. So in those days, when you ran into Carey you never knew what to expect. It was pretty unnerving, I can tell you.' She looked around and got up to fetch her cigarettes, waited until she had lit up before going on. 'Sometimes he'd carry on as though he was terrified of you and other times . . . the things he used to say! Talk about bizarre! And sometimes he'd just ignore you and talk to his voices. Most schizos hear voices, apparently, hear them and talk to them. Well, I don't know if you've ever been at close quarters with someone who's hearing voices, but believe me it can be pretty scary. I was very relieved when Mike arrived, I can tell you.'

'Was Carey ever violent?' said Thanet.

'Sometimes. Not that he ever actually attacked anyone, to my knowledge. But I do remember once he smashed in his TV with a chair. Said it was trying to get inside his head, control him. And before Mike came he tried to commit suicide more than once. Mike told me there's a terrifically high suicide rate among schizos – one in ten, I think he said. It was after the second attempt that they decided to get a live-in nurse.' She lifted a shoulder and blew out a lungful of smoke. 'It was the obvious thing to do, really. They could afford it.'

Her attitude was cold, almost callous. The suffering of everyone involved in such a desperate situation had obviously left her unmoved. There was, it seemed, only one person who mattered to Barbara Mallis and that was Barbara Mallis.

'So what about now? Is Mr Roper efficient?'

'Seems to be. Carey never goes out alone and I know Mike makes sure he really does take his medication.'

'So last night was unusual, in that Carey did get out?'

'Yes, very. Some idiot unlocked the door and didn't

relock it, I believe. Mike blames himself for not actually removing the key when he went downstairs, and let's face it, it was pretty careless of him, when the house was full of people.'

'Habit, I suppose, if that's what he always does.'

'Perhaps. Anyway, I can't imagine why they didn't think of looking in the dog kennel earlier. Carey's always been very fond of Jason and of course Jason's chiefly an outdoor dog, he's not often allowed in the house.'

Thanet couldn't visualise himself ever wanting to squeeze into a kennel with a Dobermann, but then Tess had said that the dog was 'an old softie' so perhaps it wasn't that surprising. Perhaps Carey had found comfort in proximity to the animal he loved.

'To return to the party, then,' he said. 'We've been told that Mr Jeopard was handed a note during the evening, somewhere around nine o'clock. Did you by any chance witness this incident?'

She shook her head.

'And have you recalled anything else you feel we ought to know?'

Another negative.

'Right, well, I think that's about all for the moment.' He was interested to note the relief in her eyes and the alacrity with which she jumped up. What was he missing? On the way to the door he paused. 'Oh, by the way, I forgot to ask Mr and Mrs Sylvester. Where were Tess and Mr Jeopard going to live after they were married?'

'In London.' The gleam of malice in her eyes was unmistakable. It was clear that she had taken pleasure from the thought of her employers' disappointment if Tess had moved away from the area. Was this because she had a specific grudge against them, or was her nature such that she always enjoyed the spectacle of other people's misery? Could this be why she had stayed so long in this particular household?

'And if she had married Mr Argent?'

'I believe they were house-hunting locally.'

On the way downstairs Lineham said, 'Pretty keen to get rid of us, wasn't she?'

'Yes. I wonder why?'

'And it was Mike this, Mike that, did you notice?'

'Think there might be something going on there?' Another possible reason why Barbara Mallis had stayed? Thanet wondered. And if so, had her interest been reciprocated? Personally he would as soon have curled up in bed with an anaconda, but there was no accounting for taste and both she and Roper must be starved of a social life. Certainly they must have seen a lot of each other over the last few years.

'Rather him than me,' said Lineham.

'Well, let's not jump to conclusions.'

They were back on the first-floor landing and they followed Marion Sylvester's directions to Carey's quarters. He and Roper shared a self-contained suite of rooms at one end of the first floor. The single entrance door to the premises was at one end of the landing corridor and Thanet understood why someone last night might have thought it led to a bathroom. Though surely the fact that the key was on the outside, not the inside, should have given them pause for thought? He said so to Lineham, while they waited for an answer to their knock.

'Might have had too much to drink, sir.'

'True.' Thanet sniffed. 'What's that smell?' As so often happens with smells out of context it was familiar but he could not place it.

Lineham wrinkled his nose. 'Turps.'

There was the rattle of a key in the lock, the door

opened and a more powerful waft of turpentine gushed out to meet them. Thanet had not met Roper last night and in view of what he had just been thinking about Barbara Mallis he was interested to see that the nurse was indeed a very personable man, with good physique and an air of alert competence. He was in his early forties, Thanet guessed, and was casually dressed in jeans and sweatshirt.

Introductions made, Thanet asked how Roper's charge was this morning.

'Not too bad. I've seen him better.' The voice was low pitched, slightly nasal, with a hint of cockney accent.

'He's recovered from last night's escapade, then?'

Roper shrugged. 'Don't suppose he's given it another thought.'

'Does he know about Max Jeopard's death?'

'I told him. I had to, with policemen all over the place.'

'How did he react?'

'There wasn't much reaction at all. He just looked at me for a moment, then went back to what he was doing.'

'Which was?'

'Watching television.'

'We'd like a word with him, if possible.'

Roper hesitated, then stood back. 'Try not to upset him.'

This was going to be tricky, thought Thanet. He'd never interviewed anyone with this particular mental condition before, and found that he was feeling slightly apprehensive. Don't be stupid, he told himself. Fear of mental illness, he knew, was universal, but Carey was stabilised, his nurse would be present . . . Treat him like any other witness, he told himself. Just be particularly aware of his responses, that's all, on the alert for the first sign of trouble.

Roper led them through a minute hallway into a room on the right. It was, Thanet realised with a jolt of surprise, set up as a studio. Hence the smell of turpentine. Nobody had told him Carey painted. Perhaps painting was regarded as therapeutic, part of his treatment programme? In any case it was, he thought, an excellent idea. Carey was a virtual prisoner in his own home. Something had to be done to fill in the long hours of incarceration.

Carey was of medium height and had his father's stocky build. He was standing in front of an easel with his back to them, head on one side as if considering the work in progress. To Thanet this looked a meaningless daub of shrieking colour – brilliant blue, green and purple slashed with black. Glancing about, Thanet saw that similar canvases were stacked around the walls, each one transmitting powerful waves of chaos and turbulence.

'Someone to see you, Carey,' said Roper. 'Two policemen.'

Only a twitch of the shoulder betrayed the fact that Carey had heard.

Thanet waited a moment and then walked slowly forward until he was able to see the young man's face. Carey was frowning at the painting and as Thanet watched he jabbed the brush he was holding at his palette and added another jagged black streak to the picture.

Thanet said nothing. Would Carey have any curiosity, or was his self-absorption total?

Carey shot a glance at him, so lightning-swift that Thanet almost wondered if he had imagined it.

'You've come about Max,' he said.

Thanet was startled. He didn't know what he had expected, but it wasn't this calm, rational tone. Which made what Carey said and did next all the more shocking.

He put up his arms as if winding them around someone's neck, closed his eyes in pretended ecstasy and moved his hips sinuously, as if crotch to crotch. 'Oh Max, darling,' he said, in a high-pitched voice, 'promise me you won't go away again. Promise?'

Tess, Thanet realised. At some point Carey had seen Max and Tess together.

Carey opened his eyes and said, once more in a perfectly normal, reasonable tone, 'Good riddance, if you ask me.'

'You didn't like Max?'

'He was shit. Shit. Shit, shit, shit . . .'

He was becoming increasingly agitated and Roper stepped forward to lay a soothing hand on his arm. 'OK, Carey, calm down.'

Carey jerked his arm to shake him off. 'Leave me alone. I'm fine.' He dabbed at his palette again, scarlet paint this time, and then twitched the brush at the painting. Brilliant red droplets flew from the bristles and spattered on to the canvas, like drops of blood. Some of them trickled down, others hung there, globules of viscous crimson.

'You've known Max for a long time, haven't you,' said Thanet, grimly determined to press on despite increasing doubts that there was any point in doing so.

This time Carey startled him by bursting into song, beating time to the music with his paintbrush. '"Boys and girls come out to play, the moon doth shine as bright as day,"' he sang.

'Yes, you used to play tennis with him,' said Thanet. 'I saw a photograph, downstairs. You and Tess and Anthea and Linda and –'

'Linda's ill, you know,' said Carey, interrupting him. 'I don't know what's the matter with her, but she's ill.'

'We can see the Fieldings' bungalow from our sitting-room window,' said Roper by way of explanation.

'They say I'm ill too,' Carey went on. 'Do you think I look ill?' He suddenly left the easel and walked across to a mirror on the wall. He leaned forward and peered into it. 'I look perfectly healthy to me. And all the witches agree. What do you think?'

Nonplussed by the comment about witches, which had been uttered in a perfectly matter-of-fact manner, Thanet decided to ask his questions and terminate what increasingly seemed to be a pointless exercise. 'I just wanted to ask you if you saw him last night? Max, I mean.'

Carey returned to his stance in front of the easel but did not respond.

'Or if, when you were outside – er – keeping Jason company, you saw anything at all unusual?'

'Good dog,' muttered Carey. 'What a good boy!'

Thanet gave up.

'Waste of time,' commented Lineham, when they were outside.

'We had to try.'

'What d'you think, sir? D'you think he had anything to do with it?'

'Impossible to tell. If he did, he seems to have been invisible. There were enough people looking for him. Presumably most of the guests would know him, being friends of the family. If any of them had seen him in the house they'd surely have said so.'

'Some of them must have seen him, even if it didn't register. He must have come downstairs, to get outside.'

'True.'

'He probably slipped out through the kitchen.'

'In which case . . .'

Both of them were remembering that at the other end of the corridor which led to the kitchen was the door to the pool house.

'So if he'd turned left rather than right . . .' said Lineham.

'Exactly.'

'He obviously didn't like Jeopard.'

'Not surprising. Doesn't sound as though many people did.'

They had almost reached the top of the stairs now and as they did so purposeful footsteps clacked across the parquet floor in the hall below.

Thanet put out his hand. *Wait*. They drew back a little. You could learn a lot about witnesses when they thought they were unobserved.

Barbara Mallis appeared, heading for the front door, dressed to go out in suede jacket and high heels.

Just as she was opening it another door clicked open somewhere beneath them and Marion Sylvester called out, 'Are you going anywhere near a shop that might be open?' She sounded slightly hesitant, diffident almost, about asking.

As if he thought his wife had been calling him, Ralph Sylvester appeared in the sitting-room doorway and simultaneously Barbara turned and said, 'I might be. Why?'

Her tone surprised Thanet. Surely a housekeeper would not normally address her employer in that peremptory manner? He realised that she was not aware of Sylvester's presence; the front door, which she was holding ajar, was preventing him from being in her line of vision.

'My husband would like some cigarettes, please.' There

was a slight emphasis on the first two words, and a hint of defiance, as if the fact that it was Sylvester's request made it legitimate for Marion to make it.

Without a word of acknowledgement Barbara Mallis turned on her heel and left. Below them a door softly closed. Sylvester turned and went back into the sitting room, but not before Thanet had glimpsed his face. It was grim.

'Well, well, well!' said Lineham. 'Interesting.'

'Quite. What did you make of it, Mike?'

'I'm not sure. It sounded as if Mrs Sylvester was almost afraid to ask.'

They started to descend the stairs, keeping their voices down.

'And, more to the point, as though Mrs Mallis had the power to refuse,' said Thanet.

'As if she was the one with the upper hand. In fact,' said Lineham slowly, 'almost as if she's got some sort of hold over her.'

'My thought exactly.'

'But what?' Lineham grabbed Thanet's elbow. 'Sir, look at that!' They were halfway down the stairs by now and through one of the glass panels which flanked the front door they had a clear view of Barbara Mallis driving off in the BMW convertible which Lineham had admired earlier. 'It can't be hers, surely!'

'Not exactly the sort of car you'd expect a housekeeper to drive,' said Thanet. 'Let's go and find out.'

Ralph Sylvester was still in the sitting room, standing at one of the front windows, gazing out.

Thanet joined him and was just in time to see the BMW turn out of the drive on to the road, giving him a convenient opening. 'Nice car.'

A brief conversation elicited the information he needed.

According to Sylvester Mrs Mallis had bought the car the previous year with money inherited on her father's death.

'Think that's true, sir?' said Lineham, when they were outside.

'We'll look into it. If it's not, of course, we have to ask ourselves where she did get the money from. It's not just the car, is it? That flat is over the top for a housekeeper and she must spend a pretty penny on clothes. In fact, Mike . . .'

They looked at each other.

'Blackmail?' said Lineham.

ELEVEN

'I wouldn't put it past her, would you?' said Lineham as he started the car. 'And by the look of it, it's Mrs Sylvester she's blackmailing. I wonder what she's got on her. Er . . . where now, sir?'

'Gerald Argent next, I think.'

Lineham glanced at his clipboard of names and addresses. 'He lives on the Ravenswood estate.'

This was one of the new estates which had mushroomed around the edges of Sturrenden despite the Green Belt policy supposedly followed by successive governments.

'I was wondering earlier,' said Thanet as Lineham put the car into gear and moved smoothly off down the drive, 'why Mrs Mallis had stayed so long in this job. I shouldn't have thought it was quite her cup of tea, being stuck out here in the country. I thought perhaps it was Roper who was the attraction, as we suggested earlier.'

'Well, he is a good-looking guy, and Mrs Mallis does seem to have an eye for the opposite sex, as we saw last night!'

Thanet studiously ignored the reference. 'But now I'm wondering . . . If she's got something on Mrs Sylvester and is getting her to pay up for keeping quiet about it, well, she's on to a good thing, isn't she? She wouldn't leave without good reason.'

A couple of hundred yards down the lane they saw the Sylvesters' gardener, Fielding, strolling towards them. Equipped with binoculars and briar stick he was obviously out for a Sunday afternoon walk. Thanet raised a hand in greeting and briefly envied him the freedom to enjoy it. But not for long. It was a lovely day, true, a typical March spring day with blustery winds, fluffy clouds and fat buds about to burst on every tree and hedgerow, but at the moment there was nothing he would rather be doing than pursuing this investigation. The process of delicately feeling his way into a whole new mesh of relationships was the part of his work which interested him most of all. People fascinated him and despite the long years of police work he still on the whole liked them, enjoyed meeting them and trying to understand what made them tick. And this particular case promised a rich harvest.

'Perhaps,' said Lineham suddenly, 'it's Mrs Sylvester who's having an affair with Roper! She's a pretty sexy type, isn't she, and they must see a lot of each other, living under the same roof day in, day out. And Mrs Mallis found out about it, threatened to tell Mr Sylvester.'

'Could be. Did you see Sylvester's face, in the hall, after that incident between his wife and Mrs Mallis? He knows something's going on, that's for sure. And Mrs Sylvester is definitely trying to hide something, wouldn't you agree? So perhaps that's what it is, an affair with Roper. As a matter of fact I was wondering why Roper has stayed so long, too. It must be a pretty soul-destroying job.'

'You're telling me! Those paintings!' Lineham shuddered. 'If that's what the inside of Carey's head feels like I wouldn't wish his state of mind on my worst enemy. And Roper is shut up with him month after month. I don't know how he stands it! I wonder if he ever gets a break.'

'Oh, I should think so. He'd be entitled to holidays like anyone else, I imagine. But on a day-to-day basis . . . He hasn't even got the company of colleagues to make it bearable. So he must also have a pretty powerful reason to have stuck it as long as he has, and it could be one of the women who's the attraction. Yes, I think we need to take a closer look at both Roper and Mrs Mallis. We'll put DC Martin on to it. He enjoys digging into people's backgrounds.'

They were silent for a while, mulling over what they'd heard so far today. At the beginning of a case there was so much to take in it was difficult to assimilate it all.

'Bit of a tangle, isn't it, sir,' said Lineham eventually. 'A real game of musical chairs. I've been trying to work it out. Let's see if I've got it straight. First it was Tess and Max, on and off, then it was Hartley and Anthea, then Max and Anthea, then Tess and Gerald, then Max and Tess again. Is that right?'

Thanet laughed. 'I think so. You're right, it is a tangle.'

'Mind,' said Lineham, 'I think I can understand why Max kept on backing off like that. Sounds to me as if when they were younger Tess was a bit too clinging. I suspect he felt stifled and it made him want to escape.'

'And he finally succumbed when he realised he was in danger of losing her for good.'

'And when he felt she'd got the message that he wasn't going to be tied down too much. That's the way I see it, yes.'

'I'll tell you what all this reminds me of. The Alicia Parnell case, remember?'*

'Yes I do. As I recall, that also involved a group of young people who'd been inseparable in their teens. Yes, you're right.'

'It seems to happen sometimes, doesn't it. You get a group of teenagers with a certain, what shall I call it, chemistry? between them and it seems that whatever happens in later life they never quite break away from each other, not entirely anyway. And there's often one person around whom the others seem to pivot. In that case it was the lad who committed suicide, if you remember. What was his name? Paul something? And in this, it seems to be Max Jeopard.'

'Yes. People like him seem to expect the world to revolve around them and blow me, it does!'

Thanet grinned. 'Sickening, isn't it!'

'Too right it is! No, but seriously, I'd say Mr Sylvester wasn't far off the mark when he said Max was spoilt rotten. You could tell by the way his mother talked about him that she thought the sun shone out of him. And people like that, well they seem to go through life behaving as though they've got a divine right to have their own way. And what gets me is the fact that they usually do! I mean, look at the way he waltzed in and pinched his brother's girlfriend from under his nose! And it wasn't even as though he was serious about her, he was just amusing himself because Tess wasn't around. Imagine how Hartley must have felt! It would have been bad enough hearing his mother sing Max's praises all his life without that happening! And then, a couple of years later, he does exactly the same thing to Gerald! If you ask

* Last Seen Alive

122

me it's not surprising he ended up in someone's swimming pool!'

'You are getting hot under the collar, Mike.'

'Yes, well, people like that get up my nose.'

They had reached the outskirts of Sturrenden now and Thanet fell silent to allow Lineham to negotiate the big roundabout and edge his way into the one-way system. When they were moving smoothly again he said, 'We mustn't forget Anthea, either. It's obvious she expected to take up with Max where they left off before he went away on his last trip. And you know what they say about a woman scorned.'

'Yes. "Hell hath no fury" as la Mallis says. I'm quite looking forward to meeting her, aren't you, sir? She sounds a real little spitfire. I have the feeling she really enjoyed making that scene at the party. I bet she'd rehearsed it over and over until she'd got it just right.'

'She certainly has a powerful dramatic instinct. I imagine it had all the more impact because she said so little. It's interesting that that brief incident brings her into such sharp focus. I don't know about you, but I already have a very clear picture of her. Whereas Gerald is a much more shadowy figure.'

'Though according to Mrs Mallis he still had enough gumption to cut Max dead in public, at the party.'

'True. And I'm sure she was right when she called him Mr and Mrs Sylvester's blue-eyed boy. I'm certain they would much have preferred him as a son-in-law. They'd have kept Tess close to them then, seen their grandchildren grow up . . .'

'And he's got a nice steady job as bank manager. I don't blame them. I know which I'd have chosen as a son-in-law myself.'

'Whereas if she'd married Max he'd have whisked her

off to London and given her a good deal of heartache into the bargain.'

'So what are you saying, sir? That you think it might have been Sylvester who shoved him into the pool?'

'Well, we only have Mrs Mallis's word for it so far but she did say she saw Max making a pass at more than one girl at the party. Sylvester might not have been too pleased about that.'

'I bet Jeopard thought himself irresistible!' Lineham was peering out of the window and now he swung left, entering the Ravenswood estate. Serried ranks of newly-built houses marched off in all directions. The developer had attempted to introduce variety by using half a dozen different designs and setting them back at varying distances from the road, but the effect was still depressingly uniform. Perhaps, thought Thanet, they would look better when the trees and shrubs reached maturity. At the moment there was little to soften the expanses of raw new brick.

'Maybe he was. It sounds as though he had an eye for the women. I even got the impression that Mrs Mallis was hinting he'd made a pass at her. The point is, Mike, if Sylvester saw Max flirting with other girls, saw that Tess was hurt by it, maybe he decided to tackle him about it. Say he took him into the pool house to talk because he knew they wouldn't be disturbed in there. Then they argued, it came to blows and, well, he may not have intended to push him into the pool but when it happened he certainly wasn't going to fish him out.'

'Oakleaf Crescent,' muttered Lineham. 'I'm sure it's along here somewhere. Ah yes, there it is.' He signalled and turned right, then glanced at Thanet. 'You're not suggesting the note was from Sylvester, sir? A bit unlikely, don't you think? Wouldn't he have been much more likely to have a word in his ear?'

'Not necessarily. He may have thought Max would refuse. So he might have resorted to subterfuge, sent a note which pretended to be from a woman, suggesting an assignation, on the assumption that Max would probably turn up through sheer curiosity.'

'Yes! Now that is a possibility. Though for that matter, anyone else could have done the same.'

'True. Let's hope Wakeham manages to track the note down.'

'Here we are. Number twenty-one.' Lineham pulled in neatly alongside the kerb.

Tess's erstwhile fiancé lived in a tiny mid-terrace box which looked as though it wasn't much more than one room wide and one deep.

'Bachelor pad?' said Lineham as they took the two strides which covered the concrete path to the front door. He rang the bell, which immediately burst into a truncated version of 'Home Sweet Home'.

Thanet winced. He hated doorchimes. 'Looks like it. Mrs Mallis did say he and Tess were house-hunting before Max arrived back on the scene.'

'I expect Daddy was putting up the cash,' said Lineham 'After all, he wouldn't want his little girl to have to live in a style to which she was not accustomed.'

'Oh come on, Mike. Argent must be earning a decent living. Bank managers aren't exactly paupers and I believe bank employees get preferential rates on mortgages.'

Lineham rang the bell again. 'Looks as though he's out.'

'What a pain! We'll have to come back later.' They returned to the car and Thanet glanced at his watch. Four-fifteen. 'Where does Anthea live?'

Lineham consulted his clipboard. 'Donnington.'

So they'd have to retrace their steps. Thanet groaned. 'Stupid of me. If I'd had any sense I'd have checked before we left the Sylvesters' and we could have gone there first.'

'My fault too. I did think of suggesting it.'

'Ah well, back we go then.'

But Thanet wasn't really too put out. They could have rung Argent first, to make an appointment, which would have avoided the risk of wasting time, but early on in a case Thanet often preferred to keep people guessing. Besides, the time was never entirely wasted; it was often quite useful to have a short breathing space. It gave you the opportunity to step back a little and reflect and it was always useful to get some impression of a witness's life-style. Argent's chosen career had indicated that in all probability he was a steady, careful type and to Thanet's mind his house had confirmed that predictably he was both unostentatious and prudent, the sort of man who would never run before he could walk and who would bide his time until he could achieve what he truly desired. How would such a man react when his patience apparently paid off and then his prize was snatched away from him? Was it possible that as Lineham would no doubt put it, the worm had turned? According to Barbara Mallis, Argent had originally refused the invitation to the engagement party – scarcely surprising in the circumstances. But then he had changed his mind and turned up. Why? Was it a purely masochistic impulse which had driven him to attend, or had he had something more sinister in mind than a mere snub?

Fortunately, as it was Sunday, the traffic was light. Ten minutes later they were back in Donnington. The village was small, consisting chiefly of one main street

126

and a few clusters of cottages on little side-turnings to left and right. The motor car was gradually turning far too many villages into little more than dormitories, thought Thanet; there was no village shop and even the pub looked as though it had seen more prosperous days.

Wistaria Cottage also looked as though it had come down in the world. The owner – Anthea? Her parents? A landlord? – was obviously either hard up, lazy, incapacitated or indifferent to the deterioration of his property. It was a typical Kentish cottage, mellow red brick to the first floor and tile-hung above, separated from the pavement by a rickety picket fence which badly needed a coat of paint. The two tiny patches of earth on either side of the uneven path sported a fine crop of weeds. Grimy window panes, peeling paint and rusting door knocker all added to the general air of neglect.

The woman who answered the door was wearing black leggings and a loose multicoloured tunic top in panels of different materials sewn together with blanket-stitch. The effect was as off-beat as the cheongsam last night and for a fleeting moment Thanet thought that it was Anthea. Then he registered the lines on the woman's face, the texture of skin from which the bloom of youth had faded and he realised that it must be her mother. The likeness was remarkable but this woman was in her forties.

When he told her who they were her eyes flashed. 'I don't know why you're bothering. We should be hanging out the flags, that the world has one bastard fewer in it today.'

'We have to make enquiries, Mrs Greenway. May we come in?'

She cast a defiant glance up and down the road as if to

say to the neighbours, *Yes, it's the police. So what?* Then she turned. 'Suit yourself.'

They stepped straight into a small square sitting room. It struck chill and dank, as if it were rarely used and was, Thanet thought, quite the most cluttered room he had ever seen. Every available square inch of surface on mantelpiece, windowsills and table-tops was jammed with an extraordinary collection of objects ranging from ornaments of every possible description, some broken and some intact, to shells, stones, pebbles and bits of driftwood. There were so many pictures and prints crowded together on the walls that there was virtually no wall-surface to be seen, and even the ceiling was partially concealed by bunches of dried flowers of all colours, shapes and sizes, some in woven baskets, suspended from hooks screwed into the beams. There was an all-enveloping smell of cats and Thanet counted at least three, curled up on the chairs. Lineham wrinkled his nose in distaste at Thanet as one of them jumped down and followed its mistress into an equally cluttered kitchen and finally into a glass structure built right along the back of the house, too ramshackle to be called a conservatory. Here too the windowsills were crammed with objects, this time interspersed with potted plants. A steamy warmth gushed forth to meet them, emanating from an oil convector heater. The windows were running with condensation and in here the smell of cats was overpowering. Thanet found that he was breathing through his mouth and seeking the source of the stench he traced it to several litter trays, some of which he noted to his distaste had been used more than once. Mrs Greenway was evidently of the school which considered the great outdoors to be anathema to her pets.

Restraining an impulse to rush to the door and fling it

open, he forced himself to look around, realising at once that for the second time today he was in a studio. Unlike Carey Sylvester Mrs Greenway worked in watercolour; a large table loaded with pots of brushes, boxes and tubes of paint and all the other accoutrements of a watercolourist stood in front of the window. Nearby was a smaller table with a still life set up on it, a carefully arranged group of kitchen objects on a harlequin-patterned cloth – a stainless steel kettle and saucepan, some dessert spoons and three silver eggcups.

Thanet gestured at the painting upon which she was obviously working. 'May I?'

She shrugged and nodded, her expression still hostile.

Leaning over to look at it he saw at once what he had not appreciated before, that all the objects in the still life were shiny. It dawned on him that what interested her was the reflections. Each object reflected the others, the shapes distorted by the curved surfaces, as were the diamonds of hazy colour cast up by the cloth. The degree of detail was astonishing. If part of an artist's task is to enable the viewer to look at the world with new eyes, she was certainly succeeding. He glanced up at her with respect. 'This must be incredibly difficult to paint.'

Sensing his genuine interest she thawed a little. 'It is a bit complicated, yes.'

He studied it a moment longer before straightening up. 'I believe a famous writer once said, "If it wasn't difficult everybody would be doing it."'

That amused her and she even managed a slight smile. 'I never thought of it like that but yes, I suppose that's true.'

'It must take you ages to complete a painting. This is so detailed.'

'It does, unfortunately. I'm afraid I work at a snail's pace.'

'And the fewer you finish, the fewer you have to sell.'

'If you can sell them at all!'

'Yes. I imagine it's not the easiest field in which to make a living.'

'You can say that again!'

She was now almost ready to be cooperative, thought Thanet. 'I suppose you collect all this sort of thing for your work.' He waved a hand at the crowded windowsills.

'I'm a real magpie. You just never know when something is going to come in useful.' She sat down in front of the table, swivelling the chair around to face them as if conceding that she was now ready to talk. 'There's only one spare chair, but it's warmer in here than in the sitting room. Tip the cat off, if you like.'

Thanet glanced at the basket chair to which she had referred. The cat which had followed her in was now firmly ensconced upon it, engaged in its ablutions, one leg stuck up in the air. The cushion, he noted, was plastered with cats' hairs. 'It's all right, we'll stand.'

'Or there are a couple of stools in the kitchen.'

Thanet glanced at Lineham and the sergeant went off to fetch them.

'Actually, it was your daughter we wanted to talk to.'

Her expression hardened. 'I assumed as much. But I'm afraid you're out of luck. She's terribly upset. She's still in bed, been there all day.'

The stools, Thanet was relieved to see, were made of wood and reasonably clean.

'I'm afraid we really have to talk to her.'

'Won't I do, instead? She can't tell you anything I don't know.'

'Were you at the party last night?' Thanet was pretty sure she hadn't been. He hadn't seen two Greenways on the guest list.

She shook her head.

'In that case, we really must see her.'

'She won't get up. I know she won't.'

'Would you try to convince her it would be a good idea? She'll have to talk to us sooner or later and it would be far better for her to get it over with.'

Mrs Greenway stared at him for a few moments, considering what he had said, trying to make up her mind. Then her mouth tugged down at the corners. 'I suppose you're right.' She stood up. 'All right, I'll try. But I can't promise anything.'

TWELVE

When she had gone Lineham said, 'D'you think we could open the door for a few minutes, sir, let some fresh air in?'

'Better not. She might not be too pleased and we don't want to upset her now she's come around.' Thanet sat down on one of the stools Lineham had brought.

The sergeant reluctantly followed suit. 'How can anyone live in an atmosphere like this?'

'They're used to it, presumably, don't notice it any more.'

'Don't notice it? How can anyone fail to notice it? I've spent so long holding my breath I thought I would suffocate!'

'Breathe through your mouth, Mike. And stop being such an old woman. I don't like it any more than you do but we have to do this interview and that's all there is to it.'

Lineham looked mutinous and muttered, 'We ought to get extra pay for this sort of thing.'

'Danger money you mean?' said Thanet with a grin.

Lineham gave him a sheepish look and then, his normal good humour reasserting itself, grinned back.

'What'll we do if Anthea won't come down, sir?'

'Make an appointment for her to come in to Headquarters, I suppose. Anyway, let's hope that doesn't happen. I'd much prefer to talk to her now.'

They were in luck. A few moments later Mrs Greenway returned and said, 'She's getting dressed. She'll be down shortly.'

'Good. Thank you.' Thanet waited until she had sat down and then added, 'I gather you weren't too keen on Max Jeopard.'

She grimaced. 'How did you guess!'

'Would you mind telling us why?'

'Where do I begin?'

'Oh, it's not as bad as that, surely,' said Lineham.

'You didn't know him.'

'No,' said Thanet. 'But we're learning.'

'Well, you've come to the right person. I've known Max since he was in his teens. He and Anthea used to run around in the same crowd of young people. They were always in and out of each other's houses, so one way and the other I saw quite a lot of them.'

'You're talking about Max, his brother Hartley, Tess and Carey Sylvester, your daughter Anthea, Gerald Argent and Linda Fielding?' said Thanet.

'You haven't wasted much time, have you! Yes, that's right.'

'So tell us about him,' said Thanet.

Mrs Greenway frowned. 'I always find it difficult to describe people I know well. I suppose,' she said reluctantly, 'the most striking thing about him was his, well, I suppose you'd call it charisma. He could charm the birds out of the trees, could Max. To begin with you thought, what a delightful young man! Then after a while it began to dawn on you that this façade – his politeness, good manners and so on – was all just a means to an end, that of getting his own way. Sooner or later, everybody always ended up doing what Max wanted. It took ages for me to realise this but when I did I wondered why on earth I hadn't seen it before. There's no doubt about it, he was the sort of person who thought he could get away with anything and usually did.'

Until now, thought Thanet grimly. This time he went too far.

'The girls were all dazzled by him, of course,' Mrs Greenway was saying.

'All?'

'Yes. Even Linda, and she was very different from the other two, much quieter and more retiring, and she didn't actually spend as much time with the group as Anthea and Tess. But now and then I'd catch her looking at Max and there's no doubt about it, she fancied him all right. Poor girl, she's desperately ill now, I believe. I feel so sorry for her parents, they absolutely doted on that child. What was I saying?'

'You were talking about Max's fascination for women.'

'Ah, yes. Well, Tess absolutely adored him, of course, and poor Anthea never got a look in. The curious thing about Max was that although he couldn't resist making a pass at any eligible female within arm's reach, there was really only ever one girl he was seriously interested in.'

'Tess.'

'Tess. The trouble was that, being Max, he was determined to have her on his own terms.'

'Which were?'

'That he should have complete freedom to do as he wanted. Max was a great one for having his cake and eating it. So Tess was expected to wait patiently at home while he bummed off around the world for as long or as short a time as took his fancy. I'm not surprised she got fed up with it. It was always Tess who broke off with him, you know, not the other way around. Until, eventually, he went a little too far and discovered that she'd finally given up on him and was about to marry someone else.'

'Gerald Argent.'

'Exactly. When I heard Tess and Gerald were engaged I thought, good for Gerald! I knew he'd always had his eye on Tess but while Max was around he never had a hope. And I must admit to a sneaky feeling of satisfaction that just for once Max wasn't going to get what he wanted. I should have known better! When Max came home at Christmas I think he realised this was his very last chance with Tess and he went all out to get her back. Poor Gerald never stood a chance. He was very cut up about it, I believe, or so Anthea says, anyway.'

'It wasn't the first time Max had pinched someone's girl, was it. I believe he did the same thing to his brother, with your daughter.'

'Typical!' Mrs Greenway clamped her lips together as if to prevent her angry feelings from spilling out against her will and it was immediately obvious that she had no intention of talking as freely about Anthea as she had about the others.

So, how to get her to open up? Thanet tried an oblique approach. 'Tess was away when this happened, I believe?'

'In America, yes.'

'How long had your daughter been going out with Hartley, at that time?'

'I'm not sure. I wasn't counting.'

'Weeks? Months? Years?'

'Oh, months, I'd say.'

'How many?'

'I told you, I wasn't counting!'

'At a rough guess, then?'

'Five, six, I suppose.'

'So it was quite a well-established relationship.'

'Look, if you want to find out about this, you'll just have to talk to Anthea. I'm not prepared to discuss it.'

'Discuss what?' A new voice, from the doorway. Anthea, at last. Her long dark hair was caught up into a pony-tail on the top of her head with an elastic band and she was wearing jeans and a baggy sweater with sleeves so long that only the very tips of her fingers protruded. But although her clothes were much more conventional than last night she still retained a slightly exotic quality, her slightly slanting eyes lending her a touch of the Orient absent in her mother.

'Your love life,' said Mrs Greenway, clearly attempting to shock Anthea into indignation.

Anthea yawned. 'How boring!' she said. She sauntered to the basket chair, picked up the cat and sat down, settling it on to her knee. Almost at once it began to purr.

'I think perhaps your mother is exaggerating a little,' said Thanet, introducing himself. 'I'm simply trying to find out more about Max Jeopard and naturally I have to talk to all the people who knew him.'

'No need to pussyfoot around,' said Anthea. 'No doubt you heard about the little act I put on last night. Ouch! Stop it, Tibbles!' The cat was kneading Anthea's thighs with half-extended claws.

'Act? What act?' said her mother sharply.

'Oh don't fuss, Mum.'

'I want to know what you're talking about!' Mrs Greenway glared at her daughter, willing her to give in, but Anthea wasn't budging. Her mother switched her gaze to Thanet. 'Inspector?'

But Thanet had no intention of alienating Anthea. 'Mrs Greenway, I'm sorry, but I think it would be best if you left us to talk to Anthea alone.'

'No! It wouldn't be right.'

'Oh Mum, really! I am a grown woman, not a twelve-year-old! I agree with the Inspector. It would be easier all round if you went.'

'What is it you don't want me to hear? I insist on staying!' And then, as no one responded, 'You can't turn me out of a room in my own house! I refuse to leave!'

'Very well,' said Thanet, rising. 'Miss Greenway can accompany us to Headquarters, instead.'

'Oh, for God's sake!' said Anthea in disgust. 'What a fuss about nothing! Sit down, Inspector, do. I don't want to go trailing into Sturrenden when we can get it over with more quickly here. Please, Mum, just go, will you? I promise you there's no need to worry. It's no big deal.'

'Well . . . If you're sure . . .'

'I'm sure!'

Mrs Greenway's reluctance showed in every line of her body, in her dragging footsteps and the backward glance she cast over her shoulder.

'I'm her only chick,' said Anthea with a grin when she had gone. 'She can't help it.'

'Perfectly understandable,' said Thanet. 'But now . . .'

'OK, OK, I'll tell you all about it, right? Then if there's anything more you want to ask you can fire away afterwards. I've got nothing to hide.'

'Fine.'

'It's all quite simple really,' said Anthea, with a toss of her pony-tail. 'I don't know how much you've found out

137

about Max yet but you may or may not know that until Christmas he'd been away on a really long trip, in South America. He's a travel writer so naturally he has to travel. The point is that before he went we had a bit of a thing going and I had the distinct impression that when he came back we'd take up where we left off. But we didn't. Instead, he made a beeline for Tess again and just didn't want to know, as far as I was concerned. Well, naturally, I was, to put it mildly, rather pissed off with him.' She shrugged. 'Hence the little scene last night. End of story.'

'If he's been back since Christmas why wait until last night to tell him so?'

'Oh I didn't! Oh no! I told him what I thought of him, believe me, in no uncertain terms.'

'So why tell him again, in public?'

Anthea abandoned her world-weary pose and sat up with a jerk, leaning forward in her eagerness to get them to understand, and the cat, affronted, jumped down and stalked off into the kitchen. 'But that was just the point, don't you see? *In public*. Before, I'd just spoken to him in private but this time I wanted to humiliate him in front of everyone he knew.'

'Including Tess?'

Anthea's expression changed. 'I must admit that was the one thing I felt badly about. I didn't want to hurt her and I made sure she wasn't actually in the room before I staged my protest, but I'm afraid I was so mad with him that every other consideration just went out of the window.'

'*Every* other consideration?' said Thanet quietly. 'Precisely how angry with him were you?'

She stared at him, the animation fading. Then she frowned and narrowed her eyes. 'What are you getting at? You surely aren't suggesting that I . . .? Oh no. You can't be.'

'That you pushed him into the pool?' said Thanet. 'Did you?'

'Don't be ridiculous! As far as I was concerned I'd made my point and that was it, finish!' And she made a chopping movement as if to indicate how final her severance with Max had been.

Apart from a slight puffiness beneath her eyes Anthea had so far revealed no sign of grief or regret at Max's death, thought Thanet. Yet her mother said that she was so upset she had stayed in bed all day and certainly last night she looked as though she had been crying. He distinctly remembered thinking, when he noticed her, that there went someone who had mourned Max Jeopard's passing. So, had the grief been for him, or had there been some other reason for her distress? He had to find out how she truly felt about Max in order to gauge the likelihood of her having had something to do with his death. How could he get behind this show of bravado? 'It looks as though someone did,' he said. 'By all accounts Max was a strong swimmer. No one has suggested that he'd had too much to drink, and it's unlikely that he would have slipped if he'd been in the pool house alone. We think he went there to meet someone.' Thanet glanced at Lineham, who understood at once what Thanet was trying to do, and chimed in.

'We think there was a struggle.'

'That Max slipped . . .'

'Or was pushed . . .'

'And fell into the pool . . .'

'Knocking his head on the side as he fell.'

'So he was unconscious as he went into the water.'

'And whoever it was just let him drown.'

They stopped and Lineham's last words hung in the air, with all their overtones of callousness and deliberate intent on the part of Max's assailant.

Anthea stared at the two policemen, eyes glazed, obviously visualising the scene they had conjured up. Then her lower lip began to tremble and she sucked it in, bit on it and closed her eyes as if to shut out the images in her brain. Two tears squeezed out from beneath her closed eyelids. 'Oh, God,' she said, and covered her face with her hands.

Thanet and Lineham glanced at each other, reading their own emotions mirrored in the other's face. They had achieved their aim but couldn't help feeling ashamed of themselves. Many policemen over the years build up a carapace of insensitivity which enables them to employ such tactics without the slightest qualms of conscience, but Thanet had never been able to do so – nor would he have wanted to. Somewhat pompously he told himself that he was not prepared to relinquish his humanity. At times like this, however, he wondered if somewhere along the line he had done so without even realising it. After all, Anthea had not for a moment denied her anger with Max. Should that not have been sufficient?

'Miss Greenway,' he said gently, leaning forward. 'I'm sorry. Our account was too graphic and I apologise.'

She took her hands away from her face and gave him a searching look, blinking away the tears which were still welling up.

Without a word Lineham handed her a handkerchief and she wiped her eyes before blowing her nose.

'I'll be frank with you,' said Thanet. 'The trouble is that even the most innocent of witnesses feels threatened at being questioned by the police, and resorts to defensive behaviour. It's understandable, of course, but it does get in the way, hold things up.'

'I think I see what you're getting at. I was putting it on a bit. Playing it cool.'

'Yes, but that was your way of coping,' said Thanet. 'I see that now.'

Suddenly and unexpectedly she smiled, for the first time, and Thanet saw how vital and attractive she might be in normal circumstances. 'You're much too nice to be a policeman.'

Lineham rolled his eyes. 'You wouldn't say that if you worked with him!'

'That's enough from you, Sergeant!'

They all laughed and the atmosphere lightened still further.

'OK,' said Anthea. 'Let's try again. Tell me how I can help.'

'I know it might be painful for you, but if you could tell us a bit about Max? It really is helpful to find out how different people viewed him.'

She frowned, picking at some nail varnish which had worked loose. 'It's so difficult when you know someone well,' she said, unconsciously echoing her mother. 'And I've known Max for years, ever since we were in our teens.' She shook her head. 'And I still can't believe he's . . .' She swallowed hard and dabbed at her eyes with Lineham's handkerchief. 'He was so alive, so much, well, larger than life. I know he was self-centred and big-headed but somehow, with Max, you could forgive him because, let's face it, it was justified. He had everything, you see. He was good-looking, intelligent, gifted . . . The fact that he traded on all this just seemed to fade into insignificance when you were with him. He made life so much more exciting, just by being there. That's why he was always the centre of a crowd. He was like a magnet. That was the secret of his success as a travel writer, I think. People would have opened up to him in a way that was pure gold as far as his work was concerned.' She stopped, gave a little grimace and a wry grin. 'That was his good side.'

'And his bad?'

'He was pretty ruthless really. If he wanted something he went for it, no matter who got hurt on the way.'

'And I should think,' said Lineham as they returned to the car, 'that that just about sums him up. What amazes me is that she could see all that so clearly and yet she was still crazy about him.'

'It really shouldn't surprise you, Mike. There are men like that, and women too, and no matter what they do the unfortunate souls who fall in love with them just keep coming back for more.'

'Back to Sturrenden to see Argent?' said Lineham, starting the engine. He waited for Thanet's nod before moving off. 'So what do you think, sir? Think it was her?'

'No, I don't. I may be wrong, of course. She was certainly away from the others long enough.'

Anthea had confirmed that around 9.40, while they were queueing for supper, she had left Gerald and Hartley; to go to the loo, she claimed. There had been a number of women with the same idea and she had had to wait to use the bathroom, passing the time with social chit-chat. Lineham would check the names she had given them but even so, the fact that she had been away a good fifteen or twenty minutes meant that in the general confusion of people milling around at suppertime it would be virtually impossible to pin down timings precisely.

'Now if her mother had been there . . .' said Lineham.

'I know. But she wasn't.'

'I think what made Mrs Greenway so furious with Max was that she could see all along he was only amusing himself with Anthea because Tess wasn't available. She knew Anthea was going to get hurt and there was nothing she could do about it.'

'And being proved right has given her no satisfaction. You're right, Mike.' Thanet was thinking of Bridget and her ex-boyfriend Alexander. 'It's not easy to stand by and see your children get hurt. It's bad enough when it's not intentional, when it's a love affair that just goes wrong, but when you suspect from the beginning that someone is just using your son or daughter for his own amusement and you feel helpless to prevent it ... Oh yes, I can understand how she feels, all right. But if we all went around bumping off people who had jilted our offspring there'd be mayhem.' Why, oh why hadn't they heard from Bridget? Would she ring tonight?

'Anyway, as you say, she wasn't even there.'

This time they were not disappointed. Although dusk was only just beginning to fall there were lights on in Argent's house and a couple of cars parked outside.

'That's Hartley Jeopard's Golf,' said Lineham.

'So it is. Never mind.' Thanet was already out of the car. He wasn't going to be put off now. Gerald Argent was the only member of the group they had not so far met and he was eager to do so. 'Let's see what Argent has to say for himself.'

THIRTEEN

Gerald Argent was the type you'd pass in the street without a second glance, thought Thanet as they followed him through a hall so tiny that there was barely room for more than two people to stand in it. Argent was neither short nor tall, fat nor thin, dark nor fair, and had, on first impressions, no peculiarities of physiognomy to make him stand out from the crowd. It was all the more intriguing, therefore, to enter his living room and be confronted by two shelves of cups and trophies and a number of framed photographs which clearly commemorated the occasions upon which they had been won. Apart from this touch of individuality it was a room which would, Thanet thought, be indistinguishable from hundreds of thousands of others in modern houses up and down the country, simply but adequately furnished with a sofa, two matching armchairs, some adjustable bookshelves, a television set and a CD player. At one end there was a small round modern dining table and four chairs.

Hartley Jeopard unfolded his long frame from an armchair as they came in. 'Good evening, Inspector, Sergeant. I'll be off, then, Gerald.'

'Don't be ridiculous, Hart. I don't mind you staying,

not in the least.' Argent cocked an interrogatory eyebrow at Thanet.

'It's entirely up to you,' said Thanet.

Hartley shuffled his feet. 'No, I think it would be best if I went. Tell you what, I'll go and pick up something to eat. D'you fancy Chinese?'

'Fine by me.'

'OK. Anything special?'

'Up to you.'

The display of photographs was drawing Thanet like a magnet and during this exchange he edged closer to them. The images took on definition, became recognisable. The distinctive silhouettes of ballroom dancers have become universally familiar via the medium of television. Perhaps Argent wasn't quite your Mr Average after all, he thought. Distinction in any field can only be achieved by patience, dedication, perseverance and sheer hard work. He turned to find Argent watching him, and waved a hand at the trophies. 'You must be very good at it.'

Argent shrugged. 'A lot depends on finding the right partner.'

'You obviously have.'

'We've been dancing together for a number of years now.'

'I imagine it's a pretty time-consuming hobby.'

'It does take a fair amount of time, yes. Do sit down.'

'How do boyfriends and girlfriends, husbands and wives feel about that?'

'Much as they would about any other hobby, I suppose.'

'And Miss Sylvester?'

Argent was immediately wary. 'What do you mean?'

'I was wondering how she felt about your spending so

much time with another woman, when you were engaged.'

'June isn't "another woman", as you put it, Inspector. She's my dancing partner and nothing more. As a matter of fact she's engaged herself and getting married in the autumn. Anyway, the question is irrelevant. My engagement was recently broken off as you're obviously aware. And in any case, I frankly don't see that it's any of your business.'

'Oh but it is, Mr Argent, as I'm sure you'll realise if you put your mind to it. In fact, you must think I'm pretty naïve if you imagine I don't appreciate the possible consequences of Max Jeopard's death as far as you are concerned.'

Argent's lips tightened but he did not respond.

'Yes, I see you understand me. Miss Sylvester is free again now, isn't she?'

'I refuse to discuss the matter. I think it's in very bad taste, so soon after Max's death.'

'In my view, bad taste doesn't enter into it, where murder is concerned.'

'It is definitely murder, then?'

'We're treating it as such at the moment, yes. It's difficult to see how it could be anything else. And the plain fact is that yesterday Miss Sylvester was lost to you. Now, she is attainable again, because of Max Jeopard's death.'

'So that makes me a murderer, does it!'

'Not necessarily, no. But you must see that suspicion is bound to fall upon you and it's up to you to convince us that you had nothing to do with his death.'

'Great! I thought that in this country you were innocent until proved guilty, not the other way around!'

'I didn't say that it was up to you to convince the

Court that you were innocent, just to convince us. A very different matter. I'm putting this to you quite plainly because you are obviously an intelligent man and I want you to understand that there is no point in trying to be anything less than frank with us.'

'Why should I be less than frank with you? I've nothing to hide.'

'Good!' said Thanet. 'In that case . . .' He glanced at Lineham.

The sergeant took over smoothly and while he put his questions Thanet observed Argent carefully, on the alert for the slightest sign of unease, wariness, dissemblance. When you were doing the questioning you had to concentrate so hard on what you were saying that it was not always possible to pick up these nuances. But try as he would he could detect no sign that the man was lying. Argent's account accorded with that of Anthea and Hartley: he had remained behind in the queue while the other two went off to their respective loos. He had, he claimed, collected his food and then gone to sit down while he waited for them to return.

'We understand that in the first instance you refused the invitation to the party,' said Lineham.

'I don't know why that should surprise you. I would have thought it understandable in the circumstances.'

'Quite. No, we're much more interested in why you later changed your mind.'

Argent shrugged. 'I thought about it a lot before deciding to go after all. As I saw it, the fact of the matter was that although Tess and Max would be living in London we would be bound to see each other from time to time and unless I was prepared to go through life avoiding any possibility of running into them, I might as well start as I meant to go on.'

'Your change of heart did not extend to being civil to Mr Jeopard, though.'

'My God, you have been listening to gossip, haven't you?'

'Naturally we've been talking to everyone who was present last night, yes. What else would you expect, in a murder case?'

'Snubbing someone doesn't mean to say you intend to nip off and kill them later on in the evening, does it? In fact, I'd say the opposite was true. If I'd intended to bash Max over the head and shove him into the swimming pool I'd scarcely have made it quite so obvious I wasn't on speaking terms with him, would I?'

Argent had a point, there, thought Thanet.

Lineham had picked him up quickly. 'Who said anything about bashing him on the head?'

'Nobody! But it's obvious to anyone who knew Max and has even a grain of intelligence that he must have been unconscious when he went into the water or he would have got himself out again. Hasn't anyone told you what a strong swimmer he was?'

Definitely round one to Argent, thought Thanet as they left. Despite his nondescript appearance he was clearly not a man to be underestimated. He said so, to Lineham.

'You're right there!' The sergeant was clearly smarting at having allowed Argent to gain the upper hand.

'He's either a good liar or he has nothing to hide.'

'I agree.'

'But the fact remains, he had a pretty powerful motive.'

'Too true. Tess Sylvester would be a good catch for any man. I mean, she's got everything, including an old man who's rolling in it.'

'I sometimes think you're completely lacking in romance, Mike.'

'That's what Louise says.'

'You'd better watch it! Once your wife starts saying that sort of thing you could be in big trouble.'

Lineham appeared unconcerned. 'She's been saying it since before we were married and it didn't put her off then, so why should it make any difference now? Still, maybe you're right.' He grinned and glanced at Thanet. 'You'll be asking me when I last told her I love her, next!'

Thanet laughed. 'When did you?'

On the drive back to the office they were silent, thinking. Just before they got there Lineham said, 'There is one possibility we haven't considered.'

'What?'

'That Hartley Jeopard and Argent could have been in it together. They seem pretty close.'

'Oh come on, Mike. Haven't we got enough suspects, without you scratching around for further possibilities? Besides, I think we'd both agree that this is unlikely to have been a premeditated murder and I can't really envisage a scenario in which more than Jeopard and one other person were involved.'

Back at the office there were endless reports to read and to write and it was late before Thanet managed to get away. He was tired, his back was aching as usual and all he could think of was getting into bed and sinking into oblivion. He thought that both Joan and Ben would have been in bed long since and on arriving home, therefore, he was surprised to see lights on downstairs. Bad news about Bridget? His mind clicked into higher gear as the adrenalin began to flow.

As he closed the front door Ben appeared in the living-room doorway. He'd obviously been waiting for his father to get home. But there was no sign of Joan, so this was probably nothing to do with Bridget. Thanet breathed a sigh of relief.

'Hi, Dad. I know it's late, but any chance of a word?'

'Yes, of course. The spurt of anxiety had in any case woken Thanet up. He could guess what Ben wanted to talk about and felt guilty that he had scarcely given a thought to his son's future all day. 'Fancy a cup of tea?'

'Thanks. I wouldn't mind a snack as well. You want one?'

'No, I'm not hungry. Had something in the canteen earlier. You go ahead, though.'

Thanet put the kettle on while Ben assembled the makings of one of his famous snacks: bread, margarine, cheese, tomatoes, lettuce, spring onions, cucumber. 'How's the case going, Dad?' he said.

'All right, I suppose. The first day's always a bit hectic. I can never seem to get through as much as I'd like to.'

'Sounds an interesting one, by what I heard on the news. Is it true that it happened at the victim's engagement party?'

'Yes, I'm afraid so.'

'Tough on the fiancée.'

'Quite.'

'They said he was a travel writer.'

'That's right. He'd only written one book so far, but he did pretty well out of it. As a matter of fact I've got a copy.' Thanet had shoved the book Mrs Jeopard had given him into his raincoat pocket before leaving the office and now he went to fetch it, handed it to Ben.

'*Peephole into China.* Mmm. Interesting cover,' said Ben, studying it. He turned the book over. 'This him?'

Thanet nodded. The kettle had boiled and he made the tea, then poured it.

'Looks pretty full of himself.'

Thanet made no comment and Ben, sensing that his father had said all he was prepared to say on the subject, handed the book back and picked up his sandwich and mug. 'Ready?'

They retired to the living room where the embers of a fire still glowed. Both Thanet and Joan loved an open fire and always used it in the evenings in preference to central heating.

Thanet threw a couple of logs on to it then sank back into his armchair with a sigh of relief. 'That's better. So . . . I imagine you want to talk about this new suggestion of yours.'

Ben nodded. 'We didn't have much chance to discuss it last night.' He sank his teeth enthusiastically into his sandwich.

'I know. I'm sorry.'

'It wasn't your fault. And I'm sorry, too, to spring this on you at the end of such a long day. But I don't have any choice. I really do have to make up my mind in the next day or two.'

Thanet grinned. 'I know. But I think we'd better stop apologising to each other, don't you? Now, tell me what you really feel about this and I'll try to do the same.'

Ben took another huge mouthful before replying. 'Well, I know that last night I came over a bit strong. But to be honest, Dad, I still haven't really made up my mind. I suppose I was afraid you'd be so dead set against the idea that I felt I had to present you with a cut-and-dried decision to counter what you were going to say.' He gave a shamefaced grin. 'Knowing you and Mum I should have had more sense.'

'What do you mean?'

'Well, you're not exactly heavy-handed types, are you?'

Thanet smiled. 'We try not to be. Is that a complaint?' He was endeavouring to hide his relief. There was still a chance, then, that Ben might opt for university after all.

This time there was mischief in Ben's smile. 'Well, it doesn't leave much room for adolescent revolt!'

'Is that what this is?'

'No! Well, not exactly. I suppose I feel I've just drifted into the idea of going on to university without really questioning whether or not it's what I really want.'

'And when did you decide that what you really wanted was to go into the police?'

Ben shrugged, finished demolishing his sandwich. 'Oh, I don't know. Years ago, really, if I look back. I've always been very interested in your work, as you know. But I suppose I didn't actually come out with it because in a way I didn't want to seem to be following in my father's footsteps. If you see what I mean. And then I thought, well hang on, this is ridiculous. If it's what I want, that shouldn't stop me doing it. Should it?'

'No, of course not.'

'So, what do you think?'

Thanet paused before replying. He desperately wanted not to say the wrong thing. He chose to prevaricate. 'Would you tell me first how thoroughly you've looked into this?'

Very thoroughly, he discovered. Ben knew precisely what the selection procedure involved, how long the training would be. He was also aware of the graduate entry scheme and its advantages and disadvantages. And of course he had had first-hand experience of the kind of demands police work could make on a man's domestic life, through his father. No, he certainly wasn't going into this with his eyes shut.

'So come on now, Dad. Tell me what you think.'

'All right. I'll try to be frank.' Thanet paused for a moment before continuing. 'As you know, your mother and I have always hoped that if you proved bright enough, you'd go to university. There's no point in pretending otherwise. Nor is there any point in pretending that if you don't we won't be disappointed. At the same time we both feel that it's your life and your career that's at stake and it would be wrong for us to try and impose our wishes on you. So, you have to make up your own mind and the best I can do in the way of advice is to say to you what I would say to any other bright young potential recruit who came along: that you shouldn't rush into this, that you should get some experience of life first. Maturity is a great help in the force, both in terms of relationships with the public, who don't like policemen who look wet behind the ears, and in terms of helping you personally to deal with difficult situations. So I would say go to university and take some time out for travel, either before or afterwards. Then when you've got your degree see if you still feel the same. If you do, then go ahead, and good luck to you.'

'And that really is what you'd say to anyone in my situation?'

'Definitely, yes. The other point is of course that at the moment entry is difficult. Most forces are swamped with applications. But I don't see that as a particular problem in your case. I think you'd have a pretty good chance of getting in, provided you can find a force which is recruiting and you're then prepared to wait several months before starting training.' Thanet felt that he couldn't be fairer than that.

Ben was silent, thinking over what his father had said.

'If you like,' Thanet offered, 'I could arrange for you

153

to talk, in confidence, with someone else. I'm sure the Super would be only too happy to advise you.'

Ben grinned. 'It's OK, Dad. I trust you. He'd probably only say the same as you. In fact, you're only confirming what I already suspected.' Ben heaved himself out of his chair. 'Thanks.'

Thanet was longing to ask if this meant Ben had reached a decision, but he restrained himself. *Don't push it.* As it was, the outcome looked far more promising than he had hoped.

He had just switched the light off in the sitting room and started up the stairs when the telephone rang. At this hour of the night it could only be an emergency at work or Bridget. Praying that it was the latter he hurried back down and snatched up the receiver.

Relief flooded through him at the sound of his daughter's voice.

'Dad? Oh thank goodness! I'm sorry I haven't managed to get through to you before!'

Apparently Bridget's host family in Adelaide had met her at the airport, scooped her up and borne her straight off into the outback where they were spending a few days at a holiday home lent them by a friend. This had no telephone and Bridget hadn't realised that she would therefore be incommunicado for some time. On their first trip to a town she had seized the opportunity to ring.

'I realise it must be the middle of the night there, Dad, and I'm sorry if I've woken you up, but I felt I must grab the chance.'

'Don't worry. I wasn't in bed anyway. It's a relief to hear from you. It sounds as though you're having a great time.'

'Oh, I am! Love to Mum.'

Thanet would have loved to talk to her longer but they

had agreed before Bridget left that these calls would be brief, because of the expense. Anyway, it was enough just to know that she was safe.

Thanet went to bed a much happier man and expected to go out like a light. But peace of mind, it seemed, was not enough to keep at bay the crowded impressions of the day. Always, at the beginning of a case, there was so much to think of, to remember, to plan, that he tended to find it difficult to go to sleep and tonight was no exception. They shouldn't forget, as he had said to Lineham, that Kent had been only part of Jeopard's life. He had actually lived and worked in London, when he wasn't away on his travels, and presumably had contacts there of which they as yet knew nothing. His publishers, for instance, or his literary agent, if he had one. All his papers and correspondence would be there too. Yes, they really ought to make a visit to his flat a priority. Tomorrow morning they would skim through the reports and if there was nothing urgent they would get clearance from the Met and be off. As Monday was a weekday and parking in the capital such a problem it might be best to go by train – so long as he was back in time for his visit to the chiropractor. Joan would be furious if he missed it after having had to wait for a month before getting an appointment. He wasn't looking forward to it. He didn't know exactly what chiropractors did but whatever it was he was sure it would be painful. And he really didn't think it would do any good anyway. He'd tried physiotherapists and osteopaths but none of them had really made any lasting difference. Experimentally he eased his back, wincing as pain stabbed. Well, it could be worth a try, he supposed. If there was even a thousand to one chance it might help, it would be worth taking it.

He felt as wide awake as ever. Perhaps he should read

for a while? He had brought Jeopard's book up with him. He didn't want to disturb Joan but her deep, even breathing indicated that she was sound asleep. He switched on the bedside light.

Joan stirred and sighed but did not awake and he reached for the book and studied again the inspired jacket design. Was Chinese landscape really as spectacular as that? It looked so mysterious, so exotic, kindling a longing he had never known before, to see other cultures, other climes. He'd never had the opportunity to travel, himself. He and Joan had never been able to afford really expensive holidays and when he was young it hadn't been such an accepted part of a young person's preparation for life. Nowadays it had become almost routine for youngsters to take off either before or after college or university. They even had a name for it. The gap year, they called it. And some of them, like Max Jeopard, got a taste for travel, were never again content to settle for less than constant movement, new experiences. Though very few managed to capitalise on that restlessness as Jeopard had.

Thanet turned the book over and studied Max's photograph again in the light of what he had heard about him today. Yes, there was no denying the charisma of which Anthea's mother had spoken with such bitterness, and although for some that charm evidently wore thin, for others it seemed never to have lost its power. However hard Tess had fought to struggle free of it she had always succumbed in the end, and it had been strong enough to bind Anthea to him through an absence of over two years in the hope that he would one day come back to her.

What made you tick? Thanet silently asked the smiling, confident image. And just how did you overstep the mark? What was it that cost you your life?

Perhaps this book could provide an answer, or part of one.

He opened it and began to read.

FOURTEEN

It was usually Thanet who rose first and took Joan a cup of tea in bed but next morning it was the other way around.

'What time is it?' he said, sitting up with a jerk and squinting anxiously at the clock.

'Don't worry. It's only ten to seven.' Joan sat down companionably on the edge of the bed with her tea.

'I must have slept through the alarm.'

'I'm not surprised, with such a long day yesterday. You fell asleep with the light on. Reading this, I presume.' She reached for Jeopard's book, which had fallen on to the floor.

'Yes. It's fascinating. It was written by the victim. His one and only, as it turned out. His mother gave it to me. She was so proud of him.'

'Poor woman. Imagine how she must feel.'

'Which reminds me!' said Thanet. 'Bridget rang last night.'

'Did she? Oh, good! What a relief! Is she all right?'

'Fine.' Thanet explained what had happened.

'Did Ben wait up for you, by the way? Nothing was said, but I got the impression he was going to.'

'Yes. We had quite a long talk. Did he discuss this new idea of his with you?'

Joan shook her head. 'And I wasn't going to broach the subject. I think he wanted to have a heart to heart with you first. Did you reach any conclusion?'

Thanet related the conversation. 'So it looks as though there might still be a chance he'll opt for university.'

'Oh well, we'll just have to keep our fingers crossed.' Joan was still holding the book and now she tapped it and said, 'Perhaps you ought to give him this to read. It would do him good to travel. Lovely cover, isn't it.' She turned the book over, studied Max's smiling face. 'What an attractive young man!'

'He was only twenty-nine,' said Thanet, suppressing an involuntary little spurt of jealousy. He felt ashamed of himself. Jealous of a man who was almost young enough to be his son, and a dead man, at that! Whatever next?

'What a waste! He looks as though he had a pretty good opinion of himself, though.'

'He did, by all accounts.'

Joan put down her cup, flicked through to the beginning of the first chapter and began to read aloud.

I flew into Beijing – Peking, as it is known in the Western world – three weeks to the day after the massacre in Tiananmen Square, my mind full of the sounds and images we had witnessed on our television screens: the advancing tanks, the terrified faces of the students, the shots, the screams, the blood.

Until then, we had been told, the spirit of optimism had been running high in the young people of the Chinese Republic. They had been convinced that the future was in their hands, that a new era was about to dawn, and they were confident that nothing could stem the tide of revolt against the stultifying tyranny their country had suffered for so long. Had all this hope been crushed out on that hot summer night, extinguished by the ruthless action of the elders of the old regime?

I was about to find out.

'Stirring stuff,' she commented. 'Certainly makes you want to read on.'

'Oh he was talented, no doubt about that. But now I really must get up. I've got to go to London this morning.'

'You haven't forgotten your appointment with the chiropractor?'

'How could I?' said Thanet with a grin. 'You've reminded me often enough!'

After attending the morning meeting and dealing with various administrative matters Thanet and Lineham caught the 9.45 to Victoria. The decision to travel by rail had been clinched by the news that there had been a serious accident on the M20 near Maidstone. Fortunately the train was virtually empty and they were able to talk.

A certain amount of information had come in since yesterday, though nothing particularly constructive. A little research into Sylvester's background had confirmed that he was a successful businessman, dealing in road construction and heavy plant hire. His daughter would have been a catch for any man, as Lineham had pointed out.

Wakeham had found and interviewed the waitress who had handed the note to Jeopard, but had learned nothing useful about the person who gave it to her. She had, she said, been very busy at the time. Someone had simply left it on her tray when she had gone to fetch fresh supplies of drinks. It hadn't been in an envelope, had simply been a small sheet of white paper, folded once and with Max Jeopard's name on it in capital letters. She knew who Max was because he had been pointed out to her as the prospective bridegroom. She had not waited to watch him read it and had been indignant at the suggestion that she might have taken a peek at its contents.

'Pity,' said Thanet. Ethics could sometimes be a hindrance.

Now Lineham said, 'That note. The fact that it wasn't in an envelope suggests that it was written on the spur of the moment. So I wonder where he – or she – got the paper? I mean, you don't go along to a party with a notepad in your pocket, do you?'

'Was there a pad beside the telephone in the hall?' said Thanet.

'I didn't notice, but I imagine there was.'

'Pity we didn't think of this before. We slipped up there, didn't we. I bet it's had a dozen messages scribbled on it since then.'

A further search of Jeopard's clothes had failed to produce the note and so far no trace of it had been found in the swimming pool. If its arrival had not been witnessed by several people Thanet would have begun to doubt its existence.

'There's only one explanation why it can't be found, isn't there?' said Lineham. 'The murderer must have taken it away with him.'

'But how on earth would he have got it back, if it was in Jeopard's pocket? If there was a struggle there would have been no time. Unless he jumped into the pool after Jeopard went in, of course, and took it out of his pocket while he was in the water. In which case he would have been dripping wet. And,' said Thanet, his voice rising slightly in excitement, 'someone was!'

They stared at each other. 'Sylvester!' said Lineham. 'He had to change his clothes, he told us, after going in to pull Jeopard out. But no, that won't work. That was later, much later. Jeopard had been missing for, what, half an hour by then.'

'Missing, but not necessarily dead,' said Thanet.

Lineham stared at him. 'You mean Jeopard might still have been alive when Sylvester found him?'

'It's possible, surely?'

'But that means . . . Let's work it out. Say it happened as we suggested before, and it was Sylvester who sent the note to Jeopard, pretending that it was from some girl. Sylvester didn't go to look for him until ten o'clock. Would Jeopard have hung around for twenty minutes waiting for her to show up?'

'He might have, if he was sufficiently intrigued. But there's another possibility.'

'What?'

Thanet leaned forward. 'Say the note was genuine. Say it *was* from a girl. Say it *did* suggest an assignation in the pool house, and Jeopard decided to keep the appointment.'

'And Sylvester saw her leaving, perhaps! Yes. It could have been like that! He would have been furious, to think Jeopard was messing around with another woman at his own engagement party. So there was an argument which got out of control and bingo! The rest, as they say, was history.'

'I don't know,' said Thanet, shaking his head. 'Would Jeopard really have slipped off to meet another woman on an occasion like that? Pretty unlikely, surely.'

'Depends. He strikes me as being the sort of chap who

was easily flattered and also the type who would enjoy an element of risk, of clandestine excitement, if you like. Or he might simply have turned up out of sheer curiosity.'

'But in any case, that scenario wouldn't explain the disappearance of the note, would it?'

'True. But your first suggestion would. That Sylvester engineered the whole thing.'

'Maybe. We'll just have to wait and see. It's pointless to speculate about this, really, when we haven't a shred of evidence to go on.'

Unlike the previous day it was a dull, grey morning and by the time the train pulled into Victoria station it was pouring with rain. Jeopard had lived in the maze of streets behind Victoria and in normal circumstances they would have walked there but today Thanet took one look at the weather and decided on a taxi. There was no point in getting soaked to the skin within minutes of their arrival.

A few minutes later they were deposited in front of a newish block of flats which had no pretension to style and nothing to recommend it, so far as Thanet could tell, but proximity to the main-line station.

'I'd hate to live in a place like this,' said Lineham as he worked his way through the various keys on Jeopard's key-ring to discover which one opened the street door.

'If you want to live in London it's convenient, I suppose.'

'Ah, got it,' said Lineham triumphantly as the door clicked open. 'I wouldn't,' he said as they consulted the list of flat-owners and waited for the lift. 'Want to live in London, I mean. Not if you paid me.'

'Just as well we don't all feel the same.'

Jeopard's flat was one of three on the fourth floor and

as Lineham went through his routine with the keys again the door of the flat across the landing opened a crack and an eye peered out. In the background a radio was playing.

'Who are you?' The voice was female and Thanet tried to sound his most reassuring as he turned and advanced a few steps. 'Police, madam.'

'I wondered when your lot was going to turn up. Thought you'd have been around yesterday. Give us a look at your identification.' A hand emerged through the slit.

The door was still on the chain, Thanet realised as he obligingly laid his warrant card on the outstretched palm. The hand disappeared and the door closed. He grinned at Lineham, who had by now found the key to Jeopard's flat and was waiting impatiently to go in.

Another rattle and the door opened, wide this time. 'Fancy a cuppa?' she said.

Her name was Ellie Ransome and she was tiny, less than five feet tall, with a frizz of improbably red hair and make-up so exaggerated that it wouldn't have been out of place in a circus. She was wearing a ginger-coloured Crimplene suit with a fawn blouse and misshapen down-at-heel slippers which were clearly too comfortable to throw away. Thanet judged that she was well into her sixties. He and Lineham raised eyebrows at each other as she led them into her living room. He had thought, yesterday, that Mrs Greenway's sitting room was the most crowded he had ever seen but in comparison with this it was positively uncluttered. Cardboard cartons of all shapes and sizes were stacked all around the walls from floor to ceiling, sometimes three or four deep, so that there was barely room for the little furniture the room contained. His eyes skimmed over the boxes, registering that they contained – or had contained – chiefly electrical goods of all sizes and descriptions, ranging from microwaves, television sets and CD systems to kettles, toasters and shavers. He and Lineham looked at each other again.

?

Various bizarre explanations flashed through Thanet's mind. This diminutive old woman was a receiver of stolen goods, a fence? In which case she would scarcely invite the police into the flat, surely? A pawnbroker, then? Or perhaps she simply collected empty cardboard boxes?

As if she had read his mind she cast a mischievous glance at him over her shoulder. 'They're full all right. Sit yourselves down and I'll tell you all about them in a minute.' She switched off the radio and cleared a couple of boxes from the settee. 'Shan't be a tick,' she said, heading off along the cardboard corridor to what was presumably the kitchen. 'The kettle's not long boiled, I'd just made me elevenses when I heard the lift.' She nodded at a mug on the only table, which was covered with a mess of newspapers, magazines, and scraps of paper, along with a jampot containing a number of ballpoint pens and a couple of pairs of scissors. A chair in front of it had been pushed back askew as if she had been interrupted in her task. It was obviously the hub of the room's activity. What on earth was she up to?

Thanet was longing to go and take a good look but he and Lineham obediently sat down on the space she had cleared and a few moments later she returned.

'There you are.' She handed them mugs of tea and offered them sugar, which they both refused.

She picked up her own mug and sat down at the table, swivelling to face them. 'Competitions,' she said. 'All this,' she explained, waving a hand at the boxes, the papers. 'I win them.' She looked smug. 'Got the knack, you see.'

'Competitions,' said Lineham. 'You mean when you have to tick the right answers and then write a sentence summing up why such and such is the best product in the world?'

'Got it in one!' she said.

'All this?' said Lineham. He looked slightly dazed.

'All this.'

'But how? I mean, the questions are usually easy enough to answer, but it's always the sentence that's the deciding factor, I imagine.'

'I told you. I got the knack. I just put myself into their position and tell them what they want to hear. And I'm a dab hand at jingles, I can tell you.'

'I'm amazed!' said Lineham. 'I don't know a single person who's ever actually won anything in that way.'

'That's because they don't take it serious enough. I really work at it, I can tell you. Spend hours at it, every day. It might take a week to come up with a really good sentence or slogan or whatever.'

'I've even wondered if these competitions are genuine.'

She smiled and her eyes lit up. 'Oh, they're genuine, all right. I've had some really lovely holidays, cruises and that. You name it, I've won it.' Her face fell. 'No, I tell a lie. I still haven't won a car. Or the big one.'

'The big one?' said Thanet. He knew this conversation was a waste of time but he was enjoying it immensely. Such interludes were one of the unexpected joys of his work.

'A house,' she said. 'You know, cottage in the country, with roses round the door.'

'But,' said Lineham, 'why bother to duplicate like this?

166

I mean, who wants more than one microwave, for example.'

'Oh I don't *keep* them,' she said scornfully. 'They're me income. Me old-age pension, if you like, me hedge against inflation. I win 'em, then when I need money I sell 'em.'

'You don't get much for second-hand goods, surely?' said Lineham.

'You'd be surprised. If people know they're brand new, still in the box and have never been opened ... And I always tell them, if you're not satisfied, bring it back within fourteen days and I'll give yer yer money back. They hardly ever do. I run one or two ads in the local paper every week. Never fails.'

She was really enjoying this, Thanet realised. If she lived alone, opportunities to talk about her somewhat unique talent must be rare. And Lineham was the perfect audience.

Once again she tuned in to his thoughts. 'Nice to have a bit of company for a change,' she said. 'I sometimes feel I'm the only person left alive in this dump, during the day. They all go off to work and the place is like a morgue.' She pulled a face. 'If you'll pardon the expression, in the circs. I heard about the poor lad across the way on the wireless.'

'Did you know him well?' said Thanet.

'Nah ... Scarcely passed the time of day with him. He was always polite enough, mind, not like some, these days. But he was away so much and when he was here he just shut himself up in there for hours on end. Never seemed to go out to work.'

'He worked at home, I expect,' said Lineham. 'He was a writer.'

'Really? What did he write about?'

'He'd only written one book so far,' said Thanet. 'A travel book, about China.'

'Ah . . .' Comprehension dawned. 'So that was why he was away such a lot.'

It didn't look as though she could tell them anything useful. 'So you don't know anything that might help us?'

'Ah well now, I didn't say that, did I!'

Thanet waited. Clearly she was enjoying her moment of suspense. She put down her mug and leaned forward, lowering her voice as if someone might be able to hear if she spoke too loudly. 'There was a girl, come around asking for him.'

'When was this?' said Lineham.

'Night before last. About seven.'

Saturday, then, the night Jeopard died. 'You hadn't seen her before?'

She shook her head. 'She was a foreigner. You know. Darkish.'

'Black, you mean?'

'More like sort of olive. I should think she was Italian or Spanish, something like that. Her English was hopeless, I could hardly make out what she was saying.'

'What was the gist of it?'

'She was looking for Mr Jeopard.' Ellie Ransome shrugged. 'I couldn't help her. I didn't have the foggiest where he was. So I suggested she came back next morning, yesterday.'

'And did she?'

'Yes. I was late getting up, I always have a lie-in on Sundays, so I hadn't heard then that he was dead, or I might have told her. I dunno. I might not've. It's not very nice breaking news like that, is it? Anyway, she obviously didn't know. Her English was so bad I shouldn't think she'd bother to turn the radio or telly on. I just told her I thought he must be away for the weekend and she ought to leave coming back until today. I said she ought not to come too early, so as to give him a chance to get home if he'd stayed over until this morning.'

'And has she?'

'Not yet, no.'

Thanet left his card in case the girl turned up later.

'Someone he met in South America?' said Lineham as they crossed the landing.

'Sounds likely.'

'Must be pretty keen, if she's followed him over here.'

Jeopard's flat was smaller than Ellie Ransome's and a far cry from the sophisticated bachelor apartment with which Thanet's imagination had endowed him, consisting of a cramped sitting room, a shoebox of a bedroom, a galley kitchen and a bathroom so tiny that there was barely room for the door to close when one was standing inside.

'This shouldn't take long,' said Lineham, after they had taken a quick look around. The place was minimally furnished, could almost have been any impersonal hotel room had it not been for the outsize desk, which was set at a right angle to the window and took pride of place. On it were ranged computer, printer, telephone, fax machine, neatly stacked sheaves of papers and all the other accoutrements of a writer's life.

'Looks as though he used this place chiefly for work,' said Thanet, picking up a pile of typescript and flicking through it. A cursory glance was sufficient to tell him that this was Jeopard's current oeuvre, on his experiences in South America. He had completed about 120 pages. 'I suppose he wouldn't have wanted anywhere too big, with the sort of life he led, not while he was still a bachelor, anyway. It would just have been an encumbrance.'

The wastepaper basket was overflowing and there were crumpled sheets of paper all over the floor around it. Thanet up-ended it. Most of the rubbish was discarded sheets of typescript and perforated strips torn off the edges of computer paper, but there was one interesting item, an airmail letter with a Brazilian stamp.

'Look at this, Mike,' he said, holding it up. It had been torn through, unopened. The sender's name was on the back and Thanet held the two pieces of envelope together to decipher it. 'It's from a Rosinha Gomes, with an address in somewhere called Manaus. The girl who called yesterday, no doubt. And he didn't even bother to read it.' He extracted one of the torn sheets of writing paper and peered at it. 'Don't suppose you speak Portuguese, by any chance?'

Lineham shook his head. He was working his way through the drawers of the desk.

Thanet put the letter in his pocket. He could get it translated later. 'Found anything interesting?'

'Only this.' Lineham held up an address/telephone book.

'Is his agent's number in it?' said Thanet.

Earlier attempts to ring Jeopard's publishers in order to get hold of this had been unproductive and they had decided that the offices probably didn't open until ten. It was Jeopard's agent rather than his publishers that Thanet was anxious to talk to. He suspected that he – or she, for he'd heard somewhere that the majority of literary agents were women – would have had rather more contact with Jeopard than his editor.

Lineham found several possible names with 071 telephone numbers, but it was impossible to tell which, if any, was the one they wanted. A brief session at the telephone quickly yielded results, however, and they were able to arrange an appointment for half an hour's time.

'She's called Carol Marsh,' said Lineham as they went down in the lift. 'Of Marsh and Walters Literary Agency. It's in Golden Square, just off Piccadilly.'

Thanet had never met a literary agent before and wasn't quite sure what he expected. Someone rather brash, perhaps, certainly sophisticated and probably somewhat intimidating, wearing the kind of clothes normally dubbed 'power dressing' – short skirt, silk shirt, tailored jacket. Carol Marsh was therefore a surprise, a plump woman in her forties wearing a rather drab ankle-length dress. She was carefully made-up, however, and her very short blonde hair had been expertly styled. She welcomed them with a smile appropriately tinged with sadness. 'I've never been interviewed by detectives before. It'll be a new experience. Though I could wish that it had been under pleasanter circumstances. It was such a shock, to hear of Max's death on the news yesterday.'

Her assistant was despatched for coffee and they all sat down. It was a pleasant place in which to work, thought Thanet. The sash windows overlooked the square and there were two whole walls of books.

He waved a hand at them. 'Are these all by your clients?'

She smiled and nodded. 'For my sins.'

'It must be very satisfying, to see the fruit of your labours set out before you like this.'

'Oh it is. Not a satisfaction granted to your profession, I imagine. I love my work. Most literary agents do.'

'I can imagine. To discover a new talent, foster it, see it succeed . . .'

She grimaced. 'Like poor Max, you mean. Yes. It's such a tragedy.'

Her assistant arrived with the coffee and she waited until the cups had been handed out before saying, 'He had a brilliant future before him, everyone said so.'

'He was certainly talented. I was glancing through his book last night. His mother lent it to me.'

'It did very well. I was looking forward to his next. It was on South America. He had some amazing experiences out there.'

'So I understand.'

'They would have made fascinating reading.' She sighed. 'Now it will never be finished. Such a shame. He was well on with the writing of it, I believe.'

'Yes, he was. We've just come from his flat.'

A calculating gleam came into her eyes. 'You've seen the typescript?' she said eagerly. 'How much of it was there?'

'About 120 pages.'

'I wonder if there was any more on disc.'

'I've no idea.' Thanet's tone was dismissive. A certain amount of conversation was allowable, to break the ice, but he hadn't come here to discuss Jeopard's work in progress.

She picked up his disapproval at once and echoed his thought in words. 'But you haven't come here to talk about Max's work.'

'It was obviously an important part of his life and we can't just ignore it. Had he made any enemies in his professional life, do you know?'

'Someone who hated him enough to kill him, you mean? Good grief, no! In any case, in literary circles any back-stabbing is likely to be verbal rather than physical.'

'You really cannot think of any reason why anyone should wish to harm him, or any issue over which some-one would have been likely to quarrel with him?'

She shook her head. 'No. Definitely not. Max could be irritating, true. He was rather big-headed, and the fact that he had good reason to be wasn't enough to stop him getting on your nerves, sometimes. Though . . .'

'What?'

She was hesitating. 'It's just that he did rather have an eye for the opposite sex.'

'You have someone specific in mind?'

'Well, to put it bluntly, he found women irresistible. And as he was a very attractive man, on the whole it worked both ways. Put Max in a room with a woman and he couldn't help making a pass at her. To be frank, I felt rather sorry for that fiancée of his. So far as I could see, she'd have had nothing but heartache ahead. And she's such a beautiful girl, too, she could have had anyone she chose.'

'So what are you suggesting? That there's a jealous husband somewhere in the background?'

'I'm not thinking of anyone in particular. It's just that with Max it's something that's bound to spring to mind.'

And that was really all she could tell them. To her knowledge Max had no close friendships in connection with his work and had bought his flat because he found it easier to work there than at home in Kent. He had, she said, intended keeping it on after his marriage, for this purpose.

'Complete waste of time,' said Lineham gloomily, on their way back to Victoria.

But Thanet didn't agree. Little by little he was building up a picture of Max Jeopard and the life he had led. Somewhere in that tangled web of relationships lay the solution to the mystery of his death.

Thanet was determined to leave no stone unturned until he found it.

FIFTEEN

As soon as Thanet and Lineham walked through the door at Headquarters the constable on desk duty pounced.

'Inspector! The Super wants to see you the minute you get back.'

'Oh? What about? Do you know?'

'I'm not sure. It could be something to do with the phone calls from Mrs Jeopard. She's been ringing all morning, wanting to speak to you, and in the end she asked to be put through to him. Anyway, whatever it is he's pretty worked up about it.'

'Better go straight in, then. Mike, send someone off to collect that notepad, will you? And see if you can find someone to translate this.' Thanet handed over the letter from Brazil found in Jeopard's wastepaper basket.

He hesitated for a moment before knocking on Draco's door, bracing himself. Draco in one of his moods could be pretty overwhelming.

'Come!'

Thanet had heard that tone of voice before. No doubt about it, Draco was definitely on the warpath about something. What could Mrs Jeopard have been saying to him?

'Ah, Thanet. About time too. Where the hell have you been?' Draco's dark eyes were snapping and he raked his fingers through his short curly hair – not for the first time, by the look of it; it was standing on end like a bottle brush.

'To London, sir. I did tell you I was going, at the morning meeting –'

'Yes, yes.' Draco waved an impatient hand. 'But what the devil took you so long?'

'Well it does in fact take quite some time to –'

'Oh never mind, never mind. The point is, how often have I given instructions that the families of victims are to be kept informed about what is going on?'

So that was what this was all about. Mrs Jeopard must have been complaining that she wasn't being kept up to date. This was one of Draco's current hobby-horses and on the whole Thanet was inclined to agree with him. In this instance, however, he felt somewhat aggrieved. It was only twenty-four hours since he had seen Jeopard's mother and there had been nothing as yet to report. He opened his mouth to say so, but wasn't given the chance.

Draco had jumped up and begun to pace about in front of the window: three steps to the right, pause for speech, three paces to the left. 'You know how I feel about this. It's an absolute scandal that sometimes victims' families are left completely in the dark, that cases even reach court without their being informed!'

'I agree, sir. And we never allow –'

'Mrs Jeopard has been trying to get hold of you all morning, without success. Just think what she must be going through!'

'But we –'

'How would you like it, if you were in that situation, tell me that?'

'Well naturally I'd –'

'Exactly! So the very least you could have done is get someone to ring her in your absence.'

This time Thanet made no attempt to respond. What was the point? But it seemed the Superintendent had had his say. He glared at Thanet. 'Well?'

Draco would never listen to excuses. Thanet took a deep, unobtrusive breath. 'What would I have told her, sir?' His tone was as calm, as reasonable as he could make it.

Draco stared at him, lips pursed. Then he clasped his hands behind his back. 'Don't ask me! That's your job! Something, anything, to make her feel that we're not sitting around twiddling our thumbs.'

Prudence battled with a sense of injustice and lost. 'But there really wasn't anything to tell her!'

'Then tell her that!' Draco put his hands on his desk and leaned forward, thrusting his chin out. 'Just so long as you remember that she had a right to know.' He straightened up and waggled his fingers. 'Within reason, of course. No need to dot the i's and cross the t's.'

Pointless to argue. 'I'll detail someone to give her a ring each morning, sir,' Thanet said stiffly.

The concession won, Draco sat down with a thump, pulled a file towards him and opened it. 'Good.' His tone was already absent-minded. Clearly, the interview was over.

Feeling like a schoolboy who has been unjustly accused by his headmaster Thanet left the room and walked upstairs fuming.

Lineham took one look at his face and said, 'Like that, sir, was it?'

Thanet related the conversation.

'Sounds par for the course to me,' said Lineham.

'You weren't on the receiving end! I mean, I agree with him, Mike! Victims' families should be kept up to date with what is going on. But what's the point of ringing just to say there's nothing to report?'

'You don't need to convince me, sir.'

'It's just a waste of time and manpower!'

'Well, if it'll keep him happy, it's a simple enough thing to organise. Honestly, sir, it's not worth getting so worked up about.'

'I just object to being ticked off unfairly!'

'You don't object if it's justified, then?' said Lineham with a grin.

Thanet glowered at him, then reluctantly grinned back. '*Touché*, Mike. And you're right. It's not worth getting steamed up about.' If he was honest with himself, Thanet realised, it was hurt pride that was making him react like this. He sat down at his desk. 'Anything new come in?'

'Ellie Ransome rang at about 12.30, apparently – the competition lady. So I rang back. She said the girl came back again soon after we left. She still hadn't heard that Jeopard was dead so Miss Ransome felt she had to tell her. She had hysterics on the spot. Miss Ransome took her into her flat to try and calm her down and tried to find out more about her, where she was staying and so on, but the girl was so upset and her English so poor that she was more or less incoherent. Miss Ransome gave her your card and tried to get her to understand that she really must contact us.'

'But she hasn't yet, I gather?'

Lineham shook his head.

'And this was, what?' Thanet glanced at his watch. 'Three hours ago. Hmm. Well, we'll just have to hope she does. It may not be that important, of course.'

They were soon to find out. Half an hour later the

constable on desk duty rang through to say that a Miss Gomes was asking for Thanet.

'I'll be right down.'

Thanet had pictured a tall Spanish-style beauty with an abundance of tumbling dark curls but for the second time today he was wrong. The girl who rose in response to his greeting was small, tiny in fact, and looked very young, little more than a child. She reminded Thanet of someone and almost at once he realised who it was: Tess Sylvester. She could have been Tess's younger sister. Was this what had first attracted Jeopard to her?

She looked very nervous, fearful even, and Thanet put himself out to set her at her ease, taking her into the least depressing of the interview rooms and despatching someone for a tray of coffee and biscuits.

She was wearing a short, loose raincoat and she slipped it off as she sat down. It was as she twisted to drape it over the back of her chair that Thanet saw that she was pregnant. The bulge was slight but unmistakable. He wondered if Lineham had spotted this and glanced at him, but the sergeant was fiddling with the recording equipment.

Remembering the airmail letter, so callously torn across unopened and discarded as rubbish, Thanet's opinion of the man dropped several notches further. Max must surely have been told about the pregnancy months ago.

'Now, how can we help you, Miss Gomes?'

'The woman, she tell me ... Is true?' she said. 'Max is ... 'e is dead?'

'I'm afraid so.'

Her forehead wrinkled. 'Afraid?'

This was going to be difficult. And there was no way he could get hold of an interpreter who could speak Portuguese on the spur of the moment. He would just have to do his best and try to make sure there were no misunderstandings. 'Sorry. Yes. Max is dead.'

She stared at him, her eyes huge, the tears welling up again and spilling over to trickle unheeded down her cheeks. 'I see him,' she said.

'I do not understand,' said Thanet, speaking slowly and clearly.

'I want see 'im.' Impatiently she flicked the tears away. 'Per'aps there is mistake.'

So that was it. She had come to view the body. She wasn't convinced that Jeopard was dead, Thanet realised, and wouldn't be until she had seen for herself. He shook his head. 'No mistake.'

'I see 'im,' she repeated. Her jaw set stubbornly. 'I mus'.'

'Very well,' said Thanet. If the girl was carrying Jeopard's child she surely had the right to view its father's body. He could tell she hadn't understood that he had agreed, though. He nodded emphatically. 'Yes. We will take you to see him.'

She relaxed a little, sat back and now, for the first time, picked up her cup of coffee and drank, cupping her hands around it as if to draw comfort from its warmth.

'Did you know Max long?'

She looked puzzled. 'Max long?'

Thanet tried again. 'How long did you know Max? Weeks? Months?' This was going to take some time but might be his only opportunity of talking to her and he was determined to learn as much as he could. Slowly, patiently, he extracted her story.

She lived in the city of Manaus, which was in central Brazil, on the Amazon. Max Jeopard had been brought in by some tribesmen to the hospital where she was a nurse – she was, astonishingly, twenty-two, several years older than Thanet had first thought. Her English wasn't good enough for her to explain exactly what had been wrong with Jeopard but he had been very debilitated. The next part was predictable – according to Rosinha they had fallen in love and he had flown back to England in December, promising to return as soon as possible. She had been convinced that when he did so, they would marry. But she had never heard from him again.

'He gave you his address?'

She shook her head. 'I find a . . . how you say? A letter go in it . . .'

'An envelope?'

'Yes. An envelope. Empty. In a book he leave. So I write. I write many, many time, but he no reply. And then . . .' Her hands rested gently on her stomach.

'The baby.'

Lineham's startled face told Thanet that the sergeant hadn't guessed.

'Baby. Yes.'

She had been frantic when, about a month after he left, she realised she was pregnant. Her religion barred her from having an abortion and further letters to Max telling him the news had still elicited no response. When she finally plucked up the courage to tell her parents they had thrown her out, told her they didn't want to have anything more to do with her. She knew the time would come when she wouldn't be able to work any longer and decided that her only option was to come to England and find Max. Now she didn't know what to do. She had only been able to afford a one-way ticket and her limited funds were almost gone.

Her story finished she dissolved once more into tears and Thanet and Lineham exchanged glances. How would he feel, Thanet wondered, if it were Bridget in this situation? But she wouldn't be, of course. Under no circumstances would he and Joan cast her out, as this girl's parents had done. Even allowing for a different society, a different culture, he simply couldn't understand the mentality of such people in this day and age. What was to be done?

Thanet left a policewoman sitting with the girl while he and Lineham withdrew to confer.

The sergeant was equally concerned about her. 'What are we going to do, sir? We can't just take her to the morgue, show her his body then pack her back off to London on the train. What will become of her? With no money, no work permit, nothing?'

'I agree. We must think of something.'

'Social services?'

'We could try, but I doubt that they'd regard it as their responsibility.'

'They might come up with some suggestions, though.'

'True. Better get on to them then, Mike. No, just a minute . . . I wonder . . .'

'What?'

'It might be worth a try. Tell me, how d'you think Mrs Jeopard would react to the idea of a grandchild?'

Lineham stared at him. 'You think she might take the girl in! That's a brilliant idea, sir! Max was the apple of her eye! You're right, it would be worth a try! Let's go and suggest to Miss Gomes that she meet her.'

Impulsive as ever, Lineham was already moving towards the door but Thanet caught his sleeve. 'Just a minute, Mike. Not so fast. Let's think about this. Say Mrs Jeopard does take her in. What sort of a life would she have? Would *you* like to live with the old lady?'

'No way. But I'm not young, homeless, penniless and pregnant.'

'And in the long term there'd be legal problems too, bound to be. She's only over on a short visit, remember. What happens when her visa runs out?'

'But as you say, sir, all that is in the long term. Surely the main thing at the moment is to make sure she has a roof over her head in the immediate future? And it would buy her time, to take stock of the situation and to adjust to the shock of Jeopard's death.'

'If she stays, she's bound to find out he had just got engaged to someone else.'

'True. And, OK, that'll be hard. But not as hard as finding herself on the streets.'

'All right, Mike. You win. We'll suggest it to her. But not until we've got the visit to the morgue over, first. I don't believe she can think beyond that, at the moment anyway.'

'We'll take her ourselves, sir?'

'Oh, I think so, don't you? She's got enough to cope with without being made to feel like a parcel that's being handed on from one policeman to another.'

'You think we ought to tell her about Tess?'

'I'm not sure. Probably not. We don't know yet whether Mrs Jeopard will take her in and even if she does, the girl's English is so poor it could be ages before she found out, so she'd have time to adjust to the situation gradually. No, better not to say anything about it at the moment.'

'It's odd that she hasn't yet asked any questions about how he died, don't you think?'

'I really don't believe she's accepted that he has, yet. When she's done so, and when she's got over the initial shock, that's when she'll start asking questions. But that might well not be today.'

And Thanet was right. Rosinha's reaction to the sight

of her lover's lifeless face was predictable: she fainted. When she came to she was clearly in a state of shock and inclined to go along with whatever Thanet suggested. A tiny spark of interest briefly kindled in her eyes when Max's mother was mentioned but on the brief drive out to the Jeopard house she remained silent and sunk in misery, wiping away the tears which rolled down her cheeks in a never-ending stream. It wasn't until they turned off the road under the stone archway at the entrance to the Jeopard's drive that she paid any interest at all to her surroundings.

'This is Max's 'ome?' she said, peering out of the window at the lovely old timbered house.

'Yes, Miss Gomes,' said Lineham.

Hartley's Golf was again in the garage barn, alongside the Astra.

'Hartley's here, I see,' said Thanet. He wondered how Max's brother was going to react to the arrival of Rosinha Gomes. 'He's Max's brother,' he explained to her.

She nodded. 'I know. Max tell me about 'him. 'E is, 'ow you say, with money?'

'Yes, an accountant,' said Thanet. 'Now, I think it would be best if you stay here while I go and . . .' No, no good, he could tell by the look of anxious concentration already spreading across Rosinha's face. Try again. 'You stay here, I go talk to Max's mother.'

She nodded her comprehension. 'I wait.'

Once again it was Hartley Jeopard who opened the front door. Did he look relieved when Thanet said that it was Mrs Jeopard he had come to see? Thanet couldn't make up his mind. Hartley showed him into the galleried hall, where his mother and aunt were taking afternoon tea.

'About time!' said Mrs Jeopard.

Thanet couldn't think what she meant for a moment,

then realised that she assumed he had come to make the report Draco had promised her. As if he had the time to do so in person! Some people really didn't have a clue!

'Well?' she demanded. 'Have you any news for us?'

'Not as far as the investigation is concerned.'

She opened her mouth, presumably to make some scathing comment, but Thanet jumped in first. 'But I am arranging for one of my men to be in touch with you each day, to keep you up to date. And as soon as there is anything of importance to report, I will contact you myself.'

The wind taken out of her sails, she contented herself with saying, 'Good.' She did not, however, offer him a seat.'

'But this afternoon I have come about another matter. If I could have a word with you in private, perhaps?'

'I have no secrets from my son or my sister, Inspector,' she said stiffly. 'You may speak freely.'

Thanet was surprised. He would have expected a woman in Mrs Jeopard's position, dependent upon others for her slightest need, to relish the prospect of having the small measure of power involved in knowing something they did not. 'It's up to you.' But still he hesitated. Ought he to try to persuade her to see him alone?

'Well?' she said impatiently. 'What is it?'

Mentally, Thanet shrugged. He had tried, after all. If she regretted it later, then that was her affair. He didn't feel, however, that he could remain standing while he told them about Rosinha. 'May I sit down?'

She gave a grudging nod and he chose a small upright chair, moving its position slightly so that he could see their faces. Then he gave them a brief account of how he had learned of Rosinha's existence and of her subsequent visit to Headquarters. He was hesitating over how best to break the news of her pregnancy when Mrs Jeopard interrupted his narrative.

Leaning forward, she said, 'May I assume that all this rigmarole has a point, Inspector? I really cannot see that one of my son's former girlfriends has anything to do with me!'

She had given him his opening. 'Oh but she has, Mrs Jeopard, I assure you. You see, she is carrying your grandchild.' He couldn't help a spurt of satisfaction as he saw how the news affected her: her eyes flew open wide with the shock of it and her pale skin was infused with a tide of colour from neck to temple. Her sister looked equally shocked, as did Hartley. Neither of them had said a word until this point but almost at once Hartley burst out, 'Are you sure? I mean, is it true?'

'She is certainly pregnant. That is obvious.'

'When is the baby due?' said Louisa Burke.

'In a few months, I imagine. What I haven't yet told you is that her parents have turned her out, refuse to have anything more to do with her. She used the last of her money to fly over here to see Max, relying on the fact that he would help her. Now she is virtually destitute and of course desperately upset over your son's death – still in a state of shock, in fact, after seeing his body. She insisted on doing so. Until then I don't think she really believed he was dead. I didn't feel we could put her on a train back to London in that state and in her situation. That was when I thought of you.'

'Where is she now?' said Hartley.

'Outside, in the car.'

Three startled faces glanced towards the window as if they could see through bricks and mortar to this stranger who had suddenly entered their lives. Then Mrs Jeopard spoke for the first time since he had broken the news. 'How do we know that the child is Max's?'

'You don't. Not at this stage. Later, of course, when the baby is born, this could easily be confirmed by blood tests. But frankly, I doubt that she would have flown all this way if it weren't.'

'Poor girl,' said Louisa Burke. 'What a terrible situation to be in.'

Her sister shot her an admonitory look. 'Really, Louisa, tell you any sob story and you'll swallow it hook, line and sinker! We've heard enough from Max about the conditions in central Brazil to make any tale like this suspect.'

'But why should she make it up?' said Louisa stubbornly.

'If people are desperate enough they'll try anything on,' said Hartley, ranging himself alongside his mother.

Hartley would, after all, have a lot to lose if his brother's child came on the scene, thought Thanet.

'And if her parents have kicked her out . . .' Hartley went on.

'But to be completely alone, and to come all this way . . .' said his aunt. She turned to Thanet. 'What is she like?'

'What does it matter?' snapped Mrs Jeopard, clearly exasperated by her sister's unwonted opposition. 'I hope you're not suggesting we should actually *do* anything about this.' She shot a venomous glance at Thanet. 'I really can't imagine why you should have brought this . . . girl here at all. I suppose you thought you could just shuffle off the responsibility by dumping her on our doorstep.'

'But Eleanor,' protested Louisa, determined not to give up, 'surely, if she's carrying Max's child, she *is* our responsibility. By no stretch of the imagination could she be called the Inspector's.' She gave Thanet a shy smile. 'I think it was very caring of him to bring her to us.' She ignored Eleanor's snort at the word 'caring'. 'It would have been only too easy for him just to put her on the train back to London and wash his hands of her.'

'If she was as close to Max as she claims, she's bound to know he comes from a fairly well-off family,' said Hartley. 'When she found out he was dead I bet she asked you for our address, didn't she?' he said to Thanet.

Thanet shook his head. 'She didn't ask a single question about Max's family. She was so distraught after such a shock that I think she was incapable of thinking rationally at all.'

'What did you think of her, Inspector?' said Louisa. 'Did she strike you as being the calculating type?'

'Not in the least.'

Eleanor Jeopard gave a derisory snort. 'A pretty girl can pull the wool over most men's eyes,' she said. 'Especially if she has a sob story to tell. She could have slept with dozens of men, for all we know, and the child could have been fathered by any one of them.'

Louisa Burke stood up, in an unconscious need, perhaps, to repudiate her usual subservience to her sister and underline the importance of what she was about to say. 'Have you thought what will happen, Eleanor, if we refuse to help her or have anything to do with her? With no money, what will she do? Where will she go?'

'Back on the streets, perhaps, where she probably belongs.'

How callous can you get? thought Thanet.

Louisa Burke was equally shocked. 'I can't believe you really said that, Eleanor. You'd actually be prepared to let that happen? When she might be carrying Max's child? Your grandchild, as the Inspector so rightly points out?'

Hartley intervened. 'We could pay her air fare back to Brazil.'

'And then what?' said his aunt. 'From what we hear, she has no resources there. And,' she added, turning back to her sister, 'can you really tell me that you are prepared to let her disappear into the blue? That even if her story is genuine and this is Max's baby, you're willing to lose touch with her permanently?'

This had struck home. Eleanor Jeopard's lips tightened and for the first time since Thanet had told her that Rosinha was pregnant a hint of doubt appeared in her eyes.

'Would it not be sensible,' he said, 'to play safe? As I said, when the child is born it will be a simple matter to establish whether or not Max is the father.'

She was weakening, he could tell. She was blinking rapidly and her mouth was working, her hands plucking restlessly at the mohair rug which covered her knees.

He pressed home his advantage. 'Can you risk,' he said gently, 'never knowing for certain?'

SIXTEEN

'That was what clinched it,' said Thanet. 'She knew that if she let Rosinha walk away now without even seeing her, she might lose contact with her completely and she would never know for sure if it was Max's baby. She couldn't bear the prospect of that.'

He and Lineham were driving back to Sturrenden. Mrs Jeopard had reluctantly volunteered to take Rosinha in, for the moment at least, making it clear that this was only a temporary arrangement while the situation was considered and enquiries into Rosinha's background were made, and Hartley was going to drive the girl back to London to collect her suitcase from the hotel.

Lineham grinned. 'I'd love to have seen the old bat's face when you told her.'

'I just hope we've done the right thing.'

'Stop worrying, sir! As I said before, at least the girl will now have a roof over her head.'

'But for how long, Mike? I did make it clear to Mrs Jeopard that I was pretty certain Rosinha wouldn't be allowed to stay here permanently. You'd better ring Croydon to find out what the position is. We don't want to be accused of encouraging illegal immigrants!'

'What time did you say your appointment is, with the chiropractor?'

'Five o'clock.' Thanet glanced at the dashboard clock. It was twenty to five. 'I should just make it.'

But he hadn't allowed for late-afternoon traffic. They should have gone out to the Jeopard house in separate cars, he realised, then he could have gone straight to the clinic. He didn't feel he could ask Lineham to hang about waiting for him while he kept the appointment and by the time they'd got back to Headquarters and Thanet had picked up his car it was already five past. He arrived at reception twenty minutes late.

'I'm so sorry. I do apologise. The traffic . . .'

The receptionist was middle-aged, with a round, pleasant face, wispy brown hair put up in a precarious bun and layers of flowing garments of ethnic design. She gave him a reassuring smile, revealing a set of perfectly even over-large false teeth. 'Don't worry,' she said. 'Miss Carmel has only just finished with her previous patient and you are the last for today.'

Janet Carmel was brisk and businesslike in tracksuit and training shoes. She was in her late thirties, tall and slim with straight fair hair caught back in a pony-tail and very direct blue eyes. Knowing that her profession abounded in unqualified practitioners, Thanet had taken care before making the appointment to check that she was a registered chiropractor. She had, he discovered, taken a full-time four-year course at a College of Chiropractic.

Medical history noted, he found himself stripped to his underpants, gowned and lying on his back on an examining couch which she cranked up to an appropriate height for the treatment. He had rarely felt so vulnerable. What was coming next? What, exactly, did chiropractors *do*?

'I think I've changed my mind about this,' he said with a nervous laugh.

She recognised that he wasn't entirely joking and gave a reassuring smile. 'Don't worry,' she said. 'It'll be all right, I promise.'

Believe her, Thanet told himself. She is qualified, after all.

'Now,' she said. 'I want you to extend your right arm up into the air and clench your fist. I am going to say "Hold", and try to push it down. I want you to resist the pressure if you can. Do you understand?'

'I think so.'

'Right, then.' Miss Carmel grasped his clenched fist in her left hand, inserted her right hand under Thanet's back, and simultaneously pressed her fingers against one of his vertebrae and pushed against his extended arm. 'Hold.'

Thanet successfully resisted the pressure and his arm remained in a vertical position.

'Good,' she said. 'Again.' Pressing her fingers against a different vertebra she repeated the process. He again resisted the pressure against his right arm. What on earth was this telling her? he wondered. Over and over again she went through the same motions. 'Hold . . . Hold . . . Hold.'

Thanet was beginning to think that this was a completely pointless exercise when suddenly, when she said 'Hold', his right arm seemed to lose all power of resistance and she pushed it down with ease.

'Ah,' she said, and repeated the same pressure, the same movement, this time pushing his arm down with only one finger.

'Why did it do that?' He was astounded. His mind was telling his arm to remain vertical, his body was refusing to obey.

'Because your brain knows that there is something wrong in that area. This is where your major problem is. It's as I suspected, when you told me about the original injury to your back, heaving that lawnmower into the boot of your car.'

'So what's wrong, exactly?'

'It's your sacroiliac joint, the big joint at the base of your spine. It's been strained and it's unstable. Over the years the instability has increased and because it's a major weight-bearing joint your body has had to compensate, thus putting strain on other joints. This is why your back pain has been so general.'

'So can anything be done to put it right?'

'I can certainly put it back in position. The problem is going to be getting it to stay there in the long term. As this is a long-standing injury the ligaments holding it in position have become stretched and slack so they can't hold the joint together. Your body is now used to the instability; it's been programmed to accept it, so to speak. One of the difficulties is going to be in reprogramming your brain to a different assessment of the situation.'

'That doesn't sound very optimistic.'

'I wouldn't say that. I can't promise anything, but I think there's a good chance it could be treated successfully. It would take time, though. You can't eliminate twenty years of damage in a matter of weeks.'

'So what sort of timescale are we talking about?'

'It's really impossible to tell. What I would propose is that we begin with a course of four weekly treatments, then reassess the situation. By then I should have a good idea of whether or not it's going to work.'

'But you think there's a chance that it might.'

'A good chance, yes.'

'Then I'll try it. After all those years of backache any chance is worth taking!'

'Right, then. Turn on to your right side, please.'

Apprehensively, Thanet allowed his position to be adjusted to her satisfaction, trying not to tense up in anticipation of what was coming. Relax, he told himself. Relax.

'Try to relax,' she said. Then grasping his left shoulder firmly with one hand, his right hip with the other, she performed a rocking, twisting movement which culminated in a final jerk. There was a cracking sensation at the base of his spine and it was over.

'On your back again now, please,' she said calmly.

Gingerly, Thanet turned over. His spine was still intact, it seemed.

Reverting to her diagnostic procedure she went through the same process as before. This time, to his further astonishment, when she pressed the place where his arm had formerly shown no resistance it remained firmly in the air.

'Ah, that's better,' she said, with satisfaction.

The treatment continued. At one point, to his surprise she donned rubber gloves and putting her fingers into his mouth did some uncomfortable pressure movements inside, for cranial adjustment, she told him. Finally she inserted two large wedges under his buttocks, one on each side. These, she told him, were pelvic blocks and they realigned the sacroiliac joint and stabilised it. This process would also inform his brain that this was how things should really be in that region. When he left he was to take a ten-minute walk before getting into his car, to give both brain and body time to adjust to the new situation.

Thanet walked out of the consulting room feeling dazed. He couldn't believe that someone had at last told him what, specifically, was wrong with him. Conscientiously taking his brief walk he was aware of a new ease of movement and absence of pain in his lower back. He had been warned that this might not last; after each of the first few treatments the joint would probably slip out of alignment again quite quickly. But for the first time in twenty years something constructive had actually been done to tackle what he had come to believe was an intractable problem and he felt a cautious optimism. Was it really possible that some permanent improvement could be achieved? He had arrived a sceptic and left a convert. He couldn't wait to tell Joan all about it.

He arrived home before she did and started preparations for supper. She was surprised to see him. 'I didn't expect you yet!'

'I came straight home after my appointment.'

'So how did you get on?' She took another look at his face and her eyebrows went up.

He held up his hands in a gesture of surrender and laughed. 'All right, I admit it. You were right and I was wrong!'

'Really? You mean, she actually managed to do something constructive?'

'It was amazing!'

They sat down at the kitchen table while Thanet described the experience in detail. Joan listened with complete attention, her mobile face as responsive as always. When he had finished, she said, 'Well, I'm delighted, of course, darling. Absolutely delighted. But please, don't get too excited about it. She did say she couldn't *guarantee* any long-term improvement.'

'I know. But what she did, it's made so much difference! The fascinating thing is that I wasn't expecting it to. Just the opposite, in fact, as you know. Which makes it all the more convincing, don't you see?'

'Yes, of course I do.' She got up, came around the table and kissed him. 'All the same, let's not get carried away. Let's just wait and see, shall we? I just don't want you to be disappointed if it doesn't work.'

'Talk about role reversal!' said Thanet. 'Usually I'm the one advising caution!'

His mood of euphoria lasted overnight and next morning he was up earlier than usual, delighted to find that the ever-present discomfort in his back was still considerably diminished. He felt as though he were firing on all four cylinders instead of the usual three and for once was at his desk before Lineham.

The sergeant's eyebrows went up when he saw him. 'You're looking very pleased with yourself today!'

'It's the chiropractor. She was amazing!'

'Really? That's great!' Lineham had seen at first hand how Thanet had suffered over the years and his pleasure was genuine. 'You think she really might be able to help you?'

'She says she's willing to try, and thinks there's a good chance she can. I'll tell you all about it over a pint, later, Mike. I've been trying to catch up on the reports I didn't write last night. Have a look through what's come in, will you?'

For a while both men concentrated on their work. Finally Thanet sat back and said, 'Well I think that's it. So what's new?'

'Well, I'm afraid I haven't found anyone to translate Rosinha's letter yet. Does it matter, now we've seen her?'

'Shouldn't think so. No, leave it.'

Lineham consulted his notes. 'DC Carson says the notepad was still there beside the telephone on the table in the hall at the Sylvesters' house, so he's sent it off to forensic with an urgent request for comment.'

'Good.'

'It would be terrific if they came up with something, wouldn't it?'

'Don't suppose for a minute that they will. It's a long shot, but worth trying. What else?'

'You remember Sylvester told us that Barbara Mallis said she'd inherited money from her father? Well DC Martin says the old man is still alive and kicking and living in a council flat off the Old Kent Road. He's a retired bus driver. Looks as though we were right, doesn't it? No one could afford a BMW on a housekeeper's salary.'

'I agree. We'll go and see her again. Though I doubt that we'll get anywhere. She's not the type to cave in easily. What does Martin say about Roper?'

'Ah, well, he's a different matter. You know we were wondering why he'd stayed so long with the Sylvesters? Apparently he's paid almost double the going rate. I suppose they feel it's worth it, to keep someone who really knows how to handle Carey. Also, and this is the point, he has a young sister who has psoriasis very badly – you know, that really extreme form of skin disease – and he's spending a fortune on trying to find an effective treatment for her. His mother can't speak too highly of him.'

'He could still be involved with Mrs Sylvester, though, couldn't he?'

'Yes. And if he is, Barbara Mallis would be ideally placed to find out. So if she is blackmailing Mrs Sylvester, that's probably why.'

'Maybe.' Thanet was frowning.

'What's the matter, sir?'

'I don't know, Mike. Say we're right. Say that is what's going on, and Sylvester suspects it. What possible relevance could it have to Jeopard's murder?'

'You've said yourself, sir, often enough, that you can never tell what relevance a fact might have, in a murder case.'

'True. All the same . . .'

'Sir! Look at the time!'

Draco was a stickler for punctuality and Thanet had barely one minute to get downstairs to the Superintendent's office for the morning meeting. He didn't want to risk incurring Draco's displeasure again, after yesterday, and he shot out of his chair and down the stairs as fast as he could move. Boon had evidently given up on him and gone in.

Draco's eyes went to the clock as Thanet entered. 'Ah, Thanet. We were just about to begin.'

The Superintendent took Tody and Boon briskly through their reports and listened intently to Thanet's. Then he opened a file on his desk.

Thanet's heart sank. He knew the signs. What now?

Draco sat back, steepling his fingers. 'I've been thinking about your case, Thanet. This lad Carey, the Sylvesters' son. He's a schizophrenic, you say?'

'Yes, sir.'

'You've interviewed him?'

'As best I could, sir. It was . . . rather tricky.'

'In what way?'

'Well, one second he'd be rational, the next he'd be talking nonsense.'

'Is he dangerous?'

'I don't know, sir.'

Draco gave what Thanet privately thought of as his crocodile smile; danger lurked behind it. 'Then may I suggest you find out?' He sat forward, picked up a newspaper cutting from the file in front of him and fixed Thanet with a gimlet-like stare. 'I've been doing some research. This is an article from the *Daily Telegraph*, a reputable newspaper I think you will agree, whatever the colour of your politics. Admittedly it dates from last year, at the time of that television programme about the Zito case, I expect you remember all the fuss, but all the same the facts it gives are very interesting. If you remember, Zito was killed by a diagnosed schizophrenic who had been released into the community. As a result the National Schizophrenia Fellowship collated some figures. Just listen to this. According to them, in the year following Zito's death there were seventeen cases of killings by schizophrenics, five of which were carried out by former mental hospital patients who had shown previous violent behaviour. Longer-term research had shown that over the thirty-three months up to the December before the article was written, there had been thirty-eight fatal attacks. Thirty-eight, Thanet! Over one a month!' Draco tossed the cutting on to his desk. 'I think the facts speak for themselves.'

Thanet felt bound to defend himself. 'As I understand it, sir, they are only dangerous if they don't take their medication. And Carey Sylvester is closely supervised, with a full-time nurse to look after him.'

'But I understand he escaped and was loose on the night of the murder.'

Thanet didn't like the word 'loose' in reference to Carey any more than he had when Mrs Jeopard had used it. It made the lad sound like a wild animal and he was, after all, a human being. 'Yes, sir. But –'

Draco shook his head. 'All I'm saying, Thanet, is that I

think you ought to look into this more closely. Which hospital was he in?'

Thanet realised to his chagrin that he didn't know. 'I'll find out, sir.'

Draco's hairy eyebrows arched, but showing unusual restraint he refrained from comment. He closed the file and brought the meeting abruptly to a close. But as they were on the way out he called Thanet back.

'Get this put up on the noticeboard for me, will you?'

Outside Boon said, 'What is it?'

The three of them stopped to read it. Draco's distinctive handwriting marched across the page.

You are reminded that the families of victims should always be kept up to date with what is going on in the relevant investigations.

> G. Draco

'What brought that on?' said Boon.

'Me,' said Thanet. 'Well, actually it was Jeopard's mother. She kept on ringing me up yesterday and I was in London, so she got herself put through to the Super. He hauled me over the coals as soon as I got back.'

'Hard luck,' said Boon.

It would have given Thanet tremendous satisfaction to screw the piece of paper up and toss it into the nearest wastepaper bin, but restraining himself with difficulty he handed it to the desk sergeant. 'Put this up, will you?'

Lineham looked up as Thanet came in. 'The PM is fixed for later on this morning. What's the matter, sir? Not more trouble?'

'I'm not exactly the Super's blue-eyed boy at the moment, Mike. He thinks we've been remiss in not looking into Carey's background more closely.' Thanet sat down with a thump. His back protested and he clutched it. 'Oh, no!' He hoped he hadn't dislodged the joint again.

'What?'

'Oh, nothing.' He couldn't be bothered to explain. It was too complicated. 'The trouble is, he's probably right.'

'But . . .'

'No, Mike. Put Martin on to it right away. Get him to find out all he can about Carey's medical history – which hospital he was in, how long he was there and so on. Tell him to find out which psychiatrist he was under and to make an appointment for us with him as soon as possible – this afternoon, perhaps. And make sure that Carson understands that he has to ring Mrs Jeopard every single morning to keep her happy. Tell him to use his common sense about what to tell her. With any luck, though, with Rosinha's arrival she'll have something else to occupy her mind now. Which reminds me. Did you get through to immigration at Croydon last night?'

'No. They were closed. But I spoke to them just now, while you were in the meeting.'

'And what did they say?'

SEVENTEEN

'It's not too hopeful, I'm afraid,' said Lineham, reaching for the sheet of paper on which he had made notes. 'First of all it doesn't look as though Rosinha would have applied for an entry clearance certificate which is essential as a preliminary to getting permission to stay here. If she had applied for one, giving pregnancy as a reason, she wouldn't have got it without documentation – a letter from the child's father, for instance, and we can be pretty sure from what she says that Jeopard didn't provide her with one. So she would have come into the country in the normal way. No visa is required and provided she could satisfy immigration that she was a genuine visitor and convince them that she intended to return to Brazil, there would have been no problem about entry and she would then be able to stay for six months.'

'Six months. That means she could in fact have the baby over here. Does that mean it will have British nationality?'

Lineham was shaking his head. 'No. Definitely not. Even if the father is British, unless the parents are married the child would be of Brazilian nationality and permission to stay longer than six months would be refused.'

'Ah.' Thanet could see problems looming. 'We'll have

to tell Mrs Jeopard all this. Perhaps we should have looked into the matter more thoroughly before taking Rosinha to meet her. She's going to be pretty upset if she sees her through her pregnancy and then finds the baby is whisked off to Brazil.'

'I still don't see what else we could have done.'

'In any case, it's too late now to worry about it.' Though Thanet knew that he would.

'So, what's on the agenda for this morning, sir?'

'Another visit to Mrs Mallis, I think.' Because although, as he had said to Lineham, it was difficult to see how the fact that the housekeeper might be blackmailing her employer could have any relevance to the case, Thanet's instinct kept tugging him back to the Sylvester household. Something was going on there, and he was determined to get to the bottom of it. And it was, after all, the place where the murder had happened. Why was that? he wondered. Why had Max Jeopard met his death in that particular place and at that particular time? His engagement party should have been an occasion for celebration but instead of a day for rejoicing it had become a day for dying.

As they were about to leave, however, DC Martin knocked on the door.

'About Carey Sylvester, sir . . .'

'That was quick.' Thanet sat down again.

'I got on to someone very helpful at County Hall.'

'So?'

'Well, apparently Carey would have been in the catchment area for St Augustine's, Canterbury, but that was finally closed down at the end of '93 and patients now go to the new, purpose-built wing at Sturrenden General. There are only sixty beds there and patients are admitted only if it's absolutely necessary. Someone like Carey

Sylvester, who has his own nurse, wouldn't have a chance unless something went dramatically wrong.'

'So if St Augustine's is closed, what would have happened to his medical records?'

'They go with the psychiatrist, provided he stays in Kent. If he moved out of the area, the files would go to his successor. But we're in luck, there. Dr Damon, who treated Carey, is actually in charge of this new wing at Sturrenden General. I rang his secretary to request an appointment for you and she said they'd have to discuss the matter with management first. I stressed the urgency and she promised to try and get back to me today – later on this morning, if she could.'

'Well done!' said Thanet. 'Let's hope they agree.' Even if they didn't, there would be sufficient new information to pacify Draco. And he had to admit that the Super was right, as usual. Carey's medical history was a loose end which should be followed up.

The heavy rain which had greeted them in London yesterday had moved south-east at a snail's pace and was only now clearing Sturrenden. Outside the banks of dense cloud were moving away and a brightness in the sky hinted that the sun was doing its best to break through. The country lanes were still awash with water and more than once Lineham had to slow down in order to negotiate huge puddles which had spread halfway across the road. Thanet sat gazing out at the drowned landscape and planning the best way to tackle Barbara Mallis about the suspected blackmail. She wasn't going to give in easily and admit it, that was certain. So would it be best to be polite and devious, or come straight out with the accusation? No, not the latter, he decided. That would simply put her back up and get nowhere. The softly softly approach, then.

Lineham agreed. 'Think we'll get anywhere?'

'Frankly, I doubt it. But we can try. She's the only person we know for certain is lying at the moment.'

'We've only Sylvester's word for it that she claims to have inherited money from her father. He could have got it wrong, misunderstood her, whatever . . .'

'That's true. We'll have to tread carefully, hope we can catch her out.'

As they turned into the drive of the Sylvester house the sun came out at last, illuminating it as if a spotlight had been turned on. It looked so innocent, thought Thanet. Who, passing in the lane, would ever have guessed that behind its walls murder had so recently been done?

Fielding, the gardener, was squatting by a blocked drain in front of the house. He had the cover off and was ramming a flexible metal rod down it.

'Trouble?' said Thanet.

'Too much water coming off the roof too fast,' said Fielding. 'If there's any kind of obstruction, this drain can't take it. It has a sharp bend a short way along, it's always causing problems.'

It was Tess who answered the door. The Dobermann was beside her and advanced to nose at Thanet's hand. With difficulty he prevented himself from flinching and managed to pat the dog's head. 'Good boy.'

Tess smiled. 'You see?' she said. 'I told you he'd remember you.' She looked a little better today, her eyes less bloodshot, the skin beneath less puffy.

Thanet smiled back. 'It's Mrs Mallis we've come to see.'

'She's in the kitchen.' Tess stood back to let them in.

'Thank you. We know the way.'

She nodded and turned back to the open door of the sitting room, where the television set was on. The dog's toenails clicked rhythmically on the parquet floor as he followed her.

Barbara Mallis was preparing the family's evening meal, a casserole by the look of it. She was cutting up stewing steak and dropping it into a large green Le Creuset pot. Bags of various root vegetables lay on the table. She was wearing a neat blue and white checked overall to protect her clothes and her hair was caught up into a French pleat. As usual she was carefully made up and sported a number of pieces of jewellery. In addition to earrings Thanet counted four rings and three gold necklaces of varying thicknesses and designs. He wondered how she managed to maintain her long varnished nails in such good condition.

She didn't look too pleased to see them but she invited them to sit down. 'You don't mind if I go on with this?'

'Not at all. You must spend quite a lot of time in here, with – how many? – six adults to cook for?'

'I do, yes.'

'Do you do all the cleaning too?'

'Oh no. A woman from the village comes in every day. I supervise her, do the food shopping and organise the running of the house in general. And cook, as you say.' She dropped the last batch of meat into the pot and set it on the hotplate of the Aga. It began to sizzle almost immediately and she reached across to switch on the extractor fan.

This was rather noisy and Thanet had to raise his voice. He regretted agreeing that she should continue with her preparations. 'You like the job?'

A shrug. 'It's all right.' She was stirring the meat vigorously with a wooden spoon to prevent it sticking.

How to put this tactfully? 'I imagine the Sylvesters are generous employers.'

She gave him a sharp look over her shoulder. 'I don't see that's any business of yours, Inspector.'

'I'm not sure whether it is or not.'

She removed the casserole from the heat, closed the hotplate lid and turned to face him, giving him her full attention for the first time. 'And just what, exactly, do you mean by that?'

So much for the softly softly approach. It had been naïve of him to imagine that he could approach the subject of money without putting her on the defensive. He would have had to come out into the open sooner or later and it was obviously sooner. 'How much, exactly, do you earn, Mrs Mallis?'

'I told you. I don't see that it's any of your bloody business!'

'Oh, but I'm afraid it is, Mrs Mallis. Whether you like it or not. You are living in a house where murder has been committed and –'

'You're not implying that *I* might have had anything to do with it?'

'We're keeping an open mind at the moment.'

'And what does that mean?'

'Just what I say. You were here, in the house, when Mr Jeopard died –'

'Along with about a hundred other people! Are you hounding them, too?'

'Hounding? Oh come, Mrs Mallis, don't you think that's an exaggeration?'

'No, I do not! You barge in here asking questions about my private affairs . . .'

'About your salary, specifically. Now why should that upset you so much, I wonder?'

She was silent for a moment, glaring at him. Then she said, 'I just don't see that it has anything to do with you.'

'But I disagree, I'm afraid.'

She said nothing, just waited, and he saw the muscles along her jawline ripple as she clenched her teeth.

'You see, he said, 'you present something of a mystery. And I'm afraid that we cannot afford to let mysteries go unsolved in a house where we're investigating a murder.'

Still no response.

'We couldn't help noticing, you see, that you seem to have rather an extravagant life-style for someone who lives on a housekeeper's salary. One has only to look at you to see that you spend considerable sums of money on your appearance . . .'

'I have no one else to spend it on,' she said between clenched teeth. She was containing her anger with difficulty, restraining herself only because she wanted to know exactly what cards were in his hand.

Thanet hoped the trump up his sleeve would catch her unprepared. 'Also, Sergeant Lineham and I were surprised to see how luxurious your flat is.'

'As you suggested, the Sylvesters are very generous employers,' she said. 'And they appreciate the service I give them. Ask them, they'll tell you! They just want to make sure I stay, that's all. So they provide me with a really nice flat. Big deal!'

'Then there's your car,' said Thanet. 'Sergeant Lineham is very interested in cars, aren't you, Sergeant? You noticed it right away.'

'I did,' said Lineham, nodding. 'Very nice, too.'

'But a BMW convertible?' said Thanet. 'How much does a BMW convertible cost, Sergeant, do you know?'

'I checked,' said Lineham. 'Around £26,000, for a K-reg. 325i in good condition, like Mrs Mallis's. Probably more, if it has certain extras.'

'Really? At least £26,000, then! As much as that! I

wonder how many housekeepers could afford to spend so much on a car?'

'There's always hire-purchase, of course,' said Lineham. Barbara Mallis opened her mouth, but before she could speak Lineham added, 'Something we could easily check.'

She shut it again.

'True,' said Thanet.

She really was furious at being driven into a corner like this. Her hands curled into claws at her sides as if she would like to fly at Thanet and scratch his eyes out. With a violent movement she folded her arms across her chest, as if to try and hold her anger in. 'If you must know,' she spat out, 'I bought that car with money I inherited from my father when he died a couple of years ago.'

Got you! thought Thanet. 'Really?' he said. 'How strange. I could have sworn that DC Martin said he'd actually spoken to – what was Mrs Mallis's father's name, Sergeant?'

'Waycom.'

'Yes, that's it. Waycom. An usual name, wouldn't you agree? Yes, I'm certain DC Martin said he was talking to him only yesterday. Er . . . Did you say something, ma'am?'

She had gone white, then red. 'How dare you!' she said. 'How dare you pry into my private life! You had no right!'

'Every right, I'm afraid,' said Thanet. 'And the sooner you understand that the better.' He leaned forward. 'Look, Mrs Mallis, I don't enjoy browbeating anyone . . .'

'You could have fooled me!'

'Well it's true. I don't. But sometimes I am driven to it. You must admit you're not exactly being cooperative. I'm not asking for details, just a general clarification of your financial position. All I want is the truth, pure and simple, then we'll leave you in peace.'

She stared at him, lips pressed together in a thin hard line.

Would she give in?

Thanet doubted it. She had nothing to lose, perhaps everything to gain, by remaining silent.

Her eyes narrowed then suddenly she seemed to relax. She unfolded her arms and rested her hands lightly on the metal bar of the Aga behind her. Her lips curled in a malicious little smile. 'Then you'll have to go on wanting, won't you, Inspector. And there's not a thing you can do about it.'

She was wrong, of course, but at the moment Thanet did not feel justified in pursuing the matter further. If it became necessary, he would do so. So he contented himself with lifting his hands in apparent defeat. 'It's up to you.'

Back in the car Lineham said, 'She's got something to hide, no doubt about it.'

'I agree. I'm just surprised she reacted so strongly. I'd have thought she'd realise that would make us even more suspicious.'

'You caught her by suprise, I suppose.'

'Perhaps.'

Back at Headquarters they ran into Doc Mallard hurrying down the stairs. He looked harassed.

'Ah, there you are, Luke. I'm in a bit of a rush, I'm afraid. But I thought I'd just pop in to let you know the PM didn't come up with anything unexpected. Jeopard died of asphyxia, drowning if you like, not from the blow on the temple. I expect the diatom test to confirm that.'

'Remind me what that is.'

'Sorry, I really haven't got time to explain just now. Next time I see you, perhaps.'

'Don't worry, we'll look it up. Thanks for letting us know.'

'Not at all. 'Bye.' And he was gone.

'So,' said Lineham, 'it's as we thought. He must have been unconscious when he went into the water.'

'And someone just left him to drown,' said Thanet grimly.

In the office there was a note from DC Martin on his desk. 'Good, we've got an appointment with Dr Damon at 2.30 this afternoon, Mike.'

'Great.' But Lineham had only half heard him. He had gone straight to the bookshelves and was looking something up. 'I can't remember precisely what a diatom test is, either. Ah, here we are. "Diatoms . . . microscopic algae found in water . . . In drowning, they're sucked into the lungs and during the moments of struggling they enter the bloodstream . . . Presence in body tissues proves that victim was alive when entering the water." So, conversely, their absence presumably proves he wasn't.'

'Quite.' This murder may not have been premeditated but it had certainly been intentional. He said so, to Lineham.

'I agree, sir. So which of them d'you think could be sufficiently callous to stand by and watch him drown?'

'I don't know. I don't feel we're getting anywhere at the moment, Mike. We seem to be just casting around in the hope of finding a lead, and allowing ourselves to be sidetracked by Rosinha, when we should have been concentrating on the case.'

'We couldn't just ignore her situation, could we, sir?'

'I know, I know. But what have we done today, you tell me that. What exactly have we achieved?'

'Not a lot, I admit.'

'And where do we go next? Oh come on, Mike. Let's go to the canteen and have a bite to eat.'

'Perhaps we'll strike lucky with Carey's psychiatrist this afternoon,' said Lineham as they picked up their lunchtrays.

'Perhaps,' said Thanet.

But in the mood he was in, he doubted it.

EIGHTEEN

At the hospital Lineham set off along the seemingly endless corridors with confidence. His wife Louise was now once again a Ward Sister here, as she had been before their marriage. She loved her work and had found it very hard to give up during the years when Richard and Mandy were too young to go to school. She had stuck it out, however. She was a strong character, a woman of principle, and she believed that if you chose to have children you should be prepared to look after them during those early, formative years.

'I'd hate to put them with a childminder,' she'd once said to Thanet. 'I want them to learn to behave as Mike and I want them to, not how some stranger thinks they ought to. And I couldn't bear to think that someone else was instilling her values into them instead of mine. Especially these days, when moral standards generally are so low.'

Thanet agreed with her and said so, but wished she didn't always make him feel he was being preached at. 'Why are people like Louise, who invariably believe they're in the right, so wearing?' he'd said to Joan.

Joan had laughed. 'Because they usually are right?'

In any case, Thanet had always been thankful that it was Lineham who was married to Louise, not him.

'Mike! What are you doing here? You didn't tell me you had to come to the hospital.' Louise had emerged from a door as they were passing. She looked trim and efficient in her uniform, her dark hair neatly tucked away beneath her cap.

'Didn't know myself until this morning.'

'Where are you going?'

'The new psychiatric wing.'

Louise rolled her eyes. 'Very swish.'

They chatted for a moment or two before continuing on their way. Thanet was beginning to wonder if they would ever get there when Lineham pushed his way through swing doors and they entered a new and glossier world. Sturrenden General had been built in Victorian times and although it had been modernised over the years it was still rambling, inconvenient, and badly adapted to contemporary requirements. For years there had been talk of abandoning it and building a new hospital on the outskirts of the town but the prohibitive cost of doing so, allied to a vigorous Save Our Hospital campaign, had resulted in the status quo being maintained, with various concessions to changing policy. The building of the psychiatric wing had been one of them; the closure of the older mental hospitals and the release of former mental patients into care in the community had made some new provision for those who needed hospital care essential.

They had stepped into a circular foyer with a hexagonal dome of obscured glass and short corridors leading off it like the spokes of a wheel. Over the entrance to each of these was a name – Stour, Rother, Medway, Beult, Len; Kentish rivers, Thanet realised. Was there some deep psychological significance to the fact? In the centre was a round reception desk with a green and white striped canopy suspended above it. The effect was cheerful without being over-stimulating – a carefully achieved balance, Thanet guessed.

The receptionist was young and pretty with glossy shoulder-length hair the colour of a ripe horse-chestnut. 'Ah, yes. He's expecting you. It's the third door on the left along Medway.'

Thanet's knock was answered at once.

'Come in.' The voice sounded weary.

And its owner looked it, thought Thanet as they entered.

Dr Damon and his room were in complete contrast. He was small, tired, and balding, whereas his surroundings were aggressively new and resplendent. Seated behind a huge mahogany desk in an executive-type black leather swivel chair with high back, he looked somehow diminished, as if the years of functioning in shabby outworn surroundings had left an indelible imprint upon him.

Introductions made, Thanet said, 'As you'll have gathered, this is about Carey Sylvester.'

'Yes.' Damon picked up a black ballpoint pen which lay on the file before him – Carey's file, Thanet presumed – and began to slide it through his fingers, turning it over again and again. 'I've been half-expecting you. But before we begin I must make several points clear. First, I want it understood that this discussion is entirely off the record.'

'Agreed.'

'And I also want your assurance that nothing I tell you today would be used in any future Court proceedings.' Damon laid the pen down on the desk blotter, carefully aligning it with the edge of the file.

'Understood.' Thanet could appreciate the psychiatrist's caution. He had seen enough expert witnesses put through the mill by able Counsel to appreciate why

Damon was being careful to spell out the ground rules for this interview. He himself was always very careful how any material which might subsequently be used in Court was obtained.

The telephone rang and Damon picked it up. 'Excuse me. Damon here. Sorry, no, not at the moment. Yes, as soon as I can.'

He replaced the receiver and folded his arms across his chest. 'Also, and I must make this clear although I'm sure you are already well aware of the fact, my main concern must be to safeguard my patient's privacy.'

'Yes. We appreciate that.'

'Good.' The psychiatrist unfolded his arms and sat back in his chair. 'In that case, I'll naturally do what I can to help. I assume I'm right in thinking this is about the murder on Saturday night at the Sylvesters' house?'

'Yes.'

'And you suspect that Carey is involved?'

'Not necessarily, no. He is only one of a number of suspects.'

'But I don't see how the question could arise. As I understand it, the Sylvesters employ a qualified nurse, full time, to look after Carey. I cannot, in fact, think of another single patient of mine who is so well cared for, out of hospital.'

Thanet explained how Carey had come to be wandering about. 'And unfortunately, it was just at the time of the murder.'

Damon tutted. 'What rotten luck.'

'Naturally, what we would really like is your professional opinion as to whether Carey would be capable of killing someone.' Thanet knew that there wasn't the slightest hope of getting it, but he had to ask.

'I'm sorry. You must see that I can't possibly give you an answer.'

'Would you, then, be prepared to tell us whether or not he has ever shown violent tendencies?' Another vain hope, Thanet knew.

'I'm sorry. Again, I can't help you there. What I can tell you is this: it is very difficult to make categorical statements about schizophrenics. The very nature of their illness renders them so unpredictable that it is virtually impossible to generalise.'

'Is there anything you can tell us, which might be of help?'

The telephone rang again and again Damon spoke into it briefly. Then he passed a hand over his bald head and looked thoughtfully at Thanet. 'Well, I can say this. If this murder you're investigating was premeditated you can rule Carey out. If schizophrenics commit murder it is almost invariably on impulse. That is one generalisation I can make. Usually it's because something, something which to us may seem completely irrational, triggers them off.'

'Have you any idea what that something might be, in Carey's case?' Once more there was little point in putting the question, but Thanet felt he had to.

Damon was shaking his head almost before Thanet had finished speaking. 'I can't answer that, I'm sorry.'

The telephone rang yet again. 'Damon here. Yes, I see. I'll come at once.' He was already rising. 'I'm sorry, Inspector. A minor crisis. I really must go.'

Outside Lineham said, 'Well, a fat lot of use that was.'

'I agree. All we learned really is that we can't rule Carey out and we knew that already. Still, at least the Super will be satisfied.'

But Thanet was wrong. Back at Headquarters they ran into Draco in the entrance hall.

'Ah, Thanet. Martin tells me you've been to see Carey Sylvester's psychiatrist. How did you get on?'

Thanet told him.

'And that's it? You couldn't get any more out of him than that?'

'He was being very careful, sir, covering himself in case it ever came to Court.'

'But doesn't the man realise that meanwhile we have a murderer running around loose, and it could be his precious patient?'

Thanet contented himself with a shrug. When Draco got on to his high horse there was little point in trying to present any other point of view.

'It's an absolute disgrace that in cases like this the police shouldn't have free access to information they consider relevant!' Draco stumped off along the corridor, irritation in every line of his body.

Back in his office Thanet found that somehow his hand had found its way into his pocket and emerged clutching his pipe. He looked at it wistfully. Gradually, over the years, forced by the strength of medical opinion, public disapproval of anyone who emitted clouds of smoke and, closer to home, Lineham's intense dislike of the habit, Thanet had managed to cut down on his smoking and now allowed himself the luxury of only one pipe a day, usually in the evening, after supper. But just occasionally, in times of stress or frustration, he still found himself lapsing.

He suspected that this was going to be one of those times.

Besides, he always thought best with a pipe in his mouth, especially if it was lit.

Lineham had noticed and was grinning. 'Going to give way to temptation, sir?'

'Why do I sometimes wish you didn't know me so well?'

'Oh go on, sir. Light up. Indulge yourself for once. I'll survive.' Lineham was already going through the routine they followed at such times, opening the window and propping the door ajar so as to create a through draught.

'Thanks, Mike.' Thanet fed tobacco into his pipe. 'Well, as I was saying earlier, we don't seem to be getting very far, do we?'

'Perhaps we ought to interview Carey again.'

Thanet shook his head. 'What's the point? You saw what he was like. He lives so much in a world of his own you can't be sure of the truth of anything he says. Even if he confessed I'd have serious doubts about it. No, as I see it, the only possible way in which we could be certain he was guilty would be if we found some material evidence to prove it.'

'Not much chance of that, is there!'

'Precisely. No, we'll just have to put Carey on the back burner for the moment, whether Draco likes it or not, and get on with examining all the other possibilities. Which at the moment means only one thing.' He struck a match and lit up, feeling a blissful sense of relaxation steal through his veins. All right, he told himself defiantly. So I'm addicted. As long as I keep the habit under control, as I usually do, what's the harm?

'Reports?'

Thanet nodded. 'Reports.' When there was much to do and many leads to follow it was only too easy to overlook some detail which at the time may have appeared unimportant but which in the light of subsequent knowledge proved otherwise. Although neither of them enjoyed the process, experience had taught them the value of constant reassessment so they now settled down to read their way steadily through the material which had come in so far. From time to time they would comment, discuss, but for the most part they just read, absorbed, immersing themselves in the case.

It was when Thanet was scanning his own report on the interview with the Sylvesters on Sunday morning that he remembered something which had puzzled him at the time. 'Mike?'

'Mmm?' Lineham was deep in a report.

'I've been meaning to mention it. When Mrs Sylvester was filling us in on the background of Max and Tess and the others, did you notice anything odd when she was talking about the time when Max came back for the publication of his book?'

Lineham was frowning. 'I don't know. I don't think so. Oh, hang on a minute. It's coming back to me now. Yes, now you mention it, I did. She sort of dried up, didn't she?'

'Yes. I wondered why, at the time. I think it must have been something she remembered, something she didn't like remembering. I wonder what. Of course, it might not be relevant to the case.'

'But there again, it might,' said Lineham.

They stared at each other, thinking.

'Which year was that?' said Lineham. 'When Jeopard's book was published?'

'Nineteen ninety-two. In May, I think Mrs Sylvester said.'

'And Mrs Mallis started work there in '91. When did they get Roper in to look after Carey? We know it was some time later because she was talking about what it was like before Roper arrived.' Lineham began shuffling through the reports. 'Ah, here we are.'

'What are you getting at, Mike?'

'Just that I wondered if what Mrs Sylvester was remembering might be connected with the blackmail.'

'You mean, if Mrs Sylvester was having an affair with Roper, it might have been around the time of Max's book being published that Mrs Mallis saw whatever it is that's given her a hold over her?'

'Could be . . .' Lineham was still perusing a report. 'No. That's no good. According to Martin, Roper didn't start work at the Sylvesters' until the autumn of '92.'

'Unless . . .' said Thanet slowly. A new and bizarre idea had suddenly struck him.

'Unless what?'

'It's just occurred to me. Say we're right about the blackmail, wrong about the reason.'

'Well?'

'Just think, Mike. Look at the facts.' Thanet began to tick them off on his fingers. 'Everyone's been telling us that Jeopard is not only attracted by women, but also attractive to women. As his agent said, "Put Max in a room with a woman and he couldn't help making a pass at her." What if –?'

'Mrs Sylvester!' said Lineham, suddenly seeing what Thanet was getting at. 'Yes! Could be! I mean, she's a good-looking woman if you like that type, and she's in pretty good shape for her age. And Tess was away at the time, so when Max came looking for her as Mrs Sylvester said he always did . . . You could be right, sir! And if Mrs Mallis saw them together, now that really would give her a hold over Mrs Sylvester! I mean, just think how Sylvester would feel, if he knew! He can't stand the man and not only his daughter but his wife succumbs to him!'

'Exactly, Mike. And if he found *that* out . . .'

'Some motive!'

But now Thanet was shaking his head. 'No. It's a bit far-fetched, don't you think?'

'Oh come on, sir, think of some of the things we've seen in the past. In comparison with them this is positively run-of-the mill!'

'I suppose so. The trouble is, how do we prove it?' It would be difficult if not impossible to worm such information out of any of the people involved, but Thanet knew he had to try and he was already on his feet.

'Back to the Sylvesters'?' said Lineham.

Thanet nodded. 'Back to the Sylvesters'.'

NINETEEN

This time it was Barbara Mallis who opened the door. 'Oh no, not you again!' she said.

'Relax,' said Thanet. 'It's Mrs Sylvester we've come to see this time. Is she in?'

'Just got back.'

'And Mr Sylvester?' It was only 4.45 and Thanet was hoping Sylvester would still be at work. It would be impossible to interview Mrs Sylvester on such a delicate topic with her husband present.

'He's not home yet.'

Barbara Mallis led them to the sitting-room door, tapped and stuck her head in. 'Police,' she said.

Thanet and Lineham exchanged glances. The house-keeper's lack of respect for her employer verged on insolence. If she really was blackmailing Mrs Sylvester, thought Thanet, nothing would give him greater pleasure than to see she got her just deserts.

In the sitting room the glow of a coal-effect gas fire imparted an atmosphere of cosiness to the scene. Marion Sylvester and Tess were sitting companionably together over afternoon tea – the sort of tea one rarely came across these days, Thanet noted. A splendid fruit cake with one slice cut out of it took pride of place and there were plates of sandwiches, too, and scones, jam, cream. If Tess and her mother indulged themselves in this way every day he was surprised they weren't both grossly overweight. Perhaps, in the present circumstances, it was a classic case of eating for comfort. He averted his eyes from all the goodies as his mouth began to water.

Mrs Sylvester had obviously been shopping, cheering herself up as women often do by going out to buy herself something new. There were several carrier bags lying about and she had been showing Tess her purchases – a brightly coloured skirt and jacket were draped over one end of the sofa and on the floor two pairs of shoes nestled in tissue paper in opened boxes. The faces she and Tess turned towards the two policemen were full of weary resignation.

'Would you like a cup?' said Tess, getting up with a marked lack of enthusiasm. 'I can easily make a fresh pot.'

Thanet shook his head reluctantly. He made it a rule never to accept such an offer grudgingly made. 'We'd like a word with Mrs Sylvester if we may.'

Tess looked at her mother, who nodded. 'Off you go, lovey.'

'You're sure?'

'Quite sure. Really. Take these up for me, will you?' Marion Sylvester put the lids back on the shoeboxes and scooped them up, thrusting them into Tess's arms. Then she draped the skirt and jacket on top. 'Thanks.'

'She's looking a little better today,' Thanet said, when Tess had gone.

Marion grimaced. 'She's putting a brave face on it. But I don't think she'll ever get over it, not properly. I'm afraid poor Gerald was always second best. Do sit down, for heaven's sake. I can't stand people looming over me.'

On the way over Thanet had given some thought as to the best way to broach the subject, but had come to no satisfactory conclusion. It was, whichever way you looked at it, going to be a tricky interview and he had finally decided to play it by ear.

'Mrs Sylvester,' he began, 'you will appreciate that during the course of a murder investigation we come across all sorts of things which may or may not be relevant. Some of them are, shall we say, delicate matters, and we have to look into them because we have to make up our minds whether they are or not. Relevant, that is.'

She was already looking wary. Today she was wearing cornflower blue leggings and matching sweatshirt exactly the colour of her eyes. Her figure was good and if only she didn't wear such heavy make-up she would, as Lineham had said, be an attractive woman. Thanet could understand why a womaniser like Max might have made a play for her. But she was waiting. He must press on. 'I do want to make it clear that if anything . . . private is uncovered, and proves to have nothing to do with the investigation, it will remain absolutely confidential.'

'I don't see what you're getting at, Inspector.'

But her body was betraying her. Her legs were crossed and the foot which was suspended in mid-air had begun to twitch. Thanet knew that extremities are often less controllable than facial muscles.

He persevered. 'There are two things we couldn't help noticing about your housekeeper.'

'Mrs Mallis?' Her voice was shrill and she must have realised it. Her next words were consciously in a lower register. 'What's she got to do with it? Really, Inspector, I haven't a clue what you're going on about.'

'The first,' said Thanet, ignoring the interruption, 'is that she does appear to be remarkably affluent for someone in her situation. Her car, for instance, is a much more expensive model than you'd expect a housekeeper to run.'

'I don't see what it's got to do with me, if my housekeeper chooses to spend all her money on a BMW.'

'It's puzzling to know how she can afford it.'

'If you must know,' said Marion, 'though frankly I can't see that it's any of your business, she bought it with some money she inherited.'

'From . . .?'

'From her father, dammit! Do you always go about poking and prying into people's private affairs like this?'

'Only if we feel it necessary, Mrs Sylvester. As we do, I'm afraid, in this case. So that's what she told you, is it? That she inherited the money from her father?'

'Yes.' The monosyllable was over-emphatic. There was defiance in it, and a hint of fear, too, as if she could foresee what was coming.

'Well, I'm afraid you have been grossly misled. Mrs Mallis's father is very much alive, and living in the East End – in a council flat off the Old Kent Road, if I remember rightly. That's correct, isn't it, Sergeant?'

Lineham nodded. 'He's a retired bus driver, ma'am.'

'So you see, even if he had died, which he hasn't, it doesn't sound as though he'd be in a position to leave his daughter enough money to buy a BMW.'

Marion Sylvester lifted her shoulders. 'So she got the money somewhere else. I didn't enquire further. Perhaps she won it on the pools.'

'Then why not say so?'

'How should I know?' Her voice was raised, her self-control slipping. 'If she chooses to tell lies about it, that's nothing to do with me!'

'Isn't it?' said Thanet softly.

She opened her mouth to challenge him, but she didn't dare. He guessed she was too afraid of the answer. She stared at him. He could see in her eyes what she was thinking. *He knows*, she was thinking. *He knows*.

The certainty that he was right about all this was growing all the time. But he had to get her to admit it. As he had said to Barbara Mallis earlier, he didn't enjoy browbeating anybody, but this could be crucial to the case.

'You see, the second thing which we couldn't help noticing about your housekeeper was her manner towards you, her employer. It verges on insolence, especially when she thinks she is unobserved.'

Marion jumped up. 'Sorry, but I've had just about enough of this. I don't see why I should have to put up with being interrogated in my own house. Would you please leave. Now.'

Thanet stood up. 'By all means, Mrs Sylvester. But if we do, I'm afraid I shall have to insist that you accompany us to the police station for further questioning.'

She stared at him, her look of desperation heightening the sympathy he already felt for her.

'Look,' he said gently. 'You must accept that one way or another we have to talk about this. Why don't we try to discuss it calmly? Please, sit down again, won't you?'

The flash of defiance had evaporated and her shoulders sagged in defeat as she returned slowly to her chair.

Now was the time to bring matters out into the open. 'She's blackmailing you, isn't she?'

Marion's lips tightened and her hands clenched together.

Please, let her admit it, thought Thanet.

Then, at last, when he had almost decided she was

going to persist in her denials, she took in a deep breath as if inhaling courage and gave a reluctant nod.

'Threatening to tell your husband if you didn't pay up?'

Another nod.

'And this has been going on since the May of '92?'

He saw the flash of astonishment in her eyes, that he should know so much. 'How . . . How did you find out?'

'I assume it happened when Max came looking for Tess, as he always did? She was away, wasn't she?'

'Stupid!' she whispered, shaking her head in dismay and disbelief at her own weakness, foolishness. Her voice grew louder. 'I was so stupid!' She beat one clenched fist against the palm of the other. 'Stupid, stupid, stupid! One stupid mistake, and God, how I've been paying for it ever since! It was only once, you see. He caught me at the wrong moment. I'd . . . Oh, what's the point of making excuses. It happened. And I've never been allowed to forget it, not for a single day.'

'I assume Mrs Mallis has some kind of proof with which to back up her story, should it ever come to that? What is it?'

'Another idiotic mistake,' Marion said bitterly. 'I wrote to Max, telling him it must never happen again. I was so ashamed. My husband . . . I love my husband, Inspector, I really do. He's a good man. I wouldn't hurt him for anything. And Tess . . . Oh God, there was Tess, too. She'd never forgive me. So I wrote. It was just a note, very brief, but it was difficult to write and I had several goes before I was satisfied. If only I'd burned my first attempts! Another unbelievably stupid mistake, a real catalogue of them, isn't it? But I just tore the rough drafts up and threw them in the wastepaper basket. I knew Ralph would never dream of going through my waste paper and piecing together stuff I'd thrown away and it was him I was thinking of, he was the one I didn't want to see them. I never thought of her. How naïve can you get? Oh God, this won't have to come out, will it, Inspector? You did mean what you said, about it being in confidence if it wasn't connected with the case?'

'Yes, I did.' Thanet didn't have the heart even to hint that her confession had just doubled her husband's possible motive for Jeopard's murder. But he had to prepare her in some way. 'But if it's your husband finding out that you're worried about, I think I ought to warn you . . . You remember the other day, when you were in the hall? Mrs Mallis was going out and you called after her, to ask her to pick something up?'

She nodded, afraid of what was coming.

'We were on the landing and saw what happened. You didn't realise but your husband, thinking that you were calling him, perhaps, came to the sitting-room doorway. He heard the way she spoke to you. I could see the look on his face.'

Still she said nothing, but a horrified awareness crept into her expression as she understood the significance of what Thanet was telling her.

'Yes,' he said. 'I think he knows – or at least suspects. Not the details, perhaps, but in principle.'

As he watched, tears welled up in her eyes and spilled over, running down her cheeks unheeded. 'No,' she whispered, shaking her head. 'No. You're wrong.'

'I don't think so.'

'He would have said. He would have told me.'

'Would he?' said Thanet. 'Are you sure that, like you, he didn't simply prefer to pretend it wasn't happening?'

She buried her head in her hands. 'Oh God,' she sobbed. 'What'll I do? What'll I do?'

Suddenly the door opened and Sylvester burst into the room, rushed to his wife, dropped to his knees beside her and gathered her protectively into his arms. 'It's all right, darl,' he murmured. 'It's all right. Ralphie's here now. Hush, it's all right.' He ignored the two policemen completely.

Tess must have left the door ajar, Thanet realised, burdened as she had been with her mother's purchases, and Sylvester must have been listening outside. Engrossed in the interview Thanet hadn't heard him arrive and wondered how long he had been there. Long enough for his chief emotion to be concern for his wife rather than anger that Thanet appeared to have reduced her to tears, anyway.

Lineham raised his eyebrows at Thanet and jerked his head towards the door.

Thanet shook his head. His instinct too was to leave the Sylvesters alone for a while, give them some space and privacy, but he couldn't afford to.

Now, if ever, could be the moment for the truth to come out.

TWENTY

Marion Sylvester's sobs gradually diminished and her husband fished a handkerchief out of his pocket and pushed it into her hand. Without raising her head to look at him she eased herself away a little, wiped her eyes, and blew her nose. Finally, still without meeting his gaze, she whispered, 'You heard?'

Sylvester nodded, his face grim. 'The bastard! I could – ' Awareness of what he had almost said pulled him up short and he looked uneasily at Thanet.

'And did you?' said Thanet. 'Kill him?'

'No!'

'But you knew there was something wrong between your wife and Mrs Mallis. We could tell, the other day.' And Thanet explained what they had seen.

Sylvester stood up and taking his wife gently by the hands tugged her out of her chair to sit beside him on the sofa. There he put his arm around her and she leaned into his shoulder, drawing comfort from his proximity. Her mascara was smudged, her face tear-stained, her eyelids swollen with crying and she looked subdued, but it was obviously an immense relief to her to know that her husband knew the truth and had apparently forgiven her. If Sylvester had heard her admission of what had happened between her and Max, Thanet realised, he had also heard her declaration of love for her husband, and it was obvious which mattered to him most. It was equally obvious that she still hadn't perceived the new danger in which her admission had put him.

'Something wrong, yes,' said Sylvester. 'But I didn't know what, until a few minutes ago.' He squeezed his wife's hand and gave her a loving look. 'You should have told me, darl,' he said. 'Putting yourself through all that for nothing.'

Now, for the first time, she met his gaze squarely and returned his look of affection with a tremulous smile. 'I couldn't,' she said. 'I was afraid you'd . . .'

'What? Beat you or something? Not my style, darl, you know that.'

'No, that you'd leave me,' she said.

'Leave you? You can't get rid of me as easily as that, you ought to know that by now!'

She smiled again, shook her head.

'We've only got your word for it,' said Thanet, 'that you didn't know until a few moments ago.'

'Well, you're never going to prove otherwise, are you? You couldn't, anyway, because it's true.'

'Even if it is, you must see that you are still are a prime suspect.'

'What?' cried Marion. 'Ralph is? You can't be serious!'

'Oh, but I am,' said Thanet. 'Just think about it for a moment. To begin with, you didn't like Jeopard, did you, Mr Sylvester, and you especially didn't like the way he kept messing your daughter about, blowing hot and cold so that she never knew where she was with him. Also, I believe you genuinely thought she would be unhappy with him. You suspected he'd be unfaithful to her, cause her a lot of heartache, and you couldn't bear the prospect of that. No, you much preferred the idea of having Gerald Argent as a prospective son-in-law, didn't you, and so did you, Mrs Sylvester. That was obvious, from the way you both tried to keep him out of our discussion the other day. He's so much more suitable in every way, isn't he – a nice, steady sort of bloke with a good, respectable job, and if Tess had married him she would have continued to live locally, you'd have seen a lot of her and have been able to watch your grandchildren grow up. Jeopard, on the other hand, was going to whisk her off to London where you'd hardly ever see her and, worse, would more than likely sometimes take her off on those long trips of his. She would, in short, to a greater or lesser extent be lost to you and you hated the idea of that, especially as your son, in his own way, tragically already is.

'So it seems to me quite possible that when Tess finally succumbed to his blandishments once more, broke off her engagement to Gerald and agreed to marry Max instead – and seemed so eager to do so that she was even prepared to utilise all the wedding arrangements you had already made instead of delaying matters by having to start all over again – you decided the time had come to act. I'm not saying you actually *planned* to kill him. Perhaps you thought it would be worth trying to buy him off, as so many men have done before you when confronted with unsuitable suitors for their daughters . . .' And yes, that shaft had found its mark, Thanet could tell. Was this, in fact, what had happened? Had Sylvester tried a bribe, and failed, lost his temper and shoved Jeopard in the pool instead? 'I'm right, aren't I?'

'What if you are?' said Sylvester. 'Right about trying to buy him off, that is. But wrong about everything else.'

'You didn't tell me you'd offered him money, Ralph.'

232

Sylvester patted her hand. 'No need for you to know, darl, was there? And we must make sure Tess never finds out, either. She'd never forgive me.'

'How could she find out? I'm certainly not about to tell her.'

'What do you mean, wrong about everything else?' said Thanet.

'I tried offering him a nice fat bribe over a week ago, the day after Tess told me she was going to marry him instead of Gerald. Met him in town, gave him a slap-up lunch. Offered him a hundred thou.'

Thanet saw Lineham's lips pursed in a soundless whistle.

'But it wasn't enough,' said Sylvester bitterly.

'He refused?'

'He knew which side his bread was buttered. I'm a wealthy man, Inspector. He could see that the long-term benefits would outweigh anything I offered him now. Travel writer! What sort of job is that? Money coming in in dribs and drabs and never a secure income from one year to the next! Oh no, he knew that if he married Tess I'd never see her go short, he'd have a meal ticket for life. Of course he refused.'

'Nevertheless,' said Thanet, 'you must see that all this builds up into a strong case against you.'

'Then all I can say, Inspector, as I said before, is prove it. And you never will. Not ever. Because it didn't happen.'

Thanet could see he wasn't going to get anywhere. He stood up.

'Hang on, not so fast,' said Sylvester.

Thanet raised his eyebrows.

'Before you go, we've got some unfinished business to deal with.'

'What?' said Marion.

'That woman upstairs, that's what.' Sylvester sounded savage. He stood up.

His wife clutched at his trouser leg. 'What are you going to do?'

'See she gets what she deserves, of course.'

'What do you mean exactly, Ralph?'

'Well, first I'm going to make damn sure she knows it's all out in the open now and there's no point in her trying to put anything over on you ever again, and then I'm going to tell her, with the Inspector and the Sergeant as witnesses, that we're going to take great pleasure in prosecuting her. We have got grounds, haven't we, Inspector?'

Thanet nodded. 'No doubt about that. I assume you have records of the payments you've made, somewhere, Mrs Sylvester?'

'Yes. But I don't want to! Bring it to Court, I mean.'

'Why not?' Sylvester sat down beside her again with a thump. 'You can't mean that, surely, darl, not after all she's put you through!'

'But that's just the point, don't you see? I've had enough, I really have. And to think of it all coming out in Court . . .' She shuddered. 'I couldn't bear it. I really couldn't.'

'It would all be done very discreetly, Mrs Sylvester,' said Thanet. 'In cases of blackmail we take great trouble to protect the victim, otherwise nobody would ever bring a prosecution.'

'No! All I want to do now is put it behind me! Please, Ralph. And have you thought what it would do to Tess? If it went to Court, there's no way we could keep it from her.'

Sylvester smote his forehead. 'Idiot! Damn and blast, I

hadn't thought of that! You're right, darl, of course you are. OK. If that's the way you want it, then that's the way it'll be. But you do agree that she'll have to go out on her ear, don't you? Now? Today?'

Marion nodded.

'Then humour me in this. It goes against the grain to let her off so lightly, and I'd like to put the frighteners on her, make her realise that she's only getting off by the skin of her teeth. So I want to confront her with it now, in front of the police.'

'OK, Ralph. It's up to you.'

'You're happy about that?' He gave her a searching look. She nodded again.

'Right. And you don't mind waiting, Inspector?'

'Not in the least. Quite the contrary, in fact.'

'Good.' Sylvester jumped up and marched purposefully to the door. 'Mrs Mallis?' he bellowed.

Thanet had noticed a large handbell on the table in the hall near the telephone and Sylvester went out and rang it vigorously. 'Mrs Mallis!' he shouted again. Then, more quietly, 'It's all right, Roper, there's nothing wrong. Sorry to have disturbed you.'

Roper had obviously come out on to the landing to see what all the noise was about.

Sylvester came back into the room. 'She's coming,' he said.

A moment later Barbara Mallis entered and stood just inside the door, hands folded meekly in front of her, the picture of an obedient servant. 'You rang?' she said sweetly, sarcastically. Sylvester had rung the bell so loudly it had probably been heard by the Fieldings down by the front gate.

'I certainly did.' Sylvester had taken up a stance on the hearthrug, hands clasped behind his back, chin down.

There was a pent-up ferocity in him, as if he were restraining himself with difficulty. He reminded Thanet of a bull about to charge and that made him wonder: had this latent violence erupted during an encounter with Max on Saturday night?

Now that she had had time to absorb the atmosphere in the room Barbara Mallis obviously sensed the tension and hostility. Her eyes flickered from Sylvester, to his wife, to Thanet, to Lineham and back to Sylvester again. She shifted uneasily and subtly her attitude underwent a change. Her eyes became guarded and she frowned. 'Why? What's the matter?'

'How you have the nerve to stand there and ask me that, I simply do not know!' said Sylvester. 'What the bloody hell do you think is the matter?'

Her aggression flared up in response to his. 'How should I know?'

'Blackmail, that's what's the matter! It's been going on for years, I gather.'

Barbara Mallis shot Marion a look of pure venom. 'I don't know what you're talking about.'

'Oh,' breathed Marion. 'You wicked woman. You really are a wicked, wicked woman.'

'It's interesting,' said Thanet, 'that only a short time ago Sergeant Lineham and I were querying the fact that you seemed to have so much money to throw around. Now we know where you got it from, don't we? You do realise, of course, that blackmail is a criminal offence?'

Barbara Mallis gave Marion another vicious look. 'Amazing what stories some people will dream up to make themselves the centre of attention,' she said, obviously deciding that whatever happened there would be no future for her in the Sylvester household. 'Especially bored middle-aged housewives without enough to do.'

'How dare you!' shouted Sylvester. 'I won't have you insulting my wife like that!'

Marion stood up alongside him and put a restraining hand on his arm. 'Shh, Ralph. Don't let her get to you.' She looked at the housekeeper and lifted her chin. 'Middle-aged I may be, but at least my story can be backed up by proof.'

'Proof? What proof? I always . . .' Barbara Mallis's mouth closed like a trap over the dangerous words which had almost escaped her lips.

'You always what, Mrs Mallis?' said Thanet politely. 'Always insisted on payment in cash? Is that what you were about to say?' He glanced at Marion Sylvester for confirmation.

She nodded. 'But I kept a record. Always.'

Barbara Mallis's lips tightened.

'And of course,' said Lineham, unable to resist joining in, 'we can always check your bank statements. Unless you actually kept the money under your mattress or in the wardrobe – where we'd still find some of it, I imagine – you must have paid at least some of it into the bank.'

She said nothing, but the shaft had gone home. The muscles along her jawline bulged as her teeth clenched. Then, unexpectedly, she laughed, an unpleasant, jeering sound. 'Haven't you forgotten something?'

'What?' said Sylvester.

'Your precious daughter. Tess. Have you told her, too? No. I can see you haven't. Such a pity if she were to find out, wouldn't it be?'

'Right!' said Sylvester. 'That's it!' He turned to his wife. 'We've got to do it!'

Marion shook her head. 'No.'

'But, darl . . .'

'No!' She looked at Barbara Mallis. 'I think you ought to know that we *had* decided not to prosecute.'

The housekeeper's eyes narrowed.

'Partly,' said Marion, 'because I was too much of a coward to face all this coming out in Court. But also because if it did there would be no way to prevent Tess from knowing. And she's been hurt enough. So let me tell you this. If you breathe so much as one word – no, even drop the merest, slightest hint to Tess, then I shan't hesitate to go ahead and take you to Court, however difficult I may find it. That I promise you.'

'I second that,' said Sylvester. 'And meanwhile, you can pack your bags and get out of our house. I give you one hour, no more.'

Barbara Mallis smiled. 'My contract says one month's notice. Or pay in lieu of.'

'Don't push me,' said Sylvester between clenched teeth. 'One hour. And count yourself lucky.'

She shrugged. 'Ah well, it was worth a try.' And she walked jauntily out of the room.

'What a poisonous woman!' said Lineham, expressing the feelings of all present.

'Good riddance!' said Marion. 'Oh Ralph, it's such a relief, I can't tell you! I'd never have believed that something good could come out of all this!'

'We're not out of the woods yet, darl,' said Sylvester grimly. 'Remember what the Inspector said. Somehow we've got to prove I wasn't involved in what happened to Max.'

'We will.' Marion smiled radiantly up at him. 'It'll be all right, you'll see.'

Back in the car Thanet said, 'I wish I shared her confidence. For my money, Sylvester is still at the top of the list. But it's difficult to see where to go from here.

Tell you what. The team working on the suspects' alibi checks should be finished by now. If the reports are all in perhaps it's time that we had a session putting them under a microscope.'

'But DC Penry is doing all that on the computer. It's ideal for that sort of job.'

'All right. So we'll talk to Penry, see if he's come up with anything.'

'And if he hasn't?'

'We'll see.'

Lineham groaned. 'I know what that means. And there was I thinking that was it for today, I could go home and put my feet up.'

'Come on Mike, that's not like you, where's your enthusiasm, your dedication! Personally I know I won't rest tonight until I feel satisfied that we've been over all the ground we've covered so far and haven't missed anything.'

Back at the office DC Penry was unequivocal. 'I've just finished, sir. Every piece of information with reference to the alibis is now on file. It's all collated and I've asked the computer every possible question I can think of, without positive results.'

'I wish you wouldn't talk about that machine as if it were a person,' said Thanet. The next generation of policemen would no doubt take computers for granted but personally he didn't like them, never had and never would. He conceded that they could be useful in certain cases but their major disadvantage in his view was that they were only as efficient as the person who operated them; if you didn't ask the right question you wouldn't get the right answer.

'Come on, Mike,' he said now. 'Let's see what the human computers can do.'

Lineham rolled his eyes at Penry but followed Thanet up to the office.

'Right,' said Thanet. 'I'll take Hartley, Gerald and Anthea, as they were together around supper time, and you take the Sylvesters.'

'Including Tess?'

'Including Tess. Just in case she'd had enough of his flirting and decided to have it out with him.'

'And left him to drown?'

'Mike, just get on with it, will you? And remember, we're looking for discrepancies, no matter how small, no matter how apparently unimportant.'

They settled down to work. Bentley and his team had done an excellent job, thought Thanet. He had been the perfect choice for the job. Patient, thorough, painstaking, he had made sure that all witnesses had been interviewed, even if one of his team had had to go back several times to catch them in. The reports had then all been assembled in logical order.

First came the statement of the suspects. Some time had obviously been spent with each of them, dredging through his or her memory. Checking quickly, Thanet counted that Anthea claimed to have seen or spoken to twenty-six people who might have remembered seeing her on her way to, in or on her way back from the upstairs bathroom which had been made available to female guests. Hartley had come up with eighteen names and Gerald, who had remained behind in the queue and then returned to their table, with fifteen. On each suspect's statement these names had been listed in the claimed chronological order, with approximate times beside each one.

The witnesses' statements had then also been assembled in the same chronological order. Some of them remembered seeing or speaking to Anthea/Hartley/Gerald at the times they claimed, some did not, but then that was scarcely surprising; there were a lot of people milling about and just because someone didn't happen to have noticed you at the same time as you noticed them, it didn't mean you weren't there. Anthea had actually been separated from the other two longest, Thanet noted, having left them at 9.40 and returned about 10, but again this was not unduly surprising; women always tended to take a long time in the bathroom, presumably because they were seizing the opportunity to comb their hair or repair their make-up. Hartley had been away for between ten and fifteen minutes, having left just after Anthea and returned five minutes before her – a period therefore during which both he and Gerald would theoretically have had the opportunity to slip along to the pool house. Amongst those who backed up their statements were Barbara Mallis, who had seen Anthea coming down the stairs; Fielding, who had been looking for Carey at the time but had noticed Hartley coming out of the dining room; and Marion Sylvester and Jeopard's aunt, Louisa Burke, who had noticed Gerald returning to his table just before Hartley (Gerald claimed to have been chatting in the queue for ten minutes, but the witnesses interviewed about this were vague about the length of time they had had to wait to collect their plates of food).

Thanet sat back and sighed.

Lineham looked up. 'You haven't found anything, sir?'

Thanet shook his head. 'Have you?'

'Not a thing.'

'The big problem is the timing, isn't it. We're talking about such a short period, only twenty minutes at the most, and practically everyone says they couldn't be sure of the exact time. Why should they, after all? It was a party, no one was clock-watching. Most of them relate

what they did or who they spoke to to certain events.'
Thanet shuffled through the statements, picking out
phrases and reading them aloud: '"After we were told
supper was ready"; "Before I collected the first course";
"Not long before Ralph asked me if I'd seen Max";
"After I'd been to the loo".' He tossed the papers on to
his desk in disgust.

'I know. Bentley's done his best but this chronological
order is pretty useless really. Most of it is according to
what the suspects have told us.'

Thanet shuffled the reports together. 'Right,' he said.
'That's it for tonight. I don't know about you, but my
brain feels as though it's stuffed with cotton wool. Let's
sleep on it.'

If we can, he thought gloomily as he drove home.

Matters improved, however, when he got there. Joan
came to greet him, all smiles.

'You look cheerful,' he said, giving her a half-hearted
kiss.

'Which is more than could be said of you. Case not
going well?'

Thanet sighed and shook his head.

'Well, this'll make you feel better. Ben's decided to go
to university! He's putting Bristol as his first choice.'

'Good! Excellent!' Joan was right. The news had lifted
his spirits. 'Is he in?'

'No. Come on, have something to eat. That'll cheer
you up even more.'

And once again she was right. By the time he'd con-
sumed beef casserole with dumplings and settled down to
watch television with his pipe drawing well, he was
feeling a new man. Forget the case, he told himself.
Tomorrow is another day.

It was an effort but he managed it, sitting mindlessly

through a documentary about AIDS in the Far East, followed by a play which was so boring he fell asleep.

It wasn't until he was getting into bed that he realised: as so often happened, while his conscious mind was switched off his subconscious had been working away regardless. The conviction sprang into his brain full-blown: some time today he had read, seen, heard something which he should have picked up and hadn't.

'What's the matter?' said Joan, noticing his sudden immobility.

He shook his head as if to clear it. 'I'm not sure.'

'You're feeling all right?' she said, in alarm.

'Yes, yes, I'm fine. But I've just realised that I've missed something.'

'What?'

'If I only knew!'

'Sleep on it,' said Joan. 'You've often said it's the best way.'

'Easier said than done.'

'In that case ...' she said, rolling over to face him, putting her arms around him and lifting her face to his kiss.

Thanet wasn't going to argue with that. He responded with enthusiasm.

TWENTY-ONE

After their lovemaking Thanet went out like a light and didn't wake up until the alarm went off next morning. He was in the bathroom shaving when it hit him. Of course! That was what had been bothering him last night!

The revelation had unsteadied his hand and a bright red globule of blood oozed out where he had nicked his chin. Automatically he dabbed at it with a tissue and reached for his styptic stick, his mind busy with this new discovery. Could it have any significance? The more he thought about it the more his initial excitement faded. It was probably a genuine mistake on the part of the witness and even if it wasn't, it was difficult to see its relevance. Still, it was precisely the type of discrepancy he and Lineham had been looking for last night, and as such would have to be followed up.

Of course, his memory could be playing tricks on him and he might not be remembering the statement accurately. Anxious to get to the office and find out, he speeded up his early-morning routine. He was eating a piece of toast standing up when Joan came into the kitchen. She glanced at the bare table. 'No breakfast?'

Because he never knew whether or when he would get

lunch Thanet invariably ate a good breakfast. In the early days of their marriage it had been cornflakes followed by bacon and egg, white toast, butter and marmalade. Only the marmalade had survived Joan's campaign for healthy eating, the rest having gradually been replaced by bran flakes or muesli mixed with fresh or stewed fruit and yoghurt, followed by wholemeal toast and polyunsaturated margarine. Bacon and egg were now saved as a rare treat for high days and holidays.

He shook his head. 'Something I want to check.' He kissed her, shoved the last piece of toast into his mouth and left.

He arrived at work before Lineham and was riffling through the reports, looking for the statement he wanted, when the sergeant arrived.

'Morning sir. What's up?' said Lineham, registering Thanet's air of purpose.

'Remembered something this morning, and I just want to check. Ah, here it is.' Thanet began to read. A moment later he stabbed triumphantly at the paper with his forefinger. 'I thought so. Look.' He turned the statement around and passed it across to Lineham. 'Read that.'

Lineham did so. And read it again. Then he looked up, puzzled. 'So?'

Thanet leaned back in his chair. 'I'm glad you missed it too. I was beginning to think I was slipping. But before I went to bed last night I began to think there was something I'd overlooked – you know, you just get that feeling sometimes. Then this morning I realised what it was.'

'I wish I knew what you were talking about.' Lineham glanced down at the paper he was holding. 'I still can't see that there's anything to get excited about here.'

'Well, I agree that there may be nothing in it. It could

just be a slip of the tongue. Or perhaps a misunderstanding on Bentley's part.'

'Sir!' Lineham put the paper down and folded his arms belligerently. 'If you don't tell me what you're going on about . . .'

'All right, all right.' Thanet picked up the sheet of paper. 'This is one of the statements taken to check Hartley's alibi, right?'

'Yes. Fielding's.'

'Quite. Now if you remember, Hartley says he was on his way out of the dining room when he saw Fielding.'

'Yes. Fielding was in the house looking for Carey . . . Oh.' Lineham stopped.

'Ah. You've got it.'

'Yes, I think so. It's the timing, isn't it? Fielding confirms what Hartley says. But Hartley claims to have left the dining room to go to the loo immediately after Anthea, at twenty to ten. And he was back in the dining room getting his supper, as I recall, by five to ten. Whereas it wasn't until five to ten that Roper went down to Fielding's bungalow to ask him to help look for Carey. So . . .'

'Exactly. What was Fielding doing in the house at twenty to ten?'

'I don't think we ought to get too excited about this. He could have gone in for any one of a number of legitimate reasons. One of the guests might have left the lights on, on his car. Or dropped something in the drive outside. Or –'

'Yes, yes,' said Thanet testily. 'I'm well aware that there *could* be a perfectly reasonable explanation. But in that case, why didn't Fielding tell us he'd been into the house earlier? I did specifically ask him, if you remember, and he said no, he hadn't been in until he went to look for Carey. He was quite definite about it.'

'If it was a trivial errand, perhaps it just slipped his mind.'

'Well there's only one way to find out. We'll have to ask him. What I don't understand is how we could both have missed this until now. I suppose it must be because it was Hartley's statement we were checking and we were looking at the other statements only in the light of whether or not they confirmed his. It just goes to show, though, how things can be missed. In fact, I'm just wondering if we'd better start again, go through all the other statements looking at them from a different point of view.'

Lineham groaned. 'Not now, surely. Not after that session yesterday.'

'Well, perhaps not. But if we get stuck again ... Anyway, what about you? Did you have any bright ideas in the night?'

Lineham shook his head. 'Only that I think we ought to take a closer look at the three young people, Anthea, Gerald and Hartley. They've all got strong motives and we've only interviewed them once so far. Perhaps we've been concentrating too hard on Sylvester.'

'I was thinking the same thing. Right. That's what we'll do today, then. But we'll check with Fielding first, get that sorted out.'

It was another bright March day with a brisk breeze and cotton-wool clouds chasing each other across the sky. The spring sunshine was having its effect, Thanet thought: each time they drove out to the Sylvesters' house, the haze of fresh green foliage on the hedgerows seemed to be more intense.

On the way Lineham said, 'You still haven't told me

how you got on with the chiropractor. Louise was asking me last night.'

Thanet told him, doing his best to describe the treatment. 'It was amazing!' he said. 'My brain was telling my arm to stay up but it simply wasn't obeying!'

'Incredible! Anyway, what sort of an effect has it had?'

Thanet moved experimentally in his seat, testing for aches and pains. 'At first there was an unbelievable difference. When I came out of there I felt as though I was walking on air. But I've got a nasty feeling the joint has slipped out of position again – probably yesterday, when I sat down with a thump, remember? I muttered about it at the time. Still, she said that would probably happen, to begin with. I'll just have to be more careful.'

'But she thinks she might be able to get it to stay back in position permanently?'

'She's not promising, but she's willing to try.'

'That would be great! After all this time!'

'I wish I'd gone years ago. To be frank, I wasn't expecting the treatment to do any good. I only went because Joan kept on nagging at me.'

'I bet she was pleased.'

'I told her, I was only too delighted to have been proved wrong! She –' Thanet broke off. They were nearing the Sylvester house and ahead of them in the lane, a couple of hundred yards short of the gateway, was a woman pushing a wheelchair. 'Mrs Fielding and her daughter, I should think.'

Lineham had slowed down and was signalling left. The woman had pulled in to the side, waiting for them to pass, and Thanet glimpsed Linda Fielding's face for the first time. It was covered with unsightly blotches.

'Poor girl,' said Lineham. 'It must be terrible for her parents.'

Thanet said nothing, didn't even hear what the sergeant had said. He was experiencing that unique moment in every murder case he had ever solved, when suddenly the relevant pieces of information come together, assume their true importance and reveal a solution so clear, so obvious that he wondered how he could possibly have missed seeing it before.

But no, in this case he was wrong, he must be.

'Sir?' said Lineham.

Thanet became aware that the car was parked, the engine switched off, and that he was staring fixedly through the windscreen. He turned a dazed face towards Lineham.

Knowing him so well, the sergeant saw at a glance what had happened. 'You've got it!' he said.

Thanet nodded, slowly. 'Perhaps. I'm not sure. But if so, I only wish I hadn't.'

'Well?' said Lineham. Then, as Thanet did not immediately respond. 'Don't tell me you're going to hold out on me?'

'No. I'm still trying to absorb it, that's all.'

'So?'

Thanet told him.

Lineham listened with rapt attention. His reaction was gratifying. When Thanet had finished he said, 'Beats me how you ever worked that one out. And I agree, it's just possible you could be right. But if so, how on earth are we ever going to prove it?'

'To be frank, I'm not sure I want to. But I suppose we have to try.'

They got out of the car and walked back down the drive. By now Mrs Fielding was pushing the wheelchair up the path to the front door of the bungalow and as Thanet and Lineham came up behind them the two women looked around apprehensively. Thanet was familiar with the expression 'a shadow of her former self' but felt he had never truly appreciated what it meant until he took his first proper look at the face of Linda Fielding. Superimposed upon the hollow cheeks and sunken eyes he envisaged the plump, healthy features of the girl in the tennis photograph, and his stomach twisted in sympathy as he smiled at her and introduced himself. 'I'm sorry to trouble you. I wanted a word with Mr Fielding.'

There were no answering smiles. The two women exchanged nervous glances and Mrs Fielding laid a hand on Linda's shoulder as she said, 'I'll see if he's in.'

Fielding must have heard voices and a moment later he opened the door, his welcoming look for his wife and daughter fading when he saw the two policemen.

'Could we have a word, sir?'

Fielding gave a grudging nod.

Thanet and Lineham waited while the Fieldings manoeuvred the wheelchair through the doorway, a difficult procedure as there was only an inch or so of clearance. In the hall Mrs Fielding hesitated.

'You and Linda go in the kitchen,' said Fielding. 'I won't be long.'

'Why don't we go into the kitchen?' said Thanet. 'I'm sure Miss Fielding would be more comfortable in the sitting room.'

Mrs Fielding gave him a grateful smile and removed the rug from Linda's knees. Then, with the clumsiness of those unused to such skills, she and her husband each tucked an arm under one of their daughter's and lifted her to her feet. Her slow, shuffling progress across the hall to the sitting room was painful to watch. The doorway was too narrow to admit the wheelchair, Thanet realised.

A moment or two later Fielding returned and led them into a spotlessly clean small square kitchen equipped with an old-fashioned range of cupboards, a stone sink and a drop-leaf formica-topped table with three chairs. In the inner wall was a serving hatch which was slightly open, Thanet noticed. Did this mean that Mrs Fielding and Linda would be able to overhear their conversation?

'D'you want to sit down?' said Fielding ungraciously.

'Thank you.'

Lineham was to begin the questioning and now he said, 'We just wanted to go over what you said in your statement, Mr Fielding.' He took out the photocopy he had made and handed it to Fielding. 'Perhaps you'd just glance through it.'

Fielding took a spectacle case out of his pocket and put on some steel-rimmed reading glasses. When he'd finished reading he passed the paper back to Lineham without comment.

Lineham tapped it. 'You say here that you saw Hartley Jeopard coming out of the dining room while you were looking for Carey.'

'That's right, yes.'

Lineham was shaking his head. 'That doesn't make sense.'

Fielding frowned. 'Why not?'

'Because Hartley Jeopard came out of the dining room at just after twenty to ten. He was back in the supper queue by five to ten and then remained at his table until the alarm was raised at 10.35, when his brother's body was found. Whereas you told us you didn't go into the house until after Roper came down to tell you Carey was missing, at five to ten. So how could you have seen Hartley at twenty to?'

Silence. Fielding was still frowning. He was beginning to sweat, too, Thanet noticed.

Lineham waited for a few moments and then said, 'Can you explain this, sir?'

Fielding was shaking his head. 'No. I can't. I must have been mistaken. Perhaps I didn't see him.'

'Yes, you did. Because he certainly saw you. Which is why you were questioned closely about this in the first place.'

Another silence. Then Fielding said slowly. 'Well I just don't understand it. It's a real puzzle, isn't it? I suppose I must have gone in on some errand or another. But if so, I can't remember what.' He stood up. 'I tell you what, I'll have a think about it and let you know.'

Lineham glanced at Thanet, who shook his head and said, 'I'm sorry, Mr Fielding, we can't leave it like that. You see, there's something else.'

'Something else?' Fielding glanced from Thanet to Lineham, as if wondering from which direction the blow would fall. He subsided slowly back on to his chair as if his legs would no longer bear his weight.

'Yes.'

Lineham was as puzzled as Fielding, Thanet could tell, though he was hiding it well.

Thanet hesitated, torn. Now was the moment of decision. He could go on, or he could simply shake his head and say, 'Never mind, it's of no importance,' and leave it at that. The inner man counselled compassion, but the policeman in him urged him on. The years of devotion to duty, the ingrained habit of a working life, would not allow him to falter now. If he did, he knew his conscience would give him no rest. It was after all not up to him, not up to any individual to be judge and jury, only to oil the wheels of justice. He took out his notebook, tore off a sheet of paper and handed it to Fielding, together with a biro. 'I'd like you to write something for me, please.'

The Adam's apple in Fielding's throat moved as he swallowed, nervously. 'What?'

'Write, "Meet me at 9.45 in the pool house."'

Fielding swallowed again. His weatherbeaten skin had gone the colour of uncooked pastry and his hand shook as he began to write. 'What was that? "Meet me . . ."'

'". . . at 9.45 in the pool house."' Thanet watched the biro travel laboriously across the page. Fielding's hand was shaking like that of someone with Parkinson's disease. At times like this Thanet wished he was anything but a policeman.

Fielding pushed the paper across the table.

'Thank you.' Picking it up only by the extreme tip of one corner, Thanet studied it. 'Yes.' He glanced at Lineham. 'I think we have all we need here. Have you got the sheet we tore off the telephone notepad at the house, to compare?' He was confident that by now Lineham had understood what he was doing.

'I'll get it. It's in the car.' Lineham stood up.

But Fielding was shaking his head. 'Don't bother. What's the point?' He dropped his head into his hands, clutching at it with one hand on each side as if to try to contain his despair.

Lineham raised his eyebrows at Thanet and Thanet signalled, *Wait*.

Head still bent, Fielding shook it and mumbled. 'It's obvious you know what happened.'

Neither of the policemen moved or spoke. This still wasn't enough.

Then, at last, Fielding straightened up. His eyes were bleak and his shoulders sagged, as if weighed down by sorrow. 'But it was an accident, I swear.'

Thanet realised he had been holding his breath. He nodded at Lineham, who gave the caution.

He had been right in thinking the two women in the next room had been able to overhear the conversation. While Lineham was still speaking the hatch was pushed up to its full extent and Mrs Fielding appeared. She waited until he had finished and then said quietly, and with a sad dignity, 'I think you all ought to come in here now.' Then, to her husband, 'Linda and me want to be with you.'

Fielding looked at Thanet, who assented, and in silence the three men filed next door.

Linda was sitting in an upright armchair near the hearth, where a fire burned brightly. Without her coat it was even more obvious how frail, almost skeletal, she was. More of the unsightly blotches disfigured her neck and the backs of her hands. As her father entered she gave him a loving smile and patted the end of the sofa beside her. 'Come and sit here, Dad.'

He did as she asked and Mrs Fielding sat down next to him. Wife and daughter each took one of his hands and held it. The message was clear: *divided*, *we fall*.

'We knew it would have to come out in the end,' said Mrs Fielding. Her eyes flickered to Linda. 'But we hoped it wouldn't be just yet.' In contrast with the slight frame of her husband and the fragility of her daughter she looked solid, substantial, as if she was prepared to use up every last ounce of strength she possessed to shore up her disintegrating family.

'And it really was an accident,' said Linda. She smiled at her father and squeezed his hand. 'Dad wouldn't hurt a fly.'

'But you did leave him to drown,' said Thanet, looking at Fielding.

Fielding was shaking his head. 'I still don't understand how that happened. He could swim like a fish, I've seen him, a thousand times.'

'We thought he must have banged his head on the side and knocked himself out as he went in,' said Linda. 'It's the only possible explanation.'

'You don't think Ron would have just walked out if he'd *known* Max was unconscious?' said Mrs Fielding.

Thanet looked at Fielding and their eyes met, each reading what could not openly be said.

I can't guarantee that.

I wouldn't condemn you if you had.

'Perhaps you'd better tell us what happened,' said Thanet quietly.

TWENTY-TWO

Suddenly, as if a dam had burst, the Fieldings were all speaking at once.

'I only wanted to talk to him.'

'Ron didn't mean him no harm.'

'It's all my fault,' said Linda. And, to the consternation of everyone present, dissolved into tears.

In a flurry of concern Fielding fished a handkerchief out of his pocket and thrust it into Linda's hand and Mrs Fielding got up, squatted down in front of her daughter and put her arms around her. 'Hush, lovey. That's not true. It simply isn't true.' She glanced over her shoulder at Thanet and her eyes were hard. 'If it was anyone's fault, it was his. Max's.'

'I assume it happened on the night he took Linda to the College Ball?' said Thanet.

Linda had regained her self-control and now she wiped her eyes, blew her nose and nodded.

Her mother gave her one last hug and returned to her seat. 'The pig!' she said. 'He spiked her drink and then took advantage of her. She's not used to alcohol, we don't hardly ever touch it in this house. She thought she was drinking orange juice and never knew no better until she woke up in his bed next morning. She never told us at the time, of course. I knew she was upset, but I thought it was just because he never asked her out again. So when she got this, this . . .' She shook her head.

It had to be spelt out. 'It's AIDS, isn't it,' said Thanet.

They all looked down, as if they were ashamed to admit it.

'I feel so dirty all the time,' said Linda. 'I don't know if you can understand that.'

'Understand, yes. Agree, no. As your mother says, it wasn't – isn't, your fault.'

'Intellectually I know that,' said Linda, unconsciously reminding him that unlike her parents she was university-educated. 'But emotionally it's a different matter. I think I could have found any other illness easier to bear.'

'That's why we haven't told anyone,' said her mother. 'No one around here knows what's really the matter with her. They know Linda's ill, of course, but I think they all believe it's cancer.'

'Yes, they do. At least, that's what Mrs Sylvester told me.' Thanet looked at Linda. 'And there was absolutely no doubt that Jeopard was responsible?'

'There was never anyone else,' she said. 'If it weren't for him I'd be a phenomenon. A twenty-five-year-old virgin in the nineties!'

'Linda!' said her mother, shocked by such plain speaking. This wasn't the kind of household in which sex would ever have been discussed openly, Thanet guessed.

'Mum, it's all right! I'd guess the Inspector's pretty unshockable by now. Am I right?'

'I admire the fact that you're able to joke about it,' said Thanet. 'I would find it hard to consider the situation even remotely funny.'

'If I didn't, I'd go mad at the unfairness of it all.'

'So when did you learn the diagnosis?' said Thanet.

'Not until the first lesions started to appear.' Linda looked at the blotches on her hands. 'Until then no one knew what was the matter with me. My doctor, rightly or wrongly, had never thought of testing for the AIDS virus.'

'He knew you, that's why,' said her mother. 'Knew you were a decent girl, not the type to pick up something like that.' She looked at Thanet. 'Linda's right. That's what's so awful about it. It's so unfair. It's not even as if she agreed to go to bed with Max. Then you could say that she asked for it. But Linda was innocent! Innocent!'

Her husband was nodding agreement and he patted her hand. 'No point in upsetting yourself all over again, Mother.'

'But look where it's got us!' she cried. 'Look what he's done to our family! There's Linda so ill and now you, in all this trouble. He was a wicked, wicked man and that's the truth of it. How could he do such a thing, to a girl like Linda?'

What was there to say? 'So Jeopard must have been HIV positive,' said Thanet. 'And never developed full-blown AIDS.'

'They said it can take years for that to happen and there are cases when it never does,' said Fielding. 'You can be a carrier all that time and never know it. Terrible, isn't it? We think he probably picked it up in foreign parts. We've seen programmes about it, on the telly. Those little girls in Thailand and such like . . . He was always off on his travels and the Lord alone knows what he was up to when he was away, if he could do this to a girl like our Linda.'

'But what I don't understand is why you left it until the day of the engagement party to tackle him about it,' said Thanet.

'Because we didn't know until that morning who the man was, who was responsible!' said Fielding. 'Linda would never tell us.'

'When we found out it was AIDS,' said Linda, 'I couldn't believe it at first. I mean, I'd never had a serious boyfriend. But when they told me it can take years to develop, after being infected, I realised it must have been Max. There was just no other explanation. I didn't tell Mum and Dad it was him, though. It was bad enough for them to know what was wrong with me, that I was going to die, I just felt it would be even worse if they realised they knew the man who had infected me. Better, I thought, for them to have this shadowy, anonymous person to hate than someone they could put a name and face to. But I was worried in case Max didn't know he was HIV positive – worried, that is, about all the other women he might have infected or still could infect, without even being aware of it. I could have written to him, I suppose, but somehow I wanted to do it face to face. It was wrong of me, I suppose, but I wanted to say to him, look, look what you have done to me. I wanted to punish him, make him feel guilty, acknowledge the consequences of what to him must have seemed a bit of harmless fun.'

'Harmless!' said her mother. 'Harmless!'

'Hush, Mother,' said her husband. 'Let Linda explain.'

Mrs Fielding clamped her lips together and glared, but subsided.

'That's what I feel most guilty about,' said Linda. 'If I hadn't wanted revenge, my petty little revenge, and I'd contented myself with writing a letter, then Dad wouldn't be in this position now. The excuse I gave myself for not doing so was that I wanted to ask Max about Tess. And it's true that I was worried about her, naturally.'

And not only Tess, did you but know it, thought

Thanet grimly. There was Marion Sylvester, Anthea, Rosinha and perhaps even her unborn baby, apart from countless other women Jeopard might have infected in his promiscuous way through life.

'I was pretty sure he must have slept with her, and every time I saw her it was a relief that she was still looking healthy, but this was something I wanted to ask him about, for my own peace of mind. I felt I couldn't trust him to reply, if I asked him about this in a letter.

'My other excuse, of course, was that I was feeling pretty rotten. It's been a ghastly few months, one way and the other, and I've had to conserve all my energies just to cope with day-to-day existence. But I hadn't forgotten about contacting Max. I knew it was becoming urgent, and when I went into the Hospice at the beginning of last week I realised it would have to be sooner rather than later. The next serious infection might well be the last. So I'd pretty much decided that when I came home I was going to stop hoping to tell him in person and write to him instead, and you can imagine how I felt when I did get home on Saturday morning, saw those balloons tied to the gatepost and learned why they were there. Until then I'd no idea that Tess had broken off her engagement to Gerald and was getting engaged to Max.'

'It didn't occur to us to tell her while she was in the Hospice,' said Fielding. 'To be honest, we didn't even think about it. All we were concerned about was how she was getting on, whether or not she'd be able to come home again and if so, how soon.'

'We could tell she was upset when we told her about the engagement,' said her mother. 'But she wouldn't say why. Not until the afternoon.'

'I had to think,' said Linda. 'I didn't want to have to talk to Tess about it, you see. Picking up the virus is a bit like Russian Roulette, I gather, and I was just unlucky, especially as it had only happened the once. Rather like girls who are unfortunate enough to get pregnant their first time, I suppose. Anyway, if Tess was all right I didn't want to worry her – I mean, it could give her nightmares for years, and all for nothing. So I decided the only thing to do was to stop prevaricating and talk to Max then, that day, preferably before the party. I knew that if I missed the chance I might not get another for months – perhaps not at all, and besides, what I really wanted was to get him to agree to call the engagement off, for Tess's sake, before it was officially made public. I thought, if he really loved her, he'd do it.'

'Not Max! Not if it didn't suit his book!' said Mrs Fielding grimly. 'In my opinion he always looked out for number one, first and last, never mind anyone else.'

'But I had to try, Mum, you must see that. If he refused, I was prepared to take pretty desperate measures to make him agree, threaten to tell Tess, to begin with, and then, if he still wouldn't listen, threaten to get Dad to wheel me up to the party and make a public announcement.'

Thanet could imagine what courage that would have taken and what a furore it would have created.

'Anyway, the point was, I didn't know when Max was coming down from London, so I got Dad to find out, casually, from Tess. I was hoping that if he came down early, in the afternoon, perhaps, I might manage to get a message to him, to come and see me.' She gave a wry smile. 'I thought if he saw me like this he'd realise what he'd be saving Tess from if he agreed to give her up. But unfortunately we discovered he wouldn't be arriving until the same time as everybody else. So at that point I decided that there was only one thing to do. I couldn't hope to go up to the house myself and manage to get a word with him in private, it would be too difficult to arrange, so I'd have to ask Dad to do it for me.'

'That was when she told us,' said Fielding. 'That Max was the one.'

'You must have been absolutely furious with him,' said Lineham.

'Oh, I was,' said Fielding. 'No point in denying it. We both were, weren't we, Mother?'

His wife nodded. 'Can you blame us?'

'But by the evening I'd calmed down,' said Fielding, 'and I agreed to do as Linda asked, chiefly because I could see how much it was worrying her but also because I'm fond of Tess. She's a lovely girl, isn't she, Mother, and we've seen her grown up from a toddler. I couldn't bear to think of this happening to her, too.' He glanced at Linda, raised her hand to his lips and kissed it in a strangely courtly gesture.

He was, Thanet thought, a truly gentle man. What could Jeopard have said or done to goad him beyond endurance?

Linda smiled at her father. Then she turned to Thanet with a serious look. 'So you see, it really was all my fault. If I hadn't insisted . . .'

'Shh,' said Fielding 'Don't start that again, lovey. We agreed. There's no point in trying to say who's to blame and who isn't. Your mother's right. When it comes down to it, Max brought it on himself and no one can say different.'

'So what happened, exactly, on Saturday evening?' said Lineham.

'Well, I was directing the car parking,' said Fielding. 'So it was easy for me to look out for him. But when he arrived he was in a hurry, as usual, and when I asked him if I could have a word he just brushed me off and said, yes, sure, later, and went racing off. So I decided the only thing to do was write him a note and get one of the waitresses to hand it to him. I was very busy for a while, the guests were arriving thick and fast, so I didn't have a chance until later. When I did, I nipped into the house and scribbled a message on the pad by the telephone in the hall. Well, you know about that, don't you.'

'You didn't sign it.' Thanet made this a statement, not a question. He didn't want Fielding to guess that the words he had asked him to write down had simply been an inspired guess.

'No, I didn't, deliberate, like. All the while I was parking the cars I was thinking what to say, and I decided to keep it short and simple and not to sign it so that he'd be, well, sort of intrigued. I just said something like, meet me in the pool house at 9.45, on a matter of life and death.' Fielding lifted his chin in defiance. 'Well, it was, wasn't it?'

Only too true, thought Thanet.

'I thought that would bring him, if anything would. And I was right. It did. When I got to the pool house he was already there, waiting for me.'

Thanet's imagination was setting the scene: darkness pressing against the windows; light reflecting off the water; Max, elegant and debonair in his expensive suede trousers and silk shirt; and Fielding, a complete contrast in his old cord trousers and tweed jacket.

'Fielding? What do you want?'
'I told you earlier, I wanted a word with you.'
'Well I can't speak to you now. I'm expecting someone.'
'That's me.'

263

'What do you mean? You mean, you wrote this?'

'Yes, I did.'

'Of all the bloody nerve! What the hell do you think you're up to? A matter of life and death indeed!'

'But that's true. It is. Linda's death. My daughter's. And yours, too, probably.'

'That stopped him in his tracks,' said Fielding with satisfaction. 'He was halfway to the door by then.'

'What the devil are you talking about? What do you mean, mine? Look here, are you threatening me?'

'Not in the way you think. If you do die you'll have only yourself to blame.'

'You're out of your mind, man. Raving. Let me pass.'

'Not until you hear what I have to say. Linda is dying. Dying, do you hear me? Of AIDS. And you are the only man who's ever slept with her.'

'What?'

'I said, Linda is dying of AIDS, and you're the only man who's ever slept with her. You know what that means, don't you? You're HIV positive and you've got a time-bomb ticking away inside you.'

'I don't believe you!'

'It's true. Just come and take a look at Linda and you'll see how true it is. She's in a wheelchair now, did you know that? She can hardly stand up unaided and she's spent all this week in the Hospice. The next infection she picks up will probably carry her off. And make no mistake about it, you're the one who's responsible. You, and no one else.'

'I just don't believe that. Look at me! I'm perfectly fit and healthy.'

'You may seem so, now. But just wait and see. And believe me, nothing gives me greater satisfaction than knowing that from now on for the rest of your life you're going to wake up every morning afraid to look in the mirror, for fear of seeing that first lesion. Your death warrant.'

'She's lying! She must be!'

'Don't you dare call my Linda a liar! She's worth a hundred of you any day. What sort of a man spikes a young girl's drink and then seduces her?'

'Oh, that's what she told you, is it? Well, let me tell you, she was willing. Not just willing, panting for it, d'you hear me? Your precious daughter couldn't wait to –'

'That's not true!'

'And that,' said Fielding sadly, 'was when I pushed him. He was standing near the edge of the pool saying all these terrible things about Linda and I just couldn't bear it, I just wanted to shut him up. So I gave him one great shove and walked out. I admit I was beside myself, but I swear, Inspector, that I didn't mean to kill him. I had no idea he'd hit his head on the side as he went in and I didn't look back. I just heard this almighty splash and thought, *that'll ruin your fancy clothes. How are you going to explain that away?* Then I came back home.'

'He told us what had happened,' said Linda. 'We were waiting for him, to see how he'd got on. And we all had a good laugh about it! We couldn't believe it, later, when Dad came back and told us Max had been found dead in the pool.'

Thanet shook his head gravely. 'Why didn't you tell us all this straight away?'

'Because of Linda!' said Fielding. 'If I had, everyone would have had to know why Max and me were having the argument in the first place! This terrible thing with Linda is *private*, Inspector. We haven't got much longer together and we wanted to be able to spend that time quietly, by ourselves. It takes every last ounce of energy we've got to face up to this situation day by day. We couldn't bear the prospect of all the rumpus, all the publicity. Surely you can understand that?'

'Oh yes,' said Thanet sympathetically. 'Only too well.'

'Yes,' said Linda. 'I believe you do. But there's not much hope of keeping it quiet now, is there? We must just bear it as well as we can.'

'What will happen to Ron?' said Mrs Fielding fearfully.

'Mr Fielding will have to accompany us back to Headquarters,' said Thanet. 'He will be formally charged, and have to stay there until he comes up before the Magistrates. But if we can hurry that up I think it highly probable that in these rather special circumstances he'll be released on bail. So he should be home again in a day or two.' *And you'll still be able to spend Linda's last weeks together.*

'Really?' Linda smiled, for the first time.

She was looking exhausted, he realised, was barely able to remain upright in her chair.

He was glad that he had been able to give the stricken little family at least some small grain of hope and consolation.

TWENTY-THREE

'It's a relief to get away from the office,' said Thanet, peering into the mirror. 'What do you think, love? This tie or that one?'

It was Saturday night and they were getting ready for the Dracos' party.

Joan considered, head on one side. 'The spotted one, I think.'

'You don't think it's a bit conservative for a celebration?'

Joan paused in applying her lipstick. 'If that's how you feel, why not go for something really wild? Like the one Ben gave you for Christmas?'

This was a concoction of fluorescent swirls, guaranteed to cause comment. So far Thanet had worn it only once, on Ben's birthday.

'Why not?' he said. 'It's pretty representative of my state of mind. The last few days have been a nightmare. I feel as though I've been living in a state of siege.' He took the tie out and started to put it on.

'Luke, you're not really going to wear it?'

'Why not? It was you who suggested it.'

'But I wasn't serious!'

'But I am.' Thanet finished tying the knot and stood back to study the effect. 'There. What d'you think?'

Joan closed her eyes. 'Dazzling.'

'Good!'

'What d'you mean, a state of siege? The press?'

'Partly. Though it's nothing to what the Fieldings have had to put up with.'

It had been impossible to keep Fielding's arrest quiet. It had been such an unexpected and astonishing development that the media had been on to it like a pack of hounds and the clamour for more information had been deafening. Fortunately Draco had proved unexpectedly cooperative. Perhaps his own experience through the years of his wife's illness had given him a special sympathy for the Fieldings' plight, and he had allocated Thanet extra men to protect the little family from unwarranted intrusion by the media.

'But apart from that, everyone involved in the case has been pestering me for an explanation of what happened, and the problem is, my hands are tied until it's officially confirmed that Jeopard was HIV positive.'

'Until you get the results of the test back, you mean?'

'That's right, yes.'

'And when will that be?'

'The sample wasn't sent off until Wednesday – the test isn't a routine part of a post-mortem – and it takes a week, apparently, so it'll be several more days yet.'

'But you are certain about it, aren't you? That he was HIV positive, I mean?'

'Oh yes. There's no doubt in my mind that Linda Fielding is telling the truth, poor girl. If you'd seen her, Joan . . . Every time I think of her I imagine how I'd feel if it were Bridget in that condition.'

'Well, let's hope and pray that Bridget marries a man who's never been in contact with the virus, and that she has the sense meanwhile never to have unprotected intercourse. Heaven knows she's had the message dinned into her often enough.'

'The other thing that's worrying me is all the other women who were involved with Jeopard. They all seem well at the moment, but I can tell you I'm really dreading breaking the news to them. And again, that can't be done until we have official confirmation. At the moment, as I say, everyone remotely connected with the case is completely bewildered by Fielding's arrest and can't understand why we won't give them a proper explanation. Jeopard's mother, especially, has been bombarding us with phone calls and visits and is furious that I keep fending her off. Well, you can't blame her, can you? If it had been my son, I'd feel entitled to an explanation too. But it does make life rather difficult for me.'

'I'm just off now.' Ben appeared at the door. 'Wow! Great tie, Dad!'

'Thought it was about time I gave it another airing. Where are you going tonight?'

'Disco at the Blue Moon.'

'Well, have a good time.' With difficulty Thanet refrained from adding, 'But be careful.' He'd said it often enough in the past. If Ben hadn't got the message by now he never would.

'Ditto.' And he was gone, whistling.

Thanet and Joan exchanged indulgent smiles.

'What d'you think?' she said, standing up to display her dress, which was a new one, bought especially for the occasion. It was in a fluid smoky-blue silk which deepened the colour of her eyes, emphasised the curves of breasts, waist and hips and swirled around her calves as she moved.

'Give us a twirl.'

She obliged.

'Mmm, delicious.' He put his arms around her and nibbled her neck. 'You look good enough to eat.'

'But not now!' she said, giving him a quick hug before easing herself away. 'I couldn't face doing my make-up all over again.'

'As if I would suggest it!'

Outside Joan shivered. 'I'm glad I put my thicker coat on.'

For no apparent reason the temperature had plummeted. Although dusk was falling, over to the west the sky was still stained with the remnants of what must have been a spectacular sunset – mandarin-gold, shell-pink and apricot.

'I think there'll be a frost tonight,' said Thanet.

Inside the car Joan huddled into her coat and said, 'But I still don't understand how you came to suspect Fielding in the first place. I mean, he really didn't seem to have anything to do with the case, so far as I can gather, apart from being a part of the Sylvesters' household.'

'I know. That was what was so misleading. It simply didn't occur to me that he might be involved. But once I realised, of course, the whole thing fell into place. The clues were all there, I just hadn't appreciated their significance.' He switched the heater on. 'I think the engine should be beginning to warm up by now.'

Joan waved her hand in front of the air grill. 'Yes, I can feel it.'

'Well, I knew quite early on that Linda had been one of Max and Tess's crowd. But I tended to dismiss her, partly because she doesn't seem to have been involved with them for quite some time now, partly because she wasn't at the party, and partly because Marion Sylvester had told me that Linda had really only been on the fringe of the group, she hadn't been nearly as closely involved as the others.'

'Why was that?'

'Chiefly, I think, because her background was so different – not in the social sense, the Sylvesters certainly aren't snobs by any means – but because her parents were getting on a bit when she was born and I gather that, as so often happens with only children of older parents, Linda was much more staid and reserved than her contemporaries. But as she was in the same class as Tess and Anthea at school and also because she happened to be right there, on the doorstep, she was often asked to make up a four at tennis. So she certainly knew the others fairly well, even if she'd never been close to any of them.'

'She sounds the last person Max Jeopard would take to a College Ball, from what you've told me about him.'

'In normal circumstances, I agree. But Jeopard had counted on taking Tess, you see. As I told you, when he went up to Oxford she followed him, took her secretarial course there and then stayed on, took a job there, to be near him. I suspect he wished she hadn't, that as Ralph Sylvester said, he'd probably have preferred to be footloose and fancy-free during his university days, but even so there was no real excuse for the fact that he didn't tell Tess until the end of his final term that the day after the College Ball he'd be leaving on a year-long trip to China. He must have been planning it for ages, all the travel arrangements were made. She was so upset and so furious with him that she broke it off, said she never wanted to see him again.'

'I'm not surprised! So only a few days before the Ball he found himself without a partner.'

'Exactly. And the problem was that because the Ball was being held after the end of term all the girls he knew well either had partners and were staying on especially for it, or had already gone home. So he had to think of someone who might be available at the last minute.'

'I.e. Linda.'

'Yes. She was in her first year at Bristol and might be free, not being the type to be caught up in a social whirl. Oxford terms are shorter than most other universities, so he knew she'd still be there. I should think he also counted on the fact that she would swallow her pride at being asked only at the last minute and agree to come. The Oxford College Balls really are rather special and I suppose most girls would jump at the chance. Apart from which, Anthea's mother told me she thought that as a teenager Linda had secretly had a crush on Max and if that was so I imagine Max was aware of it.'

'And she accepted the invitation.'

'She did. To her bitter regret in view of what happened. She was, of course, being the innocent she was, the perfect victim to have that sort of trick played on her.'

'What a truly despicable thing to do.'

'I know. And that it should have such disastrous and far-reaching consequences, all these years later . . .'

'Poor girl.'

'You should see her, Joan. She's such a pathetic sight. I've never actually met anyone who was really ill with AIDS before. But the moment I set eyes on her I realised what was the matter with her. The Fieldings had kept it quiet, you see. It's awful, they feel so ashamed about it. Even the Sylvesters still think that she has cancer, which is what they'd told me. And if I hadn't seen that film on AIDS I don't suppose I would have questioned it. You know the one I mean, we saw it last year.'

'The one in which the wife discovers her husband is an active homosexual and has been having unprotected intercourse with her for years, you mean?'

'That's right, yes. You remember the bit where she watches a documentary on AIDS?'

'Oh, I see!' said Joan. 'The lesions.'

'Exactly. Linda has them on her face and neck as well as her hands. I gather from Doc Mallard that they are usually even more widespread on the trunk. But they are instantly recognisable, believe me. And when I saw them, well, everything suddenly came together – the fact that Max was promiscuous, had done a lot of foreign travel, had taken Linda to a College Ball where things can often get out of hand, that Linda's illness was sufficiently serious to have reduced a strapping, healthy girl to a frail-looking creature in a wheelchair . . . From there it was only a hop, skip and a jump to suspecting her father. We were already on our way to interview him because he had been seen in the house much earlier than he claimed . . . It all just fitted.'

'Yes, I see. But how on earth did you get him to admit it? From what you're saying I gather there wasn't a shred of evidence against him?'

Thanet shook his head. 'No, there wasn't. So I played a trick on him and I'm not proud of it, I must admit. I still feel ambivalent about it. I've come up against this before in cases where I feel I'd really rather not make an arrest at all.'

'What are you suggesting? That you shouldn't have pursued the matter, that you should have just left it?'

'Perhaps. It would have bought them a little time, you see, enough for Linda to have spent her last days in peace with her parents. After her death I'm pretty sure Fielding would have owned up. He's not the sort of man who could live indefinitely with something like that on his conscience.'

'And what would you have done in the meantime? Would you have told Draco?'

'I shouldn't think so. He'd probably have insisted on having Fielding in for questioning and the whole object of the exercise would have been defeated.'

'So you'd have gone through the motions of continuing the investigation. And a number of innocent people would have been left in uncertainty for an indefinite period of time.'

'Not long, I shouldn't think.'

'All the same, I don't think you would have been very comfortable with the situation.'

'No, I'm not pretending I would. But to be honest, Joan, I can't pretend my motives in manipulating a confession were pure. I have a nasty feeling that I had to go on, I had to find out, for my own satisfaction. And to show everybody what a clever person I am. Apparently to have failed to solve the case would have made a big dent in my vanity.'

'But even if that's true, and I suspect that because you feel sorry for the Fieldings you're going too far the other way in questioning your motives, you've said over and over again that it's not for you to judge in such matters. Your job is to find out the truth and then hand it over to others to decide what to do with the culprit.'

'I know. But it's not always an easy course to follow.'

'Well, I don't really see that you had any choice. I feel you did the right thing. So stop agonising about it and tell me how you did it.'

'I suppose you're right.' Thanet was silent for a few moments, thinking, and then gave Joan a smile and said, 'Yes. Of course you are. Well, what happened was that

Mike and I played a little charade. You remember the note I told you about?'

'The one that was handed to Max at the party, which you hadn't been able to trace?'

'Yes. We knew it hadn't been in an envelope, we checked, so we guessed that someone had written it on impulse. Now, obviously, very few people carry notepaper around with them, especially to a party, so Mike came up with the idea that it might have been written on the telephone pad in the hall. One of the disadvantages of all these crime series on television is that the general public has learned too much about our techniques for catching criminals. But in this case, it was an advantage. By now most people know that we can lift from a message pad the impressions made on it by words written on a sheet that's been torn off.'

Joan was nodding. 'I'm sure you're right.'

'Yes. Well, the problem was that I'd slipped up there. It didn't occur to me – until Mike suggested it, as I say – that we should have examined the telephone pad earlier. By the time we took it away, it had been used a number of times in between, and forensic have confirmed that the important top sheet was long gone. But, and this was the point, Fielding didn't know that. I also banked on the fact that if the note had been been written on impulse for some reason – as in fact it was, because Max refused to talk to Fielding when he first requested it, on Max's arrival – then the writer wouldn't have thought of disguising his handwriting.'

'You're saying that if someone is planning to write an anonymous letter he'd probably use capital letters, whereas if he scribbles something off in a hurry he won't bother?'

'Exactly. So I tricked Fielding into thinking we had

that top sheet, the one on which his handwriting would have been indented, by getting him to write down what I guessed the message would have been, and pretending we were going to compare it.'

They had arrived at the Dracos' house, or at least as near to it as they were likely to get. The Superintendent lived in a select cul-de-sac of five large modern houses and the influx of cars spilled out into the road leading to it. Thanet pulled into the kerb and switched off the engine.

Joan made no move to get out, however. Her curiosity still wasn't entirely satisfied. 'But how did you know what to tell him to write?'

'Pure guesswork. In fact, the whole thing was a gamble. As I said, at that point, apart from the fact that Fielding was clearly under stress during the interview – and let's face it, a lot of perfectly innocent people react badly to being interviewed by the police – we didn't have a shred of proof. But again, he didn't know that.'

'And you guessed correctly!'

'Luck.'

'Stop being modest.'

'I always am, you know that!'

Joan laughed. 'I'm glad to see you're back on form. Anyway, it worked.'

'It did. Though as I say, I could almost wish it hadn't.'

'What happened to the note itself? You said you hadn't been able to find it. Did Fielding take it away with him?'

'Unlikely as it seems, yes, he did, though he didn't realise he had until the next day, when he found it in his pocket. Apparently, when he arrived in the pool house Jeopard was actually holding it in his hand, looking at it, and during their conversation thrust it at him, right into his face, to ask if he was claiming to have written it.

Fielding thinks he must have taken it, as one does if someone shoves something at you like that, and was then so engrossed in the conversation that he put it in his pocket without realising it.'

'So you've seen it?'

'No. He burned it.'

'Poor man.'

'Yes. I really do believe that he didn't look back when he walked out, and had no idea Max was knocked out when he fell into the water. When Fielding got home they actually laughed together about him pushing Max into the pool, you know. I really can't believe they'd have done that if Fielding knew what had happened.'

'Well,' said Joan, opening her door, 'let's hope he gets off lightly. Somehow I think he will.'

'I agree,' said Thanet, getting out of the car. Lightly in one way, perhaps. But the gardener and his wife would no doubt spend the rest of their days mourning the daughter they would soon so tragically lose. And what of the others – all three Sylvesters, Anthea, Rosinha, who was still with the Jeopards, perhaps even the baby? What if they too were HIV positive? How must it be, to live with the threat of AIDS poised like the sword of Damocles above one's head, always to be watching, waiting, wondering when or if it would descend? With a considerable effort he pushed them to the back of his mind. Tonight was Angharad's night and he must do nothing to dampen the mood of celebration. 'Come on,' he said, taking Joan's arm. 'Let's try now to forget about the case and enjoy ourselves.'

'A vain hope, I should think, in view of the company we'll be keeping.'

Thanet shook his head. 'Shop talk has been banned for tonight.'

As they turned the corner into the cul-de-sac the Dracos' house came into view. With light blazing from every window the jubilant message came over loud and clear. *We made it! We came through!*

The front door had been left ajar and Thanet rang the bell before pushing it open. Inside they were enveloped by light, warmth and the hubbub of a successful party well under way.

'Luke!' shouted Draco, who never used Thanet's Christian name at work. He was resplendent in bow tie and plum-coloured velvet smoking jacket. 'And Joan!' He kissed her on both cheeks with enthusiasm. 'You look absolutely ravishing!' he said, his Welsh accent even more pronounced than usual. 'Lucky men, you and me, Luke, aren't we, boyo! Let me take your coats.' He handed them to a girl in black dress and white apron, obviously hired for the occasion. 'Put these away for me, will you, *cariad*?'

Behind his back, Thanet and Joan exchanged indulgent smiles. 'He's well away!' whispered Thanet as they followed him into the sitting room.

And here they all were, the familiar faces he saw every day, cares and anxieties smoothed away, transformed by the atmosphere of rejoicing: Lineham and Louise, Doc Mallard and his wife Helen, Tody and Boon and their wives and many, many more, mingling with the Dracos' other friends.

And, above all, there was Angharad, in celebration of whose continuing survival this party was being held. Thanet had always thought she was one of the most beautiful women he had ever seen; had found it difficult to believe, when he first met her, that Draco, that near-ugly little Welshman, could have won such a prize. But he had quickly realised that their devotion to each other was equally matched, had castigated himself for so superficial a judgement, and during the years of her illness had often wondered what would happen to Draco if Angharad should die. Now, looking at her tonight, it was difficult to believe that this radiant woman had ever lost that wondrous cloud of copper-coloured hair, had ever looked as though she was holding on to life only by her fingernails.

He only wished that there was even the remotest possibility of Linda Fielding making a similar recovery.

'What's the matter?' whispered Joan, observant as ever.

He shook his head. 'Nothing.'

'Great tie!' said Lineham. 'Why don't you wear it to work?'

'Be careful!' said Thanet. 'I might.'

'That would raise the Super's eyebrows!' said Lineham.

They all laughed.

After supper they all raised their glasses in response to Draco's birthday toast to Angharad.

'And now,' he said, with the gleeful air of a conjuror about to produce an especially large rabbit out of his hat, 'we come to the *pièce de résistance* of the evening. If you'd all move across to the windows on that side . . .'

They did as they were asked, and an expectant hush fell.

Suddenly the lights went out as at the far end of the garden a match flared. With a fizzing of light, the letter A sprang at them out of the night and then, in swift succession, NGHARAD.

There were oohs and aahs. Angharad exclaimed in delight and clapped her hands. Someone began to sing, 'Happy birthday to you, happy birthday to you,' and they all joined in as rockets exploded in a myriad stars and her name hung emblazoned across the darkness.

Once again Thanet made an effort to push the thought of the Fieldings and all the others out of his mind. Tonight, he thought, it would have to be enough to know that at least one story had had a happy ending.

ONCE TOO OFTEN

To Laura, first of the next generation

ONE

Lamplight. Curtains drawn against the chill of an early October night. No sound but the crackle of the fire and the flutter of paper as Joan referred to one of her interminable lists. The atmosphere should have been conducive to creative thought, but Thanet was scowling as he sat gazing at his latest attempt with its numerous amendments and crossings out. He groaned, ripped the sheet off the pad, scrumpled it up and tossed it at the fire. He missed and it bounced back and lay on the hearthrug, a silent reproach – and a reminder, as if he needed one: three more days and she would be gone from them for ever.

'No good?' said Joan.

He shook his head. 'Hopeless. Absolutely hopeless. It's impossible! Keep it short, you said, that's the main thing. No more than, what? Five minutes?'

'Ten at the outside, I'd say.'

'All right. Ten. But it also has to be urbane, coherent, witty without being vulgar and contrive to sustain what we hope will be an atmosphere of conviviality and goodwill.

1

And to be honest, the prospect of standing up and attempting to achieve all that in front of Alexander's snooty friends and relations frightens me out of my wits!'

'Don't be unfair! How can you say they're snooty if you've never even met them? Bridget says they're all very nice, the ones she's met so far, anyway.'

'Bridget sees anything to do with Alexander through rose-coloured spectacles.'

'Isn't that only natural?' said Joan gently.

Thanet had the grace to look shamefaced. 'Yes, of course it is. It's just that . . .'

Joan put down the sheaf of papers she was holding and took his hand. 'Look, darling, don't you think that every father agonises over his speech for his daughter's wedding exactly as you are doing now? But they all manage it, somehow.'

'That's supposed to make me feel better?'

'And to be honest, no one worries very much what the father of the bride says as long as he's brief about it.'

'You've been talking to Ben.'

Ben, their son, had just gone back to Reading for the beginning of his second year of a degree in computer studies. He was due to return on Friday, to be an usher at the wedding on Saturday.

'He said the same thing, did he? There you are, then. We can't both be wrong.'

'If you're both right and nobody cares what I say, why bother to say it at all? Why don't we scrap the speeches altogether?'

Joan ignored this as he knew she would and said, 'Speaking of Ben reminds me.' She made a note. 'He said he won't be back in time to pick up his suit on Friday. We must get it at the same time as yours. Anyway, as far as your speech is concerned, I don't know what you're worrying about. The whole atmosphere of the occasion will be working in your favour. At a wedding everyone's in a cheerful mood, predisposed to enjoy themselves and be uncritical.'

'I just don't want to let Bridget down, that's all.'

Joan grinned. 'Oh come on. Admit it. It's your pride that's at stake too, isn't it?'

She was right, of course.

'Anyway, I'm sure you're getting into a state for nothing. You'll give a brilliant speech, I know you will, and I shall be proud of you. So get it over and done with. You want to be finished with it before the invasion, don't you?'

Thanet rolled his eyes. 'How many did you say we have staying here on Friday night?'

'I think it was seven, at the last count. There's the four of us, your mother, Lucy and Thomas, her fiancé. He's bringing a sleeping bag and he'll sleep on the floor in Ben's room.'

Lucy was one of the two bridesmaids, a friend who dated back to Bridget's schooldays and who now lived in York.

'I think I'll put up a camp bed at the office for the rest of the week. It'd be a lot more peaceful.'

'Coward!'

'Roll on Sunday, say I.' Thanet picked up his pen, thankful that he had only one daughter. Imagine if they'd had three or four! It didn't bear thinking about.

For over a year now, ever since Alexander had turned up on their doorstep out of the blue one Sunday morning after an absence of eighteen months, the momentum towards the wedding had been gathering pace. Thanet had found it very hard to welcome him back after the shameful way he had treated Bridget previously: a year-long relationship terminated without warning by Alexander on the grounds that he 'wasn't ready' for a long-term commitment. But Bridget had never really got over the affair and in the face of her radiant delight at Alexander's return, Thanet had been forced to capitulate; the last thing he wanted was to alienate his beloved daughter. The reservations, however, remained. If Alexander could hurt Bridget once, he could do it again.

Thanet was uneasy, too, about the fact that Alexander came from a more affluent background than their own. Although on the surface he was a good match, with a lucrative job in the City, Thanet was aware of the minefield that was the English class system and afraid that Bridget might get hurt trying to negotiate it unawares. There were undeniable advantages to the marriage, of course, not least the fact that on the strength of his mind-boggling salary Alexander had been able to take out a huge mortgage and buy a house in Richmond, apparently considered a highly desirable residential area. Bridget and Alexander had taken them to see it and Thanet had had to admit he was impressed. It was spacious, in excellent repair and even afforded a glimpse of the river from the upstairs windows. It would be a delightful area in which to live, Bridget had enthused, with both Richmond Park and the river close by.

If only, he thought now, he could somehow guarantee that she would always be as happy as this. Unrealistic, he knew, but there it was, he couldn't help feeling that way.

4

'What are you doing?' He peered at the paper on Joan's lap.

'Making a sort of timetable for the rest of the week.' She held it up.

So far as Thanet could see the lists of things to do grew longer and longer by the day. 'You'll wear yourself out.'

'Only a few more days and I'll be able to relax. Anyway, Bridget'll be back on Thursday to help.'

Bridget was spending a few days at the house in Richmond, hanging curtains and taking delivery of various household items.

Joan tapped the blank sheet of paper in front of him. 'Your speech, Luke! Honestly, you'll never get anywhere at this rate.'

The telephone rang.

'Saved by the bell,' said Thanet, jumping up with as much alacrity as his back would allow. About time he paid another visit to the chiropractor, he thought as he hurried into the hall.

It was Pater, the Station Officer.

'Sorry to disturb you, sir, but the report of a possible suspicious death has just come in, in Willow Way out at Charthurst. The woman fell downstairs, apparently, but our blokes are not too happy about the circumstances. I've notified Doc Mallard and the SOCOs.'

'Right. I'll get out there straight away.'

Thanet made a mental note of the directions Pater gave him, replaced the phone and poked his head into the sitting room.

Joan forestalled him. 'Don't tell me! Your speech is never going to get written!'

'Sorry, love. It'll have to wait.'

Already Thanet's pulse had quickened and as he drove out into the darkness of the countryside via the relatively deserted streets of Sturrenden, the small country town in Kent where he lived and worked, he felt a mounting sense of anticipation. Anxiety about Bridget's forthcoming marriage forgotten, his mind was filled with the kind of pointless speculation which he was powerless to control at the beginning of a case: what would the dead woman be like? Was her family involved? Who had called the police, and why? And what were the circumstances the police officers considered suspicious?

Charthurst was about fifteen minutes' drive from Sturrenden, a large village which had, over the past twenty years, expanded considerably to accommodate a steadily growing population; possessing the dubious benefit of a main-line station to London, it was a popular choice with commuters. At this time of night there was nobody about. Only the cars parked outside the two pubs showed that there was any social life.

Thanet turned right as instructed at the second, the Green Man. The little estate where the dead woman lived was tucked in behind it, on the edge of the village. Beyond, there was a group of farm buildings and then the road narrowed to a lane bordered by high hedges. Number 2, Willow Way was obviously the house on the right-hand corner at the entrance to the estate; police vehicles and an ambulance were clustered around and the congestion was made worse by some minor roadworks at the edge of the road immediately in front of it. Figures visible at lighted windows and a small huddle of interested spectators showed that the neighbours were taking a lively interest in what was going on.

With difficulty Thanet managed to squeeze his car in behind Doc Mallard's distinctive old Rover. It was starting to rain and he turned up his collar as Sergeant Lineham came hurrying to meet him.

'What's the story, Mike?' With weary resignation Thanet recognised the onset of a familiar churning in his gut. The moment he always dreaded was at hand and there was nothing he could do to armour himself against it. Despite every possible effort and all his years of experience nothing seemed to help him bear with fortitude that first sight of a corpse. He had long ago come to accept that it was the price he had to pay for doing the work he loved.

'The dead woman is Jessica Dander, sir.'

'The *KM* reporter?'

'Yes. Apparently there was a 999 request for an ambulance. The caller just said there'd been an accident and gave the address. Didn't give his name.'

'His?'

'That's yet to be established. Anyway, when the ambulancemen arrived they found the husband crouched over the body – in a terrible state, they said.'

'By terrible state they meant . . .?'

'Distraught.'

'This was how long afterwards?'

'The call was made at 8.11. The ambulance arrived at 8.26.'

'Pretty good response time. Right. Go on.'

'Well, they thought it all looked a bit fishy. The husband swore he'd been out for a walk, had only just got in, and found his wife lying at the bottom of the staircase. But someone – either he or someone else – had made that call. So they decided to call the police and our lot weren't too happy about it either.'

While they were talking Thanet had been looking around. Housing estates varied considerably in quality and presentation, and in his opinion this one came somewhere near the bottom of the league table. Nowadays it seemed to be only the very expensive, quality-built new houses which could find buyers, but ten years or so ago, when these had been put up, mass production equalled lower prices equalled speedy sales. Here, the builder had crammed the houses together in order to fit in as many as possible and although there was a mix of detached and semi-detached, the detached ones barely merited the description: between the wall of the garage and the house next door there was room for only the narrowest of paths. The houses were depressingly uniform in style too, and the layouts inside would be virtually identical, Thanet guessed. He was surprised. He would have expected Jessica Dander to have lived in a more upmarket area than this.

'You've spoken to the husband?'

'Only briefly. Thought I'd wait until you got here. I'm not sure that was the right thing to do, though. He's in a bit of a state and I've got a feeling he can't take much more tonight.'

'Right. Better see what he has to say then.' Thanet set off at a brisk pace up the short concrete path to the front door. *In a few moments now I'll see her. Don't think about it. Don't think about it.*

'Just one point, sir, before you speak to him.'

Thanet turned, only half listening, his mind on his imminent ordeal. 'What?'

'I know him, sir. The husband. I was at school with him.'

Thanet forced himself to concentrate. 'That could be useful. What's his name?'

'Manifest. Desmond Manifest.'

'She kept her maiden name for work, then.'

'Apparently.'

Inside the house the cramped hall was grossly over-crowded. Apart from the fact that there seemed to be far too much furniture for such a small space, Scenes-of-Crime Officers were already busy and Doc Mallard was kneeling beside the body, partly obscuring her from view. Hearing Thanet and Lineham come in he glanced up and nodded a greeting. Thanet swallowed, took a deep breath and moved forward to look.

She was lying on her back, one leg twisted awkwardly beneath her, arms outflung and head at an unnatural angle to her neck. Her eyes, a clear translucent green, had that fixed stillness which only death can impart. Never having met her and having seen only a black-and-white photograph of her at the head of her column in the *Kent Messenger*, Thanet was surprised for no good reason to see that her abundant curly hair was a deep, rich auburn, the colour of copper beech leaves in autumn. She was in her mid-thirties and, although her nose was a little too pointed and her lips too thin for her to be called beautiful, she was still a very attractive woman. She was small, no more than five feet three, he estimated, with a trim, compact figure, and was wearing clothes which looked expensive: a cinnamon-coloured silk blouse with loose sleeves caught in tightly at the wrist, and narrow dark brown velvet leggings. Already the cramps in his stomach were subsiding, his mind becoming engaged in

9

the how and why of her death. One of her brown suede high-heeled shoes was missing, he noticed. Involuntarily his gaze travelled up the staircase and Lineham, who had worked with him so long that words were often unnecessary, said, 'It's near the top.'

Perhaps a simple accident after all, then?

Mallard was getting to his feet. 'Yes, well, not much doubt about the cause of death, by the look of it, though I'll have to confirm that after the PM, of course.'

'Broken neck,' said Lineham.

'Precisely,' said Mallard. 'Severance of the spinal cord. But time of death, now that's a different matter. As you'll remember from that case last summer, the one where that oaf fell off a ladder – to general rejoicing, as I recall – spinal injuries can be tricky.'

'Ah yes, I remember,' said Lineham. 'You told us that unless the cord is completely severed the victim can live on indefinitely, although completely paralysed.'

'You only have to visit Stoke Mandeville to see that,' said Mallard. 'All those poor devils who've been knocked off their motorbikes or dived into shallow swimming pools.'

'You also said that even the slightest unskilled movement of the head by some well-meaning bystander could be enough to finish the person off,' said Thanet.

'Which is why paramedics take such extreme care in dealing with such cases,' finished Lineham.

'Bravo! Total recall!' said Mallard. 'Well, you see what I'm getting at here, then. Did anyone move her head?'

Thanet and Lineham exchanged glances.

'Her husband was kneeling beside the body when the ambulancemen arrived,' said Lineham.

'Well, you'd better check with him, then.'

'We shall, of course,' said Thanet. 'But even though you can't be precise, could you just give us some idea as to time of death?'

Mallard looked at Thanet over the top of his gold-rimmed half-moons and raised his eyebrows. 'You know I always hate committing myself at this stage, Luke.'

Thanet persisted. 'Just a rough estimate?'

Mallard shrugged. 'Oh well, if I must. Some time within the last two and a half hours, I'd say.'

Thanet glanced at his watch. Nine-twenty p.m. Between 7 and 8.26, when the ambulance arrived, then. 'Thanks, Doc, that narrows it down a bit.' Though it didn't help with the question of whether she died immediately, or later because her head had been moved. 'Where's her husband?' he asked Lineham.

The sergeant nodded at a closed door to the right of the hall. 'In there.'

'You said he's in a bad way. Has his doctor been sent for?'

'Yes. I rang straight away when I saw the way things were going. But he was out on a call. His wife said she'd give him the message as soon as he got in.'

Thanet glanced at Mallard. 'Would you mind hanging on while we interview him? In case you're needed?'

'Not at all.'

'Good. I'll just have a word with the SOCOs and then we'll go in. I assume they got all the pictures they wanted before you examined her?'

Mallard nodded.

'In that case, the ambulance can take her away. We don't want her husband to have to see her again like this, if we can help it.'

11

It was a sad fact, Thanet knew, that in cases of domestic murder the person most likely to have committed the crime was the spouse. He also knew, from long experience, that preconceived ideas could get in the way. He had no intention of condemning Manifest before he even set eyes on him.

But he was still eager to meet him.

TWO

The sitting/dining room stretched from the front of the house to the back but even so was not very large – some ten feet wide by eighteen feet long, Thanet guessed. He noticed that like the hall it was crammed full of furniture – good-quality stuff, too, though the scale was all wrong for a house like this. At the far end a long oval mahogany dining table with eight matching chairs looked ridiculously pretentious in this setting and most of the space in the rest of the room was taken up by two vast sofas and a couple of equally plump arm-chairs, all of them upholstered in expensive-looking fabrics. There was a lavish display of entertainment equipment: a huge television set and video housed in an antique-style cabinet, and a CD player with enormous loudspeakers and hundreds of CDs stored in shoulder-high vertical racks nearby. All around the walls, tables, chairs and even two sizeable desks stood cheek by jowl, with books, lamps and ornaments covering every avail-able surface. Thanet was beginning to get the picture. Either the Manifests had come down in the world, or they were living in temporary accommodation between moves.

Desmond Manifest was sitting in one of the big arm-chairs, leaning forward with elbows on knees and head in hands. He was still wearing outdoor clothes, a Barbour and a green-and-cream-checked woollen scarf. He raised a dazed face as they came in, his eyes moving slowly from one to another, coming to rest on Lineham. But he didn't speak.

Thanet dismissed the uniformed constable who had been waiting with Manifest until they arrived and then nodded at Lineham. At this stage it made sense for the sergeant to interview the man, as he knew him.

Lineham introduced Thanet and Doc Mallard and they all sat down. Manifest acknowledged them with no more than the merest flicker of an eyelid and remained in the same position as if incapable of further movement. He was a little older than his wife, a big man with heavy jowls and an unhealthy pallor which could have been due to shock. He looked as though he hadn't shaved that day and his hair straggled untidily over his collar. Definitely a man who had seen better days, Thanet thought. The interesting question was whether it was professional or domestic prob-lems which had brought about this deterioration.

'You'll appreciate we have to ask you a few questions, Des?' Lineham glanced at Thanet to check that the infor-mality was acceptable.

Thanet blinked approval.

Manifest took a while to respond but eventually he nodded slowly, sliding back in his chair and stretching his arms along the armrests. His fists, however, remained clenched.

14

'Would you tell us what happened this evening?' said Lineham.

Manifest opened his mouth as if to speak, but no sound emerged. He closed it again.

'Des?' said Lineham.

Manifest tried again. 'I . . . I went for a walk.' His voice was hoarse, as if rusty with disuse.

'How long were you out?'

No response, just a blank stare.

Lineham tried again. 'What time did you leave?'

The man's forehead creased as if the question were some immensely complicated and difficult inquiry. 'After supper.'

'Could you be a little more precise?'

Manifest compressed his lips and the frown deepened. 'I . . . I . . . Is she really dead?'

Lineham glanced at Thanet. 'I'm afraid so, Des. I'm so sorry. And I'm sorry too to have to bother you with questions at a time like this. But we really do need to know, you see.'

'She was just lying there,' whispered Manifest. 'All . . . all crumpled up. I saw her as soon as I pushed the door open. But why?' His gaze suddenly became fierce. 'I don't understand. I mean, why was he *there*? He should have been here.'

'Who? Who should have been here?'

Suddenly Manifest folded his arms across his chest and began to rock to and fro. 'Oh God, Jess, I can't bear it. Oh God, what shall I do?' He clutched at his head, then, still holding it as if to cling on to his sanity, leaned forward and continued rocking and moaning, 'Oh God oh God oh God oh God oh God oh God!'

Lineham glanced at Thanet and raised his eyebrows. Thanet looked at Mallard, who frowned, pursed his lips and shook his head. 'Sorry,' he said. 'I think you ought to stop. He needs to take a sedative and rest.'

'But he can't stay here by himself in that state,' said Thanet. 'We'll have to find someone to sit with him. See if you can get him to suggest someone, Mike.'

But Manifest was beyond reason, it seemed. Lineham could get no sense out of him.

'Any bright ideas then, Mike? You seem to know the family.'

'Only slightly. But he has got a younger brother who lives locally, I believe. His number should be in the phone book.'

'See if you can get hold of him.'

'Right.' The phone was in the hall and Lineham went off to make the call, returning a few minutes later. 'He'll be over as soon as he can.' He crossed to Manifest, who was still sitting hunched forward, face hidden. 'Des, Graham will be here soon to keep you company. But we think you ought to rest now. Dr Mallard here will give you something to help you sleep, then we'll take you upstairs.'

At the top of the stairs the door to what was obviously the main bedroom stood open but Manifest directed them with a nod towards a room at the back of the house. At first Thanet attributed this choice to a natural delicacy: Manifest did not want to sleep in a room which perhaps more than any other in the house would remind him of his wife. But Thanet changed his mind when he saw that the back bedroom, which was just as cluttered with furniture as the sitting room, bore signs of permanent occupation: one of the two single beds was already made up and there was a pair of pyjamas on the pillow. Manifest collapsed on to it and rolled over on to his side, turning his face to the wall. They covered him with the duvet from the other bed and left him.

'Separate rooms,' murmured Thanet, outside on the landing.

Lineham nodded. 'I noticed.'

'Let's take a look at the main bedroom.'

This was so crowded with furniture that there was barely room to move around the king-sized bed. Thanet counted two dressing tables as well as two double wardrobes. 'Why all the clutter?' he asked Lineham. 'Do you know?'

The sergeant pulled a face. 'Their last house was much bigger, a lovely converted oast out at Marden and I suppose they couldn't bear to get rid of it all when they had to move.'

'What happened?'

'Des was made redundant about five years ago and so far as I know he's never managed to find another job. The trouble is, he has no qualifications other than experience in the work he was doing. It's a sad story. He went straight into the City after A levels and during the Thatcher years he was really raking it in. We all thought he had it made. Then when the recession came, suddenly he was out on his ear, just like that. Turned up for work one day to find his desk had been cleared. No warning, nothing.'

As Lineham was speaking an icy chill had crept through Thanet's veins. Could the same thing happen to Alexander?

'It must be awful when you're used to earning huge sums like that, suddenly to find yourself on the dole,' said Lineham, innocent of the discomfort he was causing.

'That's terrible,' said Thanet. 'Can they do that? Kick you out without warning?'

'They can and they do, apparently. Imagine what it must be like, living on that sort of knife edge, never knowing each morning whether you're going to discover that you're suddenly a mere unemployment statistic!' Lineham was moving about the room, looking into drawers, picking up and putting down bottles and jars on one of the dressing tables. He peered at a label. 'Mmm. Chanel. She obviously had expensive tastes. It must have been a terrible shock for her, thinking she'd married a wealthy man only to find she'd suddenly become the breadwinner. I wonder how it affected their relationship. It obviously wasn't very good.' He nodded at the single set of pillows in the bed and twitched back the sheets to reveal Jessica's solitary silk nightgown, neatly folded.

'Quite. But he could have found some sort of job, surely.'

'The trouble with people in his position is that they're afraid to take low-paid work in case it doesn't look good on their CV when they're trying to find something more lucrative. So they end up doing nothing.'

'I don't think I could bear that. It must be so demoralising. Though I can understand the dilemma.' How would Alexander react, if his high-powered job were snatched away from him? And how would Bridget? With an effort Thanet forced himself to concentrate on what he was supposed to be doing. He opened a wardrobe door. The

18

array of expensive clothes inside was now explained, all purchased no doubt in better days.

'They hadn't been married that long when it happened, either,' said Lineham.

'Oh?'

'I've been trying to remember exactly when the wedding was. I think it was the year Mandy was born, so it must have been nine years ago.'

'Did you know his wife personally, then?'

'No. Oh, I met her briefly, once or twice, but that's all. Des and I were never close friends. It's just that he was in my form at school and from time to time I'd hear about him from one of the others on the grapevine. You know how it is.'

Thanet nodded. He knew. He too had been brought up and educated in Sturrenden and although he had done his stint away, had been glad to return and settle here. He loved the town, liked the area, and over the years had built up a network of acquaintances in all walks of life. News of former classmates invariably filtered back to him too, sooner or later, especially if they lived locally.

'What's his background?'

'Pretty ordinary. Working class. His father was a bus driver and they lived in a council house. Still do, I believe. He's retired now. They were both so proud of Des. It must have been a terrible blow for them when he ended up on the dole.'

'What about the brother?'

'Graham? He's a carpet-fitter. Self-employed. Very efficient. Fitted all our carpets, as a matter of fact, and I can thoroughly recommend him. Ironic, really. It was Desmond who was supposed to be the shining success but it's Graham who's managed to weather the recession relatively unscathed. Come to think of it, it was probably when Graham was laying our bedroom carpet that I heard about Des.'

While they talked they had drifted out on to the landing and now they paused at the top of the stairs to see if there was any indication of how the accident had happened. At Lineham's request Jessica's shoe had been left where it was until Thanet had seen its position. It still lay against the staircase wall, three steps down from the top.

'Doesn't seem to be any obvious reason why she should have fallen,' said Lineham. 'No frayed carpet or uneven floorboards.'

'Quite. The heel of the shoe is pretty high, though. If she turned over on it, lost her balance . . .'

'The only explanation, if it was a simple accident,' agreed Lineham. 'Of course, if she was pushed . . .'

Thanet sighed. They'd been here before, in at least two previous cases. And, he reminded himself, in both of them they'd managed to get at the truth in the end.

Downstairs Lineham picked up the telephone. 'It might be worth dialling 1471.' He listened, raising his eyebrows at Thanet and nodding as he jotted the number down. 'It's a local one,' he said. 'Do you want me to try it?'

'Might as well.'

Lineham dialled again and a moment later said, 'Ah, I believe you rang this number earlier, sir. I'm speaking from the Manifests' house. This is the police. I'm afraid there's been an accident. Would you mind confirming what time you rang? And your name and address please? Thank you. And what is your connection with this household?' He listened for a moment, then covered the receiver and said to Thanet, 'He's her brother-in-law. Rang at 7.31 according to the recorded message. Do you want me to give him the bad news?'

Thanet considered. 'Let me have a word with him. What's his name?'

'Covin. Bernard.'

Thanet took the receiver. Covin must be married to Jessica's sister, who would no doubt be able to fill them in on the dead woman. It would be useful to talk to her as soon as possible. He broke the news of Jessica's death as sympathetically as he could and arranged to see him later. He lived in Nettleton, about ten minutes' drive away.

He had just put down the receiver when the door opened and the uniformed constable looked in. 'Mr Manifest's brother is here, sir.'

'Send him in.'

The first thing you noticed about Graham Manifest was his ferocious squint. Apart from that he was a younger, fitter version of his brother. He had the same stocky build, square face and dark curly hair, but he moved lightly on his feet and it was obvious there wasn't a spare ounce of fat on him. He was wearing jeans, trainers and a dark blue anorak streaked with rain. 'This is terrible!' he said, one eye looking at Lineham and the other, apparently, at Thanet. 'Where's Des, Mike?'

Lineham introduced Thanet, then said, 'Upstairs. Asleep, we hope. He's been given a sedative.'

'How's he taking it?' As he spoke Graham slipped off the anorak and shook it. Droplets of water spattered everywhere.

'Let's go into the lounge, shall we?' Lineham waited until they were all seated before saying, 'Badly, I'm afraid.

Not surprising, of course. But people react differently, you can never tell.'

Graham was nodding. 'He always was potty about that woman.'

'You didn't like her?' said Thanet. He knew he shouldn't find the squint disconcerting, but he did. He tried to focus on Graham's good eye.

'Couldn't stand her. Oh, I know you shouldn't speak ill of the dead – though frankly I don't see why not, if they deserve it – but she was a real cow.'

'In what way?' said Lineham.

'Well, look at this place!' Graham's eyes swivelled alarmingly as he waved at the superfluous oversized furniture stacked around the walls. 'Why couldn't she have just accepted that Des had lost his cushy job and wasn't going to get another one, and made the best of it? A lot of people would be bloody grateful to have a roof over their heads, let alone a nice place like this. But no, they had to live all the time with the reminder that she was expecting him to hit the jackpot again one day soon, that this was only a temporary arrangement. I mean, look at this stuff! Poor old Des! It must be like camping out in a posh department store!'

'Are you saying she married him for his money?'

'You bet I am. She was all sweetness and light for the first few years, wasn't she?'

'And she changed, when he lost his job?'

'Well, not to begin with.' Graham was grudging. 'Not while she was still expecting him to pick up something equally well paid any minute. But as soon as she began to realise that wasn't going to happen, it was a different story. You ask Sarah – my wife. She'll tell you I'm not

22

making all this up. No, there's no doubt about it, she was bad news for Des, was our Jess.'

'Though he didn't think so, apparently,' said Thanet.

'He was always making excuses for her. She could walk all over him and he wouldn't lift a finger to help himself, and that's the truth.'

'And did she?' said Thanet. 'Walk all over him?'

Graham's good eye glared fiercely at Thanet. 'It used to make me mad, the way she treated him. "Do this, do that. Fetch this, fetch that." As if he was a pet poodle or something. I don't know how he stood it.'

And maybe, in the end, he couldn't, thought Thanet. Maybe one day, this evening in fact, Desmond Manifest had reached the point where he had had enough. He had seen his chance and the temptation had proved too much for him: one little push and he would be a free man again.

Lineham was thinking the same thing, Thanet could tell.

'We stopped coming over in the end,' said Graham. 'Unless we could be sure she wouldn't be here.'

'But it sounds as though your wife was quite friendly with her at one time,' said Thanet.

Graham pulled a face and shrugged. 'Sarah was never that keen, but she made an effort, for Des's sake. Jessica was all right on the surface, nice as pie when she wanted something or things were going her way, but you only had to cross her to see the claws underneath. She was never afraid of speaking her mind, whether it would hurt or not. I could never decide if she genuinely didn't know how the things she said affected people or if she just didn't care. Des always said it was because she'd had to learn to stick up for herself. She'd had a rotten time when she was young, he said.'

'Do you know anything about that?' said Lineham.

Graham shook his head. 'Couldn't have cared less, to tell you the truth. Just kept out of her way as much as possible.'

'Your brother said something odd when we were talking to him earlier,' said Thanet. 'He said, "I don't understand. Why was he there? He should have been here." Have you any idea what he meant or who he was referring to?'

Graham thought for a moment or two before saying, 'Haven't a clue.'

They decided to go to Covin's house in separate cars, as it was now 10.30 and Thanet couldn't see much point in returning to the Manifests' house tonight. He was pleased to find that the rain had eased off to a light drizzle. It wouldn't have been much fun floundering about unfamiliar terrain in the dark in heavy rain. Lineham said he knew the way and Thanet followed the sergeant's tail-lights through the empty lanes. In Nettleton there was no street lighting and many of the houses were already in darkness. The black-and-white timbered façade of the combined shop and post office was illuminated, however, presumably to deter prospective burglars. They passed the church at the far end of the village street, with the row of cottages opposite where Thanet had once solved one of the most fascinating cases of his career, and half a mile further on turned left at a sign saying 'HUNTER'S GREEN FARM'.

Here the road surface was covered with lumps and clods of mud from the passage of farm vehicles and there was a constant stuttering sound as Thanet's tyres picked them up and hurled them against the wheel arches. Thanet could imagine Lineham, who was very car-proud, muttering about the mess they would be making. On either side were tall hedges, concealing what lay beyond.

They passed the looming bulk of the farmhouse with lights in its upstairs windows and as directed continued up the track for several hundred yards further to a smaller house next to a number of large outbuildings. A light had been left on over the front door, presumably for their benefit. They parked in front of one of the barns and got out. Looking around Thanet could now see that they were surrounded by orchards. A fruit farm, then.

'Honestly!' said Lineham, bending down to peer at the splatters of mud on his car. 'Look at that! What a mess!'

Thanet was grinning. 'Don't be such an old woman, Mike. No harm done. You should expect to find mud in the country.'

'Preferably not on my car!' said Lineham.

'Anyway, you can't possibly see properly in this light. Do stop fussing! At least it's stopped raining.'

They started to walk towards the house but Thanet paused. 'What do you think he meant, Mike?'

Lineham understood at once. He and Thanet had worked together for so many years that they were rather like an old married couple in this respect: frequently picking up long afterwards a train of thought left unpursued earlier.

'Sounded to me as though he had expected someone, a man, to be at the house and he wasn't. Des had seen him somewhere else, somewhere he hadn't expected to see him.'

25

'Looks that way, doesn't it? What do you think of Manifest as a suspect, Mike? You know the man. Do you think he was capable of pushing her? The worm turning and all that?'

'I really couldn't say. People change. I knew him as a schoolboy. I haven't a clue what he's like now.'

There was an uncharacteristic acerbity in Lineham's tone and Thanet glanced at him uneasily. Lineham had become increasingly short-tempered of late. He was having problems with his mother again. She was tired of living alone and had been dropping stronger and stronger hints that she would like to move in with Lineham and Louise. The trouble was that neither of them could face the prospect, Louise because she was just as strong-minded as her mother-in-law and Lineham because he knew that with both women under the same roof he would constantly be the rope in a tug-of-war between them. Meanwhile the situation was deteriorating rapidly. Both women were becoming increasingly impatient with Lineham, his mother because she wasn't getting the invitation for which she was angling, Louise because Lineham was procrastinating. Thanet sympathised with his sergeant's predicament but felt that the matter would have to be resolved shortly. The strain on Lineham was beginning to tell and, sooner or later, if he didn't act, Thanet would have to sit down with him and try and get him to make a decision.

But now was not the moment. Covin must have heard their cars draw up, and had come to the door.

THREE

'Evening. Come in.' Covin stood back to let them in, then ushered them through to a sitting room which stank of cigarette smoke. It was conventionally furnished with fitted carpet, three-piece suite and the ubiquitous television set, which was tuned in to a late-night current affairs programme. A dying fire flickered in the hearth and Covin crossed to poke it and put another log on before switching the television off and inviting them to sit down. He chose what was obviously his favourite armchair – on a small table nearby stood an empty mug, a packet of cigarettes, a disposable lighter and an overflowing ashtray. He tapped out a cigarette and lit up. 'Hope you don't mind.' He flapped his hand in a futile attempt to disperse the clouds of smoke.

Thanet elected to sit on the sofa. 'It's your house,' he said, knowing that Lineham would mind, very much, but that there was nothing they could do about it.

Lineham retreated to an upright chair against the wall, as far away from Covin as he could get. He took out his notebook.

Covin gave the notebook a nervous glance. 'I'm not quite sure why you wanted to see me.' He took a deep drag at his cigarette. His fingers, Thanet noticed, were stained a deep yellow but outwardly at least his addiction didn't seem to have affected his health: his colour was good, his eyes bright and his dark hair a luxuriant curly thatch which many men of his age would envy. Thanet put him in his early fifties.

'We're just trying to fill in some background,' Thanet said reassuringly. 'Mr Manifest is naturally very distressed and has had to be sedated, and as you are married to Mrs Manifest's sister, we thought you might both be able to help us.' He laid slight emphasis on 'both' and glanced hopefully towards the door. 'I hope your wife hasn't gone to bed yet.'

'I'm afraid my wife died two years ago, Inspector.'

'I'm sorry.'

'No need to apologise. How could you be expected to know?'

'So you live here alone?' Thanet's eyes flickered towards the mantelpiece where there were a number of photographs, mostly, so far as he could make out, either of a woman and a girl or of a young girl alone, at various stages of her childhood. In the largest and most colourful picture she was posing on skis against a background of snowy mountain peaks.

'Yes.' Covin followed Thanet's glance. 'Well, most of the time, anyway.' He lit another cigarette from the stub of the old one.

'That's your daughter?'

'Yes. But she's away at university.'

'Oh, which one? My son's at university too. Reading.'

28

'So is Karen.'

'So she's just gone back.'

'Yes. This evening, as a matter of fact.'

Ben had gone yesterday. 'You must miss her.'

Covin shrugged. 'You have to put up with it, don't you?'

Thanet was trying to get the feel of the man but so far he wasn't succeeding. He certainly hadn't warmed to him and for some reason felt as though he were having to drag information out of him despite the fact that Covin had answered his questions readily enough. Thanet was sufficiently experienced to know that every good interviewer uses his own reactions to the interviewee as a tool, so he now tried to work out why Covin should be having this effect on him. Was it because the man was naturally morose or because he was used to leading a solitary life? Or was he holding back for some other reason? If so, of course, it might have absolutely no connection with their investigation.

On the other hand it might.

'This phone call you made to your sister-in-law earlier this evening, what was it about?'

'It wasn't actually about anything. I didn't get through.'

'Why didn't you leave a message on the answerphone?'

'Can't stand the things. As soon as the recorded message began, I rang off.'

'What time was this, exactly?' Though Thanet knew of course.

'I'm not sure. Is it important?'

'It could be.'

Covin stubbed out his cigarette, but it was only a few

29

moments before he was shaking another out of the packet. 'I think it must have been about half seven. I know it was just after Karen left, and I remember looking at the clock when we finished supper. It was just gone twenty past then, and she went soon afterwards.'

'Rather late for her to be leaving, wasn't it?'

'She was driving down. She borrowed my car.'

'So, what was your reason for ringing your sister-in-law?'

'Karen asked me to. She'd intended to go round to see her aunt before she went back to Reading but she just hadn't managed to, and she wanted me to ring and say sorry, give her her love.'

'How well did you know your sister-in-law, Mr Covin?'

Covin shrugged, his mouth tugged down at the corners. 'Pretty well, I suppose. We more or less brought her up.'

'You and your wife, you mean? How was that?'

'Jess's father died when she was six, in an accident at work. Eileen – my mother-in-law – got decent compensation so she didn't have to go out to work and everything was fine for a couple of years, until she got breast cancer, same as Madge, my wife. They say it's often hereditary, don't they? Anyway, Eileen struggled on for another couple of years and then she died, so Jess came to live with us. We'd been married about five years by then.'

'Your wife must have been considerably older than her sister.'

'Yes, she was. Sixteen years. She was twenty-six when her mother died.'

'So your sister-in-law had a pretty rough time, really,

losing both her father and her mother within – what? – four years of each other.'

Covin shrugged. 'I suppose so. Though you could say she was lucky she had someone to take her in. Otherwise she'd have had to go into care.'

'I have the feeling you didn't like her much, Mr Covin.'

'She wasn't the most appealing child in the world. She was always whining, clingy, wanting her own way and making a fuss if she didn't get it. And my wife was inclined to spoil her, which only made things worse.'

It didn't sound as though Covin had been the most sympathetic of father substitutes, thought Thanet. And Jessica had obviously been a source of conflict between him and his wife.

'She took advantage of my wife's good nature,' Covin went on. This obviously still rankled, even after all these years. 'She was always asking for things we couldn't afford. Had expensive tastes, even then. But when she was earning, later on, and it came to spending her own money, it was a very different story. Madge used to make excuses for her, call her thrifty, but I say she was just downright mean.'

'I understand she was quite well off for a few years at least, after she got married.'

Covin gave a bark of cynical laughter. 'Yes, and that was a laugh, when he lost his job and she found she was having to support two people on her salary instead of one.'

'You think she married him for his money?'

'Perhaps not entirely,' Covin said grudgingly. 'But I'd say it was a major factor, yes.'

'But she did stay with him.' Lineham intervened for the first time.

31

Covin looked surprised, as if he'd forgotten the sergeant was present. 'Yes. I was never quite sure why. I think to begin with she thought he'd just walk into another job pretty quickly.'

'But he didn't,' said Thanet.

'No.'

'So why do you think she did stick with him?' persisted Lineham.

'How should I know? Just waiting until a bigger fish came along, I should think.'

'You mean she was actively looking?' said Thanet.

'No idea. I told you, I didn't see enough of them to know much about their private life.'

'So you don't know if she had any boyfriends? Her husband hasn't dropped any hints?'

'No. You'd have to ask him.' Another cynical laugh. 'Though they do say the husband's often the last to know, don't they? Look, I don't want to speak out of turn, but why all the questions?'

'We always have to be careful, in cases of sudden death, Mr Covin.'

'What do you mean, careful?' Covin glanced from Thanet to Lineham and back again. 'I thought you said it was an accident?'

'I said that she had fallen down the stairs,' said Thanet.

Covin stared at him for a moment. Then in went another cigarette and this time his hand was shaking as he lit it. He inhaled deeply, then said, 'Are you implying what I think you're implying?'

'I'm not implying anything. At this stage we have no idea what happened and we shall have to wait for the post-mortem results before we are even certain of the cause of death. But meanwhile we can't afford to sit around twiddling our thumbs, just in case the matter is not as straightforward as it seems.'

Covin was puffing furiously and even though Thanet was a pipe smoker himself and used to a certain amount of tobacco smoke his eyes were beginning to sting and water. He spared a sympathetic thought for the way Lineham must be suffering.

'You're saying someone might have pushed her, aren't you?'

'I'm saying that at this point we have to keep an open mind.'

'Which is why you're asking all this stuff about Des and whether or not Jess was running around with someone else.'

'Please, Mr Covin, there's no point in jumping to conclusions, I assure you. All we're trying to do is find out as much as possible about your sister-in-law. So, if you wouldn't mind answering just a few more questions, fill in a little more background for us . . .'

'Go on, then. I've got nothing to hide.'

'I wasn't suggesting that you have.' No point in becoming exasperated. It was always a shock for witnesses to realise that they might, however marginally, be involved in a potential murder investigation and their reactions varied widely, from complete withdrawal to belligerence. 'So, if we could very briefly go back to what you were telling us. Mrs Manifest came to live with you when she was ten and stayed until . . .?'

'She started work.'

'How old would she have been then?'

'Sixteen.'

'She left school after she took her O levels, then?'

'Yes.'

'Where did she go to school?'

'Sturrenden Grammar.'

'And where did she work, when she left?'

'The *Kent Messenger*. She'd done a week's work experience there the summer before, and enjoyed it.'

Thanet was surprised that Jessica had been taken on straight from school like that. Nowadays there was such competition for reporters' jobs that he understood it was virtually impossible to get one without a degree. But it was – what? – twenty years or so since Jessica Manifest started work. Perhaps things had been different then. In any case, she probably hadn't started reporting straight away. No doubt there'd have been some kind of apprenticeship. All the same, if she had been reasonably bright, as she must have been . . . 'As a matter of interest, why didn't she stay on at school, to take her A levels?'

Covin leaned across to stub out his cigarette in the ashtray which was now so full that he had difficulty in doing so. He got up and emptied it into the fire. 'Oh, you know what kids are like at that age. She was fed up with school, wanted to start work, earn some money of her own. And, like I said, she was pretty good at getting her own way, if she really wanted something.' He didn't sit down again but stood with his back to the fire, hands clasped behind his back.

A hint that the interview had gone on long enough? Thanet had no intention of ending it until he was ready. 'Just one or two more points, then. Would you mind telling me what you did, after you finished supper this evening? That was just after twenty past seven, I believe you said?'

Covin was lighting another cigarette, but he didn't sit down. 'That's right.'

'Presumably your daughter then had to load her things into the car?'

'No, she did that earlier, before supper, so she was all ready to go.'

'So it must have been about 7.30 when she left?'

'About then, yes.'

'Then you tried to get through to your sister-in-law . . .'

'I thought I might as well do it right away, while I was thinking of it.'

'Quite. And then?'

Covin shrugged. 'Nothing much. I sat around, watched the telly.'

And that was as much as they could get out of him. There was, he assured them, nothing more to tell.

'What do you think, Mike?' said Thanet, when they were outside.

Lineham was standing with his head thrown back, taking in great gulps of fresh air. 'Honestly, I thought I was going to suffocate in there! It was the worst atmosphere I have ever been in in my entire life! And I bet our clothes absolutely reek of cigarette smoke.' He sniffed experimentally at his sleeve. 'Faugh! Disgusting. I'm certainly not leaving these indoors all night, they'll stink the house out.'

'What will you do, Mike?' said Thanet, grinning. 'Undress in the garden? That'll intrigue the neighbours. I can just see the headline . . .'

'Give over, sir.' Lineham was not amused. He stalked across to his car then turned to say, 'I bet my hair stinks, too. I'm going to have a shower before I go to bed.'

Privately, Thanet resolved to do the same. But all he said was, 'Mike! I've got the message. And believe me, I sympathise.'

'It's a wonder he's still walking around, if you ask me! He ought to be six feet under, by rights.'

'There is no justice,' agreed Thanet. 'And now, if you wouldn't mind turning your attention to the matter in hand for a few minutes . . .'

'Sorry, sir. OK. What were you saying?'

'Look, it's getting a bit chilly. Let's sit in your car for a few minutes, shall we?' He waited until they were settled before picking up on the conversation. 'I was just wondering what you thought of Covin – apart from disapproving of his smoking habits.'

'They may not be entirely irrelevant though, sir, may they?'

'What do you mean?'

'Well, you could tell he always smokes a lot, from the way the room stank, but he surely couldn't chainsmoke like that all day? Apart from anything else, it would cost an absolute fortune.'

'He did seem very tense, I agree. And Jessica obviously wasn't exactly his favourite person.'

'A bit far-fetched, though, surely, sir? I mean, what would he be doing there in the first place? And why suddenly shove her down the stairs after all these years?'

'It does seem unlikely. But we only know what he has actually told us. He may have a very powerful motive about which we know nothing at the moment. I certainly had the feeling he was holding back on something.'

'So did I.'

'What, I wonder?'

Both men were silent, thinking.

'Of course, it might have nothing to do with Jessica's death,' said Thanet. 'I suppose it could be connected with his daughter. What was her name? Karen.'

'In what way?'

'Well, it does seem odd that she's driven herself back to Reading. It isn't as though she has a car of her own. Most students I know are either driven back by their parents along with all the gear they seem to need to take with them, or they travel by public transport, looking like pack mules. But say that was what they originally intended, that her father should drive her. And then say they had a row and she walked out and drove off in a temper . . . He could be on tenterhooks in case she had an accident on the way. That could account for his being tense, and for the fact that we both felt he was holding back. He wouldn't have wanted to tell us he'd had a row with Karen, would he? He'd regard it as none of our business.'

'But she'd have arrived by now, surely.'

'Maybe. But if she hasn't rung to let him know and there's no phone in her digs so he can't ring her to find out . . .'

'Mmm. You could be right.'

'Or, let's face it, there could be half a dozen other reasons why he happens to be uptight tonight. Maybe he had a nasty letter from his bank manager this morning. Maybe he's just been sacked. Maybe he's just learned he's got some fatal disease . . .'

'Like lung cancer, for example.'

'Quite. But in any case, I think we ought to check the times he gave us with Karen. It won't do any harm. Jerry

Long's stationed in Reading now. Give him a ring in the morning.'

'With respect, is there any point, sir? Even if she does confirm that she left about 7.30, Covin would still have had plenty of time to get over to the Manifests' house, if he was involved. That anonymous 999 call didn't come in until 8.11, as I recall.'

'I know. Still, it's worth a phone call, I think.'

'OK. I'll ring him first thing. Mind, it's in Covin's favour that he made no attempt to hide the fact that he didn't like Jessica, isn't it? If he'd had anything to do with her death he'd surely have kept quiet on that score.'

Thanet pursed his lips. 'Unless he hoped that's what we'd think.'

'Bit subtle, for him, don't you think?'

'Perhaps. You know, if it weren't for that call to the emergency services we might well have accepted without question that this death was a straightforward accident. But someone made that call and according to the ambulance crew it wasn't Manifest. When they arrived at 8.26 he told them he'd only just got in.'

'If he's telling the truth.'

Never overlook the obvious, thought Thanet. Here was a marriage long gone sour, a husband sorely provoked by his wife. Perhaps they needn't have bothered to interview Covin at all. Still . . . 'First thing in the morning check the number that call was made from.'

'I can do it tonight, if you like.'

'No. It'll keep.' Thanet had had enough for one day.

At home, Joan had gone to bed, leaving the light on in the hall. Beside the telephone were two more gaily wrapped parcels which must have been dropped in during the evening. So many had arrived over the last couple of days that Bridget was going to have a positive orgy of present-opening when she got back.

These reminders of the wedding resurrected Thanet's worries about his speech and he fell asleep once again rehearsing his proposed opening. His dreams were anxiety-ridden: he was at the reception and first he found that he had mislaid his notes and then, when he finally stood up to address the blurred sea of faces which seemed to stretch away to infinity, he discovered that he had forgotten to put on his trousers.

Next morning, when he went downstairs to make their tea, he found a Post-it note stuck on the handle of the kettle saying, *Check bows on bridesmaids' dresses* and there was another on the mirror in the bathroom saying, *Ring printer.* Over the last week these little self-reminders had been appearing everywhere. The truth was that with a house to run and her full-time job as a probation officer Joan simply didn't have time to deal with all these last-minute details and the fact that she was writing them down whenever and wherever they occurred to her was a measure of the strain she was under. Bridget really should have stayed at home this week to give her a hand.

'Is there anything I can do to help?' he asked at breakfast and felt a guilty relief as she shook her head. 'Well, do try not to overdo it, darling.'

If only, Thanet thought as he started the car, Alexander's parents were less upper middle class. It was natural that he and Joan didn't want to let Bridget down in front of her new in-laws, and equally natural that this anxiety should be an extra pressure upon them both. He wasn't looking forward to meeting them for the first time at the family dinner which had been arranged for Friday evening at the Black Swan, where the Highmans would be staying and where the reception was to be held next day.

With a determined effort he put thoughts of the wedding out of his mind and tried to concentrate on the day ahead. At least it looked as though it might be fine. Overnight the clouds which had brought yesterday's rain had begun to break up and there was a promising brightness to the east.

Lineham invariably arrived at work before him and today was no exception.

'So,' said Thanet, taking off his coat. 'What's the story? Anything interesting come in from the house-to-house inquiries?' He sat down at his desk.

'A couple of things. The next-door neighbours are away for a few days, unfortunately, but another neighbour saw a red Volkswagen Polo parked just up the lane around half past seven last night. He passed it when he was coming home.'

'Any details?'

'I'm afraid not, except that it was newish. He said the back was that rounded shape which came in in '95. Apparently it was only there for a very short while – ten or fifteen minutes, he thinks. He got to thinking it was rather odd, that it should be parked there like that, and looked out again about a quarter of an hour later to check if it was still there. But it was gone.'

'Was there anyone in it?'

'First he said yes, then he said no, then he said he couldn't be sure because it was dark by then, and he was concentrating on turning into the estate.'

'Pity.'

'However,' said Lineham, and Thanet could tell that the sergeant was looking forward to imparting the next piece of information. 'Inquiries at the Green Man turned up some potentially useful stuff. Apparently, because the lane is so narrow, people often use the pub car park even if they're not paying customers, and, as you can imagine, the publican isn't too pleased about this. In fact, it makes him hopping mad, and he's taken to trying to catch them out – not always easy, partly because he's often busy behind the bar and partly because although he recognises most of the cars belonging to regular customers, when there are strangers in the pub it's hard to tell whether the cars are legitimately parked or not.

'Anyway, though none of them was there for long, last night there were three cars which didn't belong to customers – well, one was a pick-up. A white Ford. But there was also a Mercedes which he thinks he's seen around but which hasn't actually parked at the pub before, and a Nissan which is apparently a persistent offender. He'd taken the number of that one and I've checked it on the computer. Belongs to an Alistair Barcombe who lives in Sturrenden.'

'Excellent. That's a bit of luck.'

'There's more. Another neighbour says that she's seen a young man hanging around lately. She's been dithering about reporting him to the Neighbourhood Watch but she hasn't because she thinks he looks familiar and she wondered if in fact he lives somewhere on the estate and she'd be making a fool of herself. Anyway, she's sure she's seen him before somewhere, but she can't think where. Says if she does remember, she'll let us know.'

'Good. That the lot?' Thanet glanced at his watch. Time for the morning meeting. 'It'll have to wait.'

The morning meeting was Superintendent Draco's way of keeping his finger on the pulse of his domain. A fiery little Welshman, he had initially made himself unpopular by the demands he made upon his staff but gradually they had come to regard him with affectionate respect. They had supported him wholeheartedly throughout his wife's long struggle with leukaemia and had rejoiced with him when against all the odds she had made a good recovery. Draco adored her and now that she was restored to health he was back on the top of his form, crackling with energy and 'sticking his nose into everything' as Lineham frequently complained.

Today, however, the meeting was soon over. Immediately afterwards Draco was leaving for Heathrow. Since 1989, the Foreign Office had been helping Eastern European countries to establish new systems of law and order by examining existing ones and today a group of delegates from Poland was arriving on a two-day visit to study different aspects of the British criminal justice system. Extraordinarily enough, for some reason Thanet could not remember (a Polish grandmother?) Draco spoke Polish and had been asked to accompany the group as an interpreter. Within ten minutes Thanet was back in his office. He plumped down in his chair and said, 'Where were we, Mike?'

Lineham put down his pen. 'Just two more points, sir. One, Doc M. says today's impossible for the PM. Promises he'll fit it in first thing tomorrow.'

Thanet shrugged. 'Ah well, can't be helped.'

'And the other thing is, I thought you might be

interested to know that Louise was at school with Jessica Manifest – Jessica Dander, as she was then.'

Thanet sat up. Now that *was* interesting. 'Was she indeed? What does she have to say about her?'

'That Jessica didn't mix very well and had the reputation for being unsociable. There were a couple of girls she was friendly with, one in particular, a Juliet Barnes – Juliet Parker then – but on the whole she tended to keep herself to herself.'

The phone rang and Lineham picked it up. 'Jerry Long,' he mouthed at Thanet. 'Rang him earlier.'

You couldn't hope for a much swifter response than that, thought Thanet. Long must have sent someone out to see Karen Covin right away.

In fact he had gone himself, but Karen was out. He had spoken to her roommate, however, and she had said that Karen had arrived about 10.15 last night, that she had been rather subdued and her roommate suspected an argument with her father.

'Just as we thought,' said Thanet. 'Anyway, her arrival time is about right.'

'The roommate was a real chatterbox, apparently,' said Lineham. 'Jerry found it hard to get away. She says she and Karen are good friends, go on holiday together and so on. He heard all about their summer holiday hiking in Scotland, their plans to Interrail around Europe next year and go to India the year after. He asked if we'd like him to go back later and speak to Karen herself, but I said no. Was that right?'

'I think so. There doesn't seem much point at the moment. We can always get back to him if necessary. Did Louise tell you anything else of interest?'

'Well, she did say that Jessica was very bright, and that everyone expected her to go on into the sixth form and probably to university. They were all surprised when she left after her O levels.'

'Does this Juliet Barnes live locally?'

'I'm not sure. I think so, from the way Louise spoke about her. I could find out.'

'Right.'

'Do you want me to ring her now?'

'Oh no, tonight will do. We've enough on our plates for today.'

'So,' said Lineham. 'What first?'

'I think Desmond Manifest comes top of the list, don't you?'

FOUR

There was a Council transit van parked just beyond the sectioned-off area in front of the Manifests' house and two workmen were sitting inside drinking from the tops of Thermos flasks and reading tabloid newspapers. A spade and a pickaxe lay near the hole in the road as evidence of good intentions though so far as Thanet could see nothing had yet been done this morning. Beyond was parked a bright red Datsun. Had the next-door neighbours returned? Thanet wondered.

'Hard at it, as usual,' murmured Lineham as they walked past the van. 'It makes me mad,' he went on as they waited on the doorstep for a response to their ring. 'It's taxpayers' money they're wasting!'

The door was opened not by either Desmond Manifest or his brother, as Thanet had expected, but by a burly man in his sixties, with greying hair and a square face with an aggressive thrust to the jaw. Desmond's father, perhaps?

It was, and he was none too pleased to see them. 'My son isn't well enough to talk to you.' And he started to close the door on them.

Lineham acted swiftly, stepping forward to hold it open.

'Mr Manifest,' said Thanet. 'I don't think you understand. We really have to speak to your son. If he's not prepared to talk to us here, I'm afraid he'll have to accompany us back to Headquarters.'

Manifest hesitated and then grudgingly stood back to allow them in.

In the hall stood a diminutive woman with arms folded across her chest and one hand pressed to her mouth. Frightened eyes peered out at them from a shapeless nest of badly permed hair. 'It's the police,' said Manifest. 'They want to talk to Des. Is he up?'

The woman shook her head.

'Go and tell him, then.'

Without a word she turned and scuttled up the stairs.

'You'd better wait in here.'

By daylight the overcrowded sitting room looked subtly different – shabbier. Now Thanet could detect signs of wear in the upholstery, and the surfaces of the wooden pieces were slightly clouded, as if they hadn't been polished for a very long time. Strange, he thought, how possessions can say so much about their owners. These spoke of aspirations abandoned, of dreams destroyed, above all of a mistress who didn't care about them any more. And her husband? Had she cared about him? Or he about her?

Manifest senior was determined not to be hospitable. He did not invite them to sit down and stood on the threshold, arms folded, watching them intently as if he expected them to pocket the non-existent silver. His attitude was understandable, Thanet told himself, trying not to be irritated by such unwarranted hostility. The man was simply being protective. After all, how would he, Thanet, feel if Ben had suffered a mortal blow? Remember how furious he had been with Alexander when Bridget had been so hurt by his rejection?

'Mr Manifest,' he said, 'I can understand your wanting to ensure that your son is not upset any further, but we really do have to speak to him. You must see that.'

'I don't see nothing of the sort! She fell downstairs, didn't she? Simple accident. So why all the fuss? Why can't you leave well alone?'

'Look, sit down for a moment, will you? Please?' he persisted, as Manifest remained obdurate. 'Perhaps we ought to explain just why it is so important.'

Manifest moved at last, reluctantly going to perch on the edge of an upright chair against the wall near the half-open door.

Thanet glanced at Lineham and they both sat down.

'I don't suppose you're aware of the circumstances of your daughter-in-law's death,' said Thanet.

His wife entered the room. She moved so quietly Thanet hadn't heard her come downstairs. 'He's getting dressed,' she said to her husband.

He acknowledged what she had said with a nod. 'Go on,' he said to Thanet.

'Just after ten past eight last night someone phoned the emergency services.' Blast. He had forgotten to ask Lineham if he had checked the number that call was made from. And Lineham had forgotten to tell him. He glanced at the sergeant and raised his eyebrows, hoping Lineham would understand.

'That call was made from this number,' said Lineham. 'By a man.' *Sorry*, he signalled to Thanet.

47

Was it indeed? thought Thanet.

'And when the ambulance arrived at 8.26, fifteen minutes later,' Lineham went on, 'they found your son kneeling over the body. He told them he had just come in.'

'So who made that phone call?' said Manifest.

'Precisely,' said Thanet. 'So you see, the matter is not quite as straightforward as it might appear.'

'I still don't see why you have to bother Des.' Manifest glanced up at his wife, who was standing beside him, one hand on his shoulder. They looked, Thanet thought, rather as though they were posing for a Victorian photographer. 'I can't see how he can help you, if he wasn't here when it happened. I don't want him upset any more than he already is. He's in a right old state, isn't he, Iris?'

She nodded, her thin face a troubled mask.

'Though I can't say we feel the same. Do we, Mother?'

A shake of the head this time.

'You weren't fond of your daughter-in-law?' said Thanet.

'Good riddance, I say. We both do, don't we?' Manifest did not wait for a response this time before saying, 'Nothing but trouble, she brought him.'

'Trouble?'

'With her airs and her graces, wanting this, wanting that. All over him, she was, when he was doing well, but the minute he lost his job . . . He was made redundant, you see. Disgusting, the way it was done, wasn't it, Iris? Anyway, it was a different story then. Treated him like dirt, she did. You'd think she'd never heard of the marriage vows. For better or for worse, my foot! No, once he's got over the shock it'll all be for the best, you'll see.'

'Dad? What are you saying?' Desmond Manifest came in. His hair was wet from a shower but he hadn't bothered to shave and he still looked slightly dazed. He was wearing jeans and a sweatshirt.

Manifest looked discomfited. 'Nothing much, son. Just chatting to the Inspector here.'

'Yes, well, thank you, Mr Manifest. We'd like to talk to your son now.'

Manifest didn't take the hint. He remained seated, as if he were welded to the chair. His wife glanced uneasily at him and then at Thanet. She took her hand from his shoulder and started to move away but he snatched at her skirt to restrain her and gave Thanet a defiant glare.

'Alone,' said Thanet.

'We have every right to stay.'

'Dad! I'm not a child, you know.'

Ah, thought Thanet, you may not know it, but you are. To them, anyway, and always will be. 'If you'd like your parents to stay . . .?'

'No, thank you.'

'Mr Manifest?' said Thanet.

The old man rose reluctantly. 'If you want us,' he said to Desmond, 'we'll be in the kitchen.'

Desmond touched him on the shoulder. 'I know. Thanks.'

When they had gone he said, 'He means well.'

'I realise that. Please, sit down, sir.'

Desmond chose the same chair as the previous evening and glanced uneasily at Lineham, who was opening his notebook.

'There are a few points we'd like to clear up,' said Thanet. They had decided that he should conduct this

49

interview. Last night, when Manifest had been so vulnerable, it had helped that Lineham was a familiar face. This morning it could be a disadvantage. 'First of all, someone rang for an ambulance last night, from this number. Was it you?'

'No. I was wondering about that. I told you – told someone, anyway, I'm afraid it's all a bit of a blur – I'd only just got in when they arrived. Who did ring?'

'That's what we're wondering.'

'What did they say?'

Thanet glanced at Lineham.

'Just that there'd been an accident, and the address,' said the sergeant.

'I wonder who on earth it could have been. And why didn't they wait for the ambulance to arrive? And how did they . . .?' Desmond's eyes narrowed. 'Hang about . . .'

'What?'

'I was going to say, how did they get in? But I've just remembered . . . When I got home the door was open. My God, how could I have forgotten that?'

Because, thought Thanet, assuming that you're innocent, every time you've had a flashback to last night you'll have seen nothing but that image of your wife lying crumpled at the foot of the stairs. 'Because you were in a state of shock,' he said. 'But it does explain something that was puzzling me.'

'What was that?'

'Last night, you didn't say, "I saw her as soon as I opened the door." You said, "I saw her as soon as I pushed the door open." The implication is that it already was.'

'There you are, then.'

'How wide open was it?'

Manifest frowned. 'Just a few inches, I think.'

'You'd been for a walk, you said.'

'That's right.'

'How long a walk? What time did you leave?'

Manifest pressed his thumb and forefinger into his eye-sockets, then looked up, blinking as if the light were too bright for him. 'About twenty past seven.'

'And you didn't get back until twenty-five past eight?'

'So?' The first hint of aggression there.

'You were walking for over an hour.'

'I like walking.'

'Where did you go, exactly?'

'The way I usually go.'

Lineham scribbled as Manifest outlined the route. It might be necessary for someone to walk it later.

'Did you stop at all on the way?'

Something flickered behind the man's eyes and there was the merest hesitation. But it was enough to alert Thanet. 'No.' He crossed his legs and his foot twitched.

Thanet was well aware that people are more practised at controlling their facial muscles than their extremities. 'You didn't call in at a pub for a drink, for example?'

Again that hesitation. 'I was going to, but I changed my mind.'

'Oh? Why was that?'

A shrug. 'Just didn't feel like it, I suppose.'

He was lying, definitely. But why? It was worth probing a little further, irrelevant as it might seem. 'Was it the pub you usually go to?'

'Sometimes. Sometimes I go to the Green Man, down the road.'

'It depends on whether you're going for your usual walk, I suppose.'

'Yes. Look, what the devil has this got to do with . . . with . . .'

'I'm just trying to get a clearer picture of last night,' said Thanet soothingly. 'And I'm afraid that might mean asking questions about all sorts of things which appear irrelevant. Just bear with me, will you?'

Manifest didn't argue, so Thanet went on, 'So, you'd been for your usual walk. For some reason you decided not to call in at the pub as you often do – what time would that have been, by the way?'

'I'm not sure, exactly. I've never timed it.'

'Approximately, then?'

'Ten or a quarter past eight?'

'The pub is well over half way, then? You said you left here at 7.20 and if you reached the pub at 8.15 and got home again at 8.25, just before the ambulance arrived, it must be only about ten minutes' walk away from here by the shortest route.'

'Oh, I see what you mean. Yes. I never do the circuit that way around.'

'Which pub did you say it was?'

'The Harrow.'

And Manifest hadn't wanted to tell him that, either, but hadn't known how to refuse. What was going on here? 'So you got home about ten minutes later. Would you tell me what happened then? I'm sorry. I know this is going to be painful for you.'

Manifest compressed his lips, narrowed his eyes and frowned, remembering. 'So far as I can recall,' he said slowly, 'there was nothing out of the ordinary until I got close to the front door. Then I saw it was ajar and that did alarm me. Jess would never have left it open when she was alone in the house at night. I called out to her as I pushed it open and then I . . . There she . . .' Manifest swallowed hard, over and over, as if to suppress incipient nausea.

Thanet waited for a few moments while Manifest got himself under control again, then said, 'Now, I want you to think carefully. Did you touch your wife at all? Move her in any way, to even the slightest degree?'

This was very important. If he had, it was possible that Jessica might have been alive until that moment, that an understandable but fatal effort to check whether or not she really was dead, or a spontaneous gesture of despairing love, such as gathering her up in his arms, might have finally severed a badly damaged spinal cord. In which case, Manifest might in all innocence have caused her death.

But he was shaking his head emphatically. 'I saw a St John's Ambulance film once and it said if it looks as though someone's neck is broken the last thing you should do is touch them. And it was obvious right away . . . I mean, the angle of her head . . .'

'Good,' said Thanet. 'You did exactly the right thing. Now, I have to ask you this. Do you know of anyone who might want to harm your wife?'

Manifest pushed a hand wearily through his hair. 'The obvious explanation, so far as I can see, is that it was a burglary which went wrong. And even so, of course, it might have been a pure accident.'

'Quite. Well, we shall see. It's early days yet.'

Manifest hesitated, then said slowly, 'But there is one other possibility.'

'Oh? What?'

'My wife was convinced that someone had been following her lately. I'm afraid I didn't believe her – thought she was imagining things. I never saw any sign of anything like that. But perhaps I should have listened, paid more attention. If I had . . . Oh God, if I had, perhaps she'd still be alive.' And he buried his face in his hands.

Thanet and Lineham exchanged glances.

'Des,' said Lineham. 'Could you tell us a bit more about this?'

Manifest shook his head but he did straighten up again and take several deep breaths in an effort to calm down.

'Try, will you?' Lineham urged. 'It could be important.'

'There's nothing more to tell, really. She did make a complaint to the police, but nothing came of it.'

'Did she ever describe the man to you – I assume it was a man?' said Thanet

'We both assumed it was a man. But no, that was half the trouble. It was just an impression, really. A feeling she had. And twice at night she was convinced she'd seen a prowler outside, watching.'

'In the garden, you mean? Looking through the windows?'

'Once she thought she'd seen a movement in the back garden. I went outside to look, but there was no one there. And another time she thought she saw someone behind the hedge across the road. But that time I was out.'

'I see. Well, we'll look into it. There's only one other point to clear up at the moment, I think, then we'll leave you in peace. When we were talking to you last night, you said – let me see if I can remember the words exactly: "I don't understand. I mean, why was he *there?* He should have been here." What did you mean?' Thanet could tell immediately by the guarded look which had appeared in Manifest's eyes as he was speaking that another lie was coming.

'I can't imagine. I was very confused. I didn't really know what I was saying.'

'Well,' said Lineham as they walked down the path to the gate. 'I don't know what you think, but if he had anything to do with her death he's missed his vocation. He should be on the stage.'

One workman was now pecking away half-heartedly at the hole with his pickaxe while the other stood by, leaning on his spade.

'Don't overdo it, will you?' murmured Lineham after they were past them. 'On the other hand,' he went on, returning to what he was saying, 'it's obvious he was lying in his teeth when you asked him about the pub.'

'Yes. I wonder why?'

'I was thinking about that. What if he wasn't as fond of his wife as people are making out? After all, she didn't treat him too well by all accounts, did she? And what if he'd found himself another girlfriend, was in the habit of meeting her in the pub, and didn't want to mention the pub because he thought if he did we might check up and find out about her?'

'Possible. But it also occurred to me . . . You know what we were saying, about him having seen someone somewhere he hadn't expected to see him, someone he had in fact expected to be with Jessica . . . What if he'd intended calling in at the pub, but had seen – either through a window or after he'd gone in – the person he had thought would be here, and that was why he changed his mind about having a drink and came home instead?'

'Yes. That would make sense. In which case . . .'

'Quite,' said Thanet. 'We need to find out who that someone was.'

'But if that's so, why didn't he tell us about this person? What possible reason could he have for not mentioning him?'

'If we find out who, we might find out why.'

'Shall we go to the pub, ask some questions?'

'No. We'll get someone else to do that. We've got too much to do today. But first, I want to nose around here a bit. Let's take a look behind that hedge, shall we? See if there are any signs of this prowler.'

'If he exists,' said Lineham.

'Quite. If Manifest had nothing to do with his wife's death he's certainly feeding us plenty of red herrings – open front doors, watchers in the dark . . . Over that five-barred gate, I think?'

'I suppose the prowler could be the young man that neighbour mentioned.'

'That's certainly a possibility.'

'But what I don't understand,' said Lineham as they climbed the gate and worked their way along behind the hedge, 'is why Des goes out walking in the evenings, when he's got all day to do it in. It does sound as though he made a habit of it.'

'Unless he has a girlfriend, as you suggested.'

'Oh, I don't know. On second thoughts I admit the girlfriend idea is unlikely. He does seem genuinely cut up about his wife's death.'

'Perhaps it was simply that she'd got fed up with him,' said Thanet, 'and wanted the place to herself in the evenings. Remember the separate rooms? Or that he regularly went out when she had a visitor he wanted to avoid.'

'The mysterious someone!' Lineham had been poking around in the hedge with a stick and now he straightened up with a jerk. 'Yes! That makes more sense. What if it was a lover, sir?'

'And Manifest went out on the evenings he was expected, leaving him a clear field? Sounds a bit far-fetched to me.'

Over the hedge Thanet saw Desmond Manifest's father leave the house and fetch something from the Datsun. The car didn't belong to the neighbours then.

'Just say I'm right, though,' Lineham persisted. 'Say she and her lover quarrelled and he pushed her down the stairs. He panics, rings for an ambulance, then scarpers . . .'

'And Manifest gets back a quarter of an hour later, realises what has happened and decides to cover up for him? I really think we're moving into the realms of fantasy here. Anyway, it doesn't add up, Mike. If you're right about all this, the lover was sitting in the Harrow and Manifest saw him there.'

'But it all depends on the timing, sir! You said yourself that the Harrow was only ten minutes' walk away. That's only a couple of minutes by car. This chap could have arrived at the house after Des left at 7.20 and while Des was walking for the next fifty-five minutes there'd have been plenty of time for him and Jessica to have quarrelled and for him to have driven to the pub afterwards so that he was sitting there calm as you please for Des to see when he got there at 8.15!'

'True. Well, we'll see. It shouldn't be too difficult to unearth him if he exists. All this, of course, assumes that Manifest didn't do it himself.'

'I still think that unlikely. Though I agree, we shouldn't rule it out. It all depends, really, on whether he was telling the truth about the front door being open. Otherwise he might well have rung for the ambulance himself and simply have been pretending that he'd just arrived before they did. What do you think, sir?'

'At the moment I'm inclined to give him the benefit of the doubt. Doc Mallard didn't seem in any doubt that he was genuinely in a state of shock last night, and if the business about the door was a ploy to divert suspicion from himself, it was a pretty subtle one. Just to slip in that he pushed it open and leave it to us to pick up –'

'But he didn't, sir. He was the one who brought it up this morning. He wouldn't have known that you were going to mention it anyway.'

'I still think there would have been a temptation for him to make more of it last night. Anyway, it's pointless to speculate any further at this stage. Let's get a few more facts under our belt first.'

'Look at this, sir!'

Their little foray had been rewarded. At a point directly opposite the Manifests' house the ground was trampled, the grass flattened, and there were a number of cigarette butts.

'Roll your own,' said Lineham, taking a polythene bag from his pocket and slipping it over his hand so as to pick them up without touching them. 'Not many people smoke those these days.'

'We'll check to see if she did file a complaint.'

'I was wondering, sir . . . That unauthorised parking at the pub . . . You don't think the owner of that Nissan –'

'The same thought had occurred to me. What was his name?'

'Barcombe. Alistair Barcombe.'

FIVE

The owner of the Nissan lived in one of the little Victorian terraced houses on the Maidstone Road in Sturrenden. These had been built in the days when their peace would have been disturbed by nothing more intrusive than the gentle clopping of horses' hoofs and the rumble of carts, but now, in addition to local traffic, a never-ending line of lorries, cars, vans and buses streamed past on their way to the Channel ports, to the huge passenger station for the Channel Tunnel trains at Ashford, to the new industrial estates which had sprung up to the south of that town and to the Tunnel car terminus on the M20. That the beautiful county of Kent, the so-called garden of England, had become little more than a through-route to Europe, never failed to anger Thanet and all those who, like him, loved the county and had known it before so much of it had been sacrificed to the god of transport. It still boasted some of the most beautiful gardens, the most historic castles, the loveliest landscapes in England, but its long-suffering inhabitants couldn't help wondering where it was all going to end.

Double yellow lines and the narrowness of the road meant that it was impossible to park in front of the house and they had to drive some way past and turn off the main road to find somewhere to leave the car before walking back. The sun had broken through at last but Thanet scarcely noticed, he was too preoccupied with trying to take shallow breaths in order to avoid filling his lungs with the exhaust fumes with which the air seemed saturated. The houses were small, with only the narrowest of pavements to protect them from passing vehicles. Here and there an optimistic gardener had managed to gouge out a hole in which to plant a climber, but coated with the dust constantly thrown up by passing traffic the shrubs had failed to thrive.

'Don't know how people ever manage to sleep at night living on a road like this,' said Lineham as they waited for an answer to their knock, raising his voice to make himself heard over the roar of a passing lorry. 'It must be impossible to have the bedroom windows open. If you weren't deafened you'd be suffocated.'

'I suppose you get used to it,' said Thanet. 'But I agree, I'd hate it.' So often, when interviewing people in their homes, he gave heartfelt thanks for his own comfortable if modest home. Though this one, he had noted, was much cherished: the windows sparkled, the paintwork was in pristine condition, and the brass knocker, the letterbox and even the keyhole cover shone with much polishing.

'House-proud,' said Lineham, reading his mind.

Thanet nodded as the door opened.

'Mrs Barcombe?'

'Yes?' She was tall, thin and bony, clutching a duster and a spraycan of polish to her chest and was dressed like a charwoman from a forties comedy, with a turban over her hair and a floral crossover apron of the type Thanet would have expected to be virtually unobtainable nowadays. Perhaps she made them herself, he thought irrelevantly as he introduced himself.

She immediately looked alarmed. 'Police?' Her eyes darted from one to the other. 'What's happened? Is it Kevin?'

'No. Please don't worry. These are merely routine inquiries. Er . . . May we come in for a moment?'

She looked down at their feet and Thanet saw that not only was she herself wearing carpet slippers but that two more pairs, men's, were lined up to the right of the door. A thick sheet of plastic carpet protector ran down the centre of the narrow hallway. Mrs Barcombe evidently carried her war against dirt to the kind of extremes he would find impossible to live with. On the whole Thanet tried to accommodate himself to the lifestyles of those he had to interview on the principle that there was no point in arousing unnecessary antagonism, but he drew the line at taking off his shoes. He watched her struggle to overcome her desire to request just that, and waited with what he hoped was an expression of polite expectation.

Eventually she capitulated. 'I suppose so,' she said grudgingly.

They followed her through a door on the right into a sitting room where there were antimacassars and armprotectors on the three-piece suite and every surface shone, sparkled or twinkled. There was a strong smell of Brasso and furniture polish overlaid with air freshener but no evidence of any occupation – no books, newspapers, magazines, no knitting or needlework, not even a television set. Thanet guessed that the room was rarely used. Pride of place was taken by a photograph of a young man, no more than a boy really, set precisely in the centre of the mantelpiece. It was obviously a holiday snap – he was leaning against some railings with a background of beach, sea and sky. If the owner of the Nissan was Alistair Barcombe, this, presumably, was Kevin.

'Is Mr Barcombe in?'

She shook her head. 'He's at work.'

'Where is that, Mrs Barcombe?'

'Bentall's, in the High Street.'

A men's outfitters, in the town.

'May we sit down?'

She nodded and sank into a chair herself, still clutching the duster and spraycan. Comfort objects perhaps, thought Thanet. 'He drives to work?'

'No, he walks.'

Thanet waited.

She fidgeted with the duster, then said, 'It's not far into the town from here, it's not worth getting the car out. Then there's the parking. If you can find a space you have to pay through the nose for it.'

'Where do you keep your car? Some distance away, I imagine?'

'We rent a garage, round the back.'

'Does your husband take it out much in the evenings?'

'Has it been stolen or something, and smashed up? Is that what all this is about?'

'No, not at all. Does he? Take it out in the evenings?'

'Well, sometimes, yes.'

'And last night? Did he take it out last night?'

'No, he stayed in at home with me. We watched the telly.'

Thanet believed her. Which left Kevin – who, he guessed, was the apple of her eye. He would have to be careful. He stood up. Lineham, taken by surprise, was a little slow to follow and gave Thanet a questioning glance. 'Well, thank you, Mrs Barcombe,' said Thanet, smiling. 'I don't think we need to trouble you any further at the moment.' He turned away and in so doing pretended to notice the photograph for the first time. 'Is this your son? Kevin, did you say his name was?'

She was already on her feet, relief making her almost garrulous. 'Yes. Well, adopted son, as a matter of fact. We've always made a point of making no secret about that. I always think it's a mistake not to be open about it, don't you? You hear of such terrible stories when the children learn about it late in life. We told our Kevin very early on, and whatever people say to you about adoption, don't you believe it. No son of our own could have been more to us than he is, nor treated us better. He's never given us a moment's worry.'

But the shadow behind her eyes denied what she was saying.

Thanet smiled. 'I'm delighted to hear that. It's rare enough, with young people carrying on the way they do these days.' He began to move towards the door. 'Does he work locally?' His tone was casual, as if he were merely expressing a polite interest.

'At Snippers, in the High Street.'

'Oh. That's where my wife has her hair done. She started going there last year and says she's never had it cut so well in her life before.'

Mrs Barcombe looked gratified. 'That's why Kevin was so pleased to get in there. They do a really good training, he says.'

'He's apprenticed, I suppose.'

'Halfway through.'

They were on the doorstep by now, about to leave, when Thanet turned as if an afterthought had just struck him – a technique which always amused him when he watched the Columbo films but which could occasionally, as now, prove useful. 'He drives, I suppose? Kevin? And borrows your husband's car sometimes?'

But he saw at once that his tactic had failed. A tiny frown appeared on her forehead and her eyes grew wary. 'Yes. Why?'

'Did he borrow it last night, by any chance?'

She hesitated, clearly torn between a reluctance to lie and anxiety that she might incriminate her son. 'I'm not sure.' She was still holding the spraycan and now, with a sudden movement, she tucked it under her arm and began to twist the duster into a tight spiral with hands reddened and coarsened by too much unnecessary housework.

'He doesn't always ask your husband's permission, if he wants to borrow it?'

'I don't always hear. If I'm in another room or something.'

'Of course. But he did go out last night?'

'Yes.' The answer was grudging.

'And what time did he leave?'

'I'm not sure.'

'A rough estimate?'

She sucked in her breath in exasperation. 'About a quarter to eight, I suppose.'

'I see. Well, thank you again, Mrs Barcombe.' And they left her staring after them.

As soon as they were out of earshot Lineham said, 'He obviously did borrow it last night, don't you think?'

'Looks like it.' Thanet glanced at his watch. Twelve-twenty. 'We'll have a bite to eat, then go and see what he has to say.'

Over a beef-and-pickle sandwich and a pint at a nearby pub Lineham said, 'And what was all that stuff about adoption?'

'Yes, I wondered that.'

'Something gone wrong there, you think?'

'It did sound rather as though she was trying to convince herself as well as us.'

'I was surprised she mentioned it at all.'

'I don't know. It sounded to me as if she was genuine in saying they'd never made a secret of it. It all came out as though it was something she told people automatically. But as for Kevin "never giving a moment's trouble", well, I'm not so sure.'

They drove into the town centre and, leaving the car at Headquarters, walked along to Snippers. It was a unisex salon but Thanet had never set foot inside before, preferring to have his hair cut the old-fashioned way in a barber's shop with a striped pole outside. Such places were becoming harder and harder to find but Sturrenden still boasted two and Thanet had been going along month after month to the same one for longer than he cared to remember; despite Joan's occasional proddings he had no intention of abandoning a practice of such long standing. He made a mental note, *Must fit in a haircut before Saturday.*

Inside he was surprised to see that the one feature he invariably associated with salons where women had their hair done was absent. There was not a single dome-shaped hair-drier in sight. The place was open plan and several stylists were at work, cutting, wielding combs, hand driers and styling wands. All but one, an older man, were young. Pop music blared out and the air was full of the mingled scents of shampoo, hair-spray and another more acrid ammoniac smell. Thanet found it very difficult to envisage Joan fitting in to this environment. On the other hand the place obviously had a wide appeal – the clients seemed to range from teenage to elderly.

'Can I help you?' The receptionist was in her teens with tousled hair streaked with green and red. She was wearing a black top with irregularly shaped holes cut out of it, revealing unappetising glimpses of pallid skin beneath.

'We'd like a word with Kevin Barcombe, please.' Briefly, Thanet flashed his warrant card. 'Police,' he murmured. He saw no point in causing unnecessary embarrassment.

She frowned. 'I'll get him.'

After a quick word with the older man, who gave them a sharp look, she went to the back of the shop where the boy in the photograph was working not on a customer but on a model head. He was putting its hair up into an elaborate plait which began high on the back of the head and his absorption was total. He started when the girl approached him and left his work with reluctance.

'Is there anywhere private we can talk?' said Lineham, when they had introduced themselves.

'There's an exercise room upstairs. I'll have to ask Dennis.'

This was the older man, the owner presumably. He nodded and Kevin led them to an upper room equipped as a gym. Various exercise machines stood about and Lineham glanced at them with interest. 'I didn't know you had these here.'

'They're chiefly used in the evenings and at weekends. People come to work out. Look, what's all this about, then? I ain't done nothing – so far as I know, anyway.'

'We're just making some routine inquiries,' said Lineham. 'This shouldn't take long.'

'Good. It don't do my image much good, do it, to have you coming here like this?'

Thanet wondered what 'image' Kevin had of himself. Neither of his most memorable features was attractive – carrot-coloured hair and the dense crop of freckles which so often accompanies it.

'We understand you borrowed your father's car last night.'

'So? No crime in that, is there?'

But Thanet was sensing that beneath the bravado the boy was nervous. Was it possible that he really had been involved in Jessica Dander's death? Or was it simply that he had never been questioned by the police before and found the process alarming? Even innocent people often did, as Thanet was well aware.

'Of course not. Where did you go?'

'Sally's.'

A nightclub which had recently opened in a disused warehouse on the edge of town. According to Kevin he had left home at 8.15 and gone straight there. He had stayed until just after midnight, then returned home. A number of friends, he said, would confirm his story.

On the way out Thanet paused at the desk and inquired if Jessica Dander – or Jessica Manifest as she might have called herself – had been a client at Snippers. Apparently she had.

'So,' said Lineham as soon as they were outside, 'he knew her, by sight, anyway. He could be the prowler, don't you think? And if he's the prowler . . .'

'Let's not jump to conclusions, Mike. I agree, he could be. But let's get a little more evidence before making up our minds.'

'But he's involved somehow, isn't he? Otherwise, why lie about the time? There's a discrepancy of half an hour between the time he says he left home and the time his mother gave us. What's more, it covers part of the period we're looking at. Doc Mallard put the time of death between 7 and 8.26, and if Kevin left home at around 7.45 he could have been in Charthurst by eight.'

'Motive?'

Lineham grinned. 'Give me time and I'll come up with one.'

'Meanwhile we'll check the time of his arrival at Sally's, though I don't know if we'll get much joy. It's pretty popular, I believe, and usually heaving with people.'

'I'm not so sure. There might not have been many there so early in the evening. Things don't usually hot up until much later, I believe.'

'Well, we'll see.'

'So, what's next on the agenda, sir?'

'A visit to the *KM*, I think, in Maidstone.'

'Great.' Lineham loved driving, the further the better.

Thanet was relieved to have a brief respite too, to sit back and enjoy the mellowness of the early autumn landscape. This was the moment when the land was poised between one annual cycle and the next. The harvest was long since over and the year was winding down, but already some of the fields had been ploughed and sown with winter wheat, their chocolate-brown furrows etching graceful curves across the contours of the earth. Soon the tender green shoots would appear but meanwhile nature was preparing itself for its most spectacular display, the blaze of autumn colour which was already beginning to tint the patches of woodland which flanked their route.

At this time of day the roads were relatively clear and by just after 1.30 they were pulling into the car park at Maidstone Police Station in Palace Avenue. A few minutes' walk took them to the *Kent Messenger* offices which were in Middle Row, a narrow block of buildings between Maidstone High Street and Bank Street, one of the oldest streets in the town.

The reception area was light and airy with access from both streets. Behind a large square inquiry counter were two receptionists, one of them working the switchboard. The other looked up and smiled at their approach, but her expression quickly changed when she heard why they were there.

'We still can't believe it. You never think it'll happen to somebody you know.'

'You knew her well?'

Like Jessica the woman was in her thirties, with a broad, flat-featured face and short, straight blonde hair.

'Not really well. She wasn't a friend, if that's what you mean, but she had worked here for ages.' She turned to the other woman. 'Someone was saying this morning that

70

they thought Jessica had worked at the *KM* longer than anyone else here, weren't they?'

Her colleague nodded.

'So you're bound to feel it, even if you didn't particularly . . . even if you weren't particularly close.'

So the receptionist hadn't liked her. It might be worth talking to her later. Meanwhile it was time for the appointment they had made with the news editor.

'I believe Mr Anderson is expecting us.'

The receptionist rang through and within minutes Colin Anderson had arrived and was whisking them upstairs. The narrow staircase led into the main editorial office. This too was light and airy and stretched the whole width of the block, with high windows overlooking both streets. Reporters were busily tapping away at their computers or answering telephones surrounded by a sea of paper piled up on desks and overflowing from bins, cardboard boxes and wire baskets. A large map of Kent hung on the wall. Anderson nodded at an empty desk. 'That was Jessica's.'

'Perhaps we could take a look at it later.'

'Of course.'

He led them through a door at the far end of the room and up a further flight of stairs into an interview room. When they were all seated he said, 'Now, how can I help you? I'm not sure what you want of me but I gather from your visit that you are not satisfied Jessica's death was an accident. Are you treating this as a murder investigation?'

Thanet and Lineham had already agreed that as the senior officer Thanet should conduct this interview. They felt that in view of his position Anderson would expect it. So Thanet began by saying, 'First of all I would like your assurance that anything said in this interview will remain confidential. As you know, we always try to cooperate with the press and we shall continue to do so in this instance, especially as we do appreciate that you must have a particular interest in the case, since Mrs Manifest – or Miss Dander, as I suppose I should call her here – was a colleague of yours. We'll do our best to keep you up to date with developments, but I'm sure you understand that we can't release information which might prejudice the investigation.'

Anderson nodded. He was in his forties, with horn-rimmed glasses which gave him an earnest, studious air, and hair which was already receding at the temples. Like the other reporters downstairs he was in shirtsleeves. 'Understood.'

'So, yes, we have to say that we are not satisfied as yet that her death was an accident. There are one or two circumstances, which I can't reveal to you at the moment, that are giving us reason to doubt that it was.'

'So. Fire away. Jessica might not have been very popular but no one would have wished that on her.'

'She wasn't? Popular?'

'Not particularly.'

'Why was that?'

'She was a bit impatient. Offhand.'

'So she didn't have any close friends at work?'

'Not really, no. Oh, she rubbed along well enough with people but she was a bit of a loner, that's all.'

'How important are personal relationships in a place like this?'

'Well, there's a certain amount of teamwork, obviously, there has to be. But at the same time there's always rivalry,

72

even between friends. Everyone has the same aim, to get their story and their name on the front page.'

'Was Jessica ambitious?'

'To a degree, yes, you have to be in a job like this. In many ways she was a model employee. She was a good writer and she was hardworking, punctual, efficient, reliable. You always knew that if you asked her to do something it would be done thoroughly and well. Not brilliantly, perhaps, but there are plenty of times when it isn't brilliance that's needed.'

'Is that why she stayed with the same paper for so long – since she was sixteen, in fact? Because she didn't have that little extra edge of talent? It's pretty unusual to stay as long as that, isn't it?'

'Yes, it is. And yes, perhaps that was why. Maybe she didn't want to risk trying for one of the nationals.'

'Risk?'

'Perhaps she was afraid of failure. Maybe she felt secure here.'

'You think she was an insecure sort of person?'

Anderson shrugged. 'Underneath, I'd say she probably was.' He leaned back in his chair, considering, then shook his head. 'She wasn't easy to understand. She was dedicated to her work, as I say, very intense about it. But she found it difficult to ease up, she was prickly, didn't have much sense of humour, and hated being teased. On the other hand, I know she had a softer side, and this certainly came over in some of the features she wrote. They were what she was best at. Her news sense wasn't so good.'

'What do you mean by that, exactly?'

Anderson laughed, revealing two crooked front teeth. 'The classic way to explain that is to tell the story of the

73

editor and the new reporter. He sends her out to cover a wedding and when she comes back she tells him there wasn't a story. "What do you mean?" he says. "There wasn't a story because there wasn't a wedding," she says. "The bride didn't turn up."'

Thanet and Lineham laughed.

'So,' said Thanet. 'This softer side –'

The telephone rang. 'For you, Inspector,' said Anderson, handing it over.

The Manifests' next-door neighbours had returned and were at Headquarters, asking to speak to Thanet. He glanced at his watch. He was almost finished here. 'Tell them I can be back by around 2.45. Apologise for keeping them waiting and suggest they go and do a bit of shopping or something.' He handed the receiver back. What had he been saying? 'This softer side. It came over in what she wrote?'

'Yes. Especially when she was working with disabled people, or those who had suffered a tragedy or were in some terrible predicament. Nowadays our reporters do a tremendous amount of their work by phone, but sometimes we want pictures and personal interviews, and photographers who've worked on those sort of stories with Jessica tell me she was a different person when she was talking to people like that. And I suspect that was because she found it easy to relate to them, because underneath she may have felt just as vulnerable as they are. Perhaps she had a tough time as a kid, I don't know.'

'She came to the *KM* straight after her O levels. I imagine that's pretty unusual nowadays.'

'Oh yes! Very rarely happens any more. There's tremendous competition for jobs in journalism, even

74

among graduates; a prospective employer can usually pick and choose. But – what? – twenty years ago it was a different matter. The office was based at Larkfield in those days and she'd have been taken on as an editorial assistant – that's a grandiose title for someone who runs errands and makes the tea, draws up the chemists' rotas and so on. Then I imagine she'd have graduated to junior reporter, perhaps in another paper within the group, and probably have moved around a bit before ending up here.'

'How did she get on with the opposite sex?'

Anderson smiled. 'That's an interesting question.' He took off his spectacles and rubbed his eyes before putting them back on. 'She wasn't above turning on the charm when she wanted something, but she definitely didn't put out signals that she was available, so to speak.'

'Some men regard that as a challenge.'

'True.'

'But to your knowledge none of them got anywhere?'

An emphatic shake of the head. 'No. And when she married Desmond, of course, the comment was that she had obviously been saving herself for someone rather better off than a mere reporter. Not that we didn't feel sorry for her when it all fell apart.'

'Did her husband's unemployment make any difference to her work?'

'I'd say she was a little more . . . driven, I suppose is the word. I imagine she felt it was especially important that she keep her job, as she was now the breadwinner.'

'Did she ever talk about it?'

'No. If she'd wanted to, there were a number of sympathetic ears around. But we didn't feel it was up to us to broach the subject. It's a pretty sensitive issue, after all.'

Thanet thought of the made-up single bed in the Manifests' back bedroom, of the solitary pillow in the marital bed. 'We understand the situation was a considerable strain on her marriage. Do you happen to know if she looked for consolation elsewhere?'

For the first time Anderson hesitated.

'What?' said Thanet.

He chewed the inside of his lip. 'I don't want to drop anyone in it unnecessarily.'

Thanet sighed. 'There's not much point in holding anything back. We'll find out in the end anyway. It'll just take longer, that's all.'

He shrugged. 'I suppose that's true. Well, the rumour was she was having an affair with Adam Ogilvy, the estate agent.'

Thanet knew at once who he meant. Ogilvy was a well-known figure in the area. 'He drives a silver Mercedes, doesn't he?' The charge of adrenaline made it difficult for Thanet to keep his tone casual and refrain from exchanging glances with Lineham.

But Anderson was no fool. 'Yes. Why?'

'I'm sorry, I can't say at the moment.'

They learnt nothing more of interest, either from going through Jessica's desk or from talking to the receptionist, who merely confirmed what Anderson had told them about the former reporter's relationships with her work mates.

'So,' said Lineham, the minute they were out in the street. 'Adam Ogilvy, eh? Car owner number two by the look of it.'

'Yes. Looks as though you were right about the lover after all. No need to say, "I told you so"!'

Lineham grinned. 'Wouldn't dream of it, sir.'

'Though it's beyond belief that Manifest went out in the evenings so as to leave his wife's lover a clear field!'

'Sounds like it, though, from all that "Why was he there when he should have been here" stuff.'

'Well, we'll find out sooner or later, no doubt.'

'I assume we'll go and see him now? Ogilvy?'

'We have to go back to the office first.' Thanet told Lineham about the appointment with Manifest's neighbours.

'I wonder what's made them come rushing into town to see us the minute they got back,' said Lineham.

'Well, we'll soon find out.'

SIX

Back at Headquarters a uniformed constable on his way out gave them a wide grin and there was more than a hint of amusement in Pater's greeting when they inquired about Manifest's neighbours.

'The Bartons? They're in interview room four. They didn't go into the town, said they were quite happy to wait.' Pater exchanged a conspiratorial look with a colleague.

'What's going on?' said Thanet.

Pater's smile broadened. 'You can see for yourself, sir. They're . . . er . . . meditating.'

Thoroughly intrigued by now Thanet and Lineham went straight to interview room four and opened the door. The Bartons were both standing on their heads, side by side against the far wall. Their eyes were closed and they gave no sign that they had heard anyone come in. Thanet cleared his throat and when that had no effect said, 'Mr and Mrs Barton?'

Their eyes opened in unison and they righted themselves with an ease he guessed was born of long practice, landing up side by side as if awaiting further instruction. They were in their sixties and quite remarkably alike – could certainly have been taken for brother and sister. They both had slightly hooked noses, deep-set eyes and sported identical hairstyles. They were dressed alike, too, in maroon tracksuits with navy trim, and if it hadn't been for the fact that one of them was slightly smaller than the other and had two unmistakable bulges in her upper torso, Thanet might well have thought them both male. 'I believe you wanted to see me.' He introduced himself and Lineham. 'Sit down, won't you? I'm sorry to have kept you waiting.'

'Oh, not at all, Inspector. We really didn't mind. We have many ways of improving the shining hour, haven't we, Ellie?'

His wife nodded vigorously. 'It really didn't matter at all.'

Thanet waited until everyone was settled, then said, 'So, how can I help you?'

They exchanged glances and then Barton said, 'We thought we ought to come and see you –'

'About Jessica, being as we're next-door neighbours –'

'And hearing the police were involved –'

'And that it might not have been an accident.' Mrs Barton finished what turned out to be the first joint sentence of many and they looked at Thanet expectantly.

'Quite,' he said, wondering if this double act was the norm.

Barton leaned forward confidentially. 'Only being so close you can't help hearing –'

'And seeing –'

'What's going on,' finished Barton.

'Of course,' said Lineham.

Mrs Barton screwed up her face anxiously. 'We mean, we wouldn't want you to think we're the type who spend all their time –'

'Looking over the neighbours' wall.'

They gazed at Thanet earnestly.

'We quite understand,' said Thanet. 'The houses are very close together.'

'And the gardens!' said Mrs Barton. 'They're very close too. In the summer –'

'You just can't avoid overhearing.'

'And we like Desmond,' said his wife. 'He's there much more than she is – was –'

'So naturally, we see much more of him.'

'Both of us being retired.'

'Naturally,' Thanet agreed.

'And we felt sorry for him,' said Mr Barton.

Thanet felt the first quickening of his pulse. 'Oh? Why was that?'

'We're not gossips, you know,' said Mrs Barton. 'I mean, we've never breathed a word of this –'

'Not to anyone. But we think we were probably the only ones to know. And we wanted you to understand –'

'What she was really like.'

'They say the police always suspect the husband first, don't they?' Mrs Barton gave hers a fond glance. 'Though why that should be I can't imagine.'

Barton reached across to squeeze her hand. 'Not everyone is as lucky as us, my dear. And in any case, we know Desmond is in the clear.'

'He was out for a walk, he told us.'

'Lucky for him, wasn't it?'

80

'Awful for him to come back and find . . . find . . .' Mrs Barton shuddered. 'It doesn't bear thinking about.'

Patience, Thanet told himself. We'll get there in the end. Let them tell it their own way. They obviously had scruples to overcome and this was never easy.

'Still,' said her husband, 'I suppose it's not surprising, in the circumstances.'

They needed a little prod. 'What circumstances?'

There was a brief silence and then Mrs Barton leaned forward and said in a hushed tone, 'She was carrying on, you see.'

'And not behind his back, either.'

Their indignation was gathering pace.

'Openly!'

'Disgraceful, it was. The fellow would come to the house –'

'When Desmond was there –'

'When we *knew* he was there.'

'And once or twice –'

'If we were just coming back from a walk –'

'We'd see the bedroom light go on –'

'Just after he arrived –'

'And we'd see them both –'

'This man and her –'

'Both up there –'

'Bold as brass.'

'It was awful,' said Mr Barton.

'So humiliating.'

'In the end Desmond took to going out just before he arrived. We didn't blame him, did we, Ellie?'

She shook her head. 'Poor man.'

'Do you know who this man was?' said Thanet.

'Drives a great big silver car,' said Mrs Barton.

'A Mercedes.'

Ogilvy. Further confirmation that the rumour Anderson had heard was correct.

'I wonder why none of the other neighbours have mentioned him,' said Lineham.

'Television!' Mr Barton almost spat the word out. 'We won't have one in the house.'

His wife was nodding. 'Got better things to do with our time, haven't we, love.'

'And he always came in the evenings when they'd be glued to *Coronation Street* or some other such rubbish.'

'That's why we said we thought we were probably the only ones to know. We've never heard a word about it from anyone else.'

'How long had this been going on?' said Thanet.

They consulted each other with a glance.

'Four months?' said Barton.

'Four or five,' said his wife.

'Well,' said Thanet, starting to get up, 'thank you very much. We appreciate your taking the time and trouble to come in. You've been most helpful.'

They didn't move.

He sat down again. 'There's something else you wanted to tell us?'

Another wordless consultation.

Shall we?

We did agree.

'Well,' said Barton hesitantly, 'as a matter of fact there was.'

'And we're absolutely certain no one else knew about this, either.'

'We never realised such things went on.'

'Shocked, we were, that first time we found out about it.'

They stopped.

'About what?' said Thanet gently. This was hard for them, he could see that. They certainly weren't aiming for dramatic effect and there was no pleasure for them in the telling either.

But they had to make an oblique approach.

'We were in the garden, weren't we, Ellie? A lovely day it was, so peaceful.'

'We'd been working hard all afternoon –'

'And we sat down for a cup of tea.'

'And then she started,' whispered Mrs Barton. 'Shouting –'

'Screaming –'

'Terrible things.'

'Horrible.'

'They were inside at first –'

'In the kitchen –'

'But then they came out –'

'Into the garden –'

'And we heard this noise, didn't we, Bill. A sort of –'

'A thwacking sound. That's what it was.'

'At first we thought one of them was beating a carpet –'

'With one of those old-fashioned carpet beaters, you know?'

'But then we began to wonder –'

'Because it wasn't a dry thud, it was a wet thud –'

'If you see what we mean.'

'And all the while she was calling him names –'

'Saying how useless he was –'

'And the thuds were coming in between every word.'

'So naturally we couldn't help wondering what on earth was going on.'

'Desmond wasn't making a sound.'

'And there's a gap in the fence.'

'A sort of broken bit.'

'So we went and looked through.'

They paused – not, Thanet thought again, for effect. They were genuinely reluctant to say what they had seen. By now, of course, he had guessed what it was and so, he suspected, had Lineham. He gave an encouraging nod.

Mr Barton leaned forward and lowered his voice, as if by doing so he could diminish the shocking nature of what he was about to reveal. 'She was hitting him,' he said. 'With a rolled-up towel. We think it was wet.'

'It made this horrible squelchy noise every time it hit him.'

'And he was just standing there –'

'With his shoulders hunched –'

'And his hands over his head –'

'To protect it.'

'If I hadn't seen it,' said Barton, 'I wouldn't have believed it. A grown man, just standing there and taking it, like that!'

'In the end she just flung the towel on the ground and stalked back into the house. I could never feel the same about her after that.'

'When was this?' said Lineham.

'Not long after they moved in,' said Barton. 'Three years ago?'

'And this wasn't the only incident of this kind you noticed, I gather?' said Thanet.

84

'No. The only reason we're telling you is because we wanted you to know –'

'What she was like when she lost her temper.'

'Someone else might not have been so ready to put up with it –'

'Being treated like that.'

'Someone like her fancy man, for instance.'

'And if they had an argument –'

'At the top of the stairs –'

'It would only need a little push –'

'If you caught her off balance.'

'Quite,' said Thanet.

'Well,' said Lineham when they had gone. 'So Desmond was a battered husband. That's a turn-up for the book, isn't it? And what a pair! I've never seen anything like it.'

'I suppose it's called being of one mind,' said Thanet with a grin.

'You can say that again. They obviously carry on like that all the time. And I really don't think it even entered their heads that they were making things look black for Desmond!'

'I know. It certainly gives him an even stronger motive. In fact he seems to have had plenty of provocation, one way and the other.'

'She sounds a nasty bit of work to me. Flaunting her lover like that.'

Thanet grinned. 'Flaunting. That's a good old-fashioned word, Mike. But I agree. Not very nice.'

'What gets me is that he put up with it! The beatings, too! It just shows how little you know about other people. I'd never have put him down for such a wimp!'

85

'Anyway, I think we can take it now that a lot of what we guessed was correct. She did have a lover and Manifest did go out for walks in the evening because he wanted to avoid him. So let's say, for the sake of argument, that that's what happened last night, that he had nothing to do with her death and he's telling the truth when he says he went out around 7.20 and didn't get back until just before the ambulance –'

'Meanwhile lover-boy turns up on his white horse, so to speak. But he can't park in front of the house because of the hole in the road, so he parks at the pub instead, where his car is noticed by the owner.'

'Why didn't he simply park further up the road?'

Lineham's mouth turned down at the corners and he raised his shoulders. 'Because he didn't want to draw attention to himself and people in a street like that always tend to notice cars that are parked directly in front of their houses?'

'Possibly,' Thanet conceded.

'Anyway, when he gets to Jessica's house Desmond has already left. They go up to the bedroom as usual, but they have a row. They argue, she falls, he's horrified and dials 999 for an ambulance. Then he scarpers to the pub, to give himself an alibi –'

'Where he's seen by Desmond –'

'Who can't understand why he was there instead of with Jessica.'

Thanet laughed. 'Do you realise we're doing a Barton?'

'A what?'

'Finishing each other's sentences.'

Lineham grinned. 'So we are. We'll have to watch it or we'll be standing on our heads next.'

SEVEN

The distinctive purple and green 'For Sale' boards of Ogilvy and Tate were a familiar sight in the area. It was an old-established family firm with many branch offices in the larger villages around. Its main premises, in Sturrenden, occupied a prime site in the High Street, not far from Snippers. Thanet glanced into the hairdressing salon as they passed by but without actually stopping and peering in he couldn't make out if Kevin was inside or not.

The estate agent's double shop front was crammed with photographs of houses for sale. The property market had had a rough ride since the heady, hectic days of the eighties, when houses sold like hot cakes and the scramble to buy pushed prices higher and ever higher. The subsequent collapse, in 1988, had resulted in hundreds of thousands of people being left to suffer the trauma of 'negative equity', a bland-sounding term for the harrowing situation of having bought a property which was worth far less than the mortgage taken out to purchase it. During the long stagnant period which followed estate agents were forced to tighten their belts. Branch offices closed, staff were made redundant and even the giant Prudential Insurance Company decided to pull out of the property market. Things had picked up over the last year or two, especially in London and the South East, but many firms were still licking their wounds.

'I wonder how badly affected he was by the recession,' said Thanet as they paused to look in the window.

'Look at that one!' Lineham was admiring an imposing modern house 'newly completed and in a select, tranquil environment'.

'Bit out of your price range, isn't it, Mike?' Thanet peered more closely. 'I don't know, though. It has got a granny flat.'

Lineham hastily moved away and pushed open the door.

Inside there were fitted carpets and four little islands of desks where negotiators sat talking into telephones or busying themselves with paperwork. One of them slipped on his jacket and rose to greet them. He was in his late twenties, neatly dressed in pinstriped suit, white shirt and discreet tie. His look of eager welcome faded at the sight of Thanet's warrant card. 'Mr Ogilvy is out, I'm afraid.'

'When will he be back?' said Lineham.

'I don't think he'll be coming back into the office this afternoon.'

'Where is he, exactly?'

'Visiting a prospective client, near Ashford.'

Must be an important client, thought Thanet, for the boss himself to visit him.

'Will he be going straight home afterwards?'

'I imagine so, yes. I'm not sure.'

Reluctantly he handed over Ogilvy's home address.

At the door Thanet glanced back. The young man was already dialling. Ogilvy's mobile, perhaps?

'So, what now?' said Lineham.

'We'll wait. Go and see him at home. Meanwhile we might as well catch up on some paperwork and save time later.'

Thanet took advantage of the open air to light up. Apart from a few puffs in the car on the way to work this morning he hadn't had a pipe all day. To his disgust Sturrenden Police Headquarters had recently become a smoke-free zone. Smokers had first been relegated to a designated smoking area (i.e. the bar) and then, when the bar closed, found themselves ousted altogether. In the face of gentle nagging from Joan and Lineham's aversion to tobacco smoke in any shape or form he had in any case cut down substantially on his smoking but he resolutely refused to give up altogether, partly because he enjoyed it so much, but also because a core of stubbornness in him refused to be emotionally blackmailed into doing so.

Back at the office there was a message to say that the landlord of the Harrow had been out when the officer called and another attempt to interview him would be made later.

'Better get him to check if Ogilvy was there last night too.' Thanet lowered himself carefully into his chair. Over the last hour he had become increasingly conscious of the dull ache in the small of his back and now he again thought that he must try to fit in a visit to the chiropractor. Like millions of other people Thanet had suffered from back trouble for years. None of the treatments he had undergone had had any lasting beneficial effect until a year or two ago, when he had given in to Joan's urging and, without any expectation of relief, had gone to a chiropractor. To his amazement she had worked wonders for him and treatments were now very rarely necessary. This, however, he decided, especially with the wedding coming up, was one of those occasions. He glanced at his watch. Three-forty-five. Perhaps he ought to take advantage of this brief lull and give her a ring now, just in case she might be able to fit him in. He reached for the phone. He was in luck. She had just had a cancellation for four o'clock. If Inspector Thanet could come along straight away . . . 'I'll be there,' he said. A quarter of an hour later he was submitting himself to Janet Carmel's expert ministrations. She was in her thirties, tall and slim with very direct blue eyes and long fair hair braided into a thick plait. As usual she was wearing a tracksuit and training shoes.

'You've been doing very well,' she said, as she followed her usual routine of testing for the vulnerable area. 'It's five months since your last visit.'

'Amazing!' said Thanet. 'I never thought I'd go that long without needing to see you.'

'Ah,' she said. 'Yes. That's it. Turn on to your right side, please.'

Fifteen minutes later Thanet emerged, feeling as if he were walking on air.

'That woman is an absolute miracle,' he said to Lineham. 'She is just incredible.'

Lineham, who had worked with Thanet in the days when he had been severely incapacitated, grinned. 'She certainly does wonders for your temper.'

'Temper? Me? Nonsense!'

'While you were out I checked on that prowler business. Jessica did file two complaints, one on September 28th, one on October 4th. Uniformed branch investigated but with no results.'

'I wonder if it was Kevin,' said Thanet. 'Say he'd developed a thing about her, from seeing her at the salon. She was a very attractive woman.'

'Bit long in the tooth for him, though, wasn't she? He's only, what, twenty, twenty-one?'

'Oh come on, Mike, don't be naïve. Older women and younger men are all the fashion these days. And in Victorian times it was considered quite the thing, I believe, to be initiated into the mysteries of sex by a woman with a bit of experience.'

'Are you suggesting that's what happened here?'

'No, not necessarily, especially if she was already having an affair with Ogilvy. Let's face it, there's no doubt he would have been a much more attractive prospect. It does sound as though wealth was something of a magnet for her and a hairdresser's apprentice doesn't exactly fall into the right category. On the other hand, open admiration is always flattering. She might quite innocently have smiled on him a little too warmly, fed his fantasies with false hopes.'

'But surely, if it was Kevin who was following her she would have recognised him?' Lineham shrugged, answered his own question. 'Not necessarily, I suppose, if he was careful not to get too close. Well, if you're right, and he was there last night . . .'

'Who knows what he might have seen? Exactly. Which is why I want to go gently on him at the moment, until we have a clearer picture. Now, if there's nothing else, I must try and get some of these reports done before we go.'

It was a quarter to six when they turned in between the stone pillars at the entrance to the drive of Ogilvy's house.

'Wow!' said Lineham.

'Stop drooling, Mike!'

But Thanet had to admit, it really was a lovely house. As Goldilocks would have said, it was neither too big nor too small, but just right, a Georgian gem of perfect proportions, with two tall sash windows on either side of the porticoed front door and five above. Its elegance was enhanced by the simplicity of its setting, a wide straight gravelled driveway flanked by young copper beeches and terminating in a perfect turning circle in front of the house.

'I suppose in his position he had the pick of the market,' said Lineham.

'I imagine so.'

'Doesn't exactly look as though he had to tighten his belt too much over the last few years, anyway.'

'Quite.'

As they reached the circle Thanet saw that the drive branched off it, left and right, maintaining the symmetry imposed by the house, and he glimpsed outbuildings behind and a car parked in front of them beside a horse box hitched to a Land-Rover. Lineham pulled up near the front door and they got out.

'Just a moment, Mike,' said Thanet with a jerk of the head, and they walked back to the corner of the house. 'I thought so,' he said. 'It's a red Polo.'

They looked at each other, remembering the red Polo

a neighbour claimed to have seen parked near Jessica's house the night she died. 'Mrs Ogilvy's?' said Lineham. 'I wonder if it's the same one.'

'Bit too much of a coincidence, if it's not.'

'That's what I was thinking.'

The door was opened by a girl in her late teens. The perfect oval of her face was emphasised by the way she wore her dark hair, sleeked back into a pony-tail. She was casually dressed in jeans and sweatshirt and was carrying a little dark-haired girl of about two who stuck her thumb in her mouth when she saw the two strangers. Had Ogilvy taken a child bride?

'Mrs Ogilvy?' he said.

The girl laughed, showing teeth of the degree of perfection normally seen only in toothpaste advertisements. She shook her head. 'I am Chantal.'

Even in those few syllables her nationality was obvious.

'And this is Daisy,' she added, giving the baby a little bounce and planting a kiss on the top of her head.

'Hullo, Daisy,' said Thanet, smiling. The child was enchanting, with huge brown eyes and a tumble of curls tied up in a bright red ribbon.

She turned her head away and buried her face in the girl's shoulder.

'Is Mr Ogilvy at home?' Thanet thought he might not be. There was no sign of the silver Mercedes. If not, he was prepared to wait.

But Ogilvy must have put his car away because Chantal stood back and invited them in. 'I will fetch him. Wait here a moment, please.'

They were in a wide hallway with a generously proportioned staircase running up the right-hand wall. Oriental rugs glowed on polished floorboards and framed prints hung on the walls above the dado rail.

Chantal disappeared through a door on the left and they heard a murmur of voices. A few moments later she emerged with two boys of about eight and five beside her, closely followed by a man. She went off up the stairs with the three children and Ogilvy came forward to greet the two policemen. He was in his early forties, with brown hair that was over-long at the back and already thinning at the temples. He had discarded his suit jacket and his trousers were held up by braces decorated with Rupert Bears, a fun present from his wife or daughter, Thanet guessed. Despite the *déshabille* he still contrived to look well groomed: shoes highly polished, blue-and-white-striped shirt still crisp, discreetly patterned tie firmly knotted. Introductions over he led them back into the drawing room which was as beautifully proportioned as the house and elegantly furnished with a large Persian carpet, swagged and tailed curtains at the tall windows, and comfortable sofas and chairs complemented by carefully chosen pieces of antique furniture.

A woman rose and switched off the early evening news as they came in.

'My wife, Inspector. Penny, this is Inspector Thanet and Sergeant . . .?'

'Lineham.'

Mrs Ogilvy acknowledged them with a nervous nod and an attempt at a smile before returning to her seat on the sofa. She was a good ten years younger than her husband, with long straight blonde hair and speedwell-blue eyes. Thanet liked her at once. Despite her obvious anxiety there was a candour about her, an openness of expression which appealed to him. She was dressed for riding in well-cut breeches and Puffa waistcoat.

'Sit down, Inspector, please,' said her husband.

'May we have a word in private, sir?'

'That won't be necessary. My wife and I have no secrets from each other.'

Thanet glanced at Mrs Ogilvy but she wouldn't meet his eyes. She was hating this, he could tell. 'It's up to you, of course.' He and Lineham sat down.

Ogilvy stood looking at Thanet, waiting for him to speak.

Deliberately, Thanet allowed the silence to prolong itself.

Ogilvy shifted from one foot to the other, then cleared his throat. He had a high colour which Thanet thought looked distinctly unhealthy and was slightly overweight too, not drastically so but enough for his belly to bulge over the waistband of his trousers.

'How can I help you, Inspector?'

'I expect you realise why we've come.'

Ogilvy glanced uneasily at his wife who refused to look at him. She was plucking nervously at a loose thread on the arm of the sofa on which she was sitting. 'It's Jessica, I suppose,' he said. 'We heard about it on the news this morning. Though I don't quite understand why the police are involved. The report said she had fallen down the stairs.'

'That's right. But there are one or two circumstances which make us question whether it was an accident.'

Mrs Ogilvy made an inarticulate little sound and pressed her hand against her mouth.

'Such as?' said her husband.

'I'm not at liberty to say.'

Mrs Ogilvy spoke for the first time. 'Inspector . . . are you saying someone might deliberately have pushed her?'

'Let's just say we're keeping an open mind at the moment.'

Her eyes flickered to Ogilvy and back to Thanet. 'But . . . but that would mean . . .'

Thanet and Lineham exchanged the briefest of glances. *She's wondering if her husband did it.*

As if she had tuned in to their thoughts she said, with more spirit than she had shown before, 'You're surely not suggesting my husband had anything to do with it?'

'Mr Ogilvy's car was seen in the vicinity of Mrs Manifest's house around the time she died,' said Lineham.

'And so,' said Thanet softly, 'was yours, Mrs Ogilvy.' Not strictly accurate, but worth a try.

They stared at him but did not deny it.

'All right,' said Ogilvy, 'I was there. I admit it. But I only stayed ten minutes, then I left. And I assure you that she was certainly alive and kicking then.'

'What time did you arrive?'

'Seven-thirty.'

And Manifest had left at 7.20. That made sense, if he had wanted to avoid Ogilvy. 'And you left ten minutes later, you say. At 7.40, then.'

'Approximately, yes.'

'Why did you stay such a short time?'

Ogilvy shifted uncomfortably. 'I had come to a decision.' He stopped.

Thanet waited.

Ogilvy glanced at his wife. 'We . . . my wife and I . . .

we'd discussed the matter and I had decided to end my – er – relationship with Mrs Manifest.'

Translation: his wife had found out what was going on and given him an ultimatum.

'You verify this, do you, Mrs Manifest?'

'Of course.' She compressed her lips and folded her arms across her chest as if to contain the distress which this conversation was clearly causing her.

'Could we go back a little then, sir. Would you tell me exactly what happened, from the moment you arrived at the house.'

Ogilvy shrugged. 'I got there about half seven, as I said. There was a bloody great hole in the road so I couldn't park outside. I parked at the pub instead and walked back.'

'Why not park a little further up the road into the estate?' said Lineham.

'I didn't want to attract too much attention. People always notice if you park in front of their houses. They seem to think the road belongs to them. And my car isn't exactly unobtrusive.'

'Go on.'

'There really isn't much to tell.'

'Presumably you didn't walk straight in, tell Mrs Manifest you wouldn't be seeing her again and walk straight out again?'

'No, of course not.'

'Well then. In detail, please.'

'I knocked at the door,' said Ogilvy. 'She opened it. I went in. Is this enough detail for you?'

Thanet ignored the sarcasm. 'That's fine. Do go on.'

Reading between the lines of Ogilvy's no doubt heavily

edited account Thanet imagined the conversation must have gone something like this:

'Adam! It's lovely to see you.'

'No, not upstairs, Jess. Let's go in here.'

'Why?'

'I can't stay tonight.'

'Why not?'

'I . . . Look, let's sit down for a minute, shall we?'

'What's up, Adam? There's something wrong, isn't there?'

'No. Yes. Yes, there is. Penny's found out about us.'

'So? That's wonderful! Terrific! I've hated all this hole-and-corner stuff. Now we can be together at last.'

'Hang on, Jess. I never said anything about splitting up with Penny.'

'But that was what you intended, wasn't it? Eventually?'

'You don't understand. I simply can't afford to run two households. The last few years have been hell in my business. But we've managed to survive and now, at last, we're starting to pull out of it –'

'Well, that's fine, then, isn't it? I can wait a bit longer.'

'But it'll be ages before we're properly on our feet again. Years, maybe. I have to put the business first. It's what we all depend on.'

'I haven't exactly noticed you going short. You still have your house, your cars, your horses, private schools for James and Henry and no doubt Daisy in due course.'

'It's essential to keep up appearances in order to maintain confidence in the business. If people saw me selling my house, sending my kids to state schools and driving a Ford instead of a Mercedes the word would go round in no time that I was on the ropes.'

'I see. So what, exactly, are you trying to tell me? That we're finished, is that it?'

'Yes. I'm afraid so. I'm sorry, Jess.'

'Sorry! I thought we had something special, but no, it sounds as though as far as you're concerned all it comes down to in the end is money, money, money.'

'That's not true. Of course it was special!'

'But not special enough. What a fool I've been! I was just a nice little bit on the side, wasn't I? You never had any intention of giving up your wife, your children, your home and life-style for me, did you? Get out. Go on, get out.'

'Jess, don't be like this. I hoped we could still be friends.'

'Just go, Adam, will you. Now.'

'And I can assure you that, as I said before, she was absolutely fine when I left,' Ogilvy concluded.

But if Jessica had gone straight upstairs after opening the door and Ogilvy had followed her and a similar conversation had taken place at the top of the stairs instead of in the sitting room as Ogilvy claimed, it would be only too easy to imagine it ending in disaster.

'Did the telephone ring while you were there?' said Lineham.

Ogilvy stared at him. 'Yes, now you come to mention it,

it did. Soon after I got there. But she didn't answer it, said the answerphone was on.'

Not surprising that Jessica had considered her conversation with Ogilvy of more importance, thought Thanet.

'Did Mrs Manifest come to the front door with you?' said Lineham.

'No, she didn't. Why?'

'Did you shut it behind you?'

'Yes, I think so. I must have. Yes, I'm sure I did. Why?' Ogilvy asked again.

'So,' said Thanet to Mrs Ogilvy. 'Where were you while all this was going on?'

She flinched at becoming the focus of attention. 'In my car,' she said with a lift of the chin.

'Waiting for your husband, presumably.'

'Of course.'

'Why?'

'I don't understand what you mean.'

'Why were you waiting for him?'

'Well, obviously because I wanted to hear how he'd got on.'

'Why didn't you accompany him in his car, then?'

She bit her lip and glanced at her husband. It was obvious what had happened. Ogilvy had promised her that the meeting with Jessica would be brief and she had followed him to see if he had kept his word.

'I . . . I didn't make up my mind until after he had left.'

Her husband came to her rescue. 'You thought it would be nice for us to go out for a drink together afterwards, didn't you, darling? Which is what we did,' he added, turning to Thanet. 'When I came out I saw my wife's car and realised she was waiting for me.'

'Where did you go for this drink?' said Lineham, though they were already pretty certain of the answer.

'To the Harrow. You can check if you like. There weren't many customers, they'll probably remember us.'

'Why not the Green Man? Your car was already parked there.'

'We wanted to go a bit further away.'

In case Jessica or her husband came in, thought Thanet. Ogilvy wasn't to know that it was to the Harrow that Manifest usually went.

They had, he said, arrived about 7.45 and stayed until around 8.30. Manifest claimed to have passed the Harrow about 8.15, so it was just as they had thought: he had probably intended to go in but had changed his mind when he spotted Ogilvy and his wife there.

Ogilvy claimed that they had arrived home at about 8.45.

'Is there anyone who can confirm these times?' This wasn't really necessary at this stage but Thanet wanted an excuse for a word with Chantal. Nannies have a pretty good idea of what goes on in a household.

'Chantal?' said Mrs Ogilvy to her husband.

'I'll fetch her,' he said.

'I'd better come with you, to look after the children.'

'Just one more point, Mrs Ogilvy,' said Thanet quickly as she started to move towards the door. 'Could you see Mrs Manifest's front door from where you were parked?'

'No, I couldn't.'

'And after your husband came out? Did you get out of the car?'

'No. He came across to speak to me.'

101

'Which way was your car facing?'

'Towards the village.'

'So you had to turn around, to drive to the Harrow?'

'Yes.'

'Where did you turn?'

'I backed into the road leading into the estate.'

'Did you happen to notice then if the door of Mrs Manifest's house was open?'

'No. I was watching that I didn't back into some traffic cones that were in front of her house.'

'I see. Thank you.'

Lineham waited until they had gone, then said, 'He must have been crazy, to run the risk of losing all this, those lovely children and that nice wife of his.'

'Yes, I liked her too. She doesn't trust him, though, does she? Following him like that to Jessica's house. And I'd say she wouldn't put it past him to have shoved Jessica down the stairs.'

'I agree.' Footsteps could be heard on the staircase and Lineham lowered his voice. 'I wonder when she found out about them.'

Ogilvy came back in with Chantal. 'There's no need to be nervous,' he said to her. 'Just answer whatever questions the Inspector asks.' He sat down on the sofa as if to underline the fact that he had no intention of leaving.

Thanet could have insisted, but decided not to make an issue of it at the moment. He could always come back later if necessary. He suspected Chantal wasn't too keen on her employer, which could prove useful. She quickly confirmed the times of departure and arrival Ogilvy had given them and they left it at that.

'All very well,' said Lineham when they were back in

the car, 'but I'd say he definitely goes on our list. We've only his word that Jessica was alive when he left.'

'Quite. Put Bentley on to investigating his background. Mrs Ogilvy's, too.'

'You don't suspect her, surely?'

Thanet shrugged. 'Just being thorough. They could be covering up for each other.'

'So, where now, sir?'

'I think it's time we had another go at Desmond, don't you? He's got rather a lot of explaining to do.'

EIGHT

They consulted the map to work out the most likely route for Ogilvy to have taken to get to the Manifests' house in Charthurst and discovered that it went past the Harrow.

'Explains why they chose that particular pub,' said Lineham. 'It was the first one they came to on the way home. And he must have passed it many times.'

Thanet agreed. 'Might as well call in, as we're going by. It's past opening time, the landlord should be there now.'

'Though I still don't get it,' said Lineham as he started the engine. 'Just think about it. You know your wife is expecting her lover so you obligingly go out. When you get home the front door is open and you find her dead at the bottom of the stairs. Then you learn someone rang for an ambulance from your own number. I mean to say, what would you think?'

'You forget, he was confused. He'd seen Ogilvy in the Harrow with his own wife only ten minutes before.'

'It doesn't take much intelligence to work out that Ogilvy'd have had plenty of time to visit Jessica first, though, does it? I really can't see why he didn't put us on to him straight away. Especially as it would have let him off the hook himself!' Lineham shook his head. 'I just don't understand him.'

'I've a feeling there's a lot we don't yet understand about him – or about Jessica either, for that matter.'

At the Harrow the landlord confirmed that Manifest was a regular customer, calling in two or three evenings a week. 'Though Des isn't exactly what you'd call a big spender. Only ever has one drink and makes it last more than an hour, usually. Not surprising, really, being as he's on the dole. I don't mind, he's a good bloke.'

'What about last night?' said Lineham.

'Ah, now that was very peculiar. He started to come in through the door then turned around and went straight out again!'

'What did you think?'

A shrug. 'That he'd seen someone he didn't want to meet, probably. It happens.'

'Any idea who?'

'No.'

'What time was this?'

'About a quarter past eight? Something like that.'

'And were you busy at the time?'

'Not particularly.'

'So do you remember if there was anyone in at the time who wasn't a regular customer?'

'A few, yes.'

'Who, for instance?'

The man frowned. He was big and beefy and didn't look as though he'd have much trouble controlling diffi-cult clients. 'Couple of American tourists, a businessman on his way home, a commercial traveller asking if we had a room for the night . . .'

'No one else?'

'Well, there was Mr Ogilvy, the estate agent. He's not exactly a regular, I suppose, but he's not a stranger either.'

'Was he alone?'

'With his wife. At least, I assume it was his wife, hadn't seen her before, he's usually by himself. A real looker, blonde hair, blue eyes.'

'Did Mr Ogilvy see Mr Manifest?'

'Don't think so. He was sitting sideways on to the door.'

'What time did Mr Ogilvy and his wife arrive?'

Another shrug. 'I don't time people's arrivals and departures, you know!'

'Approximately, then.'

'Oh, I don't know. They'd been here a little while before Des looked in, anyway.'

'What d'you mean by "a little while"? Five minutes? Ten?'

'No. Half an hour, more like.'

This fitted what they had been told.

'You didn't happen to notice if he came by foot or by car, did you?' It had occurred to them that if Desmond had borrowed Jessica's car this would have altered the time scenario considerably.

'On foot, as usual.'

'You're sure?'

'Positive. Like I said, things were quiet and I thought it was so peculiar he hadn't come in I went across to the window to see what he was doing. The car park's around the back, as you know, but he was walking off in the direction of Charthurst.'

'You could see him clearly? It was pitch dark.'

'We're well lit up, at the front. And he always wears one of those fluorescent safety straps. It was him all right.'

Lineham left it there.

'So,' said Thanet when they were back in the car, 'neither Manifest nor Ogilvy made that phone call.'

'There are only three possibilities,' said Lineham. 'Either someone else had a key and let himself in . . .'

'Unlikely, don't you agree?'

'Yes, I do. Or, Jessica was alive when Ogilvy left, as he claims, and she later opened the door to someone else.'

'Possible.'

'Or Ogilvy did in fact kill her but didn't shut the door properly and someone else got in, found the body and made the phone call.'

Thanet sighed. 'I think you'd better stop, Mike. It seems to me there are an infinite number of possibilities and at the moment we haven't a hope in hell of proving any of them.'

In any case, they had arrived. Allowing for the stop at the pub the drive to Willow Way had taken thirteen minutes.

'Looks as though the parents have gone,' said Thanet. The red Datsun was no longer there.

'Mmm.' The hole in the road in front of the Manifests' house was still roped off and Lineham was peering into it. 'A day's work for two men and it still looks exactly the same! How do they get away with it?'

'If it annoys you so much why don't you complain to the Council? Come on, Mike,' said Thanet as he approached the front door. 'We haven't got all day. I really have to finish my speech for Saturday tonight.' He rang the bell.

107

Lineham was grinning as he hurried up the path. 'I'm looking forward to hearing it.'

'I'll remind you you said that, when Mandy gets married!'

Amanda, the younger of Lineham's two children, was nine.

'I'm not going to start worrying about that yet!'

'I shouldn't be too sure of that. The expense is unbelievable!'

'I took out an insurance when she was born,' said Lineham smugly.

'Mike, has anyone ever told you that sometimes you are completely and utterly insufferable?'

'You have, sir.'

Grins gave way to solemnity as the door opened.

'Oh, it's you,' said Manifest with weary resignation, standing back to let them in. He was wearing the same clothes as this morning and still hadn't bothered to shave. Thanet wondered what he had been doing all day. It was always difficult in a case like this to tread the tightrope between suspicion and sympathy. If Manifest had had nothing to do with his wife's death and was genuinely in mourning for her, he deserved every consideration, but they couldn't afford to allow compassion to cloud their judgement and let a possible murderer off the hook.

There was an appetising smell in the hall and Manifest walked ahead of them into a cramped kitchen which was furnished with a cheap range of units, a huge refrigerator and a flap table neatly laid for one against the wall. With three men in the room there would have been no room to move and Lineham hovered in the doorway.

'I'm sorry if we're interrupting your supper,' said Thanet.

Manifest stooped to turn off the oven on the electric cooker. 'It's all right. I'm not hungry anyway. My mother insisted on preparing it, but . . . Let's go back in the other room, shall we?'

In the sitting room Thanet came straight to the point. 'Why didn't you tell us about Mr Ogilvy?'

Manifest blinked, then sighed. 'Didn't take you long to find out, did it?'

'That's beside the point! Withholding information in a possible murder investigation is a serious matter! If someone did push your wife down those stairs, don't you want to find out who it was?'

Manifest said nothing, merely hung his head like a schoolboy being reprimanded by the headmaster and stared glumly down at his clasped hands.

'You knew he was expected last night, didn't you, Des?' said Lineham. 'And you didn't go into the Harrow for a drink because when you arrived you found he was already there. And you couldn't understand it. That was why you said, "Why was he there? He should have been here", wasn't it? We actually asked you about that this morning. So why didn't you tell us?'

There was a long pause and then Manifest raised his head and held the gaze of first one then the other. 'If your wife had been having an affair,' he said, 'would you have found it easy to say so to a bunch of policemen?'

So, it was partly loyalty to Jessica which had held him back, thought Thanet, and partly a desire to hold on to the last vestiges of his privacy. If you have just received a mortal blow the last thing you want to do is expose yourself to further humiliation. 'You're right, of course,' he said. 'I'd have hated it. On the other hand, you must see that if we are to make any progress we have to be in full possession of the facts. And we've wasted a great deal of time finding out what you could have told us in the first place.'

'I suppose I should have realised it would only be a matter of time before you did find out. Jessica wasn't exactly . . . discreet. I just wanted to give myself a bit longer to think things over.'

'What things?'

'To try to understand it all.'

'What happened last night, you mean?' said Lineham.

Manifest shook his head and sat back in his chair. 'Oddly enough, not that so much, no. More what went wrong between us.'

Thanet wasn't surprised. He had seen this before – how someone who had suffered a catastrophic blow sometimes tried to avoid thinking about it by obsessively raking over the past. The psychiatrists probably had some jargon to describe the process – displacement activity, perhaps? Nor did it surprise him that Manifest apparently wanted to talk. If what the Bartons had said was true – and Thanet could see no reason for them to lie – Manifest must have been humiliated beyond measure by her openly taking her lover to bed while he himself was in the house. Thanet didn't think Manifest would have confided this to anyone and doubted that he would do so now, but in the long, dragging days of unemployment he must have spent many an hour brooding on the situation. Now that Thanet and Lineham knew about his wife's infidelity maybe the urge to talk about it at last was irresistible. 'And did you come to any conclusions?' he said.

110

Manifest rose, walked across to the window and stood gazing out as if to get a clearer view of the past. 'Only that it was mostly my fault,' he said.

'Oh come on, Des,' said Lineham. 'It's never just one person's fault.'

'Mostly, I said.' He turned around to face them, and leaned back against the windowsill. 'I mean, look at this.' His gesture took in the cluttered room, the cramped little house, the neighbourhood. 'She didn't expect this when she married me, did she?'

'But she did promise for better or for worse,' said Lineham.

'And she stuck to me when it all fell apart! She never gave up hope, you know, that it would all come right again.'

Thanet wondered whom he was trying to convince. Himself, probably. Thanet's own guess was that Jessica had been preparing to abandon ship with Ogilvy, an altogether better prospect. He thought that in Jessica's eyes her husband had probably become irrevocably a loser. He wondered if Desmond really had been a battered husband (but again, why should the Bartons lie?) and if so, whether the abuse had begun early in the marriage when Manifest was still a success or whether it had been born of Jessica's anger and frustration at the disastrous turn of events.

'The trouble was,' said Manifest, 'that Jessica needed security. And I really do mean needed it, like most people need food and drink. And unfortunately I couldn't give it to her any longer. That was why I appreciated so much the fact that she stood by me.'

To the extent that he was prepared to put up with

111

whatever treatment she felt like dishing out? thought Thanet. 'Why was that, do you suppose? Why did she need security so much?'

Manifest lifted his shoulders. 'I imagine it was to do with the fact that she lost both her parents when she was quite young. Her father died when she was six and her mother four years later. She went to live with her sister, who was much older than she was and married by then.'

'Yes. We've talked to her brother-in-law.'

Manifest pulled a face. 'Bernard.'

'You don't like him?'

'He's all right, I suppose. I just can't stand the way he smokes like a chimney and stinks like an ashtray.'

Lineham shifted in his chair, obviously longing to voice his agreement.

'Strange that it should have affected her so profoundly,' said Thanet. 'Obviously it's pretty traumatic for a child to lose both parents one after the other but at least she did have close family to take her in. If she'd gone into a children's home and been shifted from pillar to post it would have been a different matter.'

'I know.' Manifest had relaxed considerably by now. He returned to his chair and sat down, stretching out his legs and clasping his hands loosely in his lap. 'But there it was. It took me a long time to realise that the Jessica we saw on the surface – so self-assured and confident – was quite different from the person underneath.'

'What was she like underneath, then?'

'Insecure, as I've said. Pessimistic. Gloomy. Often depressed. And angry. For a long time I couldn't understand why she would blow up about quite trivial matters and then, eventually, it dawned on me. There was this

112

constant anger always simmering away beneath the surface, just waiting to erupt the moment something triggered it off.'

Thanet thought of the scene in the garden which the Bartons had described. An anger, then, which occasionally erupted into violence. An anger which might last night have erupted at the wrong moment, against the wrong person?

'Anger about what?'

Manifest shrugged again. 'Life in general, I suppose. I've had a lot of time to think about things over the last few years but I've never reached any cut and dried conclusions. I don't suppose you ever can, as far as people are concerned. They change all the time, according to circumstances and how life treats them. Look at me, now! You'd hardly recognise me as the man I was five years ago.'

Thanet hesitated. There was something he badly wanted to ask and he didn't know if Manifest would ever again be in the mood to talk so frankly about his wife. In Thanet's experience people often regretted such confidences later and tended to withdraw. He decided to risk it. 'Look, sir, there's a question I'd like to put to you. But it could be painful.'

'Go ahead. I don't suppose it'll affect me too much. I'm still pretty numb at the moment.'

'How do you think your wife would have reacted if Ogilvy had told her that he was breaking off the affair.'

Manifest tensed. 'Did he?'

'He says he did.'

'Last night?'

'Yes.'

113

'So that was why he didn't stay long. Poor Jessica! I suppose he'd found himself someone new. He was in the Harrow with a woman.'

'That was his wife.'

'Oh. What was she doing there?'

Thanet shook his head. 'I'm sorry, I can't go into all the ins and outs of the situation now. You haven't answered my question. How do you think Mrs Manifest would have reacted?'

Manifest stared at him. 'I don't know.'

'Would she have been crushed? Or angry? Pleaded with him?'

'No! She wouldn't have pleaded! She had too much pride. And she wouldn't have wanted him to know if she was really upset. She'd have kept that till later, when she was alone. But yes, she would have been angry. Furious, in fact.' He sat up with a jerk. 'My God, is that what happened? They had a row because he was leaving her, and he shoved her down the stairs? It all makes sense now.'

'It's much too early in the investigation to jump to conclusions, sir. That's the danger of being in possession of only half the facts.' Thanet hoped he hadn't been imprudent. He didn't want Manifest to do anything rash like rushing off to accuse Ogilvy.

'But don't you see?' Manifest jumped up out of his chair and began to pace about, swerving to avoid those pieces of furniture which projected into the limited free space. 'It must have been him! He's the one who made the phone call! Then he scarpered, before the ambulance got here, so he wouldn't be involved, the bastard!'

'He assures us that your wife was alive and well when he left.'

114

'Well he would, wouldn't he!'

'And,' said Lineham, 'the phone call was made at 8.11, only a few minutes before you yourself saw him in the pub with his wife. What is more, the landlord confirms that they arrived at around the time Mr Ogilvy claims, a quarter to eight.'

But Manifest was not deterred. 'OK, so he didn't make the phone call. But he still could have been involved in her death, before he left for the pub. Someone else must have found her and rung for the ambulance.'

'Who?' said Thanet, thinking *the prowler*? 'And how would he have got in? Mr Ogilvy swears he shut the front door behind him.'

'You've only got his word for that. Maybe he didn't. Or maybe he thought he had and the latch hadn't caught. It doesn't always.'

'The point is,' said Thanet, 'that all this is speculation. We have to wait and see what the scientific evidence tells us. Then we might have a clearer picture.'

Lineham waited until the front door had shut behind them and then said, '"Poor Jessica" indeed! Imagine being sorry for your wife because her lover had given her the push! Talk about weird!'

'I think he really cared about her, in spite of everything,' said Thanet as they got into the car. 'In fact, I think he's still in love with her.'

Lineham buckled his seat-belt, started the engine and switched the lights on. Dusk was now beginning to fall. 'I don't know about that, but I do think we're beginning to get a clearer picture of what went on last night, don't you?'

'Yes. Though there are still too many gaps for my liking.'

'Of course, the fact remains that he's right about Ogilvy. He could have done it before he left for the pub.'

'Has it occurred to you the same could be said about him?' said Thanet. 'All right, we know he couldn't have made the phone call, but we've only got his word for it that he was striding about the countryside in the dark between 7.20 and 8.15. What if he set out on his walk as usual, then thought, what the hell, I've had enough of this, I'm going back to have it out with them?' Thanet could tell by the expression on Lineham's face that he didn't like this idea.

'What would be the point, sir? If they were . . . brazen enough to go to bed together with him still in the house, they're not going to listen to him if he finally loses his temper with them.'

'To relieve his feelings, get it off his chest?'

'Possible, I suppose.' But Lineham still sounded unconvinced.

'But then, when he got there, Ogilvy had already left and Jessica was by herself. But Manifest had worked himself up to the point of having it out with her and that was what he did. With tragic results.' Having put the theory into words it seemed to Thanet that it was all too likely a scenario.

But Lineham was still reluctant to accept it. 'I think I agree with what you said earlier, sir,' he said, turning the tables. 'It's too early to jump to conclusions.'

Thanet grinned inwardly. *Very neat, Mike.* Then he yawned. 'I'm sure you're right. Anyway, I don't know about you, but I think we've had enough for today.'

'Can't wait to tackle that speech, eh, sir?'

Thanet grinned. It was a pleasure to see Lineham in a good mood, engrossed in the case. The sergeant had always loved his work. Maybe this was just what he needed to give him a sufficient boost in morale to lift him out of his impasse and help him to resolve his problems at home. With any luck Thanet wouldn't have to intervene after all.

It was a cheering thought and his spirits lifted further at the thought of an evening – what was left of it – at home alone with Joan. He was therefore not very pleased to find a strange car in the drive. 'Who on earth . . .?' he muttered, as he parked in the road.

Joan must have heard his key in the lock and came out into the hall to meet him. A savoury smell made Thanet's mouth water and his stomach give a protesting rumble at the thought of nourishment being further withheld. In response to his raised eyebrows and expression of dismay as he gestured towards the sound of voices in the sitting room, Joan whispered, 'James and Marjorie. Called in with a present for Bridget.'

Thanet scowled. 'Better say hullo, I suppose.' He was fond of James and Marjorie and was normally pleased to see them, but not now, at the end of a long day, when he was tired and hungry. He put his head around the door and greeted them with a smile.

Despite their declared intention of leaving at once it was another three-quarters of an hour before they did so.

'Poor you. You must be starving.' Joan went straight into the kitchen and took his supper out of the oven. She took the cover off the plate and a delicious aroma of lamb casserole with herb dumplings filled the air.

He sat down. 'That smells good.'

Half an hour later, with a cup of coffee beside him and his pipe drawing well he was a different man.

'How's the case going?' said Joan companionably. She was stretched out full length on the sofa with her shoes off. Tonight, she had announced, she was not going to do one single chore connected with the wedding.

Thanet had always discussed his work with her. Some policemen, he knew, shut the door on their working life the minute they got home, but he had never found it possible to do that. Joan was completely trustworthy and she had often helped him to see his way through a difficult case. He knew too that it helped her to cope with the often unreasonable demands his job made upon her if she felt, in however limited a way, a part of it.

'You have your hair cut at Snippers, don't you?'

'Yes. Why?'

'I was surprised, when we went there today. I wouldn't have thought it was your kind of place.'

She laughed. 'What is my kind of place, exactly?'

'Something a bit more, well . . .'

'Conventional?'

'Perhaps, yes. All that pop music –'

'Dull?' Joan persisted.

'Of course not!'

'Fuddy-duddy, in fact?'

'Perish the thought! You know I love the way they do your hair. It suits you perfectly. It's just that the atmosphere was a bit, well, brash, I suppose.'

'I agree,' said Joan.

'You do?'

'Unreservedly. But as far as I'm concerned, I'd be prepared to put up with anything so long as they cut my hair

118

as well as they do.' Joan ran her fingers through her mass of curls. 'They're the first place I've been to that could tame this lot. Dennis is a brilliant cutter.'

'Ah so, you have Dennis, do you?'

'Yes. Why all the interest, anyway? What were you doing there?'

'One of the apprentices is hovering on the fringe of this case. Kevin Barcombe.'

'Oh yes. He's washed my hair occasionally.'

'What do you think of him?'

The silence lasted a little longer than Thanet would have expected.

'Joan?' he said.

'I'm thinking. As a matter of fact, though I haven't consciously admitted it to myself before, I don't particularly like him.'

Thanet's brain clicked into a higher gear. 'Why not?'

'That's what I was trying to work out a moment ago. And the truth is, I don't know. He just makes me feel uneasy, that's all.'

'But why? This could be important, darling. Please try to think.'

She hesitated a moment longer, then said, 'It's his eyes, I suppose.'

'Ah! "The windows of the soul", as the saying goes. What you mean is, you find him creepy.'

'Yes.'

'Because you have a nasty feeling that something rather unpleasant is going on in his mind.'

'Yes.'

'Because of the way he looks at you?' Thanet found his hackles rising.

119

'No, that's the puzzling thing, that's not it. It's nothing to do with me, specifically, which is why I haven't given it much thought. And it's not the way he looks at other women, either. No, sorry, I'm not sure what it is exactly. Just an uneasy feeling, as I said. Why the interest, anyway?'

Thanet explained and Joan said, 'So, a prowler. Now yes, that would just about fit the bill, I think.'

They talked for a while longer about the case and then Thanet said, 'The frightening thing is that for the Manifests the whole thing fell apart because of something completely outside their control.'

'Him losing his job, you mean? Why frightening?'

'You do realise that he was in the same line as Alexander, don't you?'

'Oh. I see.' Joan swung her feet on to the ground and sat up. 'So of course you're wondering, what if the same thing happened to Bridget and Alexander?'

'I can't help asking myself that. I mean, that huge mortgage they've got . . . What on earth would they do if Alexander were to turn up for work one day and, like Desmond Manifest, find his desk had been cleared – which is, I understand, how it's often done?'

'So I've heard. It must be shattering. And I've no idea what they'd do. But look, Luke, you're just going to have to accept that if it came to the worst and that did happen, they'd simply have to cope with it in their own way. If we thought of every possible thing that could go wrong for them before they've even started, we'd go mad.'

'I suppose so.'

She left the sofa and came to kneel on the floor in front of him. She took his hand. 'You're finding this very hard, aren't you? To let her go.'

It was difficult to admit it, even to himself. He sighed. 'You're right, of course.'

'It's nothing to be ashamed of! She's always been your little girl and, let's face it, she always will be, in a way. But at the same time she's a woman now, and you have to allow her to be one.'

'I know, I know, I know! I'll manage it in the end, I'm sure. If only I were happier about Alexander.'

'Alexander is all right. He's kind –'

'Kind, after the way he ditched her!'

'He was younger then. Commitment is a frightening thing. Young people these days seem to find it very difficult. If he wasn't ready for it, it was only right for him to say so. I know Bridget was hurt but far better that he should go into marriage sure in his own mind that he's doing the right thing, than rush into it too soon and always wonder if he had. But now . . . No, I think they'll be fine. He's loyal, patient, hardworking . . .' She smiled up at Thanet. 'Just like you, in fact.'

'Like me!' Thanet was astounded. The successful, glamorous Alexander, just like him! 'Rubbish!' he said.

'I mean it. Come to think of it, that's probably why Bridget chose him.'

'For a sensible woman you do talk a lot of nonsense sometimes!' But secretly, the thought pleased him and he tucked it away for future examination.

NINE

'I remember Bridget once saying to me that she had decided she wasn't going to get married at all, she was going to be a career woman,' said Thanet to his reflection. 'It goes without saying that that was before she met Alexander.' He adjusted his tie. 'In fact, she was only six years old at the time.' He paused, then consulted himself. 'Too feeble? No, I don't think so. But I must get the timing right. A pause before "In fact".'

He had stayed up late last night putting the final touches to his speech and was now running through it for the second time this morning.

'Luke? You're getting behind.' Joan was calling up the stairs.

He checked the time. So he was. He slipped his jacket on, stuffed wallet, keys, loose change, pipe and tobacco pouch into his pockets and hurried downstairs.

Joan was in the hall, putting her coat on. 'I've got to get in early,' she said. 'One of my clients is starting a new job this morning and I want to see him before he goes to work.'

'Have you had any breakfast?'

She nodded. 'A piece of toast and a cup of tea.'

'Are you all right?' Despite her evening off she was still looking tired, he thought.

'Fine. How's your back this morning?'

Thanet moved experimentally. 'Much better, thanks, after that session yesterday. When is Bridget arriving?'

'I'm not sure. Some time this afternoon, I think.'

'Good.' He kissed her. 'See you this evening, then.'

In the kitchen he made himself a cup of coffee to accompany what Joan called his breakfast cocktail, an approved (by her) mixture of various cereals, fruit and yoghurt. Except on high days and holidays bacon and eggs were a thing of the past. At first Thanet had protested about the healthy regime she had instituted but by now he had got used to it – enjoyed it, even, though he had no intention of admitting it. By twenty past eight he was in the car on his way to work enjoying a few puffs of his pipe, speech forgotten, focusing on the day ahead. It was a crisp autumn morning with clear skies, bright sunshine and a touch of frost in the air. His spirits rose. While he deplored the senseless waste of human life, the challenge of a new case always excited him. He enjoyed the way it stretched him, forced him to exercise all his skills, all his ingenuity, all his patience. He liked meeting new witnesses, working out fresh lines of inquiry and following them through to their logical conclusion. Above all he enjoyed that incomparable feeling of elation when the days of striving finally bore fruit and he knew the mystery was solved. And this time, of course, there was the added bonus that with Draco away he wouldn't have the Superintendent breathing down his neck. He wondered what new information was awaiting him on his desk. By the time he got to work Lineham would no doubt have sifted through the reports as usual.

But surprisingly, Lineham wasn't there.

Thanet checked what had come in. A neighbour who regularly walked his dog at that time had been returning home at about twenty past seven on Tuesday evening and had seen Desmond Manifest set out on his walk 'as usual'. This backed up what the landlord of the Harrow had told them.

Much more interesting was the fact that Kevin Barcombe apparently hadn't arrived at Sally's, the night-club, until around 8.30. The doorman was a client at Snippers and knew him by sight. He remembered the time because he was keeping a close eye on it; his mother had been rushed into hospital that afternoon and he had been told he could ring and inquire how she was any time after 8.30 p.m. Kevin had been the last person to come in before he made the phone call.

Thanet sat back and thought. Kevin claimed not to have left home until 8.15, but Thanet was much more inclined to believe his mother, who said he had left at 7.45. Thanet worked out a possible scenario: Kevin drives to Charthurst, arriving at about eight. By this time Ogilvy would be cosily ensconced in the Harrow with his wife. Kevin parks at the pub and takes up his post behind the hedge opposite the Manifests' house.

Then what?

Say Jessica had fallen or been pushed down the stairs during a quarrel with Ogilvy and say Ogilvy had not shut the front door properly behind him as he claimed. Manifest had said that the catch was faulty. After a few

124

minutes Kevin realises that the door is ajar. He goes to investigate, discovers the body, phones for an ambulance and leaves. Yes, the timing of the phone call would be right, and if he left immediately Kevin would have been back in Sturrenden in time to have arrived at the night-club at around 8.30.

Alternatively –

'Sorry I'm late, sir.' Lineham arrived, out of breath.

'Nice lie-in, Mike?'

'Very funny. It's my mother. She rang before breakfast, said she'd had one of her "turns". I had to go and check.'

'Of course. Was she all right?' Mrs Lineham's 'turns' had haunted Lineham throughout his working life, had almost prevented him getting married at all. It was tempting to believe that she was invariably crying wolf but she was getting old and one of these days no doubt it would be serious, even fatal. In the very nature of things it would be the one occasion when Lineham decided to ignore her cry for help. He simply couldn't risk it and Thanet sympathised.

'Yes. It was just a dizzy spell. It had more or less passed off by the time I got there.'

'Good. Listen, Mike.' Thanet related the scenario he had just visualised, studying Lineham as he did so. The sergeant looked tired, exhausted, even, with deep pouches beneath his eyes and a grey tinge to his skin. Perhaps he should speak to him about his dilemma after all. He didn't want to interfere in what was, after all, a private matter, but things couldn't go on like this. On the other hand, Lineham was still functioning efficiently. Thanet could hardly take one late arrival as an excuse to broach the subject in view of the fact that Lineham was almost invariably at his desk before anyone else and never complained about late hours or extra duty. No, he would have to wait. If Lineham started slipping up, then that would be a different matter.

The sergeant was nodding. 'Yes. It could have happened like that. But if Kevin was there, there's no reason to think he didn't do it himself. Say Ogilvy left the door open, Jessica didn't realise, Kevin saw his opportunity to get in, and took it. Jessica is in her bedroom, hears footsteps on the stairs, comes out, sees Kevin, gets frightened –'

'Et cetera et cetera. Quite. Yes, it's possible, I grant you.'

'Anything else come in, sir?'

'The PM's been confirmed for this morning, that's all.'

'So, what next?'

'I was thinking . . . I'd like to get a bit more background material. Did you get the address of that schoolfriend of Jessica's – what was her name? – from Louise?'

'Barnes, sir. Juliet Barnes. Yes, I did.' Lineham fished out his wallet and extracted a slip of paper. 'She lives at Ribbleden. But if you want to see her this morning, she works as a chiropodist in the town.'

'How convenient!'

The morning meetings conducted by Draco's deputy were always brief and before long Thanet and Lineham were stepping out into the sunshine. Another bonus of this case so far, Thanet thought, was that a number of the witnesses worked in the town. He sometimes felt he spent half his working life driving around and it was pleasant to walk along Sturrenden's picturesque High Street occasionally acknowledging a smile or a hand raised in greeting. By now it was virtually impossible for him to take even the shortest stroll through the town without seeing someone he knew.

The chiropodist's practice was based in a terraced house just off the High Street. The receptionist, a prim starchy woman in her mid-fifties, was not amused at the prospect of having Mrs Barnes's list of appointments disrupted and it took patience, persistence and diplomacy to convince her that they really did need to see her employer as soon as she had finished with her current client.

Juliet Barnes herself was a different matter and without hesitation ushered them through into her surgery. 'Aren't you married to Louise Stark?' she said to Lineham as they went.

'Yes. You were at school together, I believe.'

'That's right. I see her around occasionally.'

'So she said.'

'It's about Jessica Manifest of course, Mrs Barnes – Jessica Dander, as you knew her,' Thanet said, as soon as the door was shut behind them.

'Yes, I heard what had happened. It's dreadful, really dreadful.' She was tall and well built, statuesque almost, with broad high cheekbones, shining blonde hair cropped short and earnest hazel eyes. She was wearing a white medical coat and exuded an air of professional efficiency. 'Do sit down.' She waved a hand at the only two chairs in the room and propped herself against the windowsill.

She waited until they were seated, then said, 'But why on earth have you come to see me? I haven't seen Jess in years. Well, I've seen her, of course, round and about, but we never used to meet on purpose or spend time together.'

'We're trying to fill in on Mrs Manifest's background, actually,' said Thanet. 'And we understand that you and she were close friends, when you were at school.'

'Yes, we were, at one time. But you know what it's like when you're young. You drift in and out of friendships; some last and some don't. Ours didn't, I'm afraid.'

'We're thinking particularly of the year you took your O levels,' said Lineham.

'My goodness! That's – what? Twenty years ago now! It hardly bears thinking about!'

'I know,' said Thanet, smiling. 'But if you could cast your mind back . . .'

'I'll try. What do you want to know?' She shifted uncomfortably against the window-ledge and Lineham stood up. 'Wouldn't you prefer to sit down?'

She smiled at him. 'Very well. Thank you. Though without wishing to be unhelpful I do hope this won't take too long. I have a full list of appointments this morning and if I fall too far behind I won't get a lunch break.'

'We'll be as brief as possible,' said Thanet. 'If you would cast your mind back, then, to that summer, the summer when you were sixteen. You and Jessica were friends at that time, I believe?'

She nodded.

'Now, we understand from Sergeant Lineham's wife that Mrs Manifest – we'll call her Jessica for convenience – was very bright, and you all expected her to stay on at school to take her A levels and go on to university, that in fact everyone was surprised when she left school that summer.'

128

'Yes, that's true. I was as surprised as anyone. I mean, she'd made her A-level choices and everything.'

'So what happened, do you think? What made her change her mind?'

'I really don't know.' Juliet's forehead creased as she frowned, remembering, and her eyes narrowed as if she were peering into the past. 'All I can recall is that when school broke up at the end of that summer term I was looking forward to doing all the usual things with her – playing tennis, swimming, going for bike rides and so on. Jess was especially keen on swimming and during the previous Easter holidays we'd gone every day. But for some reason she went cold on me and whenever I rang up to suggest we go out she had some excuse ready. I was really upset about it at the time and I'd just decided I wouldn't bother about her any more when she rang to say she was going to stay with an aunt in Bristol for the rest of the holidays. Then she wrote to say she loved Bristol, it was a great city, and she much preferred living with her aunt than with her sister and brother-in-law – and who could blame her? – and she'd decided to stay on there.'

'Why do you say, "who could blame her?"'

'She couldn't stand him. Her brother-in-law. What was his name? Bernard.'

'Why not? Any particular reason?'

'Have you met him?'

'Yes.'

'Well, there you are then. He's a creep, isn't he? And that stink, those perpetual cigarettes . . .'

'Was she going to continue her studies in Bristol?'

'I don't know. But I do know that things went wrong. The aunt fell ill, so much so that Jess couldn't cope alone and Madge – that's Jess's sister – had to go and help look after her, even had to stay over Christmas. Bernard went to join them over the holiday, I believe. Anyway, when the aunt got better Madge came back but Jess stayed on. And then, a month or two later, the aunt had a relapse and died unexpectedly so Jess came back to Sturrenden.'

'To live with her sister again, I presume.'

'At first, yes. But Madge's baby had arrived by then and I think Jess felt a bit *de trop*. She landed herself a dogsbody job on the *KM* and as soon as she was earning she moved out into a bedsit in Maidstone. You had to hand it to her. She really worked her socks off – went to journalism classes at nightschool and slowly climbed the ladder until she was a fully fledged reporter. You had to admire her for that.'

An inflection in that last sentence made Thanet say, 'I sense a reservation there.'

She grimaced. 'Yes, I suppose so. To tell you the truth; one of the reasons why we lost touch is that I decided I didn't particularly like her. She was very ambitious, of course, nothing wrong in that, but she became much too materialistic for my taste.'

There was no point in asking her to elaborate. Thanet didn't want to waste her time and he felt that she had told them as much as she knew. They thanked her and left.

'Interesting,' said Thanet as they emerged on to the street.

'Yes. I wonder –' Lineham dodged to avoid a young woman with a pushchair and Thanet saw that it was the Ogilvy's nanny, Chantal, with Daisy bundled up against the autumnal chill in bright red bobble hat and miniature ski-suit.

He seized his chance and minutes later they were seated in one of Sturrenden's many teashops, ordering coffee. 'I hope we're not holding you up too much, Mademoiselle . . .?'

'Chantal, please.' The perfect teeth flashed at him again as she took a box of breadsticks from her shopping bag and presented one to Daisy, safely ensconsed in a high chair. Daisy took it and holding it like a sword swiped the air with it once or twice before taking her first bite. 'No, not at all. So long as I perform my duties I am free to do how I wish.'

'Have you been with the Ogilvys long?'

'I come when Daisy is born.' She reached out to remove Daisy's hat, smiling at her. She was obviously fond of her charge.

The coffee arrived and there was a pause while it was served.

'Au pairs don't usually stay as long as that,' said Lineham.

Chantal took a sip of her coffee and grimaced slightly. 'I did not intend to. But Penny – Mrs Ogilvy – is very kind and she offer me more money to stay. And I think, well, why not? But I must move on soon.'

'Why is that?' said Thanet. 'This coffee's not very good, is it?'

'I understand that the coffee in England is much better than it used to be. But sadly, not everywhere. You must not stay with a family more than two years,' she went on, answering his question. 'It becomes too hard to leave the children. I know I will miss Daisy so much already. I keep on putting it off.'

'Your English is excellent,' said Lineham.

Another dazzling smile. 'Thank you. I try, and Penny help me. I ask her to correct me and she does. That way, I learn.'

'You're obviously fond of her, too,' said Thanet. It was a pity, for his own purpose. The girl might be too loyal to talk.

'Yes. I am.'

'But you're not so keen on her husband.'

Chantal gave him a startled look then a rueful smile. 'Oh dear. It is so obvious, then?'

'Not at all. We are trained to notice these things. You do understand why we're interested in him, don't you?'

She frowned. 'Yes. Don't do that, *chérie*.' Daisy had started sucking the breadstick and was now wiping the chewed end up and down the front of her ski-suit, leaving brown trails. 'If you don't want any more, give it to Chantal.'

Daisy handed it over with an angelic smile and said, 'Want my book.'

Chantal wiped the little girl's hands with a damp flannel which she produced from her bag then rummaged in it again. 'Say please.'

'Please.'

Chantal's hand emerged holding a book which she duly presented to Daisy. '*The Very Hungry Caterpillar*,' she said. 'It's her favourite.'

Lineham shifted impatiently, but Thanet was happy to let Chantal set the pace. He judged, however, that she was now ready for him to be frank with her. 'You know that Mr Ogilvy was involved with the journalist who died? That he admits to visiting her that evening? And that there is a question mark over her death?'

'She fell down the stairs, didn't she? You are suggesting he might have pushed her?' Chantal's eyes opened so wide that the whites showed all around the irises.

Thanet felt he had to reassure her. 'We really don't know at present and even if he did, we don't believe for a moment that he is a danger to anyone else. In fact, there are several possible suspects. But we do need to find out as much as we can about all of them. So if there is anything you can tell us, to help us . . .?'

She shrugged. 'In France everything is so different. A mistress, *pouf*, it is no big deal, as you say. But here . . . Penny was very upset, when she find out.'

'When was that?'

'On Tuesday.'

Thanet's pulse quickened. The day of the murder.

'She go to a coffee morning and when she come home she go straight up to her bedroom and shut the door. She does not come down for lunch and when I see her later her eyes, they are red from weeping. Then, when Mr Ogilvy come home, there is a quarrel.' She paused to extricate Daisy's finger from one of the holes in her book.

Don't stop now, begged Thanet silently. 'You heard what was said?'

Chantal lifted her slim shoulders. 'I was curious,' she admitted. 'I do not like to see Penny unhappy. I wondered what had upset her. So when I hear them start to argue, yes, I listen. It is my affair, after all. If there is something wrong between the parents, it will affect the children.'

'Quite. So what did you hear?'

'I couldn't hear every word, you understand, but Penny, she was accusing him of being unfaithful and he

133

was not denying it. She was very upset, she was crying and shouting. She is not usually like that. Usually she is calm and patient.'

Thanet waited. Across the table he could see Lineham silently urging her on. Daisy was mercifully quiet at the moment but the attention span of a two-year-old is brief, as they were both aware, and the next interruption might be the signal for Chantal to decide that it was time she gave her charge her full attention again.

'She tell him he must choose between this woman and her. She say that if he choose the woman she will fight for her home and her children and he would soon find he wouldn't be able to live – how do you say? – in the style to which he was accustomed. The business, you see, has not been good during the recession. Mr Ogilvy has been very worried at times. Just after I come, two years ago, things were so bad they were talking about selling their house.'

'I see,' said Thanet. And he did.

So did Lineham. 'So,' said the sergeant, outside, after they had waved Daisy on her way, 'someone spilled the beans at that coffee morning. Mrs O. presented him with an ultimatum and he knew which side his bread was buttered. No matter what Jessica said he wouldn't have given in.'

'Let's go and have another word with him, while we're in the town,' said Thanet. 'And we mustn't forget that we have only their word for it that his wife didn't get out of her car that evening.'

'You're still wondering if she was involved?'

'It's difficult to see how she could have done it by herself,' said Thanet. 'They must have gone off together

134

afterwards, as they claim, or how could she have known he was at the Harrow?'

'She could have spotted his car there, as she went by. It is on their way home.'

'True. But I don't see how he could have missed seeing her car when he left Jessica's house. I shouldn't think people normally park there, the lane's too narrow, I think she deliberately parked where she did so that he would see her.'

'So what are you suggesting, sir?'

'Well, say she was too on edge to bear just sitting still in the car, waiting for him to come out –'

'Yes!' said Lineham eagerly. 'And say Jessica had gone straight upstairs and Ogilvy had followed and his wife saw them in the bedroom – the Bartons said Jessica often didn't bother to draw the curtains, if you remember –'

'Quite. She might not have been able to resist the temptation to go and try to break up the tête-à-tête by knocking on the door.'

'No, she wouldn't have done that, surely?'

'Who knows? She was obviously in a state about the whole business. People often act out of character when they're deeply upset, do things they would never dream of doing under normal circumstances. And if Jessica opened the door . . . No, I don't think I can believe in this scenario.' They had come to a halt outside the premises of Ogilvy and Tate. 'Anyway, let's see what Ogilvy has to say for himself, if he's in.' Thanet was studying the advertisements. 'Look, your house hasn't been sold yet.'

'My house! At that price? Ha ha.' But Lineham paused to take another look at the photograph before following Thanet inside.

This time Ogilvy was in and they were ushered straight into his office. It was furnished with high-quality office reproduction furniture, a black leather executive swivel chair behind the desk and photographs of his wife and children in silver frames. He rose with a smile as they came in. 'Inspector. How can I help you?'

His bonhomie disappeared in a flash, however, when Thanet said, 'We find you've been less than frank with us, Mr Ogilvy.'

TEN

Ogilvy's eyes darted from one to the other. 'What are you talking about?' He sat down behind his desk again as if to establish who was in charge here and flicked his fingers at a couple of chairs nearby.

Thanet and Lineham moved them so that they were facing him squarely and sat down. The battle lines were drawn. Thanet could almost hear Ogilvy thinking: *What have they found out?* 'I'm talking about your account of what happened on Tuesday evening.'

Ogilvy's eyes narrowed.

'And specifically about the conversation with your wife, before you left to visit Mrs Manifest,' said Thanet. Was that a flash of relief he saw before Ogilvy's expression hardened?

'Conversations with my wife are a private matter,' snapped the estate agent. He picked up a gold propelling pencil and began rolling it to and fro between his fingers.

'I'm afraid you'll soon discover that where murder is concerned privacy flies out of the window. And in this instance the conversation was highly relevant to our inquiry.'

'How?' The monosyllable was like a gunshot.

'When we last spoke to you you said – What, exactly, did Mr Ogilvy say, sergeant?' It wasn't that Thanet couldn't remember but that a notebook was occasionally a useful weapon against a hostile witness. It can be intimidating to realise that every word you say is a potential boomerang.

Lineham dutifully shuffled back through the pages. '"My wife and I discussed the matter and I decided to end my relationship with Mrs Manifest."'

'Quite,' said Thanet. 'A fairly bland description of what actually happened, wouldn't you agree?'

'I don't know what you're talking about.'

'Oh come, sir. We now know that Mrs Ogilvy had only found out about your affair with Mrs Manifest that morning, and naturally she was extremely upset about it. That evening you quarrelled and she presented you with an ultimatum: give Mrs Manifest up or your marriage was over. And the fact of the matter was that when it came to the crunch you weren't prepared to risk losing your beautiful home, your wife and your children for the sake of your mistress.'

'I don't know where you've been hearing all this stuff,' said Ogilvy. 'Oh, I see! It's that bloody girl, isn't it? Chantal. Interfering little b—' He cut himself off, realising perhaps that he had gone too far.

Thanet said nothing. It didn't worry him that Ogilvy had guessed the truth. When Chantal had told them about the quarrel she must have realised that this would get back to her employer. But Thanet didn't think it would have worried her too much. She was quite capable of standing up for herself and in any case it was Mrs Ogilvy who at the moment was calling the shots in that household. She would soon put a stop to it if Ogilvy tried to fire the girl. And if the worst did come to the worst, well, as Chantal had said, she intended moving on soon anyway.

'I don't know what the devil she's been telling you,' said Ogilvy, 'but all this stuff about ultimatums is a load of rubbish.' He placed the propelling pencil precisely in the centre of the tooled leather blotter before him as if squaring up his thoughts, then said, 'It was all very unfortunate, really.' His tone had changed, suddenly become confidential, and he leaned back in his chair, adopted a man-to-man, somewhat quizzical expression. 'Ironic. You see, it's true my wife was told about Jessica and me on Tuesday, at a coffee morning she went to. Some well-meaning so-called "friend", I suppose,' he added vindictively. 'But the point is, I'd already made up my mind before that to break it off that evening. Sickening, wasn't it?' *To think I almost got away with it*, his expression said.

'Very annoying for you,' said Thanet.

Unsure whether he was serious or not, Ogilvy gave him a suspicious look. 'So you see, there was no question of ultimatums or anything of that nature.'

'Why had you come to that decision, sir? To break it off with Mrs Manifest?'

'I don't see that's any of your business.'

Thanet simply raised his eyebrows, folded his arms and waited.

'Well, if you must know, I'd got a bit fed up with the way she was carrying on.'

139

'Carrying on?'

Ogilvy sighed. 'Look, it all started really because, well, to tell you the truth, I was flattered. Right from the beginning she was the one who made the running. After all, she is – was – quite well known in the area and she was a very attractive woman. And I must admit she intrigued me. She was an interesting combination, you know, of career woman and – how shall I describe it? – vulnerability. Yes, that's it. Vulnerability.'

Ogilvy looked pleased with his description, as if he had just pulled off some difficult feat of terminology.

'But?'

'But lately, well, I'd been getting more and more . . . Oh hell, this is really very difficult . . . Well, uncomfortable, about her behaviour.'

'In what way?' But Thanet could guess. How many men would enjoy going to bed with their mistress under her husband's nose, so to speak? But he wasn't going to let Ogilvy off the hook.

The estate agent shifted uncomfortably on his chair as if the seat had suddenly become too hot to sit upon. 'Put it this way. Usually, if you're sleeping with a married woman, it's all hole-and-corner stuff. Neither of you is too keen for it to get back to your partner, you know what I mean? But in this case, Jessica actually seemed to enjoy parading our . . . relationship before her husband. And to be honest, I found that downright embarrassing. Well, wouldn't you?'

'But she obviously didn't.'

'No, not in the least! That's what I mean! In fact, she actually seemed to enjoy it. Poor sod, I couldn't help feeling sorry for him.' He gave a cynical laugh. 'And that's a

140

new one, isn't it! Feeling sorry for the husband you're cheating on! All the same,' and he leaned forward across his desk and lowered his voice, 'if you really do suspect that someone pushed her down the stairs, I'd take a long hard look at Manifest if I were you.'

'You're accusing Mr Manifest of murder?'

He backtracked immediately. 'Certainly not. I mean, not necessarily.'

'Did you see any indications of violent behaviour against his wife?'

Honesty struggled with the desire to shine the spotlight anywhere but on himself. 'Well, no, not exactly. He didn't say much. Just seemed rather . . . depressed.' Another cynical little laugh. 'Not surprising, really, is it? But he must have resented the way she was carrying on. Stands to reason, doesn't it?'

'So it was her treatment of her husband that, shall we say, put you off her?'

'Well, it does make you think. I mean, if she could treat him like that . . .'

'She could treat you like that too.'

'Exactly!' Ogilvy was warming to his theme now. 'But that wasn't the only thing.'

'Oh?'

'She had a nasty temper, you know. It used to come out in all sorts of little ways, whenever she was crossed or frustrated – in a restaurant if the service was bad, for example, or if she hadn't been able to get what she wanted out of an interview. With her husband it seemed to be there all the time, ready to flare up at the slightest provocation, and I saw signs that she was beginning to lose patience with me too. She was getting very pushy, pressing me to

141

leave Pen, go and live with her. But I never did have any intention of doing that. My wife and children are the most important things in my life.'

Not so important that you wouldn't risk losing them for the cheap thrill of an affair with a woman you weren't even in love with, thought Thanet harshly, the image of Daisy in her red bobble hat and mini ski-suit fresh in his mind.

'I'm sure you know what I mean,' Ogilvy was saying. 'Have you got any children, Inspector?'

'Two,' said Thanet reluctantly.

'There you are, then.' Ogilvy gave a saccharine smile, as one family man to another. 'Anyway, I think it was beginning to dawn on Jessica that she wasn't going to get anywhere. So one way and the other . . .'

'You were getting a bit fed up with her.' Although the picture of Jessica that Ogilvy was painting was an unattractive one, and Thanet certainly couldn't condone the way she had treated her husband, he couldn't help a twinge of sympathy for her. It seemed that nothing had ever gone right for the woman. 'Speaking of your wife . . .'

Ogilvy frowned. 'What about her?'

'Is she in the habit of following you about?' Thanet deliberately chose to be offensive in the hope of provoking Ogilvy. He succeeded.

The estate agent's nostrils flared and he put his head down like a bull about to charge. 'Frankly, I don't see that it's any business of yours. Just leave my wife out of this, will you?'

'I'm afraid we can't do that, can we, sir?'

'Why not?'

'It's obvious, surely. She was there, only yards away from the spot where a murder was committed.'

Ogilvy jumped up and, resting his hands on the desk, leaned forward and said angrily, 'Not while I was there, it wasn't! I repeat, Inspector: Jessica Manifest was alive and kicking when I left her house that night. I can't prove it but if there is any justice in this world – which frankly I'm beginning to doubt – sooner or later you'll find out that I'm telling the truth. And as for my wife, she has no involvement in this whatsoever. And now, if you don't mind . . .'

Thanet didn't budge. 'If that is true you have no reason not to answer my questions. If you refuse, of course, we can only draw our own conclusions.'

Ogilvy took a deep breath, then slowly subsided on to his chair. 'Very well,' he said wearily. 'But get on with it, will you? I do have a job to do.'

'When did you first notice your wife's car?'

'Just after turning out of the front gate. She told me she'd parked there deliberately, so I couldn't miss seeing her.'

'Was she in the car or out of it?'

'In.'

Was he telling the truth or not? Thanet couldn't tell.

'When you were in the house, did you go upstairs at all?'

Ogilvy looked surprised at the sudden change of direction. 'No. Why?'

'And you're absolutely certain that you shut the front door behind you?'

'Yes! I told you!'

'Did you check that it was properly shut?'

'No. I just slammed it.'

Ogilvy couldn't hide his relief as Thanet rose.

'Well, I think that's all for the moment, sir. Thank you.'

'It's very odd,' said Lineham when they were outside, 'the more we learn about her the less I like her, but the more sorry for her I feel.'

'I know. A paradox, isn't it? Who did you put on to investigating the Ogilvys' background? Bentley? It'll be interesting to see what he turns up.'

Lineham clapped a hand to his forehead. 'Oh no! I forgot to brief him! I meant to do it first thing this morning, then I was late, of course.'

'Not like you, Mike.' Was this the first of the slip-ups Thanet had been afraid might happen? He sighed inwardly. It looked as though he was going to have to tackle Lineham about his domestic situation after all. 'Anyway, no harm done, very little time has been lost. Do it when we get back.'

They were now passing Snippers.

'There's Kevin,' said Lineham.

The boy was in the window, rearranging the wigs on some model heads with improbably classic features against a swathe of black velvet. He caught sight of the two policemen outside and Thanet glimpsed a flash of fear in his eyes before he turned away without acknowledging them and busied himself with his work. Something tweaked at Thanet's memory and his stride faltered as they moved on.

Lineham had noticed. 'What?'

Thanet shook his head. 'Nothing. Well, there was something, but I don't know what it was.'

'What sort of thing?'

'I don't know.' He frowned. What could it have been?

'I thought he looked frightened when he saw us,' said Lineham.

'So did I.' Thanet was still struggling to place what it was that had disturbed him. He took a few more steps and then paused to glance back over his shoulder. From this distance the tableau in the window of Snippers looked positively surreal, the disembodied model heads with their unnaturally perfect tresses seeming to float at different heights against the dark background. Kevin bent to pick something up and briefly his hair flamed as it caught the sun. Red hair. Suddenly Thanet understood.

Lineham, who had stepped behind him to allow a woman with a shopping trolley to pass, had cannoned into him. 'Sorry, sir!'

'My fault,' said Thanet, mind in turmoil. The tumblers in his brain were turning, click click click.

'You've realised what it was,' said Lineham, recognising that look.

'Yes, I have. Look, I know it's a bit early, but let's go and have a bite, Mike, and I'll explain.'

'Where shall we go?'

'How about the Woolsack? We haven't been there for ages.'

'Fine by me.'

Thanet chose a baguette with crispy bacon and mushrooms, Lineham a ploughman's platter. English pub food, thought Thanet, seemed to get better and better. The sergeant waited until they were seated at their table before saying eagerly, 'Well?'

145

'You can work it out for yourself, Mike, it's really very simple. Just a matter of making the right connections. Put it this way: what colour was Jessica's hair?'

'Auburn. First thing I noticed about her. Gorgeous, wasn't it?'

'And what colour is Kevin's?'

'Carrot.' Lineham's face went blank as he saw what Thanet was getting at. 'And Kevin was adopted,' he said slowly, obviously taking in the implications.

'Exactly!'

'So the reason why Jessica left school unexpectedly that summer was because she was having a baby. And that,' said Lineham, speeding up as he warmed to his theme, 'was why she wouldn't go swimming with Juliet Barnes during the summer holidays –'

'And why she went to stay with an aunt in Bristol –'

'And stayed there when the holidays were over!' finished Lineham. 'Yes, it all fits, doesn't it!'

'A bit far out, though, don't you think, Mike?'

'I'm usually the one who says that!'

There was a pause while the food was served.

Lineham loaded a piece of french bread with cheese and pickle, popped the food into his mouth and chewed thoughtfully. 'It all depends on whether Kevin really was the prowler. If he was, then you may well be right. Adopted children often seem to want to trace their biological parents, especially their mothers, when they get to Kevin's age. And if he did, he may well have been trying to pluck up the courage to tackle her. I've often thought it must be a hell of a thing, to walk up to the door of a complete stranger and say, "Hi, I'm the baby you gave up for adoption all those years ago."'

146

'And a tremendous shock for the mother, too. Mmm. This looks delicious.' The baguette was positively bulging with bacon and mushrooms and Thanet's mouth filled with anticipatory saliva. He took a huge mouthful.

'So,' Lineham went on, 'say he'd been hanging around, keeping an eye on her, watching for his moment. What time did we say he would have arrived on Tuesday evening? Around eight? Ogilvy claims to have left at twenty to, which fits with him arriving at the pub a few minutes later. Say he did leave the door open – Kevin would soon have noticed that it was ajar . . .'

Thanet had finished chewing and he swallowed. 'If she was still alive, wouldn't Jessica have noticed that it was open in the interim?'

'Not necessarily, if she stayed in the sitting room after Ogilvy walked out on her.'

'I suppose.'

'So if Kevin decided to investigate, pushed the door open . . . There are two possibilities, aren't there: Jessica was already dead, in which case he rings for an ambulance and gets out of there as fast as he can, or . . . Let me see . . . If she was in the sitting room as you suggest, she'd probably have heard him come in, so she calls out –'

'Comes into the hall –'

'Panics –'

'Runs upstairs –'

'Kevin follows, to try to reassure her –'

'She thinks he's chasing her, they struggle and –'

'That's it!' said Lineham. 'She falls.'

They both concentrated on their lunch for a few minutes, thinking.

'It could have happened like that,' said Lineham at

147

last. 'If it did, he'd have panicked himself then, made that phone call and scarpered.'

'Yes, but as far as I can see our only hope of proving beyond doubt that he was behind that hedge is a saliva test on those cigarette ends. And as yet we don't even know if he smokes.'

'Easy enough to find out.'

'True. But I think the first thing to do is tackle Jessica's brother-in-law again, find out if she really did have a baby. She was living with them at the time, he'd have had to be in the know.'

Lineham groaned. 'Let's try and catch him in the open air. I don't think I could stand another session in that stinking living room.'

'We might not have any choice.'

They decided to drop in at the office before going to see Covin and had been there only a minute or two when the door opened and Mallard bounced in. Thanet never ceased to marvel at the new lease of life which the police surgeon's second marriage had given him. For years after his first wife died of lingering cancer the little doctor had been one of the loneliest, saddest men it had ever been Thanet's misfortune to meet. He had continued to work but there had been no joy in his life and he had quickly acquired the reputation of being cranky and short-tempered. Since his marriage to the cookery writer Helen Fields a few years ago, however, he was a changed man, radiating good humour and contentment. An added bonus was that from one year to the next, he never seemed to age. It was a pity, thought Thanet now, observing the police surgeon's bright eyes, clear skin and his general air of well-being, that happiness couldn't be

148

doled out on the NHS. The geriatric wards and nursing homes would empty in no time.

'Morning both,' said Mallard, beaming. 'Thought you'd like a verbal on the PM.'

'So what's the verdict?'

'Nothing very exciting, I'm afraid, nothing unexpected. To put it in lay terms, she died of a broken neck.'

'Instantly?'

Mallard shrugged. 'Assuming that she wasn't moved after she fell, then yes. As we've said before, if anyone did move her, then it's a different story. But there's no way of telling.'

'And that's it?'

'Afraid so. Sorry I can't be of more help.' He bustled towards the door. 'Must get on.' With one hand on the doorknob he paused. 'You hoping to get this case cleared up before Saturday?'

'Ha ha,' said Thanet. 'Very funny.'

'Not going well?'

Thanet pulled a face. 'Slowly, that's all.'

'You never know. Miracles can happen. When's Bridget coming home?'

'Today.'

'Helen asked me to tell you she's finished decorating the cake, if Bridget and Joan would like to pop round to take a look.'

'Fine. Thanks, I'll tell them.'

With a wave of the hand Mallard was gone.

'Not much help there, then,' said Lineham gloomily.

'Well we didn't really expect anything else, did we? Come on, Mike. Let's go and see what Covin has to say.'

ELEVEN

'We're looking for Mr Covin.' Thanet had to raise his voice above the barking of a Labrador/Collie cross.

Covin's house was shut up and they had gone to the main house to inquire whereabouts on the farm he might be working. It was a typical Kentish farmhouse of rosy red bricks to the first floor with tilehanging above. Someone was a keen gardener: the lawns were trim, the flowerbeds immaculate and still colourful with Michaelmas daisies, late roses and dahlias. The door had been opened by one of the tallest men Thanet had ever come across. He reckoned that Covin's employer must be a good six foot five and his build matched his height. He was in his sixties with grizzled hair cropped very short and the kind of tan acquired only by those who work outdoors in all weathers. He was wearing sturdy corduroys worn thin on the thighs and knees and a padded waistcoat over a thick checked shirt. 'Quiet, Ben! Sit!' he said, and the dog subsided, reluctantly lowering its haunches on to the flagstone floor.

'Do you happen to know where Mr Covin might be, Mr . . .?' said Thanet into the blissful silence.

'Wargreave. James Wargreave,' said the farmer.

'We're investigating the death of his sister-in-law, Mr Wargreave.' Thanet produced his warrant card.

'I'm afraid you're out of luck. He's out and won't be back until around five.'

'May I ask how long he's been working for you?'

'Twenty years or so.' Wargreave frowned. 'Why? Is he in trouble?'

'Not at all. It's just that we're trying to fill in some family background. I wonder, would it inconvenience you too much if we had a brief talk?'

Wargreave stood back. 'If you think it'll help.'

There was a savoury smell in the hall and a clatter of dishes from the kitchen.

'I hope we're not interrupting your lunch.'

'Oh no, we've just finished. We were washing up.'

He took them into a square sitting room which had a comfortable lived-in air. The soft furnishings were faded and threadbare in places but there were books and newspapers and some knitting bundled up on one of the armchairs as if its owner had just put it down for a moment and would soon return.

'Who is it, James?'

A little barrel of a woman appeared in the doorway drying her hands on a tea towel. She went to stand beside her husband. Jack Sprat and his wife, thought Thanet. She couldn't have been above five feet tall and with her rosy cheeks, untidy bun and voluminous apron she was almost a caricature of a farmer's wife, a model for the illustrations in children's picture books. But her eyes were bright with intelligence as she listened to her husband's explanation and Thanet guessed that she didn't miss

151

much. Good, he thought. If anyone could sum up the Covin household, she would.

'Sit yourselves down,' she said. 'Though I can't see how we can help. We hardly knew her really, did we, James? Poor girl, what a terrible thing to happen.'

When they were all settled Thanet said, 'When, exactly, did the Covins come to work for you?'

They consulted each other with a glance.

'Nineteen seventy-eight?' said Wargreave. 'Or was it 1977?'

'It was a couple of months before Mum died, I do remember that – that was on February 27th, 1978.'

'That's right,' said her husband. 'So it must have been the beginning of January that year.'

The January after Jessica took her O levels, thought Thanet. 'And was Mrs Manifest living with them then?'

'No. She was staying with an aunt, I believe,' said Mrs Wargreave. 'Then in the spring the aunt died so she came to live with the Covins. But it was only a month or two before she moved into a bedsit, in Maidstone. You know what these teenagers are like, they all want their independence.'

'And it was more convenient for her work, of course,' said Wargreave. 'She'd found herself a job on the *Kent Messenger* and she didn't have any means of transport. She was very excited about it, I remember.'

'So you see, we hardly knew her. She never visited her sister much. I don't think she got on too well with Bernard – at least, that was my impression.'

And Thanet's impression was that Mrs Wargreave wasn't too keen on Covin either.

'How did she seem when she came here?' said Thanet.

Mrs Wargreave's forehead creased into unaccustomed folds. Smiles rather than frowns were more her line, Thanet guessed. 'In what way?'

'Was she cheerful or depressed?'

'She looked a bit peaky when she first arrived, I thought.'

Not surprising, if his theory was correct, thought Thanet. But come to think of it, why wouldn't Jessica have had an abortion? Perhaps he was barking up the wrong tree.

'But she soon picked up,' said Mrs Wargreave. 'I assumed she'd been upset by her aunt's death. She was only a young girl, after all, it must have been pretty distressing for her.'

'Where were they living before they came here?' said Lineham.

'Bernard was assistant farm manager at a farm near Headcorn,' said Wargreave. 'He went there straight from college, as I recall.'

'What was the name of his employer?'

'Pink.'

Lineham made a note.

'So he must have been working there for what, ten or twelve years?' said Thanet.

And Jessica would have been living with the Covins for six of those years, thought Thanet. Perhaps the Pinks should go on his list of people to interview. They would have seen her grow from child to teenager, might even have had some inkling of the pregnancy, if there had been one.

'Is Mr Covin a good manager?'

Wargreave shrugged. 'I've got no complaints. He's

conscientious, hardworking, honest . . . I think that's as much as one can hope for these days.'

'But Mrs Wargreave wasn't too keen on Covin, I thought,' said Lineham when they were back in the car. They would return to interview Covin later. 'Perhaps she can't stand the smell of him either. They were both non-smokers, did you notice? There wasn't an ashtray in sight.'

'Mike,' said Thanet, who had been trying to work out the best way to approach the subject, 'there's something I want to talk to you about. Pull in over there, will you?'

'There' was an empty layby and after a troubled glance at Thanet Lineham did as he was asked. He switched off the engine and silence descended.

Thanet wound down his window and took a deep breath of fresh air. There was a post-and-rail fence on their left and beyond that the ground fell away to a little valley where sheep were peacefully munching away at what was left of the grass after the long hot summer. At moments like this Thanet wondered why on earth he didn't suggest moving out into the country. Now that the children were grown and easy access to public transport was not so important, it would be perfectly feasible to make a move. Perhaps he ought to suggest it? Perhaps, with Bridget's wedding, he and Joan would move into a new phase of their life together. He became aware of Lineham's expectant silence and realised that he was merely prevaricating, reluctant to broach a difficult subject. 'I was just wondering if you'd got any closer to making a decision about your mother. I don't want to intrude on a private matter, but I am concerned about you. And apart from anything else, I feel it's beginning to interfere with your work.'

Lineham sighed. 'You're right, I know you are. It's just so difficult.'

'I appreciate that. But putting off the decision isn't going to make it any easier, is it, Mike? I'm sure that by now you've looked at the options from every possible angle.'

'And some,' said Lineham with a groan. 'The trouble is, the problem just isn't going to go away. In fact, if anything it's going to get steadily worse. I mean, let's face it, her health has been gradually deteriorating over the last few years. She keeps on asking why she can't come and live with us, and it gets harder and harder to put her off.'

'And you and Louise both agree it wouldn't work?' Thanet put the question as a matter of form. He already knew the answer.

'Louise and Mum could never live happily under the same roof! They've never got on very well, as you know. They just seem to rub each other up the wrong way.'

Because they were too alike, Thanet suspected.

'But if you do as your mother suggests, sell both houses and buy a larger one with a granny annexe – like the one we saw in Ogilvy and Tate's window . . .?'

But Lineham was shaking his head. 'I still can't see it working. We're both out all day and I think what Mum really needs is company. The truth is, she's lonely and she's bored, it's as simple as that, and living in a granny annexe wouldn't help. Apart from anything else, having been alone all day she'd want to share our evening meal and spend the evenings with us, I'm sure she would. I'm very fond of Mum, you know I am, but it would drive Louise and me round the bend, never having any privacy.'

'Then you'll just have to look for some kind of alternative solution.'

'Such as? She'd never go into a home, I'm sure of that, and in any case she doesn't need to. She's perfectly capable of looking after herself.'

'What about sheltered housing, with a warden on call?'

'We've discussed that and I don't think she'd be much better off than she is now. It's true that someone would be at hand in an emergency but I honestly don't think she'd be any happier.' Lineham sighed again, a deep, despairing sigh. 'I only hope I won't end up being a burden on my children.'

'Don't we all?' said Thanet. 'Unfortunately we all end up having very little control over that particular situation. The trouble is, the perfect answer doesn't exist, it's bound to be a matter of compromise all along the line. We just have to muddle along and try to find the best solution we can, and it isn't easy. In the end it's bound to come down to choosing the least unacceptable alternative.'

'Don't I know it!'

'Wait a minute!' said Thanet suddenly. 'I've just thought of something. I remember my mother mentioning some organisation to me that she seemed to think was very good. A friend of hers had gone into one of their homes and my mother had visited her there and was very impressed.'

'I told you, Mum would never even consider a home.'

'But these aren't conventional homes at all, not the sort where the residents sit around the walls staring at a television set all day. It's coming back to me now. For a start, they only take a small number of residents – ten at the most, I think. They're really more like family homes, for people who are still fairly independent but would benefit from some degree of being looked after and from having

156

company available to them should they want it. So far as I can recall, they have their own rooms, with their own furniture, but there's a communal dining room and sitting room and the place is run by a resident housekeeper who provides lunch and tea each day. But they're free to go shopping, go to church, visit relations, in other words live as normal a life as possible. Mum said if ever she couldn't go on living alone she'd be happy to go into one herself.'

Lineham was listening avidly but now he pulled a face. 'It all sounds too good to be true, but horribly expensive.'

'Apparently not. Mum told me that it's a charity, and that residents pay rent according to what they can afford.'

'How old is your mother now?'

'Eighty.'

'Eighty! And she still lives alone quite happily?'

'Yes. She's amazing.'

When Thanet's father had retired his parents had, like so many, decided to leave the increasingly crowded southeast and move to the West Country. They had bought a bungalow in a village near Salisbury and had settled happily into community life. Unfortunately, only four years later Thanet's father had died suddenly and unexpectedly of a heart attack and Thanet had thought his mother might return to Sturrenden to be near him and his family. Instead she had stayed on, declaring that life in Wiltshire suited her very well and she had no intention of leaving it unless she were forced to by ill health. So far, however, she had been lucky.

'She's coming to the wedding, of course?'

'Wild horses wouldn't etc.,' said Thanet, grinning. 'We offered to go and fetch her by car but no, she said she

157

always enjoyed the train journey. You can see so much more than from a car, she says. And as the Salisbury trains go into Waterloo she doesn't even need to cross London from one mainline station to another to transfer to the Sturrenden line. So we're meeting her at the station tomorrow afternoon.'

'Well, I just hope I'm as fit and active at eighty,' said Lineham. 'Anyway, what's this amazing outfit called?'

Thanet frowned. 'That's what I'm trying to remember. Something with a monastic flavour to it, I think, though it's not connected to any religious organisation. I can easily find out, anyway. I'll give her a ring when we get back.'

'Thanks, sir. It does sound good. Though whether Mum will listen or not is another matter.'

'You can but try. I think the thing to do is to emphasise the fact that it is not a normal type of residential home at all. Best of all would be to take her to look at one, let her meet some of the residents and talk to them.'

'Always assuming there is one in this area.'

'True. Perhaps it would be sensible to find out before mentioning it to her.'

'Yes. It would be infuriating to get her all interested only to find that there just aren't any around here.'

As a matter of principle, Thanet did not usually make private telephone calls from the office, but as the matter was affecting Lineham's work, on this occasion he felt justified in doing so. His mother was surprised to hear from him during working hours but at once gave him the information he needed and said how much she was looking forward to the wedding.

'Why don't you let us come and fetch you? It would only take a couple of hours.'

'Certainly not! You've got enough on your plates, I'm sure. Besides, I've already bought my ticket and I'm really looking forward to the journey.'

'See you tomorrow evening, then.'

'The Abbeyfield Society,' he said triumphantly to Lineham as he put the phone down. 'I told you it had a monastic flavour. And its headquarters are in St Albans, so you can get the number from directory enquiries.'

'Is it OK if I ring from here, sir? By the time I get home I imagine their office will be closed.'

'Go ahead. You must try and get this sorted out.' Thanet occupied himself with some paperwork while Lineham was making his call. 'Well?' he said, when the sergeant had finished.

'Some good news and some bad. The first bit of good news is that there is an Abbeyfield House in the area, in Maidstone –'

'Excellent.'

'The bad news is that there's usually a long waiting list for places, and that they don't often come up.'

'Oh.'

'You have to wait for someone to die, I suppose.'

Thanet pulled a face. 'Quite.'

'However, the other piece of good news is that they're hoping to open a new Abbeyfield House in Sturrenden in the spring of next year. Apparently they've found suitable premises and the sale is going through at the moment.'

'That's a bit of luck. So it might be possible to get your mother's name down on a waiting list.'

'Exactly! Meanwhile, I've got the number of the Maidstone house to arrange a visit if Mum would like one. I must say, they were very pleasant and helpful.'

'Good.' Thanet couldn't help feeling pleased with himself. There was a long way to go, of course, before the matter was settled. Meanwhile one of the main obstacles, he felt, was going to be the attitude of Lineham himself. 'Look, Mike,' he said, 'before you broach the subject with your mother I think you have to settle in your own mind what you feel about this yourself. If you really do think that having to share a roof with her is out of the question, you'll just have to bring yourself to be honest and say so. For one thing it's unfair to her to keep her dangling, and for another, well, to put it bluntly, as there seems to be no way of pleasing both your mother and Louise, however painful it might be you're going to have to disappoint one of them. Otherwise you're going to end up pleasing neither.' Thanet was thankful he himself had never been in that position.

'I know. I do realise that and I'm well aware that I've been burying my head in the sand because there just didn't seem to be any way out. But this really does sound a possible solution.'

'Let's keep our fingers crossed,' said Thanet.

Back at the farm they ran Covin to earth in the packing shed, which was filled with the rich, fruity aroma of ripe apples. The packers had gone home for the day and the grading machine and conveyor belt had been switched off. The shed was a high-ceilinged structure divided to provide office and communal rest room along one side. The internal walls were glazed above waist height and a light burned in the office where Covin was busy with paperwork. Predictably, he was smoking.

'Let's try and get him outside,' whispered Lineham as they knocked at the door.

160

Covin raised his head, saw them through the glass and beckoned them in.

The room smelled almost as bad as the man's sitting room but Thanet had no intention of giving Covin a psychological advantage by asking him a favour right at the beginning of the interview. Lineham would have to grin and bear it. The sergeant had left the door open and remained standing nearby. Wisps of smoke curled past him into the huge empty space beyond.

'Is this important, Inspector?' Covin hadn't got up. 'I don't want to be unhelpful, but I've been out most of the day and I've got a lot of paperwork to catch up on.' He gestured at the littered desk.

'Yes, I know. We came out to see you earlier.'

Covin frowned. 'Oh?' He removed a strand of tobacco from the tip of his tongue and wiped his finger on his trouser leg. 'What's so important?'

'We think you've been less than frank with us, Mr Covin.'

He stubbed the cigarette out in an overflowing ashtray and stood up, leaning against his desk. He folded his arms defensively. 'What are you talking about?'

An acrid smell of burning filter drifted up between them. Thanet suppressed the urge to point out that he hadn't put his cigarette out properly. The stink really was disgusting. Unobtrusively he edged away a little. 'Your sister-in-law, sir.'

There was a flicker of some emotion in Covin's eyes which, frustratingly, Thanet couldn't read. What had it been? Relief? Anger? Fear? Or perhaps it had merely been irritation?

'When we asked you why she hadn't stayed on at school

161

to take her A levels as everyone seemed to expect, you told us she was simply fed up with school and wanted to start work, earn some money of her own.'

'So?' Covin was wary now.

'That summer, the summer she was sixteen, we understand she went to stay with an aunt in Bristol.'

'That's right. Yes.'

'Why was that?'

Covin shrugged. 'It was twenty years ago! How should I know?'

'You're saying you can't remember?'

'I imagine she felt like a change.'

'But she didn't come back afterwards, did she?'

'So? She liked it there. They got on well together.'

'I want you to think very carefully before you answer my next question, Mr Covin. I strongly advise you to tell the truth this time. Otherwise . . . Well, you do understand that when we discover someone has been lying to us we tend to look rather more carefully at that person the second time around. And if he lies again . . .'

Covin said nothing.

'So what I want to ask you is, was there another reason why Jessica did not go back to school that autumn? The reason why she didn't return to Sturrenden until the following spring?'

Covin's lips tightened.

'Make no mistake about this. We are determined to find the answer, and we can, of course, do so ourselves, with a little research. But it would save time if you were prepared to be frank with us.'

Covin still remained silent but now Thanet read uncertainty in his eyes.

162

'Very well. If you're not prepared to volunteer the information, perhaps you would just confirm or deny what I suggest to you. But do bear in mind what I said. The truth will emerge, sooner or later.' Thanet paused. Covin's arms were still folded and Thanet saw the tips of the man's fingers whiten as he tightened his grip in anticipation of what was coming.

Thanet's conviction that he was right was growing by the second. 'We believe that Jessica left school unexpectedly because she was pregnant, and that she went to stay with her aunt in order to have the baby out of the area.'

Covin abruptly left the desk and blundered across the room to the window. There he remained with his back to them, staring out into the fading light.

Thanet and Lineham exchanged victorious glances.

'Mr Covin?' said Thanet.

Covin apparently came to a decision. He squared his shoulders and turned. 'Yes,' he said quietly, with a sigh. 'You're right, of course.' He went back to his desk, shook a cigarette out of the pack and lit it, inhaling as greedily as if he had been deprived of nicotine all day.

'And the baby was adopted.'

A long plume of smoke. 'Yes.'

'What sex was it?'

Drag, exhale. 'A boy.'

'And which adoption agency was used?'

Another drag. 'I've no idea. Madge arranged it all. With Jessica, of course.'

'Why were you so reluctant to tell us?'

A shrug. 'I promised.'

'Who? Jessica?'

'No. My wife. Well, it came down to Jessica in the end, I suppose. I expect she went on at Madge to get me to promise.'

'But they're both dead now,' said Lineham. 'What does it matter?'

Covin cast him a scornful glance. 'A promise is a promise. Or it is in my book. Anyway, the kid's not dead, is he?'

Point taken, thought Thanet. 'Who was the father?'

'She wouldn't tell us.'

'As a matter of interest, why didn't she have an abortion?'

'Don't ask me. Heart to hearts with Jessica weren't exactly my line, as you might have gathered last time. I just didn't want to know.'

And that, it seemed, was as much as he could tell them. But Thanet was satisfied. It was enough to move them on one step further and that was all that mattered. He was as glad as Lineham to get back into the fresh air. They lingered beside the car, breathing deeply.

'Hope that's the last time we have to interview him,' said the sergeant, 'or I'll be claiming danger money. Anyway, it looks as though you were right.'

'Partly, anyway,' said Thanet. 'We still don't know if Kevin is the son.'

'So what next?'

'We go and see his adoptive mother again for a start. See what she can tell us.'

TWELVE

'What if Kevin's there?' Once again Lineham had to shout to make himself heard over the roar of traffic thundering past as they waited for Mrs Barcombe to answer their knock. 'He should be home from work by now.'

It was six o'clock.

'We'll have to play it by ear.'

Mingled scents of furniture polish and frying onions wafted out to compete with the reek of exhaust fumes as the door opened. One of the two men was home anyway, Thanet noted: there was only a single pair of men's slippers just inside the door.

Mrs Barcombe wasn't too pleased to see them. 'Is it important? I'm just cooking the tea.' She was still wearing the crossover apron.

'We won't keep you long.'

'Who is it, Mary?' A shaft of brighter light shone along the passageway as a door at the far end opened and the silhouette of a man appeared. The smell of frying onions intensified.

She half turned. 'It's the police again.'

'What do they want?'

'How should I know?' Then with a muffled exclamation she darted along the passage and brushed past him into the kitchen.

The man advanced. 'You'd better come in,' he said with an apologetic smile. He was in his fifties, with thinning brown hair carefully brushed to conceal incipient baldness. The subservient forward tilt of his head was probably habitual, the result of years of deference to customers. He was still dressed for work in striped shirt, discreet tie and the trousers of a suit, held up by braces. Bentall's was a good-quality shop and would expect its salesmen to uphold certain standards. They would no doubt have frowned upon the woolly carpet slippers, which looked distinctly incongruous.

Although it was still light outside the sitting room was gloomy and Barcombe put the overhead light on. In the sickly glow of a low-wattage bulb the antiseptic room looked more unwelcoming than ever. Introductions over, the three men sat down.

'Just got there in time,' said Mrs Barcombe, bustling back into the room. 'You could've kept an eye on the onions, Al. Couldn't you smell they were starting to catch?' She plumped down beside him on the settee.

'Sorry, dear.'

Thanet decided to go straight to the point. They had wasted enough time and Kevin could arrive home at any minute. He wanted to talk to the boy again, but not until he'd clarified the issue with the Barcombes.

'When we were here yesterday, Mrs Barcombe, you told us that Kevin was adopted.'

Immediately deep frown lines appeared between her

166

brows and she exchanged an uneasy glance with her husband. 'That's right. What's it got to do with you?'

'Mary!' said her husband nervously. 'Just listen to what the Inspector's got to say.'

'How old was he when he came to you?'

'Six weeks. But I still don't see –'

'Bear with me, will you? When was this, exactly?'

She didn't hesitate. 'February 10th, 1978.' But despite her swift, almost automatic response, she was becoming agitated. Her bony fingers moved restlessly, rolling and unrolling a corner of her apron.

Thanet experienced a spurt of triumph and he caught Lineham's eye. *You see?*

'So he would have been born towards the end of December 1977.'

'Yes. Look, I think we've a right to know what all this is about.'

'I'm sorry, I'm not at liberty to tell you at the moment. Were you living in Sturrenden at the time?'

'We were living here, in this house. We've always lived here.'

'Which adoption agency did you use?'

She shot to her feet. 'That's it. That's enough. You have no right to come here poking and prying like this.'

'Mary.' Barcombe was on his feet too, a restraining hand on her arm.

She shook him off. 'Don't "Mary" me! I'll say what I like! Kevin's done nothing wrong!'

Thanet rose too. 'Look, Mrs Barcombe, I'm sorry. I can understand your getting upset –'

'Oh, you can, can you? I don't suppose you've ever had to put up with people coming into your home and asking questions about your private life, have you?'

The answer to that, of course, was that no, he hadn't. None of his family had ever been in trouble with the law, thank God, unlike those of other policemen he knew. 'We don't enjoy upsetting people, you know.'

'But you don't let that stop you, do you!'

And again, she was right. In his job you had to learn to put personal feeling aside. He had one last question to ask before giving up. 'Mrs Barcombe, has Kevin ever tried to trace his natural mother?'

Bullseye. He could tell by the agonised glance at her husband, by her sudden stillness.

'No!' she said wildly. 'I told you yesterday. He's never given us a moment's worry.'

Thanet remembered the shadow behind her eyes when she had said this and now he understood it. Adoptive parents, especially those who dearly love their adopted child, as she did, must always dread the moment when the questions about the natural parents start to proliferate, must always be afraid that sooner or later the tug of blood will win over the years of unselfish devotion.

In the ensuing silence the sound of a key in the front-door lock could clearly be heard.

'There's Kev,' she said, starting towards the door.

'We'll need to speak to him,' said Thanet.

She ignored him and went out, shutting the door firmly behind her. There was a murmur of voices.

Thanet nodded and Lineham went to open the door. 'We'd like a word, Kevin,' he said.

The boy came in, stripping off the anorak he was wearing. His mother put out her hand and he gave it to her. 'What's up?' he said, jauntily. But his eyes belied his tone.

168

'We'd like to speak to Kevin alone,' said Thanet.

'No!' said his mother.

'Yes,' said Thanet.

'We have every right to stay. We're his parents. Tell them, Al.'

Barcombe, who had remained silent through most of the interview and was clearly used to letting his wife rule the roost, looked uncomfortable. 'I don't think we can do that, Mary.'

'Your husband's right, Mrs Barcombe. Kevin is no longer a minor. If you prefer, we could take him away and interview him at the Station.'

'No!' she cried. Her eyes moved in desperation from one to another, seeking a way out of the dilemma and failing to find it. Then the muscles of her face sagged and her shoulders slumped as she acknowledged defeat. She turned away, hugging Kevin's anorak to her chest for comfort. 'I'll go and get your tea ready, Kev.'

'That's right, dear,' said Barcombe, putting an arm across her shoulders. 'I don't suppose they'll be long,' he murmured as they went out.

Now all that agonised emotion had been removed the room seemed very quiet. In unspoken agreement they all sat down and Kevin at once took out a tobacco pouch, extracted a packet of cigarette papers and a few strands of tobacco and proceeded to roll a cigarette. Lineham cast a glance at Thanet in which triumph at being right was mixed with despair at the prospect of being trapped in yet another smoke-filled room.

Thanet was equally certain. In his opinion, this clinched it. So few people rolled their own cigarettes these days that he simply couldn't believe that it was a

169

second person involved in the case who had stubbed out those butts behind the hedge opposite the Manifests' house. No, Kevin had been the watcher, he was now sure of that. But how to get him to admit it?

'Well now, Kevin,' he said. 'We've been doing a bit of checking up.'

'I'd've thought you had better things to do than waste your time on me.'

'It always pays to be thorough, doesn't it, sergeant?'

'Certainly does, sir.'

Lineham deserved full marks for not flinching as Kevin blew a long stream of smoke in his direction, Thanet thought. 'And in this case we've come up with one or two question marks. Now, you claim that you left home on Tuesday night around 8.15 and went straight to Sally's. But your mother says you left at 7.45 –'

'No she doesn't. She was mistaken. You ask her.'

So Kevin had persuaded his mother to change her story. 'And the doorman at Sally's said you arrived at 8.30.'

'So? What's a few minutes here or there?'

'A few minutes here or there, as you put it, may be very important indeed. You know the Green Man in Charthurst?'

The sudden change of subject caught Kevin unawares. He blinked and leaned forward to stub out his cigarette. 'I know where it is, yeah.'

'Been there lately?'

'How should I remember?'

'I'm not asking you to go back very far, Kevin. Only to Tuesday night.'

Kevin clamped his lips together, clearly in a dilemma.

170

He didn't want to incriminate himself further by lying, nor did he want to admit to anything he didn't have to.

'You see, the landlord of the Green Man has been getting pretty fed up lately because people who aren't customers keep using his car park.'

Kevin ran his tongue over his upper lip.

'So he's been keeping a record of the registration numbers of offenders. Er . . . You did say you borrowed your father's car on Tuesday night, Kevin?'

Kevin's eyes were taking on the hunted expression of a rabbit hypnotised by a stoat.

'Because one of the cars parked at the Green Man in Charthurst around eight p.m. last Tuesday night was a red Nissan.' Thanet glanced at Lineham who read out the registration number. 'That is the number of your father's car, isn't it?'

The boy licked his lips again, his freckles now in stark contrast to the pallor of his skin.

'It is, isn't it?' Thanet persisted.

'I . . .' Kevin croaked.

'Yes?'

'I went for a walk.'

'I see,' said Thanet, nodding. 'A walk.'

'I felt like one. A breath of air. After being cooped up all day.'

'Kevin.' Thanet was gentle, reproachful. 'Are you really expecting us to believe that you drove all the way to Charthurst to go for a walk in the dark?'

'It's quiet there,' said Kevin with the bravado born of desperation.

'There's plenty of quiet countryside much closer than that.'

171

A shrug. *That's my story and I'm sticking to it.*

'You knew Mrs Manifest, didn't you?'

'Not know her, exactly. She used to have her hair done at Snippers, so I've seen her in the salon.'

'You've spoken to her?'

'I've washed her hair once or twice. Look, I want to go to the toilet.'

Excellent. Kevin's bladder was playing up, a sure sign of nervousness – if Thanet needed another. Signs there already were, aplenty. Besides, Kevin's absence would give him the opportunity he had been hoping for. 'OK,' he said, with a nod at Lineham.

The two left the room and Thanet quickly took out a polythene bag and pocketed the cigarette butt.

Lineham didn't miss a trick, he noticed when they returned. The sergeant's eyes went straight to the ashtray and then met Thanet's in comprehension. Thanet was amused to find that he felt as though he had received a pat on the back.

'So,' he said when they were all settled again. 'You washed Mrs Manifest's hair occasionally. Did you like her?'

An emotion which Thanet couldn't define flashed briefly in Kevin's eyes before he shrugged and said, 'She was OK.'

'Your mother tells me you're adopted, Kevin.'

A little pulse began to beat near the corner of the boy's right eye.

'Kevin?'

'So what?'

'So I wondered if you'd ever thought of trying to trace your natural mother.'

172

'It's none of your bloody business.'

'That may well not be true.'

Kevin gave him an intense stare. 'What are you getting at?'

'If you have tried to trace her, we'd be very interested to hear what you found out.'

'I still don't see what it's got to do with you.'

Thanet was tempted to voice his suspicions straight out, but something, some unspoken restraint seemed to be operating in his brain. 'We just want to be certain that this has nothing to do with Mrs Manifest's death, that's all.'

Kevin appeared genuinely bewildered. 'I don't know what you're talking about, I really don't. How the hell could there be any connection between my natural mum and Mrs Manifest?'

The question seemed to hover in the air between them, inviting the obvious answer.

'No!' said Kevin suddenly. 'You can't be thinking . . . No!'

'What?'

'That Mrs Manifest was . . .' He stared at Thanet and suddenly, disconcertingly, began to laugh, a few sniggers at first and then, in a release of tension, a mounting crescendo of near-hysterical laughter. Tears squeezed their way between his eyelids and began to run down his cheeks and he clutched his stomach as if in pain.

Thanet and Lineham looked blankly at each other. Did this mean the collapse of their theory?

'Kev?' The door burst open and the Barcombes came in, their faces confused. 'What's the matter? What's going on?'

Kevin shook his head, still gasping and snorting with mirth.

His mother took a handkerchief from her apron pocket and thrust it into his hand. 'Here. Wipe your face.'

He did as he was told. He was gradually calming down but little hiccups of laughter kept on escaping like gas from an underground reservoir.

His parents stood watching him, one on either side.

Anyone who had seen their concerned faces would never again doubt the love which adoptive parents can feel for their child, thought Thanet.

'Mum,' he said at last, twisting his head to look up at her. 'I think you'd better hear this. The Inspector wants to know about my natural mother.'

Their eyes all turned to Thanet, Kevin's mocking, his parents' puzzled, resentful, anxious.

'But why?' said Mrs Barcombe.

'He seems to have some fancy idea that she was Jessica Dander – Jessica Manifest!' Kevin dabbed at his eyes as he succumbed to another bout of laughter.

His parents both looked astounded.

'The *KM* reporter?' said his mother.

'The one who was found dead a couple of days ago?' said his father.

'Is that true?' said Mrs Barcombe to Thanet. 'Was she his mother?'

Thanet shrugged. *Don't ask me.* Her reaction was interesting, he thought. The fact that the police were investigating Jessica's death and that they seemed to think Kevin had some connection with it was not for her the most important issue. Later, no doubt, it would be.

She looked at Kevin. Clearly there was something she was longing to know but dared not ask.

All at once Thanet understood what was going on here. Mrs Barcombe either knew or suspected that Kevin had been trying to trace his natural mother but wasn't sure if he had succeeded. It was this uncertainty that was tormenting her.

'Oh Mum,' he said. 'Get real.'

There was fear in her eyes now and her lips moved stiffly as she said, 'How can you be sure?'

He stood up suddenly, as if propelled from his chair by an invisible force. 'Because I found out who she was, didn't I.' He turned to face them all, as if to confront his own pain. 'There, now you know. I went through the whole bloody performance, didn't I, social workers, interviews, questions, questions, questions. It took for ever, months and months and then, in the end, when I finally tracked her down, what happened? She just didn't want to know.'

Relief blossomed briefly in Mrs Barcombe's face before, for Kevin's sake, she tried to hide it. 'She didn't?'

He turned away to conceal his expression. 'Nah.'

Swiftly she crossed the room and put her arm around his shoulders. They twitched, but he didn't shake her off. 'Oh Kev,' she said. 'I am sorry.'

'Yeah, well . . .' he mumbled.

'We'll need her name and address,' said Thanet. 'We'll be very discreet,' he added.

Kevin was still clutching the handkerchief his mother had given him and now he blew his nose and shrugged. 'Why not? It's no skin off my nose.' He glanced at her. No doubt he didn't want her to hear the details. 'I'll write it down for you.'

On the way back to the car Thanet stopped suddenly and banged his fist against the wall. 'What a fool! What an idiot!' Kevin's laughter still sounded in his ears.

'What do you mean?'

'Building such an elaborate structure of theory without a shred of evidence to base it on.'

'That's not true.'

'Nothing worth speaking of, anyway.'

'I don't see it that way at all. All right, so we were wrong about Jessica being his mother, but we were right about everything else. Kevin's admitted he was in Charthurst that night and we're now virtually certain that he was watching her. What's more –'

'He'll never admit it.'

'What's more, we'll now be able to prove it. It's a bit of luck you managed to get hold of that cigarette end.'

'We *hope* we'll be able to prove it.'

'Oh come on, sir. Give over. You're just feeling negative at the moment. OK, you were partly wrong. So what?'

So my pride is dented, thought Thanet. And not for the first time. Serves me right. When am I going to learn?

It was after seven o'clock and they decided to call it a day. As he drove home through a spectacular sunset Thanet made a conscious effort to slough off his dejection and forget about the case for a while. He had been looking forward to this evening. Tomorrow the house would be bursting at the seams but tonight he and Joan and Bridget would be able to spend some time together, just the three of them.

This turned out to be a vain hope. What else should he have expected? Thanet asked himself as Bridget went to answer the phone for the umpteenth time. The talk was

176

all of arrangements, arrangements, arrangements and like many a father before him he thought he would heave a sigh of relief when the whole thing was over. Still, it was a joy to see Bridget so happy.

He watched fondly as she returned to sit on the floor beside his chair. 'Just think,' he said, 'in two days' time you'll be an old married woman.' *And you won't be my daughter any more. First and foremost you'll be Alexander's wife.*

As if she had divined his thoughts she looked up and smiled. 'Don't worry, dad. We'll only be an hour away.'

An hour too much, as far as he was concerned. 'I'm looking forward to all those free lunches.'

'Breakfasts, lunches, dinners, the lot. You'll have to come up for weekends, let us educate you about London. You don't know what you've been missing all these years.'

'A new dimension to our lives,' said Joan, smiling.

'Just what I was thinking earlier,' said Thanet. But not in quite that way. Try as he would, he could see Bridget's marriage only as loss, not gain.

THIRTEEN

'What time's your fitting?' said Joan as she switched off the radio. They had been listening anxiously to the weather forecast for the weekend. Fortunately it sounded good.

'Ten o'clock,' said Bridget.

Joan had taken the day off and they were discussing their plans for the day over breakfast.

'It shouldn't take long, though,' Bridget added. 'It was only a very minor adjustment.'

'Good. Well, I suggest that after that we go on into the town and pick up the suits for your father and Ben from Moss Bros.'

'Wouldn't it be better to bring my dress home first, to hang it up straight away? And I'm not particularly keen on the idea of leaving it in the car while we go shopping. What if the car got stolen!'

'No doubt you'd expect me to mobilise the entire police force of the area to get it back in time!' said Thanet with a grin.

'Naturally!' said Joan. Then, to Bridget, 'But you're

right. Better to hang it up as soon as possible. Back here first then, before going into town.'

'What about the service sheets?'

'Done. I collected them in the lunch hour on Wednesday.'

'That's a relief.' Bridget grinned. 'The last wedding I went to they didn't arrive until the guests were actually seated in the church.'

'Poor organisation,' said Thanet. 'No chance of that, with your mother in charge.'

'Thank goodness! What time is Gran arriving?'

'Twelve-forty-five,' said Joan. Her own mother lived only a few miles away.

'Who's meeting her?' said Thanet.

'We both are, of course!' Bridget was mildly indignant.

'Then we'll come back here for lunch and try to persuade her to have a rest before everyone else arrives.'

'Good luck,' said Thanet, finishing his coffee and rising. 'She won't want to miss a thing.'

He put his coat on and went back into the kitchen to kiss them both goodbye. 'Oh, by the way, Helen says she's finished decorating the cake, if you want to go round and take a look.'

'Oh good!' said Bridget, eyes lighting up. 'She's delivering it to the Swan tomorrow morning, but I can't wait till then. I'm dying to see it.'

'We could pop in on the way back from picking up your grandmother at the station,' said Joan. 'I'm sure she'd love to see it too. I'll give Helen a ring, check she'll be in.' She followed Thanet into the hall. 'Bye, darling. You will be able to make the dinner this evening, won't you?'

179

'I'll be there,' he said. 'Stop worrying!'

'And don't forget your haircut,' she called after him.

'I won't.' When on earth was he going to fit it in? he wondered. Somehow, he must. His heart sank as he remembered that Draco was due back later on this afternoon and given the opportunity would no doubt insist on being brought up to date with every last detail. Thanet resolved to avoid the office after four p.m. if at all possible.

Lineham was back on form this morning, already immersed in a report. He looked up as Thanet came in. 'I did it, sir!'

'Did what?'

'Spoke to her. My mother. Put it to her straight, like you suggested, that it just wouldn't work, her coming to live with us.'

'How did she take it?'

Lineham grimaced. 'Better than I expected, really. But she wasn't too pleased, obviously. It's not exactly an easy thing to put tactfully.'

'Did you talk to her about the Abbeyfield organisation?'

'Yes. At first she just didn't want to know, but I kept on telling her they weren't like ordinary homes and pointing out all the advantages and in the end she did at least agree to go and look at the one in Maidstone. I rang the housekeeper there and we're going over on Sunday. She sounded really nice. They have a waiting list, so it would mean the Sturrenden one in any case, and it'll be getting on for nine months, apparently, before they get that one off the ground, so there'll be plenty of time for Mum to get used to the idea. They suggest not selling her house until she's given them at least a month's trial, and I think that's reassured her – you know, that she isn't going to be shoved off into a home against her will, that it really will be ultimately her decision.'

'What did Louise think about it?'

'She's over the moon that I'm trying to get things sorted out at last. She thinks the Abbeyfield idea sounds great. Let's hope it's all it's cracked up to be.'

'I hope so too!' said Thanet. 'Or I really will be in the doghouse.' But he trusted his mother's judgement and was confident that it would be. He nodded at the report Lineham was reading. 'Anything interesting?'

'Bentley's report on the Ogilvys,' said Lineham. 'Local opinion is that Mrs O. is an angel in disguise, pillar of the community, nothing too much trouble etc. etc. He's not so popular, though there was no specific complaint against him. People seem to agree that they had a bit of a sticky time during the recession – there were little signs like cutting back on help in the house and garden, changing her car to a cheaper model – but that things are picking up again now. She's gone back to a Polo from a Mini for instance.'

'Nothing of any use, then.'

''Fraid not.'

The telephone rang. Lineham answered; listened. 'Put her on. Hullo? Yes, I remember. Yes. Oh, have you?' He listened intently. 'Yes, I see. Thank you for letting us know. Yes, that's very helpful.' He put the phone down. 'You remember that neighbour who said she'd seen a young man hanging about and thought he looked familiar but couldn't place why?'

'Don't tell me! She has her hair cut at Snippers.'

'Exactly!'

'Doesn't really help, though, does it, Mike? I suppose it might be worth following up. Yes, better send someone out to get more details – exactly where and when it was that she noticed him around.'

Lineham made a quick note. 'Kevin keeps on cropping up, doesn't he?'

'Yes. But there's still no scientific evidence to connect him with Jessica yet.'

'There's the cigarette butt.'

'We hope.'

'So what do you reckon, sir? Which of them would you put your money on? Kevin, Desmond or Ogilvy?'

Thanet shook his head. 'Your guess is as good as mine. They all had the opportunity. On the face of it both her husband and Ogilvy had good reason to get involved in an argument with her but the very fact that Kevin was there at all is suspicious.'

'Downright creepy, if you ask me. Any man who makes a habit of lurking behind hedges to spy on a woman isn't normal.'

'I agree. There must be some kind of morbid fascination there. In which case . . . It's just occurred to me. If that is so, in view of the fact that Jessica was a public figure, he might well have made a habit of collecting stuff about her.'

'Kept a sort of scrapbook, you mean. Yes!' Lineham's face was alight with interest. 'Articles she wrote, photographs and so on. You're right.'

'The question is, which do we do first – interview him again, now that we have an independent witness to testify that she's seen him near Jessica's house on more than one occasion, or go and search his room, see if he has got anything like that stashed away?'

'His mother'd never let us search his room without a warrant.'

'No. And it would mean a Section 8.'

Both men were silent, thinking. The more usual Section 15 search warrant was easier to obtain than the Section 8 warrant, which was granted only in the case of serious crimes such as murder and if the application met certain conditions. If they applied for one, it would not be sufficient for Lineham to go before the magistrates, Thanet himself would have to do so. He must therefore be very sure of his ground.

'I think we could meet all the conditions,' he said. 'What I'm not sure about is whether we'd be justified in applying for a warrant at this juncture.'

'The trouble is, if we interview him again and he continues to deny any involvement, we'd have to let him go and he might well start feeling very nervous and decide to get rid of any incriminating material, if he has any.'

'*If* he has any. That's the trouble. We can't be sure. It's all conjecture.'

'Suspicion is all that's necessary, surely,' objected Lineham. 'After all, this is a murder case.' He began to tick the points off on his fingers. 'One: we have Jessica's belief that she was being watched, backed up by two police reports. Two: we now have an independent witness who claims to have seen Kevin lurking in the vicinity of Jessica's house. Three: we have scientific evidence to prove he had been spying on her –'

'Unconfirmed as yet. It'll be days before forensic get back to us on the saliva test.'

'Exactly! We can't afford to wait that long. Four: we have another independent witness, the pub landlord, who will swear that the Nissan has been parked at his pub on more than one occasion and that it was there on the night Jessica died. Five: Kevin actually admits that he was there, on the spot, during the period the murder was committed and so far he's only come up with the thinnest of excuses for his presence. Six: we have good reason to suspect that we might find further evidence to link him with Jessica if we search his room and that if we delay that evidence could be removed or destroyed. No, sir, there's no doubt in my mind that we'd be justified in applying for a warrant and I really don't think any magistrate is going to disagree.'

'It's true that if we interview him again before we search, he might have the opportunity to get rid of the evidence if there is any . . .' Thanet made up his mind. 'You're right, Mike. We'll go for it.' He stood up. 'Ring the Magistrates' Clerk and tell him we'll be over at 10.30. But before we do anything else today I absolutely must go and get my hair cut.' He ran his hand over the back of his neck. 'I don't like taking time off during working hours but I really can't turn up at the wedding looking like an old English sheepdog.'

'I'll do that right away.' Lineham glanced at his overflowing in-tray. Since Tuesday night routine work had been pushed aside. 'Then I'll do a bit of catching up while you're gone.'

'Right.' Thanet hurried out and set off for the barber's at a brisk pace, hoping that there wouldn't be too much of a queue. As he turned into the High Street he ran into Mallard, almost knocking him over.

'Whoa!' said the little doctor. 'Ease up.'

'Sorry! I'm in a bit of a rush.'

'I can see that!'

'I've sneaked out to get my hair cut for tomorrow. If I don't make it I'll be in real trouble at home.'

'I've been wanting a word,' said Mallard. 'And we never seem to get a chance to talk nowadays. I'll walk with you.'

They fell into step.

Mallard gave him an assessing look. 'If you could take your mind off work for two minutes . . . I was just wondering if you felt happier now, about Alexander.'

Unconsciously, Thanet's pace slowed. Apart from Joan, the Mallards were the only people to whom he had ever confessed his reservations about Alexander. He remembered an evening not long after the two young people had first started going out together when Mallard had taken him to task about this, accusing him of being prejudiced against every boyfriend that Bridget brought home simply because he didn't want to lose her. And there had been a measure of truth in that – still was, for that matter, he thought uncomfortably, remembering his thoughts last night. Mallard had also accused him of wanting someone perfect for Bridget and had pointed out that no one ever was, that such expectations were completely unrealistic. Thanet had been left to face the uncomfortable fact that his reservations arose chiefly from his own feelings of inadequacy in the face of Alexander's superior education, earning power and upper-middle-class background.

Now he felt ill at ease as he said, 'Yes, I suppose so.'

'But you're still not sure.'

'I just feel that if he could hurt her once . . . Last time she had no warning, you know. He simply dropped her,

185

out of the blue, just like that.' Thanet snapped his fingers. 'You know how upset she was. It took her ages even to begin to get over it. In fact, she never really did.'

'All the more reason, surely, to be thankful that he changed his mind and came back?'

Thanet shrugged. 'Perhaps. But you must see that it makes me a bit wary of him.'

'On the principle that if he did it once he can do it again.'

'Precisely.'

'But as I recall, Luke, the reason he gave for breaking it off on that occasion was that he felt he wasn't ready for the commitment. Leaving Bridget's feelings aside for the moment, wouldn't you regard that as a pretty responsible decision to take? Surely you'd prefer him to be sure of his feelings before marrying her, rather than rush into marriage without proper thought, like so many youngsters nowadays – as the soaring divorce rate demonstrates only too clearly?'

How can I leave Bridget's feelings aside? 'That's what Joan says.'

'Sensible woman, your wife!'

Some oranges had fallen off the display in front of a greengrocer's shop and were rolling across the pavement. They stooped to pick them up.

'Thanks,' said the shop assistant as they handed them back. 'Cheers.'

Thanet had been thinking over what Mallard had said. 'It wasn't so much the fact that he broke it off,' he said as they moved on, 'as the way he did it. It was so abrupt, such a shock for her. There'd been no warning at all.'

'According to her.'

Thanet stopped. 'What are you saying?'

'Just that there may well have been signs, but that she may not have wanted to read them. You know perfectly well that we often see only what we want to see and that love, as they say, is blind. A cliché, maybe, but none the less true.'

'I never thought of it like that,' said Thanet. They resumed their walk, which had slowed down to a snail's pace as they neared their destination. 'It's true that she was head over heels. Still is, for that matter, as I said.'

'Which is just as it should be. And in my opinion, so is he. If you ask me, Bridget is a very lucky girl.'

'You think so?'

'Oh come on, Luke! It's not very often one comes across a young man who has all of Alexander's qualities. He's hardworking, honest, sincere, likeable, very able, he's earning a good living and, to cap it all, has a sense of humour. Truthfully, now, what more could you ask?'

Thanet gave a sheepish grin. 'Not much, I suppose.'

They came to a halt beneath the barber's striped pole. Peering in, Thanet was relieved to see that there were only two people waiting.

'I tell you this,' said the little doctor. 'I've never had any children, as you know, more's the pity, but if I had had a daughter I would have been very happy to see her married to Alexander.'

'You would?'

'I swear it! And it's not often I go out on a limb like this, as you know.'

That was true. Thanet was touched by the fact that Mallard had gone out of his way to try and reassure him – and had succeeded in doing so. Somehow he felt easier in

187

his mind. He trusted Mallard's judgement; he always had. 'Thanks, Doc, I appreciate this.'

Expressions of gratitude had always embarrassed Mallard. 'See you at the church,' he said gruffly, and with a wave of his hand, was gone.

By the time Thanet got back to the office it was twenty past ten. They hurried across to the Magistrates' Court and had a brief discussion with Graham Ticeman, the Magistrates' Clerk, who satisfied himself that all the conditions pertaining to a Section 8 warrant applied. The magistrates had been alerted to the fact that an application was to be made and had agreed to hear it at the end of the current case. Meanwhile, Thanet and Lineham slipped into the courtroom and sat at the back as usual. Thanet was pleased to see that the chairman today was Felicity Merridew, a magistrate of long standing with a reputation for sound judgement and impartiality. She was a tiny woman in her sixties with neatly cropped silver hair and a remarkable air of authority for one so small of stature. They didn't have long to wait as the case was just finishing and in a matter of minutes they were taken into the retiring room to present their application.

The other two magistrates were male and towered over their chairman as they came in. She greeted Thanet and Lineham with a smile and said, 'Right, Inspector Thanet. Let's proceed.'

Thanet took the oath and then laid forth his arguments for the application. All three magistrates listened carefully. When he had finished Mrs Merridew glanced at the Clerk. 'Are you happy about this, Mr Ticeman? You've satisfied yourself that the conditions have all been met?'

'Yes, ma'am.'

'Is there any advice you wish to give?'

He shook his head.

She consulted her fellow magistrates with raised eyebrows. They too shook their heads. 'Very well, Inspector. Your application is granted.'

'Great!' said Lineham, outside.

'All right, Mike. No need to say "I told you so."' But Thanet, too, was pleased that it had gone so smoothly.

A quarter of an hour later they were knocking yet again at the Barcombes' now familiar front door. No reply. They knocked again; waited. Still no answer.

He and Lineham exchanged glances of dismay. They were all geared up to search, eager to find out if their guess was going to pay off. Thanet had no intention of forcing an entry. Perhaps she had gone shopping.

He took a step backwards to peer up at the façade of the house and felt the slipstream tug at him as a lorry passed close behind.

Lineham grabbed his arm. 'Careful, sir.'

'There's something different about the house. It's the curtains. The net curtains have been taken down. Knowing her, she probably washes them once a week.' Thanet stepped close to the window and shielded his eyes with his hand as he peered inside, but there was nothing of interest to see. The front room looked as sterile and uninviting as ever. 'Try again, Mike. Knock harder.'

Lineham did as he was asked and they both strained their ears to catch any sound of movement from within. Nothing. They were about to turn away when Lineham put his hand on Thanet's arm. 'Just a sec.'

Sure enough, a moment later the door opened. Mrs Barcombe, surprisingly, didn't look as unwelcoming as Thanet had expected. Perhaps she felt grateful to them for precipitating Kevin's outburst last night. It must be a great relief to her to know at last that there was no danger of losing him to the woman who had given him away at birth. Her attitude would change, no doubt, when she heard why they had come.

'Have you been waiting long? I was in the garden, hanging out my nets.' As usual she was wearing a crossover apron, a different one this time. With her standards of hygiene Thanet wouldn't be surprised if she had a different one for each day of the week. Her hands, he noticed, looked red and raw. Not surprising, considering the punishing routine to which she no doubt subjected them.

'We've only been here a few minutes,' he said. 'May we come in?'

'I suppose.'

Into the barren sitting room again, looking curiously denuded without its curtains.

'Actually, it's Kevin's room we've come to take a look at,' he said.

Her expression became hostile in a flash. Her only chick had been threatened. She shook her head vehemently. 'You've got no right to do that. You'd better go.' She turned to open the door, gestured them out.

'We have a search warrant, Mrs Barcombe,' said Thanet. He sympathised with her need to protect the child she loved, but there was nothing he could do about that. In a murder case it was inevitable that innocent people got hurt along the way and sadly it was often he who had to inflict the pain. Over the years he had had to resign himself to the fact that this was unavoidable but unlike some policemen he had never been able to anaesthetise himself against it.

She stared at him. It was clear that she had been completely unprepared for this and had no idea what to do. 'But why?' she said at last.

'Because we need to look at Kevin's room and we knew that you probably wouldn't allow us to do so without one.'

She shook her head. 'I didn't mean that. Last night, I was more interested in what Kev was telling me than why you were here. I tried to get him to explain, after, but he wouldn't. Just said it was all a mistake. But here you are again and now you want to search his room. I just don't understand what Kev has to do with that Jessica Dander.'

'I'm sorry,' said Thanet. And he meant it. If they were right, she had more shocks coming to her. 'You'll have to ask Kevin to explain.'

'But he won't! I told you! Please, Inspector!'

'I'm sorry,' Thanet repeated. 'I'm afraid I can't do that. And now we'd like to see Kevin's room, please.'

Defeated, she turned to lead the way upstairs.

'Just tell us where it is, Mrs Barcombe. We'd prefer you to remain downstairs.' With her obsessive tidiness he didn't want her breathing down their necks, clicking her tongue over every move they made.

'I'm afraid it's rather untidy,' she said. 'Kevin only lets me clean up once in a blue moon.'

And it was true that he needn't have worried. Her indulgence towards Kevin evidently extended even to

191

allowing him to make as much of a mess of his room as he liked.

'I'm amazed she lets him get away with this,' said Lineham, wrinkling his nose in distaste at the stale, unwashed odour as they picked their way through the dirty discarded pants, socks, shirts and jeans dropped, presumably where he took them off, all over the floor. The bedside table was cluttered with empty cans and dirty mugs with mould growing over the bottom. Motoring and fashion magazines were scattered across the unmade bed and the wastepaper basket nearby was overflowing with empty crisp packets and the wrappers of chocolate bars and biscuits.

'The power of love,' said Thanet, looking around. 'Just think what it must cost her, with her obsession for cleanliness, to leave things in this state. I have heard that adoptive parents find it harder to discipline an adopted child than one of their own, on the grounds that criticism may be taken as rejection.'

'Well I wouldn't put up with this mess from one of ours, I can tell you! Where do we start?'

'Let's kick all this stuff into a corner, to begin with.' Thanet had no intention of picking up Kevin's dirty clothes with his bare hands, but all this clutter was distracting.

That done, they set to, beginning conventionally with chest of drawers, wardrobe and bed. They examined the posters on the walls, dismantled the few framed photographs of family holidays and then moved on to a close examination of the fitted carpet, which proved to be professionally fixed with gripper rods.

'Nothing,' said Lineham gloomily, sitting back on his

heels. 'Looks as though we were wrong. There's not one single thing here to connect him to Jessica.'

Thanet glanced at the hatch in the ceiling. He could think of more than one case where a loft had yielded up interesting secrets. 'If there is anything incriminating, he wouldn't have put it where his mother was likely to come across it on one of her occasional cleans.'

Lineham followed his gaze and they scrambled to their feet.

'Wonder if there's a loft ladder,' said Lineham. The hatch was just too high for him to reach but there was a wooden chair in the corner piled with dirty jeans and T-shirts and Lineham tipped them off and positioned it below the hatch. This was hinged on one side and as he lowered it a ladder swung sweetly down. 'Great!' he said.

'If there is anything hidden up there it won't be too far in,' said Thanet. 'He wouldn't have wanted to go clump-ing about in the loft and making his parents ask questions about what he was up to.'

By now Lineham was three-quarters of the way up the ladder, standing with head and shoulders in the open-ing. 'There's a light,' he said, and switched it on.

'Well?' said Thanet impatiently. He longed to be up there himself, but the sergeant had been too quick off the mark.

'The floor is boarded for a few yards around the hatch,' said Lineham. 'And there's the usual sort of junk, boxes and bits of leftover carpet and so on.'

There was a series of scraping sounds as he moved things about. 'Hang on,' he said suddenly.

'What?'

'There's a loose section of board here.'

193

A rattling sound, and then, 'Aaah.'

'"Ah" what?' said Thanet, by now in a frenzy of suspense and impatience.

'Eureka, I think!' said Lineham.

He switched off the light and began to descend.

FOURTEEN

As Lineham came down the last few rungs he handed his find to Thanet. It consisted of two items, a blue hard-covered scrapbook with thick pages, of the type readily bought in any large newsagent's, and an orange folder. When he had stowed away the ladder and closed the hatch they both sat down on the edge of the bed to take a closer look.

'Bingo!' breathed Lineham.

And here it was, the proof they needed of Kevin's obsession with Jessica Manifest, which had begun, it seemed, some six months ago. The scrapbook opened with an article written about her last Easter on the occasion of her winning an award. Then came many more, this time written by her and obviously clipped from the *Kent Messenger*. All were dated. Interspersed with these were photograph after photograph, taken in various public places. Many of them had been cut so that only Jessica remained.

'She was right, wasn't she?' said Thanet. 'He had been following her, and for some time. He obviously took these photographs himself, mostly on Sundays, I imagine. Her husband was probably with her, that's why they've been cut.'

'Yes,' said Lineham. 'That one was taken at the County Show, don't you think?'

Thanet agreed. 'And this is in the white garden at Sissinghurst. Last June, by the look of it. The rose pergola is in full bloom.'

'And I recognise that pub too. Yes, it's the Three Chimneys at Biddenden.'

Thanet opened the folder. Here were two more articles clipped from the *KM*, both of recent date and obviously waiting to be pasted in.

'I wonder if there's any undeveloped film in his camera?' said Lineham. This was hanging over one of the knobs on the headboard of the bed. He unhooked it, opened the case and examined it. 'It's on number 16 of a 24-exposure film,' he said with satisfaction. 'With any luck there'll be more of her in here.'

'Good thinking, Mike. Write out a receipt for the camera, to give to his mother.' Thanet stood up. 'I think we've got enough to pull him in, don't you?'

Mrs Barcombe was standing at the bottom of the stairs looking anxiously up as they emerged from Kevin's room. She looked even more worried when she saw what they were carrying. 'That's Kevin's camera!' she cried. 'You can't have that!'

'Don't worry, he'll get it back,' said Thanet. 'Here's a receipt.'

She snatched it from him. 'And what have you got there?' She made a grab for the scrapbook but Lineham held it out of her reach. 'That's not Kevin's! I've never

196

seen it before!' And then, illogically, 'You've no right to take his things away!'

'We're very sorry to have disturbed you, Mrs Barcombe.' Thanet edged past her in the narrow hall. 'We're leaving now.'

It was a guilty relief to escape from her anxiety and frustration.

Outside he cast an anxious glance at the sky, which had clouded over. 'I hope the weather forecasters haven't got it wrong again. They promised us a fine weekend.' As soon as they got back to the car he radioed in to give the order for Kevin to be picked up.

Earlier Lineham had dispatched two women detectives, new but very capable additions to the team, to interview Kevin's natural mother, with strict instructions to be tactful and not to proceed if she were married and her husband or family were around. Back at the office, while they were waiting for Kevin to arrive, WDC Tanya Phillips gave them a verbal report. She was in her mid twenties, a stocky girl with an engaging smile and a mop of unruly dark curls.

'She wasn't too pleased, needless to say, when she found out we'd come about Kevin. Tried to show us the door. Fortunately we were inside by then and as there didn't seem to be anyone else around we decided it was worth persisting. When she discovered that all we wanted was verification (a) that Kevin is her son and (b) that he had contacted her recently, and that that really would be the end of the matter as far as we were concerned, she gave in.'

'And he was and he did?'

'Yes. About a month before Easter. She went on and on

197

about what a shock it had been and how he had ruined her subsequent holiday in Majorca, turning up out of the blue like that.'

'She's married?'

'Yes, with two children, a boy and a girl.'

'What's she like?' Though Thanet could guess, from the little Tanya had already said.

WDC Phillips pulled a face. 'I must say I didn't take to her, sir. A bit of a hard-faced bitch, if you want my honest opinion.'

Poor Kevin. What a disillusionment. No doubt he had woven all sorts of elaborate fantasies about what his mother would be like. 'What does her husband do?'

'I didn't ask. Should I have?'

'No, don't worry. It really doesn't matter.'

'They're quite well off, I should think. Detached house, car of her own, nice clothes, spends a lot on her hair and make-up . . .'

'I get the picture.' She hadn't wanted her nice cosy set-up disturbed. And, in a way, who could blame her?

Except that he did. He did. 'Anyway, I gather she sent Kevin packing.'

'In no uncertain terms, I should think. She just didn't want to know.'

'Right. Thanks, Tanya. About a month before Easter,' he said to Lineham when she had gone. 'That's interesting, isn't it?'

'It is, isn't it? Are you thinking what I'm thinking?'

'That he substituted one obsession for another? It does seem likely, doesn't it? It must have been a pretty shattering disappointment. He must have expended so much emotional energy in tracing her, spent so much time thinking about her . . . When all that was suddenly taken away from him he might well have needed something else to take its place.'

'Are you suggesting that Jessica Manifest was a sort of mother substitute, sir?'

'No, not at all. Well, not necessarily. Just that nature abhors a vacuum and an interest in another woman would fill his mind, prevent him from brooding on his disappointment.'

'Interesting that he should choose someone so much older than him, though.'

'Yes. The question is . . .'

'What?'

'Well, if Ogilvy did leave the door open that night and Kevin did go in . . .'

'She'd be frightened, seeing a strange man in the house.'

'Yes. But how would he see her reaction?'

'You mean, would he take it as another rejection?'

'Exactly.'

'In which case, it might have made him flip.'

'It's a possibility, isn't it?'

The phone rang and Lineham answered it. 'Kevin's here.'

'Good.' Thanet sprang to his feet. He felt eager, buoyed up with optimism, certain that at last they were about to learn what had actually happened in that quiet country backwater on Tuesday night. He tucked the scrapbook under his arm. 'Let's see what he has to say for himself.'

Kevin was slumped at the table in one of the interview rooms, arms folded protectively across his chest, his expression a mixture of sulkiness, fear and defiance.

Thanet had decided that the time for pussyfooting around was over. The hard edges of the scrapbook pressing against his side were a comforting reassurance that this time he had some powerful ammunition. He marched into the room and slammed the book down on the table.

Kevin jumped and as he recognised the scrapbook his face became the colour of tallow, the freckles standing out against his sudden pallor.

'Right!' Thanet snapped as he and Lineham sat down. 'A quiet country walk, you said, didn't you, Kevin? That's why you were in Charthurst on Tuesday night?'

Silence. The boy's eyes were riveted to the scrapbook.

'We don't like it when people lie to us, Kevin, not one little bit. It makes us suspicious, very suspicious indeed. And when they lie to us more than once, as you have . . .'

Kevin opened his mouth, then shut it again.

'Because you have, haven't you? First of all you lied to us about not going to Charthurst at all on Tuesday night, and now we find you've been lying to us again. You assured us that as far as you were concerned Jessica Dander was only another customer, and not one that you'd had much to do with at that. But now, what do we find carefully hidden away in the loft above your bedroom where you thought no one would ever find it?' Thanet opened the scrapbook. 'An article about Jessica Dander. Articles by Jessica Dander. Photographs of Jessica Dander, lots of them – private photographs, taken by you.' Thanet nodded at Lineham and the sergeant held up the camera.

'Yours, I believe,' he said.

200

Kevin leaned forward for a closer look, opened his mouth then closed it again, clearly torn between denying that the camera was his and losing an expensive object if he did so.

Cupidity won. 'What if it is?' he muttered. Then, 'You've got no right to take my things away! Stealing, that's what it is. I want to make a complaint.'

'Your mother has a receipt for the camera,' said Thanet. 'But in fact you can have it back right now, once Sergeant Lineham has removed the film.'

Lineham did so, then put the camera on the table.

Kevin snatched it up and examined it, as if looking for damage.

'We're looking forward to getting that film developed, aren't we, sergeant? So.' Thanet sat back and folded his arms. 'What have you got to say for yourself now?'

Silence. Then Kevin laid the camera carefully down and fished in the pocket of his anorak for his tin of tobacco.

'No!' snapped Thanet. 'Put that away. This isn't a cocktail party!' He leaned forward. 'I don't think you quite realise the seriousness of your position, Kevin. We're talking about murder here, the worst crime in the book. Believe me, we won't be so easily fobbed off this time. You are not going to walk out of here unless and until we know the truth – and who knows? Maybe not even then. So you'd better get on with it.'

Kevin lifted his chin and shrugged. 'OK.'

Thanet found it difficult to hide his astonishment and he sensed Lineham stir beside him. He certainly hadn't expected Kevin to cave in so quickly.

'Get me off the hook, won't it? Anyway, there's no

201

point in keeping mum any longer, is there, not now you know about, well . . .' He nodded at the scrapbook. 'I ain't done nothing wrong,' he added defiantly.

'Really.' Thanet tapped the scrapbook. 'You don't call following a woman, spying on her, frightening her, something wrong?'

'Not really. It ain't a crime, anyway, is it?'

'It soon will be.' At last there was going to be legislation to make stalking a statutory offence. Not before time, in most people's opinions. 'So tell me exactly what happened on Tuesday night.'

And out it all poured. It was as if Kevin had been longing to tell somebody his story and until now had been denied an audience. It is not very often, after all, that the average person has so dramatic a tale to tell.

Kevin had, as his mother originally stated, left the house on Tuesday evening at around 7.45. By the time he had walked to where his father's car was garaged and driven to Charthurst it was just after eight o'clock. He parked at the Green Man and, having checked that there was no one about to notice him, took up his usual position behind the hedge. As he hurried past the end of Willow Way he noticed that Jessica's front door was open.

Thanet interrupted him for the first time. 'You're sure about that?'

'Certain.'

'Go on.'

'Well, I'd only been behind the hedge a coupla minutes when this geezer comes out. He hesitates, like, on the doorstep, as if he was trying to make up his mind about something, then he hurries off down the road towards

202

the pub and a minute or two later an engine starts up and I hear a car go off.'

'It was definitely a man?'

'Yep.'

'Did you recognise him?' If Kevin had been watching Jessica for months he must by now know most of the people in her life by sight if not by name.

But if he had, he was not yet ready to say so. 'I think he was trying to make up his mind whether or not to close the door behind him.' He leaned forward eagerly. 'I been thinking about it, see. And I reckon he thought, if I leave it open, perhaps someone else'll get in and that'll muddy the waters.'

'Hmm.' Thanet was non-committal. 'Go on.'

'Well, I waited a few minutes and then I thought I'd better go take a look. Well, I mean to say, it was a bit funny, wasn't it, the front door being open like that, specially at night, in the dark. Anybody could've just walked in. And I got to thinking perhaps there was something wrong, perhaps something had happened to her . . .' His voice tailed off. 'Can I have a fag now?' he said abruptly.

'Go ahead.' Thanet was interested to note the tremor in Kevin's hands as he rolled his cigarette. He made a bad job of it too and the loose paper flared up as he struck a match to it. He guessed that despite the apparent ease with which the boy had told his story until now, Kevin was dreading the next part. 'Go on,' he said gently.

Kevin spat out a loose shred of tobacco then gave him an assessing glance. 'So I went across, didn't I? It was all quiet in the house, no radio or telly on. It was like in them films, when you've got this terrific build-up to what's going to be on the other side of the door.' He stubbed out his cigarette viciously.

It was a gesture of anger and of something more. Repudiation? But of what? Thanet wondered. Of reality, perhaps. Until the moment when Kevin had pushed open that door he had been keyed up, excited, playing a part in a drama which had no real emotional impact because it was unrelated to his feelings. But if the boy, for whatever reason, had for months been focusing his thoughts, his hopes, his aspirations perhaps, on Jessica, what a shock the sight of her lifeless body must have been.

He was right. Kevin had put his elbows on the table and buried his face in his hands. 'And there she was,' he said in a muffled voice. 'It was horrible. She was all – crumpled. Broken. I never seen a dead person before. And she was always so alive.' His head came up suddenly and Thanet experienced a powerful pang of compassion at the pain in the boy's face. 'Did you know her?' he said.

Thanet shook his head. 'Only by sight.'

'She was great,' said Kevin. 'Really great. I always used to wash her hair, you know – beautiful hair, she had, long and thick and that amazing colour . . . And we'd talk. You know the great thing about her?'

Thanet shook his head.

'She made you feel you had . . . what's the word? Potential. Yeah, that's it. Potential. As though you could do whatever you wanted to do, if you only wanted it enough and were prepared to work hard enough. She had a pretty bad time of it herself when she was little, you know.'

'Yes, I know.'

'And look how she ended up! It's not fair! It's bloody well not fair!'

'You really liked her, didn't you, Kevin?'

'Yes I bloody did! She was . . . She was . . .' He shook his head, as if Jessica's qualities defied description. '. . . great,' he finished.

'It must have been a terrible shock for you.'

'You can say that again.' Now that the worst was over Kevin's bravado was creeping back.

'Did you touch her at all, move her?'

'No!' He was horrified. 'What would have been the point? Anyone could see she was dead, with her eyes all staring like that.' He shuddered. 'All I could think of was to get out of there, quick.'

'Was it you who rang for an ambulance?'

'Yeah, it was.'

'Why?'

'What d'you mean?'

'Well, as you said, she was obviously dead, nothing could be done for her.'

'But I couldn't just walk out and do nothing, leave her there like that, could I?'

'No, I don't suppose you could.'

'And I remembered to pick up the receiver in my handkerchief,' said Kevin proudly.

Police procedurals on TV had much to answer for, thought Thanet.

Lineham shifted restlessly beside him. Thanet knew why. There was one burning question which as yet remained unanswered.

'Kevin,' he said, 'I asked you just now if you recognised

the man you saw come out of Jessica's house, but you didn't reply. Did you know who he was?'

Kevin nodded and now his face was grim. 'He's some sort of relation of hers. Farm manager at Hunter's Green Farm, over at Nettleton.'

Thanet and Lineham looked at each other. 'Bernard Covin!' said Lineham.

FIFTEEN

'That's a turn up for the book!' said Lineham, when Kevin had gone. The boy could not be shaken. The man he saw come out of Jessica's house that night was Bernard Covin, and his description of him certainly matched. His interest in Covin had first been aroused when he saw him talking to Jessica in Sturrenden High Street one day. It was obvious that they knew each other well and a couple of weeks later, after seeing Covin in a pub, he had decided to follow him home. He had eventually discovered that Covin had in fact been married to Jessica's sister, now dead.

Thanet guessed that Kevin had originally suspected that Jessica might be involved with Covin and had followed him out of jealous interest. He wondered what the boy had thought of her affair with Ogilvy. 'We'd better take another look at Covin's statement,' he said. Though he could remember perfectly well what the man had told them: Covin and his daughter had had supper together before she left to drive to Reading. She had asked him to give her aunt a ring to apologise for not having managed to visit her to say goodbye before leaving for the new term and he had done so, about 7.30. When he got Jessica's answering machine he had rung off and had then spent the rest of the evening watching television.

They both read Covin's statement through again, but found nothing new or ambiguous in it.

'Presumably, having failed to get through on the phone, he then went round instead,' said Lineham.

'But why? It was scarcely an urgent message, was it? And how did he get to Charthurst anyway?' said Thanet. 'Karen had taken his car. He must have borrowed a farm vehicle.'

They looked at each other in sudden comprehension.

'That white pick-up parked at the Green Man!' said Lineham.

'A bit slow on the uptake, weren't we?' said Thanet. 'We really ought to have followed that up before. We knew about Kevin's father's Nissan and Ogilvy's Mercedes but we just didn't follow up on the Ford.'

'I suppose that was because Covin told us his daughter had borrowed his car, so we just assumed he'd be without transport.'

Will I never learn, thought Thanet? 'Just shows how dangerous assumptions can be. And of course we're making another, in assuming it was Covin who was driving that Ford.'

'It does seem likely, though, doesn't it? He must have got there somehow.'

'We really should have made an effort to trace that pick-up before, then we might have made the connection with Covin, if there is one. Anyway, assuming it was Covin that Kevin saw come out of the house, why on earth do you suppose he left the door open?'

'Maybe Kevin's right, sir. Maybe Covin did just want to muddy the waters.'

'Which waters? Nobody even knew he was there.'

'Maybe he didn't want to ring for an ambulance himself because he didn't want to get involved, but thought that if he left the door open someone else might notice and go to investigate – which is, in fact, what happened.'

'But why bother? Presumably he knew that sooner or later her husband would come home and find her. And in fact, if she did die as the result of a quarrel or whatever, I'd have thought he'd prefer to delay the discovery of the body rather than hasten it. No, it doesn't make sense.'

'Perhaps he hoped that when the police heard the door had been left open they might think it was a burglary that went wrong.'

'The last thing a burglar would have done is leave it open, surely, and draw attention to the fact that something was amiss? And it was the fact that the door was open that alerted us to the possibility that it hadn't been a straightforward accident.'

'Perhaps he just acted unwisely on the spur of the moment. He'd have been anxious to get away. I don't suppose he'd have had time to work out all the pros and cons.'

'You're probably right, Mike. Ah well, no doubt we'll find out eventually. Anyway, as far as the case is concerned we don't seem to have got much further, do we? All we've achieved is to add one more to our list of suspects.'

'You don't think we can cross Kevin off, then?'

'I think we still ought to keep an open mind as far as he's concerned. Though I'm inclined to believe his story, aren't you?'

'Yes, I am. I imagine he didn't tell us about Covin before because he didn't want to admit to having been there in the first place.'

'Quite.'

'And at least we're gradually getting a clearer picture of what happened that night.'

'True.' But Thanet was determined to feel pessimistic. The truth was, he was still feeling put out that his beautiful theory had been proved wrong and Kevin had turned out to be someone else's son, not Jessica's. It had been such a neat, satisfying explanation. He sighed. He ought to know by now that life wasn't like that, it was muddled and messy and explanations were rarely neat and even more rarely satisfying.

'What's the matter, sir?'

'There was I, thinking we were going to have this case all nicely sewn up before the wedding, and we're practically back to square one. Come on, Mike. Let's see what culinary delights the canteen has to offer today. I don't know about you but I feel distinctly in need of nourishment.'

Over dried-up shepherd's pie and watery cabbage they chewed over Covin's involvement in the case.

'I still can't see why he went over to see her,' said Thanet for the third time. He kept on coming back to this. He dug down into his pie, seeking for any sign of mince beneath the thick topping of potato. 'It really wouldn't have mattered if he hadn't passed on Karen's message until the next day. Honestly, these caterers really ought to be prosecuted under the Trade Descriptions Act. There's barely a couple of teaspoonfuls of meat under this potato!' It was a general grumble that since the

210

canteen had switched to outside caterers standards had plummeted.

Lineham grinned. 'A dicy one, that, sir. Precisely how much mince should there be in a shepherd's pie?'

Thanet grunted, then there was silence while they both considered possible reasons for Covin's visit.

'Unless . . .' said Lineham suddenly.

'What?'

'I was thinking . . .'

'Come on, spit it out, Mike.'

'Well, I was just thinking. What if that phone call wasn't to have been a message from Karen at all. What if it had been about something else entirely?'

Thanet stared at him. 'Something sufficiently urgent for him to go over there when she failed to answer the phone, you mean? But what?'

Lineham lifted his shoulders. 'Search me. Just an idea.'

'Yes,' said Thanet slowly. All at once he was aware of the beginnings of a familiar sensation in his head, almost of pressure building. His pulse speeded up. 'Let me think, let me think,' he muttered.

'Perhaps he intended putting a note through her door?'

Intent upon trying to formulate the idea that was just beyond his grasp, Thanet scarcely heard him. He froze with his fork half way to his mouth, as illumination came.

Of course!

He automatically popped the cabbage into his mouth and chewed without tasting.

Could it be true?

'Sir?' said Lineham, alerted. He was used to Thanet's

brainwaves and had seen that look more times than he could remember.

Thanet's eyes came into focus again. 'Yes?'

'What were you thinking?'

Thanet shook his head. 'I'm not sure I want to risk telling you, after the last fiasco.'

'Oh come on, sir! You can't leave me in suspense!'

Thanet still hesitated. He didn't relish the prospect of being wrong again. But Lineham had never been one to gloat over someone else's mistakes and it really wouldn't be fair to keep him in the dark. 'All right. What if . . .?'

Lineham's eyes opened wide as Thanet explained. 'But, sir, we haven't a single shred of evidence to suggest that might be true.'

'That doesn't mean to say it isn't. We got our wires crossed in exactly the same way in the Parnell case, don't you remember?'

'Yes, I do. But Covin said –'

Thanet knew exactly what Lineham was going to say. 'I know what Covin said! But he might well have been lying about that too.'

'I suppose,' said Lineham. But it was obvious that he still wasn't convinced. 'Anyway,' he said, 'even if it is true, it might have no bearing on the case.'

'*Might* is the operative word, Mike.'

'I don't see how it could.'

'That's because we haven't got to the bottom of it all yet.' Thanet was becoming exasperated. 'You know perfectly well that something we don't understand is often explicable in the light of later evidence.'

'True.' But Lineham was still grudging.

'I think it's worth following up, anyway. We'll put Tanya on to Southport.'

Lineham knew when there was no point in arguing. 'Right, sir.'

'And then we'll go and see the Pinks.'

'The Pinks?'

'Covin's former employers, Mike. Wake up!'

'But why, sir?'

'Because they'll be able to fill us in on the background, obviously!'

'But isn't it more important to go and tackle Covin?'

'All in good time, Mike. The more weapons we have tucked under our belt the better equipped we'll be.' He stood up. 'Where did the Wargreaves say they lived?'

'Near Headcorn,' Lineham muttered, obviously convinced that Thanet was going off on a wild goose chase.

'Shouldn't be too difficult to find out exactly where.'

No more difficult than consulting the telephone directory, in fact, and half an hour later they were turning in to the entrance to Barn End Farm. Thanet was relieved to see that the clouds which had blown up earlier had cleared away. Perhaps it would be a fine day tomorrow after all.

'Must have been a step up for Covin to get the job at Hunter's Green Farm,' said Lineham as they pulled up in front of the farmhouse and got out of the car. His moods never lasted long and he was already back to his usual ebullient self.

Thanet agreed. This farmhouse was smaller and the outbuildings less extensive. There were children's toys lying about and a black-and-white puppy came bouncing around the corner of the house barking shrilly, closely

213

pursued by a little boy of about four. He stopped when he saw the strangers and, like little Daisy Ogilvy, put his thumb in his mouth.

'Hello,' said Lineham, trying to stop the puppy climbing up his trouser leg. 'Where's your mummy?'

The boy turned and ran off the way he had come. Thanet and Lineham followed. The puppy was still barking and jumping up and down at Lineham as they walked.

'He's taken a fancy to you, Mike,' said Thanet with a grin, raising his voice to make himself heard.

'Why on earth can't people keep their dogs under control?' said Lineham, trying to fend the animal off.

'I've got a nasty feeling we might be disappointed here,' said Thanet. 'If the boy's parents are the owners they'd be much too young to be the Pinks we want to see.'

'Could be the son,' said Lineham. 'The old man might have retired. Down, boy! Down!'

They had to pass the kitchen window to get to the back door. There was a young woman inside, watching them. Thanet raised a hand in greeting and she nodded but made no move to open the door. They waited a few moments and then went back to the window. She was leaning forward across the sink, waiting for them.

'Identification,' she mouthed.

Thanet nodded and they both pressed their warrant cards against the window.

A moment later she unlocked the door and opened it. She was holding the little boy by the hand. 'Sorry,' she said, raising her voice above the noise the dog was still making. 'But you can't be too careful these days, especially in a place like this. Quiet, Tess!'

The dog ignored her.

'I couldn't agree more,' said Thanet.

To Lineham's relief she bent down and seized the puppy by the collar. 'I apologise for Tess,' she said. 'She's only six months old and not very civilised yet. Just a moment.' She dragged the dog off and they heard a door open and close.

'Mrs Pink?' said Thanet when she returned, relieved to be speaking at a normal pitch again.

'Yes?' Her expression changed and she glanced from one to the other. 'There's nothing wrong, is there? My husband hasn't had an accident?'

'Oh no, not at all.'

As Lineham had suggested she was the daughter-in-law of the Pinks who had been Covin's employers. Her father-in-law had retired four years previously, and he and his wife had moved into a development of retirement homes on the edge of the village. Ten minutes later Thanet and Lineham were turning in between the imposing wrought-iron gates at the entrance to The Beeches, a retirement complex set in what had obviously once been the spacious grounds of a large Victorian house which was visible over to the left behind a screen of young trees. Such developments had sprung up everywhere over the last ten to fifteen years as it had dawned on builders that the one sector of the housing market which was going to expand rather than shrink in the immediate future was custom-built accommodation for the elderly. The complexes varied enormously in price and quality, as might be expected, but this was obviously an upmarket version, built in the local vernacular of brick and tilehanging in a setting of carefully preserved mature trees and well-kept

215

lawns and flowerbeds. Thanet and Lineham followed a curving drive to the rear of the block of buildings then made for the warden's flat. Their knock was answered by a pleasant middle-aged woman.

'It's not bad news, I hope?' she said, when Thanet had introduced himself and asked for the Pinks.

'No, not at all, I assure you.'

'Good. Only Mrs Pink isn't too well. She's not long out of hospital.'

'We'll try not to tire her.'

This seemed to satisfy her. 'I'll take you along.'

'That isn't necessary, really.'

But she insisted. 'I'd like to make sure they're not alarmed.' She smiled. 'It's not often we get a visit from the police.'

The Pinks' home was a surprise. From the outside the cottages looked small but inside they were unexpectedly spacious. The warden asked them to wait while she went in, then reappeared with an elderly man whose leathery complexion criss-crossed by a myriad of fine lines at once proclaimed that he had spent his working life in the open air, rain or shine. He greeted them apprehensively then led them through a large square sitting room into a heated conservatory where his wife was sitting with one bandaged foot propped up on a footstool. 'Here they are, dear,' he said.

'Please don't worry,' said Thanet, anxious to allay their obvious anxiety. 'The only reason we've come to see you is that we think you might be able to help us with some information about a former employee.'

As if by magic their faces cleared and Mrs Pink invited Thanet and Lineham to sit down.

'Who d'you mean?' said her husband, when they were all settled.

Thanet had arranged that Lineham would begin this interview. 'Someone who worked for you over twenty years ago, sir,' said the sergeant. 'A man called Bernard Covin.'

'Oh, I see,' said Pink. And to his wife, 'It must be about Jessica.'

'Oh,' she said. 'We heard about it on the radio.' She looked tired and drawn and from time to time would ease the bandaged foot into a new position, lifting her leg with both hands. A pair of aluminium crutches stood against the wall nearby. 'And there's an article in the *KM* today.'

Of course, it was Friday, thought Thanet. He should have remembered to check the newspaper, though he doubted that they would learn anything new from it.

'Terrible, wasn't it?' she said. 'Poor little scrap.'

Thanet realised she was remembering Jessica as the child she had known.

'You remember her, then,' said Lineham.

'Of course!' she said. 'She came to live with her sister and Bernard when her mother died. You couldn't help feeling sorry for her. She always looked as if a puff of wind would blow her away, so thin and pale she was.'

'How did she get on with her brother-in-law?'

She shrugged. 'Didn't have much to do with him, as far as I could see. Very fond of her sister she was, though. She was a lovely girl, Madge. I was sorry to see her go, when they moved away. Too good for him, I always thought.'

'I never could see why you didn't like him, myself,' said her husband. 'He was a good worker, was Bernard.'

217

Another shrug. 'I just never took to him. How is Madge?' she said to Lineham.

'She died, I'm afraid,' he said. 'Of breast cancer, I believe. A couple of years ago.'

Her face had clouded. 'Oh, I am sorry. What about her little girl? What was her name?'

'Karen. But not so little now,' said Lineham with a smile. 'She's nearly twenty and studying at Reading University.'

'Twenty!' said Mrs Pink. 'You can't credit it, the way time speeds up as you get older!'

'Did you know Karen as a baby?' said Lineham. 'We thought the Covins left here just before she was born.'

'Not before. Just after, actually. Not that Madge was here when the baby arrived, so I didn't see her until she was about three months old, when Madge brought her to see me. She was so proud of her! She'd been so excited when she found she was pregnant! They'd been married six or seven years by then, you see, and had more or less given up hope. Mind, she didn't have a very easy time. First she had terrible morning sickness and then she got high blood pressure and had to rest a lot. In fact, I hardly saw her for the last three or four months. She never went out, except when Bernard took her to the ante-natal clinic. Those were the only times I caught a glimpse of her, when she was passing in the car.'

'You didn't go and see her?'

'I tried, a few times, but she would never answer the door. In the end I gave up. I assumed she just didn't feel like socialising, that she'd no doubt get back to normal after the baby was born. As she did. She certainly seemed all right when she brought the baby to see me, as I say.'

'What did you mean, "Not that Madge was here"? Where was she?'

Thanet was glad that Lineham had picked this up.

'She was in Bristol – it was Bristol, wasn't it, Bob?'

They were well away now, engrossed in their story. Like many elderly people who don't get out much they obviously enjoyed having an audience.

Her husband nodded. 'Yes. It's all a bit complicated. Madge and Jessica had this aunt, you see, who lived in Bristol. The previous summer holidays Jessica went to stay with her and they got on so well she decided to stay on. But in the middle of December Jessica apparently rang to say the aunt had been taken ill and would Madge come and help. Well, Jessica was only sixteen so presumably Madge felt she had to go.'

'She wouldn't have been very happy about it, I imagine,' said Mrs Pink. 'She had this problem with high blood pressure, the baby was due at the beginning of January and apart from anything else she'd been very busy trying to get everything packed up ready for the move.'

'The move to Hunter's Green Farm, you mean?' said Lineham.

'Yes,' said Pink. 'Bernard had put in for the job in November and just before that phone call from Jessica he heard he'd got it. He was over the moon, of course, it was a step up for him.'

'But I shouldn't think Madge was too pleased,' Mrs Pink put in. 'It meant she'd be moving house just around the time the baby was born and I'm sure she wouldn't have felt well enough to cope.'

'The job started in the new year,' said her husband. 'So they were supposed to move on January 1st.'

'Anyway, as Bob says, Madge presumably didn't feel she had any choice and off she went to Bristol,' said Mrs Pink. 'And lo and behold, the baby chose to arrive early – probably because of all the upheaval. So just before Christmas Bernard gets a phone call to say Madge had gone into labour. Well, naturally he left right away, and the next day we heard the baby had arrived and it was a little girl.'

'Bernard stayed on for another week and then had to come home by himself to do the move.'

'The aunt was still ill, you see, so Madge felt she couldn't leave Jessica to cope alone. That was why I didn't see Karen until she was three months old.'

'So when Mrs Covin did come back she went straight to Hunter's Green Farm?' said Lineham.

'Yes.'

'And when was that?'

Mrs Pink frowned. 'I'm not sure. Early in February, I believe.'

'So the baby would have been about six weeks old.'

'Something like that, I imagine.'

So there it was. Thanet felt a thrill of triumph. He was right this time, he just knew it.

Outside Lineham said, 'All right, all right, don't say it. I was wrong!'

'We're not a hundred per cent certain yet, Mike.'

'We soon will be.'

And they were. Back at the office WDC Phillips was waiting for them, fax in hand. 'This just came through, sir.'

220

'Well?' He almost snatched it from her in his eagerness. And there it was, the proof he needed. The
information on the birth certificate was unequivocal:

Name of child: Karen Mary.
Date of birth: 21.12.77.
Name of mother: Jessica Mary Dander.

SIXTEEN

'Well done, Tanya,' said Thanet, handing the fax to Lineham. 'I didn't think you'd get a response so quickly.'

'Well, I did lay it on a bit thick, sir, the urgency, I mean. A murder case and so on. But the girl was very helpful. Apparently she deals exclusively with police inquiries. And the fact that it was an unusual surname helped.'

'Good.'

'I was a bit puzzled when you told me to ring Southport. I've never had occasion to make this sort of inquiry before and I always thought the records were held at St Catherine's House. That's where I'd have rung if you hadn't told me otherwise.'

'They only have the Index to the Register there,' said Lineham. 'And they don't deal with telephone inquiries anyway. You have to go along in person and it's always packed out. This is a much better system.'

'She said the father's name does not appear on the certificate if the child is born out of wedlock unless he agrees.'

'Presumably he didn't,' said Lineham. 'Anyway,' he said to Thanet, waving the fax, 'we got what we wanted. You were right, weren't you, sir?'

'So far, anyway.' Thanet dismissed WDC Phillips with a smile and a nod.

'Though I still can't see that it gets us any further.'

Thanet grinned. 'To be honest, Mike, neither can I, at the moment.' It had done much to restore his confidence, however, and he felt optimistic as they now set off to interview Covin. He hoped Covin would be there this time. Not wishing to put him on his guard they had deliberately refrained from ringing to check.

'Hope we won't have a wasted journey,' said Lineham, tuning in to his thoughts.

'So do I.'

But they were out of luck, it seemed. Hunter's Green Farm appeared deserted.

'I suppose they're all out in the orchards,' said Lineham.

'Let's try the packing shed.'

Inside the shed the scene was very different from yesterday evening, when they had run Covin to earth in the glass-walled office. The grading machine and conveyor belts were working and as soon as they stepped inside the hum of machinery met their ears. The rich, fruity aroma of ripe apples was even stronger and there was an atmosphere of bustle and activity. Most of the workers were women, all wearing dark green overalls and a cap-cum-headscarf which covered their hair.

'No idea,' said one of them in response to their inquiry as to Covin's whereabouts. 'Mick Landy might know.' She pointed. 'Over there.'

Landy was operating a small fork-lift truck, moving boxes of apples to stack them on pallets. 'He's gone to take his dad to the dentist's. His parents haven't got a car.' He was a very tall, lanky young man, all knees and elbows as he hunched over the controls in the confined space. He was wearing a baseball cap the wrong way around.

Landy hadn't switched off the engine and once again Thanet found himself shouting. 'Is he coming back this afternoon?'

'Yes. He said he'd be back before I knocked off.'

'Could we step into the office for a few minutes, sir?' At this rate he wouldn't have any voice left for his speech tomorrow!

'Sure.' Landy twisted the ignition key, removed his cap and wiped his forehead on the back of his sleeve. Then he led the way to the office, which still stank of Covin's cigarettes. He shut the door behind them and the noise faded to a muted roar.

'What sort of car is Mr Covin driving at the moment?' said Lineham. 'We understand his daughter has borrowed his.'

'That's right. He's using the pick-up. He often does.' Landy grinned. 'Doesn't have to pay for the petrol.'

The pick-up was white, apparently, and a Ford. Thanet and Lineham exchanged glances of satisfaction.

'Where do you live, sir? On the farm?' Lineham asked.

He was obviously thinking that if, like Covin, Landy also had a tied cottage, it was possible that he might have seen or heard Covin go out on Tuesday night.

No such luck.

'In the village. Why?'

'So you wouldn't by any chance know if Mr Covin used the pick-up on Tuesday night, after Karen left to drive to Reading?'

'What's this all about?' Landy was wary now.

Thanet felt a spurt of excitement. Landy did know, obviously, but was reluctant to say so in case it caused Covin trouble.

'Just answer the question, please, sir.'

'You'll have to ask him, won't you?'

It was a struggle for Lineham to persuade Landy to talk but he managed it in the end.

Apparently Landy had been using the pick-up on Tuesday afternoon and Covin had told him not to bother to return it until next day, but at just after 7.30 that evening he had rung to ask him to bring it back right away. He said he had arranged to go out that evening and had forgotten that Karen would be borrowing his car to drive her stuff back to Reading. It wasn't until he was ready to go that he remembered Landy had the Ford. He was already late, he said, so could Landy hurry up. He would drop him back at his own house before going on to his appointment. Landy had done as he asked.

'So how did he seem?' said Lineham.

'A bit on edge, I suppose,' said Landy reluctantly.

'Did he say where he was going?'

'Didn't say much at all. Just thanks and sorry for disturbing my evening.'

'Didn't you wonder what it was all about?'

'No point, was there? It was none of my business. If he wasn't going to tell me, I wasn't going to ask.'

'Did you see which direction he drove off in, after dropping you?'

'The Ashford direction.'

The way he would have to go to get to Charthurst.

On the point of leaving Thanet turned. 'D'you happen to know if Karen usually drove herself back to Reading at the beginning of term?'

'Funny you should ask that. No, Bernard usually takes her.'

'So, what now?' said Lineham when they were outside. 'Do we wait?'

Thanet was thinking about something else. 'I don't know,' he said. Then, putting his mind to the question, 'Yes. He's due back soon and if we went to his parents' house, we might miss him. We don't want him arriving back here in the interim and hearing from Landy that we've found out he was lying about not going out on Tuesday night. I want to catch him unprepared.' He took out his pipe and tobacco. It was too good an opportunity to miss. 'I think I'll take a little stroll down the track.'

Lineham fell into step beside him. 'Anyway,' he said, 'we now not only have an eye-witness who saw him come out of Jessica's house around the time she died, but a second witness to connect him with the pick-up and a third to swear the pick-up was parked at the pub.'

'Not *the* pick-up,' said Thanet, his thoughts still focused elsewhere. '*A* pick-up.'

'Oh, come on, sir. A *white Ford* pick-up. Isn't that enough?'

'A registration number would have been even better.'

'But it's enough to bring him in.'

'To bring him in, yes. But not to charge him, obviously.'

'D'you think this appointment he mentioned to Landy was with Jessica?'

'I shouldn't think so. She had a date with Ogilvy, so she wouldn't have arranged to see Covin as well. I doubt that he had an appointment at all, it was just an excuse he gave to Landy for wanting the pick-up in a hurry.'

'So what was suddenly so urgent?'

'Ah, now I've just been thinking about that.'

'Oh?' said Lineham.

'Yes. What if –'

'Here he comes, sir.' The pick-up had just turned into the track.

Thanet sighed. He'd just got his pipe going nicely and he'd been looking forward to trying out this new idea of his on Lineham.

'Can we talk to him outside, sir?' said Lineham as they turned to walk back. 'I don't think I can face that sitting room again.'

Thanet shook his head. 'Sorry, Mike. It would be inappropriate. Too informal.'

Covin raised a hand in salute as he drove past.

'Besides,' said Thanet, 'I should think that any minute now the farm workers will be knocking off. It would be impossible to talk with people streaming past.'

Now it was Lineham's turn to sigh.

Covin parked in front of the packing shed and came back to meet them, the inevitable cigarette dangling from his lips.

'We'd like another word, sir, if we may,' said Thanet, reluctantly knocking out his pipe on the heel of his shoe.

'No need to put your pipe out, Inspector. You're

welcome to smoke inside.' But despite the apparent geniality his eyes were wary.

Thanet smiled inwardly as he imagined Lineham's reaction if he had accepted the invitation.

Having been shut up all day the sitting room smelled worse than ever. Lineham made a little gagging sound of disgust as they went in and Thanet gave him a warning glance. He sympathised, but the sergeant really would have to learn to keep quiet about this.

Covin lit another cigarette from the stub of the one he had been smoking. 'I hope this won't take too long, Inspector. I've got things to attend to before people knock off.'

Thanet ignored this. 'Do you often drive that pick-up, sir?'

'Sometimes. Why?'

'And on Tuesday evening?'

Covin's eyes narrowed above the coils of smoke. 'What are you getting at?'

'Remind me what you said you did on Tuesday evening.'

'I told you. I had supper with my daughter and after she left I watched television.'

'All evening?'

'All evening.'

'So you claim that you definitely weren't driving that pick-up on Tuesday evening?'

'Look, what is all this about?'

'And you definitely did not visit your sister-in-law's house that night?'

'No! I said, what's this all about?'

Thanet leaned forward. 'I'll tell you what it's all about,

Mr Covin. We don't like it when witnesses lie to us, that's what. Especially when it involves something as serious as murder.'

'What do you mean?' But the bravado had gone out of Covin's voice.

'One,' said Thanet, ticking the points off on his fingers, 'we have a witness to say that far from sitting innocently at home watching television that night, you actually rang him around 7.30 on Tuesday evening to ask him to bring the pick-up over because you needed it urgently to go out. Two, the landlord at the Green Man in Charthurst swears that that same pick-up was illegally parked on his forecourt around eight o'clock that evening.' This was stretching the truth a little, but still . . . 'And three,' said Thanet with emphasis, 'we also have a witness who swears that he saw you – you, Mr Covin – coming out of your sister-in-law's house at about five past eight that evening.' He stopped.

Silence.

'Well, Mr Covin?'

'They're lying,' said Covin. His fingers were trembling as he lit up again.

'What, all of them?'

Silence again.

'I don't think a jury would be likely to accept your word against theirs, do you?'

Covin still said nothing, just puffed furiously, sucking the smoke into his lungs as if his life depended on it.

Thanet wondered what would happen if they took his cigarettes away. They couldn't do that here, of course, and anyway Thanet didn't believe in gratuitous cruelty. But back at the station, perhaps, as a last resort . . .?

'Especially when we could actually prove to them that you had already lied to us about something else.'

Covin jumped up. 'I don't have to listen to this! I'm not under arrest, am I? Right, then, that's it. Enough. I'd like you to leave now.'

'By all means,' said Thanet pleasantly, getting up with a glance at Lineham, who followed suit. 'We'll continue the interview at the Station, shall we?'

'What d'you mean?'

'Simply that you have a choice: we can continue here or there, whichever you wish. But make no mistake, Mr Covin, I have no intention of terminating this interview until I am satisfied.'

Covin stared at him, chewing the inside of his lip. Then he tossed his head in disgust, sat down and shook out yet another cigarette.

The two policemen sat down again.

'I'm glad you've decided to be cooperative,' said Thanet. 'Now, where was I?'

'You were telling Mr Covin that he wouldn't stand much chance of being believed in Court, in view of the fact that we could prove he'd lied to us about something else,' said Lineham.

'Ah yes,' said Thanet. 'That's right.' He waited. 'Aren't you going to ask what that something else was, sir?'

Covin compressed his lips as if to prevent words escaping. Clearly he was longing to ask but terrified of knowing the answer.

'Very well,' said Thanet. 'When you confirmed that your sister-in-law had given birth to an illegitimate child when she was sixteen, you told us that the baby was a boy.'

Covin stared at him, the colour seeping from his naturally ruddy complexion.

'When in fact,' said Thanet, 'it was a girl.' He nodded at Lineham, who took the fax from the pages of his notebook, unfolded it and laid it on Covin's lap.

Covin looked at it and then at Thanet. It was as if he had been struck dumb, the muscles of his face and organs of speech paralysed.

No. He was waiting, Thanet realised, to see how much more they knew. Very well. 'That was quite a smokescreen you put up, wasn't it, pretending that it was your wife who was pregnant, arranging for Jessica to go away before her pregnancy began to show and then making sure your wife was away when the baby was due so that you could go through the charade of rushing to her bedside. Just as a matter of interest, did the aunt with the convenient illness ever exist, or was she just a figment of someone's fertile imagination?'

Covin didn't answer.

'But anyway, it's all ancient history now. Twenty years is a long time. Why bother to go on lying about it now?'

Covin still didn't respond.

'Mr Covin,' said Thanet softly. 'Is Karen aware that she is adopted?'

Covin jumped. In his absorption the cigarette had burned down to his fingers. He stubbed it out and found his voice at last. He ignored Thanet's question. 'How did you find out?'

'We went to talk to your former employers, the Pinks. It wasn't too difficult to work out what had happened. Of course, at the time, the deception worked well – has continued to work, for that matter, all these years. But my guess is that on Tuesday something happened to change the situation, and that was why you went rushing over to see your sister-in-law.'

Bernard stared at him.

'Karen found out, didn't she?' said Thanet softly.

'No!' said Covin desperately. Then he buried his face in his hands. He mumbled through his fingers.

'Sorry?' said Thanet. He thought he had caught the word 'accident'. Was this a confession? He glanced at Lineham who raised his eyebrows and mouthed *Caution?*

Thanet shook his head and ignoring Lineham's puzzled frown said to Covin, 'What did you say?'

Covin sat up and reached for his cigarettes. 'I said, it was an accident,' he said wearily.

It *was* a confession.

'Sir!' said Lineham but again Thanet shook his head. 'Go on.'

'Jessica had been threatening to tell Karen,' said Covin. 'We'd all agreed from the beginning that we never would. I was afraid that if Karen found out she'd turn against me, for keeping it from her. She's . . .' He faltered and briefly his face crumpled as if he were about to dissolve into tears. 'She's all I have left now my wife is gone. I was desperate to stop her finding out, so as soon as she'd left I got Landy to bring the pick-up over and drove to Charthurst.'

Already questions were buzzing in Thanet's brain but he said nothing. There'd be plenty of time later. If Covin was willing to talk he had no intention of stopping him.

'I got there around eightish. I parked at the pub

232

because the road was up in front of Jessica's house. When she let me in –' He stopped.

'Yes?' prompted Thanet.

'I tried to persuade her to change her mind, but she wouldn't listen.' Covin was speaking more slowly now. 'In the end she told me to go –'

'Where was this conversation taking place?' Thanet interrupted for the first time.

'In the sitting room.'

'I see. Go on.'

'We were both pretty worked up by then and she ended up by saying she'd made up her mind and nothing was going to stop her. She stalked out of the room into the hall and started to go up the stairs. I followed her. I . . . I caught her by the arm and she must have lost her balance. She fell. It was horrible. I couldn't believe it. I never intended to hurt her, honestly!'

'And where was she, exactly, when she fell?'

'About halfway up, I suppose.'

'I see.' Thanet's eyes met Lineham's. The sergeant no doubt had an equally clear picture in his mind of Jessica's shoe lying against the staircase wall, three steps down from the top.

They were both startled by a slow handclap from the door of the sitting room.

'Well done, Dad. Good try.'

A girl was standing with her hands on her hips, a slight figure in jeans and sweatshirt. Karen. Knowing her parentage Thanet briefly wondered how she could have failed to notice her resemblance to her mother over all these years. There was Jessica's slightly pointed nose, and lips that were too thin for beauty. But her eyes were hazel instead of green, her hair brown not chestnut. Perhaps she had resembled her aunt, her adoptive mother, too. Genes often skipped about in the generations.

He could guess what she meant by 'good try'.

SEVENTEEN

Thanet glimpsed relief then horror on Covin's face before Covin cried 'Karen!' and erupting from his seat went rushing across to seize her by the elbow and attempt to steer her out of the room.

The horror Thanet could understand, but relief? No, that was beyond him.

Karen tried to shake him off. 'Dad! Let go!'

'I really don't think this is a good place for you to be right now, love,' said Covin. He was trying to sound calm but merely succeeded in sounding desperate.

'We have no objection to Miss Covin being present, if she wishes,' said Thanet.

Karen finally managed to free herself from Covin's grasp. 'There you are, Dad. That's all right, then.'

'Inspector,' said Covin, turning to face Thanet. 'I've changed my mind. I think it would be better to continue this interview at the Police Station.'

'I'll come with you,' said Karen. 'I think the Inspector would be interested in what I have to say.'

They all looked at Covin who seemed to shrink before their eyes. It was as if all the air had suddenly been sucked out of him.

'You won't stop me, Dad,' she said softly, and put her hand on his arm.

He looked directly into her face for the first time, a long searching look, and she stared back. The air between them was dense with emotion, charged with words unspoken, explanations long delayed. 'No,' he said finally. 'I can see I won't.'

She tucked her arm through his and led him to the sofa where they sank down on to it, side by side.

Thanet introduced himself and Lineham, before saying, 'As you've no doubt gathered, we're investigating the death of your . . . of Mrs Jessica Manifest, or Jessica Dander as she was professionally known. I don't know how much you heard just now . . .'

'Most of it,' Karen said. 'I parked around the back and came in through the back door. Dad's a shocker, he never locks it.'

'Karen –' said Covin.

'Shh,' she said, and squeezed his arm. 'You're not stupid, Inspector,' she went on. 'You wouldn't have reached your present rank if you were. So you must realise Dad's story is as full of holes as a colander.' She laid a warning hand on Covin's arm as he made a movement of protest. 'It's no good, Dad. I told you, I've made up my mind.'

'I had noticed certain discrepancies,' said Thanet.

'And I suspect you can guess why.'

'He was trying to protect you,' said Thanet, catching a reproachful glance from Lineham. *Why didn't you tell me?*

He'd have to explain, later. 'I assume you've come back to sort things out.'

'Yes. And to return the car, of course. I couldn't hang on to it indefinitely.'

'We're all ears,' said Thanet. He couldn't believe it. The case was going to be cleared up in time for the wedding after all! There was going to be no coercion, no persuasion, no manipulation, just a straightforward confession, and all he had to do was sit back and listen! The only problem was, he wasn't sure if he wanted to hear it. He suspected that this was going to be one of those cases where he understood only too well why the crime had been committed, even had a sneaking sympathy for the perpetrator.

'It all began,' said Karen, 'because my roommate and I are planning to go Interrailing around Europe next summer and I needed a passport of my own.'

And there it was, the key to the whole puzzle, something so simple and so obvious. Why on earth didn't I catch on before? thought Thanet, castigating himself. I knew about the Interrailing plans, Lineham told me, early on.

'And for that, of course, I needed my birth certificate.'

Thanet glanced at the photographs, his gaze lingering on the one of Karen in ski outfit. 'Hadn't you been abroad before?'

'Oh yes, a number of times. But first on my parents' passports, then on a group passport, for school trips. This is the first time I'd needed one of my own.'

Once again Thanet was kicking himself. He'd known about passport arrangements for children too, from personal experience, but again it hadn't clicked.

'I'd been nagging Dad to let me have my birth certificate

237

for ages but first he kept on coming up with the excuse that he hadn't had time to look, then he kept on promising to look but never seemed to get around to it. When it got to the point where I was due to leave for the new term and he still hadn't produced it I said I was fed up with waiting and I was going to send off for a copy.'

'This was on Tuesday evening?'

'Yes, at supper. So, of course, he finally had to tell me the truth.'

So far she had appeared calm, composed. Now for the first time there was a tremor in her voice.

Thanet glanced at Covin. The man hadn't said a single word, he realised, ever since his bid to continue the interview back at Headquarters had failed. Covin was hunched into a corner of the sofa staring down at his hands, the picture of defeat and grim resignation. He wasn't smoking either, Thanet noticed. Perhaps he was beyond consolation.

Someone hammered on the front door. 'Bernie?'

Thanet recognised Landy's voice.

Covin glanced at Thanet for permission before going to deal with the inquiry and there was a murmured conversation in the hall.

In the interval no one spoke. There was a tacit agreement, it seemed, to wait for Covin to return before continuing.

When he had done so Thanet said, 'The truth being . . .?' It had to be spelled out. There was no room for misunderstandings and further false assumptions at this juncture.

Karen took a deep breath and began to talk.

Thanet could imagine it all so clearly:

'Oh Dad, you promised you'd find it before I went back, you really did. I've been asking you for months.'

'I know. But there's no hurry, is there? There's plenty of time before next summer.'

'It seems as though there's plenty of time, but you know as well as I do that if I'm not here to keep on at you, you'll never get around to it. I really can't see the difficulty. There are only a limited number of places you'd have put a birth certificate, surely. I'm sorry, I really don't want to wait any longer. I think the easiest thing would be for me to send off for a copy.'

'No! There's no need for that!'

'Isn't there? When did I first ask you to look it out for me? In July? That's three months ago! No, forget it. I'll see to it myself.'

'Karen –'

'Yes?'

'I . . . To be honest . . . To tell you the truth . . . I suppose I've just been putting off the evil hour.'

'What d'you mean, "evil hour"?'

'I . . . The reason I haven't produced it . . .'

'You mean, you do know where it is? You do? So what are you trying to say?'

'I didn't want to give it to you because I knew that when you saw it . . . Oh, it was stupid of me, I know that. Like I said, I was just putting it off, that's all. Pointless!'

'Putting what off? Dad, you're frightening me! Tell me!'

'Telling you . . . telling you that you were adopted . . . Karen, love, don't look at me like that!'

239

'But why didn't you tell me before? I mean, my God, Dad, everybody, but everybody knows you should always tell adopted children the truth, right from the beginning, practically as soon as they're old enough to talk! You know, all that stuff about really really wanting a baby and picking her out because she was so special . . . What? Why are you shaking your head?'

'That's the point, love, it wasn't like that.'

'What do you mean, it wasn't like that? You mean, you didn't pick me out? What did you do? Find me under a blackberry bush or something?'

'No, of course not!'

'Well, what did you mean?'

'That's one of the reasons why we never told you. It was all so complicated. When I said "adopted" I didn't actually mean legally adopted.'

'Dad, for crying out loud! I just can't believe this is happening!'

'Calm down, love.'

'Calm down! How can you expect me to be calm? Suddenly my parents are not my parents any more and I'm not even legally adopted? So who am I? And what about my mother? Who was she? Her name must be on that certificate. I want to see it.'

'All in good time, love. I might as well tell you now, myself. She was – is – your aunt Jessica.'

'My aunt Jessica? Auntie Jessica is my mother?'

And then had come the explanations, how Madge had longed for children but after years of trying had still failed to conceive, how she had seen Jessica's baby as the

240

perfect answer, a child of her own blood, how they had managed to deceive everyone into thinking the child was theirs.

Throughout Karen's account of this conversation Covin hadn't moved. It was as if he were in a state of suspended animation, waiting for something. But for what? Thanet wondered. Simply for Karen to finish, for this painful narration to be over? But no, she had stopped talking now and that air of frozen anticipation still seemed to encase the man like a shroud.

'It must all have been a terrible shock for you,' said Thanet.

'You can say that again! To find out that my mother was really my aunt and my aunt my mother, that everyone I loved and trusted had been deceiving me since the day I was born! It was as if . . . as if . . . Oh, I don't know. As if the foundations of my world had suddenly been knocked away. How could you do that to me?' she cried, addressing her father directly for the first time since she had begun her story. 'Can you even begin to imagine how I felt – how I feel?'

Now, at last, he moved. 'I'm sorry, love,' he whispered. The look he gave her was full of contrition, true, but there was more to it than that, a hunger to *know*.

And that must be it, of course, thought Thanet. Covin was longing to find out exactly what had happened at Jessica's house that night. Thanet's guess was that after all these revelations Karen's hurt and anger had been so intense that her overwhelming need had been to go and confront her mother. No doubt she had just grabbed the keys to her father's car and taken off – and afterwards had driven straight on to Reading. No wonder her father had

241

been 'on edge', as Landy put it, when he delivered the pick-up to him.

'Anyway,' said Karen, confirming what Thanet had been thinking, 'naturally I couldn't possibly just swan off to college leaving everything in the air like that. I had to see Jessica first; there were things I really needed to know. So I just took Dad's car keys and went. I was in such a state, I can't tell you . . . I don't remember anything about the journey.'

Thanet was aware that Lineham had stirred and he could guess what the sergeant was thinking. *Not a good idea to drive when you're in that condition.* Lineham was very hot on road safety. He glanced at him, willing him to keep quiet. He didn't want to interrupt the flow of Karen's story.

Lineham must have got the message because he settled down again.

'Anyway,' she went on, 'it wasn't until I got there that it occurred to me she might not be in. It simply never entered my head. It was as if I needed to see her so much she just couldn't *not* be there, if you see what I mean. I was so relieved when I saw the lights were on and then, when she answered the door . . . It was odd. She's always been a part of my life, but it was as if I was seeing her for the first time. Not my aunt, but my *mother.*' Karen shook her head. 'I just couldn't seem to make the transition. Mum – my real mother – was dead. I couldn't speak, I just stood there.'

'*Karen? What is it? What's the matter? Come in.*'

242

EIGHTEEN

'She took me by the arm,' said Karen, 'and tugged me in. I shook her off. I couldn't bear her to touch me.'

> '*Karen, what is the matter. Look, come into the sitting room and sit down.*'
>
> '*No! I'm not here for a cosy little chat!*'
>
> '*What, then?*'
>
> '*Dad's just told me the truth.*'
>
> '*What do you mean, the truth?*'
>
> '*That you . . . That you're my . . . my mother.*'
>
> '*Oh God, no! The bastard! He swore he'd never tell!*'
>
> '*I think you'll have to be careful how you use that word around me in future. And is that all you can say, anyway? Not, "Oh, I'm so sorry, Karen, I really didn't want to hand you over to someone else like an unwanted Christmas present." Or, "It really broke my heart to give you away, but I had no choice"?*'
>
> '*Well, I'm sorry you're upset, of course I am.*'
>
> '*And that's it? You're sorry I'm upset, full stop?*'

'It'll only make things worse if I'm hypocritical about it.'

'What do you mean, hypocritical? Oh, I see. You're saying you never wanted me in the first place, right?'

'No, I'm not saying that . . .'

'Well what are you saying?'

'I suppose if I'm honest . . . Let me put it another way. How many teenagers who discover they're pregnant actually want the baby? At least I had you, didn't I? I didn't have an abortion.'

'And I'm supposed to be grateful?'

'It's better to be alive than dead, isn't it? Look, I don't think there's any point in continuing this conversation. We'll talk again when you've calmed down.'

'Don't you dare turn away from me like that! What makes you think you have the right to dictate terms anyway? Don't you think it's about time I had my say?'

'I'm not saying you shouldn't! I'm just saying that it might be better to wait to talk about this until you've calmed down.'

'Better for whom? For you, you mean! No, you're just trying to wriggle out of an uncomfortable situation, aren't you? It must be so inconvenient to have your illegitimate child turn up after all these years, asking awkward questions! Well, you needn't think you're going to get rid of me as easily as that! I came here for an explanation and I'm not leaving until I've had it!'

'All right, all right! If you insist. But please, can't we at least sit down and talk sensibly about this? I

244

really can't see why you're being so aggressive. You had a good home, didn't you? Parents who loved you?'

'Yes, of course. But . . .'

'There you are, then. I really did try to do my best for you, in the circumstances.'

'But why the charade of Mum pretending to be pregnant, all those elaborate arrangements?'

'It just seemed better that way, that's all.'

'That's no answer!'

'Well, it's all the answer you're going to get, so you might as well make up your mind to be satisfied with it!'

'How dare you say that! Don't you think I'm entitled to an explanation?'

'I'm sorry, I refuse to be interrogated like this.'

'And why have I never been told the truth until now?'

'That was the agreement. In fact, the agreement was that you never would be and Bernard never should have broken it.'

'But you must have realised I'd need to see my birth certificate at some time in my life?'

'Your birth certificate? Is that what happened? You saw your birth certificate? Oh God, how stupid can you get? Would you believe, that simply never occurred to us?'

It might seem difficult to credit, thought Thanet, but he could see how it might have come about. Preoccupation with the here and now could well have blinded them to an eventuality in the distant future.

Otherwise they could easily have overcome the problem by Jessica giving Madge's name as her own when she had the baby in Bristol. A hospital has to notify the local registrar of a baby's birth, but if the medical staff had been given the wrong information this would presumably simply have been passed on and entered on the birth certificate. And why hadn't it occurred to them later? Well, it all happened twenty years ago. They must long since have been lulled into a sense of false security, have decided that any risk of discovery was past. For the first time he wondered how Jessica must have felt, seeing her child grow up under her sister's roof, unaware of her true parentage. According to Karen's account of their conversation it hadn't bothered her in the least. It sounded as though Jessica had been entirely devoid of maternal feelings. She certainly hadn't produced any more offspring. Though it was possible that on Tuesday evening she had been so unprepared for the situation that the only way she had been able to deal with Karen's attack was by keeping a tight rein on that unpredictable temper of hers, aware that this might make her seem hard and unfeeling but prepared to take the risk. She might in any case have thought it pointless to do otherwise. It was, after all, a little late in the day for a touching mother-and-daughter reconciliation.

'Anyway, what did you mean, that was the agreement, that I would never be told the truth. What agreement?'

'The condition on which I agreed to hand you over.'

'You mean . . . Oh, I see. I understand now. You

mean, you'd really intended to have an abortion, but because Mum put pressure on you, begged you to let her have me, you agreed on condition that no one should ever know I was yours!'

'I think that just about sums it up, yes.'

'But why was it so important to you that no one should know? Why would it have been so dreadful simply to have me and let it be known that your sister was bringing me up?'

'We thought it would be confusing for you, if you knew you had two mothers, so to speak.'

'Oh come on, don't give me that! Children are brought up by their grandmothers, by stepmothers, by foster mothers . . . I'm sorry, I simply can't accept that. And it couldn't have been because of the stigma. I know it was twenty years ago, but it wasn't exactly the dark ages, was it?'

'Oh, for God's sake, Karen, do stop going on! Isn't it enough that I had you, that I made sure you had a good home, people who really cared about you? It wasn't much fun, you know, being pregnant at sixteen and having to leave school when I'd hoped to go to university.'

'Oh, tough! You could have gone later. Lots of people take a year out.'

'Some year out! Believe me, having a baby is a bit different from backpacking to India. It changes you, eats away at your motivation as far as academic work is concerned. And it's all very well burbling on about it not being the dark ages and so on, but just think how many girls still feel as I did, even now, these days, when you trip over single mothers at every turn.

247

It all depends on the individual and on her circumstances. How often do you read of some poor infant being abandoned in a telephone box or in a carrier bag on a rubbish heap? At least I made sure you were well cared for. So don't give me that stuff, don't try to minimise the problems I had and the difficulties I went through. You can't begin to imagine how it feels until it happens to you.'

'And you can't begin to imagine how it feels to be that child, can you? To know that your own mother was so ashamed of having you that she would go to any lengths to keep her pregnancy quiet.'

'I did what I thought was best.'

'"I, I, I." Yes, best for you. The truth is, Jessica, you've never really considered anyone but yourself. You are completely and utterly selfish and self-centred.'

'How dare you speak to me like that! I'm not listening to this one moment longer!'

'We'd been standing in the hall until then,' said Karen, 'but suddenly she just shot off up the stairs. I was furious and I went after her. "Oh yes, you will," I said. "There's something else I need to know." She was nearly at the top by then and suddenly she twisted around and almost spat at me. "And I can guess what that is!" she said.'

So could Thanet.

And so, too, could Covin. The man's hands suddenly clenched into fists so tightly that the knuckles gleamed white. Clearly he was bracing himself.

And then at last Thanet understood what it was that

Covin had been waiting to find out. He understood, too, why the moment Karen had flung out of the house that evening Covin had gone straight to the telephone to ring Jessica. He had not only wanted to warn her that Karen now knew the truth, he had wanted to make a desperate plea that Jessica should not tell her the rest of it. His relief at Karen's unexpected return was also now explained: he had been afraid that their estrangement might be permanent.

'I suppose you want to know who your father was. Well, you won't have far to look. Just turn around and go home again.'
'You mean –'

Covin let out a sound between a sob and a gasp and buried his head in his hands. Karen looked down at the bent head, then laid a tentative hand on his shoulder and said, 'I'm sorry, Dad. But I have to tell them how it was, so they can understand what happened.' Covin half raised his head but didn't look up at her.

'Yes. Bloody Bernard, that's who. Couldn't keep his hands off his little sister-in-law, could he.'
'No!'
'No point in screaming at me. Like it or not, it's true.'
'It's not!'

'And then, well, that was when it happened. So fast that it's still all really a blur. She swung around to climb the last couple of stairs and I grabbed for her, to try and

249

stop her. She tried to jerk aside, to avoid my hand and that . . . that was when she lost her balance and . . . and –'

Up until now Karen's composure had been remarkable. During the intervening days she must have relived the events of Tuesday night so often that she had been able to relate them almost as if they had happened to someone else. Now, at last, her control cracked. Her face contorted and Thanet glimpsed the tears which suddenly gushed from her eyes before she too buried her face in her hands. 'It was horrible,' she sobbed. 'Horrible.'

As if Karen's collapse had been a signal Covin straightened up and put his arms around her, began to rock her as if she were a child. 'Hush, love,' he said. 'Hush.'

They seemed oblivious of the presence of the two policemen.

Thanet and Lineham exchanged uncomfortable glances and Lineham raised his eyebrows, jerking his head towards the door.

Thanet hesitated. Father and daughter needed some time alone together, to begin to come to terms with what had happened. On the other hand he couldn't afford to miss the rest of Karen's story. Well, he could at least give them the illusion of privacy. He rose quietly; Lineham followed suit and silently they left the room. Thanet adjusted the door so that it was slightly ajar and they waited in the hall. He didn't like eavesdropping but in this instance felt that it was the best compromise he could make.

Karen was still crying, great gasping gulps of pent-up emotion. Covin continued to soothe her, to murmur in her ear, to stroke her back.

In view of what Thanet had just learned it did cross his mind to wonder if there was a sexual element in their embrace, but he quickly dismissed the suspicion. The solace which Karen was seeking and the tenderness displayed by Covin were, he was certain, untainted by any unnatural element.

At last her sobs abated. 'Oh Dad,' she said, 'it was horrible. I can't tell you.'

'I've been so worried about you.'

'I know. I'm sorry. I'm so sorry.'

'Shh. I'm the one who should be apologising.'

'Her face . . . Her eyes . . . I can't get them out of my mind.'

'It wasn't your fault. She must have seen how upset you were. She shouldn't have lost her temper.'

'But I said such horrible things! And I can't help thinking, over and over again, that that was the only conversation I shall ever have with my real mother, and look how it ended! I'll never forgive myself, never.'

'Karen.' Covin raised her up so that she was facing him, tilted her chin gently with one finger so that she was looking directly into his face. 'Karen. Get this straight. Madge was your mother, your true mother. Oh, not biologically perhaps, but in every other way. She certainly couldn't have loved you more if she had borne you herself.'

'I know that. I do, really. But, Dad . . .'

'What?' There was a shadow in his face now. He could tell what she was going to ask him.

'What she said . . . about you. Was it true?' She knew, really; Covin's reaction just now had been all the confirmation she required. But she still needed to hear it from him.

'Yes. But Karen – you must understand, and I swear this is the truth, it only happened the once. I was bitterly ashamed of myself at the time, but later, when it brought me you, I found I couldn't really regret it.'

'Did Mum know?'

Covin shook his head. 'Jessica always refused to tell her who your father was.'

'I've thought about it such a lot this week.' Karen put a hand up to her temple and massaged it. 'There's been so much to think about . . . Finding out I was adopted and then, well, there's no point in pretending I wasn't shocked, horrified even, at first, when Jessica told me about you. I didn't want to believe it. But later, well, that was what I wanted to tell you. Later, when it had all had time to sink in, I found I was actually glad.'

'Glad!'

'Yes. Glad that you really are my father. It meant that although at first I felt the whole of my past had been just one big lie, in fact a great big chunk of it, my relationship with you, had survived more or less intact. It's the one thing I can salvage out of all this.'

'Oh Karen, you can't imagine how relieved I am to hear you say that.'

'That was why I had to come back, to put things right with you.'

'I'm so glad you did. I was afraid I might have lost you for good.'

'You won't get rid of me as easily as that!'

The tone of the conversation had lightened so much that Thanet decided it was time to go back in. So engrossed were they with each other that they barely glanced up as he and Lineham returned to their seats

252

and he wondered if they had even registered that they had been left alone for a while.

It was time to lower the emotional temperature. 'So, Karen,' he said briskly, 'you're saying Mrs Manifest's fall was an accident.'

She nodded.

'Then why on earth didn't you say so right away?' said Covin, reaching for his cigarettes and lighting up.

Back to normal, thought Thanet.

'I just panicked, I suppose,' said Karen. 'I was in such a state I was incapable of thinking straight. And I was frightened. Although I knew it had been an accident it still felt as though it was my fault, that it was I who'd killed her.'

'Because you'd been so angry with her earlier, you mean?' said Thanet. 'Perhaps you felt as though you'd almost willed it to happen.'

'Yes, that's it exactly! I hadn't thought of it like that, but you're right.'

'But why didn't you at least call an ambulance before you left?' said her father.

'I told you. I just panicked. I was terrified. It was obvious she was dead. No one alive ever has that terrible blank, fixed stare . . . I just ran, jumped into the car and drove off.'

'I saw you,' said Covin.

'Really? Did you? I didn't realise that. I didn't see you. I think I was more or less incapable of noticing anything.'

'You went rushing across the road and into the car as I was coming around the bend in the lane behind you. I didn't know whether to follow you or not.'

Thanet could understand Covin's dilemma. He must have been torn between his desire to know whether or not

253

Jessica had told Karen he really was her father, and the need to set matters right between them.

'I thought you might be going home again,' said Covin. 'So I thought I'd better have a quick word with Jessica first.'

'Did either of you touch the body?' said Lineham.

They shook their heads in unison.

'So why didn't you ring for an ambulance, sir?' said Thanet.

'Obviously I didn't want to get involved!' said Covin. 'Just in case Karen might somehow be dragged into it. So far as I knew, no one had seen either of us there and I wanted it to stay that way. That was why I left the door open, as I found it.'

'Did I leave it open?' said Karen. 'I didn't realise.'

Such a trivial matter, thought Thanet, with such far-reaching consequences. If she hadn't, there would have been no reason for Kevin to go into the house to investigate, no phone call to arouse suspicion. It would also have saved the police a great deal of time and fruitless effort. Still, he wasn't complaining. He would be able to put the case entirely out of his mind for the wedding.

The wedding!

He glanced at his watch. Six-thirty! He would barely have time to get home and change before the dinner at the Black Swan.

Quickly he arranged for both father and daughter to come in to make their statements next morning, then wound up the interview and left.

'Why the sudden rush?' said Lineham as they hurried to the car.

Thanet explained. Then he grinned.

'What's so funny?'

'I was thinking that at least I've got a good excuse for not going back to the office, if the Super complains I haven't brought him up to date! By the way, I'm sorry I didn't put you in the picture about Karen. I was just going to tell you when Covin arrived back, remember?'

'I really couldn't understand why you wouldn't let me caution him.'

'Yes, well, I'd guessed what was coming by then.' A moment or two later, Thanet groaned. 'Oh, no!'

'What's the matter?'

'I've just remembered. I'll never be ready in time. The house will be crawling with people. The bathroom'll be permanently occupied and I'll have to keep on stopping to be sociable.'

Lineham grinned. 'I'd rather you than me.'

NINETEEN

Even from the outside, Thanet's house proclaimed that something unusual was afoot. Although it was not yet fully dark, lights blazed from uncurtained windows in every room and figures could be seen moving about inside. Thanet's parking space in the drive had been left empty but cars lined the kerb in front of the house and Thanet wondered who they could all belong to.

Inside the atmosphere was charged with that special electricity generated by a high pitch of expectation. There was noise, laughter, movement all over the house. For a moment Thanet felt himself a stranger in his own home and then Joan appeared at the top of the stairs. She was all ready to go out, in a dress he hadn't seen before. It was in one of her favourite colours, a deep, rich blue, with fluid, feminine lines which enhanced the figure she had only ever lost briefly, during her pregnancies.

'Luke!' she cried. 'There you are. I was getting worried.'

'Yes, sorry darling. I'll –'

'Dad! Hi!' said Ben, emerging from the kitchen with a tray of coffee mugs. He looked unfamiliar.

'You've had your hair cut!' Thanet said.

'So've you.'

They grinned at each other.

'Couldn't let the side down, could we?' said Ben.

'Who're all those for?' Thanet nodded at the mugs.

'Just some friends who've dropped in. And the two grandmas of course. I went and fetched Granny Bolton earlier. They're having the time of their lives.'

The grandparents on both sides were to join them at dinner.

'I'll just say hullo.' The buzz of laughter and conversation swelled as Thanet opened the living-room door.

Ben was right, he saw at once. Joan's mother and his, both also dressed ready to go out, were sitting on either side of the fire like twin icons, their faces animated as they listened to the chatter all around them. 'Some' friends was an understatement, he thought. Bridget and Ben had both attended local schools and their friends seemed to have 'dropped in' in force tonight. There were half a dozen youngsters crammed on to the settee and every inch of carpet seemed to be covered by bodies seated or supine. Thanet knew most of them and there was a chorus of greeting. His mother raised a hand to wave at him. 'I'll talk to you later, dear. You go and change now.'

Thankfully, he escaped.

'Oh, there you are, Dad!' said Bridget, emerging from her room as he went by. 'We were getting worried in case you'd been held up.' She was wearing a brief velvet dress with long tight sleeves in a green so dark it was almost black.

'You look gorgeous,' he said.

Ignoring eve-of-the-wedding convention, she and Alexander had opted to join their parents and grandparents for this initial meeting between the two sets of in-laws. Thanet had dreaded the prospect of handing Bridget over to a bridegroom with a hangover but things had changed, it seemed, since he got married. Alexander's stag 'night' had been a day's go-karting with some friends, and Bridget's had been lunch in Calais on a day trip to France. In any case, he and Joan had been relieved that the young people had opted to join them tonight. It should smooth the way.

'I see Lucy's arrived,' he said. She had been one of the familiar faces downstairs.

'Yes. I'm so glad she could get away to be bridesmaid, we've known each other such a long time. Did you meet Thomas, her fiancé?'

'No. I only put my head around the door.'

'He seems really nice. I hadn't met him before.'

'Good.'

'Luke!' called Joan impatiently.

'Coming.'

She was waiting for him in their bedroom. 'It's five past seven already,' she said. 'We really ought to leave by twenty past.'

They were supposed to be meeting the Highmans at 7.30.

'Don't fuss!' Thanet said. 'It won't matter if we're a few minutes late. It's not considered polite to be dead on time.' He spotted his hired dress suit for the wedding hanging on the back of the door. 'Good grief. Do I really have to wear that tomorrow?'

'Luke! Let's concentrate on the here and now, shall

we? Just tell me what you're going to wear tonight and I'll get it out while you have a shower. I've made sure the bathroom's free.'

'I always did think it would be nice to have a valet,' he said with a grin.

'Get a move on!' she said.

By the time he came back his clothes were all laid out on the bed. He dressed quickly and was hurrying towards the stairs when he stopped dead. Passing Bridget's room he had glimpsed a ghostly white shape in the darkness. Her wedding dress. Slowly he retraced his steps and went in.

There it was, hooked over the door of her wardrobe, shrouded in protective polythene, a symbol of the great change that was to take place in his daughter's life, in all their lives, tomorrow.

Contemplating it he was overcome by a complicated blend of emotions – a sense of loss, of yearning for the days of her childhood now gone for ever, all mixed up with a heartfelt desire for her happiness with this stranger who had stepped into their lives to steal her from them.

He sighed, shook his head, squared his shoulders. It was time to face the first stage of his ordeal.

They were all four waiting for him in the hall. Ben appeared at the living-room door. He wasn't coming with them tonight and neither were Alexander's brother and sister. The party, it was felt, would have been too unwieldy. 'Have a good time,' he said.

And, astonishingly, they did. Right from the start the evening went with a swing. Everyone was in a good mood, determined to make these new relationships work, and despite his fears Thanet found the Highmans unpretentious and very easy to get along with. They were full of praise for Bridget and he found that his fears for her future began to ease. At least she was marrying a man from a stable family background and he felt that these people would do their best to welcome her and make her feel at home in their very different social circumstances.

'There you are!' said Joan, when they had taken her mother home and they were at last back in the privacy of their own room. Downstairs the party was still going strong and Bridget had slipped in to join her friends. 'Now be honest. It wasn't as bad as you expected, was it?'

'You're just saying ,"I told you so!"'

'I certainly am. Unzip me, will you? But seriously, I really liked Alexander's parents, didn't you?'

'Yes, I did,' said Thanet, complying. 'You look wonderful in this dress.'

'I hoped you'd like it . . . So, do I take it that you're not as worried about tomorrow now?'

'Marginally less, I suppose.'

'Pessimist!' she said, slipping on her dressing gown to avoid embarrassing encounters on the way to the bathroom. When she came back she said, 'How's the case going, by the way? I didn't have time to ask you earlier. I assume there's going to be no problem tomorrow?'

'It's all over bar the shouting.'

'Already! Luke! Well done! You must be delighted.' She gave him a long look. 'No? Not delighted?'

'Well, I'm pleased it's over, yes, of course. But it was all a bit of a letdown really, a lot of work to no good purpose. It turned out to be an accident after all.'

'Really?'

260

Now it was Thanet's turn to go to the bathroom and as soon as he returned she said, 'So what happened? This week's been so hectic we've hardly had a chance to talk about it.'

'What stage was I at last time we discussed it?'

Joan got into bed, plumped up the pillows behind her and leaned back against them, obviously settling down for a long talk. 'You were asking me about Kevin and Snippers. You thought he might be involved.'

'That seems ages ago!' Thanet eyed his morning coat uneasily as he undressed. He was going to feel so self-conscious wearing it that he'd never be able to act naturally.

'It was the night before Bridget came home. Wednesday, then.'

'Only the day before yesterday! Such a lot has happened since then.'

'Tell me,' said Joan.

'You don't want to hear this now, surely. You must be exhausted.'

'I'm wide awake, as a matter of fact.'

And Thanet had to admit, she looked it.

'I'm over stimulated, probably. And there's no point in trying to go to sleep until everyone has settled down. I just hope they won't be too late getting to bed. Bridget needs her beauty sleep. No, a bed-time story is just what I need to stop me worrying about all the things that might go wrong tomorrow.'

'Nothing's going to go wrong,' said Thanet. 'And if it does, well, it'll just go down in the annals of the Thanet family as something amusing that happened at Bridget's wedding.'

'So,' she said. 'Go on. Begin, as they say, at the beginning. What made you suspect it might not be an accident in the first place?'

Thanet got into bed beside her and put his arm around her. She settled her head into the hollow of his shoulder.

'Two things really.' And he told her about the phone call and the open door, went on to explain how to begin with he had naturally suspected first Jessica's husband then her lover. 'But then we found that neither of them could have made that phone call. Believe it or not, they actually alibied each other!'

She laughed. 'Really?'

'Yes.' Thanet explained about the Ogilvys' visit to the Harrow, the landlord's testimony that he had seen Desmond Manifest open the door as if to come in, then change his mind when he saw them. 'And that was only three or four minutes after the phone call – which was made from Jessica's number, incidentally. There was no way Manifest could have got to the pub in that space of time, it's a good ten minutes' walk. And he did walk, we checked.'

'I see.'

'That didn't let either of them off the hook as far as Jessica's death was concerned, of course. Ogilvy could have killed her before going to the pub and her husband could easily have slipped back to the house after Ogilvy had left. But meanwhile I got sidetracked by Kevin. He'd borrowed his father's car that night and it had been seen parked near Jessica's house. He had admitted driving to Charthurst that evening – to go for a country walk, he said!'

'Excuses don't come much thinner than that!'

'Quite. Anyway, we already knew that he was adopted – his mother told us so the first time we interviewed her. And I'd been puzzled why Jessica, who'd been such a promising student and had been expected to stay on at school and even go to university, had left for no apparent reason at sixteen and had instead gone off to live with an aunt in Bristol. Then I realised that both Jessica and Kevin had red hair –'

'So you jumped to the conclusion that he was her illegitimate child, that he had traced her, and that this was why he had been watching her – to pluck up the courage to approach her. And, presumably, that he had done so on the night she died and it had all gone disastrously wrong.'

'Exactly.'

'All seems quite logical to me.'

'That's what I thought. And at first it seemed I was right. I went to see Bernard Covin, her brother-in-law, and he confirmed that yes, she had had a baby, a boy, and it had been put up for adoption. But as it turned out, I was wrong. When we checked we found that Kevin had already traced his natural mother, who had refused to have anything to do with him. Kevin's interest in Jessica had been precisely what we originally thought it was, a rather unhealthy obsession with her.' And Thanet told Joan about the scrapbook they had found in the loft above the boy's bedroom.

Joan made a little moue of distaste and said, 'So it had all been a waste of time.'

'Well, yes and no. I was mortified at the time, that I'd been so convinced I was on the right track.' He grinned.

'Actually, it served me right, for thinking I'd been so clever.'

'Nonsense, darling. You're always too ready to put yourself down, if you ask me.'

'You're biased,' said Thanet, dropping a kiss on the top of her head. 'Anyway, as it turned out, although I was wrong about Kevin being Jessica's son, I was in fact still heading in the right direction. When we confronted Kevin with the scrapbook, in order to get himself off the hook he told us he'd seen a man coming out of Jessica's house around about the time she died.'

'And you believed him? He wasn't just trying to save his own skin?'

'Mike and I both thought he was telling the truth.'

'Did he know who the man was?'

'Bernard Covin.'

'Aha! The brother-in-law. The plot thickens!'

'Precisely. Now there were already several things that puzzled me about Covin. We knew he had rung Jessica that evening. According to him, he had supper with his daughter Karen, Jessica's niece, who was going back to Reading that evening for the start of the new term –'

'At the university, you mean?'

'Yes.'

'Like Ben. I wonder if they know each other? Oh, sorry. Go on. Yes, she was going back to Reading that evening . . .'

'And she'd asked him to give her aunt a ring to apologise for not having managed to get over to say goodbye to her before she left.'

Joan frowned. 'Strange.'

'That's what I thought. But even more strange was the fact that when he got Jessica's answerphone he actually went over straight away to see her. We didn't discover this at first. He told us he'd stayed in watching television all evening. We believed him because we knew Karen had borrowed his car. Stupid of me.'

'So how did he get there?'

'Took one of the farm vehicles, of course. Anyway, when Kevin told us he'd seen Covin come out of Jessica's house I just couldn't stop puzzling away at why? Why ring Jessica immediately after Karen left, as if the matter was urgent, and then why go rushing over when he couldn't get a reply? Unless something had happened between him and Karen at supper that evening.'

'Some kind of argument, you mean?'

'I didn't know. Just some kind of upset. But if there had been, I thought that might explain something else which had puzzled me – why Karen had driven herself back to Reading, in her father's car.'

'You mean you'd have expected him to drive her?'

'Yes. Wouldn't you? Unless she had a car of her own, that is. But she hasn't.'

'That was odd, I agree.'

'But if they'd had a row . . .'

'Yes, I see. She might have gone rushing off on impulse.'

'Exactly. In which case, I had to ask myself what the row could have been about?'

'And as he immediately rang Jessica and then went dashing off to see her, you couldn't help thinking there must have been some connection.'

'You should have joined the police force, darling.'

'I doubt it. I still can't see what the connection might be.'

265

'That's because you don't know all the facts. But I did, and that was the point at which I began to put two and two together. I already knew Jessica's sister had tried to conceive for years before succeeding. I also knew that Jessica had had a baby while staying with an aunt in Bristol. Then I learned that while she was away her sister had gone to stay with the same aunt – who was supposedly ill – and that in fact the timing of the two births had coincided.'

'I see now! You're saying that Jessica's sister didn't really have a baby at all, that Karen Covin is Jessica's daughter and that Covin lied to you about the baby's sex. To put you off the scent, presumably. But why?'

'The adoption was an informal arrangement. And – this was the point – Karen had never been told any of this. In fact, I discovered this afternoon that Jessica only agreed not to have an abortion, but to have the baby and let her sister bring it up, if the Covins swore to secrecy. That was why they had to mount such an elaborate charade – they not only had to get Jessica out of the area so no one would suspect she was pregnant, but Madge too when her supposed baby was due. There was no way they could have got away with it otherwise.'

'Because of hospital records, health visitors and midwife's visits after the birth, you mean.'

'That's right. In fact, Madge had to stay away until some weeks after the baby was born while Covin changed his job and moved to a different area.'

'Because if they'd stayed in the same place their doctor and local midwife would have wondered why they'd never had an inkling of Madge's pregnancy.'

'Quite. I imagine they claimed their health records

had been lost in the move, so that they could make a fresh start with no questions asked.'

'Very ingenious.'

'And it worked. For twenty years.'

The front door closed quietly downstairs and a moment or two later cars started up and were driven away. Shortly afterwards there were whispers on the stairs, stealthy movements on the landing.

Joan glanced at the clock. Ten to twelve. 'Not too bad, I suppose. And they are trying to be quiet, bless them. So,' she said, 'what went wrong? Are you suggesting that the upset over supper was because Covin finally told Karen she was adopted? But why on earth should he choose that particular evening? I mean, just before she was due to go back to university for the start of a new term was hardly the best timing, was it?'

'That's what I simply couldn't understand. Until Karen herself told me. And this was really the key to the whole puzzle. Apparently she wanted to apply for a passport, and needed her birth certificate.'

'Aaah.'

'She'd been trying to get her father to hand it over for months, but he kept making excuses. So finally she told him not to bother. She said she was fed up with waiting and she would send away for a copy.'

'So then he had to tell her. He wouldn't have wanted her to find out when he wasn't around to explain. Not surprising she was upset. Is he fond of her?'

'Very.'

'I may be dim, but I still don't understand why it was so important for him to go and see Jessica that evening. What did he say, when you told him you had a witness

267

who'd seen him coming out of her house that night?' Joan yawned. Her eyelids were beginning to droop.

'He confessed.'

'What? Just like that?'

'Just like that.'

'He actually admitted he'd pushed her down the stairs?'

'Something like that.'

'Well. I'm amazed. And confused. I thought you said it was an accident.' She eased herself away from him and slid down in the bed, yawning again.

'It was.'

'Darling, you're being infuriating. Would you please spell out in words of one syllable exactly what did happen?'

Thanet was enjoying teasing her, keeping her in suspense. 'I'm sure you can work it out for yourself.'

'Luke!'

'Just think. Imagine the scene at supper that night. Covin has just told Karen the truth. She's upset, naturally, confused, angry, hurt. She feels betrayed. So she rushes out to the car. But just think: would she have driven straight to Reading?'

Joan sat up with a jerk 'She went to see Jessica!' she said triumphantly. 'And she either told Covin where she was going or he guessed that that was what she was going to do. That was why he rang Jessica, to warn her! And that was why he went racing over to Charthurst when he couldn't get through on the phone!'

Thanet grinned up at her. 'Told you you could work it out for yourself.'

'But when he got there he found that Jessica was dead. Did he actually see Karen there?'

'Not in the house. He just got there in time to see her drive away.'

'So he confessed because he was afraid she was responsible for Jessica's death. But how do you know all this? He wouldn't have told you, surely. It would have defeated the whole object of the exercise, as far as he was concerned.' She slid back down in the bed. 'In fact, I still don't understand why you say you now *know* it was an accident.'

'Because while we were interviewing Covin this afternoon, Karen arrived back.'

'And told you exactly what did happen?'

'Yes.' Thanet related Karen's story.

Joan listened in silence until Thanet got to the part where Jessica told Karen who her father was. 'Oh no!' she said. 'What a way to find out. Poor kid.'

Thanet then described how the accident had happened.

'You can see it all, can't you?' said Joan sleepily. 'Poor kid,' she repeated. 'What a dreadful few days she must have had.'

'And poor Jessica,' said Thanet. 'I've learned quite a lot about her over the last few days and I can't say I much like what I've heard. But I can't help feeling sorry for her. First she lost her father, then her mother and then when she goes to live with her sister, her brother-in-law gets her pregnant. Then, when she did at last get married, her husband loses his job and she loses her home. It must have seemed to her that sooner or later everything would be taken away from her. Perhaps that was why she hung on to her husband.'

'Mmm.'

269

'And it's only just occurred to me. Maybe that was why she had affairs. Maybe she was so convinced that sooner or later Desmond would desert her too that in some strange way she was almost compelled to try and make it happen.' Perhaps that was also why she had turned on her husband physically, if what the Bartons had said was true. 'I don't suppose she ever knew just how much he loved her, how well he understood her, and the degree to which he was therefore able to forgive her. People said, you know, that she had a very short fuse and I suppose that's understandable, after what she'd been through. Desmond told us himself that he felt she was just plain angry with the way life had treated her and that beneath the surface the anger was always simmering away, waiting to erupt.'

He glanced at Joan, expecting her to comment, but she was fast asleep.

He sighed. 'Well, I suppose you could say that on Tuesday evening it erupted once too often.'

TWENTY

'Luke? Wake up! Tea.' Joan's voice.

Thanet opened one eye and murmured his thanks. He squinted at the clock. Seven-fifteen.

She was already dressed and bustling about, drawing curtains. She peered anxiously at the sky. 'It looks as though it's going to be fine, thank goodness,' she said.

Thanet remembered. Bridget's wedding day. The prospect of his speech loomed ahead and he groaned inwardly. 'You're up early.' Usually, on Saturdays, they had a lie-in until 7.30.

'I want to give Bridget breakfast in bed today, as a special treat.'

'You'll spoil her.' But his tone was indulgent.

'Not for much longer.' She came to sit on the edge of the bed. 'Oh Luke, I do so want today to be perfect for her.'

'It will be, I'm sure. And as I said last night, if anything does go wrong, it'll be something to look back on later and laugh about.'

'But I don't want anything to go wrong! It's every mother's nightmare on her daughter's wedding day.'

'You've done everything possible to make sure it won't. You can't do more. Now why don't you just keep telling yourself that, and try to enjoy it? The one sure way of spoiling it for her is to go around looking anxiety-ridden all day!'

'You're right!' she said. She put her arms around him and gave him a hug and a lingering kiss.

'Mmm,' he said. 'You don't suppose there's time . . .'

'Not this morning. Tonight.'

'Something to look forward to!' he said with a grin. He and Joan had always enjoyed a healthy sex life.

She jumped up. 'Meanwhile, drink your tea. I'm going to prepare that breakfast tray.'

When she had gone he eyed his morning coat again. He was slowly getting used to the idea of wearing it. All the other principal actors in the drama were going to be similarly attired after all. Perhaps it wouldn't be as bad as he had feared.

He hopped out of bed, fetched the cards on which he had prepared his speech and ran through it quickly. Yes, it would do, he thought. And now it might be an idea to get into the bathroom first. Bridget had claimed it for nine o'clock so at some point there was going to be a queue.

Gradually the house began to come alive. Bridget's breakfast tray complete with ceremonial single rose in vase was taken up to her and before long the kitchen was crowded with people eating cereal, making toast and drinking cups of tea and coffee. The post arrived, with yet more cards from wellwishers, then came the bouquets, the tray of buttonholes for Thanet and the ushers. Inexorably, it seemed to Thanet, the momentum gathered pace. The ceremony was to be at midday and before long it was time for everyone to change. Joan and the bridesmaids were due to leave at 11.30 and by 11.15 he and Joan were ready in their unfamiliar finery. She was wearing a Jean Muir dress and jacket in fine aquamarine wool crepe. She had agonised over buying it. 'How can I possibly justify spending so much money on one outfit?'

'If you can't splash out on your only daughter's wedding, when can you?'

'Never?' she'd said, and laughed.

But she had given in and now, as she took a final look in the mirror, Thanet said softly, 'It was worth every penny, wasn't it?'

She smiled. 'It certainly makes me feel special enough to be the mother of the bride.'

'Mrs Thanet?' Lucy's voice. 'The taxi's here.'

'Coming.' She turned and gave Thanet a quick kiss. 'See you in the church.'

He went down with her and waved them off, then stood waiting for Bridget in the hall. The sight of her as she came downstairs, a vision in cream silk, floating veil secured by a tiara of miniature roses, brought tears to his eyes. 'You look absolutely beautiful, Sprig,' he said, reverting to her childhood nickname.

For once she didn't object to it. 'Well done, Dad,' she said with a teasing grin. 'That's what every bride wants to hear.'

En route to the church she sat serenely, clearly determined to enjoy every moment of the day. He kept on glancing at her, trying to reconcile the bride-woman beside him with the baby, the toddler, the schoolgirl she had been.

At the church they posed for photographs before moving to the entrance porch. The organ launched into the opening chords of Mendelssohn's famous wedding march and as he led her proudly down the aisle familiar, smiling faces floated past as if in a dream. He saw Alexander turn to greet her with a loving look and then the ceremony began with the solemn, time-honoured words of the traditional 1662 marriage service.

'Dearly beloved, we are gathered together here in the sight of God, and in the face of this congregation, to join together this Man and this Woman in holy matrimony . . .'

Please, let them be happy, he prayed. *Don't let them become a divorce statistic. Give them the strength to overcome the difficulties which lie ahead, the perseverance to work at their relationship when it would be so much easier to give up.*

And here was his cue, the words which for him and him alone had a very special significance: 'Who giveth this Woman to be married to this Man?'

Thanet stepped forward, took Bridget's hand and gave it to the priest, who laid it gently in Alexander's.

Look after her, Alexander, Thanet urged silently.

There, it was done. For him it was a truly significant act.

It was time, finally, to let go.

DEAD AND GONE

To Charlotte, James and Elliot

And he said, That which cometh out of the man, that defileth the man. For from within, out of the heart of men, proceed evil thoughts, adulteries, fornications, murders, Thefts, covetousness, wickedness, deceit, lasciviousness, an evil eye, blasphemy, pride, foolishness: All these evil things come from within, and defile the man.

Mark 7. 20–23.

ONE

Thanet and Joan were getting ready for bed when the telephone rang. It was just after midnight. Their eyes met. *Alexander?*

Joan was nearest and she snatched up the receiver. 'Hullo?' The tension showed in every line of her body, in the intensity of her concentration. Then she relaxed. 'It's Pater,' she said, handing Thanet the phone.

The Station Officer.

Thanet found that he had been holding his breath. 'What's the problem?' he snapped. Anxiety was making him short-tempered these days.

'Woman gone missing, sir.'

'When was this?'

'Couple of hours ago.'

'Only a couple of hours? So why all the fuss? She probably had a row with her old man and walked out to cool off.' Literally and metaphorically, thought Thanet. It was high summer, school holidays and the middle of a heatwave, a prime time – along with Christmas – for domestic disputes to escalate.

'Her "old man" is Mr Mintar, sir. Mr Ralph Mintar.'

The rising inflection in Pater's voice indicated that he expected Thanet to know who he was talking about. As indeed he did.

'The QC?'

1

'The same.'

'Ah.' Thanet had come across Mintar in court from time to time. The barrister was hardly the type to lose his head in a crisis. If he had reported his wife missing he must have good reason for concern. 'I see. So what's the story?'

'Apparently she disappeared in the middle of entertaining friends. After they finished eating they all decided to go for a swim and everyone went off to change. Only she didn't come back. It was a while before anyone noticed she wasn't there and they've been looking for her ever since.'

'And no apparent reason for her to walk out?'

'Not so far as PC Chambers could gather. And he's pretty much on the ball, as you know.'

'Quite. Well, I'd better get out there. The Super been informed?'

Superintendent Draco liked to keep his finger on the pulse of what was happening on his patch.

'He's away for the weekend, sir.'

'Of course. I forgot.' That was a relief, anyway. Draco had a nasty habit of dogging Thanet's footsteps at the start of any remotely interesting investigation. 'Contact Lineham and lay on some reinforcements, will you? What's the address?'

'Windmill Court, Paxton, sir.'

Thanet scribbled the directions down. It was all too easy to get lost in a maze of country lanes in the dark.

'Sorry, love,' he said to Joan, who was in bed by now.

She shrugged. 'Can't be helped.' But her pretended insouciance did not deceive him. She would have liked him to be with her in case there was any more news.

They were both desperately worried about their daughter Bridget, who was thirty-two weeks pregnant with her first baby and had suddenly developed toxaemia. Although Lineham's wife Louise had had similar problems when their first child was born, until a few days ago Thanet and

2

Joan hadn't known precisely what the prognosis was, but Alexander, her husband, was keeping them up to date on what was happening and they had learned fast: Bridget's blood pressure was alarmingly high and there was protein in her urine. She was therefore in danger of pre-eclampsia – fits – and the baby's oxygen supply was threatened. She had been taken into hospital for monitoring.

Thanet finished knotting his tie and went to sit on the bed, took Joan's hands in his. 'If you need me, just ring and I'll get back as soon as I can.'

She shook her head. 'I don't suppose we'll hear anything more tonight.'

'All the same . . .'

'I know.'

He kissed her and left.

Outside it was still very warm, well over twenty degrees, and Thanet took off his jacket and slung it on to the passenger seat before getting into the car. Then he wound down the window to get a breath of fresh air as he drove. At this time of night there was very little traffic about and once he plunged into the country lanes his seemed to be the only vehicle on the road.

In an attempt to damp down his worries about Bridget he tried to focus on Ralph Mintar. What did he know about him? Not a lot, it seemed. As a member of the South-Eastern Circuit Mintar was a familiar figure in courtrooms all over Kent and Sussex – less so, of course, since taking silk a few years ago. QCs travel further afield, sometimes having to stay away from home for weeks or even months at a time. Still, he didn't suppose Mintar had changed much. Always looking as though he had just had a wash and brush-up, the QC was a dapper, well-groomed figure, reticent and self-contained. He belonged to what Thanet always thought of as the softly softly school of advocacy, leading witnesses gently on from one apparently innocuous point to another until they suddenly found that they had fenced themselves in and there was no way out but the direction in which counsel had wanted them to go.

Thanet knew that in a high percentage of cases of domestic murder it is the husband who has perpetrated the crime. If the worst had happened and Mrs Mintar had come to a sticky end, Mintar would be a formidable suspect to deal with. Thanet felt the first stirrings of excitement. He hoped, of course, that she would be found alive and well, but if she wasn't, well, he had always relished a challenge.

He braked sharply to avoid a rabbit which had appeared from nowhere to scuttle across the road in front of him and had then stopped dead, transfixed by his headlights. He put the car into bottom gear and began to edge forward. *Go on, go on*, he muttered. *Move!* At last, just as he was about to brake again, it turned and dashed off into the undergrowth at the side of the lane.

He was on a slight rise here and ahead of him he could now see some scattered lights. That must be Paxton. Street lighting would be sparse, as it always was in the villages, and he guessed that there would be few people still up – though more than usual, perhaps, as it was a Saturday night. He was right. Apart from the occasional glow from an upstairs window, Paxton appeared to be sunk in slumber. The village consisted of one long, straggling street with a pub at each end, one of them opposite the church. There was also a Post Office cum general shop, increasingly a rarity nowadays as the supermarkets killed off their smaller rivals.

Thanet had memorised Pater's directions: Turn left at the far end of the village into Miller's Lane. Take the first right then the second left and it's on the right, a hundred yards past the windmill.

There was the dark bulk of the windmill now, its sails a stark silhouette against the night sky and this, no doubt about it, was Windmill Court, lit up like a cruise liner. Thanet swung in between the tall wrought-iron gates

4

and halfway up the drive pulled up for a moment to admire it. The mill owner must have been a prosperous man for he had built himself a fine dwelling. Classic in proportions and as symmetrical as a child's drawing, it looked for all the world like an elegant doll's house awaiting inspection. One half expected the front to swing open, revealing exquisitely furnished miniature rooms. As Thanet studied it someone came to peer out of one of the downstairs windows. There were no cars parked at the front so he decided to follow the drive which curved off around the left side of the house. Here, in front of a long low building which had probably once been stables, were several parked cars, one of them a patrol car. Lineham's Ford Escort was not among them, he noted. As he got out a uniformed constable hurried forward to greet him.

'Ah, Chambers,' said Thanet. 'No one else here yet?'

'No, sir. Just the two of us until now. Simmonds is inside.'

'They'll be along shortly. I gather you were first on the scene. Fill me in, will you?'

There wasn't much more to tell at this stage and as Thanet listened he looked around, taking in his surroundings. The cars were parked on a gravelled area which flanked a well-illuminated L-shaped courtyard with an ornamental well in the middle. One side of the L was a single storey extension. A granny annexe, perhaps? Someone was a keen gardener: carefully trained climbers clothed the walls, and there were numerous tubs and urns of bedding plants. A faint fragrance hung in the still, warm air.

A door opened, casting a swathe of light across the paving stones, and PC Simmonds emerged, peering into the relative darkness where Thanet and Chambers were standing. There was a woman behind him.

Thanet moved to meet them and Simmonds introduced him. 'And this is Mrs Mintar senior, sir.'

'You took your time getting here,' she said. 'And I don't

5

know what good you think just one more policeman is going to do.'

'Reinforcements will be along shortly, ma'am,' said Thanet. He was about to suggest that they go inside when, as if to prove him right, vehicles could be heard approaching and a few moments later two more police cars arrived, followed by Lineham's Escort. They'd supplied him with eight officers. Good. That would suffice for now. There was only a limited amount that they could do in the dark. If necessary they'd draft in more tomorrow.

'Excuse me for a moment, Mrs Mintar.' Thanet went to meet Lineham, pleased that the sergeant had arrived. They had worked together for so long now that he felt incomplete beginning an investigation without him.

'What's the story, sir?' said Lineham.

'I've only just got here; you probably know as much as I do at the moment. I'm about to interview the mother-in-law. Get this lot organised to do a search of the grounds, then join me.'

Thanet accompanied Mrs Mintar into the house. She led him through a well-appointed kitchen and square hall into a spacious drawing room. It was, as might be expected in a household such as this, an elegant room, furnished with well-polished antiques, luxuriously soft sofas and curtains with elaborate headings. French windows stood wide open to admit the marginally cooler night air and moths were fluttering around the lamps. Thanet crossed the room to glance outside: a broad terrace surrounded by a low brick wall with a gap opposite leading to a shallow flight of steps. Beyond, the shimmer of water. A swimming pool, by the look of it.

Mrs Mintar did not sit down. Instead, she went to the window at the front of the house and stood looking out, as if she expected her missing daughter-in-law to come strolling up the drive. 'Everyone has gone off again to look for Virginia.' There was impatience rather than anxiety in her tone. 'My son will be here shortly, I expect.'

6

'Everyone?'

She turned to face him and he saw her properly for the first time. She was older than he had first thought, he realised, well into her seventies. He should have known she would be as Mintar must be in his fifties. He had been misled by her slim, wiry figure, the vigour with which she moved and her hair, which was a deep chestnut brown without a trace of grey and was cut in a cropped, modern style. She was wearing cinnamon-coloured linen trousers and a loose long-sleeved silk tunic in the same colour. Around her neck was a leather thong from which depended an intricately carved wooden pendant. The effect was stylish, somewhat unconventional, and not exactly what Thanet would have expected of Mintar's mother. What would he have expected, if he'd thought about it? What was it that Joan called that flowery print material? Liberty lawn, that was it. Yes, made up into a dress with a high neck and full skirt. No, Mrs Mintar senior definitely wasn't the Liberty lawn type.

She sighed. 'Oh God, I suppose I'm the one who'll have to give you all the dreary details, as there's no one else here.' She turned to peer out of the window again. 'Where on earth has Ralph got to? He surely should be back by now.'

Still no word of concern about her daughter-in-law, Thanet noted. 'Meanwhile . . .' he said. Then, 'Won't you sit down, Mrs Mintar? I need as much information as you can give me.'

With one last glance down the drive she perched reluctantly on the very edge of a nearby chair. 'If I must.'

Thanet sat down facing her. 'If you could begin by telling me who "everyone" is?'

She sighed again and ticked the names off on her fingers as she spoke – long, elegant fingers with short workmanlike nails. 'My son Ralph; Virginia's sister Jane and her boyfriend Arnold something-or-other, they're down for the weekend; Howard and Marilyn Squires, our

7

next-door neighbours, they were here for dinner too; and my granddaughter Rachel and her—'

As if on cue hurried footsteps could be heard on the terrace and a young couple erupted into the room, the girl towing the man behind her.

'Gran! Have they found her?' she said, dropping his hand and rushing across to her grandmother. Thanet might just as well have been invisible.

She was in her late teens, Thanet guessed, with the type of middle-class good looks which feature in the *Harpers & Queen* portrait: regular features and long, straight, blonde hair which shone white-gold in the lamplight. She was wearing an abbreviated bright pink cotton sundress which revealed a perfectly even golden tan.

The man hung back, acknowledging Thanet with a nod. He was considerably older than the girl – in his late twenties, Thanet guessed – and had the type of good looks Thanet always associated with male models: clean-cut, chiselled features and immmaculately cut hair as fair as Rachel's. He was wearing slightly baggy dark green chinos, a pale mauve long-sleeved silk shirt – brand new, by the look of the tell-tale creases down each side of the front – canvas deck shoes and white socks. Irrationally and instinctively Thanet felt a twinge of . . . what? Dislike? Mistrust? He wasn't sure. He only knew that he was glad Bridget had never brought home anyone like this. *Oh God, Bridget . . . Please let her be all right . . .* With an effort he dragged his attention back to the matter in hand.

Mrs Mintar shook her head. 'Not yet.'

Lineham slipped unobtrusively into the room. *All organised.*

'And you've called the police!' said Rachel. 'We saw the cars. Oh, Gran . . .' The girl dropped to her knees beside the old woman and buried her head in her lap. 'I can't bear it. It's Caro, all over again.'

Thanet's eyebrows went up and he gave Mrs Mintar a questioning glance. But her attention was focused on

8

Rachel. 'Now don't talk like that, darling,' she said, stroking the girl's head. 'That simply isn't true. Your mother's only been gone a couple of hours. She'll be back soon, you'll see.'

Rachel looked up. 'But where can she *be*? Why should she just disappear like that? Where can she have *gone*?'

'Miss Mintar?' said Thanet gently.

She swung around to look at them. 'You're policemen.'

'Yes. Detective Inspector Thanet, Sturrenden CID. And this is Detective—'

She jumped up. 'A Detective Inspector! I knew it! She really has disappeared, hasn't she? Oh, Matt . . .' She whirled and ran to the man, who opened his arms to her. 'What if they never find her? Oh God, oh God, oh God, I can't bear it. It *is* Caro all over again. It is, it is, it is.' And she burst into tears, burying her face in his chest.

'What does she mean?' Thanet asked her grandmother softly. 'Who is Caro?'

Mrs Mintar shook her head irritably. 'Her sister,' she said in a low voice. 'Caroline eloped, four years ago. The circumstances are entirely different. Rachel was very upset at the time; she and Caroline were very close. All this is bound to bring it back to her.'

Headlights flashed briefly across the window. Another car was coming up the drive. Mrs Mintar hurried across to peer out. 'That may be Ralph now.'

'Dad?' said Rachel, twisting out of her boyfriend's arms. 'Perhaps he's found her!' And she dashed out.

Mrs Mintar shrugged and pulled a face. 'I'm not sure it was him.' She returned to her chair. 'We'll soon find out, no doubt.'

Thanet glanced at the man called Matt. 'And you are . . . ?'

'Matthew Agon. Rachel's fiancé.'

This last was said with a hint of defiance and a sidelong glance at old Mrs Mintar.

9

Her lips tightened but otherwise she declined to give Agon the satisfaction of reacting.

The first hint of family disapproval? Thanet wondered. Scarcely surprising, considering his own reaction to the man. 'You and Miss Mintar have been searching the garden, I suppose?'

'Yes. Pointless, really, we'd all hunted there for ages before splitting up.' Agon crossed to an armchair and sat down. 'Anyway, Rachel wanted to have another look so we did. Mr Mintar and Mr Squires both went off by car, in different directions, with Mrs Mintar's sister and her boyfriend.'

A Londoner, thought Thanet. East End, by the sound of it. And, he guessed, not really at home in this setting, although he was doing his best to appear at ease.

'Are the gardens very large?' Thanet asked the old woman.

She lifted her shoulders slightly. 'A couple of acres or so, I suppose.'

The door opened and Rachel came back in, followed by Mintar and a woman, their faces betraying their lack of success. For the first time Thanet saw the barrister less than immaculate: his hair was slightly dishevelled and the sweatshirt which he had pulled on over his open-necked shirt was inside out. The woman must be Mrs Mintar's sister – Jane, was it? She was in her early forties, he guessed, and looked both prosperous and self-possessed. Her face was too wide, nose too prominent and eyes too small for beauty, but she had taken considerable trouble over her appearance: her shoulder-length brown hair had been cut by an expert hand and she was carefully made up. She had done her best to disguise her broad shoulders, wide hips and heavy pendulous breasts with an ankle-length straight black skirt and a silk tunic top similar in style to old Mrs Mintar's in a black and white print.

'Ah,' said Mintar. 'Inspector . . . Thanet, isn't it?'

'Yes, sir. And this is Detective-Sergeant Lineham. You've had no luck, I gather?'

Mintar shook his head. 'No sign of her. Oh, sorry, this is my sister-in-law.'

She gave a brief smile of acknowledgement and said, 'Jane Simons.'

Mintar crossed to a side table where bottles, decanters and glasses stood on a silver tray, and poured himself a shot of whisky. He held up the bottle. 'Anyone?' There was no response.

Rachel had gone to perch on the arm of the chair in which her boyfriend was sitting and Thanet thought he saw a twinge of distaste cross Mintar's face as his eye fell upon them.

Mintar drank the whisky in a single gulp and poured himself another, but he put the glass down without drinking any more and, gripping the edge with both hands, leaned heavily on the table, his bowed head and hunched back eloquent of his despair. His sister-in-law, who had seated herself nearby, rose swiftly and went to put an arm around his shoulders. 'I'm sure she'll turn up, Ralph,' she said. 'There must be some perfectly reasonable explanation for her disappearance.'

'What, for example?' He twisted to face her, needing, Thanet guessed, to find a focus for his frustration. Time to intervene.

'I think it would be more constructive if you could give me some idea of what happened here this evening,' he said.

Mintar made a visible effort to pull himself together. 'Very well.' Leaving the second glass of whisky where it was, he crossed to stand in front of the fireplace with his hands clasped together behind him, dominating the room. 'Briefly,' he said, 'we had a supper party here tonight. Afterwards, most people decided to go for a swim.'

Headlights again flashed across the front window. 'That'll

be Howard,' said Mintar. He hurried out, followed by Jane Simons and Rachel.

Thanet and Lineham exchanged glances. *We're never going to get anywhere at this rate.*

Suddenly the room seemed full of people as they all came back in together. Mintar shook his head despondently. 'No joy.' He introduced the two new arrivals, both in their mid-forties: Howard Squires and Arnold Prime. They were a complete contrast to each other, the next-door neighbour being shorter and more compact of build, moving with an easy grace, Jane Simons's boyfriend well over six feet, loose limbed and gangling.

Thanet tried again. 'Mr Mintar was just giving me some idea of what happened here this evening. If you would all sit down . . . ?'

All but Mintar complied. He returned to stand before the fireplace, as if establishing his authority in the room.

'So,' said Thanet to Mintar when they were settled, 'if you would go on with what you were saying, sir . . .' Looking around, he could not prevent an inward smile: the room was beginning to resemble the denouement of an Agatha Christie mystery, the difference being that here they were at the beginning of a case, not the end, and were not even sure yet whether any crime had been committed. Though the cast was not quite complete, he realised: Mrs Squires wasn't here. He wondered why.

Mintar nodded. 'Right. Well, I was just explaining that after supper everyone except me decided to go swimming—'

'And me,' said Mrs Mintar.

'Sorry, before you go on, sir, may I just ask if there'd been any kind of . . . disagreement, during supper? Any arguments, quarrels, even?'

Headshakes all around.

Thanet saw with some concern that Rachel's hands were starting to shake. After her earlier outburst she had been very quiet and he thought she had settled down.

12

Mintar hadn't noticed and he gave a barely suppressed sigh of impatience. 'Everyone except myself – and Mother' – he corrected himself with a glance in her direction – 'decided to go swimming. I had some work to do and was glad of the chance to excuse myself. I went straight to my study and stayed there. At around a quarter to eleven Rachel came to ask me if I'd seen her mother. She told me they hadn't realised at first that Ginny wasn't around. They'd looked in all the obvious places, she said, but—'

'We couldn't find her!' Rachel burst out. 'We'd looked everywhere! And then Dad came out, and we looked all over again. We looked and we looked, but she was gone! She'd just . . . disappeared!' The shaking was more obvious now.

Her father took a few steps towards her but she didn't notice, turning her head into Matthew Agon's chest as she started to weep.

Howard Squires jumped up. 'I'll get something,' he said, and hurried out.

Thanet was interested to note a flash of pure dislike in Mrs Mintar's eyes as she watched him go.

'Howard is our family doctor,' Mintar explained.

It was pointless to continue, Thanet decided. If Virginia Mintar really had disappeared, normal procedure would in any case be to interview everyone separately. He just seemed to have been pushed into this somewhat fruitless situation by circumstances. 'I think we'll leave this for the moment, sir. Miss Mintar is obviously very distressed and I suggest she be taken to her room. We'll go and see how the men are getting on outside and then, with your permission, we'll do a preliminary search of the house.'

Mintar hesitated, then gave a weary nod and waved a hand. 'Whatever you think necessary.'

Outside in the hall Lineham rolled his eyes. 'Whew! What a crew!'

'That's one way of putting it. We'll go back out via the kitchen.'

13

'A lot of undercurrents, didn't you think, sir? The prospective son-in-law doesn't exactly seem to be the flavour of the month, does he, and as for the old lady . . . She's a real acid drop, isn't she? Didn't seem to care tuppence that her daughter-in-law has apparently vanished into thin air, so she can't have been on particularly good terms with her. And did you see the way she looked at Dr Squires as he went out?'

'He's obviously done something to upset her.'

'I'll say! And I can tell you this, I wouldn't fancy her for an enemy myself.'

'What are you saying, Mike?'

The sergeant shrugged. 'Just that if young Mrs Mintar turns out to have had a nasty accident her mother-in-law would certainly go on my list.'

'Let's not jump the gun. We've no idea yet what's happened to her.'

'Difficult to think of an innocent explanation, though, isn't it?'

'Mmm.'

'Of course, just because they all agreed there hadn't been a quarrel doesn't mean that there wasn't one, does it?' They had reached the kitchen and Lineham waved a hand. 'I mean, say she came in here to tidy up a bit before changing and someone followed her . . .'

'True.' Thanet looked around. Dishes were stacked in little piles on the work surfaces near the sink and the dishwasher stood open. He stooped to look inside. Someone had loaded in the dinner plates, knives, forks and a couple of pudding dishes, but had left the task unfinished. Five more of the latter stood on the draining board nearby. 'I wonder if it was Mrs Mintar who stacked the dishwasher. If so, it looks as though she was interrupted.'

Lineham picked up a champagne bottle which stood amidst a cluster of appropriate glasses and held it up to the light. 'Empty,' he said. 'Some kind of celebration?'

There was a tap on the window: PC Chambers was outside with several of the men.

Thanet and Lineham went out into the courtyard. 'Any luck?'

'Not so far, sir. It's difficult in the dark – lots of shrub borders and a small spinney at the far end of the garden.'

'I'm sure it must be. If no one finds anything and there's still no news of her by morning we'll put a lot more men on to it.'

But the initial search was concluded without success and after a brief search inside the house Thanet decided to call it a day. 'We'll be back first thing tomorrow,' he assured Mintar. 'Meanwhile, let's hope she turns up.'

She did, but not in the way Thanet had hoped. Next morning he was shaving when the phone call came.

'Bad news?' said Joan, as he put down the receiver.

'Mrs Mintar's body has been found. In a well in the garden.'

TWO

Lineham came hurrying across as Thanet's car drew up in the courtyard.

'You must have put your foot down, Mike.'

Lineham grinned. 'I was up and dressed and having my breakfast when I heard.'

The sergeant had always been an early riser.

'The SOCOs will be here soon,' he went on. 'I didn't see much point in taping off the whole courtyard, in view of all the people who were tramping through it last night, so I've just isolated the area around the well. I hope that's OK?'

'Fine.'

'And I've called the fire brigade. The gardener says the well's about sixty feet deep.'

'Good.' Kent no longer had an Underwater Search Unit and it wouldn't be worth calling on West Sussex for this. The fire brigade was used to cooperating with the police. Thanet glanced at a middle-aged man leaning against the wall near the door to the annexe. 'That him?'

'Yes. He found the body. And I said to notify Doc Mallard that we'd need him later. There's no point in him coming just yet. It'll take a while to get her out.'

'Quite.'

'Uh-oh, here comes Mr Mintar. Better brace yourself,

16

sir. He's on the warpath, demanding to know why the well wasn't searched last night.'

That makes two of us, thought Thanet. How could he have overlooked something so obvious? All the way over in the car he had been trying to answer that question, and the only explanation he could come up with was that he hadn't realised it was the genuine article, had thought it a purely ornamental feature. Even so . . . *Never take anything for granted,* he thought. *How often have I tried to din that into my team?*

'Here he comes.'

Mintar came charging across the courtyard, obviously seeking a focus for his anger. He had dressed in a hurry. One side of his shirt collar was tucked inside and he was wearing no socks. He was unshaven and seemed to have aged ten years overnight: every line on his face seemed to sag and his skin looked parched, as though all the youth and vigour had been irretrievably sucked out of it. Not so his eyes, which burned with fierce emotion.

'Thanet!' he said. 'About time too! I hope you're going to come up with a reason for your disgraceful negligence! Why the hell wasn't the well investigated last night? It's such an obvious place to look.'

In that case, why did you all overlook it too? But Thanet knew Mintar was right. The well should have been checked and that was that.

'You do realise that if my wife had been found then she might still be alive?'

Thanet trusted that this would prove not to be the case. Leaving aside any culpability on his part, Mrs Mintar was dead and nothing could bring her back. He hoped for her sake that death had come swiftly and mercifully.

'I assure you that I'm as concerned as you are to find out what went wrong.'

'I should hope so! In any case, you can rest assured that I shall be taking the matter up with your superiors.'

There was no point in making excuses. 'I can only apologise.'

But Mintar was not to be mollified. 'Easy enough to say that, isn't it? Words cost nothing. But they certainly won't bring her back.'

'I really am deeply sorry about your wife.'

'Yes, well, just think how you'd be feeling if it was your wife down there.' Mintar glanced at the well and perhaps it was the image which his words conjured up that unmanned him for suddenly his anger seemed to evaporate and he stopped, swallowed hard, his mouth trembling. 'You can't begin to imagine—' He turned abruptly away and blundered towards the kitchen door.

Lineham made as if to follow but Thanet stopped him. 'It wouldn't do any good at the moment. He needs to be alone for a while. Let's have a word with the gardener. What's his name?'

'Digby.'

'Going to be another scorcher, don't you think?' said Lineham as they walked across the courtyard.

Thanet agreed. Already, even so early in the morning, he could feel the heat of the sun's rays penetrating his lightweight jacket. He glanced at the cloudless sky, screwing up his eyes at the white-hot haze which surrounded the incandescent sun. He blinked to clear his vision, seeing dazzling silver discs within his eyelids.

Digby didn't look a very prepossessing character, he thought as they drew nearer. The gardener continued to lean against the wall, arms folded, watching them with a sardonic expression. He had a long lugubrious face with drooping jowls and soft pouches beneath the eyes. For one who worked out of doors his skin was surprisingly pasty, the colour of moist putty, and his wispy hair had been carefully combed across his scalp in an attempt to diguise the fact that there was little of it.

Thanet longed to bark, sergeant-major fashion, 'Stand

18

up straight when we're talking to you!' Instead he said mildly, 'Tell us what happened this morning.'

'I've told him once already,' said Digby, jerking his head at Lineham. The man managed to make the word 'him' sound like an insult.

Well educated, Thanet thought, with just a trace of Kentish accent.

'I'd like to hear it for myself. In detail, please.'

Digby sighed and shrugged. 'Suit yourself. I was crossing the courtyard when I noticed that watering can standing beside the well. It struck me as odd. Mrs Mintar was always very fussy about not leaving tools and stuff lying around. Fanatical, you might say.' He glanced around. 'This courtyard was her pride and joy and she liked to keep it shipshape.'

Thanet looked as well. He had noticed last night that a great deal of hard work and loving care had been expended on the courtyard. Mrs Mintar had obviously been very fond of flowers. Climbing roses and clematis intermingled on the house walls; there were hanging baskets overflowing with colourful annuals and an abundance of terracotta pots and tubs. 'She looked after all of this herself?'

Digby nodded. 'Except for watering the camellias, yes.' He pointed out the four big evergreen shrubs planted in wooden half barrels on either side of both kitchen and annexe doors. 'I do them, during the week, anyway. Mrs Mintar did them at weekends.'

'Why didn't she always do those?'

'It's a heavier job. We use water from the well for them.'

'Ah.' Thanet was beginning to see where this was leading.

'Why?' said Lineham.

'Lovely soft water, isn't it. Tap water around here is very hard and camellias don't like it.'

'Go on,' said Thanet.

'Well, when I picked up the can I realised it was half full. Now that was even more peculiar. I mean to say, who'd leave a can half full of water, in a heat wave? But then I thought, perhaps they'd had people around last night, and she hadn't quite finished watering when they arrived, forgot to complete the job later. And sure enough, when I checked, I found that two of the camellias were bone dry. So I thought I might as well finish the job off.'

'Very conscientious of you,' said Lineham.

Digby scowled. 'It's important to keep camellias well watered in July and August, that's when the flower buds for the following year are forming. Anyway, I used up the water in the can first then went to draw more from the well. That was when I noticed the chain wasn't across and the padlock wasn't locked – the key was still in it.'

Apparently Mrs Mintar had been fussy about safety as far as the well was concerned, dating back to when the children were small. She had therefore had a removable cover made and this was always secured by a padlock and chain.

'Let's be clear about this. You're saying the cover was on the well but that it wasn't secured in any way?'

'Yes. Anyway, I took the lid off, the bucket went down, hit bottom, as I thought, and came up empty. I knew the water was getting low, she'd been worried in case it wouldn't last the season, but not that low. So I looked down.' He shrugged. 'That was when I saw her.'

'Let's take a look,' Thanet said to Lineham. And to Digby, 'Wait here, please.'

Normally he dreaded that first sight of a corpse but this time he approached the well without the usual churning in his gut. She would, after all, be sixty feet down. The bad moments would come later, when the body was brought to the surface.

The well was in the centre of the courtyard and in mitigation of his negligence last night Thanet could see why he had mentally dismissed it as purely ornamental, for ornamental it certainly was. Surrounded by a low wall of dressed stone, it was spanned by a decorative wrought-iron arch. The bucket suspended from the roller at the centre of the arch, however, should have alerted him to the fact that it might still be in use.

In the distance vehicles could be heard approaching.

'Sounds like the fire engine,' said Lineham. He had equipped himself with a torch and he switched it on as they ducked under the tape.

Thanet's over-sensitive back muscles protested as, careful not to touch the coping, they leaned over and peered down into the darkness. Far, far down the torch beam picked out a splash of brilliant colour and a paler crescent which could be the side of her face. Yes, it was. As Thanet's eyes adjusted to the dimmer light he began to make out the shape of a half-submerged crumpled body more clearly. 'Not much doubt about it, I'm afraid, is there,' he said, straightening up.

'Notice that, sir?' Lineham nodded at a smear of what looked like blood on the inner edge of the coping. 'Bashed her head as she went over, perhaps?'

'Quite possibly.'

They stood back and he and Lineham studied the well cover which was leaning against the low wall. It was made of varnished lightweight wood with a semicircular metal handle at each side to facilitate removal. When in position it rested on a narrow ledge fashioned around the inner rim of the wall.

'How did you say it's secured?' said Lineham to Digby, who was watching them with the same sardonic twist to his mouth.

'There's a chain over on the far side permanently attached to the wall. When the cover's put back on you just run the chain through the two handles and padlock it to that staple, on this side.'

The padlock was hooked through the staple, hanging open, key still in the lock. 'Simple but effective,' said

Thanet. 'Where is that key normally kept? Somewhere handy, I imagine, if both you and Mrs Mintar had to have easy access to it.'

'On a bit of wire hooked over the rim of the bucket.'

The courtyard was suddenly full of noise and bustle as Scenes-of-Crime Officers, firemen and ambulancemen arrived simultaneously. Samples of blood were taken from the smear on the coping and then the well cover was carefully removed and stored in one of the SOCOs' cardboard boxes.

'D'you think we'll be likely to get any useful prints off it?' Thanet asked the SOCO sergeant.

The man shrugged. 'We might. Fortunately it's not rough wood, the surface is smooth and it's been varnished. When did the victim go missing?'

'Last night,' said Lineham. 'Around ten, we think.'

'In that case you might be in luck. If it had rained between then and now . . .'

'They'd have been washed off.'

'In effect, yes. It's the salts in sweat that create the prints and as rain would interact with them, either there wouldn't be any prints left or not enough to be useful.'

'Why are you taking the well cover away?'

Thanet hadn't noticed Mintar come up behind them.

'To test it for fingerprints, sir.'

'Why can't that be done on the spot? We can't have the well left uncovered, it's too dangerous.'

Thanet and Lineham looked at the SOCO sergeant, who said, 'It's best done in the lab, sir.'

'Why?'

'Because it'll be done by the superglue method.'

'What's that?'

'We put the article in a cubicle and suspend it from a wooden pole, rather like hanging washing out to dry. Then a small "boat" – a round metal tray two to three inches in diameter – with superglue in it is placed below it and heated. The fumes rise and attach themselves to the article and in fifteen to twenty minutes the fingerprints will show.'

'A pointless exercise in this case, if you ask me,' said Mintar. 'It'll be covered with prints.'

'You never know, sir,' said Lineham. 'In any case, we can't afford to miss the chance of getting a useful result.'

'I'm afraid we'll have to take the prints of everyone who was here last night,' said Thanet. 'And of Digby, of course.' How could he put this tactfully? 'Look, sir, I'm sorry, I should have said so earlier, but I'd be grateful if you would make it clear to the family that this courtyard is temporarily out of bounds.'

Mintar gave a bitter laugh. 'That includes me, I suppose. Very well.' He turned away. 'But if that lid is going to be missing for any length of time,' he said over his shoulder, 'just make sure you supply us with a temporary cover. We don't want any more accidents.'

'Just as a matter of interest,' said Lineham to the SOCO sergeant, 'how on earth did anyone discover you could use superglue like that?'

The sergeant grinned. 'Pure chance. Some characters working in a photographic department broke a plastic tray. They wanted to use it, so they stuck it together with superglue. The room was hot and when they came in next day they found the whole room plastered with visible fingerprints.'

The firemen's chief approached. 'We're ready to start the lifting operation now, Inspector.'

As there was very little water in the well they had decided a wet suit would not be necessary. Thanet and Lineham watched as a fireman in protective clothing and waders was fastened into a cradle and lowered down into the well at the end of a rope, carrying a sling in which to raise the body.

It was a lengthy operation and Mallard arrived well before they were finished. 'It's Mrs Mintar down there, I gather,' he said after they had greeted each other.

23

'Yes. D'you know her personally?'

'I've met her once or twice, but only casually. What's the story?'

Thanet told him the little they knew. 'We haven't started interviewing yet. I wanted to see her brought up first.'

'How's Bridget?' The little doctor was a longstanding family friend and had watched Thanet's children grow up. Childless himself, he had always taken a keen interest in their welfare and especially in Bridget since his second marriage to Helen Fields the cookery writer. Bridget was also a professional cook and she and Helen had spent a lot of time together, concocting and testing new recipes.

Thanet grimaced. 'Not good, I'm afraid.'

'You must be worried stiff. Which hospital is she in?

'The West Middlesex.'

'Good. That has an excellent ultrasound department. What's happening at the moment?'

'Well, they were concerned about the blood flow, apparently, so yesterday she was taken over to Queen Charlotte's, where they have a foetal assessment unit, whatever that means.'

'It means they have the most up-to-date equipment to measure the baby's heart-rate, its growth, the blood flow in the cord and also to carry out the latest and most sophisticated test, measurement of the baby's cerebral blood flow.'

'Well, all those tests were apparently normal.'

'Excellent! That's great news.'

'So she was taken back to the West Middlesex and we're waiting to see what happens next. What is that most likely to be, do you think?'

'I'd imagine she'd have two steroid injections, twelve hours apart, to mature the baby's lungs, just in case it has to be induced early. It'll take forty-eight hours or so for the lungs to mature, then it'll have a reasonably good chance of survival.'

'What do you mean by "reasonably good"?'

But Thanet wasn't to find out. While they were talking the fireman who had gone down the well had been brought back up to the surface and now they began slowly to haul up the body. In a few minutes they would see her properly for the first time. Thanet braced himself as he moved forward with Lineham and Mallard, conscious of the familiar symptoms: increased heart-rate, sweaty palms, sick feeling in the pit of his stomach. Nothing he could do, nothing he could tell himself, ever seemed to cushion the ripples of horror and dismay he invariably felt during these few moments. There was something so infinitely pathetic about the body of someone who had met a violent end. He had heard people who worked in hospices say that death could be a peaceful, even uplifting affair, but that could surely never be true for those who went unprepared to their graves. Thanet could do nothing to change that but he could and did vow afresh each time that he would do his level best to ensure that those deaths should not go unavenged.

And here she came, a limp, lifeless, sodden bundle. Gentle gloved hands reached out to protect her body from further damage as she was lifted over the wall and laid on the waiting stretcher. Thanet took several deep, unobtrusive breaths. Gradually the pounding in his ears subsided and he began to absorb what he was seeing. At first he was puzzled. Although he was certain they had never met, she looked vaguely familiar. Then he realised that it was her likeness to Rachel which was confusing him. Although disfigured by smears of dirt and an extensive graze on one side of her forehead, here were the same oval face, same bone structure, same slim, shapely body, its more mature curves mercilessly exposed to public gaze by the virtually transparent nature of the wet, clinging silk of the fuschia pink blouse and matching palazzo pants she was wearing. No underwear, Thanet noted.

'What a waste,' said one of the firemen. 'A real looker, wasn't she?'

'You'll go down again?' said Thanet to the man who had rescued her. 'I'd like a thorough search of the bottom of the well.'

The fireman nodded. 'Sure.'

Photographs taken, Thanet and Lineham waited while Doc Mallard finished his examination of the body. But the little doctor was unwilling to commit himself as to cause of death. 'You'll have to wait for the PM, I'm afraid.'

'But at a guess?'

The doctor struggled up. Thanet and Lineham knew better than to offer a helping hand and a fireman who did not was simply ignored. 'Well, as you can see for yourself it looks as though she might have banged her head on the parapet as she went over and this could well have knocked her out. Then I'd say she probably drowned. If so, the diatom test will confirm it.'

Thanet escorted Mallard back to his car then returned to the courtyard.

'More or less what we expected,' said Lineham.

'Mmm. Better ask Mr Mintar if he wants to see his wife before they take her away, I suppose.'

They found him in the kitchen. Someone had cleared up in here since last night, Thanet noticed. Mintar had been watching proceedings from the window and not surprisingly declined Thanet's invitation. 'I don't want to see her like that.'

'There's the matter of formal identification, sir.'

'Later, if you don't mind. When . . . when you've . . . When she's been . . .'

'I understand. If we could just ask you a few questions, then, sir?'

'Better come into the study.'

THREE

Mintar's study was exactly as Thanet would have expected: spacious, book-lined, carpeted, well equipped with leather-topped desk, computer equipment and expensive dark green leather desk chair. His profession was immediately obvious from the serried ranks of bound law reports, copies of Archbold and *Current Law Statutes* and from the fat briefs tied up with distinctive red tape piled on the desk. Cardboard boxes stacked up along one wall presumably contained even fatter briefs. Thanet was well aware of the quantity of paperwork generated by a complicated case.

A large tabby cat lying on the desk sat up and turned to look at them as they came in.

Mintar walked around the desk and, scooping up the cat in what was clearly an habitual gesture, slumped into his chair and stared at a photograph in front of him. He seemed unaware of the two policemen.

The cat turned around three times and then settled down and started to purr.

Absent-mindedly Mintar began to stroke it.

Thanet cleared his throat, but Mintar did not respond. 'May we sit down, sir?'

With a visible effort the barrister dragged his eyes away from the photograph.

Thanet repeated his request and Mintar stared at him

for a moment as if he were speaking in a foreign language. Then he blinked and waved a hand in invitation. 'Please do.'

Thanet drew a chair up in front of the desk and Lineham seated himself discreetly off to one side.

Mintar had returned to gazing at the photograph and suddenly he leaned forward, swung it around to face them and said savagely, 'That's why I didn't want to see her just now. That's what she was really like. And that's how I want to remember her.'

It was an enlargement of a family snap: Mintar, his wife and Rachel in tennis gear, arms linked and exuding enjoyment and well-being.

Virginia Mintar had indeed been a beautiful woman, Thanet thought. With their classical features, long blonde hair and slender figures, she and Rachel looked more like sisters than mother and daughter. 'Yes, I can understand that. Look, sir, I really am sorry to have to bother you at a time like this, but I'm sure you realise I have no choice.'

Mintar swung the photograph back around and returned to stroking the cat. 'Of course. By all means, proceed.'

'If we could begin by your telling me about yesterday?'

'Right. Yes.' A pause, while Mintar collected his thoughts. As Mrs Mintar senior had told them, Jane Simons, Virginia Mintar's sister, and her boyfriend Arnold Prime were down for the weekend. They had arrived on Friday evening and as it was Prime's first visit to Kent, Jane and the Mintars had wanted to show him something of the county. Yesterday morning Ralph Mintar and his wife had taken them to visit the world-famous gardens created by Vita Sackville-West at Sissinghurst and in the afternoon Jane and Arnold had gone off by themselves to visit Leeds Castle, reputedly 'the most beautiful castle in the world'. The Mintars had stayed at home to play tennis with their next-door neighbours, the Squires, as they often did at weekends.

'My wife is . . . was, a very good player. She took it very seriously, always had coaching during the winter months, to keep her standard up.' Mintar gave a wistful smile. 'She was a great keep fit enthusiast. Belonged to a Health Club.'

They would return to Virginia Mintar later. At the moment Thanet wanted to get the facts clear in his head. 'So this tennis party would have finished at what time?'

'Around 4.30, I suppose.'

They had then had a cup of tea together before the Squires returned home. Normally that would have been the last the Mintars saw of them that day, but as Jane and Arnold were staying, Virginia Mintar had thought it would be pleasant to have an informal supper party. The Squires had therefore been invited to return later.

'They are close friends?'

'Depends what you mean by "close". They are our nearest neighbours, we're on good terms with them and we do see quite a lot of them, yes, especially as we all enjoy a game of tennis. But that's as far as it goes.'

'So who would you say is your wife's closest friend?'

'Susan Amos,' said Mintar promptly.

Lineham took down her address.

'So what time did the Squires return last night?'

Mintar grimaced. 'They were uncomfortably prompt. Supper was to be around a quarter to eight and they were supposed to arrive in time for a drink beforehand. In fact they got here at about 7.15. Ginny was a bit put out, she hadn't finished the watering. It didn't matter too much, of course, as we know them well. It was just a bit inconvenient.'

'Where were you when they arrived?'

'Having a shower.'

'So you didn't see what your wife did in the courtyard after the Squires arrived? You don't know, for instance, whether or not she replaced the well cover before coming in?'

'No. You'd have to ask them. I only knew she hadn't finished the watering because she told me so, when she came up to let me know they were here. She asked me to remind her to do it later.'

'And did you?'

'No. I'm afraid I forgot.'

'And where were your sister-in-law and Mr Prime at the time?'

Mintar shrugged. 'In their room, I assume. They didn't get back from Leeds Castle until around 6.30, so I imagine they were changing. They came downstairs ten or fifteen minutes after me.'

'Miss Simons works in London?'

'Yes. In IT. She does something very sophisticated with computers, don't ask me what, it's far too technical for me to understand. Earns a fortune.'

'And Mr Prime?'

'He's a dentist.'

'Ah.' Why was it that dentists had such a bad press? Thanet wondered. Probably because everyone associated them with pain.

'Anyway, I hurried to finish dressing and joined Ginny and the Squires on the terrace for drinks.' He shrugged. 'Then the others came down and in a little while we had supper. We ate outside, it was such a beautiful evening.' His mouth twisted.

His wife's last, he must be thinking. 'When did Rachel and her fiancé arrive?'

Mintar gave a frown of displeasure. 'They weren't here for supper. They'd been out somewhere and they arrived just as we were finishing coffee.'

'What time would that have been?'

'Somewhere around half past nine, I should think. They'd come for a swim. They urged us all to join them. We'd only had a light meal, it was too hot to eat much, so most people said they would.'

'Not you, though.'

30

'No. I'd had one swim already, after playing tennis, and didn't particularly want to go in again. And in any case, as I told you last night, I had work to do, so I had a good excuse. Mother wasn't interested either.'

'So then what happened? If you could tell me in detail from here on, please.'

'We all got up from the table and everyone picked up something to carry into the kitchen – everyone who had eaten, that is. And we all trailed one behind the other along the corridor to the kitchen, dumped whatever we were carrying on the work surfaces and dispersed.'

'And what time was this?'

A moment's thought. 'Around ten to ten, I should think.'

'Where, exactly, did you disperse to?'

'I can't say for certain. Howard and Marilyn went home to change, I know that, but then I left to come in here. I assume Mother went back to the annexe and Jane and Arnold went upstairs, but I can't be certain.'

'And your wife?'

Mintar frowned. 'Again, I can't be sure. I imagine she would have stayed behind to load the dishwasher and clear things away in the kitchen – she liked to keep things neat and tidy.'

'So she wouldn't have been likely to leave the job half finished?'

'Definitely not, no. Why? Did she?'

'You didn't notice, then? She hadn't finished loading the dishwasher.'

'I'm afraid I was in no state to take in domestic details like that last night, Inspector. But under normal circumstances she certainly wouldn't have left the job half done.'

It was obvious that they were all thinking the same thing: *but these circumstances were far from normal.*

'Something must have interrupted her, then,' said Mintar, eyes narrowed. 'But what?'

If only we knew that, thought Thanet, we'd probably be more than halfway to a solution. 'What about Rachel and Mr Agon? What did they do when you all left the terrace?'

'Sorry, no idea. They were still there when we came in and they didn't follow us into the kitchen, that's all I know. I should think Rachel went up to her room to change and Agon went to the pool house.'

'How long have they been engaged?'

Mintar screwed up his mouth and sucked in his cheeks as though he had just bitten into a lemon and glanced at his watch. 'Approximately, let me see, twelve hours, or thereabouts.'

'They got engaged last night?'

'Yes. And no, Inspector, I can't pretend to be pleased. However, we had learned from bitter experience that it is expedient to be diplomatic in these matters, so I pretended to be delighted and said we'd crack a bottle of champagne.'

'And did you?'

'Yes.'

'You didn't mention this before.'

'No, well, I suppose I was trying to expunge it from my mind. It's all I need at the moment, to know that Rachel is serious about that . . . that shyster.'

'How did your wife feel about the engagement?'

'I never had a chance to discuss it with her, but I'm certain she would have been as upset as I was. She certainly didn't approve of the relationship.'

'This "bitter experience" . . .'

'I shouldn't have mentioned it. It is irrelevant to the matter in hand.'

Thanet sighed. 'I'm sorry, Mr Mintar, but I can't agree. With all the work you have done at the criminal bar you must be aware that in circumstances like this anything and everything to do with your family is bound to come under the spotlight.'

'Oh, God.' Mintar leaned forward and put his head in his hands. 'This is unbearable.'

Thanet said nothing and after a few moments Mintar looked up. 'Yes, I do appreciate that that is so but I don't suppose for a moment you've ever been in this position yourself or indeed have ever been suspected of having committed a crime, so I don't think you can begin to understand just how intolerable it is. Not only to lose your wife but your privacy as well and, on top of all that, to know that inevitably you are bound to be a suspect.' He held up a hand. 'No, don't try to deny it. I'm absolutely certain that Ginny's death couldn't have been an accident, there's no point in pretending that it was, and we both know how often, in cases of domestic murder, it's the nearest and dearest who are guilty. There have been all too many well-publicised cases over the last year or two to ram this fact home to us.'

'I wasn't going to deny it, sir. You're right, of course. But you really are absolutely certain it couldn't have been an accident? Your wife never had any dizzy spells, for instance?'

'Not to my knowledge, no. And I'm sure I would have known, if she had. You can check with Howard Squires, of course. And in any case, the wall around the well is too high for someone of Ginny's height to topple over without extra momentum being applied, to shift the fulcrum.' He closed his eyes for a moment. The image his words conjured up must have been painful indeed. He cleared his throat before going on. 'So I really do think that you can rule out the possibility of it having been an accident. And I'm a hundred per cent certain it couldn't have been suicide. So, incredible as it may seem, that leaves us with only one alternative, doesn't it? And needless to say, I've spent the last few hours racking my brains as to who could possibly have wished to harm her.'

'And?'

'I've got absolutely nowhere. I really cannot imagine

33

why anybody should want to . . .' Mintar's voice cracked and he stopped, took a deep breath. 'No, I'm afraid it's going to be up to you to find that out, Inspector. But believe me, I shall give you every ounce of assistance possible. That is why I have tried to be frank and honest with you – in my feelings towards Agon, for instance. I don't want you to think that I am trying to conceal anything. I have absolutely nothing to hide.'

'Thank you. It would make our job so much easier if everyone had the same attitude. But to return to what we were saying, I imagine you were referring to your other daughter's elopement.'

Mintar's eyes opened wide. 'My God, you don't waste much time, do you. How on earth did you find out about that?'

'It was Rachel, last night. She was so upset, and kept on saying her mother's disappearance was "Caro all over again." So I asked your mother what she meant.'

'I see.' Mintar sighed. 'Well, I don't think it's in the least relevant but if I must . . .' He stood up and, still carrying the cat, walked across to the window and looked out. 'There's not much to tell, really. Four years ago our elder daughter, Caroline, then just eighteen, fell in love with the gardener.' He gave a bitter little laugh. 'Very D.H. Lawrence, I'm afraid. It happens, I suppose. Her mother and I were none too pleased, as you can imagine, and tried to put a stop to it – a disastrous mistake, as it turned out. They eloped and we have never seen her since.'

'But you've been in touch?'

'No.' Mintar swung around to face them. 'And we have no idea where she is. So you can see why we were treading warily over this business with Rachel and Agon.'

'You did try to find out where she is?'

'Of course. And got absolutely nowhere. She left a note, you see, stating her intentions very clearly, so of course the police weren't very interested. Oh, they went through the motions, just to shut us up, but they got nowhere. Swain

– that was his name – had never committed an offence of any kind so they couldn't trace him through the national database, and he apparently wasn't living on benefit, so far as they could find out, so that was that. And the Salvation Army didn't get anywhere either.'

'Really?' Thanet was surprised. The Salvation Army had an excellent record in tracing missing persons and would never give up until every possible line of inquiry had been exhausted.

'No. So there was absolutely nothing we could do about it, except hope that one day Caro would relent, and get in touch. Ginny never got over it.'

'Did the young man's family live locally?'

Another cynical little laugh. 'Oh yes. His mother lives in a cottage in the woods and has the reputation of being the local witch, so you can see why we didn't exactly consider him a desirable suitor for our daughter. She was as unhelpful as she could possibly be when we were trying to get in touch with Caro, still claims she doesn't have the faintest idea where they are and in fact seems to blame Caro for the whole thing. Says she turned her son's head.'

'He's her only child?'

Mintar nodded.

'So your present gardener . . . ?'

'Digby came as Swain's replacement.'

'I see. Well, thank you for explaining, sir. Just one or two further points . . . Your mother lives in the annexe, I gather. Has she been there long?'

'Yes, for many years – ever since I got married, in fact.' For the first time Mintar's expression lightened and he gave a slight smile. 'Oh, I know what you must have been thinking – that she's an unlikely candidate for a "granny annexe". And you'd be right, of course, she is. She's more than capable of running an independent establishment of her own and lives here purely for her own convenience. Perhaps I'd better explain that she's a botanist or, perhaps more accurately, an artist who is also a qualified botanist. She's always going off on far-flung expeditions and it suits her to be able to come and go as she pleases without having to worry about security and so on. We've lived in this house since I was in my early teens and when my father died we stayed on, although it was really too big for us. Mother found it rather a burden, I think, and she was relieved when I got married and Ginny and I took it over. We converted that little wing of outbuildings into a flat for her.' Again, the faint smile. 'I think Mother regards it more as a mini Dower House than a granny annexe. The arrangement has worked out well.'

'Did she and your wife get on?'

Mintar's eyebrows shot up. 'You're surely not suggesting my mother had anything to do with what happened to Ginny?'

'I was merely inquiring. It can be a difficult situation, I believe.'

'We don't exactly live in each other's pockets. And besides, as I said, Mother is away for long periods of time. They got on perfectly well, thank you.'

The door swung open.

'Daddy?'

Rachel stood in the doorway, swaying slightly. She had obviously just awoken from the sedative Dr Squires had given her last night: her eyelids drooped, her hair was tousled and she was wearing a very short white sleepshirt and an ankle-length deep blue silk kimono embroidered with huge white waterlilies. She steadied herself with one hand against the door jamb and said, 'Why is there a fire engine outside?' She noticed Thanet and Lineham and her expression changed, became more alert. 'Have you found her?'

She obviously hadn't looked out of any of the windows overlooking the courtyard, thought Thanet.

Mintar put the cat down, hurried across the room and put his arm around her shoulders. 'Rachel.' He

36

cast an agonised glance at Thanet. *How am I going to tell her?*

Time for a tactful withdrawal. Thanet did not envy Mintar the next few minutes. He stood up. 'We'll leave you now, sir. If you could just direct us to your wife's room?'

Mintar's expression changed to – what? Thanet wondered. Something unexpected, certainly. Embarrassment, perhaps? Swiftly followed by resignation. 'Up the stairs, first on the right.' He turned to his daughter. 'Come along, darling. Let's get you back to your room.'

Still somewhat dazed, Rachel allowed herself to be shepherded up ahead of them. The two policemen tactfully waited for the door of Rachel's room to close before Lineham opened the door to her mother's bedroom. Then without warning he stopped dead on the threshold, so abruptly that Thanet bumped into him. 'Mike! Watch what you're doing. What are you playing at?'

But Lineham wasn't listening. He whistled softly. 'Just look at this, sir!' he said.

FOUR

'No-o-o-o!'

Thanet and Lineham froze as along the corridor floated a wail of despair. Mintar must have broken the news of her mother's death to Rachel.

'Poor kid,' muttered Thanet. Then, irritably, giving Lineham a little push, 'Move over then. I can't see a thing with you standing there like the rock of Gibraltar.'

Lineham moved aside and Thanet saw the reason for the sergeant's surprise – and also for Mintar's embarrassed reaction downstairs. The thought of having his wife's idiosyncracies exposed to the gaze of strangers would no doubt have made him squirm. For although the four-poster bed with its graceful hangings, the toning curtains and soft-pile carpet all proclaimed that this was the master bedroom, the room was dominated by a curious phenomenon. Piled up all around the walls right up to the ceiling, two and three deep in places, were cardboard boxes.

'Odd that none of the men commented on this last night,' said Lineham. 'What on earth do you suppose she keeps in them?' He crossed to the nearest pile, pulled out a box and peered at the lid. 'It says "T-SHIRTS, WHITE".' He opened it.

It was indeed filled with white T-shirts, mostly still in their polythene bags, all obviously unworn. Lineham picked some up, read the labels. 'Alexon, Jaeger, Ralph Lauren, Mondi . . . This lot must have cost a small fortune. Whatever did she want with them all?'

Thanet was opening another box labelled 'SWEATERS, PINK'. This too was stuffed with top-quality garments in cashmere, lambswool, angora, all made by famous brand names.

They glanced at the labels on some of the other boxes: socks, pants, waist slips, full-length slips, nightdresses, pyjamas, cardigans, tennis shorts and tops, swimsuits, all in every colour of the spectrum. Then there were the accessories – belts, scarves, shoes, handbags, and gloves. The fitted wardrobe which took up one entire wall of the room was crammed so full of dresses, suits, skirts and trousers that it must have been difficult to put anything in or take anything out.

'No one woman could get through wearing this little lot in a lifetime,' said Lineham. 'There's only one explanation, isn't there? She was a shopaholic. I saw a documentary.'

'I agree, Mike.' Thanet put out a finger to touch the folds of a silk dress. 'And I wonder why. There must have been something seriously wrong.'

'I'll say. Doesn't look as though her husband slept in here, does it?'

And it was true that although there were two sets of pillows in the bed and two bedside tables, there was no sign of a masculine presence in the room.

'There's probably a dressing room through there.' Thanet nodded at a closed door. 'Quite common in certain sections of society, I believe.'

Lineham grunted. 'Not exactly the royal family, this.' Still, he went to check. 'But you're right. All very snug.'

Thanet had a look: another fitted wardrobe, single bed, trouser press, chest of drawers with silver-backed hairbrushes, bedside table with lamp and alarm clock. He turned back to the main bedroom. 'Anyway, it would take far too long for us to go through all these boxes. We'll put some of the team on to it and just take a quick glance around for now.'

But the search revealed nothing else of any interest apart from a small worn album of photographs in the drawer of one of the bedside tables. Thanet looked through it. The snapshots were all of a girl, from babyhood to teenage years, mostly alone but sometimes with another child who was recognisably Rachel. Caroline, presumably. Mintar had said that his wife had never got over losing her. Thanet had a sudden, vivid vision of Ginny Mintar sitting up alone in the luxurious four-poster bed surrounded by all this evidence of an unquenchable thirst for fulfilment, obsessively turning over the pages of the album and mourning her lost daughter. Could there be a connection?

'I wonder why Mr Mintar never hired a private detective to find Caroline,' said Lineham, tuning in, as he so often did, to Thanet's thoughts.

'I wondered that, too. But there was something odd about his attitude to the whole business of Caroline's elopement, didn't you think?'

'In what way, sir?'

'I'm not sure. I could understand him not wanting to talk about it, but I just had the feeling he wasn't being frank with us, despite his protestations to the contrary.' Thanet replaced the album and shut the drawer.

'You're not suggesting anything sinister, are you, sir?'

'Oh no, I shouldn't think so for a minute. Though it might be worth just checking, to see what action the police did take.'

'To change the subject, it did occur to me . . .'

'What?'

'You know what you were saying about the work in the kitchen being left half done last night? And what Mr Mintar said about his wife asking him to remind her to finish the watering later? Well, I did notice that the sink is in front of the window, and that there's a clear view of the well from there. What if she was rinsing the dishes and happened to look out, remembered she hadn't done it? She'd have been busy all evening, serving supper. This might have been her first opportunity – her last, perhaps, if they were all going swimming.'

'Good point, Mike. So she thought she'd better see to it then and there, while she remembered. Then what?'

'Then she must have met someone.'

They stared at each other in silence, envisaging the scene. Thanet could see it all: Ginny Mintar hurrying across the courtyard to the well in the gathering dusk, the light from the kitchen spilling out behind her and a shadowy figure coming to meet her, or following her, perhaps . . . 'But who, I wonder?' He turned and made briskly for the door. 'Come on, Mike, we really haven't the faintest idea of what everyone was doing at the time. We've only got Mintar's assumptions to go on at the moment. We'll talk to Rachel later, when she's had a chance to calm down. Let's see if we can find Miss Simons and her boyfriend.'

They ran them to earth in the kitchen, seated at the big pine table. Jane was hunched over a mug of coffee, both hands clasped around it as though despite the heat of the day she was attempting to draw comfort from its warmth. There was a box of tissues on the table in front of her. Prime was sitting beside her, a protective arm around her shoulders. They both looked up as the two policemen entered. Jane had obviously been crying. Her eyes were bloodshot, the skin around them puffy and her mascara was badly smudged.

Not having seen Virginia Mintar until this morning, Thanet was surprised now to realise that there was a resemblance between the two sisters. It was as if Ginny's features had been blown up and distorted slightly so that whereas she had been beautiful, Jane had been aptly named. Not for the first time Thanet was struck by the

41

infinite variations of the human face. Two eyes, a nose and a mouth, and apart from identical twins no two sets of features are exactly alike. A fractional adjustment here, a tiny shift of emphasis there and the result is completely different. No wonder portrait painters find it so difficult to achieve a satisfactory likeness, he thought.

Now, looking at Jane Simons, he wondered how it must have felt, having a younger sister so much more beautiful than she. Had it made her determined to shine in other ways, academically, perhaps? She had done very well for herself as far as her career was concerned, according to Mintar. Thanet suspected too that it had made her work hard to maximise her assets. Even this morning she had taken trouble with her make-up and although her cotton dress and matching jacket in a tawny mixture of black, browns and creams looked simple enough, Joan had long since taught him that such simplicity frequently carried a high price tag. Still, he felt sorry for these two. Apart from the considerable personal loss to Jane, it must be pretty dispiriting to set off for a light-hearted summer weekend in the country and find yourself caught up in what looked like a murder inquiry. 'May we sit down?'

She nodded.

Prime had sat back a little, but left his arm resting lightly on her shoulders.

'We're so sorry about your sister,' said Thanet as he and Lineham pulled out chairs and settled themselves. 'And I really do apologise for this, but I'm afraid that there are, inevitably, questions to be asked.'

She caught her lower lip beneath her teeth. 'I still can't believe it,' she whispered.

How often had he heard this from those caught up in the aftermath of a violent death? Thanet wondered. 'But sadly, it's true,' he said. 'So while last night is still fresh in your minds . . .'

'I do understand,' she said, and Thanet saw Prime's

hand give her shoulder a little squeeze of approbation. 'What, exactly do you want to know?'

Thanet glanced at Lineham. *Take over.* He wanted to think, to observe these two. They intrigued him.

'If you would tell us about yesterday?' said the sergeant.

'What, all day?' said Prime, speaking for the first time, eyebrows climbing his bony forehead.

Thanet approved of Lineham's tactics. Talking about the earlier, innocent pleasures of the day would help Jane to relax. It did. By the time they had reached their return from Leeds Castle around 6.30 p.m. she had relinquished the coffee mug and was sitting back in her chair, one hand clasping Prime's on her shoulder.

'One small point before you go on,' said Lineham. 'Did you see Mrs Mintar when you got back?'

'No,' said Prime.

'I assume she was changing,' said Jane. 'She'd obviously done most of the preparations for supper. There were various dishes laid out on this table, with cutlery and dishes on trays, ready to be carried out.'

'Did you notice if she had been doing any watering in the courtyard?'

'Sorry, no.'

Prime also shook his head.

'Though I think I'd have noticed if the well had been uncovered,' said Jane. 'I don't *think* it was, but I can't be sure.' She looked to Prime for confirmation but he again shook his head.

'Sorry, I really don't think I would have noticed if it had been.'

Their account of the evening tallied with Mintar's and Lineham took them through it at a brisk pace until they reached the point at which they rose from the table. Then he followed the pattern which Thanet had set in his interview with Mintar and asked them to proceed in detail.

They glanced at each other.

'Well,' said Jane, 'we all picked up something to carry to the kitchen, to help clear the table. Ginny went first and we followed.'

'Along the corridor which leads from the terrace to the kitchen?'

'Yes. We deposited the various bits and pieces on worktops or the table, then Ginny started to load the dishwasher. I offered to help, but she refused, said she could manage.' Jane pulled a face. 'She was fussy about things like that. You know, all the different dishes had to go in their allotted places, and the cutlery had to go in with knives on the right, forks on the left, spoons in between.'

'She was careful about detail, then.'

'Yes. And very tidy-minded. That was why . . .'

'What?'

'Well, that was why I was surprised, later, when we were all looking for her and I came in here, to find she'd left the job half done. That was when I first began to get worried, to think that there might be something wrong.'

'Was it you who finished clearing up later?' said Thanet.

'Yes. I couldn't sleep, so after you'd gone I thought I'd tidy up. Ginny hated coming down to a mess in the morning. I . . . I thought she'd be pleased to find I'd finished up for her.' Jane's voice shook. 'Stupid, really. It was as if, by assuming she'd turn up, I'd make it happen.' Her gaze drifted to the window. 'Well she did, didn't she?' Tears filled her eyes and spilled over. 'I really still can't believe it,' she said again, shaking her head.

Prime shook a tissue out of the box on the table and handed it to her. She wiped her eyes and blew her nose. 'Sorry.'

Lineham waited a few moments, then said, 'If we could go back to where you all put the dishes down . . . What did everybody do then?'

Jane was still dabbing at her eyes. 'Let me see.' She looked to Prime for help.

He narrowed his eyes, obviously thinking back. 'Ralph left straight away, went to his study, I presume. He'd excused himself from swimming, said he had work to do. Then all of us except Ginny went back and collected the rest of the stuff from the table, took it into the kitchen. Then Howard and Marilyn went off to change and so did we.'

'Where were Rachel and her fiancé?'

Jane didn't exactly wince at the mention of Agon, but her expression hardened. 'Still on the terrace.'

'When you went back, you mean?'

'Yes. To put it crudely, they were having a good snog.'

'You don't approve of Mr Agon, Miss Simons?' said Thanet.

She pulled a face. 'Slimy toad. I most certainly do not. The sooner Rachel dumps him the better.'

'You all toasted their future in champagne, I understand?'

'Yes. It was as brief and joyless a "celebration" as I have ever experienced. I couldn't help feeling sorry for Rachel, she must have realised how her parents felt – how we all felt, for that matter. But I imagine Ralph thought he really must at least go through the motions.'

'After what happened with Rachel's sister, you mean?' said Lineham.

'You know about that? Yes.'

'So, to get back to what we were saying, what time would you say it was when you went up to change?'

They agreed that it was probably between 9.50 and 10.

'And when you got back down?'

Prime hesitated. 'It must have been about a quarter past.'

Now that was interesting, thought Thanet. Up until now they had been consulting each other all the time, but suddenly it seemed to him that they were studiously avoiding looking at each other. He wasn't sure if Lineham had noticed this or not.

He had. 'A quarter of an hour's a long time, to change into swimsuits?'

Prime shrugged. 'There was no hurry. We chatted.'

What about? Thanet wondered. There was a stiffness in Prime's voice and although his arm still lay across the back of Jane Simons's chair she had released his hand. Had they quarrelled? And if so, had it been over something which had happened at supper?

'What about?' said Lineham.

Prime pursed his lips, wagged his head from side to side. 'This and that. The evening. The other guests. The engagement. Nothing very significant.'

'How can it possibly matter what we talked about up in our room?' said Jane. And there, too, was an edge which had been absent before.

'Perhaps it doesn't,' said Lineham. *And perhaps it does.* The words hung unspoken in the air. 'So when you got to the pool, who was already there?'

Thanet noted the glint of relief in Prime's eyes before he answered: 'They were all there except for Ginny – and Ralph and Frances, of course.'

'That would be Rachel and her fiancé and Mr and Mrs Squires.'

'That's right, yes.'

'Didn't it occur to you to wonder where your sister was, Miss Simons?'

'Yes, of course. That was why I asked if anyone else had seen her.'

But she wasn't being completely frank, thought Thanet. Her eyes had that evasiveness, that veiled look which frequently denotes an attempt to lie by a person who is by nature honest.

'So you were the first person to notice she was missing.'

'Yes. But we didn't realise she was, at that point.

46

Missing. We just thought she'd been delayed for some reason.'

'Then we thought she might have changed her mind about coming for a swim, didn't we?' said Prime.

'That's right.'

It was interesting that once again they were united in their responses, Thanet thought. They evidently thought that the tricky area had been successfully negotiated.

'But we did think it was odd she hadn't come out to say so,' said Jane.

'And then someone suggested she might have gone to bed,' said Prime.

'Not that anyone took that seriously. She never went to bed early and anyway she'd never have done so without excusing herself to her guests. So then Rachel went to look for her.'

'What time would this have been?'

Again they consulted each other with a glance.

'A quarter to eleven?' said Prime.

She nodded. 'Something like that.'

'Around half an hour after you got back downstairs, then.'

Again a flash of constraint before this time they nodded in unison. 'Yes.'

'But when Rachel came back, said Virginia wasn't in her room or indeed anywhere in the house, as far as she could tell, we began to feel concerned,' said Prime. 'We decided we'd have to look for her. So we all went and threw some clothes on and began to search. The rest, you know.'

But Jane Simons hadn't exactly thrown some clothes on, thought Thanet, remembering how well groomed she had appeared last night. Even in what was beginning to seem an emergency she had been determined to look her best. Perhaps that was an uncharitable view. Perhaps she didn't feel able to face the world without her full armour on.

The door opened and Rachel came in with her father.

She was still wearing the blue silk kimono, now tightly belted around her narrow waist. Although she was very pale and, like Jane, her eyes were red and swollen, she looked fairly composed. 'Daddy says you'll need to speak to me,' she said.

Thanet and Lineham had risen. 'It can wait, Miss Mintar,' said Thanet. 'There's no rush.'

'I'd rather get it over with, if you don't mind.'

'I'll stay with you, darling,' said her father.

'No!' Then, more gently. 'Thank you, Daddy, but I'll be quite all right by myself.'

'But—'

'Daddy, please. I'm not a child any longer. Just go, will you?'

Jane Simons and Prime were already on their feet. Their relief was obvious. 'We'll go too,' she said. 'If there's anything else we can do to help . . .'

'Thank you.'

Thanet waited until they had all gone and Rachel was seated at the table. 'Would you like a cup of coffee?'

'No, thank you.'

He sat down opposite her and said, 'You're sure about this?'

She shook back her long blonde hair. 'Yes.'

'Right. We'll make it as brief as possible.'

'Take as long as you like.' The blue eyes filled with tears and she dashed them angrily away with the back of her hand. 'I want to do everything I can to help.'

FIVE

Rachel would find sympathy hard to cope with, thought Thanet. Best to be brisk and businesslike. 'Now, I understand that you and Mr Agon arrived here last night as the others were finishing their coffee. What time would that have been?'

'Around half past nine, I should think.' She was twisting a strand of hair round and round a forefinger.

Thanet took her quickly to the point where they all split up to change. 'I understand that you and your fiancé were the last to leave the terrace?'

There was a brief spark of joy in her eyes before she agreed that that was so.

It had probably been the first time that anyone had referred to Agon as her fiancé, Thanet realised, and like every newly engaged girl showing off her engagement ring, she was pleased that their new status had been acknowledged. As her aunt had said, despite the spurious celebration last night she was bound to be aware that her family was less than delighted about her choice of husband.

'So what did you do, after the table had been cleared?'

'I went up to my room to change.' She was still very tense, hanging on to the hair wound around her finger as if it were an anchor.

'And Mr Agon?'

'He changed in the pool house.'

'Which way did you go into the house? Through the corridor to the kitchen, or through the sitting room?'

'Through the drawing room. It's the quickest way into the hall.'

She wasn't correcting him, Thanet realised, just using the habitual way in which the family referred to that room. 'What about when you came back down?'

'The same.'

'And the others? Which way did they return?'

The brief, factual exchanges were beginning to have the calming effect Thanet had hoped for and now she released the lock of hair and sat back in her chair, frowning a little as she thought back. 'Well, Marilyn and Howard came through the courtyard, obviously, the same way they had gone. Jane and her man came through the—' She stopped. 'No, hang on. They came back separately. I remember wondering why they hadn't come together. I saw him come through the French windows in the drawing room but she wasn't with him. She turned up a few minutes later.'

Thanet and Lineham exchanged glances. Prime and Jane Simons had certainly given the impression that they had returned to the pool together.

'And did she come through the drawing room too?'

'I didn't notice, I'm afraid. I assume so. I just saw her getting into the pool, that's all. She asked me where Mum . . .' At this first mention of her mother, Rachel's fragile composure slipped. She swallowed, pressed her lips together and took a deep breath. 'She asked me where Mum was. Until then none of us had really noticed she wasn't there. And we still weren't worried. We knew how keen she was on leaving the kitchen spick and span. We just thought she was taking longer because she was clearing up.'

'Was it usual for her to clear everything away so thoroughly before guests had left?' Thanet tried to be tactful, not to sound critical. In his book it would have been downright rude.

'Not if it was a proper dinner party, no. But last night it was very informal, just Howard and Marilyn around for supper . . . Then when we suggested a swim, that made it even more so.'

'Yes, I see. So who was in the pool when you got back?'

'Just Matt.'

'And who arrived next?'

'Let me think.' Now that they were no longer talking about her mother she had settled down again. 'Howard, I think. Yes, Howard. He came just after me. Then Marilyn, then Jane's boyfriend. Jane was last, as I said.'

'The Squires didn't arrive together either?' Thanet groaned inwardly.

'No.'

'Was there much of a time lapse between them?'

'I honestly didn't notice.' She gestured helplessly. 'We were fooling around in the pool. If I'd known it was going to be important . . . It was only a few minutes, I should think. But I don't really know.' Once again she was becoming agitated, twisting her hands together.

Thanet said, 'Never mind, it doesn't really matter,' intending to calm her down. Instead, his words had the opposite effect.

'But it does, doesn't it?' she burst out. 'Matter. It's only just dawned on me. Dad didn't say . . . I assumed it was an accident, but I wasn't really thinking straight. It couldn't have been, could it? There's no way Mum could have fallen over that parapet. Someone . . . Someone must have . . .' She stared at him wildly. 'And you think it was one of us, don't you? That's what all these questions are about. And . . . And . . .' She stopped.

Thanet opened his mouth to speak, trying to find words of reassurance – but what reassurance could he possibly give?

Before he could say anything Rachel said, 'But why? Who could possibly want to hurt her?' She put her elbows on the table and buried her face in her hands, shaking her head. 'No, I can't believe it, I just can't.'

'That's what we have to try to find out.'

There was a silence while she digested what they had been saying. Then she looked up again. 'And all this stuff about who came back to the pool and when . . . It could have been any one of us, couldn't it? *We all came back separately.*'

'So it seems,' said Thanet with a sigh.

'So . . .' She twisted her head to gaze out of the window as if trying to see back into the past. Then, eyes full of misery, she looked back at Thanet and whispered, 'Not knowing who and why and how . . . It's going to be awful. I don't think I can bear it . . . All that uncertainty . . . And at the end of it, nothing will bring her back, will it? She's gone. Gone for ever, just like Caroline.'

'Your sister. Yes. Your father told me about that.'

'Oh, Dad. What does he care?' Her tone was bitter.

Thanet was surprised. Until now Mintar and Rachel had seemed to be on good terms. 'What do you mean?'

It seemed that the mention of Caroline had resurrected past feelings of resentment. 'He behaves as if she never existed.'

'That wasn't the impression he gave us.'

'No, well, he wouldn't, would he?'

'Why not?'

'He wouldn't want to be seen as an uncaring father. Bad for the image. When the police told us that as she was over age and had gone willingly – she left a note, you know – d'you know what he said? "Well, that's it. She's made her bed and she must lie on it. I wash my hands of her." How Victorian can you get? And he's never referred to her again to my knowledge, not once, in four years.'

Truly incredible behaviour in this day and age, Thanet had to agree. But he could now understand why Mintar had been uncomfortable, talking about Caroline. It wasn't just that the hurt had gone deep, perhaps he blamed himself for not having tried harder to find her before the trail went cold, especially if her loss had affected his wife as much as he had seemed to imply. 'That doesn't mean to say he didn't care.'

'Huh! Funny way of showing it!'

'He certainly seems to care for you.'

'I'm all he's got left now, aren't I? But I used to come pretty low in the pecking order, believe me. Mum came first, then Caro, then me. When Caro went I moved up a notch, that's all. And now . . .' She was silent a moment and then said, 'If he cared, why didn't he do something about it?'

'But he did. He contacted the Salvation Army. It wasn't his fault that they couldn't find her.'

'He did not! That was Mum! He was dead against it. They had terrible arguments about it and in the end she just went ahead and did it of her own accord. He wasn't too pleased, believe me! But by then the trail was cold, it was presumably too late and they never found her.'

Although Thanet knew that the Salvation Army frequently managed to trace people who had been missing for far longer than Caroline, he did not contradict her. What was the point? It would only cause her further distress.

'Did your sister's elopement come as a complete surprise to you all?'

'Absolutely. Of course, looking back, you could see it must have been on the cards. I mean, there'd been awful rows about Caro going out with Dick and she told me she was absolutely fed up with it. But she didn't breathe a word about eloping to anyone.'

'And no one noticed she was unusually excited or tense?'

'No. That was probably because the night she went away, Gran came back unexpectedly from Turkestan or somewhere. She had been off on one of her trips for a couple of months. She's always going on these plant-hunting expeditions, she's a botanical artist. Anyway, we knew she was due back soon but there was some sort of mix-up or misunderstanding about dates and no one was expecting her when she arrived that evening. So of course there was general fuss all around and a celebratory dinner – she always produces a bottle of champagne the night of her return.' Rachel gave a brief smile for the first time and Thanet saw how beautiful she could be when warmth and animation informed her features. 'Gran always believes in doing things in style. I hope I'm like that when I'm seventy-seven! Anyway, we were all too busy listening to her traveller's tales to pay much attention to Caroline. As soon as we'd finished dinner, which took rather longer than usual, Caro excused herself, said she had a headache.'

'You didn't look in on her later, to see how she was?'

'She'd hung her "DO NOT DISTURB" notice on the door. I didn't think anything of it, just assumed she'd gone to sleep. So it wasn't until next day that anyone realised she'd gone. By then, of course, they must have been well away.'

'Your father said your mother never got over it.' Thanet still couldn't understand why, if Mintar was so fond of his wife, he had been so set against trying to find Caroline, when it obviously meant so much to Virginia. Was it simply stiff-necked pride that had prevented him from backing down?

'No, she never did. She seemed to carry on as normal, but . . . Well, you've seen her room, haven't you?'

'All the clothes, you mean?'

'Yes. She was never like that before. Oh, she used to enjoy shopping, who doesn't, but not like that, not to that extent. I tried to get her to see she needed help, but she wouldn't acknowledge there was a problem, wouldn't even talk about it.'

54

'Did she ever think of hiring a private detective to find Caroline?'

'She actually did hire one, sometime last year. But he didn't get anywhere either. It didn't help that Dick's mother was so uncooperative.'

'Do you think she knows where they are?'

'Not by the way she behaves – she blames Caroline, you know, for causing her to lose her son. As if he hadn't had anything to do with the elopement!'

'What was he like, Dick?'

Another smile. 'Drop dead gorgeous!' she said, sounding like a normal teenager for the first time. 'In fact, I have never been able to work out how such a hideous old woman could produce anything so scrumptious. I had a terrific crush on him myself and I wasn't a bit surprised when Caro went overboard for him. I was green with envy when they started going out together.' She grimaced. 'He was a great deal more pleasant to have about the place than Digby, I can tell you.'

There was a knock at the door. Lineham answered it. The firemen had finished, apparently.

'Tell them we'll just be a few minutes,' said Thanet. He turned back to Rachel. 'Digby. Why don't you like him?'

She pulled a face again. 'Him and his camera. He gives me the creeps.'

'Camera?'

'It's his hobby. Photography. Wildlife, supposed to be. And to be fair, he is a very good photographer. He's got an exhibition on at the moment, in the branch library in the village. Not exactly the Tate, but still . . .'

'What did you mean by "supposed to be"?'

She looked uncomfortable. 'Perhaps I shouldn't have said that.'

'No, please, I'm interested.'

'Well, I'm never quite sure that he doesn't sometimes photograph people.'

'You, you mean?'

She nodded. 'I'd never sunbathe in the nude when he's around, for example. And I'm careful to choose my spot if I'm wearing a bikini.'

'Have you told your father this?'

She shook her head. 'I'm not certain about it, you see. I've never actually caught him at it. It's just a feeling I have. And the way he looks at me. Slyly. As if he knows all my secrets.' She gave a shiver of distaste.

'I'm sure your father would want to know, if you feel like that. I know I would, if it were my daughter.' At the thought of Bridget Thanet experienced another shaft of anxiety. What was happening to her now? He was suddenly overwhelmed by the need to ring Joan and find out. He rose. 'Well, thank you very much for your help, Miss Mintar—'

'Rachel. Call me Rachel.'

'Very well. Thank you, Rachel. I know it can't have been easy for you. You've been very brave.'

To his dismay he saw that the compliment had brought her to the verge of tears again and he kicked himself for not keeping the tone impersonal. Still, nothing and no one was going to keep her on an even keel for long today, he guessed.

Outside the firemen were all packed up and ready to go. Laid out neatly on a sheet of polythene was an array of objects which had been brought up from the bottom of the well. 'Anything interesting?' he said.

The fire chief shook his head. 'I shouldn't think so. Anyway, there it is. We'll leave you to it. Good luck.'

Thanet thanked them, then went and sat in the car for a few moments to ring Joan in privacy. But there was no news as yet and he returned to the well, where Lineham was studying the finds: assorted bottles and jars, some broken and some intact; various bits of shaped wood, probably pieces of ancient toys; a trowel with a broken handle; a number of pieces of clay pipes; an old biscuit tin; a little stack of broken china and some unidentifiable pieces of rusty metal.

'Nothing much there,' said the sergeant.

'Doesn't look like it.'

'So what now?'

'Mrs Mintar senior, I think. But first I'd like to take a closer look at the swimming pool, get a better idea of the lie of the land.'

They left the SOCO bagging the objects retrieved from the well, then, taking the route the Squires must have followed when returning to the pool last night, walked past the end of the annexe. This had a small, private garden of its own at the rear, Thanet saw, surrounded by a tall yew hedge which also flanked the raised terrace on to which the French windows of the drawing room opened. Below that, down a short flight of steps, lay the swimming pool. Beyond it was a tennis court and over to the left a small single-storey building.

'The pool house?' said Lineham.

They went to have a look inside. There were two changing cubicles, a shower, and a lavatory.

'Simple, but adequate,' said Thanet.

'Not so simple and more than adequate,' said Lineham, opening another door. 'Look, there's a sauna. Very nice, too.'

'Don't see the attraction, myself,' said Thanet.

'Have you ever had a sauna?'

'Can't say I have.'

'There you are, then! How can you pass judgement till you've tried it? It's great! Very relaxing.'

'Not my cup of tea.'

'You ought to give it a whirl some time, sir. You might be surprised.'

'You're not advertising a health club, Mike.'

They went outside again to take a closer look at the pool area. It was paved with non-slip tiles and, except for the side nearest to the house, was surrounded by a neatly clipped waist-high box hedge affording shelter and some degree of privacy for sunbathers. On the poolside, across one of the shorter ends, was a long roller with a heavy blue plastic pool cover rolled up on it. There were comfortable sun loungers with yellow and white striped cushions and a slatted cedarwood table with matching chairs, shaded by a large cream canvas Italian umbrella. Conscious of the sun beating down on his head, Thanet walked around to the side furthest from the house, then, turning to look back at the house, squatted down. Yes, from this side of the pool and probably to about halfway across anyone in the water would have a clear view of the drawing-room windows and the door to the corridor leading to the kitchen. Only the roof of the annexe was visible; it too must have a small terrace but the yew hedge which surrounded it shielded it from view. Mrs Mintar senior would have been able to hear the swimmers last night, but she wouldn't have been able to see them. On the other hand, some of her windows overlooked the courtyard . . .

The water lay as flat and calm as a steel mirror and its blue depths looked infinitely inviting. Thanet leaned forward to test the temperature. It felt pleasantly warm.

'Thinking of having a dip, sir?' said Lineham, eyes wide with mock innocence.

Thanet scowled and stood up. 'Old Mrs Mintar,' he said. 'Now she's had time to think, perhaps she saw or heard something last night.'

SIX

Lineham rang Mrs Mintar's doorbell.

No reply.

He rang again.

Still no response.

'Try the door,' said Thanet.

It opened. Thanet put his head in and called.

'Who is it?' A voice from the left, sounding annoyed.

'Inspector Thanet and Sergeant Lineham.'

'Go into the sitting room. I'll be out in a minute.'

The door to the sitting room stood ajar and they stepped inside. It was furnished in bright, clear colours: blues, greens and turquoise, with a touch of purple here and there. Not the room of an average seventy-seven-year-old. But then her son and granddaughter had made it clear that she was anything but that. Glazed doors stood open on to a little terrace and Thanet glimpsed a huge Chinese ceramic pot overflowing with summer bedding plants and a narrow border crammed with roses and summer-flowering perennials.

On the walls hung groups of striking botanical paintings and, as Thanet stepped across to take a closer look, he kicked something lying on the floor. He bent to pick it up. It was a small brown pill bottle. Automatically he read the label: *Glyceryl Trinitrate 300 mg. Take one as directed.*

'Looks as though she has angina,' he said to Lineham. He put the bottle on the mantelpiece.

'Wonder how that affects her expeditions.'

'Quite.' Thanet returned to the group of paintings: *Pulsatilla ambigua*, he read, *Pulsatilla occidentalis*, *Pulsatilla campanella*.

'Beautiful, aren't they?' Mrs Mintar had come into the room. 'Commonly called pasque flowers, from the French. '*Pâques*,' she explained to his uncomprehending look.

'Of course,' he said, digging into his memory. 'Easter.'

'Quite. Hence *passefleurs* – "Easter flowers".'

'Did you do these after one of your expeditions?'

She looked amused. 'You know about those. You really have learned a lot about us in a very short time, haven't you? Yes. But not one expedition. Several.'

The pill bottle was no longer on the mantelpiece, he noted. She must have removed it while he was taking another look at the paintings and was no doubt hoping they hadn't noticed it. So she didn't want them to know of her condition. Interesting. 'Do you go away often?'

'A couple of times a year. More often if I can.' Talking about her work she became more animated. 'I've been very lucky, really. Expeditions are very expensive to mount and there are always loads of botanists anxious to get out into the field. But fortunately I've got this other string to my bow, being able to draw and paint. The sponsors often want more than just a photographic record, and I've gradually carved out a niche for myself. This year, for instance, I was in South America from just after Christmas to the beginning of March and I hope to go to south-west China in November.'

'Have you always done this work?'

'Oh yes. Barristers' wives have to develop their own interests, their husband's work is so time-consuming that they'd go mad if they didn't. I would have, anyway.'

'So your husband was also in the legal profession.'

'He became a High Court judge, as a matter of fact.'

'You don't use your title?'

She made a dismissive gesture. 'I don't go in much for that sort of thing. I'd rather paddle my own canoe.'

The metaphor was apt. He could just imagine her white-water rafting down the Amazon. Though the angina must somewhat cramp her style these days – if, that is, she made any concessions to it. Which, he guessed, she probably didn't. She was the type who'd rather die on a mountain than of old age in a hospital bed. He turned back to the paintings. 'These are really lovely.'

'Thank you. I just thought they'd make an interesting group.'

'Pastel, aren't they?'

Her eyebrows rose slightly. 'Yes, they are.'

'It's unusual to see botanical paintings in pastel. I thought they were invariably in watercolour.'

'They are. The ones I do for the RHS magazine, for example, are always in watercolour. These I do for my own pleasure and they aren't strictly botanical, more interpretations of the botanical, shall we say.'

'And much more exciting, if you ask me. More ... dramatic.'

'It's very kind of you to say so. But I don't imagine you've come here to discuss my work, Inspector. I know we could stand here having an interesting conversation for the rest of the morning, but I'm sure you're anxious to get on.' *And if you're not, I am.*

She was wearing wide-legged cotton trousers and a loose cotton smock smudged with pastel dust. She must have been working when they arrived, which was, no doubt, why she had sounded so annoyed at being inter-rupted. But painting? Only a few hours after her daughter-in-law's body had been found?

'I can see you're thinking I must be pretty heartless,' she said, 'to be working under these circumstances. But there's no point in pretending that there was any love

61

lost between Virginia and myself. I am sorry for my son's sake, of course, but as far as I'm concerned it's good riddance.'

'You don't mince your words, do you?' said Thanet.

'What's the point? Waste of time, in my opinion.'

'Well, it certainly makes my job much easier.'

She shifted from one foot to the other, obviously impatient to get back to her work. She hadn't invited them to sit down and had remained standing herself.

Well, he wasn't going to be rushed, thought Thanet. It was time he made it clear who was in charge here. 'May we sit down?'

She hesitated. She was so forthright that he almost expected her to refuse, but good breeding took over and she made a grudging gesture. *If you must.* She herself perched on the very edge of an upright chair as if to emphasise the fact that she hoped the interview would be brief.

'Naturally,' said Thanet when they were all settled, 'in view of what has happened, we're trying to piece together everyone's movements yesterday.'

'Quite.' She folded her arms as if to contain her impatience. *Well, get on with it, then,* her body language shouted.

'If you would take us quickly through the day?'

'The *whole* day?'

'Please.'

She gave an exasperated sigh before beginning her account. She had stayed at home all day, apparently. She had worked in the morning and had a leisurely afternoon, going for her daily swim before settling down to read the paper. After tea she had showered and changed before joining the others for pre-supper drinks.

'What time was this?'

'About 7.30.'

'And you had drinks on the terrace?'

'That's right.'

'Which way did you go to get to the terrace? Did you

62

go outside and around the side of the annexe, via the courtyard, or is there a connecting door to the house?' Thanet was annoyed with himself that he hadn't checked this point. He did seem to remember seeing a door in the corridor leading to the kitchen which might give access to the annexe, but he hadn't investigated.

'Yes, there is a connecting door, and that was the way I went.'

'Along the corridor from the kitchen to the terrace?'

'Yes.'

Pity. 'Would you have happened to notice if the well cover was on or off at that point? You might have glanced out when you locked the front door, for example?'

'I didn't. So no, I didn't notice.'

They skipped quickly to the point where the dinner party broke up and once again Thanet heard the by now familiar account of what had happened. As the others had already told him, after carrying some dishes through to the kitchen Mrs Mintar had retired to her own quarters. 'I'd had enough of being sociable by then.'

'So then what did you do?'

'Read a book until Ralph came to ask me if I'd seen Virginia. Then, of course, I got caught up in all the commotion.'

Thanet glanced at the back wall of the sitting room, where a small window overlooked the courtyard. 'Did you hear any noises from the courtyard, between the time you got back and your son's arrival?'

She hesitated.

So there was something. 'Well?'

But still she hesitated. Then she said, 'I'm just not sure.'

'What do you mean?'

'Well, you know what it's like, when you're reading, when you're really engrossed in a book. You're often not even aware of it when someone has spoken to you directly.'

'So?'

'So I *think* I might have heard something. Voices. But as I say, I can't be certain.'

Thanet's scalp prickled. 'In the courtyard?'

She nodded.

The chances were slim but he had to ask. 'Did you recognise them, by any chance?' He was aware of Lineham's pencil poised motionless over his notebook as they awaited her answer.

'No. Definitely not.'

'Please, Mrs Mintar, do try to remember. This could be very important.'

'I'm not an idiot, Inspector, I'm aware of that! But I can't be any more specific. Believe me, I only wish I could, if only because it would help to clear up this whole mess much more quickly, and get the police out of our hair. I'm sorry, I don't mean to be rude, but I really do resent having my life disrupted like this.'

'Do you have any idea what time it was?'

'No. There really is no point in pursuing this. It's just a vague impression, that's all, which is why I hesitated to mention it in the first place.'

She was right. It seemed pointless to persist and they left. Outside Thanet glanced at his watch: 1.30. 'Come on, Mike, let's go to the pub, have a bite to eat. We'll walk. It'll clear our heads.'

'Not exactly bowed down with grief, was she?' said Lineham as they set off down the drive.

'No.'

They walked in silence for a while, thinking back over the interview, turning left after passing through the wrought-iron gates.

A little further on they came to the driveway leading up to the windmill. Thanet had noticed earlier that it had obviously been converted into a house: there were curtains at the windows and cars parked in front. 'That must be where the Squires live,' he said. 'We'll interview them next, after lunch. It'll be interesting to see what it's like inside. I've never been in a converted windmill before.'

He expected Lineham to comment, but the sergeant hadn't been listening. He was still brooding on Mrs Mintar. 'She's downright self-centred, if you ask me,' he said. 'Very wrapped up in her work. I don't suppose her son had much of a life. I bet he was dumped on a nanny most of the time and then packed off to boarding school at the earliest possible moment, while she swanned off to foreign parts.'

'Yes. And if so, that could well be why he reacted as he did when Caroline left. As a child he would probably have found it less painful to try to put his mother completely out of his mind, than make himself miserable thinking about her all the time. So when Caroline went—'

'Sir. Sorry to interrupt, but isn't that Mr Prime ahead?'

Arnold Prime's tall, loose-limbed figure was immediately recognisable. He was strolling along at a leisurely pace, hands in pockets, taking in his surroundings. 'Looks like it. Probably wanted to get away from the house for a while.'

'Don't blame him. Not exactly a fun weekend, is it?'

'That's what I was thinking earlier. Still, it could be useful to have a word with him by himself. He might be more willing to give us a frank account of his impressions of the supper party last night. He was the only outsider, after all, apart from Agon who didn't arrive until later.'

They speeded up and soon caught up with their unsuspecting quarry. 'Sorry about this, Mr Prime,' said Thanet as they came alongside. 'I expect you thought you were going to have a bit of peace and quiet. But we would like another word with you.'

Not surprisingly, Prime didn't look too pleased. But he gave a resigned shrug. 'Go ahead.'

The two policemen fell into step with him.

'All this must have ruined your weekend, sir,' said Lineham.

'I'm very sorry that Jane is so upset, obviously. But I hardly knew her sister, so I can't pretend to be grief-stricken.'

'And that is precisely why we wanted to talk to you,' said Thanet. 'You're the only person there last night who – apart from your relationship with Miss Simons – wasn't actually involved with any of those present. Up until now, everyone has been saying that the supper party was absolutely without incident, but it's very difficult to believe that nothing unusual happened.'

'Why? What bearing has that got on what happened later?'

'Oh come, Mr Prime. Aren't you being rather naïve?'

Prime compressed his lips, but said nothing.

'I suppose the theory in the family is that some intruder came along and pushed Mrs Mintar down the well?' said Lineham.

'It's a possible answer,' said Prime defensively.

'Possible, but unlikely,' said Thanet.

'Statistically, the chances are that it was someone in the family,' said Lineham.

'Or at least, someone close to them,' said Thanet. 'And if so, we have to ask ourselves not only who and why but why then? Why did whoever was responsible choose that particular moment rather than any other? Did something happen during the evening to precipitate matters? Which is why we're asking you, as an unbiased observer, if you would think back very carefully and try to recall if there was anything, anything at all which could be relevant. I know it's a lot to ask, but we really would appreciate it.'

Prime had heard them out but now he shook his head. 'I'm sorry, I really don't feel I can do that.'

'I appreciate your reluctance. Mr Mintar is your host and you are close to Miss Simons. But everyone seems to agree that Mrs Mintar's death couldn't have been an accident, so we are talking about murder. And I'm afraid that in a case of murder normal social conventions just have to be put aside. I don't want to sound pompous and talk about duty and an obligation to help the police, but the fact remains that a woman has been killed. And that you might be able to help us find out who's responsible.'

There was nothing more to say. They couldn't force Prime to talk if he didn't want to and silence fell while they let him think over what had been said.

Thanet had already taken off his jacket and slung it over his shoulder but he was still conscious of his shirt sticking to his back, of the ferocity of the sun's rays beating down upon his head. It was now the hottest part of the day and ahead of them the tarmac shimmered. Already the verges at the side of the road and the grass in the fields were turning brown and crisping in the unremitting drought. If this went on, Thanet thought, England's green and pleasant land would become green no longer and in the long term the changing climate would have a disastrous effect on the native deciduous trees. Starved of water they would surely eventually die. Perhaps in a hundred years time this landscape, which probably looked very similar now to the way it had a century ago, would have changed beyond recognition. He took out a handkerchief and mopped his forehead. Thoughts of a cold shower or, failing that, a long, cool drink danced in his head. What would the Super say, he wondered, if he turned up for work tomorrow wearing shorts, sandals and sunhat?

This entertaining fantasy was interrupted by Prime. 'Very well,' he said. 'I take your point. I'll try to help, if I can. What, exactly, do you want to know?'

Thanet looked about. They had just reached the junction of Miller's Lane with the village street. To their right, at tables set out beneath the trees on the wide pavement in front of the Dog and Thistle, a number of families were lingering over a late lunch. Otherwise, apart from a young couple with a toddler in a pushchair, Paxton dozed in an early Sunday afternoon torpor. Across the road, against the churchyard wall, was a conveniently empty bench in the shade of a huge horsechestnut tree. That long cool drink would just have to wait. 'Let's go and sit over there.'

They crossed the road and sat down. 'Well, to begin with,' said Thanet, 'can you recall any particular incident which indicated, for instance, that there was any bad feeling, any animosity or resentment between any of the other guests and Mrs Mintar? Perhaps we'd better call her by her Christian name, to avoid confusion with her mother-in-law.'

Prime frowned, pondering. Eventually he shook his head. 'Not a specific incident, no, but . . .'

'What?'

'It's difficult to put my finger on it, really. I suppose the best way I can describe it is to say that I was conscious that there were a lot of undercurrents. And they seemed mostly to centre on Virginia.'

'Could you elaborate?'

He shrugged. 'As I say, it's difficult. It's just that I was aware that there were things going on below the surface, things I didn't understand.'

'How did these undercurrents manifest themselves?'

'Innuendoes. Glances.'

'Directed at Mrs . . . at Virginia?'

'Mostly, yes.'

'Directed by whom?'

'That was the thing. By practically everybody. By her husband, certainly, by her mother-in-law – there's no love lost there, I can assure you – and even by the Squires.'

'Both of them?'

Prime shrugged again. 'I'm only telling you of my impressions.'

'Was it Virginia's behaviour at supper last night which

provoked these reactions, do you think, or were they a hangover, so to speak, of past events?'

Again a hesitation. 'It was difficult to tell. I was sitting next to her, you see, so without making a point of it I couldn't actually see her face a lot of the time.'

He was holding back on something here, Thanet was sure of it. But why? 'Did she say anything, then, to upset anyone?'

Prime sighed. 'Not that I can remember.'

But again there was a reservation in his voice. Perhaps, Thanet thought, this was because it somehow concerned Jane Simons and he didn't want to get her involved. Was this the moment to tackle him about the way the couple had misled them earlier, about their return to the pool? No. Prime was fairly relaxed at present. He didn't want to put him on the defensive until he was certain there was nothing else to be learned. 'You said just now, when you were talking about undercurrents, that they were *mostly* directed at Virginia. What others were there?'

'Well, take Mrs Mintar senior, for instance. She was sitting next to Howard Squires but I can guarantee they didn't exchange a word, all evening. And Marilyn Squires hardly took her eyes off her husband, except to look at Virginia.'

'Are you saying you think there might have been something going on between Howard Squires and Virginia? And that his wife was aware of it – or, at least, suspected it?'

'I don't know. Howard certainly spent a lot of time looking at Virginia, but then she was sitting directly opposite him. And you have to understand that Virginia was the sort of woman who automatically attracted a lot of attention from men.'

'Did she set out to do so?'

'I'd say so, yes.'

Again Prime was uncomfortable and suddenly Thanet twigged. Ten to one, Virginia Mintar had been flirting with Prime, the new man at her table. Her sister would naturally have resented this and when she and Prime went up to change for the swim, they might well have had a row about it. And that could have been why they went down again separately. More sure of his ground now he decided to go on the offensive. 'Mr Prime, why did you and Miss Simons deliberately mislead us this morning?'

'What do you mean?' He was pretending to be surprised but it was obvious that he knew what Thanet meant.

'You gave us the impression you returned to the swimming pool together.'

He had to drag the information out of Prime but he managed it eventually. His guess was right. Virginia had set her cap at her sister's boyfriend and Jane had been so upset by her behaviour that it had taken considerable effort to convince her that Prime had not been taken in by Virginia's charms.

'It must be very difficult to have a younger sister as beautiful as that,' said Thanet.

'Exactly,' said Prime eagerly. 'And Jane's past experience hasn't exactly led her to trust Virginia, as far as men are concerned. More than once, when they were younger, Virginia just waltzed in and purloined Jane's boyfriends. In fact, Jane was very reluctant to bring me down here to meet her sister and brother-in-law at all. We've been going out together for almost a year now and she's been putting it off and putting it off, making one excuse after another. In the end I managed to get her to tell me the real reason for her reluctance and persuade her that she had nothing to worry about.'

'She was afraid that Virginia would lead you astray.'

'Yes. Jane said, well, I hesitate to speak ill of the dead, but Jane said that Virginia "found it difficult to keep her hands off anything in trousers". That was the way she put it.'

'And could she? Did she? You said you were sitting next to her.'

'I must admit she did come on a bit strong. I have a fairly realistic appreciation of my charms, I think, Inspector, and I know I'm no oil painting. Beautiful women don't exactly throw themselves into my arms. But there's no doubt that Virginia was flirting with me. I'm not surprised Jane was upset.'

'What about Mr Mintar? How did he react to this?'

'He didn't seem particularly worried. As I said, he did watch his wife a lot, but I suppose if she always behaved like that he must have got used to it, over the years.'

'And the others?'

'Her mother-in-law wasn't amused, I assure you. As for the Squires, well, I just don't know what was going on there. Anyway, I was quite relieved when the young people turned up with their big news.'

'Because it provided another focus of attention?'

'Exactly. Though, as Jane told you earlier, there weren't exactly any cries of delight. Oh, Ralph put on a good enough show, I suppose, producing champagne and so on, but you'd have to have been an idiot not to see that he was really pretty miffed about it. And the same goes for Virginia and her mother-in-law too. I knew about Rachel's sister, though, so I could understand their dilemma.'

Thanet glanced at Lineham, raising his eyebrows. *Anything else you want to ask?*

Lineham shook his head.

'Thank you, sir,' said Thanet. 'You've been very helpful.'

'That's it?' Prime's relief was clear.

'For the moment. When did you intend returning to London?'

'This evening.'

'I'm afraid that won't be possible. This will apply to Miss Simons too.'

'But I have a whole list of appointments tomorrow, Inspector. I can't just cancel the lot, let my patients down without warning like that.'

'I'm sorry, sir, but I have to insist. We'll let you go back at the earliest possible moment, I assure you.'

Looking thoroughly disgruntled Prime stalked off up the village street.

'Not too happy about that, sir, was he?'

'Can't be helped.' Thanet glanced across the road. Most of the tables were now empty. 'Come on, Mike. If I have to wait any longer for a drink I shall expire.'

They both ordered bacon and mushroom baguettes and carried their drinks outside. Thanet only ever allowed himself one drink at lunchtime while he was working so in addition to a bottle of lager he ordered a glass of sparkling water with a dash of lime. The second they sat down he drank this straight off, feeling himself revive as it flooded his system. 'Ah, that's better,' he said.

Lineham was watching him with a grin. 'You were thirsty, weren't you?' He took a leisurely swallow from his glass.

'I can't imagine why you weren't.' Thanet poured out half of his lager and sat back. 'You must have the metabolism of a camel. Anyway, what do you think was going on over that meal last night?'

'Sounds to me as though our Ginny liked to have all the men at her feet. I bet you're right, and she was having an affair with Howard, who didn't like it when she switched her attentions to Jane's boyfriend. And it sounds as though Mrs Squires had a good idea of what was going on. As for poor old Mintar, doesn't sound as though he had much choice but to sit back and watch, does it?'

'And presumably her mother-in-law disapproved, which is why she is so anti-Virginia.'

'And anti-Squires, perhaps?'

'Possibly. Ah, thank you.'

Their food had arrived. It smelled delicious and Thanet's mouth watered in anticipation. He took a large mouthful, his tastebuds singing alleluia as they came into contact with the fresh, crusty bread, the warm, juicy mushrooms and crispy bacon.

'Mmm, this is a bit of all right,' mumbled Lineham.

They concentrated on eating for a while, then the sergeant said, 'Well, as I said last night, the old lady has certainly got it in for Howard. That could be why.'

'And has it occurred to you, Mike, that if there was something going on between Squires and Virginia, he could have had a major problem on his hands?'

'With his wife, you mean?'

'No. With his professional position. "Our family doctor" was what Mintar called him last night.'

'Yeees,' breathed Lineham. 'I see what you mean. Affairs with patients are strictly *verboten*.'

'Precisely. It'll be interesting to see what he has to say for himself.'

SEVEN

'Must be nice to be able to afford a place like this,' said Lineham as they toiled up the drive to the windmill. Although they had walked at a gentle pace they were still sweating by the time they had covered the short distance from the village.

'Mmm.' Thanet was wishing they had taken one of their cars instead of choosing to walk. He mopped at his forehead and paused to glance up at the distinctive structure ahead of them. Although there are a number of windmills open to the public dotted around Kent, some of them restored to working order by groups of enthusiasts or, latterly, by the KCC, he had never been this close to one before. Very few have been converted into private houses and now, of course, conservation being the order of the day, it would be virtually impossible to get planning permission.

To his untutored eye this looked a magnificent specimen. Octagonal in shape, with a base of tarred brick and the upper portion of white weatherboarding, it stood on a slight rise, dominating the surrounding countryside by virtue of its height and the distinctive silhouette of its sails. It had been maintained in excellent condition and its elegant simplicity had not been marred by inappropriate domestic embellishments such as wrought-iron coach lamps or hanging baskets.

'Better get on, Mike.'

They trudged the last few yards up to the front door but there was no reply to their knock.

'They can't be out,' said Lineham. The windows were all open and there were three cars in the drive: a BMW, a Golf and an ancient Ford Escort.

'Probably in the garden on a day like this.'

They walked around to the back of the house. Thanet was right. It was an idyllic summer Sunday afternoon scene: comfortable wicker chairs and table in the shade of an old apple tree, jug of lemonade and tall glasses. Squires and a woman, presumably the elusive Marilyn, were reading the Sunday papers and a teenage girl in a bikini was sunbathing on a rug spread out on the grass nearby.

'Sorry to disturb you,' said Thanet. 'We knocked, but there was no reply.'

Squires, who was wearing crumpled khaki shorts, polo shirt and espadrilles, jumped up with the ease and elasticity of a man who took the trouble to keep himself fit. He was in his forties, with thick brown hair which flopped over his forehead in a boyish manner. 'Ah, Inspector . . . ? I'm sorry, I can't remember your name.' He held out his hand, somehow managing to exude warmth and sincerity and at the same time maintain a gravity appropriate to the occasion.

Thanet shook it. 'Thanet. And this is Sergeant Lineham.'

'I don't believe you've met my wife. She had to go home last night, she wasn't feeling well.'

Mrs Squires smiled. 'I invariably get a headache if I go swimming after a meal. I should have known better and not given in to temptation.'

Or perhaps she hadn't wanted to leave her husband free to cavort in the pool with the delectable Virginia in a bathing suit, thought Thanet. Marilyn Squires was several years younger than her husband, he guessed, and tiny, with sharp, pointed chin, cropped black hair and a flat-chested, almost adolescent figure. She was wearing lime green shorts and halter top and huge sunglasses with tortoiseshell frames.

'And this is Sarah,' said Squires, indicating the girl, who had sat up.

She was around fifteen and looked more like her father than her mother. 'Hi,' she said.

'You'd better scoot,' Squires said to her. 'I'm sure the Inspector wants to talk business.'

She scowled. 'Must I?'

'Actually,' said Thanet, 'I'd prefer to go inside, if you don't mind. It would be cooler.' Also less informal. And he wanted to get rid of those sunglasses. He liked to see the eyes of witnesses when he was interviewing them.

'By all means.'

'A fascinating house you live in,' he said as Sarah lay down again and the rest of them trooped across the lawn and around to the front door. There appeared to be no other means of egress from the house into the garden and Thanet wondered what would happen in the event of a fire.

It was as if he had pressed a button.

'It's a Smock Mill,' said Squires enthusiastically, 'built in 1820. It was a working mill right up until just after the end of the First World War. Then it became virtually derelict until the early sixties, when it was sold and converted into a house. We bought it a couple of years ago.'

'I imagine there must be problems, converting a building like this.'

'Obviously.'

They had reached the front door and now stepped into a pleasantly cool dining hall with an ancient oak refectory table and ladder-backed rush-seated chairs. The octagonal space was bisected by a partition wall with two doors in it. Kitchen and cloakroom perhaps? There was a distant but distracting beat of pop music. Thanet was pleased to see that the sudden transition from bright sunshine to the interior of the house had made Mrs Squires remove her sunglasses. Without them she looked considerably older.

Squires went straight to the foot of an open-tread staircase against the left-hand wall. 'Edward?' he shouted. 'Turn it down a bit, will you?'

There was no response and with an apologetic grimace he ran halfway up the stairs and called again. This time the music faded.

'Sorry,' he said as he returned. 'Where were we? Ah, yes, you were asking about the problems of converting a windmill. The trickiest, of course, is how to get from one floor to the next in a building this shape.' He gestured at the staircase and Thanet could see what he meant: there was an awkwardly shaped gap between it and the wall. 'That's the obvious way of course and it does look more authentic, but as you can see it wastes a lot of space and means that on each floor the size of the living accommodation is restricted by the amount of room needed for the flight of stairs. The best solution would be to have custom-made staircases built in against the walls but that's a very expensive option and so far we've held off from launching into it – it would also involve putting in new partition walls on each floor, to enlarge the rooms, otherwise there'd be no point.'

'How many floors are there?' said Lineham.

'Two in the base – this one and the sitting room above – and three in the windmill proper. That's the section above the staging. I'll show you, if you like.'

It was clear from Lineham's face that he was longing to accept the offer, and Thanet too was sorely tempted, but that was not the reason why they were here. Squires would obviously prefer to postpone the interview as long as possible and was prepared to go on discussing windmill conversions indefinitely. 'Thank you, sir, but I think we'd better get on. Shall we conduct the interview here?'

'Oh. Yes, of course. Or we could go up to my study?'

Where you would no doubt seat yourself authoritatively behind your desk, thought Thanet. 'No, this will do very well. Shall we sit down?'

'This is a dreadful business,' said Squires, when they were all settled around the dining table.

'We still can't believe it,' said his wife. She put her hand on his lap. 'Can we, Howard?'

Had Thanet imagined the beginnings of an instinctive flinch away from her?

'No,' said Squires. 'We can't take it in.'

'And to think that Sarah was here alone last night!' she went on. 'It doesn't bear thinking about . . . You never imagine this sort of thing can happen to anyone you know, do you? It doesn't seem real, somehow.' Her eyes were beautiful, very dark, almost black, and she opened them wide as she stared at Thanet, as if begging him to tell her that actually it had all been a mistake and Virginia was alive and well.

She appeared calm but Thanet was close enough to see that the pulse in her temple was beating rapidly – too rapidly, surely. 'All too real, I'm afraid,' said Thanet. 'Which is why we must ask you some questions about last night.'

They both nodded and looked cooperative.

'Anything we can do to help,' said Squires.

As arranged, Lineham took them quickly through their movements the previous day until they reached the point at which they returned to the Mintars' house in the evening. Then he glanced at Thanet and they continued the questioning in tandem.

'You walked, I presume, being so close,' said Thanet. 'Which way did you go?'

'There's a gate in the fence which divides the two gardens,' said Squires. 'We had it put in for ease of access. Ralph is very generous and lets us use the tennis court whenever we want to, if it's free.'

'So you walked through this gate and along past the front of the Mintars' house . . .'

'And around the side into the courtyard. Yes.'

'Why didn't you knock on the front door?'

'Because Ginny had said, "Supper at about a quarter to eight and drinks on the terrace before", so we went straight around to the back of the house. It was a very informal occasion, we didn't have to announce ourselves, it wouldn't have mattered if Ralph and Ginny weren't there. We knew they'd join us when they were ready.'

'And were they? There?'

'She was doing the watering in the courtyard.'

'Where was she drawing the water from?' said Lineham. 'The tap or the well?'

They looked at each other.

'Did you notice?' Squires asked his wife.

She shook her head. 'No. I was too busy thinking she obviously hadn't expected us to be quite so early and wishing we'd delayed for ten minutes.'

'Try to think,' said Lineham. 'Where, exactly, was she when you first saw her, as you came into the court-yard?'

'Watering one of the tubs by the annexe door,' said Marilyn Squires.

So as they suspected, she had been interrupted while watering the camellias, thought Thanet. In which case the well cover would almost certainly have been off.

'That's right,' said her husband.

'So what did she do?'

'Looked up, said, "Hullo", and walked across to meet us.'

'What did she do with the watering can?'

They stared at him, trying to recall.

'I remember,' said Marilyn. 'She put it down next to the well wall, when she was halfway across.'

'And then?'

Marilyn shrugged. 'She continued on her way. She just sort of dipped to one side to put it down then went on walking.'

'So can you remember now whether the well cover was on or off?'

'I really couldn't say,' said Squires, but his wife screwed up her eyes, then closed them to concentrate.

They all waited.

'I'm trying to visualise it,' she murmured.

A further silence.

Then, 'Got it!' she said, and her eyes flew open. 'It was off!' she said triumphantly.

'You're sure?' said Thanet.

'Certain.'

Thanet saw no reason to doubt her. 'Thank you, that's a great help. Now, please consider very carefully. Assuming you're right, Mrs Squires, and the cover was off at that point, could you tell me if she replaced it while you were in the courtyard?'

They both shook their heads.

'Definitely not,' she said.

'She walked straight around to the terrace with us,' said her husband.

'What about later? Both of you must have walked through the courtyard at least – what, three times? Once on your way back here to change for the swim, once on your return to the pool, and once to come home again later on. And you, Mr Squires, must have gone to and fro yet again, to put some clothes on before helping to look for Mrs Mintar. Now, on any of those occasions did you notice whether the well cover was off or on?'

'Oh, my goodness,' said Marilyn Squires, pulling a face. 'We'll have to think.'

Silence. They were both frowning, trying to remember.

Once again she closed her eyes and Thanet watched her hopefully. Eventually she shook her head. 'It's no good. I'm sorry, I just didn't notice.'

'Nor did I,' said Squires. 'We're so used to seeing that

well we never notice it any more, it's practically become invisible.'

'Please, do give this some more thought,' said Thanet. 'It really could be important. Cast your minds back.'

A further silence. More head shakes. Then, 'Hang on,' said Howard suddenly.

'What?' said Thanet and Lineham simultaneously.

'Later on. I remember now. When we were looking for her. There was a stone in my shoe so I had to stop to remove it. I was crossing the courtyard at the time and I put my foot up on that low wall around the well to tie the lace. And I'm sure the cover was on, or I'd have noticed the black hole in front of me, because it would have been different from normal. Yes. Now I think about it, I'm sure that's right.'

'And what time was this, sir?' said Thanet.

A shrug. 'I'm not sure. It was soon after we started looking, so just after eleven, I should say.'

'You simply assumed Mrs Mintar had put the cover back on?'

'I didn't assume anything, because I hadn't noticed, earlier, that it was off! If, indeed, it was.'

Squires was becoming exasperated and it was obvious that nothing was to be gained by pursuing the matter so on Thanet's nod Lineham took them back to the beginning of the evening. With wide-eyed innocence they assured him that it had been the most congenial of occasions, that nothing untoward had happened, that all had been harmony and conviviality. But Thanet, watching closely, observed the signs: from time to time Marilyn would moisten her lips with the tip of her tongue and her husband would rub his nose or tug at his ear, all good indications that they were either lying or trying to conceal something. If Howard had indeed been involved with Virginia no doubt they were desperate to keep it quiet. As Thanet had said to Lineham, the consequences could be disastrous for Howard's career as a GP.

81

'Right,' Lineham was saying. 'Could we now move on a little. We understand that you did not return to the pool together. Is that right?'

Thanet groaned inwardly. Oh, Mike. Too soon, too sudden. The sergeant should have continued patiently moving on through the evening step by step. Then, possibly, they might have made a mistake, thought it was safe to say they had returned to the pool together. And then there would have been something to pick them up on, rattle them. Thanet was becoming more and more convinced that beneath her apparent calm Marilyn Squires was very much afraid. But of what, precisely? he wondered.

But it was too late now. The question had been asked and they were both looking disconcerted. Perhaps they had been intending to lie about it, or perhaps it was simply that they were put out to discover that Thanet and Lineham had already been checking up on their movements.

Squires was the first to recover. 'That's right,' he said, smooth as silk. 'Not that I can see it has any relevance whatsoever.'

Lineham, quite rightly, ignored the implicit request for an explanation. 'Why was that, sir?' he said, politely.

Marilyn Squires lifted thin shoulders. 'There's no mystery about it. I had a phone call. You can check, I'll give you the number, if you like.'

'Thank you. Yes, we would.'

She looked taken aback. She obviously hadn't expected him to take her up on the offer. She glanced nervously at her husband before reeling it off. 'Sturrenden 842963. It's a Mrs Bettina Leyton, a friend of mine.'

Lineham wrote it down. 'Thank you.'

'Might as well get that cleared out of the way,' said Thanet. 'Is Mrs Leyton likely to be at home now, do you think? Good. Then may we use your phone?' He nodded at the telephone on the desk.

They did not miss the implications of his request: he

wasn't going to give them a chance to get in first and prime Mrs Leyton to give the right answers.

But the information had been genuine, he discovered. Just unfortunate timing for them. As it was, Howard confirmed what Rachel had told them: he got back to the pool between 10 and 10.15 and was the first to arrive after Matt and Rachel. Marilyn arrived shortly afterwards, followed by Arnold Prime and Jane.

'They arrived back together?'

'I didn't notice,' said Squires.

'Separately,' said his wife. 'Arnold first, then Jane, a few minutes later.'

'A few?'

'Sorry, I can't be more precise.'

'Did you happen to notice which door they came through?' said Thanet, mentally crossing his fingers. Mrs Squires was obviously much more observant than her husband.

'Arnold came through the drawing-room door and Jane through the door to the corridor leading to the kitchen.'

'You're sure?'

'I was sitting on the edge of the pool facing the house at the time,' she said. 'I was still dithering about going in. As I said, I often get a headache if I swim after a meal – which is, in fact, what happened. I really should have known better.'

'Thank you,' said Thanet, rising. 'You've been most helpful.'

'All right, all right, don't say it!' said Lineham, the second they were out of earshot, holding up a hand like a traffic policeman. 'I jumped the gun there, didn't I?'

'In the event, I don't think it mattered too much,' said Thanet. 'Come on, we'll go back through the gate in the fence.'

But Lineham was annoyed with himself and kept muttering about it.

'Mike!' said Thanet sharply. 'I said, forget it. It really didn't matter. The main thing is that you realised what you'd done. Apart from which we gleaned some very useful information – about the well cover and the fact that Jane Simons returned to the pool via the kitchen, for example.'

'But—'

'I said, that's enough. If you could just try to focus on the job in hand, and tell me what you thought of those two . . .'

'Shifty!' said Lineham promptly. 'And very, very nervous. I wonder why.'

'I agree. And yet, I don't know what you thought, but I didn't think they were actually lying about anything you asked them.'

'Which means, of course,' said Lineham gloomily, 'that I couldn't have asked them the right questions, could I?'

'You asked them everything I would have asked at the moment. I suppose the answer is we just haven't found out enough, yet, to know what those right questions are. I certainly don't feel that it would have been advisable at this point to come straight out and ask him if he was having an affair with Virginia Mintar.'

'No. Perhaps that was what they were afraid of, though.'

'Or perhaps not. At this stage we've got to keep an open mind.'

'Anyway, they're hiding something, that's for sure.'

'Yes. But leaving aside the possibility of his involvement with Virginia, the point is that we have no idea whether that something is relevant to our inquiries or not. You know what people are like. They're always giving the wrong impression by trying to cover up things in which we wouldn't be even remotely interested. No doubt all will be revealed, in time.'

'So what next, sir? Do we tackle Jane Simons again?'

'Not yet.' Thanet had been thinking. 'Digby said that he

always watered the camellias during the week and Virginia Mintar did them at weekends. Which would imply that he was normally off duty on Saturdays and Sundays.'

'I see what you mean,' said Lineham. 'So what was he doing here this morning?'

'It didn't occur to me to ask. Stupid.'

'Me too.'

They were back in the courtyard by now. 'Well, it should be easy enough to find out,' said Thanet. 'We'll go and ask the old lady. She should know.'

Mrs Mintar senior was clearly annoyed to be interrupted again and her answer was brief and unequivocal. Digby never worked on Sundays, and she couldn't think what he had been doing here this morning. She slammed the door behind them the moment they turned away.

'So do we want to talk to him again at the moment?' said Lineham.

'I'm not sure. There was something about his attitude . . .' said Thanet.

'That smirk, you mean?'

'It's just that I had the feeling he thought he had the laugh on us. That he knew more than he was saying.'

'He's well placed to observe what goes on in the family.'

'Exactly.' Thanet made up his mind. 'Yes, I think we will have another word.'

But Digby was nowhere to be found. Apparently he had disappeared soon after the body had been retrieved from the well.

'Probably went home once the excitement was over,' said Thanet. 'Have you got his address?'

'Yup. Made a note this morning. He lives in the village.' Lineham leafed through his notebook. 'Here it is.'

'What would I do without you, Mike?'

It sounded as though Thanet was joking but Lineham looked gratified. They both knew Thanet meant it. They had worked together for so long that without the sergeant

Thanet felt that he was working with one arm tied behind his back. It wasn't just that Lineham was efficient over minor details like this, but that over the years he and Thanet had built up so close a rapport that there was often no need to communicate in words. A gesture, a lift of the eyebrow, or the flicker of a glance were usually enough.

It was too hot to walk into the village again so they drove. After asking directions they found Digby's cottage some two hundred yards off the main street, at the end of an unmade-up track. An ugly little building of yellow brick, it crouched alone behind an unusually tall and overgrown privet hedge.

Thanet believed that the houses in which people lived invariably had something to say about their owners and his first reaction to this one was: *What has he got to hide?* 'Is he married?' he said as they pushed open the sagging picket gate and approached the front door. Nobody had expended much love on the place. The paint on windows and door was peeling, the gutters sagged and although the little squares of lawn on either side of the path had been cut, a minimum of effort had been expended on the garden.

'No idea. What makes you ask?'

'No one seems to care much what this place looks like.'

'Maybe it's rented, and he's got a bad landlord.'

'Possibly.'

Digby didn't look too pleased to see them and stood aside only grudgingly to let them in.

By contrast with the external appearance of the place, the room into which the front door opened was, if not particularly attractive, clean and well ordered. Its most striking feature was a group of three framed black and white photographs on the wall above the fireplace. Thanet also noted well-stocked bookshelves as well as a mini CD system. Interestingly, there was only one armchair, conveniently placed for viewing the television set which was tuned in to a golf programme. Did the man never have visitors? Thanet's interest sharpened. Digby's profile was becoming more interesting by the minute: male, almost certainly unmarried, a loner . . .

Digby switched off the set. 'What do you want?' he said to Thanet. 'I've gone over it all twice already and I can't see what else I can tell you.'

'It's surprising what people can remember, when they've had time to think, sir,' said Lineham.

'Maybe I've got better things to think about,' said Digby.

They were all still standing.

'May we sit down?' said Thanet, looking around in vain for a chair.

With an exaggerated sigh Digby went into a room at the rear and came back carrying a kitchen chair and a camping stool.

The man apparently had only one chair in his kitchen, too!

Lineham set the stool against a wall and opened his notebook. 'Just one or two more questions, then, sir,' he said as he sat down, somewhat gingerly.

The stool held, however.

Thanet suppressed a grin. 'You don't usually work on Sundays, we gather, Mr Digby. Would you mind telling us why you went in this morning?'

'I'd left something in the pocket of my overalls.'

'What?'

'A couple of films.'

Thanet's eyebrows went up. It was an unexpected reply, though perhaps it shouldn't have been, in view of the photographs on the walls and what Rachel had told them.

Digby took this as disbelief and launched into an explanation. 'I bought them in the town, yesterday morning, when I had to go in to pick something up for Mr Mintar. I put them in my pocket and forgot to bring them home last night. I wanted to use them this morning.'

'Ah yes,' said Thanet. 'Miss Mintar told us that you are an accomplished photographer.' He stood up and went to take a look at the mounted prints. 'These are yours, I presume?'

'Yes.'

The photographs were very unusual. They reminded him of the puzzle photographs which one occasionally sees in newspapers and magazines, when readers are asked to identify weird-looking objects which invariably turn out to be something mundane. It was a moment or two before he realised that all three were close-ups of garden plants. One was of the unfurling leaf of a fern. In another the prominent stamens of a lily thrust themselves skywards, the petals curling elegantly back behind them like unfolding wings. The third, a study in tone of strange, twisting shapes, he failed to recognise. 'What is this one?' he asked, pointing.

'A close-up of the bark of *Acer griseum*, the Paperbark Maple.'

'Do you do all your own developing and printing?' Thanet said, still looking.

Digby's lip curled. 'Of course.' *Stupid question.*

'These really are very good. Interesting. Original.' Thanet meant it. He was aware of Lineham shifting restlessly on his stool. *Shouldn't we be getting on with it?* He returned to his chair. 'You have an exhibition on at the moment, I believe.'

'Only in the local village library. It's not exactly the National Gallery.' But Digby was obviously pleased by Thanet's compliment.

'We must drop in and take a look,' said Lineham.

'Are you interested in wildlife?'

'Some forms,' said the sergeant.

The double meaning was not lost on Digby and his expression darkened again. 'Look, could we get on?' His eyes strayed to the television set.

'Of course. You want to get back to the golf,' said

Thanet. 'Well, we won't keep you long. So, you went to the Mintars' house this morning to fetch your films. I imagine you intended just to pick them up then come straight back.'

'That's right.'

'You said it was the watering can which alerted you to the fact that something might be wrong?'

'I told you. Mrs Mintar was a very tidy-minded lady. Everything had to be just so. It was unusual, that's all. So I went to tidy it away.' He shrugged. 'It was automatic.'

'That was very conscientious of you. It was your day off, after all. A lot of people wouldn't have bothered.'

Another shrug.

'Do you see much of your employers?'

'A fair bit, I suppose.'

'A good family to work for?'

'Pretty good, yes.'

'Would you say they got on well together, Mr and Mrs Mintar?'

Digby was no fool. He saw at once where this line of questioning was leading. 'If you're thinking of trying to pin this on Mr Mintar you're way off beam,' he said at once. 'I know what you lot always say about domestic murder, but he wouldn't have harmed a hair on his wife's head. Potty about her, he was. He's a good bloke.'

'And Mrs Mintar? What was she like?'

'Very nice. Polite, appreciative, not like some.'

But Thanet had the impression that Digby was deliberately keeping his expression bland. He was, as Lineham had said, well placed to observe the comings and goings in the Mintar household. If Mintar was away a lot, as he must be, and if Virginia Mintar was as man-mad as her sister seemed to imply, perhaps she might have felt that it was safe to bring her boyfriends (lovers?) home. And if she was involved with Howard Squires, Digby would no doubt know more about it than anyone else.

'And a very attractive woman,' said Lineham.

89

There was a wary look in Digby's eyes as he said, 'So?'

'She must have had admirers.'

'If she did it was none of my business.'

'It must have been lonely for her, with Mr Mintar away so much.'

Digby shrugged.

'Was there anyone special?' said Thanet softly.

Digby compressed his lips and said nothing.

'Oh come, Mr Digby. Being there most of the time you must have been aware of any regular visitors.'

Digby rubbed the side of his nose. 'I said, none of my business, was it?'

'Not then, maybe. But it is now. Don't you want to help us find out who killed her?'

'I suppose.'

'Then please, cast your mind back and tell us if there was anyone you saw her with on a regular basis, either some time ago or more recently.'

'There's that friend of hers. Mrs Amos.' The sardonic twinkle was back in Digby's eye.

Thanet felt like shaking him. The man knew something, he was certain of it. 'What about male friends, Mr Digby?'

Digby pulled down the corners of his mouth and shook his head. 'Not to my knowledge.'

Whatever he knew, he wasn't going to tell, that was clear. Thanet tried another tack. 'Could you tell us something about her activities?'

'What activities?'

Thanet saw Lineham stir. The sergeant was finding this interview equally frustrating. 'You must have some idea where she went, whom she saw?'

'Not really.'

'You have no idea at all? She never said, "Oh, Digby, I'm just going to such and such a place. If anyone calls, tell them I hope to be back by lunchtime", for example?'

'I don't recall her ever saying exactly that, no.'

Thanet was keeping his temper with difficulty. 'Mr Digby. I don't know if you are being deliberately obstructive, but I would like to remind you that your employer, a woman whom you say you liked, has been murdered. She is dead, Mr Digby, and someone is responsible.'

'So what do you want me to say?' Digby flared up. 'I was her gardener, not her minder. She didn't give me a list of her activities, did she? I know she spent a lot of time at that Health Club. And she did an awful lot of shopping, she was always coming back with those glossy carrier bags. But apart from that . . . I imagine she went to coffee mornings, had lunch with her friends, all that sort of stuff.'

As Thanet had hoped, anger had loosened the man's tongue. Careful now, not to phrase the next question in a negative manner. 'And were there any special male friends?'

'I told you! Not to my knowledge!'

Thanet and Lineham exchanged brief glances. *He's lying.*

But perhaps now was the moment to get at the truth about another of Virginia Mintar's relationships. 'How did Mrs Mintar get on with her mother-in-law?'

Digby pounced upon the change of topic with relief. 'Ah well, now that's a very different kettle of fish.'

'Oh?'

'Always rowing, they were.'

'About what?'

'This and that.'

'Can't you be a little more precise?'

'She's an interfering old bag. Always thinking she knows best and trying to tell me what to do. She was the same with Mrs Mintar.'

'She criticised her, you mean.'

'Too right, she did!'

'About?'

'Mrs Mintar couldn't do a thing right in her eyes.'

Digby was being evasive again. But now a gleam of malice appeared in his eyes. 'As a matter of fact, they had a hell of a ding-dong yesterday.'

'Oh? When was this?'

'Lunch time. I was just knocking off and I was walking past the side of the annexe when I heard them arguing.'

'Where were they?'

'In her studio. There's a window on the side. It was wide open.'

'Could you hear what they were saying?' Thanet guessed that the temptation to eavesdrop would have been irresistible.

'I'd guess the old bag had been going on at her again about something because young Mrs Mintar was saying that if she didn't shut up and stop her nagging she'd tell Mr Mintar about her heart condition, and that would put a stop to her gallivanting off to foreign parts for good and all.'

EIGHT

Outside the heat of the day was trapped between the high hedges of the narrow lane and the interior of Lineham's car was like an oven. They opened all the doors to cool it down and waited for a few minutes before getting in.

'Ouch,' said Lineham as he touched the steering wheel. 'This is almost too hot to handle.' He switched on the blower and a stream of torrid air gushed out at them. 'If the climate goes on changing like this they'll have to start putting in air conditioning as standard.'

'Mmm.' Thanet was thinking about Digby. 'Doesn't sound as if there was much love lost between Virginia Mintar and her mother-in-law, does there?'

'Nor between Digby and the old lady, either.'

'Are you suggesting he might have been exaggerating, in order to get her into trouble?'

'It's a thought, isn't it?'

'And the row, yesterday lunchtime?'

Lineham did not answer immediately. He was pulling out into the main street. His caution, however, proved unnecessary. Not a single person was in sight. Presumably they were all, like the Squireses, prostrate in their back gardens or shut up indoors like Digby, watching television. Thanet didn't blame them. He was sweating so much that his back was sticking to the car seat and he leaned forward a little to separate them and allow air to pass between.

'Oh, I should think that bit was true enough,' said Lineham. 'I don't see how he could have known about old Mrs Mintar's heart condition otherwise.'

'No. The interesting thing is that her son obviously doesn't know and her daughter-in-law did. Now how did that come about, I wonder? It certainly doesn't seem that they were on sufficiently good terms for her to have confided in Virginia. In fact, I should have thought she'd have been anxious to keep it a total secret, for the very reason Digby mentioned.'

'No more expeditions, you mean?'

'Yes. Did you notice her whip that pill bottle out of sight when we were looking at the paintings?'

'No, I didn't.' Lineham looked chagrined. He hated to feel he had missed something.

'You weren't supposed to. It was real sleight-of-hand stuff.'

'You noticed, though, didn't you?'

Thanet ignored this. Lineham was always putting himself down. 'The point is, I should guess her work is more important to her than anything else, and those expeditions are what she enjoys most of all. The only time she seemed to come to life was when she was talking about them.'

'I agree that I can't see her telling Virginia about her condition voluntarily. Unless, of course, Virginia found out by accident – she could have had an attack while Virginia was present, for instance.'

'Possible, I suppose. But she's a tough old bird. In those circumstances, unless it was a very bad attack, I could just imagine her gritting her teeth and making an excuse to get away without letting on, so that she could take her medication in private. No, Mike, if we're right and Virginia was involved with Dr Squires I think it much more likely that that's how she found out.'

94

'Pillow talk, you mean?'

'Yes.'

Lineham tutted. 'Getting in deeper and deeper, isn't he? An affair with a patient and then breaking another patient's confidentiality . . . If he did tell her, that would explain why he's so unpopular with the old lady. She would be bound to realise how Virginia found out.'

'Quite. But this is all speculation at the moment, remember, Mike. Still, I think another word with him is next on the agenda. But leaving aside the question of how Virginia found out, we can't ignore the point Digby was making.'

'That Virginia and the old lady had a row yesterday afternoon, you mean.'

'And that Virginia was threatening to spill the beans to her husband.'

'You think that might have been a strong enough motive to shove her down the well?'

'Think about it, Mike. Mrs Mintar senior's front door is only a matter of yards away from the well and by her own admission she was in the annexe at the time. It was a hot night and she might well have left her front door open when she went in, to cool the place down. And the circumstances were ideal – it was dark, everyone was out of the way, Virginia would have been alone, the well cover was off . . . So say Virginia remembers she hadn't finished watering the camellias. She goes out to the well, bends over to pick up the watering can, or leans across to reach the bucket or whatever . . . Mrs Mintar sees her chance and grabs it. It wouldn't have taken much strength. Virginia was only slight. If she was caught off balance . . .'

'What about the voices Mrs Mintar claims to have heard in the courtyard?'

'There's no corroboration, as yet anyway. She could well have made them up, to throw us off the track.'

Lineham slammed on the brakes. They were in the

lane approaching the Squires' house now and a tabby cat had just shot across the road in front of them. 'Sorry, sir! Stupid animal,' he muttered.

'That was Mintar's cat, I think,' said Thanet. 'You wouldn't have been too popular if you'd run him over.'

'If it carries on like that it won't be long before someone does,' said Lineham. 'Shall we park in the Squires' drive, or next door?'

'Next door, I think, and we'll walk through.'

Squires was not pleased to see them again so soon but with a bad grace took them back into the hall. 'What is it this time, Inspector?' He perched on a corner of the table as if to emphasise the fact that he expected the interview to be brief and gestured to Thanet to sit down.

Thanet shook his head, remained standing. He had no intention of giving Squires the psychological advantage of looking down on him. Lineham propped himself against the wall and took out his notebook.

'We've just been to interview Digby.'

Squires looked surprised. Whatever he had expected or feared, it wasn't this. But he was intelligent enough to realise that Thanet wouldn't have used this oblique approach without good reason. 'The Mintars' gardener? So?' *What has it got to do with me?*

'Mrs Mintar senior is a patient of yours, I believe?'

Squires' expression remained impassive but his left eyelid twitched. 'Please get to the point, Inspector.'

But Thanet persisted. 'She *is* a patient of yours, isn't she?'

A terse nod. 'But I still don't see—'

'Digby apparently heard Mrs Mintar and Virginia Mintar – we'll use her Christian name to avoid confusion – arguing yesterday. He said that Virginia was threatening to tell her husband about Mrs Mintar's heart condition.'

Squires said nothing.

'Perhaps you could confirm that, Doctor?'

'Confirm what? That they were arguing? How can I? I wasn't there.'

This was wilful misunderstanding and it was an effort for Thanet to conceal his rising irritation. 'That Mrs Mintar has a heart condition,' he said.

'I *could* confirm – or deny – that, yes. But I won't. You're asking me to break patient confidentiality.'

'I don't think so. We already knew of Mrs Mintar's condition. She had dropped her bottle of pills and I picked them up. It was obvious what they were for.'

'Why bother to ask me, then? Anyway, drawing your own conclusions is one matter. My breaking patient confidentiality is another. In any case, I don't see what conceivable relevance this has to your investigation.'

'Don't you? Shall I just say that we'd have to be very stupid not to have realised that there was little love lost between Mrs Mintar and her daughter-in-law.'

Squires stared at him. 'My God,' he said. 'You're surely not suggesting that Mrs Mintar . . . That *is* what you're suggesting, isn't it?' Thanet could almost hear what the man was thinking: *If they suspect the old lady, that'll take the heat off me.*

'I think you'd agree that Mrs Mintar's work means a great deal to her?'

'Certainly.'

'And that she would be deeply disappointed if she were unable to go on any more of her plant-finding expeditions?'

'I imagine so, yes.'

'And that if she does suffer from a heart condition and the organisers knew of it, they wouldn't be too happy about allowing a seventy-seven-year-old with angina to accompany them? It would be too much of a responsibility, I imagine.'

'Such expeditions are very strenuous, I believe,' said Squires carefully.

'And that if Mr Mintar knew of his mother's condition,

he would almost certainly take steps to stop her from going?'

'Steps? Mrs Mintar is a very determined woman.'

Thanet waved a hand. 'Inform the organisers. Whatever.'

'I suppose Ralph would take fairly drastic action, yes.'

'Don't you think it's time we stopped this charade, sir? Why don't you come straight out and admit that yes, Mrs Mintar does have a heart condition.'

Squires's mouth set in stubborn lines. 'I can't do that.'

'Very well. But perhaps you can tell us something else. What interests us, you see, is how Virginia Mintar learned of her mother-in-law's state of health.'

Squires was no fool. He saw at once where this was leading and his face went blank as the shutters came down.

'They weren't exactly on the best of terms, were they?' said Thanet. 'I can't see Mrs Mintar deciding to confide in Virginia, can you? And it seems to us there's only one other way Virginia could have found out.'

Squires folded his arms across his chest as if to contain – what? Anger? Fear? Dismay? 'I hope you're not suggesting what I think you're suggesting?'

'And what would that be, sir?'

'That it was I who told her.'

'Did I suggest that? I was merely asking you for possible explanations as to how Virginia could have found out.'

'Don't give me that! And I deeply resent the implication. Surely, the very fact that I have steadfastly refused, under considerable pressure, I might say, to enlighten you on the matter, underlines the fact that I take patient confidentiality very seriously indeed.'

'You might well have acted out of concern for your patient, in the hope that somehow Mrs Mintar could be stopped from doing something you are bound to have regarded as foolhardy?'

Squires was tempted by this suggestion. Thanet saw the man consider and reject it before he said, 'Certainly not!'

'Then how could she have found out?'

'For God's sake, man, it's obvious, isn't it? The same way that you did! By accident!' Squires stopped, obviously aware that implicit in this statement was the very admission he had been trying to avoid. With an exclamation of disgust he slid off the table and went to stand with his back to them, looking out of the window.

Thanet said nothing and eventually Squires swung around. His tone was weary as he said, 'Congratulations, Inspector. Very neat.'

'So how did she find out, sir?'

Squires dragged out one of the dining chairs and slumped down on it, underlining his sense of defeat. 'She went across to see her mother-in-law one day and Mrs Mintar had an attack while she was there. She said Mrs Mintar wouldn't actually admit what was happening, but that it was obvious to anyone with a grain of intelligence. She consulted me because she wanted to know the best course of action to take should it happen again.'

He was lying, Thanet was certain of it. The doctor's prevarications had at least given him time to concoct a story – though if it weren't true, he was taking a risk: Thanet might well decide to check on it with the old lady herself. 'When was this?'

'A month or so ago.'

'Did she ask you about the wisdom of Mrs Mintar going on these trips?'

'Yes, she did. And I told Virginia that it would be most unwise for her mother-in-law to go on any more, that I had told her so, but that she wouldn't listen to me.'

'Did you know that Virginia had not informed her husband of his mother's condition?'

'No I didn't. I assumed she had.'

'Why didn't she, do you think?'

'I have absolutely no idea.'

But it was obvious, really. Knowledge of this nature was power, and power over her mother-in-law was something that Virginia Mintar would not readily have relinquished. Had she paid for it with her life? 'Well, I think that's all for the moment. Thank you, sir.'

Squires's relief that the interview was at an end was obvious, and did not escape Lineham either.

'More porkies, don't you agree, sir?' said the sergeant when they were outside again.

'Yes, I do. And plenty more where those came from, I should say.' It was marginally cooler now but the sun was still beating down from a Mediterranean sky. 'I'm absolutely parched! I only wish I'd thought to bring a bottle of water with me. I certainly shall tomorrow.'

Lineham grinned. 'I've got a Thermos in the car.'

'Anyone could tell you were a boy Scout, Mike! Lead me to it!'

While they drank the tea they discussed their next move. They both agreed: in view of what Digby had told them they would have to talk to Mrs Mintar again.

'Wonder what sort of welcome we'll get this time,' said Lineham as they approached the open door of the annexe.

'Perhaps she'll have finished painting by now and be a bit more cooperative.'

And this, to their surprise, proved to be the case. She was positively affable, taking them into the sitting room and even offering them tea. Her work must have gone well, Thanet thought, and she was on a temporary high. She had changed out of her painting gear into a flowing jade green caftan with a panel of embroidery down the front. He would have loved another cup of tea but he refused it. This could be a difficult interview and he wouldn't have felt comfortable accepting hospitality from her. 'I apologise for bothering you again,' he said.

She waved a dismissive hand. 'I'm the one who should be apologising. I'm afraid I was really rather rude this morning. You were only doing your job, after all. Shall we sit down?' She waited until they were settled and then

100

said, 'I'm afraid I'm notoriously bad-tempered when my work is interrupted.'

'I can understand that.'

'Perhaps. I think that only another creative person really can – a composer, perhaps, or a writer. When you are engaged in a creative activity of that nature you become completely absorbed in it. But it's a very special kind of absorption, very difficult to describe. It's as if you are existing on a different level, as if . . . well, as if you take a deep breath and then sink beneath the waves, don't come up for air until you have finished.' She gave an embarrassed laugh. 'I'm not explaining myself very clearly, am I?'

'Oh, but you are. It's fascinating.'

'The point I'm trying to make is that if that concentration is disrupted it's often very difficult to get back to the point where you were. The thread is broken. And I'm afraid I react very badly when that happens. So . . .' She sat back and folded her hands, the picture of attentive cooperation, '. . . tell me how I can help you this time.'

Best to delay tackling her about the row with Virginia, Thanet decided, and take advantage of her helpful mood by finding out a little more about Caroline. 'We've heard quite a bit more about Caroline's elopement this morning, both from your son and from Rachel. I believe you were here at the time?'

Her eyebrows had gone up. 'I really don't see—'

Thanet sighed. He didn't see why he should have to explain himself, but he didn't want to annoy her by being too peremptory. 'It's just that in a case like this . . .'

'A case like what, Inspector?'

'Mrs Mintar. I know that everyone here would like to believe that your daughter-in-law's death was an accident. But equally, the consensus of opinion is that it couldn't have been.'

'She could have had a heart attack and fallen in. Or a stroke. People do, even at her age.'

101

'It's possible. Unlikely, in view of the height of the wall, but possible. And if she did, the post-mortem should confirm it. But we can't afford to sit around and twiddle our thumbs while we're waiting for that. So, as I was about to say, there are two other alternatives . . .'

'Suicide and murder.'

Irascible she might be, but it was refreshing to interview a witness who didn't beat about the bush. 'Quite.'

'And as we can rule out the former . . .'

'Precisely. Furthermore, although the family would no doubt love to subscribe to the theory of a psychopath who just happened to stray into the courtyard last night and push your daughter-in-law down the well—'

'All right, all right. No need to spell it out. I'm as aware of the statistics as most, I dare say.'

'The point being that in order to work out what happened last night we have to try to understand the people involved.'

'And that includes dragging up something that happened four years ago?'

'Such events have repercussions which can last for many years, for a lifetime even. We understand that your daughter-in-law was deeply distressed by Caroline's elopement and her unhappiness is bound to have had a profound effect on her behaviour. This, in turn, would have affected those around her and their attitudes to her. Surely you can see therefore that we are bound to be interested in what happened?'

She stared at him without expression, clearly considering what he had said. 'Oh very well,' she said at last. 'If you really think it will help.'

Thanet glanced at Lineham, who pretended to consult his notebook.

'To go back to the night Caroline left, then,' the sergeant said, 'we understand you arrived back from one of your trips that very evening.'

'That's right. I got back shortly before dinner. I wasn't

expected until the following day but there'd been a real muddle over our flight booking and three of us had to come back a day early. Anyway, with the benefit of hindsight, I should have known something was up as far as Caroline was concerned.'

'What do you mean?' said Thanet.

'I suppose, having been away for some time, I was looking at everyone with a fresh eye. And Caroline was like a cat on hot bricks.'

'In what way, precisely?' said Lineham.

'She kept on glancing at her watch when she thought no one was looking, for instance. And she scarcely touched her food.'

'What did you think was the matter with her?'

'I wasn't too concerned. You know what young girls are like. If it isn't PMT it's boys. I suppose I simply assumed she was anxious to get off and meet that lout she was so keen on.'

'You didn't like him?' said Thanet.

Mrs Mintar lifted her chin. 'He simply wasn't suitable for Caroline. Their backgrounds were too different.'

Thanet could hear Lineham thinking, *What a snob!* and as he expected the sergeant couldn't resist a comment.

'They seem to have made a go of it, anyway,' said Lineham.

'Who can possibly tell? She hasn't come running back, certainly. But she took after me in many ways and she had a certain stubborn pride.'

'You're saying that even if the marriage had been a disaster she wouldn't have come home again?' said Thanet.

'Possibly.'

Thanet wondered what that said about the Mintar family. He hoped that if either of his children were ever in trouble they would know where to turn first for help and support. His stomach clenched as he thought of Bridget's current problem. One of the worst aspects of the situation was that he was absolutely powerless to do anything about it. *Oh, Bridget.*

'If they ever got married at all,' Mrs Mintar was saying, with a disapproving sniff. 'Living together seems to be much more fashionable these days.'

'I understood that both her mother and her father were very fond of Caroline.'

'Oh they were. Too much so.'

'What do you mean?'

'I think she felt stifled, found the situation at home claustrophobic. I think that was one of the reasons she kicked over the traces so thoroughly, first in making a completely unacceptable choice and then by running off with him.'

'They disapproved of him as strongly as you did?'

'Of course they did! Oh, he was a handsome creature, I grant you that, in an animal sort of way, but without a grain of refinement or intelligence. Anyone could see with half an eye that what she felt for him was purely physical and would wear off in no time at all. That was why I was all for letting the thing run its course. I could see that by making such a fuss about it Ralph would only make her more determined. Which is, of course, what happened.'

'There were rows about her seeing this man?' Lineham consulted his notebook. 'This Dick Swain?'

'Endless rows, I gather. I was away when they were at their peak, of course, but I believe my son did stop short of actually forbidding her to see him, just. Not that it made any difference in the end, she went anyway.'

'I understand he's not too happy about this engagement of Rachel's, either,' said Thanet.

'An understatement, if ever I heard one.'

'There doesn't seem to be much he can do about it.'

'Oh, I wouldn't say that. Matthew Agon is a very different kettle of fish. We can always resort to the traditional solution. In fact, I've been trying to persuade Ralph to do so. But apparently Virginia was against the idea for some reason.'

'The traditional solution?' said Lineham.

'We're talking about a financial inducement, I imagine?' said Thanet.

'That's right. Bribery. I believe in calling a spade a spade.'

Not much doubt about that! thought Thanet. 'You think it might work?'

'If it were substantial enough, yes. And it would be worth every penny, to get rid of that toad.'

'But your daughter-in-law was against it, you say? Why was that?'

'I think she was afraid it could go disastrously wrong and turn Rachel against them if Agon refused the offer and told Rachel about it. But I think Ralph had hopes of bringing her around.'

'He wouldn't have gone ahead without her agreement?'

She hesitated. 'I'm not sure, if it came to the crunch.'

She had been so cooperative that Thanet was now reluctant to broach the subject which had precipitated this second interview. It had to be done, however. How to achieve a smooth transition, though? 'Your daughter-in-law was not an amenable sort of person?'

A cynical little laugh. 'Shall we just say that she liked her own way.'

'And usually got it?'

'Usually, yes.'

'As far as her husband was concerned, you mean?'

'I didn't say that. I have no intention of discussing their relationship with you, Inspector, if that's what you're hoping.'

'What about your own relationship with her?'

'What about it?'

'You said yourself, this morning, that there was no love

lost between you, that as far as you were concerned it was good riddance.'

'So? I hope you're not suggesting what I think you're suggesting, Inspector?'

Thanet said nothing, waited.

She gave a little laugh. 'You don't seriously think that *I* was responsible for her death? An old woman like me?' She shook her head in mocking disbelief. 'I'd have thought there were far more likely candidates, wouldn't you?'

'Such as?'

'I'm afraid you'll just have to work that out for yourself.'

Was she serious, or just trying to deflect him? 'I'm merely trying to find out how deep this mutual antipathy was. Because as you've already admitted, it was mutual, wasn't it?'

'I've never pretended otherwise.'

'I have to tell you, Mrs Mintar, that you were overheard having a serious quarrel with your daughter-in-law yesterday lunchtime.'

This shook her. She stared at him and her self-control slipped long enough for him to catch a gleam of panic in her eyes before the guard went up again. Her reaction could imply guilt, of course, but he guessed that she was remembering what the row had been about and wondering if the eavesdropper had been close enough to hear what was being said. He guessed, too, that she was torn between denying the whole thing and wanting to find out exactly what Thanet knew. The need to know won. Her chin went up as she said defiantly, 'What of it?'

'Oh come, Mrs Mintar, don't pretend to be naïve. Your daughter-in-law is murdered and we find out that only hours before that you had what was described to us as "a hell of a ding-dong" with her. What are we supposed to think?'

'"A hell of a ding-dong". That could only be Digby, the creep! Typical of him, to listen in on people's private conversations! I'm right, aren't I? What lies has he been telling about me?'

'What makes you think they were lies?'

'I wouldn't trust him further than I could spit! What did he say?'

She was desperate to know if her secret was safe and Thanet couldn't help feeling sorry for her. This woman's work was her life and she was terrified of having her richest source of enjoyment and inspiration snatched away from her.

'That your daughter-in-law was threatening to tell your son that you suffer from angina.'

Her hand went defensively up to her chest as if he had dealt her a mortal blow and the colour drained from her face, leaving her skin the colour of tallow. Suddenly she looked her age.

Thanet was alarmed. In view of her condition, perhaps he should have broken the news more gently. 'Are you all right?' he said.

She compressed her lips and shook her head dismissively. 'I'm fine.' Slowly, experimentally, she lowered her hand. 'Have you told my son about this?'

'No.'

'Then I must ask you not to do so.' Her mouth twisted. 'That wretched man!'

'We already knew of your condition.' Thanet explained how.

She leaned forward, tension in every line of her body. 'You must promise not to tell Ralph!'

'If the matter has no relevance to our investigation I see no reason why we should.'

At last she relaxed, leaning her head against the back of the chair as if exhausted. 'Thank you.' After a few moments she straightened up again and gave a wry grin. 'So I really am a suspect!'

107

'It's obvious how important to you it is, that he shouldn't find out. If your daughter-in-law was threatening to tell him . . .'

She waved a hand. 'You didn't know Virginia, Inspector. It was an idle threat.'

'Why should you believe that?'

'Firstly because it was the only stick she had to beat me with and she wasn't going to throw it away in a hurry. And secondly because if she did, she might have been stuck with having me living here all the time instead of just part of the time. And believe me, that wouldn't have suited her one little bit.'

Thanet had to admit that from what he had heard of Virginia so far, this made sense. 'What was the row about?'

'The usual thing. Virginia's behaviour.'

'In what way, specifically?'

'Specifically, the way she couldn't resist throwing herself at any new man who came along, in front of my son. I couldn't bear seeing him humiliated like that.'

'In this case you are referring to . . . ?'

'Her sister's boyfriend.' She hesitated, gave Thanet an assessing look. Then she got up, strolled across to a side table, opened a heavily carved wooden box and took out a long, slim, brown, elegant cigarette. With a lift of her eyebrows and a wave of her hand she offered them one and when they shook their heads she took her time over lighting up.

Thanet guessed that in view of her angina this was a rare indulgence, the need probably triggered by the stress of the interview.

She blew out a thin stream of smoke before speaking again. 'Especially . . .' she said, deliberately.

Thanet caught the malicious gleam in her eye and could guess what was coming. She had decided to relinquish any idea of preserving family privacy in order to turn the spotlight away from herself. If she had to sacrifice her son's dignity and reveal him as a cuckold – good old-fashioned word, Thanet had always thought – then so be it.

'Yes?' he said, as she had known he would.

'I'm sure you've already worked out for yourself that it was unlikely in the extreme that I should voluntarily have told Virginia about my little problem. So of course you must have asked yourself precisely how she did find out?'

She was going to tell him about Virginia's affair with Squires! He experienced the spurt of excitement and satisfaction which invariably accompanied this turning point in an interview, when he knew that he had succeeded in manipulating a witness into revealing what s/he had every intention of concealing.

'Naturally.'

'And I suspect you have already guessed the answer.'

'Perhaps.'

'Then let's see if you've guessed correctly.'

Mrs Mintar blew out another plume of smoke and gave him a mocking, challenging grin.

But Thanet was too old a hand to be caught out like that. What if he were wrong? He smiled back, benignly. 'I'd much prefer to hear it from you,' he said.

Abruptly her expression changed and she turned to stub out her half-smoked cigarette with angry, stabbing movements. Then she returned to her chair. 'Have you got any children, Inspector?'

'Two.' His stomach clenched. What was happening to Bridget right now?

'Married?'

'One is.'

'Then I hope he or she has a faithful partner. You can't imagine what it's like to have to stand by and see your son betrayed, not once or twice but over and over again, to have to watch him watching his wife flirting shamelessly with other men. Virginia simply could not resist the temptation to exercise her charms on every new male that came her way. You should have seen her last night, with Jane's boyfriend! Smiles, fluttering eyelids, oh-so-friendly hand laid upon his thigh . . . I tell you, it was a disgusting performance. And apart from the fact that Ralph was present, it was downright embarrassing for the rest of us, and especially for Jane.' She paused, and again the malicious gleam appeared in her eye. 'The big plus, of course, was that it made that parody of a doctor squirm.'

Now they were getting to the point. 'Dr Squires, you mean.'

'Who else? I must say I did enjoy seeing him suffer, after what he did to me. Oh yes, Inspector, I can see you already know. But I will spell it out for you. Virginia knew of my condition because her lover told her. Pillow talk, no doubt. Our charming Dr Squires is not only an adulterer but he has betrayed his profession, firstly by having an affair with a patient and secondly by breaking patient confidentiality. And the infuriating thing is, I haven't been able to do a thing about it. If I complained to the General Medical Council Ralph would find out about my heart condition and I couldn't afford to risk that.'

'You could change your doctor.'

'True. And I shall. But that wouldn't have helped the current situation.'

Unless you got rid of Virginia, thought Thanet. 'How long had this affair been going on?'

A shrug. 'No idea. All I know is that when I got back at the beginning of March it didn't take me long to realise what was happening. So I must say that last night I did relish the spectacle of watching him see her flirt so outrageously with another man. Believe me, he didn't enjoy that one little bit, though he tried to hide it, of course.'

'What about his wife? Did she know about this, do you think?'

'If she didn't she must be blind or deaf. He was absolutely besotted with Virginia, couldn't keep his eyes off her.'

'But you don't actually know whether or not Mrs Squires knew?'

'Not to be positive, no. But I suspect she did. I think that, like me, she was rather enjoying seeing her husband's nose put out of joint last night.'

111

'How did Mr Prime react to these attentions?'

'I gave him ten out of ten for being Virginia-resistant.'

'He didn't respond, then.'

'Only by looking uncomfortable. But of course, this just made Virginia redouble her efforts.'

'What about her sister?'

'Jane? Oh, she was furious with Virginia, as you can imagine. She didn't actually say anything, I don't think she would have wanted to embarrass Ralph, she's very fond of him, but you could tell that underneath she was seething.' Mrs Mintar leaned back in her chair with an air of finality and waved a graceful hand, the green silk of her flowing caftan sleeve falling back to reveal a tanned, muscular arm. 'So there you have it, Inspector, the full picture. Believe me, it wasn't a very pleasant social occasion and not one that I would wish to repeat in a hurry. Not that there's any possibility of that now, of course, thank God. And then, to cap it all, Rachel came waltzing in with the news of her engagement. Ralph put a brave face on it, naturally, what else could he do? We all did. But after the charade with the champagne was over I can assure you I had no wish to prolong the evening by participating in the jolly swimming party they proposed. I couldn't wait to get back and immerse myself in a book. So consoling, the printed word, don't you think? And much less wearing than people.'

Thanet rose and Lineham followed suit. 'Well, thank you for being so frank with us, Mrs Mintar. You've been most helpful.'

'Not at all.' The sardonic gleam was back in her eye. *Given you plenty of food for thought, haven't I?*

Outside Thanet hesitated. They needed to interview Howard Squires again in the light of what Mrs Mintar had told them, but first he'd like to chew matters over with Lineham. 'Come on, Mike, let's go for a stroll, clear our minds.'

They walked down the drive and turned right, away from the village. Although it was now late afternoon the sun continued to beat mercilessly down and the air was suffocatingly hot and still. Perhaps this hadn't been a good idea after all, thought Thanet. Though he felt he really had needed to get away from the Mintars' house, to distance himself a little from the intensity of the emotional situations in which all of those involved in this crime seemed to have been locked. 'Let's see if we can find some shade.'

A couple of hundred yards further on they came to a five-barred gate conveniently shaded by a big oak tree and they stopped with sighs of relief, taking out handkerchiefs to mop at sweating foreheads.

'That's better,' said Lineham. 'Been a real scorcher today, hasn't it?'

Thanet automatically felt in his pocket for the familiar bulge of his pipe, and experienced the usual little thud of disappointment that it wasn't there. At times like this, when he wanted to relax, he still felt bereft without it. For years he had remained determined to hold out against the anti-smoking brigade but in the end, as the places where it was possible to smoke and still feel comfortable about it grew fewer and fewer, he became fed up with being made to feel a pariah. Even then he would have continued out of sheer perversity but for Bridget's pregnancy. No one these days could be unaware of the dangers of smoking near babies and the prospect of being unable to light up either in Bridget and Alexander's house – or indeed in his own home when they came to visit – was the deciding factor in making him stop. It had been a great relief to Lineham, he knew, though neither of them had ever referred to it, and the sergeant had put up with his tetchiness in the early days of deprivation without a word, look or gesture of resentment.

Now, Thanet merely sighed and joined Lineham in

113

resting his forearms along the top bar of the gate and gazing at the vista before them. The lane ran along the spine of a slight ridge and from here the land fell away in the irregular patchwork of fields bordered by hedges and punctuated by specimen trees which is the essence of the English countryside, sadly destroyed only too often in recent years by greedy farmers but, mercifully, here in this area of Kent so far preserved for posterity. Though born and brought up in Sturrenden, the small country town where he lived and worked, Thanet had always loved the countryside in general and the Kent landscape in particular. In his opinion it was some of the most beautiful in England. Earlier on in his career he had had to live elsewhere for brief periods, but he had been delighted to return to Kent and now had no intention of leaving if he could help it. He had often been berated for his lack of ambition but had steadfastly refused to climb further up the promotions ladder, knowing that the higher you scrambled the more likely it was that you would have to be prepared to move around. Anyway, in his view, the further you climbed the more desk-bound you became and the more distant from the work which had attracted you in the first place. No, he had found his niche and was content to stay in it. If it weren't for this constant, nagging anxiety over Bridget ... Perhaps he ought to ring Joan? No, what was the point? If there were any news she'd have been in touch right away. But it made him sick to the stomach to think of what Bridget must be going through now. And to know that there was very real danger for her as well as the baby ...

'You all right, sir?'

Thanet nodded, lips compressed.

'Worried about your daughter?' Lineham was aware of the situation.

'I can't help it, Mike. Well, you know what it's like. You've been through it yourself, when Louise had Richard.'

114

Lineham nodded. 'The worst of it is, you feel so help-less.'

'I just can't stop thinking about it.'

'I know. It's just there, all the time. I found the best thing was to concentrate on work.'

'You're right. I must make more of an effort. But first – I've been meaning to ask but kept on forgetting – tell me how your mother is settling in at Abbeyfield.'

Widowed young, old Mrs Lineham had had a struggle to bring up her only child and, naturally perhaps, had become fiercely possessive. Lineham had had to fight to achieve independence, firstly in his choice of career – Mrs Lineham considering police work much too dangerous – and secondly in his choice of wife, his mother recognising that in Louise she would have far too strong-minded a rival. It had always amused Thanet that his sergeant had managed to break away from one dominating woman only to choose to marry another.

The result was that Lineham spent most of his life in a balancing act, trying to reconcile the needs of each with the demands of the other, and the latest crisis had arisen last year, when the old lady had decided she no longer wished to live alone and had started angling for an invitation to move in with her son and his family – a recipe for disaster if ever there was one. For some time Lineham had prevaricated, knowing himself to be in a cleft stick, but had finally been rescued by a suggestion of Thanet's, who had via his own mother heard of an excel-lent organisation called Abbeyfield. This was a charity which provided, at very reasonable cost, accommodation for small groups of elderly people who found living alone hard to bear. Residents had their own rooms with their own furniture and as much or as little freedom and company as they wished, and there was always a resident housekeeper to keep an eye on them and to provide the main meals of the day. Although initially resistant to the idea, after visiting the Abbeyfield House in Maidstone and talking to the residents there old Mrs Lineham had soon changed her mind and had put her name down on the waiting list for the new Abbeyfield House due to open in Sturrenden this year. She had moved in a month ago.

'Fine. It's early days yet, of course, but touch wood, so far she seems to be settling in well. I can't tell you how grateful we are that you came up with the idea.'

'Don't thank me, thank my mother. Pure luck, really, that she had happened to mention it to me. Anyway, I'm glad it seems to be working out. I assume she hasn't sold her house yet?'

'No, she's hedging her bets at the moment, until she's sure she wants to stay.'

'Good.' Reluctant still to return to the topic of the murder, Thanet resumed his contemplation of the landscape. 'Did you know you can tell the age of a hedge by counting the number of native species in it, Mike? One per century.'

'No, I didn't. Not that I'd recognise them anyway.'

'Ben did a nature project. I thought it was fascinating. We used to go out counting species at weekends. Let's see if I can remember . . .' He turned to look at the hedge behind them, across the road. 'Hawthorn – the most common one; dogwood – that's the one with the reddish stems; elder; hornbeam – that goes a wonderful golden apricot colour in the autumn, hazel . . . How many's that?'

Lineham grinned. 'Five. You're showing off, sir.'

Thanet laughed. 'You're dead right, I am. But just think. Five hundred years old.'

'It's a load of rubbish if you ask me. Anyone planting a country hedge would mix up the species, and in ten years' time no one would know the difference.'

'You know the trouble with you, Mike? There is no romance in your soul!'

'And no bad thing, if you ask me. Look at that lot back

there.' Lineham jerked his head in the direction of the Mintars' house.

The sergeant obviously considered it time they got down to work again. He was right, of course.

'I don't know whether I'd quite call that romance, Mike. The emotions flying around last night were a good deal more earthy than that, don't you think?'

'There were plenty of them, anyway. Not my idea of a good night out!'

Thanet grinned. 'Nor mine. Still, we're beginning to get a pretty good picture of what went on, don't you think?'

'She's a really hard nut, that's for sure.'

'Old Mrs Mintar, you mean.'

'Yes. Coming on strong about how she couldn't discuss her son's relationships and then, the second her own neck is threatened, opening up the whole can of worms no matter what sort of light it put him in.'

'She really got up your nose, didn't she, Mike?'

'Like I said earlier, I just think she's a selfish old harridan, that's all. Whatever she says about how upset she used to get on Mr Mintar's behalf, I think that all she really cares about is herself and her work. I don't think she'd let anything stand in her way. And as you said yourself, she was perfectly placed to nip out and shove Virginia down that well. I'm sure she's strong enough. I know she's got this heart problem, but apart from that she must do an awful lot of walking and climbing with all those plant-hunting trips she goes on. Did you notice the muscles in her arm just now?'

'Yes, I did. And you may well be right. Though whether we'll ever manage to prove it, if so, I don't know.'

'There could be fingerprints on the well cover.'

'Possibly. With any luck. Though I'm not sure that would really help, in this case. Defence would argue she's had a thousand and one opportunities to put them there. But in any case it'll take days to get the results of all the comparisons through and we can't afford to hang around doing nothing. And anyway, there are a number of other likely possibilities . . .'

'True,' said Lineham reluctantly. It was obvious that old Mrs Mintar was his preferred candidate for the role of murderer.

'. . . which we have to consider,' said Thanet firmly. 'The interesting thing about last night's dinner party was the degree to which Virginia was the focal point for all that negative emotion. Just think about it, Mike. Practically everyone there – except Mr Prime, perhaps – could be said to have a motive. Next to the old lady, who I grant you comes pretty near the top of the list, there's Dr Squires. If you ask me, his motive is just as strong as hers. Imagine the power Virginia had over him – and I'm not talking only about how she was making him suffer last night, but the power over his career. If she'd chosen to blow the whistle on him, he'd have been finished. And he had the opportunity too. He and his wife returned to the pool separately, remember. What if Virginia was at the well when he came back and he grabbed his opportunity to have it out with her over her flirting with Prime?'

'There wouldn't have been time, surely, for a quarrel to escalate to that degree? According to Rachel Mrs Squires was only a few minutes behind her husband.'

'Oh, I don't know. It all depends on how angry he was when he tackled her, if that was what happened. An awful lot can happen in a few minutes. I certainly don't think we can rule it out.'

'I suppose not.'

'Then there's Mrs Squires herself . . .'

'We don't actually know, yet, whether she knew her husband was having an affair.'

'True. Though if she didn't, that meant Virginia had even more power over him, if she was threatening to spill the beans. But from what old Mrs Mintar said it just wasn't possible for Mrs Squires not to have noticed. It certainly doesn't sound as though Squires took much trouble to hide his feelings. So maybe his wife felt she couldn't stand it any longer. And she had just as much opportunity as her husband. So did Jane, who according to Prime has had to put up with this sort of behaviour from Virginia in the past. Who knows, perhaps this was the last straw?'

'I wonder if that's why Jane didn't go back down to the pool with Mr Prime? What if she told him to go on ahead because she wanted to have it out with her sister? Yes! That could be why she came out of the passageway door, not through the sitting room, which is the quickest way back to the pool! She went to the kitchen first! And if her sister had just gone out to finish the watering, she could have followed her. So they argue, Virginia Mintar laughs at her perhaps, for making a fuss, and on impulse . . . ? Jane's no lightweight, is she, sir, she'd have had no problem tipping her sister over that wall.'

'True. I must admit she doesn't strike me as the most likely possibility but all the same, you're probably right about that being why she returned to the pool through the corridor. We'll bear that in mind when we next see her. But finally we mustn't forget that last, but not least—'

'There's the husband. Yes. Nobody saw him after they'd cleared the table, until Rachel went to tell him Virginia was missing. He says he stayed in his study, but he could easily have come out again while everyone was changing. I should think he'd had it up to here with her behaviour. Why did he put up with it, that's what I want to know? I couldn't, that's for sure! Imagine what it must be like, to have to sit there and watch your wife carrying on like that!'

'Obviously he must have felt quite differently about it. Some men do. I suppose it's partly a question of temperament but I imagine it also depends on the price they're prepared to pay to keep their wives. Remember that surgeon, what was his name? The one whose wife was pushed off a balcony?'

'Mr Tarrant. Yes, I remember. You're right. His attitude was he didn't care what she did as long as she stayed with him.' Lineham shook his head. 'Beats me. I couldn't stand it.'

'No, neither could I.' Though there was no danger of his having to, with Joan, thank God. Memories flitted through Thanet's mind of the torture he had undergone at one time when Joan was away finishing her probation training and briefly he had wondered if she had indeed fallen for someone else. He had been wrong, of course, and had felt thoroughly ashamed of himself afterwards, but he found it virtually impossible to imagine how it must be to have a wife who behaved so blatantly at her and her husband's own dinner table. Surely, whatever façade Mintar presented to the world, underneath he must have suffered, found the humiliation hard to bear?

'Ah well, we mustn't stand around here all day, pleasant though it may be. Come on, Mike. Let's see if Dr S. can wriggle out of this one.'

TEN

It was marginally cooler now and Squires was mowing the lawn. He had removed his shirt, revealing a tanned, well-muscled torso without an ounce of superfluous fat. No doubt about it, he really was a good advertisement for healthy living.

'Stripes!' murmured Lineham, admiring the doctor's handiwork. 'I can never get my lawn to look like that.'

'Perhaps you ought to ask him to give you a lesson, Mike.' One of the cars was missing, Thanet noticed, the Golf.

Engrossed in his task, it was some minutes before Squires saw them. He waited until he had reached the end of a strip and then switched the mower off and came across, pulling a spotted handkerchief out of his pocket to mop at face and neck. 'Look, I don't want to be unreasonable, Inspector, but three times in one day is a bit much.'

'Sorry, I'm afraid it can't be helped,' said Thanet. 'We really do need to have another word.'

Squires compressed his lips but said nothing and once again they all trooped into the house.

'You'll have to excuse me,' said the doctor and without waiting for a response took off up the stairs.

Lineham raised his eyebrows at Thanet who said, 'Gone to wash, I imagine. Or put on a shirt. Must make you feel more vulnerable, being half naked.'

A few minutes later Squires called from the top of the stairs, 'Come up, Inspector.'

So the doctor wanted to conduct the interview on his own terms. Thanet could have refused but it wasn't worth making an issue of it.

Squires was waiting for them at the top, fully clothed and looking refreshed. There were two doors on the little landing and he led them through the left-hand one into his study, which had obviously been sliced off the sitting room. It was a narrow slot of a room with three slightly angled walls and one straight one covered with floor to ceiling bookshelves. 'Thought we might have a change of venue,' he said.

'Why not?' said Thanet amiably.

Squires sat down behind his desk, which had been positioned across the far end of the room, and gestured them to a couple of upright chairs. 'Right, then, Inspector, what can I do for you this time? Do sit down.'

'Your wife is out?'

'At the moment, yes. She's taking Sarah to a friend's house. Why, did you want to see her? She won't be long.'

'No. I was only wondering because I want to discuss a rather delicate matter and I should think you would prefer her not to be present.'

This shook him. His expression of polite inquiry changed, grew wary. 'I can't think what you mean.'

'Oh come, sir, you must realise what I'm talking about. I'm referring, of course, to your affair with Mrs Mintar.'

Silence. Thanet could see that the man was thinking furiously. *How much do they know?* Obviously, if he were to deny the affair he must do so quickly, to make his reaction believable. On the other hand, if he denied it and they somehow had incontrovertible proof of it, his credibility would be destroyed.

Squires gave a forced laugh. 'What absolute rubbish! Someone's been telling you stories, Inspector.'

So he had decided to gamble on it. A risk worth taking, probably. And it could well pay off. They had no proof, after all, only hearsay, and so far as they knew the only person who could confirm or deny the accusation was dead.

Thanet tensed. Was that the distant sound of a car door being shut? He couldn't be sure. This room was at the back of the house, on the side away from the drive. In any case, Squires obviously hadn't heard it, he was concentrating too hard on the conversation.

'Who was it?' said Squires, leaning forward, eyes narrowed. 'Virginia Mintar was a patient of mine, and such a rumour is highly defamatory. It could land me in serious trouble.'

'I can imagine,' said Thanet drily. 'But I'm afraid I can't tell you. If untrue, I can assure you that it will go no further, as far as we are concerned.'

'*If* untrue?' said Squires angrily, abandoning all pretence of affability. 'Are you questioning my word?'

'I'm simply saying that if the story is untrue you have nothing to fear on our part. But if—'

'If what? No, that simply isn't good enough, Inspector. I need to know who this person is, so that I can put a stop to this nonsense!'

'Howard?' Light footsteps could be heard running up the stairs.

Squires leaned forward and said urgently, 'Inspector—'

Concentrating on getting his timing right, Thanet continued smoothly, raising his voice, '—but if not, I really do advise you to tell your wife.'

The words hung in the air as the door swung open. Marilyn Squires stood on the threshold. She ignored the two policemen and her eyes locked with those of her husband.

Excellent, thought Thanet, she must have heard, surely. 'Ah, Mrs Squires,' he said, rising. 'We were just leaving. We'll see ourselves out.'

Lineham barely managed to hide his surprise at this abrupt end to the interview and as soon as they were outside in the hall he whispered, 'Why the sudden departure, sir? Just when we had him by the . . .'

'Shh.'

When leaving the room Thanet had shut the door loudly and then, banking on the fact that the Squires would be so caught up in the highly charged atmosphere that they wouldn't notice, had quickly released the catch again so that it rebounded a little, leaving a crack to which he now put his ear. Normally he disapproved of eavesdropping but conversations between possible suspects in a murder case were a different matter and this wouldn't be the first time he had had to resort to such tactics, sometimes with invaluable results. Having been given this heaven-sent opportunity he had no intention of missing it.

Lineham cottoned on immediately, and bent to follow suit.

Thanet was right, the Squires weren't aware of his ruse. Almost at once Marilyn's voice rang out. 'Tell me what?' Her tone was ominous, accusatory.

She already knows, thought Thanet.

Squires had obviously been thrown off balance by his wife's untimely arrival, and failed to come up with a convincing reply. 'Oh, nothing important.'

'I see. Nothing important, you say. Well, I think I can guess what the Inspector was referring to.'

Silence. Squires wasn't going to risk an answer.

Marilyn's tone changed. 'You shouldn't be so careless, my love, leaving things like this in places where other people might come across them.'

Thanet and Lineham raised eyebrows at each other. *What?*

'Where did you get that? You've been going through my pockets!'

'And I'm supposed to feel guilty about that? *I'm* supposed to feel guilty, after what you've been up to? Big joke. All's fair in love and war, you surely know that, my darling. Did you really think I didn't notice your reaction yesterday morning when this arrived? The guilty, hunted look, the swift transfer to your pocket?'

A letter, then, thought Thanet.

'I suppose you couldn't risk burning it, just in case the worst came to the worst and you should ever need it as proof of blackmail, but you really should have been more careful about where you put it.' Marilyn's tone changed, became once again charged with anger. 'How could you have been so stupid, so bloody, bloody stupid? You must have known you were putting everything – your reputation, your career, our marriage, the children's well-being – everything at risk, having an affair with a patient! And for Virginia, of all people, that worthless—'

'Shut up, do you hear me? Stop it! I won't listen to you running her down. She's dead, isn't that enough for you?'

'And being dead sanctifies her, is that it? Well, I'm sorry but I'm afraid I can't see it like that.'

'I'd just like to get my hands on the person who sent that—'

'Typical! Things are never your fault, are they? You always try to wriggle out of them by trying to cast blame elsewhere. But I'm afraid that in this case that just won't wash. And you needn't blame whoever sent this for my finding out. I'd have had to be one hundred per cent stupid, and blind into the bargain, not to have noticed what was going on. It just confirmed what I suspected, that's all. Idiotic of me, wasn't it, to hope that if I just ignored it the whole thing would eventually blow over, just fizzle out. Well it didn't, did it? And now look where you've landed us. It's obvious the police have got wind of it.'

'I'm not going to listen to any more of this!'

'That's right. That's your next tactic, isn't it? If you can't shove the blame on to someone else, just avoid the issue altogether and walk out.'

Thanet and Lineham straightened up as the door swung open. Squires came to an abrupt halt, his face a study in dismay. *How much have they heard?* Almost at once, however, he recovered. 'My God,' he said in disgust. 'A pair of eavesdroppers. I didn't think you'd stoop quite so low, Inspector.'

Thanet had no intention of being put on the defensive. 'Not as low as a witness who lies in a murder case,' he said. 'I think you owe us an explanation, don't you, sir? Please.'

And he put out an arm to usher Squires back into the room.

The doctor complied reluctantly.

'And I think we'll take that, Mrs Squires.' Thanet held out his hand. He had not missed Marilyn Squires' attempt to hide the letter behind her back.

Slowly, reluctantly, she complied but Squires was almost too quick for them. He lunged forward in an attempt to snatch it from her. 'That's my property!'

But Lineham was too quick for him. His arm shot out and he grabbed Squires' wrist just as his fingers touched the paper.

Thanet glanced at the sergeant. *Well done, Mike.* 'Thank you,' he said, taking it.

And it wasn't a letter, he now saw, but a photograph: Squires and Virginia Mintar, both in tennis gear and clearly identifiable, locked in a passionate embrace on a wooden bench beside a tennis court – the Mintars', probably. Squires' hand was invisible between her legs beneath the brief pleated skirt and there could be no doubt whatsoever about their relationship. He turned the photograph over. Printed on the back in block capitals was the message: 'WANT TO SEE THE REST? I'LL BE IN TOUCH.'

Thanet handed it to Lineham to look at.

'And this arrived yesterday morning?'

A sullen nod from Squires.

'Have you any idea who sent it?'

Squires hesitated. 'No.'

He's lying, thought Thanet. He suspects, but he's not sure. The best policy now would be to let the man stew. 'Very well, Mr Squires, we'll leave it at that for the moment. But I'm sure you realise that this puts you in a very difficult position with regard to Mrs Mintar's death and I strongly advise you to be frank with us in future. Once we know that someone has lied to us we naturally regard anything else he tells us with some suspicion. I hope that neither of you has plans to go away at present? No? Good.'

And on this ominous note Thanet left.

'That'll have put the wind up him!' said Lineham. 'His face, when he opened that door and saw us there!'

'Mmm. Who do you think sent the photograph, Mike?'

Lineham didn't hesitate. 'Digby. Rachel said she was sure he was always creeping about, spying on her. And whoever sent that photograph had to have printed it himself. It's hardly the sort of thing you'd take to Boots.'

Thanet nodded. 'My guess too.' He made up his mind. 'We'll get a search warrant in the morning, see if we can find the rest of them. Interesting that Digby didn't breathe a word about Virginia and Squires when we were interviewing him. I suppose he wasn't going to risk losing a potentially lucrative source of income.'

'No. He was far more interested in pointing the finger at the old lady.'

'Yes, he was, wasn't he? But it does occur to me, Mike . . .'

'What, sir?'

'If he really was in the habit of spying and, as we now suspect, of taking photographs, who knows what else we might turn up?'

'Ye-e-e-s!' breathed Lineham. 'You're right.'

They had reached their cars and Thanet paused to glance at his watch. Six-thirty.

'What next, sir?'

'We'll call it a day here, I think. Better get back to the office, do some reports. The Super'll expect every last detail in the morning. Actually, come to think of it, I'd better give him a ring tonight, in case he's back.'

It was a quarter to ten by the time they had finished and, anxious to put work behind him when he left the office, Thanet tried Superintendent Draco's number. The answerphone was still on and he didn't bother to leave a message. It would have to wait until tomorrow.

On the way home his anxieties about Bridget came rushing back and when he got there he was dismayed to find the house in darkness and Joan's car missing. Something must have gone wrong. Why hadn't she got in touch with him? He must ring the hospital at once.

Heart-rate accelerating he hurried into the house, switching on lights everywhere. There was a note propped against the telephone on the table in the hall. He snatched it up.

2.30. Can't stand hanging around waiting for news. Am driving up to visit Bridget in hospital. Back for supper. Love, J.

Back for supper? They usually ate around seven. Where was she? Perhaps there had been a crisis at the hospital and she was staying on? If so, she would surely have let him know? He saw that there was one message on the answerphone. Perhaps it was from her? But it wasn't, it was from Ben.

Ben, their son, who was still determined on eventually making a career in the police force, had graduated in computer studies from Reading University and was now on a VSO scheme in Africa. Thanet was annoyed and disappointed to have missed him, as living out in the wilds Ben rarely had the opportunity to get to a telephone.

'Hi, Mum, Dad. Just to let you know everything's OK. And I was wondering about Bridget, of course. Not long now, is it? I'll ring again as soon as I can. 'Bye.'

Perhaps it was just as well that they had both been out when he rang, after all. Bridget and Ben had always been close and it would be especially worrying for him if he knew what was happening, when it was so difficult for him to keep in touch. With any luck, by the next time he managed to get through it would all be over, for better or for worse.

Joan had left the hospital number beside the phone and he rang it, listening impatiently to the recorded messages and pressing the appropriate keypad numbers when necessary. At last he was through to the maternity ward. No, there was no change in Mrs Highman's condition, which was being closely monitored. Visiting hours finished at eight and the nurse had no idea whether or not Mrs Highman's mother had been in earlier. Thanet asked her to give Bridget his love and rang off.

So where was Joan? Even if she'd stayed until the end of visiting time, she should be home by now. It took only an hour and three-quarters to drive back to Sturrenden – but via the M25, the most crowded stretch of motorway in Europe. There must have been an accident. One was always hearing tales of horrendous delays because of overturned lorries, collisions on contraflows and multiple pile-ups. Please God, if there had been, Joan had not been involved.

He crossed to the window and peered out. The last remnants of light were fading from the sky. If she were simply held up, why hadn't she rung him on her mobile? He could try ringing her.

But there was no reply. Another phone call, to the police operations room, ascertained that no, there had been no major incident on the M25 and traffic was flowing normally.

Keep calm, he told himself. There's probably some

perfectly simple explanation. Perhaps she's got a puncture, or the car has broken down. Suppressing memories of the many occasions when, as a young policeman, he had had to break the news of a fatal road traffic accident to a stunned family, Thanet went into the kitchen and began to hunt around for something to prepare for supper. She would be hungry when she got home.

He was defrosting an M&S ready meal in the microwave when the phone rang. He rushed to answer it, flooded with relief when he heard her voice. 'Joan! Where are you?'

And the explanation was, after all, just as mundane as he had tried to convince himself that it might be. A puncture on the slip road leading from the M25 to the M26 had complicated a relatively simple repair job. In that situation it had been too dangerous for her to attempt to change the wheel herself and she had had to walk to the nearest telephone and call the RAC.

'Why didn't you ring them on your mobile?'

'I daren't tell you.'

'You left it behind!' exploded Thanet.

'Just as bad, I'm afraid. Flat battery! I'm using the repair man's.'

'Oh, Joan, for God's sake . . .' Thanet caught himself up. What was the point of recriminations? She was safe, that was the main thing. 'How long do you think it'll be before you get home?'

It was, in fact, almost midnight.

'Don't ever do that to me again!' he said as she walked in. He held out his arms and she came to him, laid her head against his shoulder.

'I'm sorry, Luke.'

'Never mind. You're here now, that's all that matters.' He pulled away, studied her face. 'You look exhausted. Are you hungry? I'm keeping something hot in the oven.'

She shook her head. 'It's too late and anyway I'm too

wound up for a proper meal. It was such a ghastly place to break down, Luke, the cars come whizzing around the bends on those slip roads.'

'I know. It must have been awful for you. What would you like to do now? Go straight to bed? I could bring you up some tea and toast, if you like.'

'Would you? That would be lovely.'

'Why don't you have a quick bath first, to relax you.'

'Perhaps I will.'

Joan dropped her handbag on the table and trailed wearily up the stairs. Thanet waited until he heard the bath water running out and then made the tea and toast, taking up a cup for himself.

'It's such a relief to be home, I can't tell you,' said Joan as he sat down on the edge of the bed. 'I just hate driving on the M25. And believe me, I've learned my lesson about making sure my mobile is charged up.'

'I should think so! Honestly, love—'

'I know, I know!' Joan took a bite of toast then sipped at her tea. 'Oh, this is lovely.'

'So,' said Thanet. 'Tell me how Bridget is.'

Joan pulled a face. 'She's putting a brave face on it. What else can she do? But they're obviously both worried to death, you can tell.'

'Alexander was there?'

'Oh yes, I think he's staying with her all the time he's allowed to. He's being wonderful.'

'And what, exactly, is happening at the moment? Doc Mallard was saying something about some injections she might have. To mature the baby's lungs?'

'That's right. She has to have two, twelve hours apart. She had one at ten this morning and she'll have had the second by now. After that they have to wait forty-eight hours before they induce. Then the baby should apparently have a good chance of survival.'

'It's definite that they will induce?'

'Oh I should think so, yes. There doesn't seem to

be any question of that. They just can't get her blood pressure down.' Joan shook her head and squeezed her eyes tight shut, trying hard not to cry, but despite her efforts tears began to roll down her cheeks. 'Oh Luke, I'm so frightened for her.'

Thanet moved the tray on to the floor and put his arms around her. 'I know.'

Joan pulled away, reached for a tissue and wiped her eyes, then blew her nose. 'I'm sorry, darling. There's no point in carrying on like this, is there? Tell me what you've been doing today.'

'Chasing my tail, as usual on the first day of a case. Do you ever recall Bridget mentioning a girl called Caroline Mintar? She also went to Sturrenden High, but she'd be – let me see – about three years younger than Sprig.'

Joan repeated the name. 'It does have a familiar ring. Yes. Wasn't there some sort of scandal? But it was several years after Bridget left school.'

'That's right. Four years ago. She eloped with the gardener, when she was eighteen.'

'Of course, I remember now! It was in the local paper, caused quite a stir at the time.'

'Yes, well it's her mother who was found dead this morning. Apparently she never got over it.'

'She committed suicide, you mean?'

'I don't think so, no. Everyone seems to rule that out.'

'How is her family taking it?'

'Badly. Especially as they never saw or heard from Caroline again.'

'Oh Luke, how awful.'

'Yes. And to make matters worse, Rachel, her other daughter, who is now the same age as Caroline was when she eloped, has just become engaged to someone equally unsuitable. I've met him and believe me, I'm only too thankful that Bridget never got tangled up with anyone like that. Ralph Mintar, the husband, is bound to be a suspect, of course, but I can't help feeling sorry for the poor bloke.'

'We've been very lucky so far, haven't we, Luke?'

'Yes, we have.'

Then they were both silent, thinking of Bridget.

So far.

ELEVEN

Lineham was hard at work when Thanet arrived at the office next morning. It wasn't that Thanet was late, just that the sergeant was always early.

'Morning, sir. Going to be another scorcher, by the look of it.'

'Yes. I remembered to pick up a couple of bottles of water on the way. And to bring a cool bag to put them in.'

'So did I,' said Lineham with a grin.

'Well, at least we won't get dehydrated!' Thanet sat down at his desk. 'So, anything interesting come in?'

'Doc Mallard looked in. The PM's starting around now.'

'Good. Anything else?'

'Not unless you count Tanya's interview with the local witch.'

WDC Tanya Phillips was proving to be a useful member of the team. She had been with them over a year now.

'Local witch?' Thanet remembered what Mintar had said. 'Ah, yes, the mother of the lad Caroline eloped with.'

'There's nothing relevant to our case in Tanya's report, but it's just up your street. Look.'

Thanet took the proffered paper. 'What is my street, Mike?'

'Anything a bit off-beat.'

'Mmm,' said Thanet, reading. 'I see what you mean. Real Hansel and Gretel stuff, isn't it.'

The interview with Marah Swain had been part of routine house-to-house inquiries. In the literal sense she was, like the Squires, Mintar's next-door neighbour, although her house was half a mile further on down the lane and invisible from the road, being in the middle of a clearing in a wood.

She claimed not to have seen or heard anything unusual the night of Virginia Mintar's death and appeared to be unmoved by it. At the end of the report Tanya had written: *Thoroughly uncooperative. Locally has the reputation of being a witch.*

Intrigued, Thanet called Tanya in. 'This Mrs Swain,' he said, tapping the report. 'Bit of an oddball, by the sound of it.'

'Miss, actually, sir. Apparently she's never made any secret of the fact that her son was illegitimate. But yes, you can say that again!' Tanya laughed, eyes sparkling at the memory. She was in her mid-twenties, a stocky girl with a mop of unruly dark curls. 'It wasn't exactly the easiest of interviews. I don't know if she's a bit deaf but her radio was playing full blast the whole time I was there, and requests to turn it down were simply ignored. And you ought to see the inside of that cottage! It's like something out of the Middle Ages!'

'In what way?'

'Well, it's dark and gloomy, doesn't look as though it's been cleaned for about a hundred years, with bunches of dried herbs and stuff hanging from nails all along the beams in the ceiling and every windowsill crammed with jamjars full of things I wouldn't like to examine too closely.'

Lineham grinned. 'What, frogs legs and eyeballs and suchlike?'

Tanya shuddered. 'Something like that, I imagine. As

135

I said, I didn't really want to know. And the cellar is apparently stuffed with more of the same, according to a girl I interviewed in the village. She – the girl – is married to a man who went to school with Dick Swain. The two boys used to play together after school and Dick took him down to the cellar one day. Dick's mother caught them there and was furious, apparently, forbade the boy ever to come to the house again.'

'All right, so she's a bit weird. But this comment at the end of your report . . .'

'About her being a witch, you mean?'

'Yes. Somewhat far-fetched, isn't it?'

Tanya shrugged. 'Before interviewing her I would have agreed. But now, well, I wouldn't be too sure.'

'Why?'

'She looks the part, for a start. She's got long, grey hair which straggles down over her shoulders and chest, and the way she dresses is like something out of the nineteenth century – shapeless ankle-length black skirt, woollen shawl, thick stockings and old leather boots which look as though they once belonged to a tramp. Put a witch's hat on her and sit her on a broomstick and she could model for the illustrations in a book of fairy tales any day.'

Thanet was amused at the graphic description.

'Then there's the way she looks at you, sir. Suspicious and sort of well . . .' Tanya groped for the right word. 'Malevolent, yes, that's it. Malevolent.'

'Charming!' said Lineham.

'She certainly sounds something of a throw-back,' said Thanet. 'Is she supposed to practise? If that's the right word for it?'

Another shrug. 'Rumour is that she does. Though I gather it's all very clandestine, no one would actually admit to consulting her. And frankly, I can't see anyone going there unless they were desperate. The place absolutely stinks – and I really do mean stinks! Handkerchief over the nose stuff!'

136

'Glad it was you not me, then,' said Lineham.

But Thanet rather wished he had interviewed Dick Swain's mother himself. Not that there had been any reason to do so, but Lineham was right, the off-beat always intrigued him. 'Thanks, Tanya. How's the house-to-house going?'

'Slowly, as usual. We're just on our way back out there now.'

'Good.'

When she had gone Lineham said, 'Not surprising the Mintars were dead against Caroline going out with Dick Swain, is it? Can't say I blame them. His mother doesn't sound exactly the sort of mother-in-law I'd choose for my children. And on top of that Swain was illegitimate too. I wonder who his father was? Probably the tramp she got the boots from!'

Thanet glanced at his watch. 'I'd better go.' If he wasn't careful he'd be late for the morning meeting and Draco did not take kindly to unpunctuality. Added to which, Thanet thought it quite likely he would be hauled over the coals for not having contacted Draco over the weekend. Leaving Lineham to arrange the morning's appointments, he hurried downstairs.

He made it with one minute to spare. They were all waiting for him in characteristic manner, Draco drumming his fingers impatiently on his desk, Chief Inspector Tody with his self-deprecatory half-smile, Inspector Boon with his ironic twinkle.

'Ah, Thanet,' said Draco. 'Perhaps we may now begin.' *At last*, his tone implied. He sat back in his chair, fingers steepled beneath his chin, snapping dark eyes focused on Thanet like laser beams. Even his shock of black curly hair seemed to crackle with energy. 'With a report on the Mintar case, I think.'

His tone was ominous and Thanet's heart sank. He was definitely in for it later. Why did Draco always succeed in making him feel he was back in the headmaster's study?

Still, at least the Super showed consideration in such circumstances. He was not in the habit of reprimanding his men in front of colleagues.

Succinctly, he made his report.

'So,' said Draco when he had finished, 'you seem pretty certain it wasn't suicide, or an accident.'

'I don't think it could have been, sir. Not one of the people who knew her thought it could have been suicide and the wall around the well really is too high – about the height of her hips – for it to have been an accident.'

'Even if she had a heart attack and collapsed on to it?' said Tody.

'I think in that case she'd have been found slumped across it. It's a pretty thick wall. She'd have needed extra momentum to tip right over.'

'In that case you're looking for someone pretty strong, aren't you?' said Boon.

'Not necessarily,' said Thanet. 'I don't think it would have been too difficult. She was fairly slight. One good shove would have done the trick, I should think.'

'Pointless discussion!' said Draco, who had been impatiently tapping a pencil on his desk throughout this exchange. 'Let's find out the cause of death before we start speculating. Do we know when the PM is?'

'It's taking place now, sir, I believe.'

'Good. Now, the search warrant for this photographer's place . . . I agree, it sounds a sensible idea. But to justify it before the magistrates I think we really must be certain that this is a murder case and Mrs Mintar did not die of natural causes. So again, we wait for PM results, right?'

'Yes, sir.'

After this the meeting was quickly wound up. Thanet had reached the door and was thinking that he had got away lightly after all when Draco called him back.

'Why was I not informed of Mrs Mintar's death until I arrived at work this morning?'

'You were away, sir—'

'I know I was away! But as you are well aware, I always leave a contact number.'

'To begin with we didn't realise it was so serious, sir. As I said, we thought Mrs Mintar might well turn up overnight. And then, well, we got caught up in things.'

'That is no excuse whatsoever!'

'I know. I'm sorry, sir. I did try to ring you last night—'

'There was no message on my answerphone.'

'It was late, sir. I thought it could wait until this morning.'

'*You* thought! Thanet, it is I who am in charge here. It is I who am ultimately responsible for what goes on here and it is I who make such decisions. I have made it abundantly clear in the past that if anyone so much as sneezes on my patch, I want to know, and my attitude has not changed. Is that clear?'

'Yes, sir. Perfectly.'

'What is your next move?'

'I want to see Matthew Agon, Mr Mintar's daughter's fiancé. He's the only person present when Mrs Mintar went missing that we have not yet interviewed.'

'Mr Mintar does not approve of this relationship, you said.'

'None of the family does.'

'Hmm. And after you've seen Agon?'

'I'm hoping to go and see a friend of Mrs Mintar's, sir. A Mrs Amos. I thought she might be able to help us with some background.'

'Hot on background, aren't you, Thanet?'

'I do find it helps, sir.'

'And after that?'

'I'm not sure yet, sir.' Thanet hated being pinned down like this.

But Draco wouldn't let it go. 'But probably?'

The Superintendent was punishing him for his slip-up, Thanet realised. 'Probably back to Mr Mintar's house.'

139

'And I imagine you'll then be there for some time. Most of the afternoon, perhaps?'

'I expect so, sir. Unless we're able to apply for the search warrant this morning, and it's granted. In which case—'

'It's just that I'd like to take a look at the crime scene for myself. But it needn't be a problem. We'll make it early afternoon – say around 1.30? Then you'd have plenty of time to do the search later.'

Draco breathing down his neck, the ultimate punishment. Thanet's heart sank. 'Right, sir.'

Back in the office Lineham took one look at his face and said, 'What's up, sir?'

'We are to have the honour of an on-site visit from the Super this afternoon, Mike. Entirely my fault, for not making sure he was informed about the Mintar case.'

'Ah.' Knowing that Thanet would not allow criticism of a superior officer Lineham made no further comment, but his tone spoke volumes.

'Also, we're to defer the application for a search warrant until we've heard the PM results. We'd better ask Doc Mallard to ring them through. Did you manage to fix both appointments?'

Lineham had, and they were soon on their way.

The Leisure Club where Matthew Agon worked was attached to a country house hotel. Melton Park, for centuries the home of the Purefoy family, had, like many English country houses, become in the end an impossible financial burden and when the last owner had died a few years ago death duties had been the last straw. His heir had sold up and moved to a different part of the country, declaring that he could not bear to watch the indignities his family home would undoubtedly suffer in the hands of the new owners, a consortium which specialised in running upmarket hotels.

Application had at once been made, and permission granted, for extensive improvements. Outbuildings had been converted into a glamorous indoor swimming pool and leisure complex, parkland 'landscaped' into an eighteen-hole golf course, and a range of other outdoor activities catered for.

'Ve-ry nice,' said Lineham, looking about as they walked into the reception area of the Club. No expense had been spared. In the centre was a dolphin fountain, the soothing sound of trickling water a welcome change in Thanet's opinion from the ubiquitous pop music which assaults the ear in so many public buildings these days. The terracotta floor tiles had been buffed to a soft sheen and the reception desk looked as though it had been hewn out of one huge slab of marble.

'Prepare to pay through the nose, all ye who enter here,' murmured Lineham as they approached it.

'How may I help you?'

The girl behind the desk was predictably young and pretty, presenting a suitably healthy image to clientele: shining shoulder-length blonde hair and a smile which would have enhanced any toothpaste advertisement. She was wearing a crisp white T-shirt with the club logo and the briefest of brief white shorts. Her smile dimmed a little when she heard why they were there. 'Matthew? He's coaching at the moment, but he'll be free in about twenty minutes. Perhaps you wouldn't mind waiting . . . ?' She gestured in the direction of a group of armchairs. 'I could order some coffee for you.'

The message was clear. *We don't want to upset our clients.*

But Thanet was interested to see Agon in action. He smiled benignly. 'That's very kind, but thank you, no. We'll just stroll around to the courts and wait until he's finished. Where are they exactly?'

Reluctantly she gave directions and Thanet turned away.

But Lineham lingered. 'Have you a membership leaflet?'

The gleaming white teeth reappeared. 'Of course, sir.'

141

She rummaged beneath the desk and produced one. 'If you have any queries, please don't hesitate to ask. After the initial joining fee we do prefer clients to pay by monthly direct debit. It's more convenient all round.'

'Thank you.'

Thanet waited until they were outside then said, 'Thinking of taking out a second mortgage, Mike?'

'I'd need one! Just listen to this! The joining fee is £2,000 – *two thousand quid!* And that's just for a single membership. A family membership is £3,000! And then on top of that the annual fees range from £1,000 a year to £2,000 a year, depending on which option you go for. Ah well, it's all right for some.' Lineham screwed up the leaflet and threw it into a conveniently placed waste bin.

'No point in wanting things you can never hope to get.'

'Perhaps when I win the lottery . . .'

'If, you mean. Complete waste of money, in my opinion.' Apart from which, Thanet disapproved of the whole business. In his view the winning of huge sums of money never did anyone any good and in many ways was a positive force for harm. The introduction of the National Lottery, coupled with a dramatic rise in the number of slot machines and the easing of controls in the gaming industry, had resulted in a vast increase in the number of people with gambling problems, to the degree that a charity called Gamcare had been launched to help them. He himself had never bought a lottery ticket and had no intention of doing so.

Lineham grinned but said nothing. They had already discussed the matter *ad nauseam* and he knew that nothing would change Thanet's mind. 'Looks as though there are plenty who can afford the membership fees, anyway.'

The tennis courts were tucked away at the back of the building and as they walked around the side they had a clear view of the golf course. There were small groups of golfers at every hole.

'What I can never understand,' said Lineham, 'is how they can afford to belong to a club like this if they're out there playing golf instead of working their backs off to earn enough money to join.'

Thanet laughed. 'But you know perfectly well that they are working, Mike, at least in the sense that a lot of them are making or cementing important contacts from which they hope to earn money in the future. Not that that applies to everyone who plays, of course, far from it, I'm sure. But golf in particular is notorious for that.'

'So they say. I think we're in the wrong profession.'

'Oh come on, Mike. Can you honestly say you'd rather be out there knocking a ball about and buttering people up instead of being about to interview a witness in a murder case?' It was getting hotter by the minute; Thanet took off his jacket and slung it over his shoulder.

Lineham pulled a face and followed suit. 'You're dead right. I wouldn't.'

They had turned the corner and come in view of the tennis courts.

'There he is, sir.'

Thanet put a hand on Lineham's arm to restrain him. 'Wait a minute, Mike'. He wanted to seize the opportunity to watch Agon unobserved.

On the court nearest to them Agon was coaching a slim, attractive woman in her thirties. They were both standing at the base line with their backs to the two detectives and were obviously working on the woman's service. Agon stood back and watched as she served several balls.

'You're not bringing your racquet far enough down behind, so you don't get up enough momentum,' he said. 'Look.' He demonstrated, sending a couple of balls skimming over the net at speed.

She tried again. He was right, Thanet could see.

Agon put down his racquet and went to stand behind her. 'See if you can feel what I mean.' He moved in closer and curling his left arm around her waist put his right hand over hers on the handle.

'"Feel" being the operative word,' whispered Lineham in Thanet's ear.

With a sinuous little wriggle she pressed her body back against his and turned her face sideways and upwards. It was a clear invitation. And, thought Thanet, not the first time it had been tendered – or accepted.

'Very cosy!' said Lineham.

But on this occasion Agon simply murmured something which made her laugh and they both addressed the task in hand. After demonstrating the serving movement once or twice he released her. As he did so he ran his left hand lightly up her bare thigh.

'See that, sir?'

Thanet nodded.

The woman cast a coquettish glance at Agon over her shoulder. In doing so she spotted the two men watching and her expression changed. She nodded in their direction and said something to Agon, who turned.

'Don't let us disturb you, Mr Agon,' said Thanet, raising his voice. 'We're happy to wait until you've finished.'

Agon glanced at his watch. 'I just about have.' He turned to his pupil and they had a brief conversation. The woman nodded, picked up a sweater from the bench at the side of the court, then sauntered off, hips swaying provocatively. She gave the two policemen a resentful glance as she passed.

'See you tomorrow, same time,' Agon called after her.

The most casual of nods showed that she had heard him.

'Now, Inspector,' said Agon with a cooperative smile, 'how may I help?'

Despite the heat and the exercise he looked cool and unruffled in his tennis whites. Thanet envied him his shorts and polo shirt.

'Is there somewhere cooler we could sit?'

144

Agon nodded. 'This way.'

He led them along the side of the row of tennis courts and around a bank of shrubs to a shady area where tables and chairs had been set out in front of a small rustic bar serving snacks for the convenience of club members. There were a few people sitting about.

'Fancy a coffee? Or a cold drink?' said Agon.

Much as he would have liked to accept, Thanet refused. Agon would presumably have had to pay for them, and he didn't want to be beholden to the man. He led the way to a table where they would not be overheard.

'It's about the night before last, of course,' he said, and glanced at Lineham. *Take over, Mike.*

Lineham took out his notebook.

'Ah yes,' said Agon. 'Saturday night.' And briefly, malice sparked in his eyes. 'A very interesting occasion.'

'In what way, sir?'

TWELVE

Agon ran his tongue over his lips. 'Sure you don't want a drink? No? Mind if I get myself one?'

They watched him walk across the grass to the little bar, exchanging an occasional greeting with some of the other people scattered around. One young woman put out a hand to detain him and they spoke together briefly.

'Fancies him, doesn't she?' said Lineham. 'Very popular with the ladies, our Mr Agon.'

'Looks like it. Not surprising, I suppose. He's a very good-looking young man.'

'I wonder what Rachel thinks of it. It must be very uncomfortable, being engaged to someone who's such a magnet to the opposite sex, don't you think?'

'I imagine she's so head over heels she doesn't care, just feels delighted that she's the one he's chosen. Anyway, I expect he watches his step when she's around.'

'It'll be different after they're married, I bet. He won't need to be so careful then.'

'You're a cynic, Mike. Perhaps she's the love of his life.'

Lineham gave a derisive snort. 'Think he really needs a drink, sir, or d'you think he's just playing for time while he makes up his mind what he's going to tell us?'

'A bit of both, I imagine.'

When Agon returned Thanet tried to avoid looking at

the glass of lemonade he was carrying. Tall, beaded with moisture and chinking with ice it looked far too inviting for Thanet's comfort.

Agon took a long swallow and then sat back with a sigh of satisfaction. 'Ah, that's better. It's hot work out there. Now, where were we?' He crossed his legs, resting right ankle on left knee, and looked expectantly at Lineham.

Thanet had been trying to work out what it was about the man which had provoked that immediate reaction of dislike, the night before last. It wasn't that he automatically mistrusted good-looking men. Alexander, for instance, was very good-looking. *When would there be more news of Bridget?* True, Agon's eyes were set rather close together. Was there any justification for the old adage that this denoted shiftiness? Perhaps he, Thanet, was being unfair. He must be on his guard. Prejudice clouds the judgement.

'You were going to tell us about that night, sir,' said Lineham. 'You said it was interesting.'

'Ah, yes.' Agon took another swig from his glass. 'Well, if you've been talking to the family, as I'm sure you have, you'll have gathered I'm not exactly *numero uno* around there and on Saturday night they were all shook up, as Elvis would have put it, by our little bombshell.'

'That you and Miss Mintar had just got engaged, you mean.'

'That's right. You a married man, Sergeant?' Agon eyed Lineham speculatively. 'Yes, you are. I can always tell. They have that – what? That *settled* look.'

Lineham ignored this. 'You had a little celebration, I believe? Mr Mintar opened a bottle of champagne.'

'Huh! Celebration? Wake, more like it. Oh, they put as good a face on it as they could bring themselves to, for Rachel's sake, but you didn't have to be a mind-reader to know what they were all thinking. I'm only surprised it wasn't me who ended up at the bottom of the well.'

'Oh come on, sir. Aren't you exaggerating a bit?'

147

'You weren't there, Sergeant. I was.'

'Yes, well, as I said, perhaps you could give us your account of the evening.'

Agon obliged, with the occasional snide comment. He was obviously enjoying the opportunity of openly displaying his resentment of the Mintars' attitude towards him. With Rachel, of course, he probably wouldn't dare, for fear of putting her off.

His story tallied with the others. After everyone had left the terrace he and Rachel had remained behind for a few minutes 'for obvious reasons' – he gave a salacious wink here – and had then separated. Rachel had gone into the house via the lounge, as he called it, whereas he had returned to his car to fetch his swimming trunks before changing in the pool house. He had been first into the pool, closely followed by Rachel and then the others in the order already described.

'Where had you parked your car, sir?'

'In the courtyard, as usual. Everyone parks there.'

'So to fetch your swimming things you had to walk along the side of the annexe where old Mrs Mintar lives, and across the far side of the courtyard?'

Lineham's tone was factual, low-key, and betrayed no hint of the excitement which, like Thanet, he must be feeling. Were they about to be given one last glimpse of Virginia Mintar, before she died?

Agon was looking impatient. 'Well, yes, obviously.'

'Matt!' A short, powerfully built man in tennis whites was hurrying across the grass towards them. He was swinging a racquet. 'Sorry I'm late!'

Of all the moments to be interrupted! thought Thanet. Lineham was looking equally frustrated.

Agon glanced at the two policemen. 'My next lesson.' He started to rise. 'I'm afraid you'll have to excuse me.'

Thanet couldn't believe it. Agon actually seemed to think they were going to let him walk out on them, in the middle of an interview! 'I'm afraid your client will just have to wait until we've finished, sir.'

The short man raised his eyebrows at Agon, who gave a rueful shrug. 'Sorry, Mr Martin, you heard the man. If you'd like to go on court and practise some serves I'll be with you as soon as I can.'

Martin was not amused. He glanced at his watch. 'This is very annoying. I'm pressed for time as it is. No, I can't hang around at your convenience, Agon. I'll just have to cancel.' And swinging around he headed back towards the clubhouse.

'I'm not going to be very popular with my employers,' said Agon, giving Thanet a baleful glance. 'I'm sure he'll be making a complaint.'

'I'm sorry to have inconvenienced you,' said Thanet. 'But I don't think you quite appreciate the seriousness of the matter. A woman has died, Mr Agon, and we have to try to find out how and why.'

'No need to get up on your high horse,' said Agon. 'Just let's get it over with as quickly as possible, shall we, before my next session is due to start. I don't want any more trouble.' He drank off the rest of his lemonade and put the glass down with an angry thump.

'We were talking about when you went to fetch your swimming trunks from the car,' said Lineham.

'So?'

'So we want you to think very carefully indeed,' said Thanet.

'About what?'

'Precisely what you saw and heard when you were crossing the courtyard.'

Agon shrugged. 'Nothing special.'

Thanet inwardly cursed Martin's arrival. Before, Agon had been reasonably cooperative. Now, smarting from his client's reaction, resentment was making him impatient and antagonistic. And Thanet himself hadn't helped, by being sarcastic just now. A climb-down was necessary.

'Please, sir, we really would be grateful if you'd cast your mind back and try to remember. Even the smallest thing would help.'

Agon stared at him, clearly torn between maintaining his hostile stance and getting rid of them quickly by cooperating. Prudence won. His tone changed. 'Sorry, Inspector, but I really don't think I can help you. I just went straight to the car, got my swimming stuff out, and went back to the pool house.'

'Perhaps it would help if you shut your eyes and tried to visualise the scene,' suggested Lineham.

Agon sighed and rolled his eyes, but complied. After a minute or two he said slowly, 'I think . . .'

'What?' Lineham was trying not to sound too eager.

'I'm not sure, but I think the lights were on in the kitchen.'

'And?'

'I just have the impression of someone moving about in there.'

'Would you try hard to recall who it was?'

Agon was silent for a moment longer, then shook his head and opened his eyes. 'No, sorry. It was just a vague impression and I should think I took it for granted it would be Virginia. But I certainly couldn't say for sure. I wasn't paying much attention. If I'd known it was going to be important . . .'

Familiar words indeed. Now it was Thanet's turn to sigh. Time to change tack and if he wanted to steer the interview in the way he wished it to go, it would have to be an oblique approach. He glanced at Lineham. *I'll take over now, Mike.* He knew Lineham wouldn't mind, would appreciate that he simply wanted to follow a particular line of questioning.

'How long have you been working here, sir?'

'Since last October. There's one indoor court, which we use during the winter months. A lot of people like to brush up on their strokes during the winter.'

'Virginia Mintar for one, I believe.'

Not surprisingly, perhaps, Agon's eyes grew wary. 'I did coach her for a short time earlier in the year, yes.'

'So you'd have some idea what she was like, as a person.'

'I suppose.'

'It's just that it would be useful to have an impartial view of her, from someone outside the family circle.'

Agon seemed to relax. 'You see all sorts here, and she was one of the obsessive types.'

'How do you mean?'

'Obsessive about exercise. She practically lived here – came every single day, weekends included. And not just for a quick swim. No, it would be forty-five minutes in the gym or on the tennis court and then another forty-five doing lengths in the pool.'

'We understand, from talking to other people, that Mrs Mintar was – it's difficult to put this tactfully – very interested in the opposite sex.'

'You can't expect me to gossip about members' private lives.'

Oh no? thought Thanet. Well, there were other ways of getting Agon to do just that. Time for the gloves to come off. 'And you yourself are, as I'm sure you're aware, a good-looking young man.' Deliberately, Thanet glanced across at the girl who had spoken to Agon earlier. The implication was clear, but just to be sure Agon got the message he added, 'It was quite interesting watching your coaching methods just now.'

'Now hang on a minute, what are you implying?'

'Just that two and two often make four. Mrs Mintar liked men, you're an attractive man, therefore—'

'Stop right there, Inspector. I do have some discrimination, you know. Virginia was *middle-aged*, for God's sake.'

'But still very attractive. And a lot of men like older women.'

'Well, I'm not one of them! Why eat mutton when you

151

can have lamb? That's what I always say. And believe me, there's plenty of lamb available around here.'

Poor Rachel. What have you got yourself into? 'I'd hardly expect you to admit it, would I? After all, sir, just think about it. You were actually there in the courtyard, alone, at the time she disappeared—'

'I wasn't the only one to have the opportunity!' exploded Agon.

His raised voice made heads turn and noticing this he leaned forward and hissed, 'There were plenty of others who did. I've been thinking about it and as I told you, every single one of them came back to the pool alone. And if you really want me to point a finger in the right direction, look no further than next door to the Mintars.'

Thank you, thought Thanet. It had been only too easy. 'You're surely not implying that there was something going on between Dr Squires and Mrs Mintar? She was his patient, I believe.'

'Precisely! But patient or not, it was common knowledge amongst the staff here. Not that he and Virginia weren't discreet, they were, but you could tell, all right. Dr Squires comes here every day too, to work out. I suppose it was inevitable they'd get together sooner or later. As you say, Virginia was man-mad and her old man seems to spend more time away than at home. I hate to say this about someone who was going to be my mother-in-law, but the story is, she'd worked her way through most of the available men in the Club.'

'Anyone in particular?'

'Not since I was here. It's been the doctor for months. He'd really have been for it, if anyone had blown the whistle on them. I thought he was crazy, putting himself at risk like that. But he couldn't seem to help himself. I've seen it all before. If a woman like that gets under your skin ... I steer clear of them, I can tell you. You should have seen the way she was carrying on that night, making eyes at her own sister's boyfriend!'

152

'How did Dr Squires react to that?'

'Jealous as hell. He couldn't hide it, even though his wife was there, sitting at the same table! And Virginia's sister wasn't too impressed either, I gather.'

'What do you mean?'

'Rachel overheard her aunt and Arnold arguing about it, when she went up to change. She said Jane was really upset, sounded as though she was in tears. I'm telling you, it's not surprising Virginia ended up the way she did.'

'He's right, isn't he?' said Lineham as they walked back to the car. 'It isn't really surprising, is it?' Then, with a sideways glance at Thanet, 'D'you really think Agon might have had something to do with it?'

'I doubt it. I was just trying to needle him into telling us about Squires and Virginia.'

'And you succeeded, too. He was desperate to point the finger anywhere but at himself.'

'Yes. All the same, I don't think we ought to rule him out.'

'Cold-hearted bastard, isn't he, sir? "I prefer lamb to mutton", indeed. And "there's plenty of lamb available around here, believe me"! I suppose that's what Rachel is. A lamb to the slaughter, more like, poor kid. Are you still calling me a cynic, as far as he's concerned?'

'I have to concede there, Mike.'

'I tell you what did occur to me, sir, while you were questioning him.'

They had reached the car and they got in.

'What?'

'That we might just be wrong about Digby being the blackmailer. Seems to me Agon's such a nasty bit of work he'd fit the bill nicely.'

'The thought did cross my mind, I must admit. If we're wrong about Digby, that's where we'll focus next. But I still think Digby's the best bet, because of the photographs. I'm sure you're right about them having been developed and printed at home.' Thanet glanced at his watch. Eleven o'clock. Time was getting on, if they wanted that search warrant. 'Surely we ought to have heard from Doc Mallard by now?'

'He did say he'd ring, as soon as they were through.'

'What time's our appointment with Mrs Amos?'

'Eleven-fifteen.'

'And where does she live?'

'Badger's Close in Bickenden.'

The next village. 'We're in comfortable time, then.' Thanet debated with himself whether or not to ring Mallard, but decided against it. If Mallard had said he would ring as soon as he could, he would. 'Right, Mike. Let's go.'

THIRTEEN

The three impressive modern houses in Badger's Close, Bickenden, had obviously been built in the former grounds of an older house which now looked distinctly forlorn in its truncated garden. They were constructed of traditional building materials – rosy red brick and Kentish peg tiles, their double garages disguised as farm buildings in dark-stained wood. An incongruous touch was that the gardens of each were surrounded by a high brick wall with spiked railings on top, terminating in tall wrought-iron gates with an intercom system built into one of the brick pillars which flanked them. A sign of the times, Thanet supposed.

'Oh ye-e-s!' said Lineham in admiration. 'Now one of those would just suit me down to the ground!'

'Hard luck, Mike. You missed your chance, last year.'

When old Mrs Lineham had been agitating to move in with the young couple, the carrot had been that she and Lineham would both sell their houses and put the money together to buy just such a house as these.

Lineham said nothing but they both knew that it would have been too high a price to pay.

On the gatepost of Mrs Amos's house was a small, neat notice: 'Susan A. Designs'.

'What does she design?' said Thanet.

'No idea. But she did say she'd be in her studio, around the back.'

155

Interesting, thought Thanet. That was one preconception out of the window. He hadn't given much thought to Virginia Mintar's friend, but had nevertheless assumed that she would have enjoyed much the same hedonistic lifestyle. He certainly hadn't expected her to be a working woman with her own business. How often had he told his men never to make assumptions? The truth was, one made them automatically, without even realising one was doing so. Perhaps there were further surprises in store.

After a brief exchange over the intercom the gates swung slowly open and they followed the path which led around one side of the house. Here there was a single-storey projecting wing similar to that in which old Mrs Mintar lived, but smaller in scale. Thanet guessed that Susan Amos had adapted a granny annexe for her own use.

And yes, the woman who opened the door did not fit his mental picture of her. He had expected someone slim, elegant, well groomed and carefully made up, and Susan Amos was none of these things. Scruffy jeans strained across over-large hips and thighs, her dark hair was an untidy bush as if she had spent the morning running her hands through it and her face was devoid of make-up. Not surprisingly she looked as though she had scarcely slept the last two nights and her manner as she invited them in was subdued. The one striking thing about her was the beautiful knitted jacket she was wearing. Tutored by Joan, who loved such things but could rarely afford them, Thanet recognised that this was no chainstore creation. A knitwear designer, then? He remembered that years ago he had interviewed an actress who utilised her 'resting' periods by knitting picture sweaters, at a time when such things were fashionable. He had bought one for Joan, and still remembered her delight when he had presented it to her.

His first glimpse of Susan Amos's studio confirmed his guess. Around the walls were pinned sketches of sweaters and jackets, with swatches of wool attached, and one whole side of the studio up to shoulder height was taken up by what he guessed was a custom-made fitment of drawers labelled with the names of all the colours of the rainbow. One of the lower drawers stood open, displaying an astounding array of green wool in every hue, tone and texture. Above the unit four samples of her finished work were displayed on a neutral background. They were truly stunning. One jacket in particular caught his eye. A brilliant kaleidoscope of summer flowers danced across a background of many shades and textures of deep blue, purple, and rich, dark greens. There and then he made up his mind. He would buy it for Joan for Christmas, regardless of the cost. She would absolutely love it!

'Sir?' Lineham was looking at him expectantly.

'Oh, sorry. I was admiring your work, Mrs Amos. It's beautiful.'

She smiled briefly. 'Thank you. Do sit down.' She gestured at a couple of upright chairs and returned to the chair in front of a computer, its screen filled by a screensaver of shooting stars.

'Thank you for agreeing to see us.'

Lineham's mobile rang. He excused himself and went out.

Doc Mallard? Thanet wondered. Best not to start the interview until the sergeant returned, in case they had to break off. Anyway, perched on the edge of her chair with her legs twisted around each other and her hands clasped together so tightly that the knuckles showed white, Mrs Amos looked so tense that she would almost certainly be incapable of talking about Virginia in the way he had hoped. He would spend the time trying to get her to relax.

'We'll just wait, to start, until my sergeant comes back. Meanwhile, I hope you don't mind my asking, but what sort of prices do you charge? That jacket, for instance . . . ?'

157

Ouch! he thought, as she told him. 'Do you sell direct, or only through retail outlets?'

'No, I sell direct too. Some of my customers come back over and over again.'

'I can imagine.' He hesitated. Would it be unprofessional to broach the subject now? Was it possible that such a request could be construed as an inducement to talk freely? No, surely not. There was absolutely no indication whatsoever that Mrs Amos was involved in Virginia's death. Still, perhaps he ought to wait, come back another time? But then he might risk losing the jacket to another customer. He glanced at it again, wavering. He could just *see* Joan in it. He made up his mind. 'Look, I know this is absolutely nothing to do with the reason for our visit, but would you be willing to sell that one to me? I know my wife would absolutely love it.'

She smiled again, more warmly, this time. 'Of course. I do run a business, after all.'

'We can attend to the details later, then.' Thanet glanced at the door. Lineham was taking longer than he had expected. 'Do you knit your designs yourself?'

'Oh no, I'd never have time. I employ a number of experienced knitters. Most of them love knitting but have run out of people to knit for, so to speak. And I also have a part-time secretary.'

'And you do your designing on the computer?'

'Yes. I took the plunge last year and I must say it's absolutely wonderful. It's so easy to alter and adjust until you get everything exactly right.' She was loosening up perceptibly, relieved perhaps that he hadn't dived straight into talking about Virginia. 'Look, I'll show you.' And she swung her chair around to face the screen.

Thanet got up and went to stand beside her.

'This is the design I'm working on at the moment. The beauty of this software package is that each element of the design is laid on to one transparent sheet, so to speak, and can be positioned wherever I like on the screen.' She was demonstrating as she talked. 'You see? And if I want to remove it, I can sort of peel it off, without affecting the rest of the design. Like this.'

'Amazing!' said Thanet.

'It means I never have to—'

Lineham came back into the room. 'Sorry to interrupt, sir, but could I have a word?'

Thanet excused himself and they went outside, Thanet eager to hear what the sergeant had to say. There was a familiar air of suppressed excitement about Lineham which must denote some interesting new development. Knowing the sergeant so well, however, he guessed that Lineham would keep it until last. He was right.

Apparently Doc Mallard had rung to confirm the opinion given after his initial inspection of Virginia's body: death had been due to asphyxia by drowning and she had probably been unconscious when she hit the water, due to the severe blow to the side of her forehead.

That was a relief, thought Thanet. Ever since Virginia's body had been found he had been haunted by the fear that if only he'd had the well searched on Saturday night, she might have been found alive. But if she had been unconscious when she went in it was more than likely that she was dead even before he first arrived on the scene.

The injury, Lineham was saying, was consistent with her head having struck the stone coping and no doubt blood samples taken at the time would confirm this.

'We hope,' said Thanet. 'Come on, Mike, spit it out, there's something more, isn't there? I can tell.'

'Bruises,' said Lineham with satisfaction. 'On both arms, just above her wrists. Fingermarks, in fact. Doc M. reckons someone grabbed her with force. We couldn't see them when they brought her up out of the well because she was wearing that long-sleeved blouse.'

Thanet had a sudden, vivid mental picture of Virginia at that moment, the wet silk of blouse and pants clinging to every luscious curve of her body.

'And there's another on her right hip,' Lineham was saying. 'The Doc wouldn't commit himself, you know what he's like, but he did agree that it was consistent with her having been shoved against the coping, just before she went over.'

So it was as they thought. Virginia had been attacked, and with some violence, too. It gave Thanet no satisfaction to know this, except insofar as any uncertainty about the manner of her death had now been removed. 'Not much doubt about it then, is there?' he said grimly.

Swiftly he arranged for an application for the warrant to search Digby's house to be made and then they returned to Susan Amos.

She was in exactly the same position as when Thanet had left her and he guessed she had done nothing in the interval except stare blankly at the screen.

She swung slowly back around as they entered and shook her head. 'I simply can't believe that Virginia is dead. I just don't understand how it can have happened.'

'That's what we're determined to find out,' said Thanet.

His new sense of purpose must have shown in his tone of voice because she looked at him sharply. 'What do you mean?' She glanced from him to Lineham. 'Something's happened, hasn't it?'

'It's just been confirmed that Mrs Mintar's death was no accident – that there was a struggle before she was thrown down the well.'

Her eyes widened with shock and her hand flew up to her throat. 'Oh no,' she whispered. 'Oh God, Ginny ... How awful. How terrible ...' She reached blindly into her pocket for a handkerchief as tears suddenly welled up and overflowed, then swung her chair around so that her back was towards them.

Thanet gave her a few minutes and then said, 'Mrs Amos, I can see how upset you are, but we really do need your help. When we arranged this appointment we only suspected what we now know for certain.'

160

She wiped her eyes, blew her nose and swivelled back to face them, making a visible effort to pull herself together. 'What is it you want from me?'

'We're trying to gather together as much information as possible about Mrs Mintar – we'll call her Virginia too, if you don't mind, to distinguish her from her mother-in-law – and we understand that you and she had been friends for some time.'

She nodded. 'We do go back a long way. We were at school together.'

'So tell us about her,' said Thanet softly.

Susan Amos stared at him, blew her nose once more and put her handkerchief away. Then she raked back her hair in what was clearly an habitual gesture. 'Most people didn't understand her, you know. They just saw what Virginia wanted them to see, the social butterfly who lived for pleasure. But she wasn't like that at all underneath.'

'What was she like?'

Susan hesitated. 'Vulnerable,' she said at last. 'And that was why she put up such a smokescreen. She felt she couldn't afford to let people know that, or they'd hurt her.'

'Why? Had something specific happened, to make her feel that way?'

Susan gave him a long, penetrating look. Clearly she was wondering how much to tell him.

Thanet waited and then, when she did not continue, said, 'I can see you're wondering how on earth this can be relevant to Virginia's death, but believe me, it might well be.'

But she still held back and he leaned forward and said softly, 'Mrs Amos. Sometime on Saturday night Virginia must have said or done something to precipitate what happened to her. The more we learn about her and the better we get to understand her, the more likely it is that we might work out what that something was. And that might help us to find out who killed her.'

She thought about what he had said for a moment or two and then stood up. 'Right,' she said. 'I'll do whatever I can to help, of course I will. But it's obviously going to take some time. Would you like some coffee? I could do with a cup myself.'

She needed an interval in which to recover from the shock, Thanet realised. 'Thank you,' he said.

In a few minutes she returned with a tray bearing a cafetière and three mugs.

'Real coffee!' said Thanet, pleased to see that she looked much calmer. 'What a treat.'

She waited until they were all settled and then she sat back, nursing her mug in both hands.

'You asked if anything specific had happened to make her so vulnerable. And the answer is yes, several things. The first, to my knowledge anyway, was when we were fourteen. You have to understand that Virginia absolutely adored her father. He always made a tremendous fuss of her, taking her on outings, buying her presents and so on. He was so good-looking, too, real romantic hero stuff, we all used to swoon over him . . . Then suddenly, without warning, he just walked out on them – on Virginia and her mother – and they never saw him again. Virginia was absolutely shattered, I can tell you. She always felt it must have been her fault – children often do in those circumstances, I believe.'

'Why? Had she been giving him a hard time?'

'No worse than most teenagers, I imagine. But she couldn't see it that way.'

'She must have realised her parents weren't getting on, surely?' said Lineham.

'Apparently not. I think half the trouble was that her mother was such a doormat he left out of sheer boredom. And that's why Virginia was so unprepared for it to happen, why it was such a shattering experience for her. I mean, if there had been endless rows it wouldn't have been such a shock, would it?'

'And he said nothing to her about leaving, before he went?' Couldn't face her, probably, thought Thanet. What a coward!

'Not a hint. She just went home one day and found he'd gone, moved out lock, stock and barrel. She couldn't believe what her mother was telling her. Apparently she ran straight upstairs to her parents' bedroom and threw open the doors to his wardrobe. And it was completely empty. "There wasn't even a hanger left!" she said, when she was telling me about it later, and the tears were pouring down her face. "It's almost as though he never existed."'

'Poor kid,' said Lineham. 'What a rotten thing to do.'

'She just went to pieces at school. She was quite bright, you know, there'd even been talk of accelerated O levels, but her work took a nose-dive and never recovered. She just couldn't concentrate, used to spend all her time staring out of the window. And nothing any of the teachers said to her made any difference. To give them credit, they really did try to help her, to make allowances, but it didn't help in the slightest. No, I don't think she ever got over it. And it certainly changed her.'

'In what way?'

'Until then she'd always been a carefree, happy-go-lucky sort of person, very lively and cheerful. After her father left, she was much quieter, more withdrawn. Well, that was understandable, of course. But then a bit later on she changed again. She became, well, rather wild, I suppose. She didn't seem to care whether she got into trouble at school, no matter how many warnings or punishments she was given, and at home she was so rude to her mother I really felt sorry for the poor woman. Eventually the girls at school got fed up with it, started to avoid her and give her the cold shoulder, and one day I said to her, "Look, Ginny, if you go on like this you'll soon have no friends left. I've just about had enough myself." And that did seem to make a difference. But in some respects that attitude never left her.'

'Behaving as if she didn't care what people thought, you mean?'

'Yes.'

'And as if she didn't care how her behaviour affected them?' said Thanet gently. He knew it might be difficult for Susan to admit this, if true.

And indeed, she did hesitate before saying with a sigh, 'I suppose so, yes.'

'And am I right in thinking this especially applied to men?'

Susan gave him one of those long looks. 'I really don't like doing this, you know.'

'Yes, I do know. I'm sure I'd feel exactly the same if it were my closest friend who'd been killed. It's somehow all right to talk about their good points but not to reveal their weaknesses. It's not only that we feel disloyal or as though we're talking about them behind their backs, but also that the dead can't defend themselves. They have no right of reply.'

'That's it, exactly.' She sat in silence for a minute or two and Thanet let her. If Susan was to continue to talk freely it would only be by her own choice. At last she stirred and said, 'I still can't believe she's dead. She was such a . . . vibrant person. It's so sad, to think of all that vitality just . . . snuffed out.' Her tears had started to flow again and she dabbed at them impatiently. 'I'm sorry. This doesn't help, I know. What were you asking me, before we digressed?'

'About Virginia's attitude to men.'

She compressed her lips and shook her head. 'There's no point in pretending she treated them well. She didn't. In fact, I often wondered . . .'

'What?'

'If she was paying out the male sex in general for what her father did to her.'

'Not an unusual thing to happen, I believe.'

'And it was so easy for her, too. You didn't know her, but she had this sort of magnetic attraction. Men couldn't resist her. I've seen it happen over and over again. And she couldn't resist trying to prove her power over them. It's as if she was driven to it. She told me once, she regarded every new man who came along as a challenge. And when she was tired of them, she just dropped them. I think it was almost a matter of principle with her, to be the first one to end the affair. I don't think she ever truly loved any one of them, in fact I'm not sure if she was capable of it. It was so sad, really. She never knew what loving someone was really like. There was something in her which made her hold back – the fear of rejection, I suppose. She told me once that she hoped she never would fall in love because she simply couldn't bear the thought of the pain she would have to endure if he left her.'

And when she was tired of them, she just dropped them. A recipe for disaster if ever there was one, thought Thanet.

'What about her husband?' said Lineham.

'She was fond of Ralph, I'm sure, but her relationship with him was different. She would never have left him, he was her anchor, and she needed him. All the same, it was almost as if . . . How shall I put it? Almost as if she was constantly driven to test him, to see if he, too, would finally give up on her and leave. From little things she said I'm certain she felt guilty about it, but she couldn't seem to stop.'

'And did he ever show any sign of leaving her?'

Susan shook her head. 'No. I think Ralph understood her very well. Also, he's pretty realistic. His job takes him away for months at a time, as I'm sure you know, and he was well aware that Ginny wasn't the sort of girl to sit around twiddling her thumbs while she waited for him to come home. As long as she was still there when he did, that was all that mattered to him.'

'Even so, it couldn't have been easy for him, to sit by while his wife flirted with other men.'

'If you're thinking Ralph could have pushed her down that well, forget it. He'd never have hurt her. Never.'

Thanet could see that there was no point in pursuing that line. 'So, her father's abandonment affected her deeply. But you said there were other things . . .'

'Two, in fact.'

'So what were they?'

FOURTEEN

Susan stood up and stretched, placing her palms as support on the small of her back and leaning backwards. 'Sorry, I get so stiff, sitting,' she said.

Thanet knew how she felt. How many thousands of times had he himself tried to ease an aching back with just that movement? He had suffered from back problems for years and although regular visits to the chiropractor ensured that the pain was never as severe or chronic as it had once been, he could nevertheless sympathise with a fellow sufferer.

'I think I'll stand up for a while,' she said. She walked across to the window and leaned against the sill, facing them. 'If you want to understand Ginny you have to appreciate that although you wouldn't have expected it, from looking at her, she was in fact a very maternal person. Her children mattered to her more than anyone or anything else. And she was a brilliant mother – patient, loving, willing to take endless trouble on their behalf. That was why what happened was so tragic.'

'Caroline's elopement, you mean?' said Lineham.

'That too, later, yes. But you obviously don't know about the baby . . . ? No? Well, Ginny was only eighteen when she got married. It was January 1976. I remember that because I'd just gone up to university, the previous September. Ginny had failed most of her O levels and left school at sixteen, but somehow we never lost touch. She wasn't qualified for anything, of course, but she did look gorgeous and had a great sense of style, so she got a job in an exclusive little boutique, which seemed to suit her very well. Anyway, to cut a long story short she met Ralph and they got married. His mother wasn't too happy about it. I expect you'll have gathered that she and Ginny didn't exactly hit it off, and of course Ginny was very young. I think what sugared the pill as far as Mrs Mintar senior was concerned was Ralph's suggestion that he and Ginny take over Windmill Court and convert that single-storey wing of outbuildings into a self-contained flat for her. Apparently ever since Ralph's father died she'd been complaining about the inconvenience of maintaining that house, especially as she was away such a lot on her plant-finding expeditions. I suppose she felt she had to keep it ticking over for Ralph's sake.

'Anyway, Ginny became pregnant right away and to my surprise she was delighted about it, told me she felt that at last she'd have someone of her very own to love. But sadly it all went wrong. The baby was born severely handicapped – its brain hadn't developed properly – and it only lived for a few hours. Ginny was devastated.'

Please God that wouldn't happen to Bridget's baby! Once again Thanet was having to force himself to concentrate. The mere mention of babies these days sent his mind scurrying off to that bed in the maternity ward where his daughter was lying, helplessly awaiting developments.

'I was away at university at the time, of course, and didn't see her until Christmas, by which time she was pregnant again – against her doctor's advice, I might add. However, all went well and Caroline was born. Ginny was ecstatic, but I don't think she ever got over losing the first one. She was a girl, too. And of course, that's why she's worked for MENCAP all these years.'

'She worked for MENCAP? We didn't know that.'

'She didn't exactly shout about it but she's been on the committee ever since. She was particularly good at fund-raising. And once a week she'd go along to the Wednesday club – that's a social evening where mentally handicapped adults mix with ordinary people. They have Scottish dancing and play simple games. If you'd seen Ginny there . . . I think she felt that any one of them could have been the baby she lost. And they all adored her.'

So, thought Thanet. Over twenty years of selfless commitment. An entirely new light on Virginia's character.

'But then, of course,' said Susan, leaving the windowsill to return to her chair, 'came the next disaster, Caroline's elopement. You've obviously heard about that. And this time . . . You've seen all the stuff piled up in Ginny's room, I imagine?'

Thanet nodded.

'After Caroline went it was as if . . .' Susan shook her head sorrowfully. 'You know I said Ginny went haywire after her father left? Well this time it was ten times worse, as if she'd finally flipped. She seemed to lose all restraint, take all the brakes off, so that everything she did was over the top. The shopping is a typical example. She'd always loved clothes and enjoyed buying them but now, well, you'll have seen for yourself, it was a compulsion, an obsession, a sickness. She'd always enjoyed going to the Health Club, but now it wasn't just a daily twenty-minute swim it was three-quarters of an hour or an hour – on top of a session in the gym or an hour's tennis. And as for—' Susan broke off.

Thanet guessed what she had been going to say. 'As for men . . . ?'

Susan pressed her lips together as if to forbid herself to elaborate, but it was obvious that Thanet had hit the mark.

'But Caroline's elopement was – how long ago?' said Lineham. 'Four years?'

Susan nodded.

'You'd have thought she'd have begun to get over it by now.'

'Precisely. But that was the trouble. She didn't. If anything she was getting worse.'

'Didn't anyone suggest she tried to get help?' said Thanet.

'Of course! I know Ralph did, because she told me so. And God knows I tried often enough. But she just wouldn't listen, didn't want to know. "Stop fussing, Sue," she'd say. "I'm perfectly all right!"'

'What about Mr Mintar?' said Thanet. 'How did he react to Caroline's elopement?'

'Well, that was half the trouble, of course. Caroline was Ralph's favourite, you see, no doubt about that, so it must have hit him really hard too. But he just isn't one to wear his heart on his sleeve and his way of coping was simply to shut out the memory of her altogether. He said as far as he was concerned she had made her bed and she would have to lie on it. He didn't want to hear her name mentioned again.'

'Impossible, surely!' said Lineham.

'Maybe. But it certainly didn't help Ginny – or Rachel either, for that matter – to have to pretend Caro had never existed. If Ginny and Ralph had been able to, well, grieve together, it would have helped her no end, I'm sure. As it was she just had to bottle it all up most of the time and I think that was why this bizarre behaviour began to build up. I kept hoping that she would gradually adjust, come to terms with the fact that Caroline was gone for good, but she never could. She even employed a private detective to try and track her down at one time, you know, but it was no good. The pair of them seemed to have vanished into thin air. And lately, of course, this business with Rachel hasn't helped. Neither she nor Ralph were happy about Rachel's latest choice of boyfriend. Poor Ginny! Rachel only got back from a year away in Switzerland in June, and Ginny was so looking forward to having her home again. She hadn't wanted her to go away to finishing school in the first place, but Ralph insisted. And then, before she'd been back five minutes, Rachel had taken up with this tennis coach.'

'He's her fiancé now. They apparently got engaged on Saturday night, broke the news to Rachel's parents that evening.'

'Oh no!' Susan breathed. 'Engaged. Oh, my God. How did Ginny and Ralph react, do you know?'

'Opened a bottle of champagne, I gather.'

'They had no choice, I imagine. What else could they do? They wouldn't have dared risk driving Rachel away too. Oh, poor Ginny,' Susan repeated. 'It's unbelievable. Absolutely the last thing she needed.'

Had he known all this before, Thanet thought, he might have been more willing to accept that Virginia had thrown herself down that well in despair. But the conclusion to be drawn from those bruises left little room for doubt.

'Why didn't Virginia like Rachel's boyfriend? Did she say?'

'She thought Rachel was too young for a serious relationship with anyone, but apart from that, she didn't trust him, thought he had an eye to the main chance and probably saw Rachel as a good prospect. He hasn't a penny to his name, I believe. Also, she thought he was too free with his attentions to other young women at the Club. He'd been around for a while before Rachel came home, and Ginny had had plenty of opportunity to observe him.'

'He gave her some coaching, I believe.'

'Did he? That must have been when I was away. Our elder daughter lives in New Zealand and we went over there for an extended trip last winter, didn't get back until April.'

'Wasn't that difficult for your business?'

'It did require a colossal amount of organisation before I went, to keep things ticking over in my absence. But

171

you have to get your priorities right. My daughter was expecting her first baby and there were problems.'

Babies again, thought Thanet. They seemed to crop up all the time. 'Everything was all right, I hope?'

She looked surprised that he had asked. 'Yes. After a few traumas on the way.'

'Good ... Virginia didn't by any chance hint that there'd been anything between her and Matthew Agon, did she?' If there had been, it would have been to Susan that Virginia would have been most likely to mention it.

She laughed. 'Oh no. He was much too young. She wasn't in favour of toy-boys, as she called them, thought it would be degrading to have everyone pointing and whispering.'

'But she wasn't averse to causing gossip, surely. We understand her affair with Dr Squires is common knowledge at the Health Club.'

'So you know about that. Well, that's different. Matt Agon is young enough to be her son, isn't he? Frankly, I think Howard Squires was absolutely crazy to carry on with a patient like that, but there you are. Some men seem to lose all common sense when they get involved with a woman like Ginny. But that's their affair, isn't it?'

'When did she become involved with him, do you know?'

'Not really. While I was away. It was certainly going strong by the time I got back.'

'Several months ago at least, then. From what you said, about her always liking to be the one to end the affair, it was due to come to an end soon.'

'I agree. And if he does get away with it, he'll be a lucky man. Let's hope he has more common sense in future.'

'She didn't by any chance tell you she was going to break it off with him, did she?' If she had, thought Thanet, what stronger motive could they look for? The prospect of losing her, together with the outrageous way in which she had flirted with her sister's boyfriend on

Saturday night, might have been enough to provoke a row in which Squires might have lost his temper.

But Susan was shaking her head. 'But that doesn't mean she didn't. My God, do you think that's what might have happened?' She was looking aghast.

'At the moment we have absolutely no idea. It's all pure speculation. There are a number of possibilities.'

'Well, I hope you get him, whoever he is!' she cried, suddenly passionate. 'I may not always have approved of her behaviour, but she hasn't had an easy time and she certainly didn't deserve this!'

'No,' said Thanet, his tone sombre. 'Of course she didn't.' He rose. 'I think we've taken up enough of your time, Mrs Amos. You've been immensely helpful. Er . . . Before I go . . . ?' And he nodded at the jacket he had chosen.

'Oh, of course.'

The negotiation was swiftly completed. 'Christmas shopping,' Thanet said to Lineham with a somewhat shamefaced grin as they walked back to the car.

'Already? You'll be buying your Christmas cards in the January sales next!'

'Joan'll love it. I didn't want to miss the chance.'

'Just pulling your leg, sir. Bet it was a bit pricey, though.'

'It's good to push the boat out from time to time,' said Thanet, trying not to think just how far he'd pushed it this time. Anyway, he didn't care. He was delighted with his purchase. He glanced at his watch. Twenty past twelve. 'We'll go back to the Dog and Thistle for a bite to eat, before meeting the Super.'

They carried their drinks outside to a table on the wide pavement again. Here beneath the trees they were at least shaded from the fierce heat of the noonday sun. Considering himself briefly off duty, Thanet loosened his tie and undid the top button of his shirt, making a mental note to remember to do it up again. It wouldn't do for the Super to catch him like this. Draco, he was sure, would not allow himself such laxity under any circumstances.

While they waited for the food to arrive they were silent, mulling over the interview with Susan Amos.

'I still can't believe that Mr Mintar was perfectly happy for his wife to carry on like that,' said Lineham eventually.

'Difficult to accept, I agree.'

'And you know what they say about worms turning.' Lineham was warming to his theme. 'Maybe the provocation on Saturday was just too much. Perhaps the pressure had been building up all day. The four of them had been out together earlier, remember, to Sissinghurst. What if she'd been making a play for Mr Prime then, too?'

'Possible, I agree.'

'So Mr Mintar may already have been angry with her, before the dinner party even started. And then on top of all that there was the shock of Rachel's engagement and the strain of having to go through the charade of being pleased . . . Maybe that's it, sir! Maybe he thought that in view of this latest development, they had to act quickly if they were to get rid of Agon before his position became too entrenched. He'd been wanting to pay him off, remember, but his wife was against it. Maybe he grabbed the first opportunity to tackle her about it, while everyone was off changing. We've only his word that he was in his study the whole time. So maybe he went back, had a row with her about it and suddenly it was all too much and he just snapped . . .'

'Could have happened like that, I agree.'

The food arrived and they tucked in. Lineham had chosen the bacon and mushroom baguettes again, while Thanet had opted for home-cooked roast beef with English mustard. It was good, too, the meat thickly sliced and succulent, the mustard freshly made.

'Mmm. I must bring Louise here sometime,' said Lineham. 'Of course,' he went on, 'you could argue that a lot of this applies to Virginia's sister, too. She might have had enough, as well. After all, from what Mr Prime said, it was far from the first time Virginia had had a go at pinching Jane's boyfriends – and had usually succeeded too, by the sound of it, to the degree that she'd put off bringing him here to meet Virginia as long as she possibly could. Not surprising, I suppose. Jane's no oil painting is she?'

'I'll risk a cliché and say you shouldn't judge a book by its cover, Mike.'

'Maybe. But when a woman like Virginia throws herself at you, it must be a big temptation.'

'Obviously one that Prime was strong-minded enough to resist.'

'But Jane wasn't to know that, was she? After all, she's no spring chicken. Maybe she felt Prime was her last chance, and imagined him slipping away from her like others had done in the past. Rachel told Agon that Jane had been really upset, remember, that she'd heard her crying. And Jane and Prime were there for the whole weekend, there was all day Sunday yet to come. Maybe Jane felt she couldn't face it, if Virginia was going to carry on in the same way, and like we said decided to have it out with her. Marilyn Squires was pretty definite about her coming out of the door leading to the kitchen corridor.'

'If she was telling the truth.'

'You think she might not have been?'

'No, I'm inclined to believe her. Anyway, we'll have to interview Jane again, obviously. But it's just occurred to me . . .'

'What?' Lineham stopped chewing.

'Mr Mintar. I wonder how ambitious he is. His father was a High Court judge. What if he aspires to the Bench too?'

'I don't see what you're getting at.'

'Well, it sounds to me as though in that respect Virginia could have been a considerable liability.'

'The way she carried on with men, you mean?'

'Her blatant flirting, yes. Hardly proper behaviour for the wife of a prospective High Court judge, wouldn't you agree?'

'Are you suggesting he might deliberately have set out to kill her on Saturday?'

'No, not at all. But it could have been an underlying reason for him to have been fed up with her, don't you think?' Thanet was keeping an eye on the time. He wanted to be at the Mintars' house ahead of Draco. He did up his top button and tightened his tie. 'Come on, Mike, we'd better go. Mustn't keep the Super waiting, must we? No,' he went on as they walked to the car, 'I think that whoever committed this crime did it on the spur of the moment.'

'I agree,' said Lineham. 'But to change the subject, I wonder how long it'll take to get that search warrant.'

'I expect it'll have come through by the time we've finished at the Mintars'. By the way, I've been thinking, Mike.'

'What?'

'Young Rachel. I feel sorry for her. She's had a rotten time. She's obviously still very upset about losing her sister, you could tell from her behaviour the night before last, and now, on top of that, this terrible thing has happened to her mother.'

'So? We're doing all we can.'

'To find out who was responsible for the murder, yes. But what about Caroline?'

'You want to have another shot at finding her?'

'Why not? It was four years ago, I know, which in one way will make things more difficult, as the trail will be cold. But in another way the lapse of time might help. For one thing she and young Swain might have become more careless as time has gone on, and not be taking as much trouble to cover their tracks. Also, her attitude might have changed, she might not be so hardened against

176

her parents now. And apart from anything else, she has a right to know what has happened to her mother. So yes, I'd say another effort is called for, wouldn't you?'

'Who'll you put on to it?'

'Tanya, I think. It'll give her something to get her teeth into.' Thanet was conscious of time ticking away. It was twenty past one already. Perhaps they had lingered too long over lunch. He had a sudden vision of Draco standing waiting for them in the courtyard, feet planted firmly apart, stopwatch in hand. 'Better put your foot down, Mike. We don't want to be late.'

FIFTEEN

It was twenty-five past one when they pulled up at the Mintars' house.

'No sign of the Super yet,' said Lineham.

'No,' said Thanet with satisfaction. He was watching Digby, who had just emerged from a door at the far end of the coach-house carrying a ball of green twine and a bundle of bamboo canes. At least they'd know where to find him when the search warrant came through.

At 1.30 precisely the car radio crackled into life. There was a message from Superintendent Draco: something had cropped up and he would be unable to keep their appointment. Instead, Inspector Thanet was expected to report to him for an update at five o'clock sharp.

'Bet he never intended to turn up,' said Lineham. 'Just keeping us on our toes, isn't he?'

'I'm not grumbling,' said Thanet, glad of the reprieve. Lineham was probably right.

'So, who first?' said Lineham as they got out of the car.

'Jane Simons, I think,' said Thanet. 'If we can find her, that is. And after that, Mr Mintar.'

The back door stood open but they had to knock twice before Mintar appeared, clutching a white linen napkin and looking even worse than he had yesterday. He was wearing the same clothes and Thanet guessed he had probably slept in them. There were food stains down the front of his shirt and he still hadn't shaved. Those who knew the dapper well-groomed QC only from his courtroom appearances would scarcely have recognised the man.

For a moment or two he stood looking blankly at Thanet as though he'd never seen him before and couldn't imagine what he was doing there. Then came a gleam of recognition. 'Oh, it's you, Thanet,' he said in a lifeless monotone. 'We were just finishing lunch.'

'I'd like another word with you later, sir, if you don't mind. But first, if I could speak to Miss Simons . . . ?'

Mintar seemed to rouse himself. 'I gather you've nothing of moment to tell me?' And suddenly he was his former self, fixing Thanet with that familiar penetrating stare.

'There was one thing, sir.' Thanet had intended waiting to impart this piece of information until the beginning of his interview but Mintar's question had put him on the spot. 'The PM took place this morning—'

'And?' The word shot out like a bullet.

Thanet told him about the bruising, their certainty that Virginia's death had been murder.

Mintar's face was bleak. 'I see,' he said, the words little more than a whisper. He turned away. 'I'll fetch my sister-in-law.'

'Taken a nose-dive hasn't he, sir?' said Lineham softly when he had gone. 'All the same, I wouldn't fancy having to face him in Court.'

'Better keep on the right side of the law then, hadn't you!'

It was a few minutes before Jane Simons appeared and Thanet guessed that Mintar had been breaking the news of the PM results to the others.

'You wanted to see me?' She was looking shaken but was much more composed than the last time they had seen her. The only residual hint of yesterday's tears was a slight puffiness around the eyes.

179

'Just one or two more questions,' said Thanet. 'I'm glad to see you're feeling a little better,' he added as they all sat down. No need as yet to be too heavy-handed, he decided. In any case, she would have had plenty of time to prepare her story. Prime would almost certainly have told her the gist of his conversation with them on the way into the village yesterday morning, including the fact that he had had to admit that he and Jane had returned separately to the pool. 'We've been talking to everyone who was present at the dinner party on Saturday,' he said, 'getting a clearer picture of the sequence of events that evening. Miss Simons, why did you and Mr Prime give us the impression that you returned to the pool together?'

She caught her lower lip beneath her teeth in an expression of troubled innocence. 'Yes, Arnold told me you'd got the wrong idea about that. I'm sorry. We didn't intend to mislead you.'

'We understand that you had an argument, while you were up in your room, and that you were rather upset.'

'My God,' she said, with a flash of hostility. 'You have been poking about, haven't you?'

'We've had to. Your sister is dead, Miss Simons, and it's our job to try to find out why.'

She compressed her lips. 'I know. I'm sorry.'

Genuinely contrite? Thanet wondered. Or merely politic?

'If you've picked up that much,' she said, 'you've probably gathered what the argument was about. I know you're not supposed to speak ill of the dead but I've always thought that a rather mealy-mouthed attitude. There's good and bad in all of us and my sister was no exception, as I'm sure you're finding out. That doesn't mean to say I wasn't fond of her, I was. She was my sister, after all. But there's no point in trying to deny that she was a terrible flirt. I honestly don't think she could help herself. She simply couldn't resist trying to charm every man who came along. And that, of course, included my boyfriend. I suppose I was taking my resentment of her behaviour out on him, poor man. Very unfair of me, I'd be the first to admit.'

'And you no doubt decided to take her to task about it?'

She lifted her heavy shoulders. She was wearing a sleeveless sundress and Thanet saw the muscles in her upper arms ripple. She could have tipped Virginia into that well with ease, he thought.

'Why deny it?' she said.

'So what did you do?'

'Finished changing, went down to the kitchen. I knew Ginny would still be there.'

Thanet's pulse accelerated. 'And was she?'

'No. I was surprised, I must admit. As I told you yesterday, she was a stickler for getting everything ship-shape. It wasn't like her to leave the clearing away half finished. It was only later, when we realised she was missing, that I began to wonder about it, think that perhaps she had been interrupted.'

'So what did you do?'

'Went on out to the pool, of course. If she wasn't there, too bad. What I had to say to her could wait.'

'You didn't look for her?'

'No. I assumed she'd decided to swim first, finish clearing up later, and had gone up to change. I couldn't be bothered to go back upstairs.'

'Did you look out of the kitchen window?'

'No. Why should I?'

'It didn't occur to you she might have gone outside?'

'It never entered my head! Ralph said he wondered if she might have gone out to finish watering the camellias – apparently Howard and Marilyn arrived before she'd finished – but I'm no gardener, haven't even got a window box, so the idea of going out to water the garden in the middle of entertaining guests? It's just too bizarre! No, I just glanced around, saw she wasn't there, and went out to join the others.'

'Please, would you try to think back . . . When you glanced around, did you see or even glimpse someone, something, anything out of that window? Any movement . . . ?'

'No!' she cried. 'Nothing! If I had, it would have caught my eye and I'd probably have paused to take a better look. But it was pretty dark by then, remember, and I was in a lighted room. I know there are lights in the courtyard but it would still be pretty dim out there, by comparison.' She paused. 'Even so, do you think if I had looked, I might have seen something? Been able to help her? Even perhaps have prevented it?' She gave Thanet a quick, agonised glance, then lowered her eyelids as if to prevent herself from reading an affirmative in his eyes.

Thanet shook his head. 'Impossible to tell, I'm afraid. We don't even know the precise time it happened.'

'I just can't take it in. I mean . . . murders are what happen to other people, aren't they? You read about them in the newspapers, or see them in the news on television. And although you might think oh, how awful, how dreadful, the *reality* of it doesn't come home to you. And then, when it does happen to someone close to you, that sense of unreality persists. I mean, you know it's happening but you still can't believe it. Do you see what I mean?' She paused and then said, 'You will catch him, Inspector, won't you?'

'We'll do our level best, believe me.' Thanet rose. 'Now, I was going to have a word with Mr Mintar.'

'Yes. He said to go along to his study. You know where it is?'

'Thank you. Yes.'

Mintar was sitting behind his desk, his expression grim, the cat on his lap. It turned its head to give them an enigmatic stare as they came in. Mintar waved a hand. 'Do sit down.' He was looking much more alert. No doubt the shock of hearing the post-mortem result had jolted him out of his earlier almost trance-like state.

When they were settled he said, 'So I was right. It was murder. Not that it gives me any satisfaction whatsoever to say so.' His hand was moving in long, regular strokes along the cat's back from the top of its head to the tip of its tail and its purrs were a basso profundo accompaniment to what he was saying. 'And as I also said yesterday, as the husband of the victim I suppose I am, like many an unfortunate wretch before me, the prime suspect.'

'One of them, yes.' Pointless to deny it.

'Since then I have of course begun to think more rationally about the whole business and realised what my wife was doing out there at that time of night. If you remember, I told you she asked me to remind her to finish the watering later. She was obsessive about those camellias.'

Mintar's gaze strayed to the photograph on the desk and briefly his icy self-control faltered: his voice grew husky and the skin of his face seemed to quiver, as if it were having difficulty in containing the emotions threatening to erupt from beneath the surface. He cleared his throat and held up his hand as Thanet opened his mouth to speak. 'No, let me finish. The other thing I wanted to say is that although, yesterday, I told you that I would be open and honest with you, hold nothing back, I was in fact less than frank, out of misplaced loyalty to my wife.'

It was obvious what Mintar was referring to, but he had nothing to lose by taking the initiative. He must have realised that it wouldn't take Thanet long to put two and two together. 'You're referring to your wife's affair with Dr Squires.' A statement, not a question.

Mintar sighed. 'So you already know. I might have guessed. But I said "misplaced" because I've come to the conclusion that in the circumstances, in some topsy-turvy way I actually owe it to her to speak of it. Whoever killed her has to be found and I vehemently deny that it was I.

183

Not that at this stage I would expect you to believe me, but I wish to make my position quite clear.'

Grammatical even in the grip of emotion, Thanet noted. Habitual precision of speech dies hard.

'Ergo,' Mintar was saying, 'it must have been someone else. The big question is, who?'

'Are you suggesting it might have been Dr Squires?'

'Oh come, Thanet, I'm sure you've already worked out for yourself that if I come top of the list, he must surely come second. And with a woman as beautiful as my wife' – again he glanced at the photograph – 'a *crime passionnel* is bound to be on the cards.'

He gave the cat one final stroke, set it gently down on the floor beside his chair and then leaned forward as if to emphasise the importance of what he was about to say. The cat stood for a moment, its tail twitching angrily, then stalked off and jumped up on to the windowsill where it proceeded to wash itself. Mintar said, 'And that is the point, Thanet. My wife was beautiful, exceptionally so, but beauty can be a burden as well as an asset and brings with it its own special disadvantages. Virginia . . .' His voice grew husky again. '. . . Virginia was like a flame to a moth, men couldn't help being attracted to her nor, unfortunately, she to them.' He cleared his throat, then added briskly, 'I'm sure you must already have asked yourself why I put up with this sort of behaviour, but the fact of the matter is, I would have done anything, put up with anything, to keep her.'

Mintar sat back as if the hardest part of his confession was over. 'My work, as you must be aware, takes me away from home for sometimes months at a time. What was Ginny supposed to do while I was away? Sit at home, knitting? She developed her own interests, of course she did, barristers' wives have to if they are to survive, but unfortunately they were not enough for her. Because what most people didn't realise was that underneath she was very insecure. She needed, absolutely had to

184

have, constant reassurance that she mattered, that she was special. And I simply couldn't give that to her, if I was away for half the year. I understood that and was prepared to turn a blind eye to her affairs with other men, so long as she always came back to me in the end, was always there when I did come home. You see? I really am being absolutely frank with you now. I'd never have dreamt I would say these things to anyone, let alone to strangers. But needs must. I just want you to understand that if you are considering my supposed motive to be jealousy, then you couldn't be more wrong.'

'What about ambition?'

'As a motive? What on earth can you . . . ?' Mintar broke off, but not before Thanet caught the flash of anger. 'Oh, I see! You are suggesting that my wife's behaviour could have compromised my chances? Well, all I can say is that if you offered me a straight choice between a seat in the High Court and Virginia, then there's no doubt in my mind which I would have chosen. One's years on the Bench are brief and I always hoped that as she grew older, Virginia's behaviour would become increasingly moderate. Besides, I would never have contemplated old age without her through choice.' Abruptly he stood up and crossed to look out of the window and Thanet guessed that he was struggling to regain control. They were all three aware that that choice had now been taken away from him, once and for all.

It was time for a change of direction. 'You told us yesterday that your wife never got over Caroline's elopement, and since then we've seen the effects of this for ourselves.'

Mintar swung around, scooping up the cat again as he did so, obviously surprised at the sudden switch. His eyes narrowed. 'What has that got to do with it?'

'I don't know,' Thanet admitted. 'I'm not sure at this stage that it has the least relevance. But it did affect your wife's behaviour and it must have been some aspect of her

185

behaviour that sparked off this attack. At this stage I am simply trying to assimilate as much information as possible and then later perhaps I shall begin to understand what went wrong.'

'So what do you want to know?' Mintar returned to his desk and sat down again.

Thanet had already decided that at this stage he would say nothing about making a further attempt to trace Caroline. He wanted a free hand and suspected that Mintar might object to such a search, as he apparently had in the past. 'You said that Dick Swain's mother was "as unhelpful as she could possibly be" when you tried to find out where the young people had gone. You went to see her as soon as you found out what had happened, I assume?'

'Of course. Immediately after finding Caroline's note, next morning. I didn't expect to find them there, naturally, but I did hope she might know where they'd gone. But she wouldn't even let me into the house, slammed the door in my face.'

'You tried again later?'

'Certainly. That same evening, when I thought she might have calmed down. But with no more success. I just got a torrent of abuse. She was blaming Caroline for the whole thing, saying she had turned her son's head and calling her all sorts of filthy names. I might add that the police got no further than I did.'

'What about some time later, when she really might have been more cooperative? Did you ever make another attempt?'

'No. What was the point? There was no reason to think her attitude might have changed. In fact I thought it would be better, less painful, if we tried to put Caroline out of our minds altogether. It didn't work, though. Virginia was inconsolable, it seemed . . . Just a moment . . .' Once again he gave Thanet one of those piercing stares. 'All these questions . . .' He stopped, and his eyes grew distant. Then he shook his head as if to clear it. 'Sorry, go on.'

'What were you going to say, sir?'

'Nothing. It doesn't matter.'

Thanet was suspicious but Mintar obviously wasn't going to tell him. 'I understand Caroline left a note. May I see it?'

Mintar hesitated before depositing the cat on the floor again and taking a key ring from his pocket. Then he bent to unlock one of the bottom drawers of his desk, took out an envelope and handed it to Thanet.

And here, thought Thanet as he took out the letter, was the evidence that however much Mintar had apparently hardened his heart against his favourite daughter, underneath he had grieved as bitterly as his wife. The flimsy piece of paper was virtually disintegrating from much handling and from being folded and refolded countless times over the past four years. Thanet glanced at Mintar and found him watching and as he caught his eye the QC looked away, no doubt aware that Thanet had appreciated the significance of the condition of the piece of paper he was holding. He focused on what Caroline had written.

Sorry, I can't stand this any longer. I'm going away with Dick. Please don't try to find me.

And then, below, smudged with tears:

I do love you all.
Caroline

Handling it very carefully, Thanet laid the letter on the desk, tempted after all to mention his decision to make a further attempt to find her. No, better not to, in case they didn't get anywhere. But he was at least now reasonably sure that should they be successful Caroline would get a warm reception from her father, despite the smokescreen he had put up. 'There's just one other question I want to

187

ask you at present, something that puzzles me. I understand that you were very much in favour of trying to buy
Agon off, but—'

'Shh!' Mintar looked at the door and hissed, 'Keep
your voice down, for God's sake! If Rachel should hear . . .
How the hell you found that out, I can't imagine!'

Thanet lowered his voice. 'Sorry, sir.' And he meant it.
The last thing he wanted was to cause further distress to
Rachel. 'I wasn't thinking. But as I understand it, your
wife was against it. Did she say why?'

Mintar leaned forward, speaking in a near whisper. 'I
think she was afraid – and I must admit she had a point –
that he might consider Rachel a greater prize and refuse.
And that if he did, he might tell her what we'd done. In
which case . . .'

'It might set Rachel against you too. I see. Yes. That
makes sense.'

Outside again Thanet said to Lineham, 'You were very
quiet in there, Mike. Didn't utter a word.'

'Thought you were doing fine without my help, sir,'
said Lineham with a grin.

'Let's check on that search warrant.'

It had been granted and Thanet arranged to meet the
team at Digby's house in fifteen minutes.

'Come on, Mike, let's go and pick him up. I think
Mr Digby would rather enjoy a ride in a police car,
don't you?'

Lineham gave an anticipatory smile. 'This should be
interesting.'

Digby was not amused at being dragged away from his
work. 'What'll Mr Mintar say? I can't walk out just like
that, can I?'

'I'm sure Mr Mintar would have no objection whatsoever.' But he would doubtless have asked plenty of
awkward questions, which was why Thanet had no intention of asking his permission.

'Am I being arrested?'

'Certainly not, sir. We just need your help in our inquiries.'

'So I could refuse?'

'You could. But I really don't think that would be a good idea, do you? It might give us the wrong impression, even put ideas into our heads.'

Reluctantly Digby got into the car. 'Where are we going, anyway?'

Lineham grinned. 'You're going to give us a guided tour.'

'Of what?'

'Of your house, of course.'

Digby lunged for the door handle but Lineham had had the foresight to activate the safety locks. 'You have no right, without a search warrant!'

'Got one,' said the sergeant.

'Where is it, then? I demand to see it!'

'All in good time, sir,' said Thanet. 'I assure you, this is all legal and above board. The search will go ahead with or without your cooperation.'

Digby lapsed into a glowering silence which lasted until they pulled up in the lane outside his house. As they drew up four officers got out of a waiting police car.

'Ah, reinforcements,' said Thanet. 'Actually, I don't think you'll all be needed. As you can see, the house is very small, we'd be falling over ourselves.'

The warrant was produced and inspected and Digby capitulated, unlocking the door with an ill grace.

'Now,' said Thanet when they were inside. 'The dark-room is upstairs, I presume?'

'I don't want you mucking about with my equipment!'

'Your equipment will be treated with every respect. In fact, it's not so much your equipment we're interested in, but what you produce with it.'

'You're wasting your time! There's nothing illegal! Nothing pornographic or anything like that!'

'Well, we shall see,' said Thanet. 'But of course, it's not

189

always the material itself that's important, it's the use you make of it.'

'I don't know what you mean. What are you talking about?'

But Digby understood only too well. Thanet could read it in his eyes, could even hear the beginnings of resignation in his tone of voice. Thanet didn't bother to reply, just indicated that Tanya and Lineham should accompany him and set off up the narrow staircase. Digby was left downstairs with Carson.

There were only two bedrooms. As in so many old cottages with limited upstairs accommodation, the bathroom – if there was one – would have been built on downstairs, at the back. Digby's bedroom, furnished in minimal fashion with single bed, a scuffed and battered chest of drawers and a bedside table, overlooked the dreary front garden. A curtain slung across one corner concealed his scanty collection of clothes. No effort whatsoever had been made to render the room attractive.

The room at the back, a state of the art darkroom, was a very different matter. This, obviously, was where Digby's money went. Three tall narrow chests of drawers – custom-made? Thanet wondered – accommodated his prints and negatives. It didn't take long to find what they were looking for. It stood to reason that if Digby stored incriminating material in his darkroom he wasn't going to leave it lying around where a casual search would bring it to light, especially as he had some reputation as a photographer locally and this room would be a prime target for burglars.

They therefore began by removing the drawers and examining them to see if anything had been taped underneath. It was Lineham who struck lucky. 'Sir!' he said.

It was a brown manila envelope and a glance at the first photograph told Thanet that his guess had been right. Digby's net had spread beyond Squires and Virginia.

Digby had been taking a risk. He must have been standing on the terrace just outside the French windows of the drawing room of the Mintars' house – Thanet recognised the furnishings. If either of the two people in the photograph had glanced up they could surely not have failed to catch sight of him, but they were far too engrossed in each other.

They were lying on one of the big sofas, making love. Digby must coolly have waited for a moment when both of their profiles were clearly visible. No one could have mistaken Agon's male-model good looks, that cap of shining blonde hair.

At first Thanet thought the woman was Rachel but then he looked more closely. He glanced up at Lineham, seeking confirmation.

The sergeant nodded, eyes sparkling with the pleasure of suspicion verified. 'Virginia Mintar,' he said.

SIXTEEN

Tanya stopped searching and came to look over Thanet's shoulder as he shuffled through the rest of the photographs in the envelope. They were all more of the same: Matthew Agon and Virginia in compromising positions. The negatives were there too.

'Wonder what Rachel would think if she saw these,' said Lineham.

'Or Mintar, for that matter.'

'From what he's told us, he might not be too surprised,' said Lineham.

'In that case, couldn't they be used as ammunition for him to get rid of the sleaze?' said Tanya. 'No, perhaps not. If he threatened to show them to Rachel, Agon would probably tell him to go ahead, banking on the fact that her father wouldn't want to upset her – or, for that matter, show her mother up in a bad light. But then again, Mr Mintar might feel it would be worth it, to save her from marrying a character like that.'

'Difficult to tell,' said Thanet. He'd have to think about whether or not to show these to Mintar. 'Meanwhile, let's see if we can turn up anything else. The photographs of Squires and Virginia are bound to be somewhere.'

They were, along with several other caches of similar photographs of couples Thanet had never seen before.

'Wonder how many of these he's trying to squeeze money out of,' said Lineham in disgust.

'Well, if this investigation achieves nothing else, it should save a lot of people a great deal of heartache,' said Tanya.

'By the way, talking of heartache, Tanya, I was thinking . . .' said Thanet.

Tanya looked delighted to be given the task of trying to trace Caroline. 'Just up my street, sir,' she said.

'Good. You can get started on it right away, as soon as you've finished here. I'd like you and Carson to stay on, make sure there's nothing we've missed. If Digby is blackmailing any of these people, there should be some kind of evidence somewhere. He may well have destroyed correspondence, if there ever was any, but you might take a look at his bank statements, for instance. He didn't buy all this equipment on a gardener's salary.'

Leaving Tanya to it Thanet and Lineham went downstairs.

The fear in Digby's eyes as he caught sight of the incriminating manila envelopes was plain for all to see.

'Proper little paparazzo, aren't you?' said Lineham, holding them up.

'Where did you get those?' cried Digby. 'I've never seen them in my life before!'

'Don't try to put one over on us!' said Thanet. 'Who else would have taped them to the underside of those drawers?'

'I've been set up!' said Digby. 'You must have planted them yourselves.'

'Who d'you think the Court would believe?' said Lineham. 'You or the three police officers present when they were found?'

'Anyway,' said Digby, 'there's no law against taking photographs, is there?'

'Unless they are obscene,' said Thanet. 'Or blackmail is involved.'

Digby erupted out of his chair and Carson moved quickly to put a hand on his shoulder to restrain him. 'Blackmail! What blackmail? You can't pin that on me!'

'Really?' said Thanet grimly. 'We'll see about that. Tell the others I want him taken in for questioning,' he said to Carson. 'Then you join Tanya upstairs. She'll tell you what we're looking for.'

Ignoring Digby's protests he and Lineham left.

'Let him stew,' said Thanet as they got into the car. 'He can have a taste of his own medicine.'

'He deserves all he gets,' said Lineham. 'Rachel was right, wasn't she? He's a real slimeball.' He glanced at the envelopes. 'Had quite a haul there, didn't we?'

'Certainly did. Tanya's right. This should save a lot of people a great deal of heartache.'

'Will we try to trace them?'

'I doubt it. Where would we start? Unless Tanya and Carson come up with anything, of course. Otherwise it would be too time-consuming and a drain on resources. Anyway, if he is actively engaged in blackmailing any of them, no doubt they'll realise something's happened when the demands stop coming, and there'll be sighs of relief all round.'

'So where now, sir? Agon?'

'Oh I think so, yes.'

This time the receptionist's smile was definitely forced. 'He's coaching again, I'm afraid.' Once again she offered coffee while they waited and once again they refused. As they left she reached for the telephone.

'Looks as though he might be in trouble with the management,' said Lineham. 'Not very good for the Club image, is it, having the police around.'

'Am I supposed to cry?' said Thanet.

This time it was a man Agon was coaching.

'Doesn't look too pleased to see us, does he?' said Lineham, as they sat down on a bench to watch. 'I suppose this is how his affair with Virginia Mintar started.'

'Probably. Almost certainly it was here that she met him.'

'And it must have been going on while Rachel was in Switzerland and Mrs Amos was in New Zealand.'

'Quite.'

Thanet wasn't sure if Agon deliberately kept them waiting but it was a good half an hour before the lesson finished. Thanet didn't mind. There was nothing particularly urgent awaiting his attention and it was good to sit here in the shade, listening to the soothing *thock* of racquet against ball.

Agon finally said goodbye to his client then strolled across, slinging a towel around his neck and wiping his forehead with one end. 'I didn't expect to see you here again, Inspector.'

I bet you didn't, thought Thanet.

'I thought I'd answered every question you asked as fully as possible.'

'Let's go and sit at one of the tables,' said Thanet.

'I really have nothing more to add,' Agon insisted.

Thanet said nothing, just led the way.

When they were settled he said, 'You've been less than frank with us, haven't you, Mr Agon?'

'Oh?' Agon's eyes were wary. 'In what respect?'

'Middle-aged, I think you called Mrs Mintar,' said Lineham. 'And, if I recall your exact words, "Why eat mutton when you can have lamb?" Am I right?'

'What are you getting at?'

Agon still looked unruffled. As far as he knew, of course, the only person who could confirm or deny that he and Virginia had an affair was Virginia herself, and she was dead.

Lineham put the manila envelope on the table. 'This,' he said.

Agon's eyes flicked to the envelope then from one face to the other. The calm certainty he must have read there rattled him. 'What is it?'

For reply Lineham took the photographs out of the envelope and, slowly and deliberately, spread them out across the table, in front of Agon and facing him so that he could not possibly misread their contents. Then he sat back and folded his arms.

'My God!' said Agon. He looked aghast. 'Where the hell did you get these? Who took them? I'll have his guts for garters!'

'So, you recognise yourself,' said Lineham. 'And, of course, the lady.'

Agon was silent for a few moments, still studying the photographs. Then, astonishingly, he smiled, a smug, self-satisfied, somewhat prurient smile. 'Actually, you know,' he said, 'they're really rather good.'

'Mr Agon,' said Thanet, intervening for the first time. 'I don't think you quite appreciate the seriousness of your position. Mrs Mintar is dead. Somebody killed her. Now we find that you have lied to us about having an affair with her.'

'Oh no!' said Agon vehemently, leaning forward to emphasise his objection. 'You needn't try and pin that on me! All this was months ago.'

'So why lie to us?' said Lineham, sweeping the photographs together and putting them back in the envelope.

'Well, obviously because I didn't want to seem involved.'

'Implying that you were.'

'No! It was over, done with. I just didn't see the point in bringing it up.'

'Rather a naïve point of view, don't you think?' said Thanet. 'It seems to us much more likely that you didn't want us to know because you hoped we never would find out, especially as no one else seemed to know about it. Incidentally, why was it kept so quiet? We haven't had the impression that Mrs Mintar was exactly secretive about her affairs.'

'She thought people might laugh at her,' Agon said sulkily. 'Because I was so much younger.'

This bore out what Susan Amos had told them.

'Many women would regard it as something of a triumph, to have a younger man in tow,' said Lineham.

'Not Virginia,' said Agon. 'Anyway, I saw no point in telling you, in case you got ideas. And I was right, wasn't I? Though how you think an affair which finished months ago could possibly have made me tip her down a well on Saturday beats me.'

'Unless . . .' said Thanet.

'What?'

'We know of at least one person who is being blackmailed by the character who took these,' said Lineham, tapping the envelope with one fingernail.

'So?'

'What if he was also blackmailing Mrs Mintar?' said Thanet.

'I don't see what you're getting at.'

'Rachel Mintar's a good catch, isn't she?' said Lineham.

'I resent that remark! I love Rachel and she loves me!'

'Resent it or not, it's true. And you admitted to us yourself that her parents weren't exactly over the moon about it.'

'I still don't see—' Agon burst out, and then, as heads at nearby tables turned, in a fierce whisper: 'I still don't see what you're getting at. What have me and Rachel got to do with what happened on Saturday?'

'Possibly quite a lot,' said Thanet. 'Because something else happened on Saturday, didn't it? You and Rachel announced your engagement.'

'So?' said Agon again.

'So maybe this galvanised Mrs Mintar into action.'

'What sort of action?'

Thanet shrugged. 'Just say, for the sake of argument, that whoever took these photographs was blackmailing Virginia Mintar too. Maybe she decided to tell you about it.'

'What would have been the point of that? I mean, what would she have hoped to achieve?'

'She could have threatened to show them to Rachel?'

'You're barking up the wrong tree! I never saw those photographs before in my life! I never even knew they existed until you put them on the table just now.'

'Unfortunately,' said Thanet as they walked away, 'I believed him, didn't you? I'd swear he'd never set eyes on them before.'

'Inspector!' Agon was running after them.

They turned.

'There won't be any need for Rachel to know about this, will there?'

'I'm afraid I can't give you any guarantees,' said Thanet. 'We have no idea as yet what will or will not be considered relevant to our inquiry.'

'But if it isn't relevant?' said Agon eagerly.

'I'm sorry, I just can't commit myself on that, one way or the other.'

'Now look—' said Agon angrily.

'No, sir. You look. This is a murder inquiry and I refuse to have my hands tied by any member of the public wishing to restrict my behaviour for his own convenience.'

'If looks could kill,' said Lineham as they went on their way, 'you'd be dead as a doornail. Though why a doornail should be dead I can't imagine.'

'Brewer would tell you, no doubt.'

'Who's he?'

'It, Mike. Brewer's *Dictionary of Phrase and Fable*. Wait till Richard's on his Os and As, it's amazing what you'll pick up. Anyway, d'you agree with what I was saying, before we were interrupted?'

'That Agon didn't know those photos existed, you mean? Unless he's a brilliant actor, yes, unfortunately. He wouldn't have been so completely confident before we showed them to him, otherwise.'

198

'Quite.' They were silent for a while, thinking, and it was not until they were in the car that Thanet said, 'I think we might be barking up the wrong tree as far as Agon is concerned, Mike. We must remember that for all we know Virginia was also unaware that those photographs existed. And the problem is, I can't see why else she would have gone out to talk to him in the first place, can you?'

'Perhaps the fact that Rachel had actually gone as far as getting engaged made her reconsider trying to buy Agon off.'

'But her original objection would still have held good, surely, Mike – Agon might have told Rachel her mother had tried to bribe him to leave and turned her against Virginia. No, I don't think she would have risked it.'

'What if she'd threatened to tell Rachel about the affair, then?'

'The same applies, surely. She'd still be running the risk of losing Rachel, if for a different reason. What engaged girl would enjoy being told her mother's been sleeping with her fiancé? The fact is, the poor woman was in a real dilemma as far as Rachel was concerned. Whatever course of action she took to try to get rid of Agon might also have resulted in alienating Rachel, the very thing she wished to avoid.'

'Well, I don't think we ought to give up on Agon,' said Lineham, his mouth setting in stubborn lines. 'If we found his fingerprints on the well cover, for instance . . .'

'Let's hope the lab gets a move on,' said Thanet. 'And no, we certainly won't cross him off our list. But I wouldn't say he's exactly at the top of it, either.'

'So, what now, sir?'

Thanet glanced at his watch. Another hour before he had to report to Draco. But there was no definite lead he wanted to follow up at the moment. On impulse he said to Lineham, 'I think we'll pay a visit to the resident witch.'

'What for?' Lineham grinned. 'Because she intrigues you, I suppose.'

'Well, she is involved, so to speak.'

'Marginally, perhaps.'

'All right, marginally. But involved nevertheless. After all, if her son hadn't eloped with Caroline, who knows? Virginia might still be alive.'

'How d'you work that out?'

'Stop being so logical, Mike, and just drive, will you?'

Lineham drove.

There was no proper driveway to Marah Swain's cottage, just a rough track turning off to the right about half a mile beyond the Mintars' house. Branches of overhanging trees brushed the roof of the car as Lineham drove slowly and carefully along it. The ground was rock hard, the ruts baked solid by the unremitting heat of the past weeks.

'Can't be doing the suspension much good,' the sergeant grumbled.

Thanet suppressed a smile. Lineham was always fussing over his car.

A couple of hundred yards in from the road the track swung to the left and Lineham jammed on his brakes as they rounded the bend. Here the track narrowed to little more than a path and the way ahead was blocked by another car. 'Great!' he muttered. 'We'll have to reverse all the way back, I suppose.'

'Isn't that Mr Mintar's car?' said Thanet.

'So it is!'

The driver's door of the dark green 5 series BMW hung open and the keys still swung in the ignition.

'Begging for trouble, that is!' said Lineham.

Thanet did not reply. The message of urgency conveyed by the open door and the abandoned car had made him recall their last conversation with Mintar. He suddenly realised what it might have been that Mintar had refused to tell him. He snatched the keys out of the ignition and set off up the track at a run. 'Come on, Mike.'

'What?' said Lineham, catching up, bewildered by Thanet's sudden haste.

'I've just – realised – the conclusion – Mintar might have drawn – from the questions – we were asking,' puffed Thanet. He was more out of condition than he thought.

'What?' said Lineham again.

'He said – Marah Swain held Caroline – to blame – for losing her son. Mintar might have thought – we suspected her – of killing his wife.'

'Out of revenge, you mean?'

'Oldest motive – in the world, Mike. If she couldn't – take it out on Caroline – she'd take it out – on her mother instead.'

'Sir! Listen!'

They paused, to do so. Ahead of them there was the sound of banging and shouting. They took off again and a moment or two later came in sight of the house.

Thanet saw at once what Tanya meant. Crouched in the middle of a clearing, solidly built of Kentish ragstone, it had a secretive, almost sinister air. Despite its seclusion grimy net curtains hung at the four tiny windows – all of them, like the front door, firmly shut despite the heat of the day.

'Open – this – bloody door! Open it! Open – this – bloody door!' Mintar's shouts were punctuated by thumps. He was so intent on what he was doing and was making so much noise that he didn't hear them approach and started visibly when Thanet laid a hand on his arm.

'Not much point in that, is there, sir? She's obviously not going to open up.' Now that Mintar had stopped shouting Thanet could hear a radio playing loudly inside the house. Tanya had mentioned this earlier, he remembered.

Mintar stared at him dully, his mind still focused elsewhere. Then, slowly, Thanet felt the tension in the man's arm begin to seep away. Out of the corner of his eye he saw the net at one of the downstairs windows twitch. She was watching, then.

'What were you hoping to achieve, sir?'

Mintar shook his head in despair. 'She knows more than she's telling us. She knows where Caroline is, I'm sure of it. And Caro has a right to be told about her mother! I . . . I . . .' Mintar turned his head away, ashamed no doubt of the tears which threatened to fall.

Thanet saw that he had been wrong. He had mis-judged the man. Despair over the death of his wife had loosened the constraints of convention which Mintar normally imposed upon himself, causing this uncharac-teristic behaviour. It was not revenge the man sought, but consolation, from the daughter he had lost and mourned in secret. He, Thanet, should have told Mintar of their plans to make a further attempt to trace her. 'What did you propose to do, sir, shake the information out of her? That's not the way to go about it. Besides, I've already put one of my best officers on to trying to find Caroline. I agree with you, she needs to be told about her mother's death. So why don't you let Sergeant Lineham escort you back to the house and let me see what I can do here?'

Mintar nodded meekly and without a word turned away and followed Lineham back across the clearing.

Thanet waited until they were out of sight. Then he knocked loudly at the door and waited.

No response.

He knocked again, and called, 'Police, Miss Swain. I need a word.'

A moment later there was the sound of bolts being drawn back and the door opened a crack. The noise from the radio increased and a whiff of foul air drifted out as an eye appeared, with a wisp of grey hair above. He remembered what Tanya had said about the smell and recalled her description of Marah Swain: '. . . *long grey hair which straggles down over her shoulders and chest . . . dresses like something out of the nineteenth century – shapeless ankle-length black skirt, woollen shawl, thick stockings and old leather boots . . .* He held his identification up to the narrow gap and, raising his voice in case she was deaf as Tanya had suggested, introduced himself. 'I'd like to talk to you.'

'I've got nothing to say.' The voice was rusty, as if rarely used.

'Just a few more questions . . .'

'I told that girl all I know, which is nothing.'

'I just wanted to—'

The door opened a fraction wider, emitting a further gust of throat-gagging odours, and the woman thrust her chin aggressively forward, eyes flashing malevolently. 'I told you, I have nothing to say! Go away! You're trespassing! Get off my property! Go on, get off!' And she slammed the door in his face.

Thanet stared at it for a moment, then turned away, frustrated. It was rare indeed for him to be refused admittance, but there was nothing he could do about it at the moment. He hoped he hadn't made things more difficult for Tanya if she needed to interview Marah Swain again, and wondered how she had managed to get inside the house in the first place. Perhaps the old woman didn't feel as threatened by a female?

Anyway, he consoled himself as he made his way back to Ralph Mintar's car, even five minutes in that cottage would have been too long for comfort, judging by the smell. You'd have to be pretty desperate to enlist Marah Swain's reputed powers as a witch. How could anyone live in such foul air, breathe it in without becoming ill? And what could it be, that could emit that stomach-churning, foetid stench? Thanet's imagination provided him with visions of wisps of steam rising from simmering cauldrons filled with stinking brews.

Poor Mintar. How would any parents feel, if their child proposed such a prospective mother-in-law as that?

Still, feeling sorry for the man did not remove him from the list of suspects.

SEVENTEEN

'Any news?' said Thanet, the moment he arrived home.

Joan was in the kitchen, finishing the preparations for supper. She shook her head. 'No change.'

He kissed her before sitting down heavily on one of the kitchen chairs. It had been a tiring day, culminating in a punishing session with Draco who had wanted chapter and verse of every single interview they had done. Then, of course, there had been a lengthy stint on reports. 'Did Alexander ring?'

'Yes. Unless the situation changes it sounds as though they're planning to go ahead with the induction on Wednesday morning.'

'As we thought, then.'

'Yes.'

So, there'd be another day of waiting and worrying to get through before anything happened, thought Thanet wearily.

'Come on,' said Joan. 'Supper's ready. You look as though you could do with some refuelling.'

They ate in companionable silence for a while and then began to talk about each other's day. Joan told him about a seminar she was running on victim support groups and he brought her up to date on the Mintar case. After he had told her about the interview with Susan Amos (reminding himself that at some point he had to remember to smuggle into the house the jacket he had bought Joan for Christmas), Joan sighed and said, 'How sad. First her father left her, then her baby died, then Caroline eloped and she never saw or heard from her again . . . She probably felt that sooner or later everyone she loved would leave her – and she must have felt she had to walk on eggshells as far as Rachel and this man Agon were concerned, in case she lost her too.'

'I haven't told you the worst of it yet. Virginia and Agon had an affair, back in the spring.'

'Oh, no!'

'I'm afraid so. Rachel was at a finishing school in Switzerland at the time, so wouldn't have known about it, and Susan Amos was in New Zealand. Added to which, it sounds as though they kept it pretty quiet – Susan said Virginia didn't usually go in for younger men because she was afraid of people laughing at her behind her back.'

'She must have been terrified of Rachel finding out and turning against her! What a mess!'

'Quite. So her hands really were tied, as far as getting rid of Agon was concerned.'

'And it was her own fault! How she must have kicked herself, for landing herself in that particular situation. And how she must have hated the idea of him marrying Rachel. Imagine what it must be like, having a son-in-law you'd slept with!'

'Quite. Mind, it didn't surprise me in the least, given that by all accounts Virginia was very fond of men and Agon is a very handsome specimen, if you like the Adonis type. I've seen him in action with one of his pupils and believe me, she was loving every minute of it.'

'Sounds to me as though Virginia was always looking for love but never managed to find it,' said Joan as she began to gather up the dishes.

Thanet rose to help her. 'I'm not so sure. According to Susan, Virginia didn't really ever want to fall in love, for fear of getting hurt if he should leave her. That was

205

why none of her affairs lasted long – she always wanted to get in first, be the one to end them.'

'I'd guess she never forgave her father for abandoning her like that, and has spent her life taking it out on the male sex in general.' Joan set the dishes down beside the sink and began to load the dishwasher.

Thanet put the kettle on. 'That's exactly what Susan said. She also said that Virginia once confessed to her that she couldn't resist trying to prove her power over men, it was as if she was driven to it. She looked on every new man who came along as a challenge. As I said, she even tried it on with her own sister's boyfriend – and not for the first time, either. Apparently Jane had been putting off bringing Arnold Prime to meet Virginia for ages, for fear that once again Virginia would ruin things for her.'

'And she was flirting with this man over dinner, in front of her husband, you say? How on earth did he put up with it?'

'Beats me! Though he does seem remarkably understanding about the way she carried on, says he didn't care as long as she stayed with him, and in view of the fact that he's away for such long stretches of time it would have been unreasonable to expect her to live like a nun.'

'Carrying on while he's away is surely a very different matter from rubbing his nose in it at his own dinner table. I really can't believe he could just sit there and not mind.'

'I agree.'

'Though it does sound typical behaviour for a woman like her, someone who has a low opinion of herself and actually expects that sooner or later everyone she cares about will walk out on her. It's as though they have to push the person they're testing beyond the limits of endurance, just to prove to themselves that they're right, that what they fear will eventually happen. I've seen it over and over again, in my work. And of course, a lot of people just can't take it. Often they do walk out – or snap.'

'You're suggesting this is what might have happened with Mintar?'

Joan shrugged. 'I can't say. I haven't met him, you have. But it's one of the options you're considering, surely.'

'Yes, of course.'

They went on discussing Virginia for some time. Joan's insights were often invaluable to Thanet but this time no new light was shed and he went to bed feeling that there were so many people with just cause for animosity towards Virginia that unless some sound scientific evidence turned up there was little hope of ever discovering who had engaged her in that fatal struggle.

He said so to Lineham, when he arrived at the office next morning.

'Not like you to be so pessimistic, sir.'

Thanet sighed. 'One has to be realistic, Mike. Just think about it. Every single one of these people had the opportunity. They all – apart from Mintar, who was supposedly alone in his study – came back to the pool alone. Three of them – Agon and both of the Squires – actually had to pass through the courtyard, and the old lady had ready access to it and indeed was better placed than anyone to choose her moment. And Jane, by her own admission, returned to the pool via the kitchen. As for motive, well, I think we can count Rachel and Arnold Prime out, I can't see any possible reason why either of them should want to get rid of Virginia, can you?'

'I agree with you about Prime. And I'd like to agree with you about Rachel. But it's only just occurred to me . . . What if she'd just found out her mother had had an affair with Agon and they quarrelled about it?'

Thanet shook his head. 'You mean, she found out after the engagement was announced? There's never been any hint that her attitude to her mother was any different from usual during the earlier part of the evening.'

'I suppose if she did find out, yes, it would have to have been later.'

'But how would she have found out? Who would have told her?'

Lineham thought. 'No, you're right. I haven't really thought it through. We've already agreed that Virginia wouldn't have told her and it's hardly likely that Agon would have, is it?' Lineham put on an assumed voice. '"Oh, by the way, darling, did I mention I had an affair with your mother while you were in Switzerland? You don't really mind, do you?" No, I can't really see him owning up in any circumstances unless it was absolutely unavoidable.'

'Quite. So, leaving Rachel and Arnold Prime out of it, if you think about motive . . .'

'They're all in the same boat, aren't they? Mintar and Howard Squires must have been as jealous as hell, ditto Mrs Squires and Jane, and despite what she says the old lady must have been terrified that Virginia would tell Mintar about her illness. And however much Agon pooh-poohs the idea, he must have been afraid that Virginia would tell Rachel about the affair and Rachel would dump him. Look at what he stood to lose! There's a load of money sloshing around in that household and Agon probably thinks that in view of the fact that Caroline seems to have disappeared off the face of the earth, Rachel stands to scoop the lot when her old man drops off his perch.'

'Mmm. In which case he probably has a nasty shock coming to him.' Thanet had no doubt that like himself Lineham was remembering how distraught Mintar had been, the previous afternoon at Marah Swain's house. 'It's obvious that whatever front Mintar might have put up in the past, Caroline's very much still in the picture as far as he's concerned. But to get back to the point, Mike. The fact remains that unless we get some scientific evidence, there's not much hope of nailing any one of them.'

'Sir, I hate to interrupt your train of thought, but isn't it time you were on your way to the morning meeting?'

Thanet glanced at his watch and shot to his feet. It really would not do to be late this morning and give Draco further cause for complaint. 'Thanks, Mike!'

Once again he made it with seconds to spare.

'This is becoming a habit, Thanet.'

'Sorry, sir. Lot to catch up on.'

'Perhaps you would be so kind as to fill the others in on the progress of the Mintar investigation?'

I will not allow myself to be needled. And there was surely nothing in his subsequent report with which Draco could find fault, he thought as he finished speaking.

He was wrong.

'Any comments?' said Draco, looking from Tody to Boon. They shook their heads.

'Questions?' Draco was tapping his desk impatiently with the end of a Biro. His expression was that of a schoolmaster whose pupils were letting him down.

'Where d'you hope to go from here?' Tody asked Thanet, ever the good boy of the class.

'We were in the process of discussing that when we had to break off for this meeting.'

'Well, it seems to me that there is one glaring omission in what you have been doing,' said Draco. He sat back in his executive-style black leather chair and fixed Thanet with a beady stare.

Thanet's heart sank and he tried not to sound too defensive as he said, 'Oh? What's that, sir?'

'Evidence,' said Draco. 'Or rather, the lack of it.'

Trust Draco to put his finger directly on the weak spot, thought Thanet. 'Yes, sir. We are aware of that.'

'So what are you doing about it?'

Not a lot. 'That was the very point we were discussing, sir.'

'It's not discussion we need, Thanet, it's action. It's all very well being airy-fairy, going around interviewing

209

suspects and hoping to solve the case by making up your mind who did it and then persuading him to confess, but you know as well as I do that confessions can be retracted and that the only hope of getting a conviction is to back up theory with facts, and preferably facts which are incontrovertible and not capable of varying interpretations. So I suggest you give this matter very serious consideration. Evidence, Thanet. Go to it. Evidence.'

Inwardly seething – all the more so because he knew Draco was right – Thanet went upstairs and sat down at his desk.

'Rough time, sir?' said Lineham sympathetically.

'Nothing that wasn't justified, I regret to say.' Thanet relayed Draco's instructions. 'So let's put our minds to it.'

'He can't expect us to manufacture evidence out of thin air!' said Lineham.

They sat in frustrated silence for a few minutes and then Thanet snapped his fingers, making Lineham jump. 'Got it!'

'What?'

'We collect every single item of clothing worn by all the suspects on Saturday night – including swimsuits, towels and bath robes, if used – and send them to the lab to see if there is any crossmatching with what Virginia was wearing, either from her to them or vice versa. And on top of that we chase forensic to see if there was any other evidence found on her – hairs and suchlike, in case we need to collect samples.'

'You can't be serious, sir!'

'Dead serious, Mike.'

'But we can't ask the lab to run tests on all that lot just on the off chance! They'll go spare!'

'Why not? At least the Super won't then be able to say that we're not making an effort.'

'But the cost!'

'Justified, surely, if it helps us solve the case?'

'A bit over the top, though, surely?'

'Certainly not.' Thanet sat back with a glint in his eye and folded his arms as though preparing already to defend himself against criticism. 'We'll say it's upon the Super's direct instructions. After all, if he's not prepared to wait for us to narrow it down to one or perhaps two suspects then he can hardly complain if we do exactly as he says and collect all the evidence we can lay our hands on.'

Lineham raised one eyebrow, but made no further comment. Both of them knew that Draco would complain and complain vociferously – and that Thanet would play the innocent, claiming only to have been following orders to the letter.

'We'll put as many officers as necessary on to it,' said Thanet. 'One per suspect. And who knows? It might work.'

'Whatever you say, sir.'

During the subsequent briefing Thanet noticed that Tanya was missing. 'Where is she?' he demanded.

'Following up something to do with Caroline,' said Carson.

'Oh, I see. Fine. On your way then, everyone.'

There was a general exodus.

'What about us, sir?' said Lineham.

'We wait for inspiration,' said Thanet. 'As soon as all the stuff comes in we brace ourselves for complaints from the lab at the same time as pleading for swift results. Meanwhile, we catch up on some of the backlog of paperwork.'

He had often found that when he was stuck, detaching his mind completely from the case he was working on brought surprising results. But in this particular instance the results came from an unexpected direction. It was late morning when Tanya came knocking at his door.

'Well?' he said eagerly. He could tell from her expression that she had news for him.

'I think I may have traced her, sir.' She was positively glowing with justifiable pride.

'Well done!' said Thanet.

'Brilliant!' said Lineham.

'You said "may",' said Thanet. He waved her to a seat. 'Begin at the beginning, as they say.'

'Well, the first time I went to interview Marah Swain I happened to notice a postcard propped up on the beam over that big old fireplace she's got. It stood out because it was the only piece of paper in the room – there were no books or newspapers or calendars or letters, anything like that. So when you asked me, yesterday, to have another go at tracing Caroline, I thought, what if that card was from her son, and she's not letting on to the Mintars that she knows where they are because she's that sort of person – I mean, I shouldn't think she's the type to care less about saving anyone grief. In fact I'm not sure she wouldn't deliberately hold back the information out of pure spite. So anyway, I thought it might be worth going back and seeing if I could take a closer look at that card.'

'And did she let you in?' said Lineham.

'She wouldn't let us put a toe over the threshold,' said Thanet. 'In fact, I wondered how on earth you'd managed to get in in the first place.'

Tanya looked smug. 'Well, on the first occasion I caught her unawares. The front door was open and when there was no reply to my knock I just walked in. She probably hadn't heard, with that radio blasting out. Anyway, she was in the room at the back and looked very put out to see me, but short of actually manhandling me out there was little she could do about it.'

'I'm surprised she didn't,' said Thanet, 'judging by our reception yesterday.'

'But I did realise there could be a problem today,' said Tanya, 'so I was a bit sneaky, I'm afraid. I said I wasn't there in my official capacity, that I'd come because I'd heard she was good with herbal remedies and I wondered if she could help me.'

'What did you say was wrong with you?' said Lineham.

'Menstrual problems,' said Tanya. 'I thought that might be the sort of thing she could claim to cure.'

'And?' said the sergeant.

'It worked!' said Tanya triumphantly. 'Not that it was exactly what I would call an enjoyable experience. I really think the woman must be deaf because once again the radio was playing far too loudly and I practically had to shout to make myself heard. And on top of that, the smell was worse than ever today.' Tanya wrinkled her nose. 'She'd had all the doors and windows shut and it was truly appalling. I really cannot imagine what it is that stinks like that. I tell you what it reminded me of – some of the disgusting hole-in-the-ground type lavatories I've come across, on really rough holidays abroad, but multiplied a hundred times over and overlaid with stinks from the concoctions she brews up.'

Tanya had a predilection for holidays in primitive, out-of-the-way places.

'You didn't smell it, Mike,' said Thanet. 'It is truly indescribably awful. If you ask me, Tanya, you deserve a medal for going in there a second time.'

'Perhaps that's what it is,' said Lineham. 'A hole-in-the-ground latrine which she hardly ever bothers to empty, in the room at the back.'

'Anyway,' said Tanya, 'I saw right away that the postcard was still there. So I told her what my problem supposedly was, laying it on a bit thick and trying at the same time to get a look at the postcard without seeming to show any interest in it. But it was hopeless – the place is so dark and murky, I shouldn't think the windows have been cleaned in living memory and the walls are a sort of nicotine colour, discoloured I imagine with smoke and accumulated dirt. So I laid on a bit of drama. I hadn't noticed a well outside and there was no tap in the room so I assumed it must be in the scullery place at the back and I pretended to feel faint and asked for a glass of water. I wasn't sure if she'd fall for it but she did and the minute she was out of sight I grabbed the card and managed to see where it was from. There was a message on the back but I didn't dare take the time to read that. I put it back in exactly the same position and was sitting with my head between my knees when she came back a second or two later. She was very quick, I don't think she liked leaving me alone in there even that long.'

'Well done!' said Lineham in admiration.

Tanya pulled a face. 'Of course, I then had to drink from the glass. It was probably crawling with germs so if I go down with a stomach upset you'll know why.'

'And where was the card from?' said Thanet.

'Callender, in Scotland. So I rang the police station there and inquired if they knew of a Richard or Dick Swain in the area. It's a smallish town, so I was hoping they might.'

'And did they?'

She shook her head. 'But they said they'd look into it, do their best to help. Anyway, they just rang back to say they'd found his name on the electoral roll. Apparently there's a biggish house not far from the town and he lives in the lodge. I imagine he's the gardener there.'

'Married?'

She nodded, eyes sparkling. 'So they said, yes.'

'Excellent.' This would be good news indeed for Mintar and Rachel. But prudence dictated that something should be checked first. 'Did they actually tell you the Christian name of his wife?'

Tanya looked crestfallen. 'No. I was so excited they'd found him I didn't ask. I should have checked, shouldn't I?'

'It might be a good idea.'

She left in a rush.

'Well,' said Lineham. 'There's a turn-up for the book.'

'Hold your horses, Mike. We're not certain yet. It could be pure coincidence.'

'What, another Richard Swain living in Callender, where the card came from? Some coincidence!'

'Coincidences happen.'

It was a few minutes before Tanya returned. Even before she spoke, her disappointment was evident. 'His wife's name is Fiona,' she said.

There was a brief silence while Thanet and Lineham assimilated this piece of information.

'Then assuming we have the right Dick Swain,' said Lineham slowly, 'whatever happened to Caroline?'

EIGHTEEN

It was Thanet who broke the speculative silence which ensued. 'Let's not jump to conclusions,' he said. 'There are various possibilities.'

'Such as?' said Lineham.

'Well, for a start, as you yourself implied, we could have the wrong Dick Swain.'

'A bit of a coincidence, if it was, surely,' said Tanya.

'That's what I said.' Lineham was nodding agreement.

'Nevertheless, a possibility,' said Thanet. 'And there are others. Caroline might have changed her name to Fiona – she might have felt . . . new life, new identity.'

'Or Fiona might even be her second name,' suggested Tanya.

'True. You'd better check.'

'I suppose it's possible that Caroline started off with Dick Swain but they found it didn't work out and both moved on to pastures new,' said Lineham.

Now Tanya was nodding agreement. 'Yes. Four years is a long time, after all, and living with someone is very different from having a love affair.'

'Especially as they came from such very different backgrounds,' said Thanet.

'And forbidden fruit is often much more attractive than eating it every day,' said Lineham.

Thanet suppressed a grin. It wasn't like Lineham to be

so poetic. But he had a point. All in all, it seemed a likely explanation. Caroline's original attachment to Swain may well have been strengthened by the fact that her parents disapproved of it.

'But in that case,' said Tanya, 'wouldn't she have returned home?'

Both men thought about that.

'I don't know,' said Lineham. 'She might have felt it would have been too much of a climb-down.'

'To play the prodigal daughter, you mean?' said Thanet. 'Possibly. We don't really know enough about her to be able to judge.'

'If she did take off on her own it'll be like looking for a needle in a haystack,' said Tanya gloomily. 'We wouldn't have a clue where to begin.'

'But, of course,' said Thanet, 'we do also have to accept that something could have happened to her, either before she met Dick Swain that night, or after she started living with him.'

'If it was after, the Callender police would have to be involved in any investigation,' said Tanya.

'Quite. But if it was before . . .'

'Surely,' said Lineham, 'if it happened before she met him that night, if she simply didn't turn up, he'd have come looking for her? And he himself would not have gone at all.'

'I disagree,' said Tanya. 'If he thought she'd changed her mind about eloping he might have been so fed up he took off anyway.'

'Possible,' agreed Thanet. 'Obviously, the first thing we have to do is make sure we've got the right man – get him on the phone and talk to him. I'd like to speak to him myself. Then we'll take it from there. You'd better start trying, Tanya. He might well be out at work, of course, but you'll be bound to get through eventually.'

'Right, sir.'

'D'you think we ought to tell Mr Mintar about this?' said Lineham, when she had gone.

'Not yet. Let's try and find out a bit more, first. I don't see any point in either raising his hopes or frightening him unnecessarily. He's got enough on his plate at the moment.'

'You think she might be dead, sir?'

'What's the point of speculating, Mike? Let's wait and see, shall we?'

But Lineham couldn't leave it alone.

'Because if so, do you think the two murders might be connected, or do you see them as separate issues?'

'How can we possibly tell?' Thanet was becoming exasperated.

'If something did happen to her on her way to meet him, we'd have the devil of a job to find out what it was. The trail would be stone cold.'

'It doesn't take a genius to work that out! Let's hope the eventuality doesn't arise. I said, leave it, Mike! Obviously it's a potentially serious situation but we can't say more than that at the moment. In any case, I'd better go down and give the Super an update or he'll be complaining about being kept in the dark again.'

Draco listened with his usual concentration. 'You're right,' he said when Thanet had finished. 'Talk to Swain first then take it from there. I agree that the most likely explanation is that she found him too much to stomach at close quarters and moved on to pastures new. Let's hope so, anyway. Keep me posted – and meanwhile, don't forget you're conducting a murder investigation. Done anything about evidence yet?'

'Well in hand, sir.' Thanet had difficulty in keeping a straight face and on the way back upstairs allowed himself the luxury of a broad grin.

'You're looking more cheerful, sir,' said Lineham.

'Not really. I'm afraid we've got a frustrating time ahead.'

He was right. They did. He had set things in motion and now they had to sit back and wait. Very early on in their careers policemen learn to cultivate patience but Thanet always found it especially frustrating to be entirely dependent upon the activities of others to provide him with further impetus in an investigation. There was invariably work to do, of course, dangling ends of other cases to be tied up, but today he found it virtually impossible to concentrate. He felt in limbo, as if everything were on hold. He saw little point in further interviews with any of the suspects in the Mintar case until he had some material evidence, if only the merest scrap, to guide him in one direction or another. And it was equally pointless to speculate on Caroline's fate or discuss how best to proceed in finding out what had happened to her until they were certain that she was in fact missing. He wondered how Mintar would react if this proved to be the case. According to other witnesses, the QC had for the last four years been behaving as though Caroline were dead and gone, but that episode at Marah Swain's house yesterday had convinced Thanet that this was just a front, a mechanism by which Mintar had attempted to cut himself off from the pain of believing that she might still be alive and had not cared enough about her family to get in touch. If she really were dead, had been dead all along . . . It didn't bear thinking about. To lose, in effect, wife and daughter within the space of a few days and on top of that to be suspected of killing one of them . . . Tentatively, Thanet tried to imagine what it would be like, but in view of Bridget's current vulnerability it was too painful and he gave up; he tried to immerse himself in routine, failed once more, and found his thoughts going round and round in the same vicious circle yet again.

It would have helped to find relief in activity but he dared not go out in case Tanya managed to get through to Dick Swain. Swain might well be out at work but if her guess was right and the fact that he lived in the lodge of a big house meant that he was employed to work on the estate, he might well drop in from time to time or hear the telephone ring as he was passing by. And the truth was that as time went on and Thanet had more and more time to brood he was becoming increasingly concerned that something had indeed happened to Caroline on the night she eloped. It was, after all, surely unlikely that she would have allowed four whole years to go by without so much as a phone call to her parents, to let them know that she was all right and give them the opportunity to heal the breach between them. By all accounts she had been a much loved daughter, on good terms with them until she fell for Swain. Staring at the phone, willing the call to come through, Thanet compared himself with wry amusement to a love-sick teenager to whom the ringing of the telephone was the most longed-for sound in the world.

The occasional interruption was a welcome relief. At one point Tanya put her head around the door to tell him that Caroline's second name had been Anne. So that was one possibility out of the window. And as he had predicted, the laboratory manager was kicking up a fuss over the amount of stuff Thanet's team was bringing in for examination. Lineham had to field more than one irate phone call and eventually Thanet said, 'Let me speak to her.' He was, he realised, spoiling for a fight, ready to do anything, in fact, to relieve the tension that was steadily building up in him. Careful now, he told himself. It would be pointless and counter-productive to antagonise her.

'Hullo, Veronica. Luke Thanet here. Look, I really must apologise about this. I do appreciate how fed up you must be to have this avalanche descend upon you, but as DS Lineham says, the Super is insisting that we concentrate on finding some useful scientific evidence and I can't see any other way to get it. Unless . . .' He allowed a thoughtful pause.

'What?' The voice at the other end was understandably eager.

Faced with that mountain of time-consuming work, who could blame her? thought Thanet. 'I understand the fingerprint comparisons with those on the well cover aren't ready yet?'

'Not yet, no. Yours isn't the only case we're dealing with, you know, Luke. We do have other matters to attend to – in fact we're absolutely snowed under at the moment. Which is why—'

'There wouldn't be any way of hurrying them up, would there?'

'Why, specifically?'

'It's just occurred to me . . . If one of them gave us a definite lead, you might not have to bother with most of the stuff that's been coming in today.'

'I see what you mean. Yes.' A long-suffering sigh. 'Well, I suppose I could try to expedite matters a little on that front . . .'

'If you could, that would be great!'

'But I hope you realise that this puts me in a very diffi-cult position. You're not the only one breathing down my neck, you know.'

'I appreciate that, Veronica. But this way—'

'Oh God. Here's another load of stuff arriving. Look, I can't promise anything, but I'll see what we can do.'

And the connection was cut.

'Very neat,' said Lineham, grinning.

'Had to hurry them up somehow, didn't we?'

But the small glow of satisfaction soon faded and it was back to waiting again.

It was five o'clock when Tanya again put her head around the door. 'I've got through at last,' she said. 'To Mrs Swain. Her husband's not there. D'you want to talk to her?'

Thanet nodded and picked up the phone. 'Mrs Swain?'

'Yes.'

Even in that single monosyllable Thanet detected a Scottish accent and his heart sank.

'Mrs Richard Swain?'

'Yes. What is it? What's wrong?'

'Nothing. Please don't be alarmed. I don't know if DC Phillips explained, but we're trying to trace a Mr Richard Swain in the hope that he might be able to give us some information in connection with an investigation we're conducting. I wonder if we could just check that we have the right Mr Swain. Is your husband normally called Dick?'

'Yes, he is.'

'Do you happen to know how long he has been living in Callender?'

'About four years, I think. Something like that, anyway. We met three years ago, and he'd been here a wee while before that. If there's nothing wrong, why are you asking all these questions? Is he in trouble?'

'No, not at all. It's just something we need to clarify, that's all. If you could just bear with me a little longer . . . Could you tell me if he originally came from Kent?'

'Yes, he did. He was raised in a village called Paxton. Why can't you tell me what all this is about?'

So they did have the right man. Good. 'I'm sorry, I can't do that. No doubt your husband will explain, when I've spoken to him. What time will he be back, do you know?'

'Not until sometime tomorrow. He's away to the Midlands overnight visiting nurseries, choosing plants to order in the autumn for Mr McNeil.'

His employer, Thanet presumed. 'Can I get in touch with him?'

'I'm afraid not. I don't know where he'll be staying. He said he'd find a bed and breakfast place. He's travelling around, you see.'

'Will he be ringing you tonight?'

'I don't think so, no. It's only the one night he's away.'

'Well, if he does, would you ask him to ring me? And if not, could you get him to ring the minute he gets back

222

tomorrow?' Thanet dictated his office and home numbers and rang off.

Then he gave up and went home.

But for once he did not find his usual consolation there. Both he and Joan were too on edge about Bridget to be able to relax and it was a relief finally to go to bed, switch off the light and know that tomorrow should bring an end to the waiting and answers to the interminable questions which tormented them: *Would Bridget be all right? Would the baby be all right? Would it be healthy, perfectly formed? Would its internal organs be properly developed? What would be its chances of survival? How would Bridget react if anything went wrong?*

But nothing would go wrong, Thanet told himself fiercely. It was a good hospital and she was in expert hands. Because of the complications they were keeping a close eye on her. Everything would be all right.

Joan too was finding it difficult to get to sleep. Normally they slept back to back but tonight, needing her proximity, Thanet turned on to his left side and curled himself around her. She responded at once, snuggling in close to him, but whereas the natural consequence of such a manoeuvre would normally have been that they made love, this time neither of them had the heart for it. With their daughter in such a potentially dangerous situation it just wouldn't have felt right, that's all.

Thanet's arm tightened around Joan's waist. 'She's in good hands,' he whispered. 'She'll be fine.'

'I know.'

But the fact that they couldn't be certain continued to torment them through the night.

Next morning Thanet was shaving when the telephone rang. He jumped and nicked himself. 'Damn,' he whispered, dabbing at the drop of blood which oozed out and reaching for the styptic stick. Joan had answered the phone in the hall downstairs and he went to the top of the staircase. 'What?' he said, almost afraid to ask.

'Alexander,' she said, putting the phone down. 'Just

confirming that they're going ahead with the induction this morning.'

'Good.' It was a relief to be certain that one way or the other the matter should be resolved before too long. Thanet felt he couldn't have faced another day like yesterday. As it was today promised to be action-packed. Dick Swain should be ringing back and with any luck Veronica might come up with some useful information on the fingerprint comparisons.

One look at Lineham's face when he got in was enough to tell him something important had come up.

'What's up?' he said.

'Good morning to you too, sir.'

'Mike! Come on, what have we got?'

'Veronica Day has been on the phone. She'll be sending the paperwork over later, but she thought we'd want to know. They've come up with a match.'

'Any use?'

'Pretty significant, in the circumstances. If you remember, there's a metal handle at each side of the well cover to pick it up by and no doubt that's how both Mrs Mintar and Digby would have lifted it off and replaced it. But whoever put it back that night wasn't used to handling it and no doubt they were in a hurry too. So they didn't use the handles, simply grabbed it by the edges. I'm sure you'll agree that there's only one way two full sets of four fingerprints could have been found on the under edges of the well cover, with thumb-prints in the appropriate positions on the top—'

'Get on with it, Mike. So, whose?'

But Lineham was enjoying keeping him in suspense. 'According to Veronica Day, although some of the prints are blurred several of them are clear enough to make the match conclusive . . .'

'Mike! Whose?'

Lineham told him.

NINETEEN

'Right,' said Thanet. 'As soon as the morning meeting's over we'll be on our way. I don't suppose Dick Swain's rung in yet?'

Lineham shook his head. 'I thought his wife said he wouldn't be home until later on this morning.'

'She did. We'll probably be back by then. It's just that I don't want to take this particular call on my mobile – it could be at an inconvenient moment and there may be too many distractions. Tell Tanya if he calls while we're out I'll ring him back as soon as I can.'

Before going downstairs to the meeting Thanet rang Veronica Day to thank her for expediting the matter of the fingerprints and to request that the lab now focus on one particular set of clothes. 'I'm hoping to bring the suspect in this morning and if you could find anything which indicates contact with the victim, that would be an enormous help.'

A resigned sigh. 'I'll see what we can do.'

Thanet's news about the fingerprints at once restored him to Draco's good books. 'Excellent, Thanet, excellent. I knew things would start to move once you really focused your mind on getting some evidence.'

Thanet forbore to point out that they had been waiting for these particular results for days.

'You'll be anxious to get on with it, then. Well, I won't delay you. Well done.'

'We haven't got a confession yet, sir.'

Draco smiled benignly. 'You will, I'm sure, Thanet. You will.'

I hope, thought Thanet as he hurried back upstairs. You could never count on it. Already he was working out tactics. Perhaps it would be better to send someone to bring the suspect in? But no, he didn't see why he should deny himself the pleasure of seeing that self-assured façade crumble when it became apparent that this time an arrest was being made.

Lineham jumped up eagerly as Thanet entered the room.

'Right, Mike, let's go. Did you check his whereabouts?'

'Not expected at work till ten, sir.'

'Good. We'll pay him a little home visit, then. Where does he live?'

'Palmerston Row.'

'Does he, now. That brings back memories. Remember the Julie Holmes case?'

This was one of the first murder investigations Thanet and Lineham had worked on together.

'I remember them all, sir.'

He probably did, too, thought Thanet indulgently. Lineham's enthusiasm for his work had never waned. Although he himself had not returned to the area for more years than he cared to count, he found that it was little changed. The mean little back-to-back Victorian terraced houses still looked seedy, furtive almost, despite the attempts to smarten them up with inappropriate replacement windows and mass-produced front doors from DIY stores. Number twenty-nine displayed no such signs of proud ownership. Peeling paintwork, grimy windows and the row of bells beside the front door indicated that it was probably divided up into bedsitters by a parsimonious landlord.

Lineham rang the appropriate bell and they waited.

No response.

'Probably still in bed,' said the sergeant, putting his finger back on the bell and leaving it there.

A minute or two later there were sounds from inside and the door opened a crack. 'For God's sake stop making that filthy row!' A double-take. 'Oh, it's you, Inspector.'

'Yes, it's us. May we come in?'

A reluctant step backwards. 'If you must.'

Lineham was right. Agon had obviously just got out of bed. He was naked except for a pair of boxer shorts patterned all over with hearts. A present from Rachel? Thanet wondered. Or from her mother?

Agon padded up the stairs ahead of them, his bare feet soundless on the threadbare carpet. No daylight filtered into the narrow hall and staircase and the light from the unshaded low-wattage bulb at the top was obviously on a timer; as he reached the top it went off. He cursed and switched it on again before turning right.

His bedsitter was at the front, overlooking the road, probably one of the largest rooms in the house. It was furnished with the bare essentials: single bed, sagging armchair, cheap deal wardrobe and a rudimentary kitchen area – table, plastic washing-up bowl and gas ring. The microwave and television set, no doubt his own, stood out by virtue of their newness and only his clothes, visible through the open door of the wardrobe, showed any degree of care – presumably because they were important to his image. Otherwise, the place was littered with the detritus of careless living: there were used mugs everywhere and empty takeaway cartons on the floor beside the chair, forks and spoons still in them. There was a stale, frowsty smell in the air which Thanet thought probably emanated not only from the residue of food in the cartons but from what looked like a pile of dirty washing on the floor in one corner. A glance at Lineham's face told Thanet what the sergeant was thinking. *What a slob!* Thanet wondered if Agon had ever brought Rachel here. He doubted it.

Agon thrust his arms into a striped towelling dressing gown, kicked a pair of dirty socks into the pile and scooped up the cartons before dropping them into a waste bin. 'Wasn't expecting visitors,' he said.

'So I see. A bit of a contrast to your fiancée's house, isn't it?'

'I don't see what business that is of yours.' Agon folded his arms defiantly.

'Oh, but it is very much our business, sir.' Thanet nodded at Lineham.

'Matthew Agon, I am arresting you on suspicion of the murder of Virginia Mintar . . .' Lineham went on to deliver the caution.

Agon raked a hand through his hair and his mouth dropped open. 'On suspicion of murder? I don't believe it! On what grounds?'

At this point Thanet knew he had a choice. He could either proceed with the interview here or take Agon back to Headquarters for questioning. Agon was no fool and if Thanet took him in the tennis coach would probably insist on a solicitor being present. Here, this might not occur to him.

'Why don't we all sit down and discuss it?' he said.

'Oh no, you don't,' said Agon. 'I know my rights. If I'm being arrested, I'm not saying another word without a solicitor present.'

Thanet caught a rueful glance from Lineham. *Nice try, sir.* 'Very well. That's up to you. So if you wouldn't mind getting dressed . . .'

Agon ran a hand over his chin. 'I haven't even had a chance to shave yet.'

'We don't mind, do we, Sergeant?'

'No, not at all.'

'Well I bloody well do!'

'You use an electric razor, sir?'

'So what?'

'Then you can bring it with you. We wouldn't like you to feel uncomfortable, would we, Sergeant.'

'And if you don't mind I'd like to pee as well.'

'I think we might accommodate you there, sir. Sergeant Lineham will go with you.'

Agon scowled but seemed to accept that he had no choice.

Back at Headquarters they put him in an interview room and left him to organise his legal representation.

'We'll let him sweat for a while,' said Thanet. 'Let's go and see if Dick Swain has rung.' He glanced at his watch. Ten-fifteen. He wondered how Bridget was getting on. It would be some time before they heard anything, he supposed.

'Not yet,' said Tanya, in response to their inquiry about Swain, so they settled down to wait. Half an hour later they were still discussing tactics for the forthcoming interview with Agon when the call came through.

'Mr Swain?' Thanet indicated that Lineham should listen in to the conversation and then introduced himself before quickly establishing that this was indeed the Dick Swain they were looking for.

'What the hell is all this about? You ring up out of the blue, frightening my wife out of her wits . . .'

'I'm sorry if she was alarmed. I did tell her that there was no reason to be.'

'Well, she was. Is. So what's the story?'

'You remember Caroline Mintar?'

'Yeah.' At once his tone was wary.

Thanet cursed the fact that this conversation was being conducted by phone. You could learn so much from looking at a witness while speaking to him. Facial expressions, gestures, movements of hands and feet were all signals, unspoken indications of what the person being interviewed was thinking and feeling. Over the phone you had to rely on tone of voice alone and subtleties were usually lost. 'We are trying to trace her. I'm afraid her mother has died and we're sure Caroline would want to know.'

'So what's it got to do with me?'

'The last time her family had any communication from Caroline was when she left home four years ago, leaving a note to say that you and she had gone away together.'

Silence, so prolonged that Thanet said, 'Mr Swain? Are you still there?'

'Yes.' Swain sounded shaken, the belligerence gone. 'I'm just trying to take in what you're saying.'

'What do you mean?'

'Let me get this straight. For the last four years her family has believed that Caroline was with me?'

'Yes.' It was obvious what was coming.

'Well, she isn't. She never has been. That night . . .'

'What?'

'She never turned up. I waited and waited, but when she didn't come I thought she'd changed her mind. Her family was dead against me. And I was all packed up and ready to go, so I thought, what the hell, I'm not staying around here. I'm off to make a fresh start somewhere else.'

'So why Scotland?'

'Paid for the tickets, hadn't I? We were going to Gretna Green. Big romantic stuff.' Even four years later and presumably happily married to someone else, the residual bitterness could still be heard in his voice.

'You never tried to get in touch with her?'

'Nah. What would have been the point? We had our chance and she blew it. That was that, as far as I was concerned . . . But look here, if she did leave that night, where the hell did she go? You say her family hasn't heard a word from her since?'

'No. As far as they were concerned she had gone off with you and that was all they knew. They tried to trace

230

you both in the interim but without success. They had no idea where to start looking.'

'So what happened to her?'

'That's what we're beginning to worry about.'

'I mean, if she came away, leaving a note . . . But like I said, I waited and waited . . .'

'I suspect she didn't turn up because her grandmother unexpectedly returned home that evening a day early from a long trip abroad, and traditionally they always have a family celebration on those occasions. I imagine Caroline wouldn't have been able to get away as early as she intended without arousing suspicion. Her grandmother says she was like a cat on hot bricks all through dinner. Where were you supposed to meet?'

'In the lane, at the entrance to her drive. I had an old van . . . I even had her bag in the back, she'd given it to me ahead of time so no one would see her leaving with it that night.'

'With her clothes in, you mean.'

'Yeah.'

'What did you do with it? The bag?'

'Chucked it in the river when I got to London.'

'Bit drastic, wasn't it?'

'I was bloody well pissed off, wasn't I. The train got in to Charing Cross and—'

'Just a minute,' Thanet cut in. 'You said you were driving your van.'

'I was. To begin with. Broke down, didn't I, just after Dartford. I tell you, it wasn't exactly the best night of my life. So I hitched a lift to the nearest station. And don't ask me why I didn't just leave her bag in the back of the van because I couldn't tell you. I think at that point I must still have been hoping she'd somehow catch up with me. But by the time I got to London I'd seen how stupid that was, and it's only a few steps from Charing Cross down to the river so I thought, what the hell? It was sort of a . . .' Swain groped for the word, and found it triumphantly, '. . . a symbolic gesture, you might say.'

'Yes, I see.' And Thanet did.

'Look, I'm sorry I can't help you. I would if I could, honest. You will try and find her? Let me know, if you do? I feel sort of . . . responsible, even if I'm not, if you see what I mean.'

'Yes, of course. I'm afraid we shall have to request that your local police verify your wife's identity.'

A brief silence, then, 'Yeah, I see. Sure. That'll be OK.'

'Good.' Thanet thanked him and rang off.

He and Lineham looked at each other.

'Doesn't look too good, does it, sir.'

'I'm afraid not.'

The telephone rang and Lineham answered it. He covered the receiver. 'Mr Agon's brief is here and complaining about being kept waiting, sir.'

'Tell him we'll be right down. That was quick!' said Thanet as they went downstairs.

'Double quick time!' agreed Lineham.

The 'him' was in fact a 'her', they discovered. Thanet had come across her in Court, an attractive young woman in her early thirties and a recent arrival in the firm of Wylie, Bassett and Protheroe, a leading firm of solicitors in the town. Thanet had had dealings with Oliver Bassett, the senior partner, on several occasions. He was surprised to see Barbara Summers here, though. Her normal field was juveniles and family matters. Since when had Agon been her client? Thanet wondered. Then, catching the smug, almost possessive glance which Agon cast at her while Thanet was greeting her, realised that in all probability their relationship until now had been that of coach and pupil. Faced with the urgent necessity of summoning legal representation, what more natural than that Agon should have thought of a solicitor he knew? This would also explain why he had been able to get hold of her so quickly. He would be used to snapping his fingers and have his female clients come running. A glance at her left hand told Thanet that Ms Summers was unmarried and no doubt as susceptible to Agon's charms as any other member of her sex.

Barbara Summers caught Thanet's sudden look of comprehension and her lips tightened. 'Let's not waste time, Inspector.'

'As you wish.'

Lineham started the recording and began the interview by repeating the caution. Thanet was careful to play by the book and wanted it on tape. *You do not have to say anything. But it may harm your defence if you do not mention when questioned something which you later rely on in court. Anything you do say may be given in evidence.*

'Now then, Mr Agon,' said Thanet. 'You must understand that you are in a very serious position.'

'My client is well aware of that and so am I,' said Barbara Summers coldly. 'We wish to know the grounds upon which you have made this preposterous arrest.'

'All in good time, Ms Summers. These things can't be rushed. I don't know how *au fait* you are with the situation . . . ?'

'Mr Agon has explained it to me.'

'Good. Then you will know that prior to his engagement to Miss Rachel Mintar, he had an affair with her mother, Mrs Virginia Mintar, in connection with whose murder he has now been arrested. I'm sure he has also told you that we have photographic evidence of this affair.'

'Yes, Mr Agon has given me a very full and frank account of all this. And he wishes it to be put on record that Mrs Mintar was the initiator of that affair. She, in effect, seduced him.'

Looking at Agon leaning back with apparent nonchalance in his chair, legs stretched out in front of him, genitals bulging in his tight jeans, Thanet wondered

233

what a jury would make of this claim. The man couldn't help but exude sexuality and it was difficult to imagine him playing a passive role in any love affair. 'I see,' he said drily.

'And he also wishes to point out that he has absolutely no motive for committing this crime.'

'Perhaps one will emerge,' said Thanet. 'As you yourself were not present that night, Ms Summers, it might be helpful for me to set the scene for you.'

'Helpful to whom?

'To you.'

'I'm not here to listen to stories, Inspector, simply to reiterate that these charges against my client have no foundation and should be dropped forthwith.'

'In that case, hearing what I have to say should merely strengthen your conviction of his innocence. From his point of view, would that not be a constructive course of action?' Thanet was rather enjoying this sparring. Both of them knew that he wasn't going to leave this room until he had said what he wanted to say and that she would continue to go through the motions of putting obstacles in his path. It was all part of the process, in some ways almost a kind of bizarre foreplay to the real action to come.

She gave a long-suffering sigh. 'Very well, then. If we must.'

Thanet gave a brief account of the dinner party, of Rachel's and Agon's arrival with the announcement of their engagement, and of the so-called celebration which followed.

Barbara Summers was becoming increasingly restless. 'Really, Inspector, is all this relevant?'

Thanet was terse. 'Highly.' He waited a moment for a further objection but none came, so he continued his summary of events. When he got to the point where the table was cleared and everyone dispersed, he stopped. 'And this, of course, is where we get to the interesting

234

part. Perhaps I should explain that the kitchen courtyard was Virginia Mintar's pride and joy. She took particular care of four large camellias in tubs, to the extent that she always insisted that they were watered with water from the well, tap water being too hard for them. Except at weekends it was the gardener's job to do so, but this was a Saturday and she was actually engaged in this somewhat laborious task when Dr and Mrs Squires arrived. Naturally she stopped what she was doing and went to greet them, putting her watering can down beside the well wall with the intention of finishing the job later. In fact, she asked her husband to remind her to do so. Consequently, and with tragic consequences for her, she did not at that time replace the well cover, which was normally secured in position by a padlock and chain. Mrs Squires confirms that the cover was left off.'

Thanet had been watching Agon closely. The tennis coach had been feigning boredom, turning his head from time to time to gaze out of the window and examining his fingernails, one of which seemed to engage his attention. But now, for the first time, Thanet got a reaction: Agon seemed to freeze – so briefly that Thanet could almost have thought he had imagined it. But he hadn't, he was certain. Had Agon suddenly realised where this might be leading?

'Later, soon after they realised that Mrs Mintar was missing and started looking for her, Mr Squires is pretty certain that the cover was back in its usual position. We think that whoever replaced it pushed Mrs Mintar down the well before doing so but was obviously not familiar with the arrangements for securing it. Next morning, when the gardener noticed that the watering had not been finished, the padlock and chain were not in position.' Thanet paused to give weight to his next words.

'To fetch your swimming costume from the car, you, sir, had to walk right past that well.'

As yet Agon had not said a single word throughout

but as Thanet had hoped this stung him into speech. He sat up with a jerk and gave a derisory laugh. 'And that's why I've been arrested? Just because I walked past the bloody well? Anyone could have replaced that cover! Anyone! For all you know Virginia might have thought it was dangerous to leave it uncovered and put the cover back herself, intending to fix the padlock and chain later. The same goes for old Mrs Mintar – her front door is only a few yards away and it's quite likely she noticed the well was uncovered when she went back after dinner. And Dr Squires and his wife had to walk past it too, both of them – twice, in fact. Once on the way home to change into their swimming things and once on the way back. What's more, they actually knew the cover had been left off – you said so yourself.'

Thanet again allowed a telling pause before saying quietly, 'But their fingerprints are not on the well cover, Mr Agon. Yours are, where you picked it up. A full set from each hand. Thumb-prints on top, fingerprints underneath.'

TWENTY

Almost before the words were out of his mouth realisation hit Thanet with a jolt which caused his heartbeat to accelerate and the blood to pound in his ears. How could he have been so stupid, so incredibly short-sighted? The truth was, he had been so delighted to have something positive to go on at last that he hadn't thought the matter through sufficiently. It gave him little comfort to think that both Lineham and Draco had fallen into the same trap. For it was suddenly obvious to him what Agon's response would be and he, Thanet, would be defenceless against it. What should he do? Get out of here fast and think again was the answer, before Agon had time to respond.

He was on the point of getting up and Agon was opening his mouth to speak when help came from an unexpected quarter.

Barbara Summers laid a restraining hand on Agon's arm and shook her head to silence him. 'I should like to confer with my client,' she said.

'Very well,' said Thanet, on a rush of relief. He nodded at Lineham who terminated the interview and switched the recorder off.

'Talk about being saved by the bell!' he said, the moment they were out of the room. He headed up the stairs two at a time and Lineham raced after him.

'What do you mean, sir? What's the hurry?'

'I've got to speak to Veronica. Let's pray she'll come up with something. If not, we'll just have to try and find an excuse for not carrying on with the interview until she does.' Already Thanet was dialling. 'And what if she doesn't? What a fiasco! I could kick myself, I really could.'

'Sir—'

'You still haven't seen it, have you, Mike? Not that I can blame you. It only just hit me, down there, the moment I told him about his fingerprints being on the well cover . . . Honestly, you really would think that after all these years I'd have seen this coming!'

'What? I still don't know what you're talking about!' Lineham's face betrayed his frustration.

'Oh, sorry, Mike, it's just that – Hullo? Veronica Day, please . . . Veronica? Luke Thanet here. Look, I don't suppose by any chance you've – You were? You have? What?' Thanet sank down on to his chair, the receiver pressed to his ear, listening intently. 'That's terrific!' he said at last. 'Really tremendous. I can't tell you how grateful I am. Thank you, I owe you one. You really have saved my bacon.' *Or stopped me making a fool of myself, anyway.* 'What a relief!' he said to Lineham as he put the phone down.

The sergeant folded his arms and gave Thanet an accusing stare. 'If you wouldn't mind telling me what all that was about . . .' he said.

'Mike, I'm sorry, I really am. As I was saying, it was when I was telling Agon about his prints being on the well cover that I suddenly realised he could come up with a perfectly simple explanation . . . All he had to say was that when he went to get his swimming things he'd noticed the cover was still off, thought it looked dangerous, especially as it was beginning to get dark by then, and put it back on for safety's sake. And there'd be no way of proving that Virginia wasn't already down

238

there when he did so, or even that someone didn't come along later and remove it again.'

'Unlikely, surely.'

'Oh come on, a good defence counsel would make mincemeat of us and you know it. The truth is, I did what I'm always telling you lot not to do – i.e. rush ahead without stopping to think things through. That was why I was so anxious to speak to Veronica just now. As you know, I asked her earlier to give the clothes Agon was wearing that night priority and guess what?'

'They found something? What?'

Thanet told him.

A broad grin spread across Lineham's face. 'Let's see him wriggle out of that one.'

'Yes, but let's not rush into it this time. Let's think of ways he might.'

Twenty minutes later the interview was resumed. Agon was looking smug and confident again, Thanet noted.

'My client wishes to make a statement,' said Barbara Summers.

Here we go, thought Thanet.

And indeed, Agon's explanation was just as he had predicted. 'So,' he said when Agon had finished, 'you're saying in effect that your conscience wouldn't allow you to leave the well uncovered in case there was an accident.'

'That's right.' Agon was positively glowing with self-righteousness.

'So why didn't that same conscience tell you to own up to having handled it until now, when you've been forced to do so?'

'That is perfectly obvious, surely,' said Barbara Summers. 'In the circumstances my client was afraid that such an admission would place him under suspicion. As he had acted from the highest of motives he felt that this would be unfair and unreasonable, and he was not inclined to risk it. Of course he now regrets that he didn't give you a full and frank account in

the first place, and wishes to apologise for misleading you.'

'A full and frank account . . .' said Thanet. 'I'm afraid
I'm not convinced of that.'

'What do you mean?' she said.

'That shirt you were wearing on Saturday night, Mr
Agon. Pale mauve, as I recall, and very stylish . . .'

Agon looked surprised at the sudden change of subject
but couldn't resist the appeal to his vanity.

'Ralph Lauren,' he said.

'Pretty new, too, I'd guess. When, exactly, did you
buy it?'

Agon glanced uneasily at his solicitor.

'Why do you want to know?' she said.

'It's a simple question,' said Thanet. 'If your client is
innocent, as he claims, he should have no problem in
supplying the answer – though I should warn him that it
would be unwise to try to mislead us. These things can
be checked, as I'm sure you are aware.'

'Saturday morning,' said Agon.

'And where?'

'Maidstone. At a shop in the High Street. But I don't
see—'

'Let's be quite clear about this. You are saying that you
bought the shirt you were wearing on Saturday night, the
night Virginia Mintar was murdered, that same morning,
in Maidstone?'

Barbara Summers broke in. 'Look, what is the point of
all this, Inspector?'

'The point is this, Ms Summers. In view of the fact that
Mr Agon admits to having had an affair with Virginia
Mintar, I wanted to be quite certain that he could not
claim to have worn that shirt on any occasion when he
was engaged in intimate contact with her. You see, while
you were conferring with your client just now, I was in
my office speaking to the manager of our laboratory.'
He looked at Agon. 'If you remember, yesterday you

were asked to hand over the clothes you were wearing on Saturday night to one of our officers, for examination.'

Agon had guessed what Thanet might be leading up to. He was now looking apprehensive and the colour was draining from his face, his healthy tan taking on a yellowish, jaundiced hue.

'She has just told me that two of Virginia's hairs were caught up in the cuff button on the left-hand sleeve of your shirt, Mr Agon. Perhaps you wouldn't mind explaining how they got there?'

Agon stared at Thanet and then glanced at Barbara Summers. She was watching him, eyes narrowed and lips pressed together in a hard, unforgiving line. '*We're waiting.*'

'I've no idea what you're talking about,' he said, summoning up a degree of bravado.

'You'll have to do better than that, I'm afraid,' said Thanet.

'If it's true, then it must have happened by accident.'

'Oh? When?'

A shrug.

'And how?'

Still no response. Agon was looking sullen, frustrated.

'Come now, it's unlikely you would have forgotten, surely? A woman's hair gets caught in your cuff button and you don't even remember the incident? Presumably you would have had to release it – and in front of half a dozen other people, too.' Thanet turned to Lineham. 'Make a note, Sergeant. We must check with the others.' And, to Agon, 'You must have been sitting next to Virginia Mintar, of course.'

Again, no response.

'Were you? Again, we can easily check.'

Thanet waited a moment and then said, 'You may choose not to answer these questions now, Mr Agon, but I'm afraid you won't get away with remaining silent in Court. Sooner or later the truth will come out.' He

241

paused to allow what he had said to sink in, then went on, 'I'm aware, of course, that there might have been mitigating circumstances – provocation, even. You've told me yourself that the Mintars didn't approve of your relationship with Rachel and had been upset by the announcement of your engagement – as I recall you even said that it was surprising it wasn't you who had ended up at the bottom of the well. Sergeant Lineham here asked if you weren't perhaps exaggerating and you said, and I quote, "You weren't there, Sergeant. I was."'

'So?' The word was forced out of him reluctantly.

'So I'm simply saying that it wouldn't have been surprising if, seeing you cross the courtyard to your car, Virginia Mintar had seized the opportunity to try and get you to back out of it.' He paused again. 'She offered you money, didn't she?'

A flicker in Agon's eyes told Thanet he was right. 'How much?' he said. 'Twenty thousand? Thirty thousand? No? Fifty thousand, then? Even more? My word, Mr Agon, don't tell me you passed up the opportunity to be a rich man? How very noble of you!' Thanet leaned forward. 'So how did she react, when you refused? She must have been desperate. What happened? She came at you, didn't she? And you grabbed her by the wrists, to fend her off—'

'I had to!' Agon burst out. 'It was self-defence!'

There was a brief, charged silence as they all absorbed what was tantamount to a confession. Thanet couldn't resist a brief, exultant glance at Lineham. *We did it!*

Then Agon turned to Barbara Summers, sitting as if turned to stone beside him. 'It wasn't my fault,' he said, his eyes begging her to believe him. 'She came at me like a madwoman. I had to stop her!'

'Tell us exactly what happened,' Thanet said. 'From the beginning.'

Agon squeezed his eyes shut, massaged his right temple and shook his head as if to clear it of emotional turmoil. Then, picking his words with care, he began to talk.

It had all happened very much in the way Thanet had described. Virginia had called out to Agon as he was taking his sports bag out of the car. They had walked towards each other across the courtyard, meeting in the middle, beside the well.

Listening intently to Agon's account of the subsequent conversation Thanet imagined it had gone something like this:

'I wanted a word in private.'

'What about?'

'Don't play the innocent, Matt! You must have realised that little charade back there was all for Rachel's sake.'

'I do appreciate that I wouldn't exactly be your first choice of son-in-law. In the circumstances.'

'Exactly. So we – Ralph and I – were wondering if anything might make you reconsider, break off the engagement?'

'Such as?'

'Shall we say, a substantial financial inducement?'

'What did you have in mind?'

'Say, fifty thousand pounds?'

'No way.'

'Seventy-five, then? No? A hundred?'

'Look, you can stop right there, Ginny. You'll just have to come to terms with the fact that I love Rachel and Rachel loves me. She's over eighteen and she can make up her own mind about who she's going to marry. Afterwards, well, then you and Ralph can continue to keep her – us – in the style to which she is accustomed.'

'You needn't think you'd get a penny from us!'

'Oh come on, Ginny, I can't believe that. Be realistic. Ralph wouldn't like to see his only daughter living in squalor in a bedsitter or going hungry, for that matter, and neither would you.'

'But just think what you could do with that kind of

243

money, Matt! You could go anywhere you liked, stay in the best hotels . . .'

'But for how long? Sooner or later the cash would run out and I'd be back to square one. No, I really think it's time to settle down. I rather fancy myself as a family man.'

'Family man? You? Never in a thousand years!'

'Just wait and see.'

'Not on your life! Can't you get it into your head that there's no way we're going to let this happen?'

'And how, precisely, do you propose to prevent it?'

'By telling Rachel about the affair you had with me, of course. I didn't want to, naturally, if there was any way of avoiding it—'

'I bet you didn't! Mummy wouldn't want her little girl to think she's been a big bad mummy, would she?'

'But if I have to, I will. That's just a risk I'd have to take.'

'Then I shall deny it. Who d'you think she's going to believe? Who d'you think she's going to want to believe? After all, there's something pretty disgusting about a woman of your age shagging a young lad like me, isn't there? Especially if she happens to be your mother . . .'

'Then I told her a few home truths,' said Agon, finishing his account of the conversation. 'And that was when she came at me.'

Thanet could imagine how cruelly provocative those 'home truths' had been – must have been, to make Virginia react as she had, if Agon's account was to be believed.

'She was like a wildcat, hissing and spitting, fingers hooked like claws . . .'

Propelled by pent-up fury, frustration and fear, Thanet imagined.

'She was going for my face and I grabbed her wrists, to hold her off.'

244

Ah yes, thought Thanet. So that was it. Agon had had at all costs to protect his one priceless asset, his incredible good looks. Damage them and much of his power over women, the charm upon which he relied so heavily, would be lost.

'But she was like an eel, twisting and turning, and all the time trying to reach my face with those disgustingly long fingernails of hers. I thought, if I could just manage to turn her away from me and pin her against the well wall while I secured her hands behind her back . . . But it all went wrong. I gave her one almighty twist and before I knew it, she was gone . . .'

His imagination supplied Thanet with an echo of the splash as Virginia's body hit the water. 'And then?' he said grimly.

'And then, what? That was it.'

'I see. You had no idea whether she was alive or dead but you simply replaced the cover and walked away, went back and enjoyed the swimming party. The jury's going to love that.'

Agon looked from Thanet's face to Lineham's and then, finally, to Barbara Summers's, reading the same expression of condemnation in each. His jaw set and he said doggedly, 'It was self-defence, I tell you.'

Thanet nodded at Lineham. 'Charge him,' he said, in disgust.

TWENTY-ONE

'Agon? And Virginia? That's incredible!' Mintar's mouth twisted in revulsion and he buried his face in his hands, shaking his head in disbelief. 'How could she?' he groaned.

Thanet wasn't sure that Mintar had even taken in properly the fact that Agon had been charged with Virginia's murder. Thanet had tried to be tactful but nothing could disguise the sordid nature of the whole affair and Mintar had obviously focused on the fact that his wife had slept with the man his daughter was engaged to – a man whom Mintar abhorred and who was moreover young enough to be Virginia's son. And there was of course more bad news yet to impart. How was Mintar going to react to the news of Caroline's disappearance? Now that they knew the barrister was innocent Thanet's sympathy for him was unbounded. By now he would have expected the man to have begun to pull himself together just a little, but so far there was no sign of this. Increasingly haggard, careworn and unkempt with every day that passed, Thanet thought that Mintar's colleagues would scarcely have recognised him if they saw him in the street, and he had to admit he was both surprised and puzzled; he would have expected Mintar to have more steel in him.

'I'm sorry to bring such bad news, sir. This must be an awful blow to you.'

'And Rachel!' Mintar raised his head. 'How is she going to take all this?'

How indeed? thought Thanet.

There was silence for a few moments and then Mintar said with a weary sigh, 'Well, I suppose the only good thing that can come out of all this is that she will at last see what Agon is really like, and that will be the end of it.'

Thanet sincerely hoped Mintar was right. In affairs of the heart young girls frequently failed to follow the dictates of reason. Still, Rachel had obviously loved her mother and been very distressed by her disappearance, so perhaps he, Thanet, was being unduly pessimistic. In any case, there was no doubt about it, both she and her father were going to have a very bad time when all this came out in Court. Meanwhile . . .

'Let's hope so,' he said. 'Meanwhile, I'm afraid there's more bad news.'

'What?' Mintar's tone was flat, his eyes dull. He obviously felt that after what he had just been told, no news could possibly be of interest to him.

Someone tapped at the door and opened it: Rachel.

Thanet cast a warning glance at Mintar. *Don't tell her about Agon yet.* That was one conversation which needed to be conducted in privacy. 'Ah, Rachel,' he said, preempting any questions she might ask, 'just the person I wanted to talk to. You might be able to help.'

'Me? How?'

She was, Thanet was glad to see, looking much better. Just as well, in the circumstances. She was going to need all the resilience she possessed today. 'I was just going to tell your father—'

'Bad news, Rach, he said.' Mintar put out a hand to her and she crossed to stand beside him. Still seated, he put his arm around her waist and pulled her to him. *We'll face this together.*

'About Mummy?' she said fearfully.

'About your sister.' Thanet looked at Mintar. 'You

remember I told you yesterday that we were making another attempt to find Caroline?'

Mintar and Rachel exchanged apprehensive glances. 'What do you mean, bad news?' said Mintar.

'We have finally managed to trace Dick Swain.'

They both looked stunned for a moment and then Rachel burst out, 'But that's marvellous! Brilliant! Where are they?'

Her father said warily, 'Why should that be bad news, Inspector?'

'Because Caroline is not with him. He is living in Scotland and I spoke to him myself this morning. He tells me that on the night they were supposed to have eloped she never turned up and he was so fed up about it he decided to take off by himself, leave without her.'

They both stared at Thanet in silent disbelief. Thanet found it impossible to read Mintar's reaction, so complex were the emotions which chased each other across his face: incredulity, obviously, and then – what? Relief? Excitement? Perhaps. And finally, as the implications dawned, anxiety and finally fear.

'But that's not possible!' Mintar said at last. He released Rachel and stood up. He began to pace about in agitation and it was obvious he was thinking furiously. Finally he stopped and said vehemently, 'The man's lying, he must be!'

'He's been married for the last three years to someone else – I've spoken to her, too, a very nice young Scotswoman.'

'Then where's Caroline? What's he done to her? If any harm has come to her . . . You're not letting the matter rest, I hope?'

'Of course not! If necessary we shall ask the police where he is living to investigate at that end. But the obvious thing to do is begin here.'

Rachel hadn't said a word, was still standing frozen with shock. Now she whispered, 'But if she isn't there, where is she?' She turned to her father. 'Dad, where is she? *Where is she*?' Her fragile composure was fast disintegrating again and her father put his arms around her and held her close.

'Shh,' he said, soothing her, stroking her back, her hair. 'Shh. This isn't going to help Caroline, is it?'

She took a deep breath, straightened her shoulders and pulled away from him a little. 'No,' she said, 'it isn't.' She looked at Thanet. 'What did you mean, I might be able to help?'

'Perhaps we could try to talk about this calmly,' said Thanet. 'If you would both sit down?'

Without being asked, Lineham fetched an upright chair and set it down beside Mintar's. When father and daughter were both settled, he said in response to Thanet's nod, 'We just wanted to ask a few questions about the night she left, miss.'

'I don't understand any of this. She said in her note she was going away with Dick.'

'We know that,' said Thanet. 'There doesn't seem to be any doubt about what she intended to do that night. But on the face of it, it seems that she didn't do it.'

'And we think we might know what went wrong,' said Lineham. 'If you remember, that same evening your grandmother arrived home unexpectedly, a day early, from one of her expeditions. She tells us that on such occasions it is usual to have a family celebration and that that night was no exception.'

'That's true,' said Mintar. 'But what's that got to do with Caroline's disappearance?'

'We think that in all probability this meant that Caroline wasn't able to get away as early as she intended and that when she therefore did not show up Dick Swain simply thought she had changed her mind and, as he was all packed up and ready to leave, he decided to do so anyway.'

'And he never tried to contact her again?'

249

'He says not,' said Thanet, 'that he decided to put the whole affair behind him. I had the impression, though he didn't actually say so, that with hindsight he suspected it wouldn't have worked anyway.'

Rachel had been listening intently and now she suddenly said, 'You're right! I remember now . . .'

Everyone looked at her. 'What?' they all said, together.

'Normally Caroline was pleased when Gran came home. We both were. It's such fun. Gran is always full of stories and usually brings us all really exciting presents. I'd forgotten until just now, but that night Caroline was really put out, said she'd made other plans. She even said she thought she'd give dinner a miss, but I told her she couldn't possibly do that, Gran would be too upset. So she stayed . . .' Rachel stared at Thanet with an expression of dawning horror. 'So this is all my fault, isn't it? If I hadn't persuaded her to change her mind, she'd have gone off with Dick and she'd still be living with him. But now, we haven't got a clue what happened to her. If he didn't wait for her, she'd surely have just come home again, wouldn't she?'

'Or have gone to his house to look for him.' Mintar was looking grim and now he stood up again, as if propelled by an invisible force. 'This time I'm going to get the truth out of that bloody woman if I have to knock the door down!'

'You'll do no such thing, sir!' Thanet was on his feet too. 'It wouldn't help Rachel to get yourself into trouble, would it? Besides, we're ahead of you in your thinking. Our first move will obviously be to interview Dick Swain's mother and, as she has been so uncooperative in the past, we have even taken the trouble to obtain a search warrant and bring reinforcements with us in case we need to make a forcible entry. I just wanted to put you in the picture first.'

'Good!' said Mintar. 'Then I'm coming with you! I want to hear what she has to say for herself the minute she says it!'

Thanet hesitated. He should have foreseen this, he realised. In Mintar's position he would feel exactly the same.

And judging by the mulish expression on Mintar's face, nothing short of physical restraint would stop him.

'Very well,' he said with a sigh. 'But I must insist that you give me your word not to interfere in any way.'

'I promise.'

Rachel jumped up. 'I'm coming too.'

'No!' said Thanet and Mintar together.

'Why not?' she cried.

'It wouldn't be appropriate,' said her father.

An argument ensued, resulting in Rachel's departure in tears, slamming the door behind her.

'Perhaps I should have agreed,' said Mintar, looking after her. 'I hate to see her upset like that. God knows, she has enough to put up with at the moment. And we haven't even told her Agon has been arrested yet! I shudder to think how she's going to take that.'

'I know. I'm afraid she's in for a very tough time. But it's better for her to stay here at the moment. It could get ugly, judging by Miss Swain's past behaviour.'

The courtyard seemed full of police cars, though there were in fact only two beside Lineham's. In view of the fact that it was only one solitary woman they wanted to question, Thanet had debated with Lineham whether even two would be one too many, but in the end he had opted for the former. He was devoutly hoping that the show of force would be sufficient to ensure that no actual force would be necessary. Now, as the little procession set off down the drive and turned right for the short journey, the doubts reared up again: was he taking a sledgehammer to crack a nut? No, crack that nut he must. It really was absolutely essential to interview Marah Swain and find out whether or not she had seen Caroline that night and it was quite on the cards that once again she would flatly refuse to talk to them. Much as he disliked the idea, it seemed to him that if she wouldn't cooperate this time the only solution was to try to frighten her into doing so and hope that should he succeed he would be able to tell whether or not she was lying.

251

As pre-arranged, they all left their cars on the road and walked up the narrow track, Thanet equipped with loud-hailer and some of the officers carrying the heavy metal cylinder with side handles which is the contemporary version of the battering-ram. They had instructions to make sure that it and they were visible from the cottage windows, but to keep well back until called to action. *Please God, let me not be making a fool of myself.*

Even beneath the trees it was hot and still, the silence broken only by the shuffle of their feet in the leaves which, parched and crisped by the unremitting heat, were already falling prematurely from trees starved of moisture.

When they reached the clearing they stopped. With door and windows still shut fast the cottage continued to exude that air of brooding menace which had so affected Thanet yesterday. It looked impregnable, a symbol of the intractable mystery which surrounded Caroline's disappearance. Well, he was soon going to change all that, thought Thanet grimly, his jaw setting in a determined line. He nodded, and his men fanned out around that section of the perimeter facing the cottage, with the steel enforcer in a prominent position. Mintar hung back as requested; Thanet didn't want the sight of him to encourage Marah Swain to refuse them entry. Then, adrenalin beginning to pump through his system, he and Lineham crossed the clearing and knocked at the door. Once again there was that tell-tale twitch of the curtain at one of the downstairs windows and now that they were close to the house he could again hear the radio playing. Did she ever switch it off, he wondered?

Lineham knocked again. 'Police. Open up.'

No reaction.

Further knocking produced no result and Thanet walked halfway back across the clearing and spoke through the loud-hailer. 'Open the door, Miss Swain. We know you're in there.'

Still no reaction.

Thanet gestured to the men carrying the enforcer and they moved forward a few steps. Then he tried again. 'Look out of your window, Miss Swain. As you see, we have the means to make a forcible entry, and the warrant to justify its use, if you continue to refuse to let us in. You don't really want us to break your door down, do you? Because that's what's going to happen, in just a few minutes from now.'

He paused, to give her time to absorb this. *Come on, open up! Open up!*

But still she refused to cooperate. Ah well, he told himself, I've given her plenty of opportunity . . . He raised the loud-hailer again. 'Right,' he said. 'I'm going to count to ten, then we are coming in. One, two . . .' He waved the men forward and they advanced as he counted. '. . . seven, eight, nine . . .'

Relief gushed through him as at last the door swung slowly open. Essential as it may have been to gain entry he knew that if they had had to break in his self-respect would have been badly dented. He handed the hailer to one of his men and then he and Lineham stepped inside.

So intent had he been on getting access, Thanet had temporarily forgotten about the smell. Sour, rank and stomach-turning, it almost stopped him in his tracks. He saw Lineham falter beside him before they both moved on.

Marah Swain was standing squarely in the middle of the room, defiance in every line of her stance, legs planted slightly apart, arms folded across her chest, head slightly down as if about to charge. Her long grey hair probably hadn't been cut in years and straggled in greasy wisps down to her breasts and halfway down her back. It was the first time Thanet had seen her properly and she was wearing the ankle-length black skirt, woollen shawl and old cracked-leather boots described by Tanya. He wondered if she ever changed her clothes and was reminded of a book he had once read in which it was described how in remoter country districts in the nineteenth century children used

253

to be greased all over before being sown into their under-clothes for the duration of the winter. For that matter, the whole room seemed to exist in a time-warp. Tanya had not exaggerated: *It's like something out of the Middle Ages . . . doesn't look as though it's been cleaned for about a hundred years, with bunches of dried herbs and stuff hanging from nails all along the beams in the ceiling and every windowsill crammed with jamjars full of things I wouldn't like to examine too closely.* In the background a Radio Kent announcer launched incongruously into the lunchtime news.

'What's all the fuss about, then?' she said.

'It's you who has caused all the fuss, as you put it,' said Thanet. 'If you'd let us in quietly in the first place none of this would have been necessary.'

'Why should I let in any old Tom, Dick and Harry just because they ask to? It's my house, I've got every right to refuse.'

'Not in this case,' said Lineham, producing the search warrant. He held it out to her but she refused to budge and he was forced to advance and hold it out for her inspection.

She gave it only the most cursory of glances, then shrugged. 'Go ahead,' she said. 'Search all you like.'

'Before we do, there are one or two questions we want to ask,' said Thanet. Normally at this point in an interview he would attempt to make it less confrontational by suggesting they sit down but a brief glance around the room convinced him he would prefer to remain standing. Both the cushion on the only armchair and the stained and filthy cover on the sofa repelled rather than invited relaxation. Besides, Marah Swain gave the impression that she would in any case have refused to budge. Her solid bulk looked as though it had almost taken root in the spot where she was standing.

'About Caroline Mintar,' he said.

'Oh, her,' she said, and spat on the floor.

The gobbet landed near Lineham's foot and Thanet

awarded him full marks for self-restraint; the sergeant didn't even flinch.

The light pouring in through the doorway was briefly blotted out and Thanet glanced back over his shoulder to see what was going on. Mintar was now standing just inside the room. Obviously his need to know what was happening had got the better of him. Thanet hoped he was going to keep his promise and stay out of the proceedings. 'Yes, her,' he said, turning back to face the old woman.

'The bitch!' she said.

'It has always been understood that she and your son went away together, but we've now spoken to him—'

'To Dick?' For the first time, her expression altered. It was avid with curiosity. 'You talked to Dick?'

'Yes, this morning. And he tells us—'

'How is he? Is he all right?'

'All in good time, Miss Swain. He told me that Caroline never turned up that night and he went away without her. We know that she was delayed, but that she left home as intended. We assume that when she didn't find him at their prearranged meeting place, she would have come here looking for him.'

'Well, you assume wrong! And even if she had, I'd have sent her packing!'

Thanet's heart sank. The woman was lying, he was certain of it. This wasn't looking good for Caroline.

Marah Swain was still speaking. 'If it hadn't been for her, my Dick would never have gone away and left me.' She stopped suddenly and looked at Mintar, and an expression of extreme malevolence narrowed her eyes and twisted her mouth. 'Your Dick too, eh, *lover*?'

It took a few moments for the implications to sink in.

Mintar, Dick Swain's father?

A glance at Mintar's stricken face confirmed the truth of it and Thanet looked in disbelief from the QC now avoiding his eye to the woman standing triumphantly with arms akimbo. Impossible to imagine a coupling between

255

these two, but then there was no telling what Marah had looked like all those years ago. Difficult as it might be to believe, perhaps in her youth she had simply been a buxom country girl, as fresh as a daisy and with all that flower's innocent charm.

But of course the worst of it was that this meant Dick and Caroline were brother and sister. Which explained so much – why Mintar had been so dead against Caroline's association with Swain, why he had been so devastated by her elopement, why he had refused to take more than the most cursory steps to find her, why he had preferred to try to pretend she had never existed rather than confess the truth to his family and face up to the fact that it was he who was really responsible for the disastrous consequences of that liaison long ago.

Thanet's sympathy for the man dissolved like snow in summer. The truth was that loss of face had been more important to Mintar than his daughter's welfare and Thanet found that unforgivable. If the QC had only had the courage to tell Caroline the truth as soon as she started to show a serious interest in Swain, then none of this would have happened. She would never have left home and Virginia would have been saved from the worst of her excesses and might even still be alive.

Thanet stared at Mintar in horrified disbelief. *How could you have allowed this to happen?*

After one shamefaced glance at Thanet Mintar rallied and retaliated, evidently feeling that there was now nothing to be gained by keeping his promise not to interfere. 'You're lying about Caroline, Marah,' he said harshly. 'Tell us what really happened that night.'

'I did. I have. I never saw hide nor hair of her. Believe me or not, as you choose.'

'We choose not to,' said Thanet grimly. And then, to Lineham. 'Get four more officers in here, Sergeant. We're going to take this place apart.'

'Carry on!' she said, folding her arms again and shifting

256

slightly to firm up her stance, as if to indicate that nothing was going to make her budge, physically or mentally. 'Search away! I don't know what you think you're going to find!'

'That remains to be seen,' said Thanet as the officers, three men and a woman, came in. He wasn't sure himself what he was looking for. Just some indication that Caroline had been here that night, he supposed, though how realistic an expectation that was after the passage of four years, he had no idea. He only knew that the woman standing there like an immovable obstacle was not going to defeat him if he could possibly help it. 'And turn that wretched radio off!' he said to Lineham, as the presenter launched into an interview with a local celebrity. 'I can't hear myself think!'

'Now,' he said into the ensuing silence. And paused. Surely he had heard something? What? He cocked his head, listening intently.

The others looked at each other, puzzled, and Lineham opened his mouth to speak.

Thanet put up his hand. 'Shh!'

But there was nothing, only a tense, expectant silence as they all waited for they knew not what. Thanet relaxed, shook his head and was about to go on speaking when the sound came again, just the faintest metallic chink. Glancing around, he saw that this time they had heard it too.

And then, in a flash, he remembered. Understood.

He looked at Marah Swain, standing as if carved in stone in the centre of the room and she read the knowledge in his eyes, raised her head slightly and gave him a defiant stare. His gaze moved down to her feet, squarely planted on a thick, multicoloured rag rug of the type once common in poorer country households. He advanced upon her. 'Move aside,' he said.

She stood her ground and he gestured to his men, who seized her by the arms. She went limp and they were forced to drag her back, a dead weight, her heels rucking up the

257

rag mat. Now they could all see what he had suspected: there was a trapdoor beneath it.

Thanet went down on his knees and shoved the rug aside. He seized the iron ring folded down into a recess at one side of the door and lifted, swung it back and almost gagged as an even more powerful, suffocating stench gushed up to meet him, filling his nose, his mouth, his lungs. Wooden steps fell away into the darkness. 'A torch,' he gasped, looking up at Lineham. 'I need a torch!'

'A torch,' repeated the sergeant, looking at Marah Swain, but she simply turned her head away, refusing to answer. A quick glance around failed to reveal one and on a bright summer's day like this no one had thought to bring one along. An officer was dispatched to fetch as many as he could muster from the cars on the road but Thanet couldn't wait for his return. Tying his handkerchief over nose and mouth he automatically dug into a pocket for the matchbox which of course wasn't there. Since he had stopped smoking he never bothered to carry one. 'Anyone got a match?'

One of the men fumbled in his pocket and produced a lighter.

Thanet snatched it from him and then, taking a deep breath of the relatively fresh air in the room, he descended half a dozen steps before lighting it. Holding it at arm's length he peered into the blackness surrounding him.

The hairs at the back of his neck prickled as in the far corner of the cellar, where the darkness was most profound, something moved. There was that sound again, but louder this time and now he could identify it: the clink of metal on stone.

Then, so faintly as to be almost inaudible, there came a whisper. 'Please, help me,' it said.

TWENTY-TWO

'You ought to have seen the state she was in . . .' Thanet shuddered, remembering.

It was late that same evening and he and Joan were sitting in the garden, enjoying the cool of the day. Thanet was savouring the pleasure of a case brought to a satisfactory conclusion and the opportunity to relax without feeling the unremitting pressure of a serious investigation hanging over his head. If it weren't for the anxiety over Bridget his happiness would have been unalloyed, but she was now well advanced in labour and the portable telephone lay to hand on the table between their coffee cups, a constant reminder of the all-important event that was taking place some sixty miles away.

Over supper Thanet had been telling Joan about the events of the day and had just reached their dramatic conclusion. Now he shook his head in pity at the memory of Caroline's plight. 'Honestly, Joan, she was barely recognisable as a human being. She was chained to the wall like a criminal in a medieval dungeon, lying on this disgustingly filthy mattress. I shouldn't think she'd seen soap and water since the day she left home, and her clothes were in tatters – I imagine they were the same ones she was wearing that evening. Her hair was so matted I should think it will probably all have to be cut off, and when I picked her up she was so thin it felt as though she might just fall apart in my arms. It was like lifting a bundle of bones. We've all seen photographs of the survivors of the Nazi prison camps but believe me, when you are faced by the reality . . . And that smell . . . I don't think I shall ever forget it.' Even now, despite the fact that the minute he got home he had stripped off, consigned his clothes to the dustbin and taken as hot a shower as he could bear, that cloying, noxious odour still seemed to clog his nostrils, obstruct his breathing and surround him like a miasma.

'The chain was long enough to enable her to move a few feet away from the mattress but no further, and she was surrounded by piles of excrement. Everywhere you moved, you stepped in it, and she was caked in it – she was too weak to stand up so if she got out of bed I imagine she had to crawl.'

Joan had been listening in horrified fascination. 'I've come across some pretty awful behaviour in my clients, but nothing quite as horrendous as this. How can anyone treat another human being like that? It's beyond belief!'

'But sadly, this kind of thing does occasionally happen. Over the years I've read of such cases from time to time and presumably there are many more that never come to light.'

'But why do people do it?'

Thanet shrugged. 'For various reasons, apparently. I remember reading of two separate instances in the United States when women had been locked up for years in bomb shelters because jealous husbands convinced them that there had been a nuclear war. And there have been some pretty dreadful cases in remote country areas when people – men as well as women – have been locked away for as long as thirty or forty years.'

'You're right, I'd forgotten. It's coming back to me now. I remember reading ages ago about the case of an Italian woman in her sixties who had been kept locked up by her relations since she was a young woman because, they said, she was "different" after an illness and they had decided to keep her hidden – to preserve "family dignity and honour", was the way they put it, as I recall!'

'It's virtually impossible to understand the mentality of people like that, isn't it, especially when there's collusion and more than one person is involved.'

'But in this case it was just Marah Swain.'

'Yes. She's such a strange woman. In many ways she's a relic of a past age, a throw-back, if you like, and as such quite outside the normal parameters of acceptable behaviour today.'

'But that's no excuse, surely!'

'Of course not. There *is* no excuse for treating another human being like that. Reasons, perhaps; excuses, no.'

'Her reason being that she blamed Caroline for leading her son astray and ultimately driving him away?'

'Partly, yes. But I did wonder, from something she said . . . Though I don't know, perhaps I'm attributing too civilised a motive to her.'

'Civilised? I'd have thought that was the last word you'd ever apply to her, from what you've been saying. What can you mean?'

'Well, after we found Caroline, Marah said very little, in fact. But as Mintar carried the girl out she did call after him, "They had to be stopped, see. Not natural, was it?"'

'Oh, I see. You're talking about the incest. Though we don't actually know that there ever was any, do we?'

Thanet shook his head. 'Not *know*. Suspect, perhaps.'

'Still, you think she might have felt she couldn't allow it either to go on or to happen, whichever the case may be?'

Another shrug. 'I can't think what else she meant.'

'But she needn't have *kept* Caroline locked up, surely?'

'I don't know. You think about it. When would she have let her go? There would never have been a right time. Besides, I think her desire for revenge was and still is just as strong a reason for keeping Caroline there, if not stronger. She showed absolutely no shame or remorse for what she had done, or pity for Caroline's condition. Just imagine what that poor girl must have gone through! It takes a pretty tough person to survive intact four years of straightforward solitary confinement, let alone under the conditions of filth, near-starvation and total darkness that Caroline had to put up with . . .'

Joan shivered. 'It doesn't bear thinking about. I suppose it's too early to have any idea how well she'll recover?'

'Physically, do you mean? Or mentally?'

'Both, I suppose.'

'I was talking to Doc Mallard about that this afternoon. He heard what had happened and called in at the hospital to see how Caroline was. According to him the human body has an amazing ability to adapt to food deprivation and survive, which is why, during the war, so many prisoners of war did just that. After initial loss of weight the metabolism stabilises, apparently.'

'But aren't there possible long-term effects – like infertility, for instance?'

'Sadly, yes.'

Reminded of Bridget they both glanced at the telephone. When would it ring?

'Doc Mallard mentioned that, but he didn't go into it. I suppose in Caroline's case they'll just have to wait and see. But he does think her eyes will gradually get back to normal.'

'I suppose she couldn't stand the light, after so long in darkness.'

'She couldn't bear to open them at all. We had to cover them, to protect them.'

'Poor girl. What a dreadful, dreadful ordeal.'

'At least she's in good hands now.' Caroline had been taken straight off to hospital. 'I'm sure her father will make certain she gets every care. But as for her mental state, well, who can tell? In any case, it's bound to take time.'

'I can't imagine how she could ever forget an experience like that. And her father was there when you brought her up, you say? How did he react, when he saw the state she was in?'

'He was absolutely shattered, as you can imagine.' Thanet could remember only too vividly the shock, horror, disbelief in Mintar's face as he looked at the stinking, filthy, skeletal figure lying limply in Thanet's arms and whispered his daughter's name. '*Caroline?*' He remembered too the way Mintar had without hesitation or repugnance taken her from him and after one piercing glance of accusation and reproach at Marah Swain, borne his pathetic burden tenderly away. He had sat down to wait for the ambulance in the shade of the trees at the far side of the clearing, cradling his daughter with the gentleness of a mother nursing her newborn baby.

'But what made you guess, about Caroline being in the cellar?'

Thanet considered, shrugged. 'Pure luck, really.'

'Oh come on, Luke! You're being modest again.'

'No, really. Marah Swain had the radio on, you see, and it was getting on my nerves so I asked Mike to turn it off. If I hadn't . . . Well, I don't know. Perhaps one of us would have remembered a cellar being mentioned, eventually. Tanya heard about it during routine questioning of someone in the village whose husband had been friendly with Dick Swain as a boy.

'Anyway, when the radio was turned off I thought I heard something. No one else had, but we all listened. Then it came again and this time they all heard it. And then I did remember the cellar, and suddenly realised why it was that Marah had planted herself bang in the middle of the room and hadn't budged ever since we came in.'

'And that had struck you as odd?'

'Yes, it had. Everything about her body language said, whatever happens you are not going to make me move from this particular spot. She was standing on one of those thick rag mats people used to make out of old clothes.'

'I know the sort you mean. They were made with a fat metal hook, from strips of material. I saw someone demonstrating how to make them once at a country fair.'

'Anyway, it was there to cover the trapdoor, of course, and, together with the radio which was invariably playing, it would have been pretty effective at muffling sounds from below. Poor Caroline's voice is so weak now that she would never have been able to make herself heard anyway and I imagine in the early days Marah would have had no compunction about gagging her if anyone came. I should think that apart from those who want to buy one of Marah's home-made remedies very few visitors ever go to that house. In any case, we actually had to manhandle her, to drag her away from that trapdoor.'

They were both silent for a while, thinking, then Thanet said, 'You know, before we found Caroline, when it dawned on me what Marah was saying, that Mintar was Dick's father, I couldn't feel any sympathy for the man, but when I saw the way he looked at Caroline, the tenderness with which he took and handled her despite that terrible smell . . .'

'Imagine how he must have felt, seeing his daughter in that state!'

Once again they both looked at the telephone lying on the table before them, willing it to bring an end to the interminable waiting.

'So what did you mean, you couldn't feel any sympathy for him?'

'It's obvious, surely. If you think about it, he was the one who was really responsible for the whole disastrous sequence of events.'

'By seducing Marah in the first place, you mean?'

'Partly that, yes. Though looking at her now, I must confess I find it virtually impossible to imagine them as lovers.'

'He didn't deny it, though?'

'Oh no, not at all.'

'Well, there was nothing very unusual about what he did. I'm not condoning it, of course, but throughout the ages young men have sown their wild oats and usually done their best to avoid the consequences. What I don't understand is why it didn't come out in the first place – and why it's remained a secret all these years.'

'Ah, well, I can answer that. Lineham and I followed the ambulance to the hospital.' Thanet was recalling now the horrified expressions on the faces of the nurses when they had seen the state Caroline was in. Caroline herself had uttered not a single word since the moment of her discovery; indeed, but for the tears which oozed from beneath her closed eyelids, had appeared incapable of showing any emotion either. Her father had remained equally silent and it wasn't until she had been delivered into expert hands that Mintar had finally collapsed on to a chair in the relatives' room and, burying his head in his hands, had groaned, 'It's all my fault, Thanet, isn't it? Oh God, I can't bear it . . . Caroline . . .' And then, his defences eroded by distress, fear and guilt and driven, evidently, by the need to tell someone, anyone, the true facts of the story which he had kept bottled up for more than twenty-five years, he had poured out the whole sorry tale.

Thanet realised that Joan was patiently waiting for him to go on. 'I had a long talk with Mintar while Caroline was being examined and those were two of the questions I asked him. Apparently this affair with Marah – if it could be called that – took place just after he had passed his bar finals. He blames his euphoric mood for what happened. He'd been sharing a flat in London while he was studying and had come down to spend a few weeks at home before taking up his pupillage in Chambers in the Middle Temple. I suspect that after keeping his nose to the grindstone for so long he was ready for a bit of fun before launching into the next stage of his career. I'm surprised he didn't take off and do some travelling, but of course it wasn't as much the done thing then as it is now. And apparently his mother was just back from a trip and had indicated she expected him to spend some time with her. Anyway, the fact of the matter was that entertainment was a little thin on the ground in Paxton, so he spent a lot of time walking. So, apparently, did Marah. She inherited her interest in herbs from her mother. She and Marah used to scour the fields and hedgerows most days for the ones she wanted and after she died Marah continued the habit. Mintar had known Marah for years, her father was the Mintars' gardener, and now one thing led to another. I imagine the truth is he was bored and she was just, well, available, I suppose. He doesn't try to excuse his behaviour.

'Soon afterwards he went back to London to start his pupillage. He was nearing the end of it and was hoping shortly to be invited to become a full member of Chambers when, on a visit home for a weekend, he ran into Marah and she told him she was pregnant. It was far too late for an abortion by then. I don't know if she was rather naïvely hoping he might marry her but in any case, when he made it clear that this was definitely not on the cards, she demanded some sort of compensation and threatened to tell his father and even to visit his "office", as she called it, if it wasn't forthcoming.'

'I get the picture,' said Joan. 'Daddy was a High Court judge, so there would be hell to pay if he heard his son had fathered a child with the gardener's daughter, especially one as unprepossessing as Marah. And Mintar's Chambers wouldn't be exactly happy about it either, to put it mildly. The bar's a pretty stuffy profession when it comes to that sort of thing, I imagine.'

'And as you say, especially when the girl is someone like Marah. Imagining her turning up in Chambers was a nightmare scenario. Mintar suspected he would lose his chance of a place and was afraid he'd become a laughing-stock and wouldn't get one elsewhere either if the news got around. All in all, he saw the prospect of his career being blighted before it ever got off the ground. His problem was that he didn't really have much to offer her as an inducement to keep quiet. He had a small allowance from his father, enough just to keep him ticking over until he started to earn some money, but his prospects for the foreseeable future were pretty slim. In those days young barristers invariably had a hard time of it waiting for work to trickle down to them and when it did the fees were not very high. It's not like nowadays when if you're lucky enough to get into a good set of Chambers you'll probably be offered a pupillage award to smooth your path. So he racked his brains desperately to try to think of a bribe that would keep her quiet.'

'Quite a problem!'

'Exactly. But in the end he did come up with a solution. Marah has lived in that cottage for so long everyone assumes it belongs to her, but it doesn't, it's actually part of the Windmill Court property. He promised her that if she remained quiet about his being the father of her child, he would not only pay her a small weekly allowance but would give her the right to live in the cottage rent free for the rest of her life.'

'But he had no right to promise her any such thing, surely? The cottage may be his now but at that time it would have belonged to his father. And even if his father died, it could then have been passed on to his mother.'

'True. But in the event, that didn't happen. Perhaps he already knew of some family trust or arrangement whereby the property would go straight to him on his father's death. I don't know any more than I've told you. Anyway, he admits he banked on the fact that Marah was too unsophisticated to question his right to dispose of the cottage as he wished and he was right. She seemed perfectly satisfied with his offer and the legal-looking document he drew up and presented to her. After all, a roof over your head for life is not to be sniffed at.'

'But what if *her* father had died before Mintar inherited? Wouldn't the cottage have been required for his successor as gardener? How would Mintar have persuaded his father to let her stay on by herself?'

Thanet shrugged. 'No idea. I suppose he thought he'd cross that hurdle if he came to it. In the event, presumably he was lucky and it never happened. The arrangement seems to have worked perfectly all these years until now.'

'But why was she satisfied with the promise of living in the house rent-free? After all, she had him over a barrel, didn't she? Why didn't she stick out for ownership?'

'I asked him that. He thought it might simply have been that it never entered her head. It wasn't as though it was her idea to use the house as a bargaining position, it was his proposal in the first place and he said she was very taken with the suggestion. He was still very nervous that she might think of demanding ownership, of course, and that would have put him in an impossible position. For one thing, as you so rightly pointed out, the cottage wasn't his to dispose of, and for another, even if it had been, it would have been a disastrous move to make. Once it was hers she could have broadcast the truth of Dick's parentage whenever she liked and there would have been nothing he could do about it. This way, they were on equal terms and each had a hold over the other. If she spilled the beans he could turn her out and if he reneged on the agreement she could make sure he paid for it.'

'So why did she suddenly decide to go back on the arrangement this afternoon?'

'I think she realised the game was up and she had nothing to lose by telling us. When inquiries were made about Caroline in the past she'd always managed to fob people off, but this time she could see how determined we were to find out what had happened to the girl. She must have realised that when we did, it was more than likely that the secret of Dick's parentage would come to light. Also, I think that, as I said, even after all this time she was still burning with rage against Caroline and she needed to lash out one last time and vent her anger on someone. Mintar was the perfect target and she couldn't resist the temptation of humiliating him in front of witnesses.'

Joan pulled a face. 'Charming!'

'Quite. And I must say, I think he deserved it. Because what I find unforgivable as far as he's concerned is the fact that if only he'd had the guts to own up to being Dick's father when Caroline and Dick started going out together, none of this need have happened. There'd certainly have been no elopement, Caroline would never have had to endure that terrible incarceration and – who knows? – perhaps Virginia might still be alive.'

They both started as the phone rang.

Joan snatched it up. 'Alexander?' She nodded vigorously at Thanet then listened intently. 'A girl? That's wonderful! And everything's all right? Oh, what a relief! And how's Bridget? Oh? An emergency caesarian? Oh dear! So how is she now? Oh, good. Excellent. Yes, I see. Oh . . . Oh . . . Good . . . Yes . . . I see . . . We'll have to keep our fingers crossed then. Yes. Well, we'll ring the hospital in the morning and come up to see them both tomorrow evening, if all is well. Give her our love, won't you. 'Bye.' Joan put down the receiver and turned to Thanet, eyes filled with tears. 'You heard all that?'

Thanet nodded speechlessly, having himself run the gamut of emotions from elation and relief to fear and back again to relief throughout the brief call.

Joan filled in the details for him. 'The baby is one and a half kilos – that's about three pounds, five ounces, and an excellent weight for thirty-three weeks, apparently. She's been examined by a paediatrician and he says she's in very good shape. She's had to go to the Special Care Baby Unit, but that's routine with premature babies and no cause for alarm.'

When she had finished, Thanet jumped up. 'Just wait there,' he said. A few minutes later he returned with glasses and a bottle of champagne in a cooler. 'I put this on ice earlier,' he said, with a grin stretching from ear to ear. 'As an act of faith. But before I open it . . .' He disappeared into the house again and came back with a parcel. 'I bought this for Christmas,' he said, 'but I just can't wait that long to give it to you. And now seems as appropriate a moment as any.'

'Oh Luke, how exciting! I love unexpected presents!'

He watched indulgently as she unwrapped the jacket and it tumbled out on to her lap, a kaleidoscope of sumptuous colour.

'Oh!' she breathed, holding it up to admire it. Then she looked at him and again there were tears in her eyes. 'It's absolutely beautiful! Wherever did you find it?'

'That's a secret.'

She put her arms around his neck and kissed him. 'I love it, I really do. Thank you, darling!'

'Thought you would,' he said, smugly. 'And now . . .' The cork popped, the foam spilled out in the time-honoured way, and they raised brimming glasses in a toast.

'To the next generation!' he said.

TWENTY-THREE

In the aftermath of the case there was a mountain of paperwork to deal with and Thanet and Lineham spent much of the following day glued to their desks. By 4.30 Thanet had had enough. 'I'm going to look in at the hospital, see how Caroline's doing.'

Lineham nodded, grinned, and said, 'OK, Grandad.'

Thanet had been swamped with congratulations once the news got around and took the teasing in good part. 'That's enough of that, Mike!'

'Are you going up to see Bridget tonight, sir?'

'Try and stop me!'

Lineham opened a drawer in his desk and took out a gaily wrapped parcel. 'Would you give her this, with love from us both?'

'Of course,' said Thanet, touched. 'But how did you manage to produce it so quickly?'

'Had it in the drawer for a week or more,' confessed Lineham with an uncharacteristically shy smile. 'Louise said she'd played safe and chosen yellow.'

'I'm sure Bridget will be delighted. Thank you, Mike. And tell Louise we really appreciate it.'

'Louise went through much the same performance as Bridget herself, with Richard.'

'I remember. I must say, it's such a relief it's all over.'

'I know just how you feel.'

Thanet drove to Sturrenden General and before leaving the car locked the parcel in the boot. The trouble with being a policeman was that you saw thieves and villains lurking behind every bush.

The Sister recognised Thanet immediately. She had been on duty yesterday when Caroline was brought in.

'How is she?' he said.

She pulled a face. 'Put it this way: she'll survive, no question of that, but as to whether she'll ever completely recover . . . But it's early days yet. We'll just have to wait and see how she goes on. At the moment we're trying to get some nourishment into her, but we have to be very careful, take it very slowly.'

'Yes, of course.'

'Her father was talking about moving her to a private hospital or taking her home and hiring nurses to look after her, but we advised against it, for the moment anyway, and he seems to have given up the idea.'

'Is she talking at all?'

'Just a few words. Most of the time she just lies there, staring into space.'

'Has her sister seen her yet?'

'Yes. She's with her now, as a matter of fact. She's been here all day, she and her father. We did try to prepare her, but she was terribly upset when she first saw Caroline, as you can imagine.'

'Yes, I can.' Thanet's tone was grim. Rachel had a great deal to be upset about at the moment and he wondered how she was bearing up.

'And that was *after* we'd cleaned her up. Honestly, Inspector, in all my years in the nursing profession I've never seen anything like the state she was in. I don't think I shall ever forget it.'

'I know. I don't think any of us will.'

'Anyway, as I say, she's in no danger now and we're doing all we can for her.' The Sister's eyes were straying to the paperwork awaiting her attention.

Thanet took the hint. 'I'm sure. May I see her?'

'Of course.' A nurse was called to take him to Caroline's room. She was the only patient in a little side ward with two beds in it. She was lying flat on her back and Thanet suspected that she was asleep, as she didn't move a muscle as he came in. He couldn't be sure, though, as she was wearing dark glasses. Rachel and Mintar were sitting one on either side of her, holding her hands. They glanced up and smiled briefly at him as he came in. Thanet went to stand beside the bed and take a closer look at the patient.

At least today Caroline was recognisable as a human being, he thought, even though she did look as though she were in the final stages of anorexia. She was so thin that her body scarcely mounded the bedclothes and the shape of her skull was clearly discernible. Her skin was unnaturally pale, with a greyish hue, and still pitted with dirt despite the cleansing processes to which she must have been subjected. Although they had not shaved her head as Thanet had feared they might, only scanty wisps of hair remained and alopecia, caused no doubt by prolonged malnutrition, disfigured her scalp. She was a truly pathetic figure and Thanet's heart went out to her for the suffering she had undergone and the long, slow difficult road ahead of her, back to anything resembling normality.

He sensed that Mintar was watching him but when he glanced up the barrister's eyes fell away. Thanet guessed that he was still overwhelmed with remorse.

Caroline must have woken up because her head turned slightly on the pillow. Her father leaned forward and said softly, 'This is Inspector Thanet, Caro. He was the one who found you.'

Her lips moved and they all strained to hear. 'I know,' she whispered. She released Rachel's hand and opened hers to Thanet, raising one finger to beckon him closer.

He clasped the little bundle of bones, conscious of

their fragility, and leaned forward in response to the slight pressure he felt. When her fingers relaxed, he stopped, now close enough to see her eyes through the dark lenses. She was gazing up at him as if trying to memorise his features. Then her lips moved again and he turned his head slightly the better to hear what she was about to say.

'Thank you,' she whispered. And her fingers tightened again upon his. 'Thank you.'

He smiled warmly at her, squeezed her hand and said, 'Just get well again quickly.'

He saw that slow tears had begun to slide down the sides of her cheeks and he released her hand, straightened up and glanced at Rachel, who reached for a tissue and dabbed them gently away.

Although Rachel looked pale and strained, with dark circles beneath her eyes, she seemed to be coping well, Thanet thought. It was obvious that her concern for her adored sister was engaging all her emotional energy at present and perhaps having Caroline restored to her was at least in some measure consoling her for having in effect lost both mother and fiancé within the space of a few days.

Mintar had risen. 'We can never thank you enough,' he said. His eyes, too, were full of tears.

'No,' said Rachel, chiming in.

Thanet shook his head. He hadn't come here for this. 'I must go,' he said. 'I just wanted to check on her progress.' And he escaped, to avoid further embarrassment.

Later, on the way to London, loaded with gifts for Bridget and the baby, he told Joan about this little scene and said, 'I'm not sure he'll be quite so grateful when he fully realises the consequences of all this.'

'When it's all made public, you mean?'

'Yes. Well, it'll all have to come out in Court, won't it? There'll be two cases, not one, remember. Agon will be standing trial too. As for Marah . . . I can just imagine Mintar's colleagues looking at her in the dock and thinking, how *could* he? It'll all be a tremendous scandal in legal circles and I should think he can forget about a seat on the Bench, in the High or any other kind of Court.'

'What will she be charged with?'

'False imprisonment, almost certainly.'

'And what sort of sentence will she get?'

'Years, I imagine.'

They were silent for a while and then Thanet said, 'No, I'm being unjust. He'll always be thankful we found her, no doubt about that. And who knows? Perhaps the fact that at last he is going to have to pay in personal terms for his lack of courage will alleviate just a little the shame and guilt which at the moment is eating him up. I think he'd got to the point where he couldn't live with his conscience any longer. Remember how Mike and I found him trying to batter Marah's door down in an attempt to discover what had happened to Caroline?'

'Yes. You said all along you couldn't understand why he hadn't persisted in his efforts to trace her.'

'I know. But once we learned Dick was his son, of course . . . Well, obviously, if he had managed to find her he'd have had to own up, not only to Caroline but to her mother, too. And I imagine that apart from anything else he just couldn't face the possibility of losing Virginia.'

'And he lost her in the end anyway. I was thinking, what you said last night . . . You really think she might still be alive if he'd had the guts to admit that Dick was his son when Caroline first started going out with him?'

'I think it more than likely, yes.' They had left the M20 for the M23 and were now approaching the link with the M25. Thanet fell silent as he fed into the stream of traffic in the nearside lane and it was a few minutes before he went on. 'Everyone seems to agree that it was Caroline's elopement that seemed to push Virginia over the edge. It was if she just cast aside those internal restraints we all live by. She'd always enjoyed shopping, for example, but now it became an obsession. Ditto with her exercising. She'd always been attractive to men and had affairs but according to what her sister told Arnold Prime, she now "couldn't keep her hands off anything in trousers", was the way Jane apparently put it. She even eventually broke one of her own last taboos and had an affair with a much younger man. And it was this, finally, that was her undoing.'

Ever since his confession and against his solicitor's advice, Matt Agon hadn't stopped trying to justify himself. Apparently Virginia's spell had bound him fast and for the first time in his life he had proposed marriage, begging her to leave her husband. She had simply laughed at him and, consistent in this respect at least, had at once broken off their relationship.

Thanet was pretty certain – though of course Agon hadn't said so – that the tennis coach had seen ensnaring Rachel as the perfect revenge for this humiliating rejection. Thanet suspected too that it was partly Agon's residual anger with Virginia that had caused him to react so violently when she attacked him.

'You're probably right,' said Joan, when Thanet had finished telling her all this. 'A man like that, used to making easy conquests, would take it pretty hard when the one woman he's ever really fallen for laughs in his face when he proposes to her.'

'My mistake was in more or less dismissing Agon as a suspect,' said Thanet. 'And that was because I seriously underestimated Virginia's love for Rachel.'

'Her one remaining child.'

'Exactly. I thought, you see, that she wouldn't have dared offer to buy Agon off in case he told Rachel about it and Rachel turned against her. And I should think that initially that was true. But when it came to the crunch, when Agon actually proposed to Rachel and was accepted, Virginia was prepared to go to any

276

lengths to get rid of him, regardless of the cost to herself.'

Briefly he imagined the scene the night of Virginia's death: Virginia clearing up in the kitchen, glancing out of the window and seeing Agon crossing the courtyard to his car, calling out to him on impulse, anxious to do something, anything, to get her daughter out of his clutches. 'When Agon turned down the very substantial bribe she offered she played her last remaining card and threatened to tell Rachel of her own affair with him. She must have known that if she did it would almost certainly alienate Rachel but by then she was desperate. He said he would flatly deny it had ever happened, that Rachel would certainly take his word against hers, especially in view of the fact that Virginia was so old. He ended up by telling her what he called "a few home truths". I imagine they were pretty cruel, and I think it was these insults, combined with sheer frustration that Virginia had just seen her last hope of saving Rachel fly out of the window, that made her go for him.'

'And having thrown her down the well he just put the cover back on and walked off, not knowing if she was alive or dead!'

'Precisely. It's not too difficult to believe. I should think Agon has spent his life looking after number one. If he'd gone for help, he'd have had to explain how the accident – if you could call it that – had happened in the first place. Far easier to pretend it never had.'

They were now approaching the A3 turn-off and Thanet signalled and eased into the inner lane.

Joan waited until he had negotiated the complicated roundabout at the top of the slip road before saying, 'You've sometimes said that in domestic murders like this it is often in the character of the victim that the seeds of his own destruction lie. Would you say that was true in this instance?'

'Partly, I suppose. But I also think that in Virginia's

277

case circumstances conspired against her. I know that on the surface she seemed to have everything any woman could want – plenty of money, a lovely house and luxurious life-style, – but it wasn't material satisfaction she was looking for. One after another all the people she loved most were taken away from her and every time it happened she slipped a little more out of control.'

'Except her husband.'

'True. But although she always came back to him, needed him as a sort of anchor, I don't think she could have cared very deeply for him or she surely wouldn't have treated him the way she did. No, it was her children she truly loved and ultimately it was that love which was her undoing. So I suppose it was her emotional make-up and her husband's moral cowardice that proved the fatal combination.'

Joan sighed. 'And it's their children who are going to have to pay for it.'

'I'm afraid so. Poor Caroline was doomed from the moment she fell for Dick. Even if the elopement hadn't gone so drastically wrong, she'd still have spent years in an incestuous relationship and if they'd had children—'

'I simply cannot understand how her father was prepared to bury his head in the sand and just let that happen!'

But Thanet was still thinking of Caroline. 'It never ceases to amaze me how sometimes the most trivial of events can have such far-reaching consequences.'

'What do you mean?'

'Well, you wouldn't think that the fact that a grandmother returned one day early from a trip abroad would trigger off a tragic mistiming worthy of a Hardy novel, would you?'

'If you put it like that, no.'

'Hang on a minute.' They had just turned off the A3 into Roehampton Lane. 'Did Alexander give you directions to the hospital?'

'Yes.' Joan was rummaging in her handbag. 'Here they are.'

'We'd better concentrate, then.' Thanet never felt more of a country bumpkin than when driving in London.

Twenty minutes later he was turning into a hospital car park for the second time that day, but on this occasion his heart was light and full of joyous anticipation.

Laden with champagne, gifts for Bridget and the baby and the biggest teddy bear Thanet had ever seen they navigated the corridors of the hospital to the maternity ward, where they found Bridget in a little room of her own – a privilege accorded to those who had undergone a caesarian, apparently. And there was a cot beside the bed! The baby must be making good progress, then.

Thanet was also glad to see that now all the anxiety was over, although she still looked rather pale, Bridget's natural ebullience had surfaced once more. Both she and Alexander were understandably glowing with pride and delight. He and Joan tiptoed across to peer into the rather unusual cot, a kind of perspex box.

'They call it a bassinet,' said Bridget. 'It's used for premature babies, to keep their temperature up.'

'She's got your mouth,' Joan said to Bridget.

Bridget laughed, then winced, clutching her abdomen. 'Oh, don't make me laugh, whatever else you do! Alexander's mum says she's got Alexander's!'

'Have you decided what to call her yet?'

'Margaret Anna.'

Joan flushed with pleasure. Margaret was her mother's name. 'Your grandmother will be thrilled.'

'But we shall call her Meg. Would you like to pick her up?'

'Oh, is that allowed?'

'Of course. Just for a few minutes anyway.'

Alexander, Thanet saw, had produced a video camera and now filmed the scene as Joan carefully lifted up the

279

feather weight bundle and cradled her for a few minutes before handing her to Thanet.

He laid his cheek against the soft down of the baby's head and inhaled the distinctive, milky scent of new life, admired the perfection of her tiny features. He glanced at Joan and as their eyes met he knew that she too was remembering the moments when they had held their own first-born, now a mother herself. Suddenly he saw himself in a new light, as a link in the chain which joined one generation to another, stretching back into the obscurity of past ages and ahead into the unknown future.

As he laid his new granddaughter back in the cot he said a brief prayer for her health and safety, then turned to watch, smiling, as Bridget began to unwrap her parcels.

At this moment, he thought, there was nowhere on earth that he would rather be.